MW01107847

USA TODAY BESTSELLING AUTHOR

DALE MAYER

—BY—
DEATH

BOOK 1-3 OF DEATH SERIES

BY DEATH BOOKS 1–3
Beverly Dale Mayer
Valley Publishing Ltd.

Copyright © 2012, 2013, 2015
Second Edition © 2022

ISBN-13: 978-1-988315-86-7
Print Edition

About This Boxed Set

Touched by Death

Digging up the dead isn't the best way to lay ghosts to rest …

Anthropologist Jade Hansen had been touched by death once before. While in Haiti one year ago, she'd lost her unborn child, and the devastation nearly took her sanity in the time that followed. Getting back to work means facing the grief that's all but destroyed her. Determined to be strong, she returns to Haiti with a mortuary team to recover the bodies of an American family from a mass grave, following a devastating earthquake.

Dane Chester is an independent contractor, who willingly puts his life on hold to help rebuild the sleepy town of Jacmel, after the natural disaster all but razed it. He's staying with his sibling while Dane volunteers his services in the group effort, but finds himself put off by his brother's pregnant wife and her relatives. Wanting to do good for those who lost so much from the quake creates a tug of war within him, given the unexpected family strife. Selfishly he wants nothing more than to go home, … until he meets Jade, who, at first sight, makes him realize what's been missing in his own life for so long.

Jade's mortuary team begins work, but, from the start, everything that can go wrong does. As anthropologists, they've all faced the very human horrors of situations like this before. But something else is at work at this mass grave site—something malevolent that none of them can explain—yet equally can't shake the communal disquiet. Rather than laying her ghosts to rest where she suffered such loss, Jade finds herself confronting death all over again. This time her grief is mingled with an unnerving dose of terror—and this incredible man Dane, who unexpectedly awakens her heart to love again, is somehow right in the middle of it all.

Haunted by Death

Meg Pearce is haunted by a death that may never be explained, … and so she can never truly be healed. During the summer before she started college, she and her boyfriend went on a camping trip that ended with one of their friends disappearing. In one fell swoop of destruction, she lost not only a friend but her own innocence, her future, her best friend and lover, her everything.

Seventeen years later, Meg's career as an anthropologist drives her to seek understanding about why things happen and the answers for human behavior. Those questions that torment her have her returning to the same campsite of the tragedy that defined her life. A part of her hopes to solve the mystery that has plagued her for most of her adult years. Ultimately she longs to find a way to deal with the loss. Instead of gaining closure though, she stumbles onto a gruesome discovery that has her reeling back to the darkest time in her existence.

Detective Chad Ingram has spent the last seventeen years attempting to solve a stone-cold mystery—one that also stole his life and his true love.

Death seems supernaturally determined to shake up their lives for good or evil—only this time, Meg and Chad are both in the crossfire.

Chilled by Death

After losing two close friends three years ago in a snowboarding accident, Stacy Carter has become a loner and can't seem to make peace with this loss, not when Death intrudes upon her personal life again and takes two more people she loves. Meeting new people and trying to make a normal life for herself proves to be harder than anything else she's done. Meanwhile, in her career, being a forensic pathologist puts her in close contact with the dead. While fascinating and never dull, it isn't exactly a cozy conversation starter. When her brother tries to coax her out for a mountain vacation to help her heal, she has reservations, even as she tells herself rationally that she needs to face this. Reservations and rationale, however, were in short supply the last time she saw Royce O'Connell at that mountain ...

Royce is floored when Stacy finally returns to the spot where she lost her two best friends, intending to deal with the depression that she's battled for some time. Royce and Stacy have been longtime friends, but Royce wants so much more between them. Yet he's well aware that he blew their last time together. Stacy makes it clear she's not looking for reconciliation. However, he can't help seeing her reappearance in their tight-knit group as a second chance, maybe his *only* chance.

Out in their winter wonderland, the vacation atmosphere shifts from merry to mayhem in a hurry, when they come across a dead man. Then, not long afterward, Stacy's brother goes missing. The nightmare is only just beginning, as the realization settles in that they can't trust anyone.

Maybe not even each other ...

Sign up to be notified of all Dale's releases here!

https://geni.us/DaleNews

USA TODAY BESTSELLING AUTHOR

DALE MAYER

TOUCHED
BY
DEATH

BOOK ONE OF BY DEATH SERIES

Prologue

I N PERFECT SYMPHONY the clouds swayed in the sky, wrapping the moon in protective cotton wool, as the ground shook and trembled beneath the sleepy town of Jacmel in the south of Haiti.

Mother Nature growled and raged, over and over again.

As if she knew the secrets long kept hidden in the hills behind the small town.

As if she knew about the injustices done.

As if she knew this had to stop.

She gave one last mighty shove, and the earth cracked open.

Trees toppled, their roots ripped from the ground in hapless destruction. Large rocks tumbled, as their foundations were wiped out from below. Everything fell to the force of Mother Nature—at long last exposing old secrets to the light.

When the clouds moved from their protective stance, the moon glared upon the result of Mother Nature's game of fifty-two-card pickup with the Devil. The lunar light shone on bones long picked clean—now newly exposed to the sky.

The ground undulated one last time. The surrounding hillside shuddered, sending a light dusting of earth and rock to rebury the gruesome evidence.

As if the sins of man were too much for even the moon to see.

FIVE DAYS LATER, a tractor with a bucket on the front—hastily called into service—groaned, as it carried yet another load of the town's dead to a large grave. Herman, the tractor driver, was beyond pain and grief and death. He focused on the gritty details of plain survival. Five days of heat and exposure hadn't been kind to the dead—or to the living. Survival had become a grim business, and rotting bodies needed to be buried, or disease would crush them further. So many dead. No money. No time. No help.

No choice.

His neighbor, John, lifted the last small corpse from the dump truck's deposit on the ground to the loader's bucket. He pulled off one work glove, straightened the makeshift mask tied around his mouth and nose, and shouted, "Good to go!"

Herman popped the gear shift forward, then swore and prayed that Bertha would survive the job given her. He trundled forward. "Come on, girl." He patted the stick shift in his hand. "I need you to get it done. If you quit on me, I ain't gonna make it through this." And that was no joke. He knew for damn sure that he wouldn't if ol' Bertha didn't. *Bad business this.* He had respect for the dead. Every one of his family and friends had received a proper send-off, a decent burial—as was fitting. Until this earthquake.

Pain clutched his heart and squeezed. So many dead.

He'd lost his wife, one son, and two grandkids this last week. Sex and age hadn't mattered here. Mother Nature hadn't cared. She'd wiped them all out.

John, the only other person who'd stepped up to help, had been lucky. His young wife and her family had survived the devastation. Living out of town had helped. That also contributed to his motivation to help out. This mass grave butted against his wife's family's land, so it made sense for John to ensure this grave was closed over, right and proper.

Many people could be trekking here on All Souls' Day, as families came to honor their dead. Then again, complete families had been buried together. There might not be anyone left to mourn.

Herman would come and visit. Too many people remained here to forget.

HERMAN TUGGED AT the old T-shirt tied around his nose and mouth, his sun-blackened skin blending with the poor light. Nothing kept the smell out. He'd already gone through a half-dozen pairs of gloves. But, without the makeshift bandanna, each breath caught in his chest, making him gag. His clothes would have to be burned after this. No way to rid them of the smell of death.

Bertha struggled forward. Darkness hid the evidence of what they were doing. What he'd done. He only hoped he wouldn't have too many more loads to haul.

In the aftermath of the earthquake, everyone had been numb, in shock, or frozen with grief. No one could make decisions. No military arrived to take care of the problem. The government buildings and staff had been as decimated as the rest of the population.

Herman refused to leave his people lying exposed like that. Determined to do what he could, he'd taken command and had done something. Something so awful that he couldn't close his eyes without seeing the stares of the dead—blaming him.

So far, close to sixty people had gone into this pit. The natural depression, a ready-made burial spot, was a godsend to the desperate survivors, a fast answer to the bloated dead rotting on the sidewalks. Herman didn't know how many more were to come, maybe hundreds. Later, much later, if someone cared, they could open this mass grave and do the right thing. But not now. Now they had to get on with the business of survival.

Mother Nature was a bitch.

Chapter 1

One Year Later ...

JADE HANSEN TWISTED in her sleep at her Seattle, Washington, apartment, while a nightmare across the ocean took over her. Her sweaty panicked body searched for a way out of the endless nightmare of bloated bodies, desperate people, and cries for help—pleas that would never get answered. She turned in the fog as one more person, caught among the fallen rocks, cried out to her. Jade came face-to-face with a woman—blood congealed in her hair and streaked down the side of her face, a chunk of concrete crushing her legs. She begged for Jade to find her son.

Screaming, Jade took off to the safety of the tent, the tent filled with the dead ... and the living who searched for their families.

She couldn't help them all.

She couldn't help any of them.

She couldn't even help herself.

With tears streaming down her face, Jade woke in a panic, as if the demons of her nightmare had followed her into the present.

Shuddering, she recognized the hanging lamp overhead as the one in her apartment. The Aztec print couch she'd fallen asleep on was hers, a gift from her brother. And she finally understood that the evening's in-depth television coverage of a recent small earthquake in Haiti had been the trigger for her nightmare.

Jade curled into a ball, pulling her throw higher up on her neck. She winced at the images still flashing on the news. Another earthquake in Haiti. Only a little one this time. Not that the size mattered. The memories of her one and only humanitarian trip to that area, after the major earthquake almost one year ago, had etched themselves permanently into her brain. A horrible time, a praying-on-your-knees-for-help kind of horrible time. In Haiti, nightmares had destroyed her sleep. The shortage of food for those suffering had destroyed her appetite.

She'd lost weight over there, but nothing compared to the pounds that had slipped off after her return home. Sure, that had been almost one year ago too. It didn't matter. With the nightmare fresh in her mind, it felt like only days.

So much pain and suffering. *So much torment.* She couldn't stop it. She couldn't even begin to make it right. There'd been nothing she could do to help—or so little relative to the scope of the problem that it might as well have been nothing. If she'd been offered a ride out of that hell on any given day, she would have jumped over her colleagues to grab it.

She wasn't proud of that.

In fact, it made her feel small and ashamed. Her colleagues had done so much better.

She'd wanted to be better. She'd tried to be better.

She'd failed. Failed her colleagues. The victims. And herself.

The memories still haunted her.

She had had her nice safe lab job in Seattle. She drove to work every day in a nice car and returned home every night to her clean, safe apartment with running water, heat, and electricity. All the comforts denied the Haitians still struggling through the devastation from twelve months ago.

After she'd locked her front door behind her that first day home, the tears had started to pour. It seemed she'd been crying ever since.

Her life had gone from bad to worse for a while, before she'd picked herself up—somewhat.

And now another earthquake.

If a small one like that triggered Jade's memories, what was the reality doing to all those poor people still living the horror?

Her phone rang.

She ignored it.

It wouldn't quit. Finally she couldn't stand it, so picked up her cell. She didn't even bother to check the caller ID. Duncan called every night at nine. "I'm fine, Duncan."

"Hey, kitten." Her brother's pet name for her made her smile, as he'd probably intended. She used to be like him. Upbeat, funny, and carefree. Until life had dumped her on her ass at the top of the slide and had given her a hard kick downhill. She wasn't sure she'd hit bottom now either.

"I've got a job proposition for you."

His cheerful voice made her want to smile. The job proposition didn't. "I don't want to hear it."

He laughed, a buoyant sound that rang around the room. He never failed to raise her spirits. The effect just didn't hang around after his calls. "Maybe you don't, but maybe you do. How will you know if you don't hear it? It's a good one."

His wheedling tone made her smile in spite of her horrible mood. "Not if I don't want to hear it."

"You don't know what you want."

Jade groaned. "If I don't know, then how do you?"

His laughter pealed again.

She shook her head and felt the lightness—the joyful spirit that was her brother—ease the ache in her soul. "I know you keep trying to save me, Duncan, but I'm fine."

The laughter and joy cut off suddenly. Duncan's voice, sober and sad, whispered, "No. No, you're not."

Tears choked her. She rubbed her eyes. She wouldn't cry, damn it. Not tonight. Not *again* tonight.

"This has to stop, Jade. You'll collapse, and I don't want that to happen." Love slipped through her phone, making it harder to hold back the tears. Jade didn't trust herself to speak. She sniffled ever-so-slightly.

"I know you're hurting inside. I feel it, and I hurt for you."

"I know," she whispered, starting to shake, knowing she had to stop—only she didn't know how. And once again couldn't deal with it. "Look. I'm really tired. I need to get to bed. I'll talk to you tomorrow."

She didn't give him a chance to say goodbye and disconnected instead. And the tears rolled. Hot and steady, they streamed down her cheeks. She snuggled back into the couch and let them run.

The point of stopping them was long gone. Besides, she no longer knew how.

"HEY, DANE, THAT guy phoned again," John called out.

"Yeah, which guy?" Dane walked over to stand beside his step-brother, who'd stopped by the hospital construction site for a visit.

"The guy about the grave," John said.

Dane tugged off his hard hat to wipe the sweat running down his forehead. Christ, it was hot and humid here in Haiti. He surveyed the construction site in front of them. Not bad at all. They were ahead of schedule, but completion of the new wing was still months away.

Jacmel hadn't recovered from the last big earthquake, and, with smaller ones continually causing setbacks, the country would be years getting back on its feet.

It had taken weeks to convince John to let Dane come over after the big quake. When he'd realized how badly in need the town was, Dane had stepped in to help. John's small engine repair shop had been decimated in one of the smaller, more recent earthquakes, yet he refused to let Dane repair it. John had said he wanted to fix things himself.

John added, "Remember? They called before and want to open the mass grave to retrieve some guy's family?"

Dane glanced at his brother. Only the two of them were left in the family. Both stubborn. Independent. And family oriented. It had only taken that one phone call with something odd in John's voice to catch Dane's attention. He'd put his Seattle construction business in the hands of his capable foreman, an old school friend, and, without his brother's invite, Dane had flown to Haiti two days later. That had been months ago.

Shielding his eyes from the hot sun, Dane said, "I have to admit. The never-ending sunshine and warm, dry weather is hardly a hardship. Of course we haven't hit the humid summer season yet."

"See? Isn't this much better than the wet misery of the coast? Seattle is probably still buried in snow—even in March." John grinned, with satisfaction.

Dane couldn't argue that. His foreman had been complaining of just that in their last phone call. "Not everyone hates the rain like you do."

"Come on. Admit it." John smacked Dane's shoulder. A cloud of dust rose, making him step back hurriedly. "You love it here."

"I love visiting you, and, of course, I adore Tasha." Dane grinned over his white lie. Tasha obviously adored his brother, so that was good enough for Dane. It had, after all, been the call of family that had brought Dane here.

John had a terrible history with relationships. His long-time high school sweetheart had walked out the door of her home one day, just weeks before graduation, and had never returned. A few years later, John had married the witchy Elise. That marriage had been a walking disaster right from the wedding reception. Dane couldn't stand the woman, and the feeling had been mutual. John was just a big teddy bear, who attracted unscrupulous people.

Unfortunately Elise died in a car crash.

After that fiasco, John disappeared for years, before finally setting up housekeeping with Tasha in Haiti. Dane's antennae went off at that, and, given John's past, Dane could be forgiven for worrying about his brother. Only John appeared to have stabilized, flourishing even. Dane had been delighted.

The major earthquake had changed all that, sending John back into the same morose, angry man as before. So Dane was happy to see the joking John appear at times.

"Hey, are you in there?"

Dane started.

John smirked at him, a sign his lighthearted kid brother was showing through the more cynical angry one of recent years. "What's the matter? Felice getting to you?"

Heat washed over Dane's neck and face. Felice was too hot, too willing, and way too young. She was also the daughter of one of Tasha's friends who'd visited yesterday. He didn't know the specific laws in Haiti relating to that sort of thing. Still, he was pretty damn sure he'd get jail time back home, and that was deterrent enough for him. "She needs to be locked away for a few years."

"Not here. Girls her age are often married and pregnant." John added thoughtfully, "And not likely in that order."

Dane shook his head. "As long as it's not to me."

John changed the subject abruptly. "What should I do about the call? ... About this guy's request for help at the mass grave site? Sounds crazy to me."

Easily following the lightning shift of his brother's mind, Dane asked, "What's to do? He's a grieving man. His request isn't unreasonable. And it's done all the time."

John visibly shuddered. "I never expected to feel so strongly about it, but, after that earthquake last year? ... I don't know, Dane. I saw too much death. More than I should have—more than anyone should have. It seems wrong to dig up those poor earthquake victims again."

"You've been living here too long. Some weird Haitian beliefs are rubbing off on you."

John snickered, making Dane laugh. "Or not long enough. According to Tasha, Mother Earth claimed them, and she won't be happy if she's forced to give them up again."

With a sigh of disgust, Dane said, "That's crazy talk. This guy lost his family. He wants to take the three of them home to Seattle and to bury them properly. He needs closure. That's all. What's so wrong about that?"

John kicked a stray rock in the dirt. "I don't know that anything is wrong with it. I guess if it were me and mine, I'd want to take them home too. However, it's a mass grave. There are other bodies to consider, other families who will be hurt."

"Really?" Dane stared at him. "Like *how mass?*"

John shot him a look, before grimacing and staring off to the horizon. "I stopped counting at sixty. We did what we had to do. The dead? ... They were everywhere. Herman, our old neighbor, used his front loader to transport them. ... Christ, it was bad."

Dane scrunched his face.

John rushed to explain. "I saw children playing beside bloated bodies. They'd become dulled to them because there were so many. Oh, don't blame the children. They stayed close to the people they knew because they had no one else. That a dead mother or sibling lay within a few feet didn't seem to matter. Even dead, they were a comfort."

Dane closed his eyes, as terrible images flooded his mind. He couldn't imagine the horror. "I wasn't judging. I just can't envision what you went through. And to think of children sitting there, so lost and alone? ... Well, ... it's a terrible thought."

Shadows darkened John's brown eyes.

Dane was sorry for what John had been through. "That's the thing about family." Dane patted John on the shoulder and noticed his brother cringe.

"So you think this guy should be allowed to come in and remove his kin?" John wasn't backing away from this one.

"I don't have any say in this. I wasn't aware that you did either. I'm sure this man has already gone through the authorities. I'd suggest that you accept that this will happen, whether you want it to or not. The team of specialists should be here soon. When they arrive, be nice to them. Helpful. They will probably be there for a day or two, a week or two max. Then they'll be gone, leaving the others to rest in peace."

"It's not that easy."

"I know. Other people's loved ones are in that grave. Maybe someone should suggest that all the victims be identified." Dane pursed his lips and nodded his head, pleased with his idea. "Reburied properly. This guy has money. Maybe some of it should be put toward assisting the community to help them deal with the disaster. Granted, that will take more time."

John shook his head. "You don't understand the full scope of the problem here. Hundreds of bodies could be there. We just kept putting them in, then piling dirt and rocks on top to ensure they weren't disturbed. We probably went overboard on that part."

Dane blanched. "Hundreds?" He swallowed heavily. "Okay, so maybe the team will need a little longer. Still, something could be done for the other remains." Dane winced. "Or at least for the remains they can find and identify, while they search for the ones they are shipping back to Seattle."

John stared at him and gulped. "That's not helping."

"Yeah. I know. Sorry about that."

The two men stared at the half-completed hospital building in front of them. Dane took an involuntary step back. Right now the damn thing resembled a skeleton, reaching out of the ground.

Chapter 2

J ADE GROANED AND closed her eyes. A Saturday, and still she'd awakened early. What was the point of having a morning to sleep in if her body didn't get the memo? Sometimes life just sucked.

Surprisingly she drifted back to sleep.

The phone woke her hours later. She stretched out an arm, trying to find her cell, all without having to disturb her comfortable position. "Hello," she mumbled.

"Jade, I let you push me off last night but not today." Duncan spoke hurriedly. "This guy with the job wants an answer, and he wants one now. It's important. Are you awake?"

Jade huddled deeper under the covers. "No. I don't want to hear it. Leave me alone."

"Won't happen. I'm coming over," he said firmly. "Get up and have a shower. I'll bring the coffee. Be there in twenty." The call cut off.

Jade rolled over on her back and stared at the ceiling. *What the hell?*

Twenty minutes later, she slipped on socks, just as the doorbell rang. Opening the door, hairbrush in hand, she frowned. Her brother wasn't alone.

A thin man of average height and wearing coke-bottle-thick glasses stood beside Duncan. He had an overstuffed folder in his hands.

Damn it. She glared at her brother, snagged one of the coffee cups out of his hand and turned her back on them.

"Don't worry about her. She's always grumpy in the morning." Duncan motioned the stranger inside. "This is Tony Maholland. Tony, my sister, Jade."

Jade shot her brother an irritated look. Good manners dictated she at least smile politely at the man standing awkwardly behind Duncan. Exasperated, she said, "Oh, come in and sit down, for heaven's sake. You're giving me a kink in my neck."

"Jade, be nice. Good thing I warned Tony about you."

"Why?" she shot back, leading the way to the small kitchen. "You aren't being nice to me."

Duncan pulled out a chair for Tony, who stood uncomfortably beside them. He twisted a second one around and sat on it backward to face her. "Everything I do is because I love you. We don't always know what we need in life, and sometimes loving someone means making the hard choices for them."

She sat with a *thump*, glared at him, her instincts on high alert. She wouldn't like what was coming. Duncan never backed away from a fight, and he'd always been the kind of brother to lead her down the right path—whether she wanted to go there or not.

"Jade, I need to talk to you. And I need you to *listen*."

"I don't think I want to."

Compassion filled his eyes, and her brother leaned toward her. Instinctively she pulled back slightly. Wary. Duncan was a counselor—helping people was his passion. He couldn't help himself. She loved him but hated when all that do-gooder energy was turned her way.

"I want you to return to Haiti. And Tony will help you get there."

Jade's heart dropped, her stomach clenched, and tears welled in her eyes. "No," she whispered. "I can't go back."

"I'll even go there with you."

Wordless, Jade stared at her beloved brother. *He would too.* She knew he'd drop everything to help her get through this.

He placed his hand on her knee and squeezed gently. "You have to deal with this. Only then can you move on."

"Haiti? But that's where it all started." She stared down at her clenched fists. How did going back make any sense?

Duncan caught and held her hands in his. "I know."

His words, so simple and so powerful. And so not helpful.

"Excuse me." Tony leaned forward, his gaze shifting between the two of them. "Duncan, I can see this is personal, and I can't begin to understand what's really going on here, but I'm not sure she's the right person for the job. We need someone who can handle themselves down there—not people carrying personal baggage."

Jade agreed with a slight nod.

Duncan, however, grinned at the stranger. "Well put, Tony. However, remember this. *Everyone* has baggage. At least with my sister, you will know up front what the problem is. So this is the scoop. My sister went down to Haiti as a part of the Disaster Mortuary Operations Response Team. She was there precisely three weeks. She endured physical attacks on her person, unbelievable emotional trauma due to the massive number of deaths she had to deal with, and her spirit took a major hit. The experience changed her. It was as if she'd been touched by Death himself."

With an apologetic look at Jade, Duncan continued. "She was pregnant at the time. When she came home, her fiancé couldn't deal, and he bolted. About three weeks after his departure, she lost the baby."

Jade winced. Duncan hadn't said anything wrong; he hadn't exaggerated or minimized the truth. However, laid bare like that, even she could see how, although life had certainly been shitty, it was something she should have and still could recover from.

If she cared to.

Her soul was weary. That was close to explaining the way she felt. She'd been unprepared for the horror and devastation in Haiti. The need and desperation of the people. Her inability to fix ... any of it.

The normalcy of her existence after her return home had only amplified it. Her guilt. Her failure. Her life.

"She's always a professional. That won't be an issue. Haiti, itself, wasn't the problem. It just started the problem. She has to face Haiti, before her depression declines into something more than she can deal with. Besides, she's got the perfect skill set and experience, as you well know. Plus, she's available on short notice."

Depression? She stared at Duncan, her attention snagging on that one word. That was it. One simple word? Then she remembered a period in Duncan's life, just after their father had died. She'd been away in college several years by that time, buffered from the emotional element, but Duncan had been there, taking the full blast of guilt from their father's suicide.

"Is that what you felt?" She hadn't known. Not really. How could she have? To understand such darkness, such sadness in others, she had to experience these emotions first herself. *Shit.* So typical. Was everyone blind to what didn't immediately affect them? Duncan had had it hard then too, and she hadn't noticed.

"Oh yes. The thing is, sis, you can honor the grief you feel for the loss of your child and for the horror you felt for all those people in Haiti, but you can't let this beat you. You need to pick yourself up and to grab hold of the reins of your life. Reacting to a stimulus is one thing—wallowing is another thing entirely. When you know what you're doing and choose to do nothing, then ..." He sat back, his gaze warm and caring. "Whereas Tony is offering you a chance to step up and out of this place ... and to move forward."

Tony leaned forward. "Uh, *maybe* I'm offering this chance."

Duncan and Jade ignored him.

Jade traveled from one realization to another, as they slid through her, lighting all the dark places she'd clung to in her mind. Her grief *was* real and *was* valid. Her distress was also justified. She had a right to feel the way she did. Validation was empowering. Her anger at her fiancé wasn't something she had a problem honoring. ... Still, not doing something about this hollowness inside? ... Duncan was right.

That was not acceptable.

She sat back, as understanding dawned. "And—now that I do know, ... and don't do anything about it—it's self-pity?"

He grinned, pride and love shining at her. "Exactly. And now that you do know, you can't continue on the same path. And by your own words ..."

She winced, hearing her voice from past conversations. *I don't do self-pity.* She closed her eyes and dropped her head back. "Not fair. I don't know that I can do Haiti again."

"Maybe this time you could see the healing. The people who have turned their lives around and moved on. You could find the positive and let that heal you too."

She groaned. "You're so into that New Age mumbo jumbo."

"It's me."

She couldn't argue that. Abruptly she turned to face Tony. "What's the job?"

Surprised, and looking a little disturbed, he answered, "My client wants to retrieve three members of his family from a mass grave and bring them home. The team leader on the project is Dr. Bruce McLeod."

"Mass grave?" That didn't bother her. She'd done those before. It was true; she knew she handled death well. She just didn't handle the *people dying* part so well—especially on a large scale. "How mass?"

He peered over the rim of his glasses. "We have it on good authority that close to one hundred people are buried in a grave outside of Jacmel."

Jacmel. She racked her head for the little geographical information she'd allowed to rattle around inside. The opposite side of Port-au-Prince, where she'd been last time. Where her life had been flattened. "Is his family Haitian?"

Tony tilted his head, a curious look on his face. "Yes. Does it matter?"

"No. Identification would be easier if we're looking for three Caucasians in a mix of dark-haired Haitians, for example. After a year, hair will likely still be attached, making identification easier."

"My understanding is that the grave contains mostly locals, with a few tourists who were there at the time."

She nodded. She liked the idea of doing something to help someone. This could work. Close to—but not the same as—what she'd been through before. She'd been stronger going into it back then. But she'd also been unprepared. She'd be neither of those things this time. "How long?"

"As long as it takes to get the job done. My client isn't worried about the cost, within reason, and he's willing to have the other bodies in the grave identified and processed along with his family. The team will leave the information with whatever officials are in place to help identify those victims. The local families will then have the choice of what to do."

"That's generous. What about reburial of the others for the families with no money?"

Tony grimaced. "This is obviously a sensitive issue, and we're working toward a happy resolution for everyone. It may not be possible to identify everyone, and it's quite possible that many, if not all, of those people will be reburied in the same grave. And though he's generous, the expenditures must fit in his budget."

Duncan leaned back and shoved his hands into the front pockets of his faded jeans. "Whew. That'll be some job."

Shooting him a mocking look, Jade asked, "Still willing to come with me?"

He brightened. "Absolutely. I can travel and socialize, while you work."

Her leg shot out and connected with his ankle.

"Hey, I was just kidding." He shifted out of the way, sending her an injured look.

The happy relief in his eyes made her realize just how much he had been hoping she'd come around to his way of thinking. "You'd better be."

"If I could give you a few more details," Tony interrupted. "You'll leave in one week. The plan is to give it three months and reassess. We've been assured this is a decent time frame for our needs. Some adjustments may come down the road, depending on the progress."

He glanced at his notebook. "Of course, ... as I said, a budget is in place. So ..." He narrowed his gaze at her. "We'll work out many of the details over there."

"I have a job here. Remember? I'd have to give notice, ... not to mention I'd have no job when I return home." She frowned. She couldn't walk out on her boss on such short notice like that. Neither could she afford to be jobless when she returned in three months. Relief swept through her. No way she could go. She opened her mouth to say just that, when Duncan spoke first.

"Now don't get mad, Jade. However, I've spoken with Gerard already, after Tony and I discussed the issue in greater depth."

"*You what?*" Her voice came out as an incredulous squeak. "You called my boss? Are you nuts? I'm lucky he didn't fire me yesterday."

Duncan grinned. "On the contrary. And don't forget. He and I go way back. He actually liked the idea. He thought this placement might just do the trick for you."

Now her astonishment turned to anger. Like a too-old rubber band, her emotions seemed to stretch thin and snap easily. "I don't like you talking about me behind my back."

"Then don't act in such a way that the people who care about you feel they need to get involved secretly."

"Whatever." She shot him a fulminating look. Why did big brothers only come in arrogant, high-handed models? Her anger flowed, until he spoke again.

"He cares, and so do I. The bottom line is, you can leave for three months, and your job will be here when you get back."

Her protests died on her tongue. She was too weary to continue the fight. A fight she knew he'd win. Her brother did love her. It was hard to argue with her self-proclaimed savior. Besides, he was right. She couldn't continue on the same self-destructive path. Someone had to do something.

That someone had been him.

Now it was up to her.

DANE WALKED TOWARD the main house, tucking his T-shirt into faded jeans, admiring the play of the sun on the bright trumpet-like flowers bouncing in the breeze. Haiti had a lot to offer. At least this area. The countryside was green and lush, the rolling hills and white beaches some of the nicest he'd ever seen. The people were wholesome and strong in faith, even after the disasters they'd faced. He'd loved his time here.

It was coming to an end; he knew that. His future didn't lie here. He knew he'd wake up one day and know it was time to go home. He hoped it would be after the birth of his niece or nephew.

"Aren't you up early today?" His brother's voice came from the vicinity of the patio.

"Look who's talking." Dane grinned at his brother, unshaven and tousled, huddling over a large mug of coffee. "Bad night?"

"Tasha said the baby was playing soccer with her bladder all night. She must have gotten out of bed a dozen times."

Dane barely held in his laughter. "Ah, the joys of impending fatherhood." He walked toward the kitchen door. "Did you leave any coffee in the pot?"

"I left some. I don't know that Tasha did."

Dane grimaced. Tasha was pretty reasonable most of the time, but he'd been witness to a few of her *I'm pregnant, don't mess with me* moments. And they seemed to be more frequent now. He stuck his head inside first, gauged the small room to be empty, and strode over to the coffeepot, where he quickly grabbed a cupful and made a fast exit.

Back outside, his brother chuckled. "Made it, I see. She's gone back to bed anyway, so I imagine you're safe enough."

"You could have told me that before I went in there, thinking I was risking my life." Dane pulled over the second wooden chair and sat down to enjoy the morning.

"*Nah*, if I have to risk my life, you might as well too."

"There's a brother for you." The two sat in companionable silence. Dane marveled at a location where the weather every day remained a comfortable seventy-five to eighty degrees. He knew it fluctuated sometimes, but, during his stay, it had been remarkably consistent.

Suddenly Tasha stormed outside, the door slamming behind her. Dane took one look at the building fury on her face, blinked, and turned slightly away. John would have to deal with this one.

"They can't come. You tell them that they can't do this. It ain't right." She shifted into a spat of guttural Creole, making Dane grateful for his less-than-rudimentary understanding of the language.

John closed his eyes briefly, then opened them and faced his Haitian wife, while Dane looked on. "Now, honey. We've been over this. Just because I say they can't come won't stop them."

"Why not? That property is ours."

"No, it's not." John's weary voice went over ground that he had obviously covered many times.

Dane took a sip of coffee and tried not to show any interest. Tasha's black hair stood on end; her face was puffy, her dark skin splotchy. Her large belly, covered by an old stretched-out T-shirt that hung low, covered the bulk of the goofy boxer shorts she wore. Dane had been around other pregnant women, just none that reacted like Tasha. The longer he stayed, the more he worried about his sister-in-law's mental and emotional health. John never seemed to notice. Love had to be blind.

"Honey, I've told you before. That land borders the family land, but it's not ours."

"It's land we've used since forever. It should be ours." She pouted and collapsed on the arm of his chair beside him, the tempest over for now. "We think of it as ours."

John grinned and tugged her closer. "Except it isn't. I know you think it's wrong. However, you might want to try to see their point of view for a moment. If that were your family thrown into a large pit in another country, wouldn't you want to bring them home? Have a place where you could visit them? Talk to them? Grieve for them?"

She frowned. "I understand that. I'm not heartless. I feel sorry for the family. ... I do. What about all the other people buried there though? Some of them could be friends. Family. I don't know who's buried there. I do know it's bad luck to wake the dead. We need to honor their souls and let them rest."

"Maybe we can do something for the other people too. And no one is talking about waking the dead. We're hoping to give the dead—and the living—peace. We've gone over this. It's in progress, and we can't stop it."

"I still want to."

Dane buried his smile in his thick ceramic mug. She sounded more like a truculent child now. He could see her point, but his brother was right. The process had already started. By this time next week, the grave would be open.

She'd see then. Nothing bad would come of this.

Chapter 3

T HE HEAT HIT her first. Jade had forgotten how strong and heavy
the air smelled. Being March, the humidity shouldn't be bad until
they were almost finished with the job here. Jade stepped out of the
airport in Port-au-Prince and walked the tarmac toward the waiting
vehicles. Now she almost wished her brother was beside her, but she
had arrived with the rest of the team. So Duncan and she had both
decided it would be better if he came in a month or so.

She took a deep breath. Christ. She was really here.

The team consisted of seven members. A smallish-enough group
to get to know but big enough to get the job done.

Besides Bruce, the leader, and Jade herself, there was Dr. Mike, a
forensic anthropologist, but with more degrees than she had herself.
Plus Meg Pearce, who had some social anthropology degree and a
psychology degree, if Jade remembered correctly. Two other men—
Stephen and Wilson—would double as computer nerds and would
work at the grave site. A third female rounded out the group, Susan,
but Jade had forgotten the details on her.

It wouldn't take long to get to know each other, Jade hoped.
Meeting new people wasn't normally an issue for her, but this last year
of hermit living hadn't been productive in that sense. She was nervous.
And that was stupid. She was good at what she did. She wanted to
help on this project. She could do this.

And she'd almost convinced herself.

Taking several deep breaths, she allowed herself to really look at
the area. The last time she'd flown in with the army. She'd been
whisked in and whisked out and had worked most of the time behind
tight security. This time the team had taken a commercial flight.
When they landed, no army, no police—no security of any kind—met
them.

Intense blue skies smiled down on her. She almost believed everything would be all right.

Almost.

Her gaze wandered the surrounding areas, as her team made their way to the rental vehicles. Some things hadn't changed. Collapsed buildings still dotted the terrain; abandoned vehicles had been dragged off the main roads to clog fields and side roads. The biggest differences were the lack of bodies decorating the landscape and the roads were now passable.

It took a good ten minutes—with her gaze darting from side to side, searching for bodies and hoping not to find them—before Jade finally believed that death wouldn't plague her every step. She breathed a sigh of relief, feeling the almost unbearable tension draining from her system.

Haiti was obviously in recovery mode.

Thank God.

They planned to stay outside of the city center for the night to wait for gear, supplies, and mainly the paperwork. They would continue on to Jacmel in the morning.

"Come on, Jade. Stop gawking. We'll get time to sightsee later." Meg, one of the forensic anthropologists on the team, grinned at her. Tall, slim, and energetic, Meg's initial friendliness had enfolded Jade, easing the uncertainty of her decision.

Meg waved toward the three SUVs leased for the duration of the job. The team climbed into the vehicles and, within an hour, were booked in at a small and homey hotel. It appeared to have survived the earthquake unscathed. Complete streets were ripped apart in other parts of the city. Some portions were buried under collapsed buildings while others were perfect. So much of the city had been leveled. but there were pockets, like around the hotel, that appeared untouched.

The tent cities were new. The garbage lining the streets, the alleys, the sidewalks still remained the same. It was as if many people were stuck in a time warp, unable to move forward and to leave the disaster behind.

Mother Nature had a hit-and-miss hate thing going on.

After dinner, Meg and Jade stood outside the hotel and surveyed the streets for signs of progress. Stores were open, doing a brisk business. Port-au-Prince had been a thriving metropolis at one time. Jade didn't think recovery had restored that level of economic progress and stability. Poverty had always been a major part of life here. It looked to be the same. Not that she'd spent any time sightseeing on her last trip. There'd been nothing nice to see back then.

"Wow. Looks like the area still needs time to recover economically. Although I guess it's better than it was a year ago." Meg sat on the stone fence, her long jean-clad legs swinging loose. She ran a hand through her short brunette hair. She glanced over at Jade. "Are you ready for this?"

"Ready for what?" Jade asked absentmindedly, her focus on the surrounding scene, so similar and yet so different from before. She leaned against the stone fence and looked at her colleague.

"This life without electronics—although I did bring my phone. So, if you ever wanted to make a call, let me know."

"And I brought my laptop, so ditto," Jade added.

Meg nodded. "So, are you ready for the job we're here to do? It's not likely to be much fun." Meg pointed to the wreckage of cars heaped off to one side, surrounded by tall weeds. "I didn't expect to see this level of refuse strewn about. It's easy to be unaware of what's required in a country's recovery, unless you're actually on location."

"True enough. No, the job isn't likely to be much fun, but it'll be meaningful." Jade smiled, her heart lighter already. Her words had been instinctive, coming from her heart. The job had purpose, not as necessary for the masses as her previous one to Haiti, but still important. And not the same urgency or panic to this second visit. That helped to keep Jade calm and focused.

"Come on. We need to go to bed, if we want to get an early start."

They wandered into the hotel, saying good night to the other team members. At their rooms, Jade was pleasantly surprised to see she had a room to herself. Three women and four men were on the team. The others seemed normal and upbeat; Jade found herself relaxing and looking forward to her time here.

She said good night to Meg and opened her door. A maid in the hallway glanced at her shyly and handed over several towels.

Jade really was back in Haiti—where it all began.

MORNING DAWNED BRIGHT and sunny. Jade opened her eyes, staring at the same ceiling she'd stared at for over half the night. A heavy knock sounded on her door, followed by a bright, cheerful Meg calling out, "Rise and shine. It's a whole new day. We're pulling out in an hour. Get moving, and you'll have time for a shower and food. Otherwise you'll have to choose."

Jade heard her new friend bouncing down the stairs. At least one of them was in a good mood. Still, Meg's excitement was infectious. Twenty minutes later, after a fast shower and dressing, Jade poured coffee for herself in the small dining room. The rest of the team was boisterous and chewing through their meals.

"Good morning, Jade. Did you sleep well? Lovely rooms, aren't they?" Dr. Mike Chandler smiled at her, as he served himself fluffy scrambled eggs. Thankfully he didn't appear to need an answer. "Take a seat. Take a seat."

She grabbed the empty chair next to him. He looked to be in his sixties, with white hair and an aura of ageless wisdom, as if he'd seen a lot of life, and yet still found something to smile about. He looked to be someone she'd enjoy getting to know.

The waitress came around bearing food, generously heaped on her plate. "French toast? I thought we'd be eating fried bananas—or is it plantains here?—and orange juice-soaked French bread?"

"You can have that another time, if you want. I ordered this for everyone. You won't get much work done on a fried banana or two."

"I've never tried them," Jade protested, reaching for her knife and fork.

"And you won't today either. Better eat. We're rolling in ten." He finished his meal and stood to leave. Several other members followed.

Alone with only Meg at the table, Jade said, "Wow, everyone is in such a good mood."

Meg grinned at her. "Now if only we could cheer you up."

Jade sat back and gave her a sheepish smile. "I'm feeling better. Don't worry."

"Feeling better, yes. Feeling good, no. We'll fix that." She motioned to Jade's empty plate. "If you're done, let's go."

Caught in the general mood of everyone else, Jade found her doubts and worries from the night before drifting away. She raced after Meg and the others.

DANE AND JOHN watched the vehicles park outside the picket fence. Dust billowed behind them. Three SUVs—heavily loaded from the look of them.

The doors opened, and several smiling people hopped out and approached the brothers.

An older man with a beard said, "Excuse me, we're looking for Peppe or Emile Jacinte."

John pursed his lips, studying the newcomers. "They are my father-in-law and brother-in-law. Are you the mortuary team?"

Several people gathered around the speaker. The older man winced. "Yes, that's one way of putting it. I'm Dr. Bruce McLeod, and this is my group of specialists." He motioned to the rest of the group.

"Right. Well, Peppe is, ... well, he's not quite the right person to talk to, and Emile is at work already."

Dr. McLeod frowned. "We were hoping to get specific directions to the grave site, so as to evaluate the equipment we've brought with us."

A tall, lean, cheerful brunette in the group spoke first. "Could *you* show us the way to the site perhaps? We understand it borders this property."

Dane glanced over at John to see him glancing at the house. If Tasha found out John had helped them, well ...

"I'll take them, John." Dane turned to the strangers, ignoring the look of relief on John's face. "I'm Dane Chester, and this is my brother, John. His wife is Peppe's daughter. The grave site borders the family property."

The group broke into smiles and introductions as he approached them. Better to go now before Tasha saw them, though she'd have to deal with this sometime. It might be easier on her if the team had already settled in, before Tasha was forced to face them.

"It's in this direction." As they turned in the right direction, he considered the problem of parking. "Let's walk from here, and you can assess a clearing down the road a bit for parking and unloading. There isn't a road, but the path is wide and well-traveled."

They fell into a group and walked beside him.

Dane added, "John's wife's family isn't used to this many foreigners at once. How many of you are there?"

The same tall brunette spoke. "Seven on the team."

The oldest-looking man of the group walked beside Dane. "Plus one or two from the company will probably go back and forth from the States to check on our progress."

"*Progress*. Right." His lips quirked. "You do realize that not everyone is happy about what you're doing?" He felt their surprise more than saw any signs of it.

The brunette spoke again. "We hoped that people would understand."

Dane nodded. "Some will, though many more may be against having the grave opened—or *waking the dead*, as they'd call it."

"Are you Haitian?"

Dane spun around to gaze at the small blonde with a serious, almost haunted look on her face. His skin got plenty of sun with the work he did, yet he figured the locals deemed him a foreigner easy enough. He studied her for a moment, then answered, "No. I'm from Seattle, Washington. I own a construction company there, thankfully now manned by a very capable foreman." He shrugged self-consciously. "So, when I came to visit my brother and saw the destruction, I had to stay and help out."

Several people made comments in response. Dane ignored most, his gaze locked on the tiny blonde with such a serious look, who'd walked up beside him. Somehow he needed to see the reaction on her face. Her gaze stayed shuttered, but her lips quirked.

She murmured, "It's hard to *not* do something."

He was glad she understood. He wasn't sure of the undercurrents in her voice but felt like he'd said something right.

It took close to twenty minutes to get to the clearing. He pointed out the vast area to the others. "This is the best place for parking and unloading."

His gaze landed on the blonde again. She stilled at his words. Or was it from his gaze? Everyone else continued to talk around him. There were only seven of them, and he'd heard their initial introductions, but it was hard to keep them all straight. He didn't bother trying to remember names. Except for one.

Her name was Jade.

Several team members wandered the space, talking among themselves about logistics. He listened with half an ear. Jade stood quietly at his side.

He cast around, searching for something to say. "What brings you here?"

Her gaze, deep and dark, never shifted. She answered, "Sometimes you can't run away and hide. No matter how hard you try."

With that cryptic remark, she moved off to join the others, leaving him to stare after her, intrigued.

JADE STRUGGLED AGAINST the onslaught of emotions, while she stood and watched the team. She was really here.

Their guide had been a surprise. Tall and rangy, he reminded her of the lean cowboys she'd grown up with in Montana. Her family's move to Seattle hadn't erased the memories of weathered men, who loved the long hours they worked outdoors. Dane appeared to be—at least at first glance—of the same breed.

She wandered the clearing, listening, waiting for the next step. That had little to do with her.

"Anything to add, Jade?"

She glanced over at Meg. "Nothing until we actually see the grave site and understand what we're up against."

Dr. Mike agreed. "You're right. We need to consider the whole picture." He turned to Dane. "Can you show us, please?"

Moving off in that long-legged style, Dane led them to a well-worn path through the rocks and brush—one she hadn't noticed before. The group followed in single file. She fell into the last place.

Tall spindly trees grew on either side. The path was almost wide enough to drive on, and that was something to consider, although she was pretty sure the locals wouldn't appreciate that level of damage to their site. She didn't doubt they considered it their place.

She rounded the last corner and almost walked into Meg and Dr. Mike. She stepped around them, their silence seeping into her thoughts.

Oh, no.

She stilled and stared.

They'd been told that a cave-in had presented a natural depression and that the men had used the surrounding rocks and dirt to finish the job. The hilled area stretched for what appeared to be one hundred feet, crossing the path and ending at a large pile of rocks and stones at the base of a hillside. Strategically placed rock steps allowed friends and family easy access when they visited.

No one had said anything about the large cross or the many wreaths on display—or the wildflowers strewn across the area. Some of the flowers appeared to have been deliberately planted, and others appeared to be gifts from Mother Nature. Wild roses also grew rampant.

This wasn't a deserted mass burial ground. This was a well-tended and beloved grave site.

"This could be a problem," Jade noted.

The other team members murmured their agreement.

Dane asked, curiosity in his voice, "Why?"

Jade answered, "There's a difference between a mass burial ground and a beloved grave site. This place is beloved." She felt his hard gaze, wondered at it, then dismissed it as not her problem. She had her own issues to deal with.

"You didn't expect this?" Dane asked.

"No," Dr. Mike answered. "Not really. We've all seen large grave sites. Not all of them are a place of worship. Obviously people here, ... at least one person, comes on a regular basis."

"Possibly. I've never seen anyone though. Not that I've been looking."

Several of the team members stared at each other and then at him. "Are there other ways in and out of here?"

Dane shrugged. "Presumably. There's a lot of country here. I don't know all the access points."

"Have you heard anyone say anything against us coming here? We've tried to be low-key about our work but ..." Dr. Mike opened his arms expressively.

"Not everyone understands. My sister-in-law is one of those, but then she's pregnant, and everything appears to upset her lately."

Meg nodded in commiseration. "And she probably knows some of the people buried here."

"And, if she's Haitian," Dr. Mike said, in his professor voice, "her beliefs could be very strong about disturbing the dead."

Dane grimaced at both comments. "Both of those apply here. For myself, I understand. If my family were in here, I'd want to take them home too."

Bruce waved his clipboard to gain everyone's attention. "Right. Okay, everyone. I think we have a good idea of logistics. What we need to do is plan a workspace and see if we can get that much established." He turned to Dane. "Any idea who buried these people here? It would be helpful if we had some idea of how far down or in we need to go."

"If this is full, we may not have enough supplies." Bruce jotted down a few notes. "We can get more, if necessary. I'm concerned about getting mobile labs. It would be less disturbing if we could work here on-site. Otherwise we should look at moving the bodies closer to town."

Dr. Mike wandered the area. He studied the size and scope of the grave. "We've got several sites in town scoped out, depending on our needs. And we may need to use all of them. Depends on the number of bodies. After all this time, the skeletons *should* be clean. But we won't know for sure until we open the grave."

Jade suggested, "I don't know how feasible this would be, but one or two reefer trucks could work well. We don't want to disturb the locals any more than we have to. The temperature can be adjusted as needed, and it's a lockable mobile storage solution. If the bones are clean—and we won't know until we start—then storage won't be a problem. The remains can be kept in boxes in the reefer."

Bruce considered the options. "Tony has ordered body bags over boxes, considering the unknown state of the bodies. The clearing is tight but not impossible. At least one truck could be backed in there."

Body bags were more expensive, but, as cost wasn't an issue, she'd be happy to have them. Honestly, Jade could work with either. "Our labs could be along the same lines. ATCO trailers come to mind."

"That's what they used in Katrina," Meg said, her hands on her hips, considering the issue.

Bruce glanced at the clipboard in his hands. "We do have the use of a lab trailer used by past medical teams."

Knowing she had little to do with their setup's where and how, Jade clambered over the rock pile to read the inscription on the huge cross. Her French sucked. Meg hopped up beside her and translated it. "*To those who have gone this road before,*" she read aloud. "Weird."

"Different, certainly." Dane climbed the rocks to stand on a large boulder and to survey the rubble. "You'll need some heavy equipment," he noted.

"That could be fun. The town is strapped as it is." Jade wandered past several wreaths to another cross with the same inscription. Dane stayed where he was, but she felt his gaze on her back as she wandered.

"True, except equipment is available, if you know where to look."

She glanced at him. "Like from you? I believe you said you're in construction," she said politely. Jade turned around to see Stephen and Wilson, the lab techs who doubled as computer geeks and laborers, walking back toward the path.

Bruce joined them. "I think the question was lost earlier, so I'll ask again. Do you know who buried these people?" Bruce asked.

Dane fisted his hands on his hips. "Herman, a local, ran the front loader that made the trips here from the clearing, and my brother helped as well. Herman committed suicide a month later, and my brother's had a hard time ever since and refuses to talk about that time of his life. I'd like to avoid bringing him in on this, if possible. As I mentioned before, his wife is very against this project."

"Would you know how deep they buried them?"

Dane shook his head. "No. If I'd done it, I probably would have started at the path and worked in from the side. The original cave-in couldn't have been too deep or too big."

"That means there's probably no organization in the grave," Bruce muttered.

Jade hunched her shoulders. The bodies would have been tossed and crisscrossed as they landed. They could be dealing with one to ten at a time. "If we work in from one spot, instead of trying to expose the top of the grave, we might have better control on how many are exposed at one time."

"Except they'll just keep coming, … and we'd have no way to know whether we were gaining enough ground or if another year could be required. In fact, I think Tony—our boss back in Seattle—anticipated some sort of organization to the burials. Men to one side, children with mothers, … that sort of thing."

Dane grimaced. "Not from the little bit of information I've managed to get out of my brother. It was tough. The bodies were collected throughout town by trucks, then brought here, loaded in the tractor bucket, and dumped."

Jade nodded. "That's fairly typical. The town was lucky to have those two men take on the job. It's a hard thing for anyone to do."

Bruce put away his clipboard. "Let's head back to town. I need to make some calls and to see what we can do to get this moving forward. Jade, what about you? Any thoughts?"

"I think, if possible, we need to leave the space as close to the same condition as we found it. It won't be possible to replicate placement of the rocks and the flowers that will be destroyed. If I photograph the area before we begin, we can replace any items when we're done."

"Once we get into this job, everything will look different. Pictures would be helpful," Meg piped up, studying the grave.

"They are necessary actually. We always document everything—before, during, and after." Bruce motioned to the grave. "I'd appreciate it if you'd do the photography, Jade, as it would save me a job. Try to be methodical and do several panoramic photos so we can lay the photos out and see everything displayed at once. We might use the digital ones for mapping a grid even."

That made sense. Jade unpacked her Canon SLR and set about checking the light. She'd been into photography for years. Her hobby might help her get through the coming days.

The two team leaders left in one SUV; the others stayed on-site.

Jade lost herself in her art. *Click.* Twisting and turning. *Click.* Turning slightly again. *Click.* She regulated her movements and took shot after shot, as she systematically covered the burial site. The cross.

The wreaths. Another smaller wreath off to one side—older and mostly destroyed by the weather.

She went closer. *Click.* Walked close enough to lean over it and took a picture of the inscription, recognizing it as a repeat of what was on the others.

For all those who have gone before. Again. Now how weird was that? Maybe it was a common saying over here. It wasn't one she recognized, although it reminded her of an old *Star Trek* saying from TV. She grinned at her fanciful thought and continued to shoot the area.

"Are you done?"

Startled, she spun around and lost her footing. She ended on her backside, landing on a pile of small rocks. "Ouch."

"Sorry, I didn't mean to scare you." Dane stood above her, a large capable hand outstretched to help her to her feet. "Are you okay?"

"I'm fine." She scrambled up, ignoring his hand, and gave him a reassuring smile, as she stepped onto another rock, slightly farther back. "Rough ground, that's all."

"Plus, you were focused on your pictures. Did you find anything interesting?"

"Another cross, although it's older than that one." She pointed to the big one ahead. "Or made out of older wood?" she guessed.

"True enough. Supplies being as short as they were, I'm sure everything was commissioned into use."

She watched Dane bend down and read the inscription. "Interesting saying. I can ask Tasha, my sister-in-law, if she knows it. It might have special meaning to the region."

"Better ask someone else. She might get a tad upset, considering it's on this grave."

Dane winced. "Her brother works for me. I'll mention it to Emile."

Jade finished taking the pictures. She'd snapped her way through several hundred, without even thinking about it. Chances were, she'd only keep a couple dozen or crop out portions of some others. Thank heavens for the digital age.

Finished, she clambered down the rocks to where Dane and Meg were now talking. Jade swiped her cheeks and forehead on her sleeve. The heat would take some adjusting to. "I think that's got it."

"Good. Let's get to the hotel and check in. The others left already."

"Isn't it lunchtime soon?" Jade complained, her stomach rumbling on cue.

"Yes, and we'll need hours to set up and to consider how we want to establish a grid. We can check in, grab lunch, and come back later, if need be."

"Good. Hopefully they'll find a small loader. At least to take a layer off the top and to open one side. That's probably the best way to start, but—"

"That's in an ideal circumstance—which this isn't. A secondary grave is another option. I'll mention it to Dr. Mike and Bruce."

"It would be cheaper, if the numbers get out of hand."

Dane walked beside them to the SUV. "Tell Bruce, if he can't find a loader, I can rent him one of mine for a couple days—to get started."

Meg smiled. "Thank you. That's very helpful." She hopped in and closed the driver's door. Jade walked around, giving Dane a wide berth, and opened the passenger door. As she jumped in, she realized she'd lost her lens cap. She looked back frantically, as Meg started the SUV.

Dane held it out. "Here. You dropped this."

"Thanks." She closed her door and reached her hand through the window.

He dropped the cap into her palm. Their fingers brushed together ever-so-slightly. Energy sparked, like a static shock.

Startled, she pulled her fingers back and stared at him in surprise.

He grinned. "See you later."

Meg reversed the SUV and turned it around, then headed back into town.

Jade refused to look over her shoulder at him as they drove away.

But she wanted to.

Chapter 4

"**J**ADE? HEY, ARE you okay?" Meg poked Jade's jean-clad leg, as Meg drove the SUV away from Dane.

"I'm fine." Jade gave her a wan smile, hating the tiredness sliding through her body. She needed her strength back fully to deal with the job ahead. And she knew stress from the thought of coming back was the root cause. Food would help. And a good night's sleep. "I got a shock from his hand, when he gave me the cap."

Meg, her gaze back on the road, gave a half snort. "Not surprised. He couldn't take his eyes off you."

Jade snickered. "I doubt it. He was just being polite."

"*Uh-uh*. No way. That man is seriously hooked on you. His reaction was badass."

"Wow." Jade laughed, her spirits brightening. "I'd expect to hear something like that from a teenager. Sounds a little odd coming from you."

Meg relaxed slightly, the smile on her face natural and cheerful. "That's my inner child. Actually I can probably blame my nephews for corrupting me. They're all of thirteen and fifteen, and are they a handful."

Sinking deeper into the SUV cushions, Jade smirked. "Sounds about right. Kids are good for your soul."

"True enough. I'm just not ready to stop gallivanting around the world long enough to have any of my own. What about you?"

Jade's heart froze. A question she hadn't expected—but should have. Any one of the team might have asked this personal question, and Jade should have prepared an answer. Coughing slightly to cover her pause, she tried to joke about it. "No father to donate."

"I hear you. Who wants to be a single mother in today's world?" She tossed a wide grin at Jade. "I'm thinking Dane would be interested in that position."

Shaking her head, Jade let Meg ramble into a tale about her sister's first marriage that ended in divorce.

This area of Haiti was new to Jade, but it resembled every other part she'd visited. The same broken buildings dotted the landscape; the same weeds crept between fallen chunks of cement, and people navigated around as best they could. The same poverty coated the country, even here. So accustomed to the devastation, most people no longer noticed the state of their lives.

Sad but also reassuring. Life did carry on—in spite of everything. "People are resilient, aren't they?"

Meg glanced at her curiously. "That they are. Haiti is slowly recovering." She pointed to a group of laughing teens standing beside a broken wall. "Look at them. They're moving forward, finding a new normal in spite of what they've been through."

"*Hmm.* I found it hard enough to deal with life after being here last time. I came over on a mortuary team after the big quake. I thought long and hard before taking this job."

Meg smiled in understanding. "It would have been harder to adapt to the abrupt change from one situation to another. Staying here day in and day out, this would have quickly become 'normal.' For you, however, the contrast would have been unbearably hard to deal with."

"You have so got that right. What are you, a shrink?"

"Not really. However, understanding human psychology is paramount in my work." Silence filled the cab for several minutes, as Meg pulled the SUV into the hotel parking lot. "Coming here was probably one of the smarter things you've done, you know?"

Gathering her purse and camera, Jade paused to look at her. "How so?"

"Because you'll find closure this time." With that parting shot, she hopped out of the SUV and slammed the door.

Jade followed slowly. Closure would be good—on many fronts.

DANE STRUGGLED TO like his sister-in-law. He could give her some leeway because she was pregnant. A little more leeway for being upset over the current set of events with the grave, but how much leeway did she get before she came under the heading of disgruntled witch?

He was trying, honestly he was. He'd wanted to love her, to feel secure about John's future with her. Right now, every minute Dane spent with Tasha, she grated on his nerves something awful. He should move into town, give them more space. Living in the cabin at the back of the property and even having coffee with them was too close—for everyone.

Knowing Tasha and John wouldn't notice, Dane grabbed his coffee and slipped out to the patio to enjoy the cooler evening air. The sounds of their argument followed him.

"I don't care how logical it is. I don't want you to have anything to do with it. It's not safe. For you or for me."

"Tasha, I've gone over this several times. Nothing is dangerous in what they're doing. It's perfectly safe."

"Waking the dead is dangerous. This isn't just about you. You're putting me and the baby at risk—not to mention Peppe and Emile."

John, weary but so patient that Dane had to give him kudos for his superhuman effort, said, "I'm also not helping them. Dane will rent them a piece of equipment. That's all."

"And that's too much," she complained.

Dane turned and strolled down to his cabin. He'd heard enough. She could argue all she wanted, but he had no plans to rescind his offer to Bruce. Yet Dane understood the pain and the trauma on both sides. That wouldn't stop the job from happening, so he might as well help, so it could be completed faster. Then everyone would get what they wanted.

The deal would be done.

Besides, Dane wanted to get to know Jade better.

FOUR DAYS OF running around, trips back and forth, problems and tech trouble, and finally, it was the day.

Jade stood off to one side and watched as Dane navigated his smallest loader through the small spindly trees to the grave site. He'd wanted to be the one driving, in order to minimize the environmental damage. He had a good crew working for him. However, he insisted this location required his delicate touch.

It took two tries to navigate one corner to avoid cutting down a tree. Trees were no longer an abundant resource in Haiti, and so every remaining one was precious.

Dane backed up and wiggled the large machine in degrees, and, as delicately as diapering a baby, he maneuvered it to the right angle and swung right, onto the straight path.

Nice.

Jade watched him carefully take the machine to where the rocks met the path before shutting it down.

"Are we ready?" he asked, without getting out. "Has everything been logged, photographed, and removed?"

Bruce walked over and hopped onto the machine to speak to Dane, their heads bent together, as they discussed the plan of attack. Jade knew it would take the bulk of the day to remove the top layer off this portion of the grave. At that point, Dane would open a ten-foot-wide working space from the path side, and they'd work left to right until they ran out of bodies. At which point they'd move into the hill to look for the rest of them.

She knew all that, but it didn't settle her nerves at this point. Four of the team were scheduled to have the day off, but no one had taken it. They'd all showed up for this symbolic beginning.

Dr. Mike climbed on top of the grave, as high as he could stand against the hillside and started work on the project with a prayer. Everyone bowed their heads. Jade found herself repeating his words quietly in her head. *Amen.*

Dane started the loader.

It took almost an hour for him just to get a few buckets off the top. Meg wandered over to where Jade stood. "I'll head into town for lunch. How about joining Susan and me for a girls' afternoon of sightseeing and shopping? Nothing we can do here. Not today and most likely not until late tomorrow—if then."

It was a good idea. A little light relief before the real work started tomorrow. "Now that sounds great."

With a wave of her hand to the men, Jade followed Meg and Susan. Jade could really use some lightweight work clothes. She'd forgotten how badly the heat affected her here. T-shirts and shorts were the uniform of choice; a half dozen of each would be perfect.

The women headed for the Iron Market and the few shops open along the way. The elegant mansions and townhomes spoke of days gone by. Once glorious in their regal bearing and bright colors, these buildings had taken a major knock from Mother Nature. Still, even with the damage from the earthquake, Jacmel was a tourist destination like no other. At least here, obvious revitalization attempts to get the city back on its feet were seen.

The afternoon zipped by at a rapid pace—full of shopping, laughter, and fun as the women ran from shop to shop and stall to stall, buying a few items to make their job a little brighter and more comfortable. Jade was delighted to find several brightly colored T-shirts and cotton pants in a beige-khaki color. They would withstand a lot of wear and tear. At one brightly festooned stall, she found several hair clips, big enough to hold her heavy blond hair off her neck.

If she'd had a little longer to prepare and to pack, she'd have gotten a haircut. As it was, the clips would do for now. She could always get it cut here, if she couldn't stand the heat. Meg's short brunette curls looked perfect. And Susan's fine black bob that stopped at her chin also looked comfortable.

"Now that has to feel better." Meg patted Jade's hair clip. "Nice. Now I almost wish I had long hair myself. Almost." She grinned and picked up several clips. "I bet my sister would love a couple."

"Later, when it's time to go home. Too much to pack this early."

"You're right." Meg put it back with a sigh. "Too bad though."

As they headed back to the SUV, Susan stopped at another brightly colored stall, one festooned with odd-looking handmade dolls. An old short and squat woman—wearing so many necklaces, they almost obliterated the sight of her red blouse underneath—worked at the booth. The woman's black gaze latched onto Jade and never let go.

Jade moved to the other side of Susan in an effort to get away from that piercing stare. And came too close to the weird-looking straw and cloth dolls. She noticed the papier-mâché looking ones painted in black with weird markings ... and many other items she couldn't begin to recognize. "What are these things?"

"Vodou paraphernalia."

Jade shuddered and took several steps back. "Not for me, thanks."

Susan shook her head vigorously. "No. You don't get it. This stuff is for good luck. Used to ward off bad spirits."

With a second shudder, Jade moved several steps back, shaking her hands in front of her. "I still don't want one."

Susan grinned and plucked her choice off the top of the stall. "Well, I do. Just what we need for the grave work."

The transaction was done in silence. The old woman accepting the money never took her eyes off Jade. Unsettled, Jade did everything to avoid her. She wished Susan would hurry.

Finally they were done, and Jade turned to leave. The old woman moved off her stool so quickly that Jade never would have believed it possible, if she hadn't seen it herself. Before Jade could back away, the old woman grabbed her by the arm.

"Danger stalks you. You see it, but you don't understand it. Careful. Or you will join those who have gone before." She dropped Jade's arm and returned to her stool beside her cart.

Jade froze. So shocked and horrified by the crone's touch, Jade hardly understood what the old woman had said.

Meg grabbed her arm. "Come on," she hissed. "Forget about her. Let's get back to the SUV."

Susan snagged Jade's other arm, so the three walked back, linked together.

"That was too weird," Meg said. "I'm glad you got a doll, Susan. Good luck is just what we need."

JADE HAD HOPED the odd event would be over once they'd left the market, only Susan mentioned it at dinner that night.

"No way. She actually used *those* words?" Wilson stared at Jade curiously.

"Yeah," Meg confirmed, with a delicate shudder. "That so upped the freaky factor."

"This old lady never said a word to me the whole time I was buying that thing, and she never looked at anyone except Jade," Susan complained.

Dr. Mike studied Jade, his gray eyes serious. "She didn't bother you, did she? The Haitian culture is full of various superstitions. Their belief system is littered with them."

"It was kinda weird, although nothing I can't handle," Jade said casually, cutting a piece of fish, hoping her nonchalance satisfied their intense looks.

"We need to find out what that phrase means."

Marie, the hotel night manager, walked in to ensure everything was all right and to see if they needed anything. Bruce brought up the old woman at the market and her prophecies.

After quickly crossing herself, Marie stared at Jade. "Magrim. She is very well-known. She is very wise. Very accurate. Ms. Jade, you need to be careful." Crossing herself again, she almost ran out of the dining room.

Silence filled the room. Not a person clinked a fork or spoke. Everyone stared at Jade.

She was compelled to break the uneasy silence. "*Great.* I always wanted to be famous. Hadn't planned on it happening this way."

"Well, I don't believe in that stuff. The old woman was just trying to scare you into buying one of her dolls."

Jade brightened at Bruce's words. That actually sounded reasonable, as street sellers would do anything for a sale. Everyone resumed talking at once. Thankfully several different conversations took flight, and the awkward moment passed.

Dinner finished with coffee outside and an update on the day's progress at the burial site.

"So we should be ready to get started by about ten. We have one reefer trailer set up to receive bodies already. The lab trailer is to be delivered early in the morning. If the weather is cooperative, we might do some work outside. I presume you've determined a system of some sort for working through the numbers?"

"Somewhat," Meg answered. "Although that'll be a work in progress."

Susan asked, "What about DNA testing? I know we'd hoped to find a lab here—"

Bruce shook his head. "They can't handle it here. We'll ship the samples back to Seattle for testing."

Sinking farther into her chair, Susan winced. "I'd hoped we'd get results faster than that."

"We can only process the bodies as fast as we can. Then it's up to the lab. At least they'll go to a private lab."

"Does Haiti have a database of survivors' DNA? Some way we can test the dead against the living?"

Stepping in, Dr. Mike said, "No. They don't have that capability or the resources. Bruce asked the local authorities to put out the word that anyone interested in locating their loved ones needs to come and give samples at our local clinic we will set up soon. We'll have the samples shipped to Seattle, typed, and the results entered into our own database, hopefully to match with that of family members."

"If we rebury all of them before we have the results, they may have to be dug up again. That's not good."

Bruce nodded. "We'll give Jade's suggestion to give reefer trucks a try first. The decomp should have the bodies down to just bones and teeth by now, but it's never that clean."

"Even then, decomp inside the bones will continue beyond a visual examination. So we're better off with refrigeration capabilities." Jade smiled apologetically. "As a backup, an alternative burial site would be good."

She took a sip of water, thinking. "Because we're processing everyone in that grave, it'll take time. It would be much easier if we were just looking for say, … an adult female and a female child. Then the others could be moved to one end of the grave as we sorted through them all. As we're processing everyone, well, it'll be more complicated."

His grin flashed.

Jade hadn't noticed how personable Bruce was. That head of red hair and beard surrounded a smile that offered quick praise. A nice man. She grinned back.

The discussion moved into logistics. As they returned to their rooms for the night, the old woman crowded her way back into Jade's mind. What had her words meant?

She walked over to her bags and pulled out her laptop. She turned it on and opened a Word document. She realized something was beyond prophetic about Magrim's words. Repeating them aloud, she typed. "*Danger stalks you. You sense it, but you don't understand it. Careful. Or you will join those who have gone before.*"

Scary shit. She sat back and studied what she'd written. Just what did Magrim mean by them? No doubt in Jade's mind that the old woman thought she had seen a vision of some kind. Or she was a very good fake.

What danger stalked Jade? And was it a coincidence that Magrim had used some of the same words that were carved on the crosses at the mass grave?

Chapter 5

THE NEXT MORNING Jade immersed herself in work in the lab trailer. She set about organizing a viable production line plan. DNA samples needed to be taken, along with photos, and then identifying marks must be charted, plus measurements and dental impressions. She could hope the work on each case would take approximately two hours, though possibly twice that long would be required. Really no way to know until she started. They would also need help moving the bodies from the grave site to the lab trailer and to the reefer or from the reefer to the lab trailer, if the team became backlogged.

Had Bruce considered labor—as in hiring a couple young men to help with the physical moving of the body bags? She wasn't expecting them to be heavy, but they needed to be held together as much as possible. She'd have to remember to ask him.

They had ninety body bags stored under the trailer. It was anybody's guess whether that was enough or not. If the body count were higher, and the bones completely clean, then the surplus skeletons could be packed in boxes. She wasn't expecting them to be that clean though.

Finally, as organized as she could be, she stood in the lab trailer and surveyed her workspace. There wasn't much. No air-conditioning. No heat. No power. No running water—that was an issue. Antiseptic smells permeated the space after her major scrubbing session. No microwave or coffeepot. Even she'd been perturbed by that. Everything else needed for a lab was here.

This was definitely a case of making do with what they had. What she needed now were bodies.

She walked to the front steps and stood outside. The forecast for heavy rain hadn't come through. Thank heavens. Things were rough enough now, but hurricanes, floods, or another earthquake would shut them down—not to mention what it would do to the Haitians who were barely surviving now.

"Jade, they're getting close," Meg called to her from the path.

"Coming." She locked the trailer—without knowing why—pocketed the keys and raced over. Two security guards were posted today, just in case the locals decided to lodge an on-site protest. So far only Dane was here, working the tractor.

Good. She wandered in closer. Dane had sliced the top off the burial mound and had taken a good ten-foot-wide chunk out at the path. He'd also gone in a solid six feet.

He waved, nimbly backed out the machine to one side, and shut it off. Opening the door, he hopped down.

Bruce walked over to Dane, and Dr. Mike joined them.

Meg nudged Jade, and the two women headed over to see what the discussion was.

Several men, locals from the look of them, came out of the woods with shovels in their hands.

"What's up?" Jade asked.

"Dane says it's time for shovels." Dr. Mike walked around the backhoe and returned with two shovels in each hand.

Jade grinned and put her hands behind her back. "Never did find a shovel to fit my hand," she explained.

"Well, you could always try one of these. … However, I'm sorry to say, I don't have enough to go around." He laughed and handed out shovels to Bruce, Stephen, and Wilson. Dr. Mike kept one for himself. "The hired help are only here for today to help us cut down the top. Then we're on our own."

Jade walked over to the newly dug space. Uneasiness rested heavily on her shoulders. Her gaze landed on the cross laid carefully off to one side, until they were done. Magrim's warning came to mind. Jade shivered, her apprehension growing about this massive grave that she hadn't felt before.

She'd worked for morgues and labs for years. She'd seen plenty of Death's work. Too much.

On every project an initial sense of awe, a respect for the dead, was recognized at the moment just before starting work. This respect was healthy and comforting.

Today was different. When Jade thought about the task at hand, instead of awe, her feelings resembled dread. She didn't know why. She only had the old witch woman's words to blame.

"Ready?" Dr. Mike stood beside her, surveying the rocks. The odor creeping out of the ground told them what they would confirm within minutes.

"Sure. Why not." She stepped off to one side and took a closer look at the pile in front. She frowned.

Red. Just a small amount tucked between rocks on the left.

"What's that?" She stepped forward and bent down.

"Here, let us in. We've got the tools." With gloves on, two men stepped forward to move boulders, while two others used shovels to move the smaller stuff out of the way.

It took a good ten minutes to open the space.

They'd found their first set of remains.

Everyone stopped, and heads bowed for a moment of silence. Then, in unspoken accord, those in the business of identifying the dead began their work.

The portable stretcher stood nearby, with an unzipped body bag on top. The red was a T-shirt, holding a set of ribs more or less in place. The rocks were removed completely, before the body was shifted. Even then the hips and leg bones separated inside the crumbling shorts. The skull—tufts of black hair plastered into the dirt—sat nearby. For the most part, Mother Nature had done a decent job. Most of the bones were bare. A few ligaments and tendons vainly tried to connect the bones, and the odd clump of tissue was exposed.

"Glad to see the condition this one is in. Won't help with identification, however."

"Yeah, I didn't expect much would be left by now in this climate." Bruce slipped a hard plastic sheet under a foot in a fairly successful attempt to keep its bones together. He moved it carefully to the body bag and came back for the second one. "The first one is always the worst."

"*Hmm.*" Jade couldn't agree more and was relieved to know the general condition of the bodies they'd be working with. Much easier to detach emotionally and to get on with the scientific duties when decomp was this far along.

"There, I think that is it."

Bruce already had a second body bag out for the next that lay directly under the first. And it went that way for hours. Body upon body upon body. Even standing at the open slash in the earth, Jade could see no less than seven skeletons exposed, or partially exposed, in the open air.

Nothing to do but continue to dig in.

She came to a stop several hours later, when a bottle of water was shoved in her face.

Jade straightened, groaning at her screaming muscles. "Oh, thank you."

"We have to drink lots of liquids. We're not used to the climate here." Meg was sweating profusely, as she took a long drink of bottled water.

Jade sat down on a large rock to unscrew the sealed top and tried to settle her queasy stomach. She drank half the bottle in her first drink. Wiping her mouth, she grinned at the look on Meg's face. "I just streaked dirt-turned-mud across my face, didn't I?"

"Absolutely." Meg's face shone through a layer of dust. "You look like the rest of us."

"And we all look like we've been playing in the sandbox."

"At least we've gotten a good start this morning." Meg sat down beside her. "Bruce has gone to town to pick up lunches for all of us. He's planning for the hotel to provide bagged lunches, if possible, starting tomorrow."

Jade shrugged. "As long as there's lots of it, I don't care where it comes from."

"You do like your groceries, don't you?" Meg shook her head and laughed.

"Yep." Speaking of which, she reached into her pocket and pulled out a badly melted chocolate bar. She ripped it open and took a decent-sized bite, licking the melted chocolate off her fingers. Meg just stared. Jade offered the bar to her.

"No, I'm good. Besides, lunch is on its way."

"Just not fast enough." Jade alternated chocolate with her water, and, by the time she had reached the end of both, her stomach felt better. She'd been fine for the first hour; then the smells had hit. The queasiness grew after that. Add in the heat ... and she had a problem. Meg's water break had been timed perfectly.

"Ready to do a bit more?"

Jade tilted the bottle for the last few drops and stood. "Yes. Let's get this last one over to the trailer. Enough people are here that we could start in the lab this afternoon."

They walked over to the men, where Dr. Mike zipped a body bag closed as they arrived. "Hello, ladies. This is a small one. Can you move it?"

"Absolutely. When you say small, are you saying a child?" Jade refused to look down on the bag, her gaze locked on Dr. Mike's dirt-smeared face. He looked ready for a break too.

"Yes. The third one so far. All three females."

Jade pursed her lips. What ages were they looking for again? Tony had mentioned something about it back in Seattle, but she hadn't been the most clear-headed then. "And we're looking for a six-year-old female, correct?"

Dr. Mike nodded. "Yes. And the mother was twenty-eight and the father, thirty."

Jade tucked away that information for later. She bent down and lifted one end of the stretcher. Meg grabbed the other end, and they headed to the reefer, as the call came that lunch had arrived.

JADE WIPED THE sweat from her forehead. The sheer physicality of the job wore her down. After lunch, she'd returned to the burial site to help with the excavation. Many bodies were falling apart, as the team sifted through the pile, and the most important thing was to move the exposed ones.

Another three must be moved before they could close off the area again. In theory, the best approach would be to finish the bodies they already had in the trailer, before digging up more.

"Another hour with any luck." Bruce grinned at the look on her face. "I'm hoping we don't find more spare parts at the bottom."

Jade shook her head. "I know. That last couple appeared to be a lot of puzzle pieces and not a whole lot of cohesion. It won't be easy to find and match all the corresponding parts."

"We can only do the best we can." Bruce carefully laid out another body bag and started to place the uppermost skeleton inside the bag. "At least this one appears complete. I think the last one is still missing the right hand."

"We'll find it."

They worked companionably for the next hour. Finally they opened what should be the last body bag of the day. At least she hoped it would be. She was more than ready for a hot shower and something to breathe other than the smell of death. Her back ached from the constant bending. The end of this workday couldn't come fast enough.

Digging deeper into her reserves, she helped Bruce pack the last exposed set of bones. The two of them carefully lifted the rib cage and carried it to the waiting body bag. Straightening, she couldn't hold back a slight moan.

"Long day, huh?"

She offered him a tired smile. "Yes, but productive." Turning back to the grave, she lifted the left leg, and it separated from the knee in her hand. "Damn."

"It's been happening all day. Most of these at the bottom don't even have connective tissue."

"I shouldn't have picked it up that way. Just tired at this point." She wiped her forehead on her sleeve, grateful for the easing of the afternoon heat. A breeze had wafted through the valley earlier, but that had long disappeared.

"To be expected. I'll get the rest of this." Bruce motioned to the big rocks. "Sit and take a break."

Jade dropped her head back and stared at the blue sky. It had to be close to six o'clock. She closed her eyes for a long moment and took several deep breaths, hoping for a second wind.

Opening them again, she watched as Bruce carefully retrieved each tarsal and metatarsal lying loose on the ground. *Almost there.*

God, she couldn't wait to leave the site. She stared down the path toward the trailers. Another fifteen, maybe twenty minutes, and they would be on their way.

"There, that should do it."

She gently laid the tiny bones in the body bag and zipped it closed.

"Come look at this." Bruce frowned at her. "I know you're tired. Lord knows, so am I. Only ... I'm not sure this is the last one." Bruce bent over the grave site, slightly to the left of where they'd plucked the last skeleton.

"Another one?" She knew it made sense for another one to be exposed, considering how many could be in here, and she knew they couldn't leave it that way.

"I think so. Only it's a layer down."

An odd silence filled the air. She studied the frozen look on his face. "Bruce? What's the matter?"

"We'll see in a minute." He stood and took a smooth stride—one she resented after the way her body was reacting—and snatched up a shovel. He gently dug into the ground near the foot. He didn't attempt to remove dirt; instead he wobbled the tool back and forth several times and gently lifted dirt from around the foot.

The small rocks and gravel on top fell away. The bone shifted slightly to one side in the rotted too-large sandal. She leaned closer to get a better look and realized she was blocking the light. She climbed around to the other side, taking a wide path to avoid disturbing the shifting ground. "Would they have put a layer of dirt in *after* they'd put in so many bodies?"

Bruce didn't look up. "I don't know. The dirt could just as easily have fallen in on top from the sides, as the loader moved back and forth with each trip." Bruce put the shovel in a new spot and wiggled the dirt again. "There. Do you see what I see?"

Jade bent down and brushed the dirt away from the skeleton with her gloved hand—her fourth or fifth pair of gloves today.

Bruce knelt across from her and carefully removed the dirt from his side of the foot.

She did the same on her side. She gasped, leaning closer. "What," she whispered, "is that?"

"I'll remove a bit more, and then we'll see for sure."

She waited and watched. Her stomach churned. She worried her bottom lip, hating the silence that had fallen. The breeze had whistled over and around the hill for most of the day. And when the wind had calmed, birds or small animals rustled in the undergrowth. She stood to stretch out the kinks and glanced around. The place was deserted. Silence had fallen on the valley, a silence that only highlighted the sound of gentle scrapes of spade on rock.

The shadows lengthened around them. Jade swallowed hard, grateful she was here with Bruce and not Meg. Something about a strong male presence made her feel better. Not that she was a wimp. However, right now, tired and worn out, she felt that way. "And?"

"Almost." He eased away some more dirt and shifted around slightly to attack the mound from the other side.

She stepped out of his way. "Where did everyone else go?"

A laugh escaped him; he stared at her, his big grin splitting his dusty face.

She couldn't believe he hadn't shaved off his thick red beard. That had to be hot as hell.

"They've probably gone back to the hotel to grab all the hot water before us."

She groaned comically, happy to have an excuse to ease the tension twisting inside. "They would too, wouldn't they?"

"Hell yeah." His boisterous laugh rolled across the rocks. "Hold on. Almost done. ... And I'm sure the hotel is equipped with enough hot water for us."

"I'm not so sure. If you're wrong, you're sacrificing your shower for me."

He grinned. "Like hell—" His voice cut off in shock.

She heard a weird jangle and dropped to one knee beside him to peer at the mix of bone, cloth, and … Her breath caught. Her mind rebelled. She whispered—barely loud enough to be heard—"*Dear God.* What is that?"

"Look for yourself." He pointed where the tibia widened at the end. A few ligaments still connected to the foot were now slightly askew inside the shoe. Bits of cloth clung to the ankle and footwear.

Oh God. Her stomach heaved uncontrollably. Jade lurched off to one side, where her lunch made a hasty exit. After a long moment, when she was sure no more was to come, she spun around to face Bruce.

He waited for her, a worried look on his face. "Are you okay?"

She glanced back at the leg bone. She didn't know how to answer.

A chain lay twisted around the lower leg of the female skeleton.

Securely attached at the ankle was a rusted iron … manacle.

Chapter 6

T HE DINNER CONVERSATION rippled on around Jade, as if she were a mere rock in a swiftly flowing river. That suited her. Mental exhaustion and stress had added to her physical deterioration during the day. Numbness had settled in.

"Hey, Jade, tough day? You look like you're ready for bed."

With a wan smile in Susan's direction, Jade couldn't help but agree. "That's where I'm going after this."

Dr. Mike studied her face in concern. "Don't overdo it out there. You're more valuable in the lab than doing grunt work."

Keeping an eye on the staff was part of his job, so Jade didn't take his comments too close to heart. He was a compassionate man, all too willing to help out himself, if need be. "I hear you. We've reached the point where I'll be in the lab from now on."

"See that you are."

Meg gave her a curious smile. Jade didn't know whether she should mention what she and Bruce had found or not. She shot a questioning look at Bruce.

He shrugged, then began to explain. "Part of the reason for her fatigue is the emotional stress caused by the last victim we found—after everyone else had left."

Bruce directed his comments to Dr. Mike. "We left the last set of bones we found, in the ground, covered with dirt and rock. We needed to consider the situation before proceeding. I believe this is an adult female. The shoe is still there on the foot. We don't know about other clothing. We only uncovered a foot and ankle." He put down his fork and took a long drink of water.

Watching him closely, Jade empathized when he swallowed heavily.

At the site, the horror and implications of what they'd discovered had quickly overtaken them both. They'd covered what they'd found and had then left—silently. They'd not spoken of it on their way back and had separated at the hotel entrance to get showered and ready for dinner.

Jade glanced around, noticed that the room reserved for their meals had a door that could be closed. Hopping up, she walked over. She realized no one was close enough to hear them, yet felt compelled to shut it anyway.

Bruce waited until she'd retaken her seat. He gave her a nod of thanks and elaborated. "This discussion stays with us. It's possible we'll have to bring the authorities into the mix, but they may also not have the manpower nor the interest in pursuing our findings."

"Like what?" Susan leaned forward. "Tell us. The suspense is killing me."

"The woman we found had a manacle and chain attached to her ankle."

Jade had to clarify. "She'd most likely been a prisoner at the time of her death."

"What?"

"Good Lord."

Everyone sat back and stared, their gazes going from Jade to Bruce. Both nodded.

"Now you understand the problem. We need to figure out our next step," Bruce said, before taking another drink.

"Are we thinking she was murdered?" Meg's gaze stared at Bruce.

Bruce shook his head. "We can't say that—at least at this point. And, although Dr. Mike is qualified to make that determination back home, we have no authority here."

"Besides, she could have been killed by the earthquake or an infection, like any of the others. She might have been a prisoner. That doesn't mean the person responsible …" Jade added an afterthought, "… killed her. She could have been chained in a basement or shed and died in the earthquake—the same as everyone else buried here."

"Is it really possible that no one noticed the chain when she was thrown in?"

"Definitely—and there could be several legitimate reasons for that, including the time of day she was placed in the grave, where she was found, and even who found her. She might have been wrapped tight, concealing the chain." Bruce lifted his coffee cup and took a long sip. "Or no one cared. Think about it. If you have a woman chained somewhere, and she dies in a natural disaster, what will you do? You still have to dispose of the body. You still have to do it quickly, and, for all we know, this person lost other people too—ones he cared about. There was essentially no law at the time, no one to care what you did."

"God what a horrible thought." Meg shuddered. "Remember that serial killer, John Gacy? Didn't he bury a mess of boys in his basement and around the yard? What if this guy was a serial killer? What if her 'owner' was killed in the earthquake too? Anyone finding her wouldn't have understood or known what to do. They'd have been all too happy to dispose of her body, where no one would ask questions," she added, with relish.

Jade winced. "What better place than a mass grave where every-one is more concerned about expediting the burial of the rotting bodies and where no one is checking to see what killed them?"

Dr. Mike held up a hand. "Whoa. That's letting your imagina-tion go way too far. All we know is that this woman was buried with a chain around her ankle. Now Haiti has some pretty disturbing rituals and beliefs when compared to Western ways, and we can't just jump in here and assume foul play. Maybe by burying her with a chain, someone was hoping to keep her soul chained here."

"Not that that is a great improvement, but I take your meaning. We can't assume anything at this time." After that, Jade stayed quiet and listened as the conversation rose and fell. The various hypotheses and suggestions kept them all busy.

They might not have the facts; still, Jade didn't need anyone tell-ing her that this was bad news. She already knew it was.

Whoever that woman was, she hadn't had an easy ending to her difficult life.

SEVERAL DAYS LATER Dane drove up to the lab trailers and parked. He waved at Bruce, who stood outside the reefer truck, then walked over to see him.

"Hey, Dane. Good to see you. I wanted to thank you. Using your heavy equipment definitely lightened our load and improved the process."

Dane smiled at Bruce—an amiable caring person doing a very difficult job. So far, Bruce had done well keeping the lid on this project. Dane had heard only minimal grumbling about this place among his workers. Dane had stopped by to see how the team was progressing. And maybe check on Jade.

He asked, "How are you guys getting along with the language?"

His own French was only passable and his Creole—a gibberish mixture of Spanish, French, Portuguese, and English—was just about as bad. If it weren't for his English-speaking foreman, he'd be hiring translators. Thankfully enough English was spoken here that Dane could get by.

Bruce grinned. "I'm amazed at how easy it is to understand the locals with a little bit of this and a little bit of that. I would have said I was only fluent in English, except I did take French and Spanish in high school. Who'd have thought I'd remember any of it?"

"Wish mine were better. Any trouble with the locals over the grave?"

"Everything is quiet—just the way we like it. We're hoping our free medical clinic in town will appease some of their worries. Plus we are willing to help out the locals with identification and burial of these people in any way we can. The DNA testing will take some time though, especially without DNA donors from surviving family members." Bruce shrugged. "Since when did anything like this go quickly?"

"I can't imagine the cost myself."

"No, but, if I had the money, and one of my family were buried there, I'd understand spending it this way. I lost my sister to leukemia years ago, and it gave my mother unending comfort to go to her grave to visit with her. She still makes the weekly trip, even though we lost my sister a dozen years ago."

Dane walked over and sat down on the boulder beside Bruce. "Understandable."

"Absolutely. We've pulled out over fifteen so far and are processing as fast as we can. Hopefully families will step forward and help us identify these people and give us direction for reburial. Otherwise, the remains will be reburied here." Bruce waved his hand toward the grave. "Maybe they'll erect a more formal monument, although I don't know. ... The people here live simply and don't need the same trappings that Americans tend to feel are necessary."

Dane studied the view in front of him. Peppe, Tasha's father, lived in the original Jacinte homestead just on the other side of the large clump of trees on the left. Dane couldn't help but wonder what the old guy thought about Bruce and his team's quest or if Peppe even understood what was happening.

Dane nodded. "Haitians have strong beliefs, though life here is basic. More about survival than anything else. I'm a little more sensitive to this issue as my sister-in-law is beyond distressed about this whole thing. Because she's pregnant, no one wants to upset her."

Both men shared a commiserating glance.

"Yeah, don't have any kids myself," Bruce replied. "However, some women go through pregnancy just fine, and then a few seem to change personalities over the nine months. Easy to see something like this tipping the balance."

"Right now," Dane explained, "my concern is more for my brother's sake than hers. Maybe that's not fair, and I'm sorry if that comes across as harsh. Tasha's personality shift in the last week or two makes it hard to be sympathetic." Dane grimaced. Talk about an understatement. "That sounds cold, and I don't mean it to be. My brother, John, he's being incredibly patient. Still, I don't know how long he can handle the tension. I would have said something way before this. Guess that's why I'm not married."

Bruce chuckled. "Yeah, me too."

Not knowing how to broach the subject, but really wanting to know the answer to the question that plagued him, Dane asked, "So … are other members of the team married? Can't be too easy to do this job and to leave a family behind." He bent his head to study his shoes. And waited.

"No one is married, though having a committed relationship is a big help for individual members when it comes to dealing with this type of work. I believe the easiest way to deal with death on a regular basis is to have a way to affirm life."

Bruce studied Dane's face, his grin widening. "Just for your information, all three women are single, and, although Meg, the tall brunette, appears to have a long-term relationship, she jumped at the chance to come here."

Dane smiled slightly.

Bruce continued, his voice light and tinged with humor. "Now Jade, the short blonde, appears to have a solemn attitude toward life, and I don't believe she is in a long-term relationship. … And then there is Susan—our bubbly black-haired technician. She's also single."

Dane almost winced. Damn, Bruce appeared to be really enjoying this. "Well-put about Jade. Life appears to be a serious business to her."

"Yes, she's quiet, yet focused and dedicated, and I love workers like that. She's determined to do right by everyone in that grave and to find each of them their home."

"*Hmm.*"

"She could do with a bit of cheering too. So if you want to stop

DALE MAYER

by her trailer and say 'hi,' feel free. Isolation isn't good for her. She tends to be a loner most of the time anyway. Hard to break her out of her shell."

Trying for a noncommittal shrug of his shoulders, and knowing he'd failed, Dane gave it up. Pretense wasn't his style anyway. Besides, he really wanted to get to know Jade better. He stood. "Good. I'll stop by there after I'm loaded."

Dane walked away, aware Bruce watched him. Bruce was just looking out for his team. Was protective of them. That was fine. Dane could handle a little scrutiny. He had nothing to hide.

THE SOUND OF heavy machinery broke her concentration. Jade lifted her head from her workbench and frowned. Was Dane here?

She paused to straighten, wincing as her back crackled and popped. She needed to change the height of her worktable, or she'd resemble a hunchback by the end of this job.

At the open door, she watched Dane maneuver the big machine onto a trailer he kept parked here. He made it look easy, as he handled the equipment. As he hopped out, she gave him a small wave.

"Hey," he said in greeting. "Didn't expect to see you here." He walked toward her, that long loose-limbed stride eating the distance in seconds.

She watched appreciatively. "This is where you'll find me most of the time. The others will come and go from the hotel and the site. I'm likely to be a permanent fixture here."

"How are you making out?" He peered around the corner of the door. "Dark in here."

She stepped out of the way, so he could get a better view. "I have lights, only they're not very bright."

He shook his head. "You'll go blind in here over the long term."

A small laugh escaped. "Good thing three months isn't that long. I was actually hoping to move some of my work outside if I could, only that's not practical. There's no standing room, let alone a large enough deck or tables out here."

He backed up several feet, then walked around outside, looking at the simple plywood steps leading to the doorway. "*Hmm.*"

Jade walked down the steps and joined him, facing the trailer, trying to see what he saw. "*Hmm*? What does that mean?"

"I have a small portable porch with steps that attaches to my work trailers—for when we're on-site. It's not pretty, and it's really only meant to provide a bit of extra space, but it's handy. I could exchange your steps for that set." He walked closer, then glanced at her. "With a sheet of plywood on top of the railing you'd have a workspace. Not pretty but …"

Waving her arms around the area, she pointed out, "Do you see anything pretty here? The conditions are rough, but our equipment is top-notch."

His face lit with understanding. "That's all that counts. The job isn't nice to begin with, so get in, get it done, and then get out, right?"

She smiled. "Right."

His gaze stayed on her face longer than necessary.

She flushed at the naked appreciation revealed in his gaze. It had been a long time since she'd seen that kind of look in a man's eyes. She kinda liked it. Actually, she liked it a lot. A shy smile slipped out.

His gaze deepened, warmed. After a long moment, he cleared his throat. "You should get out for a walk every day too. Being inside with poor light like that, well …" He frowned at the dim light showing from the doorway of the trailer.

"Thanks, *Dad*."

Her teasing tone wiped the frown off his face. He laughed. "Ouch. I guess I deserved that, didn't I?"

"Maybe." She enjoyed the bantering. "Well, maybe not. You are closer to my brother in age."

"Well, thanks for small blessings." He studied her face. "I tell you what. I'll forgive you if you let me buy you a coffee."

She felt her face warm. Inside she was delighted at both the invitation and the idea of a fresh brewed java. "Coffee? Is there a place to get a decent cup?" Maybe staying here for three months wouldn't be such a hardship after all. Her smile brightened.

"Ah, there is, if you know where to find it. It would be my pleasure to introduce you to the pleasures of Jacmel."

She laughed. "I can't wait."

Chapter 7

JADE WATCHED AS the truck and trailer, loaded with his machinery, pulled slowly out of the clearing. With the lab trailers parked as close against the rocks as possible, she figured Dane had almost enough room to make the turn in one go. Again his smooth exit showed his exceptional handling skills.

She hated to see him leave. At the same time, he confused her, stirred feelings she hadn't expected to feel, ... at least not here. Not now. The competent air he projected was seductive. That wasn't unusual; power in all forms attracted her.

A year ago she'd lost her own power. She was determined to make this trip work. To regain her power. To regain herself. To regain her soul.

Dane seemed understated, simple, exuded quiet control—a man to have in a tight corner. A man who wouldn't walk out and leave someone hurting.

The opposite of her fiancé.

Ex-fiancé. She doubted Dane would have trouble making simple decisions in life. Like what to have on a pizza or where to go for a special meal. Her ex would whine for hours when she brought him in on the little decisions. However, when she dared to have an opinion on more important things, like the type of vehicle she'd like to buy— watch out. He'd thrown a hissy fit over that and had stomped her choice into the ground. She'd shelved her decision on vehicles. Good thing, ... considering.

She knew her brother hadn't been impressed with her choice of a partner, and thankfully Duncan hadn't dared to comment when that same partner bolted.

Her mental state wouldn't have withstood the criticism from outside herself.

How had so much changed in a week? She now sat out in the countryside of Haiti—a place she'd sworn she'd never return to—was active in a job she also thought she'd never have accepted, and had actually studied the muscular butt of one of the most attractive men she'd come across in weeks, make that months. On top of all that, she realized she hadn't cried since leaving home.

It was hard to admit, but she'd been so ensconced in her private prison, she hadn't realized that her prison had been a safety net to stop her from stepping back into the real world. She had needed that time ... in the beginning. But she'd been more than capable of moving on months ago. Instead she'd chosen to stay a prisoner in her own shell, rather than face the real world. How long would she have stayed there, if not for Duncan and this job?

She returned inside to continue her work with the adult male currently on her table. Meg had taken DNA samples earlier, while Jade did dental impressions. The body had been checked and charted, photos taken. This skeleton was complete. The victim had been wearing socks, heavy in nylon, encased in runners of some synthetic material that had helped hold the feet together. This male was young, maybe nineteen or twenty. He'd suffered a break to his right arm a long time ago.

Jade recorded everything she could see to identify him. A few personal effects found near the remains would go down on his chart but would also be entered into a main database in case they weren't his. The skeletons were so fragile that rings fell off fingers and the contents of any pockets could have fallen through to the body below, as the material holding them decomposed.

He'd had no wallet, watch, keys, or cell phone. Then again, most bodies had been stripped of anything useful. She'd seen that on her first visit. Pillaging had been rampant.

Straightening, she reached for her checklist and marked off the last few items. Everything would help family members, when trying to recall identifying marks and characteristics of loved ones.

As she slowly packed the remains back into the black body bag, she carefully checked the bones for other breaks or marks she might have missed the first time and added those to the chart. Once everything was back in the bag lying on the cart, she rolled it over to the door for safekeeping, until someone else came to help move it to the reefer.

In this way, she could operate on her own for a long time.

She had a second bag ready and waiting on the other side of her table. After opening the bag wide, she pulled the ends of it down over the stretcher's sides and started laying out the bones of a small girl on her table. She grabbed a new numbered checklist and wrote that same number in white permanent marker at the top of the body bag.

And started anew.

It wasn't just a slow job. She would also call it a careful one, particularly when she could be looking at one of the three people destined to return to Seattle. A child's skeleton lay in front of her, the bones clean and bare.

She quickly determined the child was female, and the skeleton was relatively complete. She'd been wearing a sundress in a red to orange color. Jade grabbed a magnifying glass and used it to identify stars on the material. She made a notation of it, added a quick sketch to her page, before beginning the slow job of cataloging the details of the child. Her left leg was broken, most likely as a result of the earthquake, and her skull showed a small fracture on the left side.

Jade spent the next hour learning every detail she could from the small skeleton. She found a piece of plastic between the largest toes on the right foot and not on the other. Her best deduction, based on the bright blue color of the plastic, was that the child had been wearing flip-flops at the time of her death. Testing for these details wasn't an issue on this job. No money. No time. No need.

Footsteps approaching the open door were followed by Meg's cheerful voice. "Hey, how's the work going?"

Jade smiled at her. "It's moving. Not too quickly. I'm trying to be really thorough, so I won't have to do this twice."

"I hear you there. The smell isn't too bad in here." Meg dropped her purse over by Jade's on the corner of the counter. Her light sweater was dumped on top. "Have you done the dental impression?"

"Nope." Jade looked down at the body on her table. "That's next."

Scooping up gloves on her way, Meg walked toward her, her work boots clumping on the thin floor. "Right. Then I'll work on the DNA, while you do that. Is the rest done on this one?"

"No." Jade reached for the silicone, then walked over and made the dental impression. "I'm not sure why we're doing dental. How many of the kids here would have been to dentists?"

"Lots of them. Especially our girl. She had X-rays done when she visited her grandpa last time. They'll be used to confirm identity."

"Makes sense." The two women worked together silently, until each finished the job at hand.

Jade grabbed her checklist for the little girl and marked off the completed steps. "Okay, she's done too." Writing out a toe tag, she attached it with an elastic band around the bottom of the small tibia and zipped the bag closed. She'd deliberately placed the bones at the top end of the bag and rolled the excess plastic up at the bottom.

Working with bags was different than with boxes. When she could, she laid out the remains properly and folded under the spare plastic. It felt better to her. More respectful. Plus this allowed for immediate visual confirmation of a child.

Not everyone's system ... but this worked for her.

Grabbing the cart, Jade pushed the stretcher toward the door. Meg walked behind her. "Let's move her first."

Lifting gently, they transferred the two sets of processed remains to the reefer truck. Inside the truck, they shifted the little girl first. Jade had added a simple system to let them know, without opening bags or searching for charts, that this was a female child. They would try to keep females on one side and males on the other, with children separated off as much as they could—given they didn't know how the population would break down into each demographic until they were done. Lifting the second body bag, they placed it on the male side of the refrigerator truck.

Like everything here, their system had to be flexible. The conditions were rough, and they didn't have the amenities they'd like to have. As Jade checked her marking system to ensure it conformed, she asked Meg, "How are the men doing?"

"Dr. Mike is ranting that he needs to get into the labs, but he's been busy securing more equipment for us. Bruce and Susan have been in town all day at the clinic, and Stephen and Wilson were at the site, shoveling to remove more of the top layer."

"Good. Stephen's doing the database too, isn't he?"

Meg nodded.

Jade was quite good with databases. In fact, she half expected those skills to be called into service soon.

Meg frowned, brushing a hand through her curls. She rearranged the body bags, until she was happy with them. "Are you ready? We can take one back now, if you want."

Jade looked at her watch. "When, what, and how are we getting lunch today?"

"I think bagged lunches were supposed to be here. If not, I can bring something back for you. I have to run the morning's samples to the refrigerator Bruce had delivered to the hotel."

They checked but couldn't find anything edible on-site. Once Jade realized it would be at least an hour before she could eat, she suggested, "Let's move another body bag into the lab. I'll keep working until you come back to feed me." She patted her tummy, a big grin on her face.

Meg shook her head. "You and your stomach."

Jade flashed her coworker a big grin again. "Hey, I lost a ton of weight when I was here last time. I can't afford to lose any more."

"I'll say. You're too thin now. Are you sure you don't have worms?"

The discussion degenerated from there, as they laughed and teased each other. But they transferred another bag onto Jade's table, using the portable stretchers. Right now, it looked like the reefer truck system might work out fine.

Stephen and Wilson had taken over looking after the reefer trucks—with a maintenance guy at the end of the phone, should they have trouble. They had a backup generator large enough to handle any issues, should a problem arise. On top of their temperature concerns, condensation was becoming a problem.

At that thought, Jade checked the temperature gauge outside the reefer truck. It was normal. Good thing, considering the daytime temperatures of Haiti. She frowned. "Have to keep an eye on the temperature."

Meg stepped over. "True, but it's fine now."

They returned to the lab. "If you want to grab those samples and go, I'll get to work on the next one."

"What you mean is, I should go grab *you* lunch. The samples could stay here a little longer for all you care." Meg shook her head. "As if I don't get your ploy."

"I imagine Stephen and Wilson must be starving too."

"Not likely. You're the only one starving around here." She looked toward the grave site. "I suppose I should check with them." She shook her head. "Ten years of postsecondary, another eight years of valuable experience, and I'm doing lunch runs."

Jade laughed. "And just think of the wage you're pulling in to do them."

"Good point." Meg strode down the path, her tall slim frame disappearing quickly out of sight.

Jade turned back to her lab, wishing they had the databases set up already. Database work was Stephen's domain. Still, Jade had to handwrite, then enter each chart, and she found she missed her email access out here. The computers with internet were at the hotel. She'd seriously considered upgrading her electronics before leaving Seattle but then decided that the reception could be hit-or-miss on location, so had decided not to bother.

Frowning, she stood at the door to the lab and surveyed the long narrow room. The room would do fine for now. Just as her return to Haiti was working out fine.

Surprisingly.

She'd been busy enough that she hadn't had to worry about depression or grief overwhelming her. The team had been overwhelmingly accepting. Jade no longer worried about her placement here. She belonged. This had been the right decision. If she'd realized a change in focus would allow her to heal, she might not have wasted the last six months of her life.

Jade grinned. She missed Duncan. She'd make time to send him a long email tonight. He had to be worrying about her. She'd come a long way toward recovery. Sure there'd been some back-and-forth with her emotions. They could flare at the oddest times, but she was fine right now.

He deserved to know that.

EMILE HAD CALLED in sick for work today to check out the grave site and damn near shit his pants when Dane pulled in here. Damn good thing Emile had hidden behind the trees close to his father's cabin. This end of the property was heavier in vegetation than the rest, being part of the original plantation. He'd planned on just checking out the mass grave, seeing what they were doing.

He'd spied two men working on the burial ground with shovels. He shuddered. No way he could do that job.

Then he'd seen the tall brunette drive off, leaving the little blonde to work all alone in a small trailer with only one door.

Alone. In Haiti—where the normal trappings of civilization had been stripped clean, where animal instincts were laid bare by the destruction. Sure, some of those trappings had been quickly replaced but only by some. Others had reacted wildly to the chaos—like during wartimes—raping the women they could and killing others over food. Life had gone animalistic in those first few weeks. They'd calmed down some—actually a lot. But that didn't mean any of the men had forgotten that feeling of being what they truly were. *Predators.*

Leaving young, pretty white women alone and unprotected? Now that was asking for those predatory instincts to go on a rampage all over again.

From what he'd seen, it looked like Dane had his eyes on the little one. Emile had watched the two of them when they were talking outside the trailer. The little one was skittish, but Dane was making all the right moves, moving slowly, staking his claim.

He could appreciate that. Besides, Dane *was* the boss. He should have first pick.

That left the tall one for him.

He couldn't help himself; he licked his lips and watched, as she walked along the path and clambered over the rocks to where the two men were shoveling. Both greeted her as he'd hoped. Just casually friendly. *Good.* No sign of proprietary ownership. *Idiots.* They worked beside two single women and hadn't he seen a third the other day? He cast his mind back, pretty sure he'd seen a darker-haired woman with them too. Although he didn't know that any were single. Not that it mattered for his purposes.

Honestly, if a man couldn't protect what was his, then he deserved to lose it.

And the woman? Well, according to his father, she didn't get a say in the matter.

Chapter 8

THE NEXT MORNING Jade decided there was no use putting it off any longer. She needed to work on their *prisoner girl*. The authorities had come, had had a long talk with Dr. Mike, taken a few notes and pictures, and then left.

At that point, the woman had been removed from the grave as carefully as glass slivers from skin. Jade had documented every step, taken photos at each stage. It was only right that she continue the job. She knew how to follow procedures, but she wasn't a forensic anthropologist like Dr. Mike. Someone told her that he'd also worked for a dozen years as Chief Medical Examiner in Dallas. She doubted there was much he hadn't seen in his career.

Taking a deep breath, she pulled the cart to her worktable and gently unzipped the body bag. The remains had been wrapped in something at one time—a sheet maybe. Almost nothing was left now.

Using her brush, she cleaned off the top of the body and was struck by the feminine bits and pieces of material that emerged. Bits of pink ruffles, pink pleats in the skirt—stiffened and dried—its original prettiness now a macabre imitation. Jade grabbed her camera and started taking pictures, while the body still remain in the bag. She'd taken several at the grave site, unable to throw off the concern that this was a crime scene—maybe not a killing site but definitely a dumping site.

She worked steadily for several hours.

"Hey." Meg walked into the room, a brown bag in her hand, and a tall take-out cup in the other. "Wow, it's warm in here. I brought food."

Jade fired a wide grin at her. "Great. I'm starved."

With an eye roll, Meg said, "See? I didn't even make you ask today. Besides, Dr. Mike and Bruce are looking at the grave site. They'll be here over lunch too."

"Oh, good. I have our poor prisoner girl on the table. I'm hoping for a few more answers when I consult with Dr. Mike."

"Interesting." Meg stepped over to stare at the skeleton. "She looks young." Pulling on gloves, Meg bent over, then gently opened the girl's mouth to check her teeth. "Full dentition with the wisdom just crowning in the back. She could be anywhere from twelve to eighteen for that matter. How is the fusing of the bones?" She took a magnifying glass to the radius. "Not fused at the bone plate yet." Checking the cranium next, she straightened and frowned. "Cranial sutures are still evident."

Meg glanced over at Jade. "I'm thinking a female, a teenager, approximately fifteen to seventeen years of age. Pretty rough sutures at that."

Jade pursed her lips. "That matches my guess."

"Interesting age."

"Especially here. Girls are often married by then."

Studying the bones, Meg asked, "Is she complete?"

"Yes. Appears to be." Jade tossed her gloves in the garbage. She pulled a Sani-Wipe from the dispenser and cleaned her hands thoroughly. Then, opening her brown bag lunch, she pulled out a container with rice, beans, and vegetables. She dug in. It was food, hot and tasty. They'd been offered sandwiches for lunch, but the team preferred to eat local fare. Turning back to Meg, Jade pointed out the remnants of the clothing she'd removed from the skeleton.

Meg let out a long whistle. "Pleats. Wow. I'm guessing it's the multiple layers of synthetic clothing that kept those from deteriorating."

Jade shrugged. "Possibly. I can't analyze the material properly here. However, it looks that way. No jewelry on the body."

"Interesting." She bent over the head area, then reached out a finger and checked the collarbone.

"Broken and healed."

"Agreed."

Jade munched happily. When her food was gone, she reached into the bag and pulled out a banana that she finished in six bites. She peered into the bag again, hoping for something else.

"I guess we need to get you a double-size lunch from now on." Laughter filled Meg's voice.

Catching her humorous look, Jade smirked. "Good idea." She tucked the container back in the bag and put it by the door.

Meg shook her head. "I'll work on getting the DNA samples and might as well take the dental impression too—unless you want to?"

"Go for it. I'm still charting."

"Right. We're hoping to take over the extra dining room at the back of the hotel for a communication room."

"Yeah, that side of the work is backing up." Jade motioned to her laptop, open and running, beside her. "I just emptied my flashcard, so I can take more pictures. I'll need hours to go through the ones I've already taken."

Meg studied the small workspace Jade was bent over. "Maybe we should have one person working in the lab in the morning, while the other does the computer work, and then switch?"

Jade walked around the small space, as she considered the options. There weren't many. "The thing is, I'm not sure anyone should be left alone out here for long periods. I'm not worried about being alone, but it's just common sense to stay together. And, if we're in pairs, we need to make them useful working pairs."

Meg cast a glance through the open door. "I'm not sure we should ever work alone. Sometimes it's like I'm being watched. It's a weird feeling."

Jade glanced up at her, then at the open door. She shrugged. "It could be the locals watching what we're doing."

"True enough." Meg reached for her tools.

The afternoon passed quickly, as they figured out a rhythm to sharing this space.

Working on prisoner girl took longer, as they used tweezers, brushes, and magnifying glasses most of the time. They needed to collect all the evidence there was. Once completed, they replaced her carefully in the same bag—after they'd upended it, just in case they'd missed anything. The bag had been empty, and Jade made a note of that on the chart. The two women then moved her to the reefer trailer.

Jade stood and studied the layout. It was anyone's guess if they had enough space for the contents of the mass grave.

At the sound of an engine, they both walked outside. "Looks like Dane's here again. What's he got in the back?"

Dane, driving a full-size black pickup, backed toward the lab trailer, kicking dust everywhere.

The women retreated slightly. Jade coughed once, then took a drink from her water bottle. "Oh my gosh. He mentioned something about exchanging our small steps for a big deck he had at another site. We were discussing the lack of natural light in the trailer and how nice it would be to do some of the work outside. Fresh air and all that." She tried to make sense of the jumble of wood in the truck's bed.

Meg dropped her gloves on the stretcher. "And it looks like he's a man of his word. Got to love that."

"And he's not alone."

The two women waited until the truck stopped, before walking over to see who'd come with him. Dane hopped out, looking devastating in jeans and his snug T-shirt, rippling across his chest. He smiled. "As you can see, I didn't forget."

"Thank you. I'd forgotten about it." Jade smiled at the silent Haitian by his side. He was smaller than Dane, dustier, with dark skin. "Hi."

He inclined his head but stayed silent. His black eyes watched her closely. She walked over to Dane.

Dane shot her a look. "I hadn't." He walked around to the back of the truck and dropped the tailgate. "They're in several interlocking pieces." He studied the set currently on her lab trailer. "Emile, give me a hand moving these out of the way."

The women stepped back to stand in the doorway while the two men lifted the old set of steps and moved it off to one side. Unloading the largest piece of the new set first, they butted it up against the trailer. They then grabbed the second half and lowered it into position. Large squares of decking were laid down on top.

And just like that she had a small porch. Jade bounced on her toes. "Is it safe to stand on?"

"Absolutely."

DANE WATCHED JADE run up and down the steps, like a kid at a new playground. And all because of such a simple thing. Her lab coat bounced as she moved. She had to be dying in the heat with jeans and a T-shirt underneath. But then, in her place, he would also want an extra layer or two between him and the skeletons she worked on every day.

She laughed.

He grinned. Good. She was way too serious. If something like this gave her a kick, then he was all for it. Meg followed Jade to stand on the little deck. It appeared bigger with the two women on it.

"Will that work for you?" Dane asked.

Jade smiled, and her eyes gleamed. "Thank you. This will work nicely. If I do nothing more than stand here and grab fresh air and sunshine for five minutes at a time, it's a help."

"Good." Motioning to Emile, they lifted the small set of steps and loaded it into the back of the truck. Dane walked to the front of the cab and opened the door to retrieve something. He turned around, a big grin on his face, his hands full.

"And speaking of coffee …" He held out two large take-out cups. Steam rose from the small opening in the top of the lid.

"*Ohhhh*." Delight lit up their faces.

He grinned as the women almost danced in place. "See? I keep my promises."

"And that makes you a very special soul." Jade accepted a cup and sniffed the small vent. "Wow. What is this?"

"It's a Haitian version of a cappuccino."

Jade inhaled again. "Really? Where did you find it?"

Dane grinned. "I told you I would show you the hidden gems of this area."

"Hidden is right." She took a tiny sip and sighed happily. "Thank you. It's lovely."

Dane held out the second cup to Meg. "Are you also a coffee fanatic?"

She accepted the cup gracefully. "I enjoy it, but I'm not crazy like she is. And I only eat a quarter of what she does."

"I'm not that bad." Jade smiled at Dane. "Don't let her scare you."

Dane walked back to his truck. "It would take more than a hungry female to scare me off."

Stephen and Wilson came around the corner of the rocks, dust covering their weary faces. They waved cheerfully. When Stephen spied Emile, his smile became more formal. He walked over and held out his hand.

"Hi, I'm Stephen."

Emile reached out and shook his hand. "Emile."

"Hey, you're Dane's brother-in-law, right?"

Emile frowned and glanced over at Dane.

Grinning, Dane answered, "He means you are related to my brother's family. The answer is yes, Emile is Tasha's brother."

"Ah." But Emile didn't smile with understanding.

Stephen stepped back, as Wilson walked over with a bottle of water in his hand.

Dane watched as each person spoke. Emile, like his sister, Tasha, was quiet—reticent with strangers. Still, he handled himself well in this context. He didn't exactly smile; he did, however, gradually lose his stiffness.

Dane turned his attention to Stephen. "Is Bruce around?"

Stephen shook his head. "Bruce has gone to the authorities to update them on the progress here and to let them know about our clinic opening in town, giving free doctor's visits and hoping to get people to agree to giving a DNA sample, so we can match some of the victims."

"Clinic?" Emile struggled with his English, so Stephen explained. A strange look stretched across Emile's face that had Dane wondering, … but Emile was a simple soul, so Dane let it go.

Though apparently Emile wasn't as simple as Emile's father, Peppe, whose mental health had deteriorated rapidly over the last few years. The necessary level of care was not available here for someone like him, and, according to John, Tasha wouldn't let Peppe go to a home anyway. Emile was supposed to take care of his father now. However, according to John, that wasn't happening.

Dane hated it, but it wasn't his place to interfere. He'd made his opinion of the situation clear. To no avail. He'd rather eat a bullet than sit in his own shit though.

Another reason to go home soon. It wasn't in his nature to let an injustice like that go on and on.

Neither had it been in John's nature years ago. What had the ensuing years done to him?

SITTING IN THE truck on the way back, Emile cast a wary glance at Dane, his boss. Questions burned in his mind. Only he didn't want to cross that invisible line between boss and employee. "Now those are good-looking women."

Dane tossed him a grin. "They are, aren't they?"

"Smart to help out. I would too." Emile twisted in his seat to stare out the back window. The women were gone from view. He turned around as the truck approached his home.

"Nothing stopping you. You live right around the corner from the site. Although I guess they aren't always there. And you work elsewhere." Dane nodded and turned a sharp corner.

"Exactly. You're the boss. You can come during working hours. Emile has to come after work, when women are long gone." He grinned. "Maybe Emile needs to stay home sick."

Dane laughed. "Well, at least I'd know where to find you to haul your ass back to the job." He shifted gears and made a right turn to John's house. "Those women are hard to ignore."

"Me, I like brunettes. Tall brunettes." Emile grinned.

"Me, I like blondes. Short, tiny blondes."

Emile laughed, a hoarse roughness to his voice. "Then again, I like all women."

As Dane pulled the truck to a stop in front of the main house, he smirked. "What's not to like?"

Emile hopped out and headed inside for dinner. He knew what there was *not* to like.

Women who didn't know their place.

Chapter 9

U NLOCKING THE LAB door, Jade accidentally swung her laptop bag against the side table as she entered and jarred the microscope. "Shit."

She'd woken late, barely made it for breakfast, and still hadn't gotten on track for the morning. She'd also been shortchanged on her coffee, and that was bad news. For everyone.

The air inside was stifling, so she opened the door wide. Sighing, she dumped her bags down on the floor and walked over to turn on the lights.

She frowned and looked around the lab. *What was different?*

Meg had been the last to leave and had closed the lab yesterday. It didn't feel like the same lab at the moment. *How odd was that?* The tools weren't arranged as Jade would have laid them out. Neither did her chair sit where it normally sat.

Was it because she hadn't been the last one here yesterday?

Must be. The door had been locked. She walked over to check the door mechanism. It didn't appear to have been touched or tampered with in any way. The windows had been left open though. Normally they closed and locked them when they left. The equipment inside was expensive and could be hocked for some serious money, if someone knew where to sell it.

They'd been tight with security on the first couple days. Then, when problems hadn't developed, they'd grown lax.

That needed to change.

A proverbial list maker herself, Jade booted up her laptop, then opened a new document to create a checklist for opening and closing the lab at the end of the day. She couldn't print it off here. That would have to wait until she returned to the hotel.

Dr. Mike showed up an hour later, coffee in his hand. But only one. "You dare bring java in here and not bring enough for everyone!" She shook her head in disgust.

Solemnly he held the cup out to her. "Actually, it's for you."

Shamefaced, she accepted the treat. "See? That's what happens when I'm deprived in the morning. I turn into a real bitch. I am sorry."

"*Nah.* Figured you'd run late this morning. Besides, I'm here to go over our prisoner girl. Can you point her out for me? I'll have Wilson give me hand bringing her over. Also," he said, looking around, "is there a space in here for me to work?"

"I'm just finishing this boy, and I need to enter the information into the computer, so this table will be clear in a couple minutes."

"Perfect." He nodded. "I'll grab the others to give us a hand when you're done."

Jade quickly cleaned off the table and brought out the prisoner girl's chart. They really should have some name for the poor woman. Jade pondered that for a second, remembering the plants flourishing around the grave site. She smiled and gave the prisoner girl the moniker of Rose and wrote it on the chart.

Stephen and Wilson entered, carrying Rose.

Grabbing her laptop, Jade headed to the far end of the trailer and tried to focus on her own work. It was hard to ignore what Dr. Mike was doing though. Not that there could be much to say about the condition of a body after an earthquake.

An hour went by.

Finally she couldn't wait any longer. She wandered over to his end of the lab on the pretext of grabbing her forgotten water bottle. In the silence, every move she made sounded extra loud. She waited impatiently, hoping he'd notice her presence. No such luck. She had to ask, "So did you find anything?"

"*Hmm.*"

She stared at his bent head, then leaned in for a closer look at what he was studying. "What's that?"

"Good question. The chains weren't put on after her death, as someone suggested. In fact, I'll say she'd been wearing them for a while."

Jade's stomach dropped. *Uh-oh.* She waited impatiently, until she couldn't stay silent any longer. "Anything else?"

"Lots. But not necessarily conclusive. See here?" He pointed to the neck area. "Her neck was broken."

"Which could have happened during the earthquake."

Dr. Mike bent for a closer look. "True enough but the hyoid bone has been crushed, and that's usually caused by strangulation."

Jade swallowed. Hard. "What about other injuries?"

"I'm working on it."

"Right."

Stephen blasted through the doorway, wide-eyed and gasping for breath, his emotions ravaged by ... something.

Jade shook her head, as she went to his side. "Stephen, talk to me."

He took a deep breath, as Dr. Mike joined her.

Stephen struggled to breathe normally. "You need to see this."

Dr. Mike raised his brows. "All right. Let's go."

They exited the small trailer and headed toward the path.

"Hey, where are you all going?" Wilson called out from the reefer truck. He slammed the door closed, turning to face them.

Pointing to the grave site, Jade said, "Stephen found something he wants us to look at."

"I'm coming too." Wilson jumped down the steps, then raced to catch up.

The grave site looked the same as always when they approached. In fact, she'd half-expected to see natives, lodging a protest over their arrival or something, given Stephen's reaction.

"It's over here. I wasn't sure when I first started. Now there can be no doubt."

Frowning, they gathered around the spot in question. A path had been dug through the pile, almost to the other side. Enough to be sure that no other bodies were in the heap of rock. After opening the grave in the middle, the plan had been to dig out the lower part of the pile on the left, until they'd found everything to be found, then move to the right side.

Remains lay exposed.

"What am I looking at?" Jade asked in confusion.

"Exactly the question I was hoping you'd answer for me," Stephen demanded, explaining further. "I found more skeletons. But cleaner, older, deeper in the ground than the others we've found to date. These appear to have been covered by a thick layer of dirt and rocks. As if they were in a layer below the mass grave."

Dr. Mike shrugged his shoulders. "Some of the dirt would have slid down on top of the first bodies when they were dumping in more. This was done in a hurry by people without the skills to do it right. Hell, they might have done that deliberately, if there were a break between loads of bodies. That would actually be practical. They would have to keep the predators out somehow."

"True," Stephen agreed. "But why would these victims dumped in here be so clean and be buried with chains?"

Chains?

The color bleached from Dr. Mike's face. He could barely get the words out. "More? Are you saying that you've found *more* people with chains on them? This doesn't make sense."

"It does if you don't look at this simply as a pile of earthquake victims. Sorry, but what we have here is no longer so simple."

Jade bent down to take a closer look. Stephen had opened a six-foot square. The remains and dirt had long married together into a brown sandy mess. Only the white of bones showed.

Coiling away from several of the bones were rusty-linked rings, ending in thick manacles.

Jade stared as Dr. Mike pointed out at least two sets of links crumpled in and over the top of each other. "We'll need to treat this site carefully."

Dr. Mike nodded. "Still, chains are not definitive proof. Again we can't let our imaginations run away from us here. There are possibilities other than foul play." He sighed heavily. "However, I'm really struggling to find a good one. ... I think this should wait until Bruce returns. We'll need to treat this as a potential crime scene—just in case."

Jade cringed inside. She wished there was another way. "And how about an expert on Haitian culture? Surely we can ask someone about this."

Stephen snorted. "Be serious, Jade. What can *we* ask? This isn't exactly the type of question that you ask to start a conversation. *So ...*" He mimicked a heavy Texan drawl, as if he were asking the authorities, "*Do you keep your whole family in chains—or just the women?*"

Jade winced at the images that refused to stop prodding the back of her mind. "I had worse thoughts going through my head." She took a deep breath. "I was thinking of the sex market. What if someone kidnapped young women for the slave trade in Asia or Malaysia?"

All the men stopped and stared at her.

"Now that's not a nice concept." Wilson ran one hand through his dust-covered hair and stared at her. "Why would you even think of something so nasty?"

"Because it's a huge problem. We all want to bury our heads but, just because we can't see it, doesn't mean it isn't happening all around us. After a disaster like what happened in Haiti, children were snatched off the streets, and, as always, young women are the prime victims."

"And this is as good a place as any to stop." Dr. Mike stepped in as the voice of reason. "No way to know exactly what we have here, not until we remove everything and analyze it."

"Just in case, we need to photograph this site and all the stages of our work here, until we have these bodies out and safely inside." Jade faced Dr. Mike. "Speaking of safe, has anyone considered security on the site, while we're working here?"

Stephen said, "Bruce requested more money be budgeted for security. I don't know what the end result is. Why?"

Looking around, Jade shrugged self-consciously. "I don't know if there is foul play involved here or not, but if people hear about what we've found …"

Dr. Mike clambered over several rocks. "You think that the person responsible might find out? That's highly unlikely, isn't it? Not everyone knows what we're doing."

"Sure," said Stephen. "About as likely as finding a bunch of chained women in a grave intended for victims of an earthquake disaster."

Jade stood up. She glanced back toward the trailers, barely visible through the rocks. "Bruce said he'd be here around noon today." She took a long drink. "He was hoping you'd have information on Rose, that first woman with the chains."

"Right. That's why I'll go work on her right now." Dr. Mike rotated his shoulders.

Closing the lid on her water bottle, Jade nodded. "And I'll photograph what we have so far here. Then, when Bruce arrives, we'll proceed."

Relief lit Dr. Mike's face. "Good plan."

Jade walked down with him and retrieved her camera. As soon as she returned to the grave site, she adjusted her camera for the light and started with close-up pictures from all sides.

Stephen watched her for a few minutes. "Fine. I'll grab a bottle of water then. The dust here fills my lungs and dries my throat."

"Grab me one while you're there, please." Jade focused and shot, changed her position and did it all over again. She tried not to think about the poor people in front of her. But her mind twisted through the endless possibilities. How did they end up in chains?

The stillness around her settled in. Jade felt as if she were being watched. She glanced around, wondering how long Stephen had been gone.

Weird. She continued to photograph their findings. Then, because she couldn't get the feeling out of her mind, she refocused her camera and started taking pictures of the surrounding woods. Just a nice series of shots showing that no one was there. By the time she turned back around again, Stephen stood beside her, grinning.

"And you are doing what?"

She smiled. "Sightseeing."

JADE STUDIED THEIR new communications room at the hotel and immediately laid claim to a small portable table, where she set about creating a workspace beside the window that overlooked the gardens. This space was a hell of an improvement. It was twice as large as the space they had before, boasted big bay windows that let in lots of natural light, and came with several large tables. Bruce had decided that they needed a more secure area at the hotel for work. This had been the perfect solution. Nice.

Now if only there was an answer to the on-site security issue.

Knowing she needed as much computer time as possible, she focused on her charts, as the others moved around her.

"Couldn't find yourself any better spot to be in the way, huh?" Bruce grinned at her, pointing to the empty bookshelf along the wall behind her.

"Nope. Figured this offered optimal irritation."

"You're probably right." Stephen came over and dumped on the floor a large box of binders, destined for the bookcase behind her. "When you get a chance, you can put these on those." He patted her gently on the shoulder, before disappearing again.

She shook her head and entered the information Dr. Mike had added to Rose's file. Holding the chart in her hand, she puzzled over the handwritten notes. Dr. Mike's writing was damn near impossible to read. He also didn't do computers well. But, according to all accounts, he was a hell of a doctor.

"Hello, Jade. How are you?"

Surprised by the strange voice calling out to her, Jade glanced around and frowned. *Accountant Tony.* She should have expected to see him at some point. Still, his arrival on their moving day was a surprise—just not a good one. Though their relationship had been civil so far, she hadn't been at her best during their first meeting, and he hadn't been enthusiastic about her joining the team. He'd been desperate to complete the hiring quickly and, with Duncan's urging, had finally agreed to give her the position—with a warning he'd be keeping an eye on how she handled the job.

Still, she was here. And that made him her boss. "Hello, Tony. I didn't know you were coming."

"I'll be in and out several times over the next few months."

She smiled politely. That made sense. A lot of money was being piped into this recovery. "To be expected."

"How are you handling your job?"

Was there something off in his voice? She studied his face, looking for anything other than general interest. "I'm doing well, thank you. The job is interesting, and, once we get properly set up, I can see we'll make a lot of headway."

"Are you finding it difficult to be here?"

Raising one eyebrow, Jade shook her head slightly. "Not at all. Haiti has moved forward—plus the job is *very* different—not many similarities between the two experiences at all." She shrugged her shoulders. "Things are good."

He appeared to be about to speak, then thought better of it, and left. She stared at the empty doorway for a long time.

Had he told anyone about their first meeting? Maybe not all of it, but someone must know to keep an eye on her.

She would appreciate it if her problems stayed private. But then Tony had a job to do too. Did he consider her a liability? Or was he just checking in on his investment?

Retrieving the chart again, she held it under the light to try and decipher Dr. Mike's notes.

It took almost as long to do the charts as to process each body. But when *didn't* paperwork take longer? She searched through her downloaded picture folder to locate the ones for Rose's case file. Jade attached over forty, wanting to be thorough, in case the police followed up. She finally turned to the last file.

Where had everyone gone?

"Are you done yet?"

Dressed in a long brightly colored cotton dress, Meg looked so relaxed, so beautiful, Jade sighed. She wished she could wear dresses like that. But she was so short, and the longer dresses only made her look shorter.

Then her eye caught sight of the wonderful ice cream and banana concoction in Meg's hands. Jade straightened, her stomach growling. "Is that for me?"

"Hell no." Meg laughed and took another bite. "Go get your own."

"Where? Are you guys eating without letting me know? I've been working hard in here."

"It was lunchtime a good half hour ago. Your stomach always lets you know."

Jade checked her computer. "Shit. I almost missed it." She bolted to the dining room, followed by the sound of Meg's laughter. Jade heaped her plate with something that looked like fish again. The rest of the team sat, eating and talking around tables. No one had made a new place for Tony, so he'd picked Jade's chair. *Of course.*

Shrugging it off, Jade took the only spare chair, Meg's spot, and focused on the food in front of her.

"Hungry?" Tony asked curiously, watching her eat.

She couldn't be eating that much more than everyone else surely? It only looked bad because she was the only one with food on her plate. She nodded and ate several more bites. She had taken rather a lot.

"Jade has a healthy appetite." Bruce smirked. "I think she eats more than me. And where she puts it, I don't know."

That started off a major joking fest—with Jade being the brunt of it. She took it good-naturedly. As it was, even with all she'd been eating, she could swear she was losing more weight, or her shorts had stretched. Not good. The weight loss might be because of the high temperatures here. She didn't know.

As long as she didn't get sick, she didn't really care.

"I think she has worms."

Shocked, fork halfway to her mouth, Jade stared at Stephen in astonishment.

"What? That would be the first thing I'd have checked." He grinned at her. Then forked a large bite into his mouth.

She gasped mockingly, "Are you implying I'm a bitch?"

"Well …"

Snatching up her napkin, she crumpled it into a ball and threw it at him. "Be nice."

He held out his hands. "Mercy. I wouldn't think such a thing, honest."

Jade rolled her eyes at him and finished the food on her plate. Replete, she pushed back the empty plate and sighed happily. Then she finally clued in on the conversation around her. Bruce had stopped in to speak to the authorities. "What did they say?" Jade asked.

"In short, they don't want to hear about supposition. If we have any proof of a crime, then we're to contact them, but otherwise don't bother them. I'm not surprised actually. They're swamped with more pressing problems."

Dr. Mike interjected, "I think their resources are stretched to the max. They have their hands full, dealing with current crimes instead of possible crimes from a year ago—if not longer."

Bruce agreed. "Exactly. They did say that chains are not part of any Haitian burial tradition—to their knowledge."

Surprise lit Susan's face. "Here I was so sure it was an after-death ritual."

"Apparently not."

"Do we proceed as if this is a crime scene?" Stephen asked, a frown creasing his forehead.

Studying him, Jade realized she'd enjoyed Stephen's company these past weeks. He was her age, and, unlike Bruce and Dr. Mike, who were her superiors, Stephen was easy to talk to. She could see a nice friendship developing here.

"Why is one way different than another way?" Tony asked, not at all happy with the situation. "We're not here to solve crimes. We're here to find the remains of this man's family members and take them home. Quick and simple."

Jade had been on the verge of saying something but closed her mouth. She didn't want to rock the boat. Tony was right. CSI personnel they weren't—and he paid the bills. She winced. True, they couldn't justify spending more time on the manacled bodies than on the others, but, if they didn't, who would?

"Someone needs to consider these people." Wilson lounged back in his chair, his face a study of exasperation and anger. He glared at Tony. "We understand that you and your clients are footing the bills for this job, but, from the first, our understanding was that we'd do what we could for the others in the grave as well. Surely, being as meticulous as possible isn't beyond the scope of our job? Reporting a crime scene and possible victims shouldn't be either." A small tic played at the corner of his mouth.

Jade held her breath, waiting.

"As long as they are given the same consideration as everyone else and not costing additional monies to process, then there is no problem," Tony said stiffly.

"And if a little more money is required to properly process these people, then what?" Wilson challenged.

Jade winced at the aggression but agreed with her team member.

"I can't okay any expenses that aren't within the parameters we first set out," Tony responded primly. "Bruce knows exactly what those are. I expect him to enforce those limits."

Bruce grimaced. "Thanks for passing the buck."

Tony stood. "I have no intention of doing that. Just make sure you don't either. You are all here to do a job for my client. That is all. Nothing more and nothing less. The other people in that grave are to be processed, entered into a database, and reburied in the same grave, if no one claims them. Discussion finished."

He strode out of the room, leaving the rest of them to stare uncomfortably at each other.

Wilson snorted. "That went well, didn't it?"

Dr. Mike shook his head. "Or not."

NO LIGHTS. NO guards. No brains. So much gear and equipment left for the taking. Emile knew many men who would have cleaned out the trailers in no time. Although, if Emile told them about the dead bodies, he wasn't sure anyone would touch a thing. His people had respect for the dead.

The hills cast long shadows, though the moon offered him lots of light for walking the clearing. Not that he needed it. He'd spent his life here. The darkness held no secrets from him.

Avoiding the big reefer truck, he wandered to the lab trailer, quickly picking the lock as he had the night before. The women fascinated him. He'd never had a white woman. Their skin was so silvery and looked so soft. In the sun, they almost glowed. At first he'd checked out the little blonde more closely but decided to back off—figured one woman for the boss and one for him was good enough.

Besides the bigger one would offer more fight. She was older, more experienced, and a little less likely to be controlled, … and that was fine with him. He wasn't his old man.

As his boss didn't like fighting, the quiet one would suit him. He always walked away when Tasha and John got into it. Tasha would not let a day go by without letting everyone around her know exactly how she felt. She'd always been like that. Easy and fast on opinions and bossy to boot—only she was family. There was only so much Emile could do to change her attitude.

He wandered around the inside of the trailer, intrigued and repelled at the same time. How could they do what they did? They didn't see it as wrong—he understood that. But to stand here day after day and touch dead people? No, that just wasn't right. He walked over to the entrance to stand on the small porch.

He couldn't understand the women working in here.

Tasha would never touch a corpse. Then she did only what she wanted to anyway. Their father had tried to rein her in a long time ago, but, with the death of their mother, Tasha had gained the upper hand, and look at his father now. Christ, Emile would rather jump off a cliff than finish life like his old man. Speaking of which, ... he stared off in the direction of Peppe's cabin. Chances were the old man hadn't had anything to eat all day. Damn Tasha for passing that job to him.

Emile hated dealing with his father. Sure Tasha was pregnant, but women had been having babies since time began, and other women managed to get their work done too. Why couldn't she?

Because she refused.

Well, he straightened—enlightened. Then so would he refuse. Damn weakling John could do it. He never refused Tasha anything. He could take care of Peppe too.

Grimacing, Emile remembered Peppe from last night. The old man had been sitting in soiled clothes. Emile had thrown down his food and had walked out. He wouldn't clean the old man's ass again. Once had been too much for him.

Damn women's work.

Well, he wouldn't do it anymore. And, if Tasha or John wouldn't take care of it, ... Emile's gaze glowed with inspiration, as he stared at the mass grave. Then he'd find someone who would.

Chapter 10

WHEN JADE ARRIVED the next morning, Dane's dusty black truck sat in front of the lab trailer. He leaned against the truck bed, waiting. Her heart smiled. She was such an idiot. Yet she couldn't deny that he made her feel like a woman again.

Good thing. Her self-absorption and self-enforced seclusion had shut down her hormones, as she'd allowed anger and hurt to dominate. No longer.

"About time you got here." His big grin warmed her heart. Dane opened the door of his truck, and reached in. "What do you think you're on, Haitian time or something?"

She laughed. "*Nah*, boss checked in yesterday. Meetings with him put us behind schedule."

With a regal dip of his head, he pulled out two cups of coffee. "And, as a boss, I understand the benefits of keeping workers happy. So one is for you." He presented her with a cup.

"*Woo-hoo*. You are a definite keeper. Thank you." She shuffled her bags, so she could take it.

His eyes darkened. "Glad you're so easily pleased."

She grinned. "Often the simplest things in life …" She dropped her bags at the door and brought out her keys. She inserted the key into the lock but realized—when she turned the key—she'd actually locked it. The door had been unlocked. She frowned and pushed it open.

"Problem?"

"The door wasn't locked. It should have been," she declared, her gaze sweeping the interior. The equipment was all here, at least what she saw at first glance. Nothing appeared disturbed—other than what could be attributed to Meg or Dr. Mike, who had worked here the afternoon before.

"Someone forget to lock up?" Dane stayed on the porch, poking his head inside. "It looks the same."

"I don't know. The equipment is set out slightly different. I didn't close yesterday, so can't say if the others moved things or not." She wandered to the back and then down the far side. She shrugged her shoulder. "I can't see anything missing. It just feels off again."

"Again?" His voice sharpened. "This has happened before?"

She gazed back at him over her shoulder. "Yes. This is the second time. I can't pinpoint what's wrong. It's more a sense of things not being quite right." She shrugged and walked back out to the small porch. She took a sip of coffee.

"I thought they would bring in security guards?"

Blowing the steam off her cup, she nodded. "I did too. Might have something to do with our moneyman-slash-boss who's here now. I don't think he likes the added expense."

"Then maybe he should be told about this to get approval for the security funding."

She gave him a sideways look. "I'm not sure that would make a difference."

Dane's cheeks hollowed out, his jaw jutting forward. "It damn well should. You shouldn't be out here alone."

He was worried about her. She smiled. It had been a long time since anyone other than Duncan had given a damn about her safety. "I'm not normally. One of the others will be here in an hour or so."

"That's not good enough. It's not that this part of the country has a higher crime rate than the rest, but you've opened a controversy with this mass grave, and you're foreigners, and you have expensive equipment and facilities. That makes you and these trailers a target."

She grimaced. "I know. I'll talk to them."

His jaw squared, he planted his legs slightly apart. "Today."

She glared at him, liking the power of his personality, just not so much when it was turned her way. "Fine. Can we leave it for now? Thanks."

Studying her face, he gave one decisive nod. "Sure, I have to go to work anyway. Unless you want me to stick around until someone else arrives?"

"No. I'll be fine."

He smiled and turned to leave.

"Thanks for bringing the coffee," she called out, as he descended the steps and got into his truck.

With a wave, he drove off.

Her good mood restored, Jade headed inside. After making sure nothing was missing, she went to the reefer to double-check the chart numbers. She left the reefer door open to allow for more light, as she wandered the rows of dead. So far the numbering system appeared to be working.

"Jade? Are you in here?"

Startled, Jade bolted upright from her bent-over position and spun around. "Jesus, Stephen, you scared me."

"What are you doing?" He peered around the door and grinned at her, as she walked toward him. "There you are."

"Hey. I was cross-checking the numbers on the bags." Jade hopped out of the reefer truck and waited, while Stephen closed and locked the door.

"Wilson went to town with Dr. Mike instead, leaving me free to get back to work. I'm going up to the grave site." Stephen patted the metal handle. "Bruce is heading this way in a few minutes."

She smiled. "I'll go back to the lab and wait for him."

Stephen took off, whistling, and Jade busied herself around the lab for the few minutes she had alone. Before she had time to puzzle through the feeling she'd had in the trailer earlier, she heard the sound of yet another vehicle. This one an SUV.

Bruce.

He waved as he drove closer to the lab trailer. Jade walked to the railing to greet him. "Hey."

Hopping out, he climbed the steps and walked around the new porch. "I like the new addition. From Dane, I understand?"

She wandered around the small space, appreciating the simple two-by-four construction. "Yes, a simple switch for a few weeks."

"It looks good."

"Any word on overnight security for this place?"

"Tony has vetoed the idea for now. Why?"

Oh, shit. She explained about the unlocked door and the weird feeling. "Did he give a reason?"

"*Not in the budget.*" Bruce gave her a mocking look. "We'll need to follow protocol, as we shut down every night. To know that we've locked up properly."

"Why is everything all of a sudden about money?" She watched as Bruce walked the tiny porch, still grinning his approval regarding this upgrade.

"Because our moneyman is here on the spot. It's easier to deal with them when they are a long way away. But, when they are here, they're all about control, power, ... and saving money."

"And because they pay our salaries, we are all about compliance?"

She frowned. "Part of the reason I was interested in coming was the good we'd be doing. It's hard to see that come down to number-crunching."

He studied her face. "I understand how you feel, and I think this is only temporary. Once Tony goes back home, that negativity will ease back, as everything returns to normal." He entered the lab and dropped his bag on the counter. "I'm going up to the grave site. Are you coming?"

"Absolutely." The walk only took ten minutes, taking them from the large clearing, down a path, to an opening that showed the valley. It was gorgeous country. Add in the sunshine and the easy-to-tolerate temperatures, and it was no wonder Haiti was a popular tourist destination. At least it had been. The earthquake had made a dent in that.

Stephen met them at the spot where he'd found the newest remains in chains. He'd taken the tarps off the exposed area and had moved some more of the rocks that surrounded the bones. They stood and studied the big job in front of them.

"Is Tony coming here? This morning? He should see this himself," Stephen suggested.

Yet Jade doubted anyone was ready to bring Tony in on this issue.

Bruce laughed. "Not likely. Not willingly." He looked from them to the grave and back again. "He won't know the difference between these or any other set of bones. I suggest we excavate very carefully—and tell the authorities if our suspicions are confirmed. If and only if we have forensic evidence of foul play, it will be our duty to bring someone official in on this."

Stephen nodded. "I don't see how we can't. I can't just ignore this. If what we see here is what we think it is, I will tell someone. Then, if the authorities need help dealing with these bones, they'll have my free labor."

Jade had to agree with that. "We'll process this as we would any of the bodies. That won't take any more time or money than the others. Once processed, the information is there to turn over to the police, if necessary." As Bruce went to open his mouth, she added, "Or I will process them on my own time in the evening. I'll volunteer my labor, just like Stephen suggested."

"Okay, before we go a little nuts on this, why don't we start the processing and see how long it takes us to do these few bodies? We'll measure that against the time it takes to do the same number of the other bodies," Bruce suggested. "If this takes longer, we'll all stay one night and work together to make up the time."

Stephen and Jade looked at each other. Jade smiled and added, "Works for me."

"Good, then let's get started."

Jade ran to the lab to retrieve her camera, while Bruce grabbed the closest shovel. Two bodies. At least that's all they'd found today. Tomorrow, unfortunately, could be a whole different story.

When lunch arrived, in the form of Meg and brown bags, Jade was more than happy to head back to the hotel and handle her paperwork for the rest of the afternoon.

JADE CALLED HER brother later that night and dumped the story on him. Jade sat in their new office space with the windows open. A cool breeze wafted in, circling around and blowing back out again.

His stunned silence sat heavy on the phone line. "Shit. This was supposed to take your mind off your own problems."

She laughed. "Well, it did that."

"Sure. As much as I'd love to see you find justice for these victims, remember that they are dead, and you are not. Don't do anything that will put you in danger."

"I won't." But she wasn't so sure she could follow through. There were too many unanswered questions. Who knew where this would lead?

"What's the matter? What's happened? Are you in danger now?" His sharp voice snapped through the phone line, pulling her back to their conversation.

She rushed to reassure him. Her poor brother had done enough worrying over her lately. "No. Of course not. No. I'm fine. Everything here is fine. Honest. Don't worry about me."

A doubtful silence filled the lines. "I held off coming to Haiti to give you some time. I'm thinking it might be time to come over …"

"Now, don't you go off on in panic," Jade said. "Come for a visit if you want, just not because of this. I'm okay."

"And you damn well better stay that way."

She grinned. "I will. I love you too."

"Good. That's the first time you've said that since you were in Haiti last time."

She went quiet inside. How sad. Just another example of how

self-absorbed she'd been. Damn her selfish soul. After a moment, she said softly, "I'm sorry. I've given you a lot of grief and worry recently, haven't I?"

His voice warmed. "No. Don't ever think that. You have been through a lot. You're entitled."

And she had been. But that time was over. This Haiti trip *had* been good for her. She hadn't expected these results. Certainly not the sense of things being back to normal. Not this fast. She knew there would be relapses, particularly when she returned home, but this trip had forced a paradigm shift, and she'd grown with it.

His joyous laugh came through so clear and sharp, she leaned back and closed her eyes. She missed this. Missed him. Her brother had been such a mainstay in her life, a stalwart support. She was blessed. And had so forgotten to see and to appreciate the good in her life because she had been locked in her self-imposed prison of pain and misery.

Instead of walking away, he'd been shining at her side for so long and so consistently that she'd become accustomed to it. She'd forgotten to appreciate his presence.

Not anymore.

"You are the best brother anyone could have, and I am so grateful that you don't belong to anyone else but me." Tears collected in the corners of her eyes, and, despite her best attempts, she sniffled.

"Jesus, Jade. You're killing me here."

Smiling through her tears, she said, "Sorry, I know you don't like emotionalism, but I just needed to say that."

"And needed to say it at a time that I can't wrap you in my arms and hug you." His voice deepened with emotion. "I love you, kitten. I don't know what's going on over there. If anything happens to you, I'll be heartbroken. You know that, right?"

"Yeah, I do." She sniffled harder. "I didn't mean to get into this right now, but all those dead women …"

"I know." He sighed heavily. "Wish I could help. I'd do anything to stop you from ever being traumatized again."

"I would too. And we don't know for sure that our theories are correct. *Yet.* We need to find out the truth—or what we can, while working here. That's on the table for tomorrow."

"Then you call me tomorrow. When you get back to the hotel, give me a quick call. Just a 'Hi, Duncan, had a great day, love ya' kind of call. So I know you're okay."

"I'll be fine," she insisted. She stood and wandered to the window, loving the cool night air and the sultry darkness that was so distinctive to this part of the world. If the phone cord reached, she'd have sat out on the patio, surrounded by the gardens. She'd been truly blessed to have the chance to come back here. Maybe she could think more charitably of Tony for granting her this opportunity.

"Good. Glad to hear that. But I won't be. Not unless you call."

"You're an idiot." She smiled, then chuckled. "But I will do as you ask."

"Good, and remember that this idiot loves you." His voice changed, became more teasing. "Speaking of love, any men over there making your hormones sing?"

She gasped, caught by surprise at the sudden topic change. Even though he couldn't see her, she shook her head. "No one. Don't be an idiot." *Okay, so there was Dane. Did he count?*

"I'm not convinced. Your voice says something different. Someone has caught your attention. And I, for one, couldn't be happier."

Sighing, she added, "No, there isn't, but believe what you will."

"I will. Don't worry. I will."

She could see his grin in her mind. "Idiot," she repeated affectionately. "I'm ready for bed now. Have a good tomorrow."

"I will, just promise to call me. I'll be waiting."

"Got it. Now, goodbye."

They rang off, leaving her sitting now, with a silly smile on her face.

She really did miss that big teddy bear of a brother. He was a good man.

"Now that is a lovely smile on your face." Bruce and Stephen walked into the office. "What are you doing working at this hour?"

She held up the hotel phone. "I'm not working. Just calling my brother." She grinned. "Or you could say, I'm doing as he requested and checking in with my brother."

Bruce sat down in the chair beside her. "Oh, he's protective, is he? That's probably a wise thing."

"There's just the two of us, so protective comes naturally to him." And she missed him.

"What does he do?" Stephen sat down at the computer next to her.

She stretched her back and rotated her neck. Something about bending over the tables in the lab had kinked her spine. The table was probably at the wrong height. "He's a counselor for kids at risk."

Stephen turned to look at her. "Wow. Good for him. That can't be an easy job."

"No, it isn't. Still, he's very good at it."

Bruce added in, "That's no surprise. You're also very good at what you do."

The compliment, out of the blue, surprised her. "Thanks," she said, a squeak of shock in her voice.

He looked taken aback. "You're welcome. It's true. And what I expect from every team member here." He lifted a sheaf of papers and walked out, after saying good night.

Stephen rolled his eyes as Bruce left. "Yeah, we're all just one big happy family."

Chapter 11

HEAD DOWN, JADE shifted the camera lens, as she detailed the story of the next set of bones on her lab table. She had no idea how many pictures she'd taken so far.

Dr. Mike had been working at the second table all morning. Something was wrong. He'd been muttering for hours, as he pored over his work. That couldn't be good.

Dr. Mike's face had gone stiff and cold within minutes of starting on the first of the manacled bodies. Jade had been too concerned to bother him. He'd tell her soon enough. Ten minutes ago, the two of them had returned one set of remains to the reefer and brought the next one out. He never said a word, except to ask for her help to make the switch.

Bending lower, she snapped several more photos of the small breastbone, all but pulverized. She moved around, taking as many pictures as necessary, enjoying the calm silence of the room, despite the job she had to do.

She moved to the far side of the body bag and put down her camera. Time to move on to the next step. She charted the injuries, as she found them, and took out her measuring tape. She didn't think this boy could have been more than five or six years old. His bones had a stick-thin look to them.

Her heart ached for him. At least he would have died quickly. Not like the last one she'd processed.

The day's work hadn't been too bad; still they had a long road ahead of them. Susan was helping Bruce at the team's free clinic two mornings a week. So far only one person had shown up, looking for their loved ones. Matching families to bodies would take time.

Dr. Mike sighed heavily.

Jade straightened, and stretched her arms over her head. "Problems?" she asked him gently. She glanced yet again at the open windows. Without a breeze the air hung heavy and hot.

He glanced at her and nodded. "Oh, I think maybe."

She walked to his table to see what he was working on. "What is it?"

"She was in the ground longer than the earthquake victims. Much longer. Possibly even as long as a decade." He pointed to the skeleton in front of him. "She died from blunt force trauma to the head."

"Meaning?"

"I don't know. Everyone that we've found in that mass grave had something in common. Especially their estimated time of death. All died within a short window, and, of course, we're using the earthquake to help determine that time. Then come these other remains." He shrugged. "All we can do is record the differences. Maybe there was an earlier grave under the mass grave. The countryside is full of small cemeteries. It could be a coincidence—not out of the realm of possibility.

"So one possibility is that these victims were from an earlier ca- lamity, and it was easier to just bury more on top. We'd been told a cave had collapsed, creating a natural depression. That cave-in could have been an old grave site splitting open instead."

He groaned slightly, as he shifted his position. "Another possibil- ity is the earthquake could have opened another grave somewhere else, and the responders used the mass grave as a place to dispose of bodies that needed a new home. Again, not something that is necessarily a crime."

"And, if it's all guesswork, then we still don't have any evidence to bring to the authorities, do we?"

"I can only compile the information and present it to them. Will they care?" He raised his shoulders in a tired shrug. "I highly doubt it."

"Have you examined all the women? Did they all have the same cause of death?"

Dr. Mike stretched his arms. "These two died of blunt force trauma to the head." He stood and walked around, shaking out his arms. "But the first one we found was strangled."

"The first one we found died more recently than the others, right?" Jade frowned, beyond confused. "So the chain around their ankles is similar, yet the cause of death is different? Over a ten-year period? I wonder why? Different killers?"

Jade paced the small trailer, trying to find a reasonable explana- tion, but the pieces weren't adding up to anything other than criminal activity. "Of all the things that I keep coming back to, it was the absolute chaos and panic I saw when I was here right after the big earthquake. People were left to die, slowly and painfully. The dead were sometimes cut up in order to move them out of the way. In other cases, it was easier to kill trapped victims quickly than watch them die slowly. Chaos ruled. People were also being killed to gain food and blankets. Brother killed brother—out of compassion and for sheer survival."

Dr. Mike stroked his chin in a movement she'd come to equate with slow, thoughtful thinking. "Except in this case, there were no missing limbs."

Jade agreed. "I've found enough crushed limbs to confirm plenty are in the mix."

"So, for a moment, we have a mystery. Not a crime, but a mystery." He took off his gloves and put them into the garbage can. "I need a drink of water and some fresh air. There is a little too much death in here for the moment."

"Are you done? Do you want to move the body back over to the reefer?"

"No, I'm not quite finished." He motioned toward her stretcher. "If yours is, can you process this one while I take a break?"

"I'll need another half hour at least to finish this one." Jade stopped, looked at her watch, and frowned. "I think Meg will be arriving soon with our lunch. Normally we switch at this time. However, if you'd like, I can stay and process yours this afternoon."

"If you wouldn't mind, I'd appreciate it. Although, if Tony finds out …"

Uh-oh. "I thought he left this morning?"

"He and Bruce were going over personnel files."

Jade grimaced. *Great.* She wasn't sure Tony was happy with his decision to have her here. She understood his reluctance. … Initially she might have agreed with his decision. Not now. Now she had a vested interest in finishing this job. They'd been here almost three weeks. They could see the end of the job within three months. She wanted to see it through.

Oddly enough, the more involved in these deaths she became, the more accepting she was of the loss of her own child.

At least she felt she was. Time did wonders for healing the pain. And closure here could bring her more closure once she returned home.

DANE HAD TAPPED every idea he could come up with and still did not have a decent excuse for going home at noon. So then he drove right past John and Tasha's driveway. He left a trail of dust floating toward John's small house. Dust. Another thing that was sure to be pissing off Tasha. Not that Dane could blame her. For years there'd been minimal traffic on this road. Now there were several vehicles a day.

Coming here to the mass grave was stupid because Jade had probably left already. She'd said something about switching off with Meg in the afternoons now. He parked, surprised to see two SUVs here. He checked his watch—after 2:00 p.m.

She'd be gone.

He strode over to poke his head into the lab.

"Hey, Dane," Meg called out cheerfully. "Haven't seen you in a few days. How have you been?"

"I'm doing all right. Just stopping in to see how things are going here. To see if you need the heavy equipment back again." He hoped not; it was off doing a job on the other side of town and wouldn't get back here anytime soon. Peering into the back, he was surprised to see as many people as there were. Tight quarters.

Meg turned to the back. "Hey, Dr. Mike. Dane's here. Any idea if you need the loader back today or tomorrow?"

Dane walked up the steps and went inside, surprised to see Jade working at the far end. "Hi, Jade. Didn't expect to see you here."

She lifted her head from whatever she'd been working on so intently and smiled. "Don't suppose you brought coffee, did you?"

He laughed. With her hair back in a clip, she looked like a teenager. "Sorry. If I'd known you'd be here, then I'd have stopped and picked up some. I thought you'd be at the hotel, sipping your own brew by now."

"Should be," she said cheerfully. "Dr. Mike asked me to stay and help out."

"Good for me." Dane smiled broadly.

She flushed charmingly and laughed. "That's nice of you."

Another of their SUVs drove up. "Looks like Bruce has arrived," Dane noted.

Dr. Mike came over to join them at the door. "Oh, no, Tony is with him." He glanced back at the body Jade had been working on. With his voice lowered almost to a whisper, he asked, "Are you finished with that one?"

She shook her head. "Not really. Could use another half hour, maybe even an hour." She waffled as she considered the work left. "Do you want me to pack it up unfinished or finish it while Bruce and Tony go to the grave site?"

He brightened.

Meg suggested, "Let's process it together quickly."

They didn't waste any more time but raced back to the end of the trailer and started work.

Dane pursed his lips and watched with interest. He caught Dr. Mike's look.

Dr. Mike grinned and said, "He's the boss, the big moneyman. Thinks things should be going faster and not cost so much."

"Right. That sounds familiar." And it did. Dane knew many clients who were constantly watching that bottom line—even to the detriment of a project. He turned to watch the men get out of the SUV.

Bruce had a weary patience surrounding him, as if he'd heard everything more times than he wanted to and still didn't like the end result.

"Hi, Bruce." Dane walked over to greet the men. He figured the women needed some extra time to finish off whatever they were working on. He smiled at Bruce. "Don't you look a little on the tired side. ... Heat getting to you?"

"Just a little. How are things with you, Dane? Business good?"

"Business will always be good here." With a casual friendliness, he added, "Just lacking the funding to do what needs to be done right."

Bruce rolled his eyes. "I hear you on that one."

Tony walked around the SUV to stand beside Bruce. He held a thick folder, clipboard, and pen in his hands. *The moneyman.* Talk about a cliché. Dane could have picked him out of a crowd. He smiled politely. "Hello, welcome to Haiti."

Bruce introduced them. "This is Tony. Tony, this is Dane Carver. He helped us in the beginning with the loader."

Tony's face thinned. "Right. Pretty expensive day rates too."

So *not.* Dane was in business here. He'd pulled the equipment off another job to give them a head start. He wouldn't listen to this crap. Dane smiled grimly. "Feel free to find someone else. If you can. Equipment is scarce right now."

Bruce interrupted hurriedly. "Sorry, Dane. We certainly appreciated your help. Tony doesn't understand some of the costs related to this business."

Tony's glare was hot and lethal. "I've been doing this job for a long time, thank you," he said stiffly. "Now maybe we could start with a look at the grave site itself. If I could put that into perspective, I'd understand the need for machinery in the first place."

"That's a good idea," Dane agreed. Honestly Bruce should have taken him there on the first day. If Tony had no idea of the size of this grave that they were talking about, then of course he didn't understand the need for heavy equipment. "I'll walk up with you. I want to check on the progress."

Bruce led the way. Dane looked back once to see Dr. Mike still standing in the open doorway. Dane lifted a hand. Dr. Mike grinned and waved happily. Someone else was happy to see them leaving.

Turning the corner to fully see the mass grave, Dane stepped up to walk beside Bruce—in time to hear Tony catch his breath.

"A little different than you expected?" Dane asked, as he studied Tony's face intently. Shock, horror even—and maybe an understanding of the enormity of the problem.

"This is full of bodies?" Tony gulped. "It's huge." He lifted a shaky hand and rubbed a handkerchief across his forehead. "Good God, how many bodies are we talking here?"

"We're not sure exactly," Bruce replied. "We've brought out close to forty already but could be one hundred more ... or only ten." He turned to face Tony. "Now you see why we need a storage solution. Either more refrigerator trucks or another location in town and a truck to haul things back and forth."

Tony stood and stared. He wiped his forehead again. "I had no idea." He brought out a camera from his pocket and quickly snapped off a couple pictures. "This will be something to show my client at least. The first set of photos didn't capture the scope of this site."

"Is he having second thoughts about the cost?" asked Bruce curiously.

Dane turned his attention from the grave site, where the two young men were working, to the conversation at his side.

Tony shook his head vehemently. "No. He's growing impatient. Everything is underway, yet he still doesn't have his family home. We've found several possibilities but have to wait for the DNA results to confirm."

With his hands on his hips, Bruce studied Tony's face. "We did say it would take months for us to get the bodies tested and confirmed."

"He knows that." Tony stuffed his camera away in his bag and brought out his clipboard. "Obviously heavy equipment was necessary to get started, and I can see that might be required again—even if only to refill this space. Okay, so that's no problem. I guess I'd better see the labs as well."

A much brighter-looking Bruce led Tony back down the path. He winked at Dane as he walked past.

Stephen walked over. "Now that they are leaving, it's safe to come over and say hi."

Dane motioned to the retreating men. "No one likes him, huh?"

Stephen snickered. "Nah. Tony's probably all right, just caught in the middle."

"True enough." Dane watched the others navigate the rocky path down to the lab trailers. "Speaking of which, did Bruce get security in for overnight?"

"*Nah.* Tony vetoed it."

Dane said goodbye hurriedly and raced back down the slopes. Security was mandatory.

They were too open here, too alone. Someone had to keep an eye on the place—and on Jade, when Dane couldn't.

JADE FOCUSED ON getting these poor women finished and out of the way. The light in the trailer was poor at the best of times. Urgency made her fingers thick and her actions awkward. She swore several times under her breath.

Meg wasn't faring any better.

Finally Jade stopped and stared at her. "Is she done?"

"Even if she isn't, I'd say let's get her back to the reefer and now."

Of like minds, they raced through the last steps, and, this time, Jade took off the paper sheet that she'd placed under the skeleton, while Meg processed it, just in case any evidence had dropped off. She started to fold it carefully, then realized they'd missed a hair. Pointing it out to Meg, she used tweezers to retrieve it and to bag it. For the moment, the little bag was tucked inside the body bag, which was zipped closed.

Both of them breathed a sigh of relief when the woman was secure again—from prying eyes and from Tony, whose voice they heard coming their way.

"Let's get her moved over." Meg shifted the bag slightly to sit better on their portable stretcher. "Out of sight and all that." Throwing her chart and white marker on top, Jade grabbed the other end and headed for the door.

Dr. Mike glanced from them to the bag and to the end of the room. Relief bloomed across his face. "Thanks," he whispered.

Bruce's voice boomed outside the trailer. "This is the lab trailer. In here we're processing the remains." There was a slight pause, then the sounds of heavy boots climbing the steps.

"Damn it," Jade whispered. They'd almost made it out. Still could actually. "Watch out. We're coming through with a stretcher," she called out loudly.

"Thanks for the warning," Bruce called back, and the men backed down from the small porch, as Jade came around the corner.

In a simple maneuver that they'd perfected with practice, Jade made it onto the porch, with Meg bringing up the rear. Smiling politely at the three men standing and waiting, Jade said, "Thanks, gentlemen." They walked over to the reefer truck. She rested her end of the stretcher on the steps and moved to open the door.

Dane raced over. "Let me grab the door."

She grinned. "We've done this many times, so it's not as if we can't, but a helping hand is always welcome." Jade picked up her end of the stretcher again and waited for Dane to open the door and then to move out of the way.

"Thanks, Dane." Meg smiled, as she walked up the stairs behind Jade.

Once inside, they moved the skeleton to the far end of the room and put her crosswise on the shelf. "Whew." Jade looked back to the door, where Dane peered in at them. "Glad we made it this far."

"As much as I'd love to hide away in here"—Meg handed her the white marker and the chart—"I'd better go speak with the bosses. Do your magic, then join us."

"Yeah, I'm *thrilled*." Jade watched Meg walk out and stop to speak with Dane. Then she disappeared around the corner of the trailer. Popping the top off the marker, Jade marked the bag as per her system and added a small series of interconnecting loops. *Chains.*

She straightened. No need to take another skeleton over. Dr. Mike probably had enough to work on this afternoon. Jade walked to the open door and closed it, checking the temperature as she did so.

"Everything all right in there?" asked Dane curiously. "You were a long time."

"I had to mark the bag with her chart ID." She smiled at him. "Are you taking the afternoon off? We don't get to see you often at this hour."

He snorted. "I wish. I'm on the way to the site right now. I had hoped that maybe I could convince you to go out for dinner with me this weekend."

Her eyebrows shot up. It was all she could do to stop her jaw from dropping. She stopped halfway down the stairs and stared at him.

His laughter rolled out easily. "Sorry, I've caught you off guard. So does that mean *no*?"

She shook her head, laughing self-consciously. "My reaction is not a reflection on you. It's a reflection on me. It's been a long time since I've been asked out."

"Then it's not a *no*?" He tilted his head and studied her.

She flushed. "No, it's not a *no*. It's a *yes*." *Crap*. She was handling this badly. She tried again. "Thank you, Dane. I'd love to go out for dinner with you." She smirked. "Is that better? I'm a little rusty."

He grinned. "Much better, thanks. So Saturday or Friday? Don't know what your schedule is like."

"*Hmm*. My personal life is just so full now. *Not*. Either works, but maybe Friday is better. There's talk of a team hike on Saturday, and I have no idea when we'd make it back to the hotel." She winced comically. "Or what shape I might be in afterward."

"Any idea where you're going?"

"No. Dr. Mike mentioned a couple ideas he wanted to check out further. I personally would love to spend some time out on the water."

"I know a couple tour operators who work out of Port-au-Prince. However, I'd have to ask around for local ones." As they walked toward the lab trailer, Dane added, "We'll figure it out. We'll be here for a few months so there's time to work in a few trips."

"I might also stay a little longer after this job is done. Several other team members have mentioned doing the same."

Dane's phone beeped. He pulled it from his pocket, checked the text, and sighed. "Back to work I go. Friday at seven, if that works for you?"

"Sounds good. Thanks." She watched him stride to the truck, hop in, and take off. Dane left a cloud of dust in his wake. Wafting her hand in front of her face, she walked to the lab trailer.

"We're not sightseeing on the job, are we?" Tony stood on the lab porch, watching her. "I'd hate to have to remind anyone that you are all here to work and not just to set up your social life."

She rounded on him. "I highly doubt anyone on this team is under any misunderstanding as to why we're here." She wanted to say something cutting, but Bruce's worried face, just behind Tony, stopped her.

Tony loved power and control. She had no ax to grind with him. He'd given her the chance to come back and to face her demons. Although they weren't exactly gone, she was triumphing over them.

She owed him. She'd never cheated a boss before, and she wasn't about to start now. "Bruce, if you're done in there, I'll pack up the charts and head back to the office to start on the paperwork."

He nodded. "That's fine. I know you stayed late here to finish up, so thanks."

She shrugged it off. "Not a problem. Whatever works to get the job done, right?" She brushed past the two men, wishing the small deck were four times larger. Too many people were here now. She packed up her stuff and grabbed the charts, before saying goodbye to Meg and Dr. Mike.

Outside, she hopped into the SUV she'd driven to work and left, without saying another word.

As she pulled away, she noticed Tony was writing notes on his chart. *Brownie points or demerit points?* She hadn't been joking. Whatever worked for the team and the job worked for her. Still, she wanted to see this job through to the end, and, if he wanted to, Tony had the ability to prevent that.

She couldn't wait for the week to be over at this rate. *Friday.* That put a smile on her face. Wait until she told Duncan. He'd be worried and delighted. A real date. Wow.

THE GREASY CABIN window wouldn't let any light in again. Old Peppe had used his sleeve on the glass yesterday to try and wipe it, so he could see outside. He looked around for the binoculars that he knew were here somewhere.

He saw movement through the trees—barely. So many people on-site today. *Why? What had they found?* Surely nothing too important. He'd watched as they'd thrown body after body into that grave originally. Nasty business that. He'd wanted to help, but, not being as strong any longer, especially with his mind wandering the way it did, no one trusted him with anything. In fact, no one even came and talked to him anymore.

He was a prisoner in his own home. Dependent on his son for food. And his daughter? … *Well,* he hadn't even seen her hardly since the quake.

He missed his old life. The brief glimpses of better days. His wife's death had devastated him. He didn't even remember how long ago that had been. Tasha had been a teenager then, Emile not much older. Peppe couldn't function on his own for a long time after she died. His kids had suffered, and he was sorry for that. He loved them. He didn't understand why they hated him so much now.

He sighed and rubbed his beard. He hated the damn thing, and, when he could, he took scissors to it. Speaking of cutting it, he grabbed the dinner knife beside him and started sawing away. He threw the chunks of hair on the floor. His daughter should be coming to clean soon. At least he thought she would be. He couldn't remember the last time he'd seen her sweep the floor, but, in the back of his mind, he saw her with a broom. So she must have. She needed to come soon.

Damn useless child.

He'd taught her better than that. *Hadn't he?* Surely he had. He'd give her *what for* the next time he saw her. And that damn useless son of his. How about he come and swing a broom?

Then again, Peppe himself had never been lazy. He could manage a damn broom himself.

He stood and walked to the doorway, where the broom should be, and opened the door. He couldn't find a broom. At least he didn't see one. Damn kids. What had they done with it?

He shuffled outside and sniffed the air. Something strong assailed his nose, so he turned back to the house. *That smell was coming from inside?* Horrible. He'd really have to say something when someone showed up. Damn, he was hungry.

He left the door open and wandered back into the small kitchen to check for what there was to eat. Stale and crusty pasta and peanut butter. At least that's what he thought it was. Opening the jar he sniffed the contents and almost heaved. He tossed the jar in the garbage, watching as it hit the closed garbage can lid and bounced to the floor. The garbage was too full. It needed to go out.

He headed back to the front door, frustrated by his life. He needed them to come. *And now.* There was his cane, leaning against the front door. He'd been looking for it for a while now.

Figured one of them had taken it.

"Hey, Dad."

Finally. Someone. He stared at the face so familiar and yet so strange. "Do I know you?"

"Yes, I'm your son, Emile."

The overly exaggerated patience in his voice pissed off Peppe.

"Says who? I wasn't born yesterday. How do I know you're my son?" He tottered forward. "Why does this place stink so bad? It's worse than the dump."

"This place has turned into a dump. Dad. You need to go change your pants."

"What's wrong with them? My wife got these for me. Who do you think you are?"

The young man rubbed a weary hand over his face. "I can't do this anymore. You don't even know us. So you won't miss us, will you?" He looked around at the mess on the floor and in the tiny kitchen. "We'll have to burn this place after you're gone."

"I'm not going anywhere. If you can't keep this place clean, then go get one of those women and have her do it." He muttered to himself. "Your mother would die if she saw this mess."

"She's dead, remember? From cancer. Made Tasha and I promise to look after you."

"Well, you haven't, have you? Look at this place. Where's Tasha? She should be here, taking care of me. The least you could do is bring me a damn broom so I can sweep, if you're too lazy to do it."

"Right. Tasha is in a bad way. She can't come. As for your request for a broom, you are leaning on it right now. So that doesn't make a whole lot of sense."

"I am not. Don't you try to make out like I'm crazy," he screamed. "I will not tolerate that kind of disrespect in my own home. Do you hear me?"

"Absolutely. So you don't want this rice and chicken then, *huh*? 'Cause, if you're starting your screaming fits again, I won't leave this food. In fact, I'll just walk away and hope you're not breathing by the time I check back in. Got it?"

The two men glared at each other, fury and stubbornness etched on matching faces.

And just like that, the storm blew over.

His face wreathed in smiles, Peppe said, "I love chicken. Thanks. What's in the jar?"

Emile groaned and held them out. "Your favorite—peanut butter."

Chapter 12

B EFORE TONY LEFT, he pulled Jade aside in the hotel lobby. The heat from outside penetrated through the large double doors.

"If you are having trouble handling this project or staying focused on the job, I will pull you off. This isn't a holiday, no matter what you think with your sightseeing tours and dates. We have a job to do, and I want it done right. I'm not a fool. Just because I can't be here all the time, realize that someone is keeping an eye on you. I need to ensure you're handling yourself here."

He walked away, leaving Jade in shock, staring at his retreating back. "What the hell was that all about?"

"What?" Bruce walked in the other door. "Did you say something?"

"I'm not sure what just happened." She motioned in the direction Tony disappeared. "Let me ask you something. Have I ever given you the impression that this job was too much for me mentally? Or that my social life is stopping me from doing my job?" At the astonished look on his face, some of the panic calmed, and she added, shaking her head, "Anything at all that made you consider I don't belong here?"

"No, of course not. Not a thing. Why?" An understanding settled into his eyes, and he glanced out the empty door. "Was that Tony by any chance? Warning you? I am sorry. He's a bit of an overkill kind of guy."

"Ya think?" She studied his face. Would Bruce be honest? "He didn't ask you to keep an eye on my mental state?"

Bruce shook his head. "Absolutely not. I don't understand where he would have gotten that idea in the first place." Bruce frowned, scratching his chin.

"I do unfortunately, and you would have had to been there at the time to understand fully but ..." She gave him a quick rundown on how she and Tony had met and the possible reasons behind his trepidation now. "The thing is, I've been here for over three weeks, and I hardly think I've let anyone down."

He patted her shoulder. "No, you haven't. Tony is nothing if not thorough. But I wouldn't let that worry you. There is always a team member assigned to keep an eye on the team—physically, emotionally, and mentally. So let them, and just be your normal happy self. Don't let Tony upset you."

"Will you be as happy to see him leave as the rest of us will be?" She shouldn't have asked. Bruce was the team leader. It wasn't fair to put him on the spot like that.

Bruce laughed. "Have to remember that people like Tony make the money flow. Either to us or away from us. We need them, and they need us. The partnership usually works." He grinned, more relaxed than she'd seen him in days. "It's still nice to see the boss leave for a while. Everyone will relax again and can work that much better."

"Unless we find another bunch of skeletons whose deaths appear a little suspicious."

"But he doesn't know about those, so it doesn't matter." He raised an eyebrow at her. "Right?"

"I don't know about what?" Tony stood in the doorway, his suit-cases in his hand. "Are you talking about me?"

"No," said Jade, a calm smile on her face. "We were talking about Dane and the fact that he doesn't know any charters or tour guides in this town."

Tony's face lightened. "Good. Well then, I'm off. Should be back in a few weeks to a month, depending on problems and progress." He gave a perfunctory smile. "Goodbye and good luck." Then he disappeared.

Jade stared at Bruce, who stared back. Afraid Tony might still be around the corner, he mouthed back, *Thank you.*

"You're welcome."

They watched from the lobby as Stephen drove to the front of the hotel in a company SUV. Tony got in. While they watched, Tony was driven away.

"Thank God for that," she said.

"Amen."

WHEN DANE FINALLY made it back to his brother's house the next day, he asked himself once again if it might be time to leave Haiti. The sense of finality had been growing steadily. The hospital wing he was working on wasn't complete, yet it wasn't that far off. The interior finishing always took longer than expected. Much of the stuff they needed had to be ordered in. Dane's Seattle office was handling most of that. Dane had a good foreman here. He might go home and fly back and forth until the job was done. He'd originally hoped to remain long enough to see his niece or nephew born. Now he didn't think he'd make it that long.

He wouldn't mind being gone from this family scene. As much as he enjoyed rustic living, he would appreciate running water again. He'd been told the property used to be a lively and profitable farm, until the soil had been overworked and the creek running through the property had dried up. He didn't think the property had provided Peppe's family a living in a long time. He'd learned that Peppe had been employed as a builder at one time, and, unlike many other natives, his kids had gone to school—at least for a while.

John didn't go into too much detail as to how he'd met Tasha or what they lived on. Tasha had worked in one of the bed-and-breakfasts in town, and Dane suspected that had been the extent of their income. Except for stuff she made and sold to tourists. And since the earthquake a year ago, John's business had failed.

As much as Dane loved his brother, John didn't appear to be bringing in much—if anything. And that was yet another area John wouldn't discuss. His brother took on mostly small jobs now to pay the bills—not that he'd seen John go to work much.

At this point, Dane figured that the money he paid them to stay in the cabin at the back of the property was what the entire family was living on.

His brother seemed happy enough, at least on the surface—only Dane didn't know how John could be. Was it the pregnancy that had turned his sister-in-law into a crazy shrew or something else—like this damn grave thing? Dane didn't know. At this point, he made a habit of staying late at work and leaving again early in the morning. And ate out often and showered at the hospital. He'd made arrangements to shower there, to avoid going home. Money bought almost anything here. Dane would have spent a lot more to minimize the time he spent listening to her berate his brother.

Tasha's appearance had started to slip as well. Her hair was unkempt instead of contained in the long braid she'd worn when he had first arrived. Her face was unwashed, more often than not. And her clothes? ... Had she changed them in the last week?

He immediately felt guilty for not being more understanding.

He'd heard pregnancy could do things to families and that pregnancies could be incredibly stressful. Dane just didn't understand this change in Tasha because, according to John, she'd been fine for the first three and even four months. These days it was as if whatever control she'd had over herself had come loose. He felt sorry for her. But even sorrier for his brother.

Dane shook his head, as he walked to the kitchen door. She was at it again. Their argument carried easily on the air.

"Damn it, John. Emile says he can't look after Peppe. I need you to go give him his food. Emile did it yesterday."

"And why can't Emile give him his meal today? Peppe's his father."

"I'm sure he has a reason. What's your reason for not wanting to help out? I do all the cooking here, as it is. You don't work anymore. ... You could start doing that again too. When was the last time you cooked a meal?"

John's long-suffering sigh didn't go unnoticed.

She started in on him again. "Oh, don't start that again. I hardly ask you to do anything around here, and, the minute I do, you start complaining. Well, stop. Emile isn't home, and Peppe needs food."

Dane opened the door, wondering when Tasha was due. Another six to eight weeks? Dane shook his head, as he studied the beaten look on his brother's face through the open door. "I'll tell you what, Tasha. I'll go with you, and you can introduce me to your father," Dane offered, stepping through the doorway.

Horror flicked across her face. "What? No. No. I can't. I mean, I'm not feeling well." She dropped the food tray onto the table beside John and fled.

Dane stared, open-mouthed, then turned to face his brother, who looked equally surprised. "Well, that didn't go as expected."

John stood. "That's the story of my life right now. Nothing I say is received the way I expect it to." He glared down at the tray. "This Peppe-Emile thing is driving me nuts. Emile is Peppe's son. He should be the one to do this."

Dane didn't have an argument for that. He didn't know how bad the situation really was. He'd only seen Peppe a couple times since he'd been here, and the old man appeared more or less normal each time. Apparently things had deteriorated. "True enough. Still something is going on here if neither child wants to help the parent."

"I want him in a home. I haven't found a place, and Tasha fights the idea, but neither will she deal with him." John ran a weary hand down his face. "You even suggest that she should go see her father, and she bursts into tears."

"Perhaps she can't stand to see how badly he's deteriorating?"

"I don't know what the problem is. She won't tell me." His hands fisted, then relaxed on his hips.

Dane looked around the small kitchen. Pots sat on the table. He didn't know if food was in them or not. He was glad he was taking Jade out tonight.

He glanced down at the plate prepared for Peppe. It looked like rice and beans. Looking around the kitchen, Dane realized how old and faded everything was. Definitely in need of a new coat of paint and new flooring. Another sign their financial troubles might be bigger than he'd initially believed. There'd been money here at one time. Not for a while though. Probably not since the death of Tasha's mother. They weren't at the level of poverty he saw rampant all over the rest of the country, but things hadn't been good here in a long time.

How had John made a living here before? As much as Dane would love to help, how could he? He had given his brother money when he'd first arrived to help him rebuild his business and to help out when the baby came. He gave them money for room and board—and yet didn't eat here.

So, if things were that tight, there'd be no money for Peppe's care either. "How expensive would it be to hire a local to care for him? Surely that would be a minor cost, given the economy right now?"

John's mouth twisted. He walked over to stare out the window. "I don't know. I mentioned something about hiring a woman to come and help out, only Tasha just got a weird look on her face and said, *No women.* Now I've seen for myself that Peppe can be in tough shape from one day to the next, and I know that Emile has lost his temper more than a couple times when he found his father had soiled himself. Apparently his father hadn't even noticed. Some furniture had to be thrown out one time."

Dane tried hard but couldn't quite contain the wrinkle of disgust. It wasn't Peppe's fault. He needed help and shouldn't be living alone. Usually in a case like this, the job fell to the family members, but, if they wouldn't or couldn't, then someone had to be hired to do the job.

"I don't think you have much choice. You can't leave him like that. If Emile and Tasha won't do it, then hire a man. Let him go there once a day and clean Peppe—give him a shave and a hot meal. I don't know what all else he needs. Surely, with so many out of work, you could find a brawny man with the right disposition to help out?"

John turned to face him.

Dane hated his brother's whipped-puppy look and the glimmer of hope sliding into the back of his eyes. Dane understood the situation John faced, but sometimes hard decisions had to be made. John would be a father soon. He needed to step forward and to be a man.

Dane couldn't resist pushing the point home. Not that John would listen. "John, if Peppe's children aren't capable of making a decision, then you have to step in and make it for them."

Straightening his back, John sighed. "I know that. Really. It's just not that simple. I need the pregnancy to be over and to have my Tasha back. I don't know what's eating away at her. It's most likely just hormones, but she's so volatile right now."

"Be that as it may, you can't leave Peppe like this. If it were your father, how would you feel?"

John snorted. "That old soldier boy would have walked off a bridge before ending up like Peppe."

"I highly doubt any of us would choose to live Peppe's not-so-golden years. I do know that we all deserve respect and to keep our dignity at times like this—and Peppe, if he really knew and understood, would be horrified."

John stared down at the tray and then back at his brother. "Do you want to come with me? Let's take a look and see how bad it really is."

"Hell no, I don't want to—but I will." Dane grinned at the dark look shooting his way. "Come on. Let's go face the Devil himself."

SUSAN CORNERED JADE in the computer room in the late afternoon. Jade had barely managed to get back to her charts, after the relief she felt at Tony's departure. Still, the work had to be done, and, now that she didn't have anyone watching over her—at least no one sitting here in the room watching over her—she wanted to plow through the charts.

"Hey. How is the paperwork going?" Susan dropped her bag on her computer station and took a tissue from her pocket.

It seemed she'd brought dozens of small tissue packets with her. "Are you getting sick?"

"I'd better not be. Tony asked me the same question." Susan grimaced, as Jade twisted her face. "Yeah, he made a good impression on all of us, *huh*? Anyway, he reminded me that no sick days were negotiated into the contract, and, if I wasn't capable of working because of an illness, he'd be forced to replace me."

Jade gasped. "What an asshole." She slapped the chart down on the desk beside her and turned to face Susan. "Did he just come here to upset everyone? 'Cause he succeeded. I am so glad he's gone."

"I second that. What did he do to you?" Susan asked curiously, pulling back her chair and sitting down heavily.

"He made a similar comment about my mental health, afraid that all these deaths would send me off the deep end ... or some such bullshit."

Susan snorted. "Isn't this a fine time to worry about that?"

"I know. We're almost a month into this. If I was going to lose it, I'd have done it when we first found those bones and chains."

Susan shivered and then sneezed. After a moment, she added, "Maybe I should go lie down. I'd hate to have this get any worse."

"Yes, you should. It's Friday. We've put in lots of overtime already. Go. Rest and come back on Monday, happy and healthy."

With a watery grin, the woman picked up her bag again. "Okay, you've convinced me. Besides, it's not as if we haven't worked every weekend so far."

"True enough. And this weekend won't be any different." Jade watched as Susan made a hasty exit, sneezing several times on the way. She returned to her workload.

Meg walked in five minutes later. "So are you excited?"

"*Hmm?*" Jade stared at her. "What did you say?"

"I asked if you were excited. About tonight? Your hot date with Dane?"

Jade flushed. She'd been trying to keep the date out of her mind all day. She found it a little hard to function with the butterflies rolling around inside. She didn't know what to expect, and her clothing choices were beyond limited. But then she didn't want to get hung up on that either. "I'm happy to be going out. Just not so secure in the whole *date* thing."

"Aha. If you haven't been dating for a while, I can see how that might be a little daunting. Still, you must get a lot of male attention. You're gorgeous."

Jade stared at her. Then laughed. "Aren't you a comic?"

Meg walked over and sat down beside her. "You, my dear, need to work on your self-esteem. What happened to knock that down?"

The question caught Jade sideways. She leaned back to look at the woman she'd come to view as a friend. "I'm not so sure that it's been knocked down as much as knocked back a pace or two. I had a bad breakup close to one year ago and haven't ventured into that realm since."

Tilting her head sideways, Meg smiled compassionately. "That's a decent amount of time. You don't appear to be too upset over it now."

Was she? Not heartbroken, at least not now. In fact, Jade could honestly say that she'd had a lucky escape—at least from him. Other things that happened at the same time were more painful.

"No. I was angry for a long time, but that's dissipated." She shrugged. "I'm saddened at the way everything ended."

"And now Dane is in your life."

Jade grinned. "Right. At least for tonight."

"Hey, he lives in Seattle, where you live too, and he packs a load of sex appeal into that lean rangy body, doesn't he?"

"Yeah, he does that." She'd had a hell of a time falling asleep last night because of it. Damn, he looked good. That just brought back another worry. "Sex isn't an issue on a first date, is it?"

Meg raised her eyebrows. "Sex should never be an issue. It happens on some first dates, if everything is hot-hot and hotter. If that's the case, then go for it. Otherwise, it shouldn't even come up." She grinned. "Although it's a good sign if it does."

Jade smirked, as she shook her head. "It's been a few years since my last relationship started. I'd forgotten the initial heat of attraction."

"That should have been a bad sign about your previous relationship if the heat didn't last long. So Dane has got your juices flowing, has he?"

"Hell, he's probably had every female in Haiti paying attention to him." Jade said it with humor but didn't know how she felt about that.

"Hot males don't make bad mates. They are often very loyal. My partner and I have been together for a decade now. I still love him, and he's still the best-looking guy I've ever seen." Meg's smile saddened. "That's the only thing about this job. I hate being away from home."

"No wish to settle down and to start a family?"

"We've discussed it, but it's never the right time."

Meg slouched back in her chair, seemingly unaware of her own natural beauty. Then that was probably one of the reasons Jade had clicked with her so fast. She was natural, without pretention.

Jade shook her head again. "Don't think there is any one right time. If you have a strong foundation, you may want to think on it. You're what? … Thirty-three or thirty-four?"

"Thirty-seven and turning thirty-eight in a few months. I know the clock's ticking, but that's not the best determining factor. I'd rather know that gallivanting off on these jaunts is out of my system, so I'm content to stay home as a mom. I want to look forward to that stage of my journey, instead of feeling tied down by it."

"That's reasonable. At least then you'll be ready inside." Jade looked down at the stacks of charts in front of her. She might have to work all weekend to get caught up at this rate.

"*Hmm.* What about you? No desire to have kids? Although you have more time than I do." Meg smiled.

Inside, Jade winced. "Yes, I still have time. I've thought about it a lot. I was engaged, looking forward to starting a family. It's amazing how much your perspective changes after a breakup."

"Breakups are always tough. If you didn't make it to the married part, chances are you're much better off without him."

Jade agreed. She *was* so much better off. "I know that now, but that's the thing. When you're in a relationship, it's hard to see what you really do have. You're too close, so to speak."

"True enough. Just don't take that kind of baggage on your date tonight. Dane looks like he's the kind of guy who gets out and enjoys life a little. Sounds like you could use the extra attention."

Jade nodded. "I'm looking forward to that."

THE TREK TO Peppe's cabin took only a few minutes. They walked past a clump of spindly trees, their steps sounding loudly on the hard-packed dirt path. Dane stopped and turned around. "I thought he was a lot farther away. Although that's a good thing." He grinned. "I actually have plans for tonight."

John stared at him in astonishment. "Really? Who is she?"

Dane shook his head. "Not sure I want to say. I haven't let a lady get close like this in a long time. I'm taking her out tonight."

"Really? Wow!" He might have been planning to say more, but they'd reached the cabin door. No sounds came from within. John climbed the first and then the second step, before turning back to his brother. "All joking aside, … Peppe isn't quite right. I know I haven't said too much about him. It's complicated. He has good days and bad days, but his good days are often hard to distinguish from the others now." John turned to Dane quickly, uneasily. "I don't know what shape he'll be in.

Dane looked at the cabin door from behind his brother. The

porch out front was wide, but the cabin had to be decades old. If it was sound, then age was no problem, but this building could also use some help. *Damn.* He needed to have a serious talk with his brother. "My question is, why is this such an issue?" He strode in front of his brother, opened the door, and reeled backward. "Oh, for Christ's sake."

His arm came up to protect his nose. He stumbled backward and down the steps, coughing. After a moment, he bent over his knees and took several deep breaths. "What is that smell? Jesus, John. Please tell me the old man isn't living in that."

"The place has been cleaned several times, but that damn smell never goes away." John winced. He stood with his back to the door, staring back the way they'd come. "That's why I can't do this. I'm standing here now because I can't force myself to go inside. How sad is that?"

Dane took several deep breaths, trying to clear his head. "Damn it, John. Leaving someone to live in that sewer is criminal. If you won't do something about this, then I will." He fisted his hands on his hips. "But you won't like my methods. I'll call in the authorities over this."

John snorted. "Like they'll give a shit. This isn't the States, Dane. We don't have the same regulatory bodies here as are back home." He grunted. "Besides, Tasha would never forgive you. Or me. They look after their own here."

Home? That's the first he'd heard his brother refer to the US as home. Did his brother want to return to Seattle? Take his family with him? Dane would have to give that some thought. In the meantime, this mess had to be dealt with. "That's fine, *if* they do look after their own. Living in this cabin can't be good for anyone. Damn it, John, stand up and be a man."

John shuddered, releasing a deep breath. His shoulders sagged, and he closed his eyes briefly. "Fine. I will look for someone tomorrow, and I just won't tell her."

"You'll have to hire more than one person, or you won't keep the first one. This place needs to be burned. It's unbelievable."

John turned to face the open door and frowned. "I wonder why Peppe hasn't come out. He never misses a good fight."

"Then go in and see. For all you know, the old man died from the rot in there."

Shooting his brother a dark look, John took a deep breath and raced inside. He came out several minutes later, gasping for air. "He's not here. I wonder if he's taken off again?"

Dane snorted. "Hell, I wouldn't stay in there either. Does he go out much?" Dane spun around, wondering where the hell the old man could have disappeared to. If he carried the aroma of this cabin, they should smell him miles away.

"He's been on his own for a long time, so I have no idea. I've avoided coming here for months. But, from what Emile and Tasha have said, he used to take off for weeks on end."

Dane hopped up, took a deep breath, pinched his nose, and walked into the small cabin. There was no sign of the old man. His bed was empty, the one chair in the place ... empty. Nothing but dirt, trash, waste. He shuddered. Unable to hold his breath any longer, he bolted outside. "Whew. That is beyond rank, John."

"Tasha said Emile had been shaving and washing the old man." John turned back to stare inside the small cabin. "I wonder if Tasha knows Emile hasn't been looking after him?"

"He's her brother. She has to know what he's like." Dane stepped several steps farther away, gasping for clean air. "Hell, I know what Emile's like, and I can tell you that he does the minimum at every turn. If he can get out of a job, he will, and, if he can get away with a half-assed job, then consider that done too."

John shuddered. "I wonder if he's even been feeding him?"

"I'd say, chances are, he started out with good intentions a few months ago, whenever Tasha quit looking after Peppe, and then Emile's done less and less each trip back here. That's probably why Peppe's taken off."

John's face twisted.

"What?" Dane puzzled why John wouldn't meet his gaze.

"Tasha quit looking after her father a long time ago. She's using her pregnancy as an excuse to get out of coming to help with her father for right now, but she had a broken leg before that, remember? Anyway, I don't think she's cared for him for close to a year, not since the big quake, I think."

Staring at the woods around them, Dane shook his head. "Why? I don't understand. I'm trying, John, but your new family is a little weird."

"I know. The thing is, you don't realize just how weird until something happens. It's like the earthquake changed things. She wasn't like this a couple years ago. I loved her so much then."

"*Then?*" Dane jumped on that one word. It went along with John's earlier comment about *back home.*

John ran his right hand over his short dark hair. "I didn't mean that. It's just that she was more loveable back then. I feel like I live in a war zone. Each day I have to work hard at being tolerant and patient. Sometimes I'm not sure I'll make it to the end of the pregnancy."

"As it is, I didn't think you had it in you to be this patient. I don't think I could be." Dane meant it. He thought he'd been a very patient man, until he'd seen his brother's tolerance. His brother was a bloody saint.

"I have to find a way to make this all work. I can't lose it all *again*."

It was that one word—*again*—that broke Dane's heart. "Damn it, John. You have to stop letting the past haunt you. You won't lose Tasha. Just because you lost Elise in a car accident, that doesn't mean you'll lose every woman you love. You don't have to lose anything or anyone. If this isn't working out, you need to take another look and figure out how to make it work."

"I know. ... I know," John cried out. "Why do you think I've been paralyzed with inactivity on the Peppe issue? And it's the same for my company. I'm bankrupt. My marriage is on the rocks, and I don't know how to save it. My child is due to be born in a month, and I don't know how to make that a good thing. I can't stand my li—"

John's voice cut out, as if sliced by a knife. He stared at Dane, horrified. "Oh God. I didn't say that, did I?"

Dane's heart broke. "Yes, you did." He pursed his lips and thought about what John had really said. "How much of your problem is because you don't know what you really want?" John appeared to not want anything he currently had—but had he figured that out yet? Some truths had to be reached on their own. God help John, if he decided that to be true.

John lifted a trembling hand. "Probably everything. I should never have started my own company. I'm not cut out for it. I need a job that pays decent and lets me go home to my family every day. I can't keep doing this." John plunked down on the bottom step of Peppe's cabin. "I haven't told Tasha that no money's left. No business is left."

"That's why you've been so patient and let her walk all over you?"

He nodded. "I feel like I'm coming apart at the seams. I've been waiting for the right time to discuss it, but it never comes."

"Jesus, John, there is no right time for bad news. You have to tell her." Dane groaned and stared at the festering cabin in front of him. "That's why you haven't done anything about Peppe. You don't have the money, do you? What about the chunk I gave you?"

Gazing at his brother with a defeated look, John shook his head. "No. It's all gone."

Chapter 13

MIKE STARED AT the bones, the poor light in the lab trailer derailing his progress. He hadn't left with the others, even though it was the end of work on a Friday afternoon—their time for beer out on the garden patio. And beer would be good right now. Not to mention he'd planned on talking to them about the hike he had in mind. Only he hadn't had a chance to check the options yet.

This mess with the manacles and bones sitting on his table had to be sorted out first.

He didn't know what to do with the information he had. The authorities didn't care. The local people didn't appear to care. So few people had shown up for DNA tests that he was beginning to suspect all their processing would be for naught. They could have just created a second grave site right beside the first one and moved over the bodies that didn't fit the parameters of the ones they were looking for. Would have cut the work in half.

Damn it. He knew these manacled women had been murdered. He'd bet his thirty-year reputation on it. And no one cared. *That's what hurt the most. All these women mistreated, captive for who knows how long? … And then they'd been murdered. And no one cared.*

And the details his team unearthed weren't required or welcome because, as far as the police were concerned, this wasn't something they would follow up on.

In the US, there would have been teams of specialists digging out this site to determine the type of dirt above and around, collecting the bugs, etc. Here, there was only him—and his team. And he didn't have the necessary equipment to collect all the evidence and to record all the details.

Tony had been adamant. Pass over the information to the authorities and get off the case. He'd said, *There's no joy in being the bearer of the bad news here. They won't thank us, not with the thousands of people unaccounted for here. Let it go. Process and move on.*

Speaking to the empty trailer, Mike said, "Right. And what about justice for these women?"

He walked over to the front of the trailer and stuck his head out. When he looked around, he heard something rustling in the woods, only he couldn't see anyone.

"Hey, Doc."

Mike squinted. John's brother-in-law walked toward him. *Emile.* Dressed for the heat in a tank top and blue jeans—the uniform of choice the world over—he strolled toward the lab trailer.

"Hi. Are you looking for Dane?"

"*Nah,* I know where he is. We're all looking for my father, who's gone wandering. He's not quite right in the head and gets lost easily." Emile's gaze shifted from the lab trailer to the rocks surrounding the clearing.

"Oh, dear. I haven't seen him around. Sorry." Mike couldn't help but glance around the clearing at the same time.

Emile shoved his hands into his pockets. "No problem. I figured you were here, so I asked."

Mike hesitated. He hated to ask the young man, but a few minutes of his help would be huge. He needed to get the remains stored away. "Hey, while you're here, would you mind giving me a hand moving a few things over to the other trailer?"

Emile's face twisted. "As long as it's not bodies. I don't hold on touching the dead."

"It is bones, only you won't have to touch them. I already have them in sealed bags on the stretchers." His words rushed out to reassure Emile. "I just need you to grab an end and help me move them to the other trailer."

Emile looked like he wanted to refuse but couldn't figure out how. Mike pressed his advantage. "Honest. A five-minute job—not even that. I can't leave them here over the weekend. They need to be locked in the reefer truck."

Emile's face scrunched in horror.

Mike spoke faster, before Emile could run as far and as fast as he could in the opposite direction. "I promise. You won't even see them. They are packed up. They're so small I can even put them both on the same stretcher." He stared hopefully at Emile. "Please."

Emile stared around, as if hoping someone else would show.

"There's no one else. It has to be you."

Emile's shoulders sagged. "One trip—and I don't touch anything but the stretcher handles."

"Done." Mike brightened. "Let's do it right now. It'll be over in five minutes."

Emile, once the decision was made, followed along willingly enough. He grabbed the one end of the stretcher and waited while Mike shifted the bags and laid them on top of each other. Mike grabbed his end of the stretcher. "Okay, here we go."

He'd been right. The trip took about two minutes. And Emile, true to his word, refused to help open doors or touch the bags. Mike shook his head, trying hard to understand. Not everyone could handle his profession. Death freaked out so many people.

Too bad. Everyone came to the same end, regardless of how hard they tried to avoid it.

"Thanks, Emile. I can take it from here."

Emile backed away from the freezer trailer as if afraid he'd be bagged and laid next to the others. Mike watched him almost hyperventilate with relief.

"Hey, are you all right?" He walked down to check on him.

Emile glanced back. "Yeah. I'm okay. Just don't want to be in there." He motioned toward the trailer. "Have these ones been identified now?"

"Not yet." Mike looked back down the long interior. "We have lots to do."

"What about the ones we just brought over. Are they done?"

"They've been processed, just not identified." Mike walked out the rest of the way and slammed the heavy door shut. He slid across the bolt closure and snapped on the big lock.

"Most are on one side. We put those on the opposite side," Emile pressed.

"Yeah." Mike gave him a weary smile. "Those ones are special."

Emile's gaze narrowed. "Why? Are they not all special?"

With a long look at the grave site and the bodies that still waited to be uncovered, Mike couldn't help but agree with him. "That is so true. Yet even in a large grave like that, some are different." Mike headed back to the lab. "Thank you for the help."

Emile followed him back to the lab trailer and glanced around the small room. "Lots of equipment. Not much space."

"Yeah. That should be our new logo." Mike glanced up at him with a smile—in time to see horror scrunch Emile's face. "What is it? What's wrong?"

Emile pointed to the floor, where they'd moved the stretcher. "What's that?"

Bending down, Mike found two chain links that must have fallen out from one of the women's body bags. The rusty iron clanged as he placed the links into a clear bag. "Damn. I missed these. I wonder which bag they came from."

Emile's face paled. He straightened and raced outside.

"Thanks again for your help, Emile," Mike called after him.

He never responded. Mike walked outside, sealing the chain in a small plastic bag. Emile was bent over a bush off to one side. *Uh-oh.*

As Mike watched, Emile coughed and spewed again. Mike stepped back to give him some privacy. *Damn.* He hadn't meant to upset him. Some people just didn't handle this stuff well. He set about putting the piece of chain away properly.

He walked out to check on him a few minutes later, but Emile had left.

Mike hoped he'd find his father. This wasn't a good place to go missing. Then again, this grave was right next to the old man's property, and he'd lived here for decades. He probably knew every rock and tree in the area. Positioned in the rocks and hills as their camp was, the sun had long disappeared behind the greenery, throwing lengthening shadows and weird fingers of light through the area.

Straightening, Mike stretched out his sore back and shoulders. Lord, he was tired. Long day. Long week actually. He double-checked the temperature and the lock on the reefer, before heading over to lock the lab trailer.

Time to leave.

EMILE SLIPPED AROUND the rocks, watching as the old man left the smaller trailer. Emile's mouth still smarted from the sour retchings of his stomach. How could people work in there? Touching the dead, violating their bodies, their souls. He shuddered.

How wrong could life get? He'd thought things had been bad after that big earthquake. He'd seen things that still gave him nightmares. He'd watched things people had done to each other in the name of survival.

Survival also had little to do with some of what he'd witnessed. Predators had preyed on the dead, the living, and those caught in between. He'd seen thieves empty pockets, steal shoes, grab anything that could be removed, and run to the next body, alive or dead. It hadn't mattered.

The things Emile had seen in town had been unbelievably difficult. And none of it touched on the horror of what he'd found later. Something so awful, so terrible, he couldn't stop thinking about it since. He'd had to clean up the mess, and doing something to protect another had seemed right at the time—until he'd been seen.

His stomach dry heaved with the painful memories.

He hadn't been the same since.

Then the horror had turned to fascination, and that scared him even more. The very idea had settled into his psyche and had rooted, then had sprouted into another horrible concept, only this time he was a part of it.

He shuddered.

He couldn't do that to a woman.

He shouldn't do that to a woman.

But he would—if he got the chance.

With one last look at the empty lab trailers, and the place he'd find two unprotected women, he refocused on finding his old man.

Damn him, anyway.

THE BEAUTIFUL EVENING and cool breeze blowing over Jade's heated skin made warmth blossom inside her. She sighed happily. Her hotel room held a lightness that she enjoyed, and it certainly beat the afternoon mugginess that had settled in today.

She'd spent all week in a state of nervous anticipation. Now that the time for her date had arrived, she was listening for vehicles, checking out every unusual sound, and doing lots of heavy sighing. Much to Meg's amusement.

For tonight, Jade had chosen her one decent sundress and a light sweater, just in case a wind came up. Sandals and a little light makeup too. Why she'd brought makeup when she almost never wore it, she didn't know. She'd been thinking ahead obviously. Plus she thought it was a good sign that she wanted to look special for Dane, … and that made her smile.

She missed the closeness, the specialness that came when she was part of a loving twosome. Even if it had been a long time ago. Even if it hadn't stood the test of time and trauma.

At the same time, trust and confidence were now bigger considerations for Jade before entering a new relationship.

Dane made her heart warm; she'd be happy to see where this went. Actually she'd be more than happy to help it along. He did make her hormones pay attention. She'd always enjoyed sex. She hadn't missed it because she'd been so busy being mad and hurt. Now, however, a part of her was raring to make up for lost time. How contrary could she be?

Still, the butterflies in her stomach wouldn't calm down, and honestly, she was starving again. She hoped he'd planned for a decent meal. She took a deep breath and walked downstairs to the lobby.

Dane walked in the front door as she reached the front desk. The sight of him stopped Jade in her tracks. *Damn.* He looked beyond good. Black jeans and a white cotton shirt with a stand-up collar. Only it wasn't the clothes that caused her breath to hitch. It was the way he wore them.

She sighed. All that casual muscle and grace. Like a lion roaming his territory. He knew how he looked, was proud of it, and didn't need to show off to be appreciated.

"Hi." Dane stopped in front of her, a warm welcome on his face. His eyes ran appreciatively over her.

Yeah, he was good for her self-confidence. "Hi. You didn't tell me what we were doing or where we're going, and I only have a limited wardrobe with me, so—"

"You look great. Come on. Let's get out of here." He put an arm over her shoulders and walked her out to his truck. "We're heading to a place my brother told me about."

"Perfect. I haven't been anywhere here, so it will be new and different."

"Good. I like an adventurous spirit." He opened the truck door and helped her up to the passenger seat. After walking around to the other side, he hopped in and started the engine.

She buckled her seat belt and settled in for the drive. "Adventure is nice. Life has been a little depressing lately."

"We can fix that. That's one thing I learned in my time here. Every day is a gift. Haiti has been through so much that sometimes we all need to work a little harder to find the good in the bad."

Jade glanced at him. He drove the same as he did everything else. Capably and with restrained power. *Sexy.* She sighed. Lord, she had it bad. When she'd decided to move on with her life, she'd done so with a vengeance.

"Problems?" He frowned, glancing over at her quickly.

"No. I've been thinking the same thing about Haiti. Everyone here has been through so much. It makes our lives back home look easy in comparison. It's been good coming back here. I needed to see the progress."

"Coming back? Were you here before?" He turned the truck around the next corner and headed for one of the main roads.

"I was here in the aftermath of the big earthquake. Did a three-week stint with a mortuary team then. It was brutal. Emotionally and physically."

He whistled softly and gunned the truck forward. "Then let's show you some of the better sights of Haiti and replace those more painful memories with beautiful ones. Help you to put these old memories where they belong—in the past."

Chapter 14

THE QUIET DIGNITY of the small restaurant surprised Jade. As if it were proud to be standing after all these years. Old, distinguished, and family run, the restaurant had the bulk of its seating area under the open sky on decks of different levels. Jade and Dane sat on an outside edge, surrounded by brightly colored hanging lanterns. Several other tables full of diners were discreetly placed throughout. Small screens offered privacy, while allowing almost everyone a view of the sleepy harbor. The tang of the salty ocean mixed with the heavenly smells coming from the kitchen.

Beaches were everywhere here—gorgeous blue water, smooth sand, with the locals working their boats from one side of the bay to the other. Not the typical resort beach but a working, living, breathing part-of-the-people beach.

Now that work had settled into a routine, Jade would like to take a day off every weekend and explore. Going out on a date, like tonight, was a wonderful way to start her new plan.

While they watched, the sky slipped through a rainbow of colors. The sunset shifted and changed so quickly, she couldn't take her eyes off it. "I've never seen anything so beautiful," she murmured. Warmth wrapped around her heart. She wasn't lying. Right now everything felt perfect. She smiled, turned her face up to the evening sky, and closed her eyes.

"Neither have I."

Startled, she turned to face him. "Sorry?"

"I haven't seen anything so beautiful either."

Only he was staring right at her. Heat swamped her cheeks, as she blushed like a schoolgirl. "Wow, thanks." She gave a light laugh. "I'm not used to flattery."

"And why is that?" His curious gaze studied her face. "You're seriously gorgeous, you know?"

Flustered from his sincerity, she answered with a soft smile,

"Thank you again. I haven't been out much in the last year, and I've forgotten how to accept a compliment."

"Nursing a broken heart?"

Her fingers tapped a tempo on the table, as she tried to sort out the best thing to say. "Not quite. Started that way. Now it's a matter of not allowing my history to dictate my future. In other words, not to see my ex and his deficits in every man."

"Ouch." He winced.

A giggle escaped. She clapped a hand over her mouth, staring at him in astonishment. He gave a shout of laughter. When her merriment calmed, she said, "Sorry, I was trying to be honest, only maybe that was too honest. I'm not judging you, and, if I were, you've already got him beat by a mile. So let's change the subject. This evening is too nice to ruin."

Deep-blue eyes gazed into hers. He reached across the table and clasped her hand in his. "Nicely put. And you're right. It is too nice an evening for such conversation. However, I am sorry about the bad experiences."

"Everyone has them." She smiled down at their hands. His so rough and strong, working man's hands. Hers so soft and small—she lived in surgical gloves. Yet their hands fit together like interlocking puzzle pieces. She stroked the long line of his thumb, loving his instant response, as her hand was captured between both of his.

"I don't know," Dane replied. "My life hasn't been filled with drama or heartache."

His tone held no suggestion of anything dark in his history. No censorship either. She searched his gaze. "No bad breakups?"

Dane frowned and stared down at his fingers, clenching automatically.

Her fingers, of their own volition, squeezed back. She didn't want him to be alone with bad memories. As she had been. "Yeah. That's what I mean."

He looked at her in surprise. Then understanding lit the depths of his gaze. "Not me. My brother. He's the reason for whatever you were assuming. He's been through some seriously bad periods in his life. I thought he'd found better times."

"John?"

Dane nodded. "Just the two of us are left, so I tend to keep an eye on him, although he's obviously an adult." Dane shrugged self-consciously. "Family. You can't let them wallow."

Jade laughed, a warm smile blooming across her face. "Isn't that the truth? You sound just like my brother, Duncan. I'm here because of him. He convinced me to come back."

"It was *that* bad?" Dane searched her face. "John won't talk about it much."

"It's not easy. Duncan wanted me to spew everything too. Only talking about it actually made it all come alive again. I had to relive stuff I'd rather not see again."

Dane leaned back, though his index finger gently stroked the back of her hand. "I'm sorry. Sorry that so many people suffered. I never considered the impact on volunteers and rescuers." He stared off at the sunset.

From the look on his face, Jade didn't think he was enjoying Mother Nature's artwork.

"John has slipped back into someone I barely recognize. The things he's doing—or rather, not doing—" Dane shook his head. "It's hard to stand by and to let life happen to those you love."

"Duncan basically said the same thing to me." She studied their interlocking fingers. That felt right somehow. She hadn't expected to feel anything in Haiti, except pain and anguish. She'd been wrong, and Duncan had been right. She'd have to remember to tell him that. "I'll call my brother tomorrow and tell him that he's the best brother anyone could have."

Dane chuckled. "See? That's the difference between having a little sister versus a little brother. John would die before saying something like that."

"That's a guy thing. Duncan pushed and prodded me for months now. He deserves to know that I'm healing."

"Absolutely. What does he do?"

She gave him a quick rundown, turning the conversation to more generic issues. Several hours later, after they'd worked through many topics, dinner, and dessert, Dane looked at her and asked, "Do you want to go back to the hotel now or would you like to walk down by the water?" He pointed out a path that led to the beach via the side of the restaurant.

"Oh, perfect. I'd love to go for a walk. I'm in no hurry to return."

She waited by the path, as he took care of the bill. When he walked over, he slipped an arm around her shoulders and led her to the water's edge.

Tonight was about magic. About possibilities. About the future.

They spent a sensual hour in the moonlight, with water lapping at the shore, as they walked close together, discussing anything that came up. By the time they came to a small wooden bench, Jade realized how much she'd learned about Dane and his character. The more she learned, the more she liked and respected the man. He reminded her of Duncan.

She sat down on the bench, tugging him down beside her. "I'm having a wonderful evening tonight. I know we have to leave soon, but this is truly special."

He grinned. "Glad you've enjoyed it. Maybe we can do it again."

"Absolutely." She'd love to repeat this evening—several times if possible.

"If you don't have any plans for tomorrow, maybe we can go for coffee or take a walk. Something simple."

She smiled. "That would be lovely."

PARKED OUTSIDE HER hotel twenty minutes later, Dane studied her fine-boned features, the delicate blush of color. She didn't have the same suntan that most of her other team members sported, probably because she worked in the lab so much. He loved the relaxed peacefulness he read on her face tonight.

Jade often looked like life was a serious business, ... one that reaped few rewards. He wanted to show her how much fun life could be. How good relationships could be. How good the two of them could be. If she gave them, ... *him*, a chance.

But he didn't want to scare her off.

Somewhere in all of this, he needed her to feel comfortable with him. For her to move at her own pace. For her to be in control.

He leaned back in the driver's seat, turned slightly to face her, and opened his arms, waiting to see what she would do.

When she smiled shyly, it made his heart melt.

She slid across the bench seat and snuggled close. She grasped both sides of his face, then stretched up slowly, oh-so-slowly, and put her lips against his. In a kiss so gentle, so special, it almost broke his heart. Gently stroking her arms with one hand, the other moved soothingly down and across her back and tucked her against his chest.

He felt a shiver slide down her back, so he drew her in closer, warming her slowly beneath his caressing hands. He wanted her. Had wanted her since he had first laid eyes on her. And a little cuddling in the truck was a great prelude, except he was no untried kid. He wanted so much more. And not in the truck, like two crazed teenagers. She deserved a soft bed and all the trappings that were possible for their first night together. And him? Well, he deserved time. Time to savor her, to explore, to enjoy. He moaned softly against her lips.

She pulled back slightly and smiled at him. "That's your good-night kiss."

He smiled slowly, wickedly. "Fine, then here's *your* goodnight kiss," he whispered, caressing her lips with his breath. His warm hands slid up her back to comb through her silky hair, anchoring her in place. Then he lowered his head. He didn't ravish; he didn't take. He coaxed, soothed, and enticed. When she sagged against him, he pulled back slightly, dropping his forehead against hers. "If you're going in alone, you need to go now."

She smiled and nuzzled against his face and chin. "And if I don't?"

"Then you'll be going in with company. And I don't want to cheat either of us by rushing you at this stage. If you need time, I'm happy to move slowly—well, as slowly as we can go when we're short on time." He laughed self-consciously.

She laughed too, a soft joyous sound that enchanted even as he questioned it.

"What part was funny?"

"Slightly slow is good, but I'm finding I'm much less affected than I thought I was." She dropped a kiss on his chin.

His breath caught. *Damn.* Images ripped through his mind. He almost groaned aloud. "Meaning?"

"I might be okay with quick, but this voice of reason is telling me to slow down slightly." She retreated, a regretful smile on her face. "Have to say, I'm not comfortable with sex on the first date. No matter how tempting."

He kissed the tip of her nose, before she retreated out of reach. "Tempting? So how about dinner tomorrow? The next day? The day after?"

Her gaze widened.

He rushed in with words. "I want to spend as much time with you as I can. To find out what we have. So think about me. About there being an *us*. And, if a weekend away appeals, give me some dates that work, and I'll set it up."

She laughed. "So I get to decide?"

"Absolutely. I can get away any weekend. Your schedule is a little different. I'm serious about seeing you after we return to the States too, but I'd like to spend as much time as we can together here."

Dane's cell rang, interrupting the intimate moment. Jade slid back slightly to give him room. She'd been snuggled tightly against him, and he hated the immediate coolness that drifted into the space. He wanted to tug her back, but the moment was lost.

He pulled out his phone, wondered at the number on display, and answered it.

DANE TWISTED ON the front seat of his truck and clicked a button on his phone. "I've just put the call on Speaker. It's Bruce. Something's wrong."

Jade's eyes widened, and she cast a glance out her window toward the hotel. "Bruce, what's up?"

"Have you seen or heard from Dr. Mike?"

The anxiety level coming through the phone made Jade's stomach knot and her throat catch. "Not since lunchtime. I worked in the office here at the hotel all afternoon. I don't think he'd returned by the time I left tonight."

"Right. He's not answering his phone. He's got one of the SUVs, and we don't know where he is."

She swallowed and stared at Dane. Dr. Mike wasn't old, but anything could have happened. "Could he have gone out for dinner or into town for a little fun after a tough week? It is Friday night."

"Maybe." Bruce's doubtful voice didn't put any credence to her theory though. "He should be back, if he went for dinner."

"What time is it?"

"Almost midnight."

Dane pointed at his lit watch display to confirm the time. "Wow. I had no idea it was so late. What do you want me to do?"

"I don't know. I can hardly raise an alarm just because he didn't come back from the job site and isn't answering his phone. So I guess we wait." He sighed heavily. "But I don't like it."

"We're in the truck, almost at the hotel," she lied, rolling her eyes at the wicked grin that flashed on Dane's face. "We can take a run past the site, if you'd like us to check for him there. Just to ensure he's not still working. You know how he felt about processing those remains."

Bruce's voice brightened. "Hey, I never thought about that. Maybe that's what he's doing. But he should have answered his phone then."

"Not if his battery is dead. Besides, I don't think Dane will mind driving out there with me." She glanced over at Dane, who nodded in agreement. "Dr. Mike may also have stopped in at the authorities to talk to someone, ... and that could take hours."

"You're right." Bruce paused. "He could be anywhere. I'm just paranoid."

"Better than uncaring. We'll take a drive to the lab to be sure." She disconnected the call and handed the phone back to Dane. "Sorry, I guess I should consider picking up a cell phone of my own while here."

He started the engine. "I gather Dr. Mike is missing?"

"I don't know that he's missing, but no one's seen him in hours, and he's not answering his phone."

Dane pulled the truck onto the main road. "I know it's none of my business, however, what's with the going-to-the-authorities business?"

"Dr. Mike found something—well, we all did actually—that raised a few questions." She smiled apologetically. "I'm not at liberty to say what, but Bruce stopped and spoke with the police yesterday. Said they weren't too bothered." She frowned. "They told him, if we came across definite proof, then we could come back and talk to them again."

Dane raised an eyebrow at her, before turning his attention to maneuver through the surprising amount of traffic for a Friday night. "*Hmm.* Drop a bomb like that, then don't fill in the details. Okay. I don't like it, but I can understand you not being able to speak freely." He thought for a moment. "I don't know how effective the police are here at this time. They are dealing with high-priority issues that affect their people *now*. If whatever you found is associated with the grave from a year ago, ... I don't think it'll be a priority."

"True enough." She shrugged. "It's easy to judge. From their perspective, we waltzed in here with fancy degrees and equipment and tore open a grave that everyone had been happy enough to leave alone. Now we want to make waves because of a few of the bodies."

"A few. So not an isolated case?" Dane frowned. "That's not great."

"Nope." The sky had taken on a dark-on-darker splotching look. Stars had all but disappeared behind clouds. She pointed it out. "I hate to say anything superstitious, but now the sky's almost angry looking."

He laughed. "Wait until you've been here a bit longer. I've never known such a people for their rituals and beliefs. Tasha helps her cousins make and sell these little eerie dolls and totems to the tourists.

The house is full of them in various stages. I honestly don't know why anyone would pay good money for them."

Jade shuddered and told him what Magrim had said to her that day she'd gone shopping. "What freaked me out the most was the weird look in her eyes when delivering the message."

"Did you believe her?" Dane raised an eyebrow, as he studied her face.

Shifting uncomfortably, Jade wished she hadn't brought it up. "I didn't *not* believe her. Her message was just so weird." Jade quoted, "*Danger stalks you. You see it, but you don't understand it. Careful. Or you will join those who have gone before.*" She shuddered again. "If I'd gone to a séance or something else as ridiculous, then I'd have tossed it off as a marketing ploy. However, the hotel manager says Magrim is for real, and I'd better watch my back." She shivered in the slightly cooled air. Magrim, murder victims, and now a missing Dr. Mike. Not an uplifting series of events.

"Well, I wouldn't let her worry you. Just be careful. If anything suspicious is going on at the grave site, then you don't want the news to get out. Things are still pretty primitive here—the laws, minimal. People disappear all the time."

Horrified, she stared at him. Swallowing hard, she asked, "Like Dr. Mike?"

DANE DROVE FAST in the building darkness. He had bright headlights and great night vision, and he pushed the truck to eat through the miles. Though she was quiet, he could tell Jade was beyond freaked out. He should not have said anything about disappearances. Still, if something had gone wrong, no point in sugarcoating it. Bruce hadn't brought in the necessary security, and there could already be one casualty.

He hoped he was wrong.

"Do you have to drive this fast?" Her timid voice penetrated his thoughts.

"Sorry." He eased back on the gas. "I'm used to it, and I know the roads."

"I thought you might have been angry at something," she said in a small voice.

Startled, he looked over at her. "In a way I am. But not at you. I texted my brother to see if they'd found his father-in-law earlier, and your conversation about Dr. Mike reminded of that conversation."

"What? Is he missing too?"

He kept his gaze focused on the road ahead, as he answered slowly, hesitantly. "Not really. He's walked away from home again, something he's done many times over the last few years. It's more worrisome now, as he's not himself mentally anymore. I spent time looking for him earlier, before I picked you up. Now the family doesn't want me involved. They don't like what I was saying."

"Saying?"

He felt the intensity of her gaze, rather than saw it. "Yeah. You know, like call in a search party, notify the authorities. Basics." Dane turned to watch the shock develop on her face. She was so open and expressive, she'd make a lousy poker player.

"And they didn't want to get help to find him? Why not?" she asked incredulously.

"Beats me. I expected more from John. That's what I meant earlier. He's changed—and not in a good way. Or maybe he's been this way for years, and I haven't seen it because we've not had much to do with each other over the last decade."

"Do you think he's influenced by his new family?"

"I suspect so. Tasha was muttering something at the kitchen table when I left. Looked like she was creating more of those damn dolls."

"Yuck." Jade explained what she'd learned about Vodou from Susan. "The ones I've seen were beyond freaky."

"The ones she was working on today were just papier-mâché, from the looks of it." He turned his attention back to navigating through the potholes on the road. "I didn't ask. I remember once, when I first arrived, I made a comment that she didn't like. Not sure if she took exception to what I said or to the way I said it. It was the first time I'd seen the temperamental side of her ..."

"And you've seen plenty since?"

"Yeah, you could say that. John says the pregnancy isn't easy on her."

"Oh."

A weird silence filled the cab. *Uh-oh.* He glanced sideways at her. "What did I say?"

"Nothing."

Now that was a lie. He didn't need to see her face to know something was wrong. "Yes, I did. You're different. As if I said something offensive."

She avoided his gaze, staring out into the dark of night instead.

"It's not you. It's me. I lost a baby a year ago, and sometimes I'm a little sensitive."

He sighed. "I am sorry. I didn't know."

"How could you? I didn't tell you."

Her voice was lighter, but still she wasn't saying something. "Was that related to the bad breakup?"

"Yeah. I can't say the breakup caused the miscarriage, as I was pretty broken up over everything going on in my life at that time—but my ex came to me in the hospital to let me know that he wasn't upset about the loss, as my mental state was questionable. And maybe I should seek help."

"Bastard." Soft and deadly, his voice hardened with fury. "There is no excuse for that kind of stuff. Why are people such assholes anyway?"

Her voice, when she answered, was soft, contemplative. "I'd like to think he was hurting from the loss of our child."

"Losing the baby would have been rough, but it wasn't your fault."

"Maybe it was." She shifted uncomfortably on the seat. "I hadn't been home from Haiti for very long, and I wasn't handling that experience well. It had been a terrible trip. I felt so guilty because I had a comfortable home, and the poor people here had no place to go." She stared out the window.

He had to lean closer to hear her next words.

"Worse, I wanted to stay home."

"Which is understandable." At the lack of a response, he added, "And you've stayed home since?"

She laughed. "Yeah. Until my brother forced me to face my fears, and you know what? I found out that it's much easier to let go than I thought."

He couldn't get his mind wrapped around what she'd been through already. But, as long as she was handling it and moving on, then he was good. Emotional women, as he was learning from Tasha, weren't the easiest to be around. He wouldn't expect caterwauling and screaming from Jade, but one never knew what existed underneath.

The rocks shone in the headlights as he pulled into the small clearing. "No SUV."

She frowned. "I see that. I'll check the doors, as I'm here anyway."

He drove to the small porch, his headlights shining on the front door. Jade hopped out and went to check the lock. Giving him a thumbs-up, she went to the refrigerator truck.

On her way back, she told him. "Both are locked tight. I want to walk to the grave site and confirm he isn't lying injured somewhere."

"If he was, his vehicle would be here."

"Not if it was stolen." She raised an eyebrow.

She was right. He turned off the truck, hopped out, and pocketed the keys. "Let's go."

There was enough moonlight to show them the way. He reached for her arm and tucked it against his anyway. He didn't want her falling and hurting herself. The path was uneven and rocky in good light, and, with poor light, this path could be an ankle breaker. In a few minutes they reached the grave site.

"I don't see anything." Then again he hadn't brought a flashlight.

Jade motioned to the rocks in front of them. "I'll climb up to make sure. At least that way, I can have a good look around."

Dane moved first. He stepped onto the first big boulder and then onto the second and the third. He held out his hand and helped her up beside him each time. The moonlight cast an eerie glow on the rocks and created squat blue shadows off others. "I don't see anyone here."

She stared around at the empty vastness surrounded by dark trees and hills. "I guess you're right. It was a faint hope. I just thought that maybe ..."

"It only took us a minute to be sure. Now we are. Are you good to go back to the hotel now?"

"I guess. What about you? Do you want to check in with your brother? See if they found the old man?"

"I'll text him."

Jade released his hand and made her way down to ground level. She walked around while he sent his brother a text. He waited for a moment, then sent a second one. "He's not answering."

She turned to stare at him. "Do you want to stop on the way back and check in?"

He stared at her. What he wanted was to spend the night with her, and that wouldn't happen, ... not this weekend. Next weekend— who knew? He did not want to take her to John's house because she'd be party to any scene that developed there. Perhaps an ugly scene he didn't want to expose her to. Lately there'd been plenty of those. "No, I'll take you to the hotel first."

She shrugged and walked to the clearing and his truck. She stopped abruptly and pointed to something in the rocks, over by the property line. "What's that red spot in the rocks, just below the tree line?"

He frowned, barely making out what she was talking about. "Let's find out."

She led the way. The moon slunk behind the clouds, dimming their vision yet again. Dane hopped over several rocks and came down beside the crumpled figure in front of him. "Shit."

"What is it?" She reached his side, as he answered.

"It's not *what*, but *who*. ... It's Emile."

Chapter 15

JADE WOULD LIKE to think that, in emergency situations, life in Haiti would move at top speed. Only they couldn't raise anyone on the phone when they tried to get help. She didn't understand it. Bruce's line immediately went to voice mail. John wasn't answering. And the cloud cover was building, dimming their natural light even further. "So now what?"

"I think he's coming around," Dane said, bending down. "Emile. It's Dane. Can you hear me?"

Emile groaned softly. Jade watched as Dane ran his hands over Emile, looking for injuries. "He's lying at an odd angle, but I can't find anything broken." He lifted his hand, rubbing his fingers together, peering more closely under the dim moonlight. "There's blood on the back of his head."

"Poor man. It's so damn dark here we can't see anything clearly anyway." She turned to the path. "I'll go grab a flashlight from the trailers." She stopped. "I don't have the trailer keys with me."

"I'm not sure that's an issue. He's waking up now."

She crouched in front of the two of them. "Did you check the back of his head? Perhaps he fell on the rocks and hit his head?"

"Yeah, blood is here and on the ground beneath him. Head injuries can really bleed." Dane glanced at her and nodded. "He was probably searching for his father and fell."

"Let's hope he's not too badly hurt." As she watched, Emile opened his eyes, his gaze widening as he took in his location. Took in them.

"I'm fine." Emile tried to lurch to his feet and fell sideways. Dane lunged to catch him before he fell again. "Hey, take it easy. You've hit your head on a rock."

"Is that why it feels like a watermelon about to explode?"

Dane grinned at Emile's truculent tone.

Jade didn't know how to compare him to what was normal. The

few times she'd seen Emile, he'd been reserved and not terribly communicative—about the same as now.

"Sit and relax for a moment or two."

Jade watched as Dane forcibly pressed Emile onto the closest rock. "Do you know what happened?"

"*Huh*?" Emile peered up at Dane. "What happened?"

"That's what I'm asking you. Do you know what happened to you? What were you doing here?"

"I hit my head, you said."

Oh, dear. Emile wasn't connecting the dots. Jade peered into his eyes. Concussions were nothing to make light of, and neither were head wounds. "We should take him to the hospital."

"Hospital?" Emile reared upward, swaying slightly. "No hospital. Home. Emile go home."

"Okay. Home it is. Come on. Let's see if we can get you to my truck."

Jade watched as Dane half-lifted the much smaller man over the rough rocks to the path. She accepted the keys from Dane and ran ahead to unlock the doors.

Emile settled into the passenger side. Jade ran around and slid into the middle seat and buckled him in. Dane started the truck. Just hearing the engine turn over and seeing the headlights come on made her sigh with relief. Enough had gone wrong tonight, and her skin prickled with foreboding.

Taking the road slowly, Dane bounced the truck to John's gravel driveway and pulled in as close to the kitchen door as he could. Lights were on inside. "Wait, Emile. I'm coming around."

Emile didn't say much, and his breath was raspy and unsteady.

Jade whispered, "Dane, he doesn't look so good. We should take him straight to the hospital."

"I know." Grimly, Dane headed around the truck and instead of coming to the passenger door, he knocked hard and went into his brother's house. A cry, several shouts, followed by heavy footsteps could be heard as John, Tasha, and Dane raced back to the truck. Jade stayed quiet, while Tasha howled over her brother's condition.

John tried to comfort her. Dane tried to talk them into taking Emile to the hospital to get checked out, except, when the hospital was mentioned, Tasha started screaming at the top of her lungs.

Jade had never seen anything like it. Actually that wasn't true. She'd seen too much like it in the aftermath of the earthquake. "Dane?" He couldn't hear her.

It occurred to her that Bruce was a doctor. In fact several of the team were doctors. Surely one could come and take a look? Their professional opinion might sway this emotional, nonsensical reaction. Jade hopped out of the truck and walked over to Dane, standing still, staring at the sky in frustration. She tugged on his sleeve and pulled him aside slightly. "Call Bruce. He's a doctor. He won't mind helping out. You've helped us."

His face brightened. He pulled out his cell phone and made the call. Walking away a distance, Jade studied the very pregnant Tasha in front of her. She looked worse than her brother.

Her hair was mussed and hung lank—her eyes wild.

Jade couldn't quite see the whole picture, but she figured Meg would know what to do or suggest, *if Meg were here.* Jade ran to Dane. "Have him bring Meg, if she's there."

Dane frowned at her and repeated her request. After closing his phone, he asked, "Why Meg?"

"She's a doctor and a psychologist of some sort too. I can't remember exactly what her degrees are."

He stared at her, not comprehending.

With a quick glance in Tasha's direction, she lowered her voice. "Something's not right with Tasha."

His eyes widened, and he turned to study his sister-in-law. Grim lines settled in. "She really doesn't look very good, does she?"

"No."

"Let's hope someone can help. Things are deteriorating on all sides here." Even as he finished speaking, Emile slumped. "Hey, watch him!" He raced over to Emile's side and helped John, who was struggling to hold Emile upright beside the truck.

"I'm fine. Leave me alone." Emile staggered, tried to swat away their hands, and stumbled to the door.

The two men stayed close, managing to get Emile inside. Tasha stood outside and stared at the moon. As Jade approached warily, she heard Tasha muttering under her breath.

"Tasha, come inside. Let's go in and sit down. Get you off your feet," Jade suggested gently.

But Tasha just turned her head, and her black eyes, wide and dark as obsidian, latched onto Jade. "It's too late."

"What's too late? Are you feeling okay?" Jade couldn't hide her concern now. Fear radiated around Tasha. From the size of Tasha's belly, Jade guessed she wasn't far off her due date, a month, ... two at the most. Jade gently put an arm around Tasha's shoulders and urged

Tasha into the house.

Tasha went meekly. Jade led her to the first chair they came across. The men had Emile reclining on the couch. A plaid blanket had been thrown over him.

Another brightly colored blanket lay over a second chair. Jade picked it up and draped it around Tasha's shoulders, then gave her a quick hug. She gently patted Tasha's distended belly.

There was no response. Lucky baby, it was getting to sleep through this nightmare.

Jade felt beyond useless, as she wandered the kitchen area, waiting. She noticed no teakettle here.

As she turned back to the two brothers, who argued in the middle of the living room, she stopped and felt her insides pinch. She looked and noticed the small three- or four-inch-high papier-mâché dolls hanging to dry on lengths of cord throughout the living room and eating area. Like the ones in the market. Tasha reached up and offered one to Jade. Not wanting to offend the woman, Jade accepted one and put it in her pocket. For the first time, Tasha smiled at her. Briefly. Then her face went blank again.

Creepy. ... She remembered the old woman's warning in the market and felt a shiver across her back, when she felt the bulge in her pocket. She'd throw away the doll at the first chance she got, good or bad magic be damned.

Jade gulped loudly, her hand leaving her pocket to massage her tight neck. In the middle of the living room, under a doll hanging low enough to tease his hair, Dane argued violently with his brother.

His brother, shorter, chunkier, younger, was arguing back just as strongly. She didn't want to know what it was about but couldn't help overhearing because her choices were either to stay in the small house and watch or to go outside and to leave Tasha alone. A sidelong glance toward the silent woman showed no change.

"He needs to go to the hospital," Dane stated.

"He won't go," John replied.

"He's unconscious now. He doesn't have any say in the matter."

"He'll be pissed when he wakes up."

"That won't matter because he may not wake up if he doesn't go." Dane ran his fingers through his hair, and his elbow accidentally hit the doll hanging above him. He glanced and half ducked. "If it's the money that's bothering you, forget about it. I'll cover it, if I have to." He spun around throwing his hands up in the air in frustration. And stopped. "What the ... ?" He gazed around the living room, as if seeing it for the first time. "Jesus, there are even more of them now."

"Yeah, I commented on them earlier, and she started screaming that it was all my fault," John said. "That everything bad that happens is because the grave had been opened." He stared at his now-almost-catatonic wife, a bitter look crossing his face. "I'm wondering if maybe *she's* to blame for everything instead."

Jade gasped softly.

Holding out his hands, John closed his eyes. "I'm sorry. I don't mean that. But God, Dane, I don't know what to do anymore."

"Jesus. This is like a bad zombie movie."

John ran a weary hand down his face and dropped down on the arm of the couch at Emile's feet. "Yeah, only this isn't fiction. When Tasha found out about Peppe disappearing, she really went off the rails. I didn't understand half of what she was saying. Just something about me not understanding how bad it could get, if something came out of the grave. I figured she was talking about bad spirits, but I don't know if that's what concerns her about Peppe's disappearance or not. And, no, we still haven't found Peppe." He stared at Dane with bloodshot eyes. "I don't know what the hell is going on anymore. Things are so out of control."

"Ya think? Look at your wife, for Christ's sake."

"I know." John closed his eyes. Worry pleated his forehead. "She's fallen to pieces over Peppe and Emile."

"Then stay strong. Get someone over here to help her. What about her aunt, cousins? Isn't there someone, anyone?"

"I have tried to contact several people. So far I can't reach anyone." John turned and walked over to Tasha. He crouched down in front of her. "Tasha? Honey? Look at me."

Tasha raised her head and stared at John. Tears leaked down her cheeks. He pulled her into his arms. "Oh, honey. It'll be okay. Take it easy."

She tucked her head into his shoulder, as he rocked her gently back and forth.

Jade walked over to Dane. "Bruce should be here soon."

Dane slipped an arm around her shoulders and tucked her close. He dropped a kiss on the top of her head. "Sorry. Not a great end to the evening."

"Not your fault." Appreciating the warmth and comfort he offered, she relaxed against him.

Lights of an approaching vehicle flashed in the window. "Oh, thank God. That should be them." She almost ran outside, Dane at her heels.

Bruce hopped out of the SUV, and Jade groaned with relief to see Meg in the passenger side. "Hi, Jade. Did you find Dr. Mike? And how's Emile?"

"Unfortunately no. We didn't find Dr. Mike. We went to the grave in case he'd fallen on the rocks. Instead that's what must have happened to Emile, while he was looking for his father. Emile was talking and walking with assistance but refused to go to a hospital. We brought him here and called you. So you've heard nothing on Dr. Mike either?"

Bruce shook his head. "No, not yet. Where is Emile?"

"Inside." Dane led the way.

Jade stayed behind. "Thanks for coming, Meg. I'm sorry about Dr. Mike. This has been a terrible evening."

Reaching out and giving Jade a quick hug, Meg said, "I'm glad to help. I just don't understand why I'm needed."

"It's Tasha, John's pregnant wife. And I don't know what you can do for her." Jade shook her head. "Something is definitely not right there."

"Mentally or physically?"

"Both. Add in emotionally too." She led Meg toward the kitchen door. "There's a weird smell to her—I don't know. It's way beyond me." Taking in a deep breath, she added, "I'm afraid there's something wrong with the baby."

Meg's gaze sharpened. "Where is Tasha?"

"In the living room, with Emile. Also, as you walk in, take a close look at the inside of the house. Especially the ceiling." Jade shrugged. "I need you to see it for yourself."

Meg walked through the open door. "Whatever you say."

Jade followed behind. She watched Meg take several steps toward the living room ... and falter. She came to a stop and studied the shadowed interior and the closed curtains, but especially the dolls. The house was small, cozy even, but gave off an eerie darkness, suggesting something was not right.

Jade whispered, "See?"

"Very interesting," Meg murmured.

Jade stepped around her and motioned toward Tasha. "Now look at the mom."

Meg directed her gaze at Tasha, who rocked in the big easy chair, a shuttered look closing her face down. Meg approached slowly.

"Tasha? My name is Meg." Crouching in front of the pregnant

woman, she tried to study her face, but Tasha dropped her chin lower.

Jade stepped off to one side, where she could keep an eye on both patients. Bruce was bent over, checking Emile's eyes.

Dane stood guard, while John chewed his fingers. Dane's comments repeated in her mind, and now she understood his concern. John obviously wasn't stepping up to the plate with his wife's emotional breakdown. In fact, he appeared close to sliding into one himself.

She couldn't help but think back to Duncan and how he must have felt, watching her decline. Still, with his help, she'd pulled herself up, so there was hope John would too. Now, if only they could find Dr. Mike. She glanced out into the dark night. The thought of him lost was bad enough, but, after finding Emile tonight, she couldn't help worrying that Dr. Mike might be in a similar situation.

She sidled over to Tasha and Meg. Tasha still wasn't talking.

Jade crouched beside Meg and asked, "What do you think?"

"She needs help. Serious help." Meg studied the large belly, her hand pressed gently, lower down. "How far along is she?"

"I think seven, … almost eight months. I can double-check with the baby's father, if you need to know exactly."

"She needs emergency medical care and fast." Meg stood and motioned toward John. "Is this man the baby's father?"

"Yes, come on." She led Meg to the men. "John, this is Meg," she said, with a bright smile. "She's another member of the team."

John's face scrunched. He attempted to step away in the small room but backed against a wall in the overly crowded space. "Hi. Thanks for coming by to help Emile."

Meg, her voice as gentle as a summer breeze, said, "I didn't come for Emile. I came to see your wife."

John's eyes widened. "Tasha? Why? What's wrong with my wife?"

Meg raised an eyebrow, as she glanced behind him to Dane.

Dane stepped around him, so he could face his brother. "John. You know something's wrong."

"You called this woman in?" John's voice sounded as if he didn't know whether he should be outraged or thankful.

"Theoretically, yes. I did, at Jade's request."

"Jade?" John frowned, as if he couldn't place who she was.

Jade grimaced and gave a small wave. "That's me, remember? Your wife and your child need help, John. Now."

Fear visibly shivered over his body, and his eyes panicked. "Is she having the baby now?"

Meg reached out a gentle hand. "She isn't having the baby right now, although ..." Meg looked back at the woman rocking silently in the chair. "Well, she needs emergency medical attention."

"That's good then. She'll be much better once she has the baby. Everything will be back to normal then." He made a wide sweep with his arm, taking in Emile and Tasha. Eagerness lit his face, and Jade's heart broke. She didn't think it would be that easy to fix this.

"We need to call an ambulance or whatever service is available here. If it can't get here fast, we need to take her to the closest hospital." Meg spoke to John in a calm voice.

His eyes widened in skepticism. "No. No, she'd never allow that. You don't understand. She, *they*, don't trust in doctors—not like we do. She'll have the baby at home. She planned for it." He spun to his brother. "Dane, you know that. I explained that."

"No. You tried to explain, but I didn't understand. I *don't* understand. I see that they want their own spiritual leaders, and that's fine. Call them. See if there's anything they can do. We're telling you that you need to get medical help for Tasha and Emile—and *now*."

Meg added, "You don't want to hurt the baby, John. And Tasha needs help."

Before their eyes, they saw John crumble.

"No. It wasn't supposed to be like this. I don't know what to do," he cried out.

Bruce walked over. "How long to get an ambulance here?"

Dane shrugged. "Ten, twenty minutes? I don't really know. Depends on how busy they are."

Bruce's face pinched. "Call them, please." He cast a scathing look at John. "You're no longer making the decisions here. Your brother-in-law is going to the hospital." He stopped and studied Tasha for a long moment. "Meg? One patient or two?"

"Two, actually three. The baby is in trouble too."

Both looked to Dane. He nodded and opened his cell phone to make the call. Bruce stood beside him, giving the medical details to the EMT service.

Jade wrapped her arm around John and moved him to the closest chair. "John, sit here for a bit."

"What?" Dazed and confused, John blinked several times.

Jade frowned and glanced around. Dane was just pocketing his phone. She walked over, calling to him softly. "Dane?"

He met her gaze, then followed the tilt of her head, his eyes lighting on his brother's features. Dane's face turned grim. "What's the matter now?"

"Your brother. Is it possible he could have drugs or something in his system?"

"Not drugs. At least I don't think so." He bent down and studied his brother. "Hey, John. Stay with me here. You don't look so good."

"I'm fine. A little shaken, that's all." He tried to smile but failed miserably. "I'm okay." This time his assertion was stronger. Not quite strong enough to be believable but he was pulling himself up. "And I don't do drugs." He glared at Jade, as if she were the cause of all his problems. "Neither does Tasha."

"Glad to hear it. Stay alert, please, or you'll be the next patient."

"I'm fine." His temper shone through, strong and defiant.

Jade was satisfied with that reaction. Better fire than ice. She left the brothers to work things out, while she checked with Bruce on Emile. Emile's color had slid from white to dead white. "Shit. He does not look good."

"No. Not at all. Where the hell is that ambulance?" Bruce stood watch, a careful eye on Emile.

"It's only been ten minutes."

Bruce placed a hand on Emile's wrist again, checking the pulse, his frown deepening. "They'd better get here soon, or they won't have to rush on their way back."

Jade winced. "That close, *huh*?"

He gave her a sharp nod. Jade hastened over to Meg, who was attempting to wash Tasha's face. "How's she doing?"

"No change. She's almost catatonic."

"Will that affect the baby?"

Meg frowned and gently cleaned Tasha's cheek. Tasha didn't respond at all. "The baby is very calm. Too calm."

"Any idea what could cause this?"

Meg sighed and gave her a sad smile. "Unfortunately a lot of things. I don't know if there is something physical going on here, but even emotionally … Her father is missing, her brother injured …" Meg shrugged. "Some people just snap, others give up, and then there are those who go inside, where they can't feel the pain. It's way too early to make any kind of deduction."

Meg went to the kitchen sink and rinsed her cloth. She came back and finished cleaning Tasha's face, then did her hands. She turned Tasha's hands over and studied the chewed nails. In one spot they'd been gnawed so low she had dried blood in the corners.

Meg and Jade exchanged grim looks. Jade noticed a change in the room. Something was different. Too quiet. Emile's harsh, raspy breathing had become staggered, erratic. He was having trouble breathing. "Shit!"

Bruce returned to Emile's side, just as loud sirens filled the air. Meg's eyes opened wide. Jade raced to the kitchen door. "It's the ambulance." Doors slammed outside. "Thank God. They must have been close when they got the call."

The ambulance parked beside the SUV. Two men hopped out, one carried a large bag. Jade joined them. "Hurry, please. He's having trouble breathing."

The pair ran into the house.

Jade stayed outside, gulping in the clean, fresh night air. The house smelled terrible to her—of stale sweat and fear and something strongly herbal. Maybe it was from the doll-making materials?

While they worked on Emile, Jade walked around outside, praying and hoping for Emile's recovery. She didn't know what had happened to Tasha. She hoped she'd be okay. Her baby needed her. But was the baby okay?

The moon hid behind the clouds above, dimming Jade's view of the property. The darkness provided an appropriate background to the horrible events of the night.

"How are you doing?" Dane strode toward her, his arms open. "I'm in the way in there."

She ran into his embrace. "I'm fine. Wish things were different though."

He leaned back slightly, so he could see her face. "Yeah, same here." He sounded so sorrowful, so despondent, she squeezed him tightly. He held her close, dropping his chin to rest on her head, and they just stayed like that, in the darkness, for a long moment. "I'm glad you're here," he whispered.

Just then the kitchen door opened, and one of the men ran to the ambulance. He pulled out a stretcher, dropped the legs, locked them in place and raced to the house again.

"I always feel like I should do something in situations like this, but I never quite know what," Jade muttered.

"Me, too." They stared at the house and the sounds coming from within.

She added, "How sad that John has to take care of both of them."

"I know. He's almost a patient himself."

"I'm glad you can see that too." She shifted back. "What about his missing father-in-law?"

Dane ran his fingers through his hair. "Who knows? I'll try and talk to John when this calms down a little bit."

Jade watched in silence as the two patients were transferred to the ambulance in two separate trips. After Tasha was brought out, Meg walked over to Jade, a weary sadness on her face. Jade met her gaze with the burning question in her eyes. Meg shook her head once.

Jade gasped. She bit her lip and wrapped her arms tightly around her stomach.

Dane reached out to stroke her shoulder. Leaning down, he whispered, "What?"

She shook her head violently. "Not now," she whispered. John walked beside Bruce, but either he didn't understand Meg's motion or couldn't take much more.

Dane dropped his arm from Jade's shoulder and walked over to his brother. "John, do you want me to take you to the hospital?"

"I'm going in the ambulance." John gave Dane a tight smile. "Would you mind following?"

"I'm right behind you." Dane fished the keys from his pocket and watched with the rest of the group, as the ambulance flicked on its lights and sirens and took off into the night.

Dane turned to Meg and Bruce. "Thank you."

Bruce shook his head. "Sorry the prognosis isn't better."

"I didn't hear. ... Is Emile that bad?"

Bruce sighed. "He might pull through, if they can stop the bleeding fast enough. He's young and strong."

Dane winced. "I guess that was quite the blow to the head."

"Not at all. Even a light fall can cause this kind of trauma." He rotated his neck. "I'm thinking Emile will recover. Tasha now? ... I don't know."

Dane's eyes widened. "What? I don't understand."

Meg sighed. "I don't know how she's doing mentally. As for her baby? Well, ... we couldn't find a heartbeat."

PEPPE DUCKED BELOW the old dead mango tree close to Tasha's house. Wide enough to hide him, close enough to see the flashing lights and the crowd of strangers moving in and out of his daughter's house. Darkness had long descended. He'd forgotten how long before. He crouched lower. His stomach growled. He couldn't remember when he'd eaten last. Surely his kids would bring him a meal soon.

Not Emile. Something was wrong with Emile. Peppe squeezed his eyes shut. What happened? Yelling, fighting, ropes. Running. He opened his eyes again, moisture collecting in the corners. Why couldn't he remember anything?

As he asked the questions, visions of Emile's anger and more yelling swept through his mind. They'd both been so angry. He thought his son had done something wrong. Again. But he was a good kid, just always getting into scrapes. Fighting over nothing.

Peppe didn't know what the fight had been about this time. But Emile didn't deserve whatever had happened to him. As Peppe watched the activity at Tasha's house, the moisture in his eyes dripping down his cheek, the stretcher was loaded into the ambulance.

Emile didn't deserve this. He was a good boy.

The stretcher came back out and went into the house. He straightened—fear sending icicles down his back. He hated doctors. All of them. They'd taken his money and had let his beloved wife die. They'd smiled and said they'd help. ... Instead he'd gone broke, trying to keep her alive. In the end, she'd still died, and the bills had continued to come.

He huddled deeper in the darkness. The flashing lights hurt his eyes. Made his head ache. Made him confused.

It was hard to keep watching the house. Small groups of people clustered around. He glanced around the property. It was still his place. But he didn't know who everyone was. What were they doing here?

They didn't belong here.

Neither did all the vehicles.

He squinted. The stretcher came back out.

Tasha. He perked up. The baby was coming. He would be a grandpa.

His enthusiasm fell. His wife hadn't gone to any hospital. She'd delivered their two children just fine at home.

So why was Tasha on the stretcher?

That bastard who'd married his daughter stood beside the ambulance. John. He was to blame for all of this. Things had been good before he'd come. Now look at this mess. Even worse had been John's brother, ... and all those strangers digging their noses in where they didn't belong.

Shivers racked his thin frame.

Maybe they were all to blame.

Chapter 16

J ADE FELT THE sun shining on her face and tried to open her eyes. Grit and dried tears had mingled to damn-near seal them shut. She yawned and burrowed deeper into the blankets. Thank God it was Saturday. She didn't want to go anywhere.

Her body felt like wax that had poured itself into bed, then hardened overnight.

Memories slammed into her heart, as she opened her eyes and stared across the empty room. Last night ...

Emile. Tasha and the baby.

Her eyes burned. No tears were left. She'd cried herself to sleep, asking herself and God why it had happened this way. *Why the baby?* She could deal with Emile and his sister and their father, if the news turned out to be bad. But the baby? The unborn baby. Just like hers. Only worse because Tasha had been seven or eight months along. To lose a baby at that stage?

Had Tasha known? Would that, along with her father's disappearance and then Emile's injury, have ensured her mental slide downward? Even a healthy mind would break under far less.

God knows Jade had struggled over the loss of her baby.

A light knock sounded on her door.

"Hello? ... Jade, it's Meg. May I come in?"

Jade groaned softly, as she forced her aching limbs to action, grabbed her robe, and walked to the door. She unlocked and opened it.

Meg smiled at her, looking marginally better than Jade felt. "Hey. Tough night, *huh?*"

"That's an understatement." Realizing she hadn't opened the door fully, Jade motioned her coworker inside. "Sorry. I only woke up a few minutes ago."

"Good for you. I woke up at six, as usual."

Closing the door behind her, Jade added, "I normally would have but ..."

"Yeah." Meg looked around the small room. "This room is the twin to mine."

"Is it? Makes sense, I suppose." Jade could sense Meg had a purpose to her visit. Jade walked back to her bed and crawled under the covers, waiting for Meg to get around to the main topic.

"I have an update." Meg took a deep breath. "Tasha's baby is dead. Usually when a fetus dies, the body aborts it. In some rare cases, the body continues to ignore the fact, until it can't be ignored any longer."

Poor Tasha. Blinking several times to hold back her hot tears, Jade tilted her head back and thought about Meg's news. Regaining control, she looked her colleague in the eye. "So you're saying the baby has been dead for a while?"

Meg winced. "Yes. In the US, an autopsy would likely be done to find the cause. Here, I don't know what happens." Rotating her neck as if to ease some stiffness, she continued. "Emile is alive. They think they've stopped the bleeding. It's still touch-and-go for him though."

Swallowing hard, Jade couldn't do much more than nod to acknowledge Meg's words. She didn't trust herself to speak.

"Tasha ..." Meg stopped. "Tasha goes into surgery this morning and will undergo a psych evaluation when she's healthier. The bottom line is, there's been no change. She's not talking, eating, or acknowledging the world around her in any way."

Jade couldn't help wincing. "Poor John."

"Yes." Sitting in the single chair, Meg rested her feet on the corner of the bed. "I've also spoken to Dane. I wanted to know if there was anything I could do for his family."

"And? Is there?" Jade leaned forward.

Meg slumped back. "No. John's a mess. Dane said he'd call you or stop by here later, if he can. He's sticking close to his brother."

"He was worried about John's mental state before this."

"It's out of our hands." The two women sat in depressed silence.

Then Jade remembered. "Any idea if their father has been found?"

The two women stared at each other, frowning. Meg shook her head slowly. "I forgot to ask."

"I ask because of Tasha. Dane said Peppe isn't right in the head. Makes me wonder if Tasha has a heredity issue here." Jade considered Tasha's life. "Not that what she's been through isn't enough to make anyone retreat inside."

"Any idea how old Peppe is or how long he's been like this?" Meg asked.

"No. You'll have to get Dane to ask John." As much as she wanted to laze around the hotel today, Jade couldn't stand the thought of the old man out there, wandering around lost. "We should also sort out if he's in need of finding or if he's home and fine."

"Yes. Do you want to call Dane, or should I?"

"I will." Jade threw back the covers. "As soon as I have my shower and get dressed. We might as well meet in the dining room and figure out what's next."

"I'll see you there." Meg tossed her cell phone on the bed for Jade to use, before walking to the door.

"Hey, Meg. Where was Dr. Mike last night? Did anyone ask him?"

A funny look crossed her face. "I haven't spoken to him. Haven't heard anything."

"He's back though—isn't he?" Dread edged Jade's words.

"I don't know. Things got a bit crazy last night. I'll find out." Meg rushed out, leaving Jade standing in the middle of the room, shocked.

DANE STRETCHED OUT his long legs on the stone patio to his cabin, tilting his face to the morning sun. Sleep had been hard to come by when he had finally collapsed on his bed in the wee hours of the morning. The few hours he'd managed hadn't helped much; he still felt worn out. Not the ending he'd hoped for.

His cell phone rang. He checked the number before answering. Meg's—therefore, hopefully Jade.

"Hi, Dane."

Jade's warm voice flooded his senses. Damn, it was good to hear her voice. "Good morning. How are you today?"

"Better than most of the people involved in last night's emergencies. I have several reasons for calling. First, how is John? Second, did anyone ever find Peppe?"

Peppe? Shit, Dane hadn't given that crazy old man a second thought. Not after last night's chaos. "Peppe might have come back overnight. We're just up, so I'll walk over and check in a few minutes. John is okay, but not good—still, he's holding on."

"Not a good night for any of us."

"Yes. The doctors didn't say much." Dane checked his watch. "Tasha should be out of surgery by now. We might know more soon."

The kitchen door slammed shut. He spun around to see John walking down the garden path, head bent in the morning sunlight, hands in his pockets. "I'll call you back."

Dane disconnected the call and tucked his phone back into his jeans pocket and hurried to catch up with his brother.

JADE WALKED BACK to the hotel patio table, where Meg sat waiting. Bruce came out to join them. "Dane says he'll walk over and check on Peppe and will call us back."

Bruce scrunched his face, as he pulled a chair back to sit. "What a mess."

"That's one way to put it." Jade lifted her cup of coffee, letting the steam waft upward to bathe her eyes. The shower had helped but not enough. She still ached inside, as if she were a faded version of herself. In direct contrast the thick bushes beside her were many shades of vibrant green, their branches lively in the breeze. Typical of so much of the vegetation here, it took her breath away.

"Dr. Mike's still missing," Bruce said. "I've contacted the authorities and will be heading there shortly to give them Dr. Mike's photo. He has to be missing for twenty-four hours before they'll do anything official. However, because of the work we've been doing and the missing SUV involved, they'll look into it earlier." He grimaced. "I've also contacted Tony—to give him the heads-up."

"Oh, joy," Jade muttered. "Will Tony return?"

Settling back into his chair, Bruce took a sip of his coffee, before answering in a grim voice. "No. Not at this point. He does want to know, as soon as possible, whether he needs to find a replacement."

"What!" Meg stared at him in shock. "A replacement? For Dr. Mike? Are you serious? Surely that's jumping the gun?"

"Tony is thinking of the project and his client. If Dr. Mike is injured or missing or ... anything else, then Tony needs to find a replacement." Bruce's gaze went from Meg to Jade. "It's not unreasonable, given the schedule. But we aren't going there yet."

Jade shuddered and walked off a ways. She could see both sides regarding Tony's concern, but that didn't mean she wanted to contemplate anything nasty. Last night had been enough drama for a long time. "Let's hope he went on a bender and is sleeping it off in the

SUV somewhere."

"Dr. Mike doesn't drink."

Jade spun around, raising her hands in the air. "Then maybe he found a lady friend or something. Let's remain positive, please."

"Right. I'm heading out now. I don't know what you two are planning to do today, but, if it involves searching for Peppe and Dr. Mike, please wake our two party animals and get them involved. Leave Susan alone. She needs to rest. Maybe she can throw the flu that's plaguing her."

Jade shook her head, a small grin on her face. "Is that what Stephen and Wilson were doing? Partying? We were so busy last night that I never gave them a thought."

"Me neither. Which is why we dropped the ball on Dr. Mike," Meg said tiredly.

Bruce leaned over slightly, so he could meet Meg's gaze. "Don't think that. We didn't drop the ball. Priorities shifted, due to emergencies. I'll go to the authorities right now. We'll find him."

Meg stood, as he walked back inside the hotel. She motioned to Jade. "Why don't you bring your coffee and join me in the conference room? If I stay out here, this morning sun will put me back to sleep."

Talking quietly, they walked inside to their desks and turned on their computers. Meg's phone rang. She checked the number and handed it over to Jade. "Dane. You might as well answer it."

Jade's heart lightened. "Hello, Dane."

"Hey. Too bad you don't have your own cell phone. I wouldn't have to keep bothering Meg this way."

She heard the smile in his voice that said he wasn't too bothered by the inconvenience. Still, he had a point. If she wanted privacy, she'd have to get a phone for the duration of her time here.

"Anyway, Peppe is not in his cabin. The door is open now, and it wasn't left that way yesterday. John believes Peppe came home last night and was probably confused and scared off by the sirens. We'll keep an eye out for him."

"Oh, that sounds reasonable." In fact, that was excellent news. They could focus on Dr. Mike now. "How is John holding up?"

Dane's voice flattened. "He's coping somewhat. He opened up a little, admitted that he and Tasha had been having problems for a bit. At the time he figured that was because she was upset that he allowed you to work on the grave."

Jade wrinkled her nose. "Yeah, I can see that. Relationships being what they are." Meg looked at her, an eyebrow raised. Jade continued.

"Let us know if there are any developments with Peppe. We'll turn our attention to finding Dr. Mike."

"What? Dr. Mike didn't come home?" he asked, his voice rising.

Jade had forgotten what they'd been doing when they'd found Emile. "No. There's no sign of him or the SUV. Bruce left a few minutes ago to speak with the police."

"*Hmm.* While I look for Peppe, I'll keep an eye out for him too. Let me know if there is anything we can do to help *you.*"

"I'll get back to you on that," Jade promised, then hung up. She quickly filled Meg in on the latest developments.

Meg brightened. "If Peppe had seen the ambulance take his kids away, then he'll be confused and upset. I can see him going into hiding. That doesn't mean he's not in need of care though." She thought for a moment. "Any idea what happened to Tasha and Emile's mother?"

"No. I never thought to ask." Jade stared down at the phone, wondering if she should call Dane back. Some family history would be good to know.

"Not to worry. It's not our problem."

She stared at Meg. "You're right. Yet somehow it seems like it is."

Chapter 17

T HE TEAM DISCUSSED the previous night's events over lunch, when Bruce returned.

Susan walked in slowly, just behind him. She fielded all the questions with a smile. "I'm feeling a little better. Thanks, everyone. Apparently I missed lots of excitement last night."

Jade shook her head. "And you were the lucky one there."

Pulling out her chair, Susan sat down next to Stephen. She frowned. "Not really. I think someone tried to break into my room last night."

"What?" A chorus of cries erupted from the table.

"Really?" Meg stared at her in horror. "What happened?"

"I'm not exactly sure. I took some decongestants to try and throw this cold. Those things always knock me out." She sighed, reached for her coffee cup, and took a sip. "I woke up in the night, everything was dark. But I heard movement in my room."

"Jesus." Jade so didn't want to think about what could have happened. "Did he just leave? On his own?"

Susan nodded. "I coughed a couple times, sat up to clear my throat, and this shadow detached from the wall. Then the door opened, and this person went out. Had a hard time getting back to sleep after that. The front desk sent someone up to check the lock for me."

Stephen growled. "That had better not happen again. We've got enough problems, without worrying about intruders while we sleep."

Susan gave him a wan smile. "I did get up and lock my door. Figured I must have forgotten to before climbing into bed.

At that, Bruce highlighted something they all knew but found easy to forget. "Remember, people. This area is incredibly poor. Lock up your belongings. The hotel has a safe, if you want to make use of it. And be sure to check that you've locked your room doors at all times."

Everyone had something to say. Jade sat back and listened. She couldn't believe the shitty luck the team had been having lately.

Bruce gave everyone another moment, then held up his hand. "Now on to my news. We're in luck. There's a tracking device on the SUV. The police called the rental company. Apparently, with the unrest in Haiti in the last year, thefts were up, along with every other crime imaginable. In order to keep their rental fleet insured, they'd been forced to boost their security measures." He pulled out a chair and sat. "I handed over all the paperwork on the leases, and they're doing their thing as we speak."

"Oh, wow. That is great news." Jade sat up straight. She'd never considered a tracking device.

Bruce's phone rang. He answered, gesturing for silence. The room fell quiet. He put the phone on Speaker. "Hi, did you find him?"

"We found the SUV. However there's no sign of your missing person."

Worry lined Bruce's face. "He's not there? Could he be anywhere nearby? A hotel or restaurant, something?"

"The SUV isn't far from where you're staying. There is no sign of damage or forced entry to the SUV. It was unlocked but still full of equipment. It looks as if the driver just got up and walked away. It is near a popular hiking spot. Would he have gone for a hike on the spur of the moment and not told anyone?"

Silence.

Stephen spoke first. "He's a hiker, but I can't imagine him going without letting any of us know what he was doing. He'd found a couple trails that the team would discuss, then pick one to do this weekend, but that's after we'd planned and prepared for it."

"Right. Can you please meet us at the vehicle, so we can confirm nothing has been stolen?"

Jade scratched down the location, as it came rattling through the phone.

"We'll be there in fifteen minutes." Bruce disconnected and tucked his cell back into his pants pocket.

"I want to go with you," Jade said quietly. She really didn't want to go, but she wanted to be a second pair of eyes, making sure that no one missed anything. Dr. Mike was a good man. She'd do what she could for him.

"So do I." Meg stood up.

Susan started to cough. Everyone stopped to look at her in concern. When she could, she said, "I *want* to go, but …"

Stephen pointed a finger at her. "Bed. That's the only place you're going. And lock the door behind you this time."

"I think we all want to go." Stephen raised an eyebrow at Wilson, who nodded. "Good, that's settled. We're all going." Everyone stood and headed for the vehicles. As Meg walked past Bruce, she nudged him in the arm. "We're all in this together. If Dr. Mike is in trouble, we all want to help. Accept it."

Bruce smiled and fell into step beside her. "It's good to know that the team has bonded so well in such a short time."

"Isn't it though? Susan hasn't been as involved as much, but she seems happy to be with us."

Stephen interrupted them, as he came up behind them. "Any update on the patients?"

Meg filled him in.

Stephen winced. "That's tough on everyone."

When they reached the SUV, all of them clambered in ahead of Bruce. He shook his head. "Eager or what?"

"Anxious," corrected Jade. "Dr. Mike is family. We're all family."

Bruce stopped, studied her serious face for a moment, and then smiled. "Thanks. That's the nicest thing anyone has said to me in a long time."

He hopped in and started the engine.

"It's the truth," Jade added to the thoughtful silence in the car. "We may not have been here together for long, yet bonds have started. It's up to us how we want them to continue." With those profound words, she sat back, quiet again.

Meg reached out and gave her a hug. "Thanks, sis."

Jade chuckled.

"Hey, pass the hugs around. No keeping them just up front," Stephen protested from the back row.

The jovial atmosphere kept the darkness at bay. At least until they pulled into the location they'd been given and saw the SUV parked in a small gravel lot at the foot of a large hill. Boulders piled high at the base of it, and there was no sign of Dr. Mike.

The laughter shut off like a faucet, replaced by grim silence.

"Shit." Stephen's word echoed loudly through the small space, as Bruce stopped the engine.

"I don't get it." Jade opened the sliding door and hopped out. The others stepped out behind her. They were in a small parking lot, off the main road. They saw one police car and two officers standing at the SUV, waiting. She couldn't help the horrible sinking feeling in her stomach. The SUV doors were closed, and the SUV looked deserted. She walked toward it slowly. The closer she got, the worse she felt.

Bruce walked over to speak with the officers, and the rest of them trooped over to check the SUV. One officer left Bruce and walked over to talk with the others.

"Was the door open when you found it?" Stephen asked.

"All doors were unlocked. Lucky everything didn't get stolen." The officer stood off to one side, watching the group.

"Weird," Wilson piped up, checking out the front passenger side.

"Not weird. *Bad*. Dr. Mike was particularly careful about his equipment." Meg was adamant.

Jade had to agree. "He might have gone hiking. He might be out there injured." She pivoted around, looking for any sign of him.

"He'd have said something, invited one of us along," Stephen protested. "I don't see him going out hiking anyway, at least not alone, and not late in the afternoon. And he has a cell, if he needed help." He opened the driver's side and looked inside.

"No, not hiking, but it makes total sense to come and check out a hike before suggesting it for everyone this weekend." Wilson shrugged. "That's what I'd do."

Jade frowned. "The only way he'd leave the doors unlocked and go on foot from here is if he thought someone needed him—or if someone forced him to."

"There goes that wild imagination of yours." Stephen's voice didn't hold any humor. If anything, it sounded like he was searching for another answer—any other answer. He hopped in the SUV to check the contents in the back. A moment later, he popped his head out. "I can't see anything missing or different about the SUV. Anyone else?" He jumped out the back door and stood with his hands on his hips and studied the SUV's exterior. "Meg, do you want to take a look?"

Meg obliged. Jade stood at the open rear doors and studied the stacks of boxes in the back of the SUV. A small stain looked suspiciously like blood on the corner of one box.

She shook her head. There went her imagination again. She had no reason to assume something bad just because of a tiny brown spot. "Is this blood?" Jade asked.

Meg moved in for a closer look. "What if someone found him injured? They'd take him to the hospital, right? It's not like they'd just leave him here."

Meg poked her head around the stack of boxes. "It is blood, but it's not enough to indicate anything. Still, that's not a bad idea. We spent so much time in the hospital last night, yet I never thought to check if Dr. Mike had been brought in.

Wilson called over, "Hey, Bruce, did you contact the hospital?"

Bruce shook his head. "I checked last night. I haven't yet this morning."

The younger officer beside him pulled out his cell and moved off a few paces. "I'll do that right now."

Everyone stood quietly, waiting, hoping. The officer returned within a few minutes. "No one has been admitted in the last twenty-four hours fitting that description."

"Okay, if he's not at the hospital and he's not in the SUV, what are our options for finding him?" Bruce asked.

Meg stood, hands on her hips, frowning at the vehicle. "A search party to start from here?"

Wilson rubbed his hands eagerly. "I volunteer."

"Except that he may have been mugged, and the vehicle just dumped here. Although that doesn't make any sense, as this area is facing incredible poverty. The SUV would have been stripped," Jade pointed out.

Wilson walked closer to the path to check it out, while Stephen turned to the officer. "Will the rental company's tracking system tell us where the SUV has been? So we can see where Dr. Mike may have driven?"

Bruce frowned. "They'd have told us if they had, wouldn't they?"

Stephen shrugged. "Depends on the system they're using. Tracking isn't the same as built-in GPS, I don't think. But then I don't know."

"It's just another phone call." The cop added, "I'll have someone at the station make that one. If there is any information, we'll get it."

Stephen nodded his head, then asked the cop, "Can we take the SUV back? It's full of our gear."

"We've processed it already. Lifted a couple fingerprints that we'll run. No confirmed blood or anything else suspicious." He shrugged. "We don't have a crime at the moment. We *might* have a missing person."

Meg frowned.

Jade could understand. No one knew what to do or where to start.

Wilson spoke up. He stood slightly apart from the group, staring at the woods to the far side. "Let's think about this. We're at the base of a popular hiking spot. Dr. Mike had several hikes in mind for this weekend. On top of that, we're not far from the grave site, are we?"

Jade gazed in the direction he pointed. All she saw was a small mountain with boulders at the bottom and a path twisting its way up the side to where it disappeared in the brush and small bushes. "I wouldn't know. I'm horrible with that kind of stuff."

Bruce walked over to study the same patch of hills and woods. "We can't be that far. I've driven around this area a little bit." He turned back to the others. "Anyone have a map?"

"Why does it matter where the grave site is?" Jade asked.

Wilson replied, "Because Dr. Mike could have walked over that hill to the lab."

"Why?" Meg asked, joining them. "When the SUV is here? Besides, Jade and Dane checked the mass grave last night." The first officer came back with an open map in his hands. Stephen and Bruce clustered around him.

"So I stop here, park, and then hike over that small mountain to the grave site when it'll be dark soon—for fun? Does that make any sense to you?" Jade asked, as she stared at the men in astonishment.

Meg shook her head violently. "Walk away from a working SUV to a spot you *think* is on the other side, … a decent climb from the grave site? With no wheels and without letting anyone know? No way. Not in this lifetime."

"I'd so do that," Wilson stated, a grim smile on his face. "Honestly I *have* done things like that. Except either I would return to the SUV or I'd call for a ride, once I made it to the other side—if not before—to let someone know where to bring the cold beer."

The grin on Stephen's face said he agreed with Wilson.

Jade shook her head. "So … we'll have to hike over there, if only to ensure he didn't do just that and get stuck somewhere along the way?"

Stephen laughed, while nodding.

The two women stared at each other. "Men."

"I hear you." Jade couldn't think of one woman in her life who would do what Wilson described. Not in a million years.

Bruce walked over with the one officer to speak with the other one. He returned a few minutes later. "It appears to be about a two- or maybe three-hour hike over the top."

The five team members turned to stare at the sparsely treed hillside. Shaking his head, Bruce said, "So, I suggest Wilson and I do the hike. Stephen, why don't you meet us on the other side in a couple hours? We've got water and phones."

Jade jutted out her chin. "Two of you aren't enough. Wilson can go with you too, and Meg and I can meet you at the grave site afterward." She turned to the two officers. "What about organizing a search party?"

Both officers simply shook their heads and stepped back.

"They don't have the manpower, and, even if they did, they don't have enough evidence to prove that Dr. Mike is even missing," Bruce explained. "So Jade and Meg can each drive an SUV back to the hotel. They can leave Dr. Mike's parked there, then meet us at the grave site."

Leaving the rest of the words unspoken, Wilson walked over to the first SUV and pulled out his backpack. He hefted it over one shoulder and turned toward the hillside. "Come on. Let's go. We've only got an estimate of how long this will take. It could take us twice that."

"Good thing it's a nice day for a hike." A grinning Stephen walked past, his camera in hand.

Jade and Meg watched until the men disappeared from sight. Meg had the foresight to speak to the police before they took off; she got their contact information, in case the three men didn't show up as planned. After they were left alone, Jade hopped into Dr. Mike's SUV. Meg fired up the other SUV and led the way back.

Maybe this day would turn out to have a happy ending after all.

DANE WATCHED HIS brother pace from the living room into the kitchen and back again. He let him do it a couple more times before deciding that maybe he'd worked off enough energy to talk. "What's going through your head?"

John spun around and looked at him, his face flushed with temper.

Good, he'd get this out, one way or another, and, if they had to resort to fists, like old times, well, then that's what they would do. Dane stood and shifted his weight to the balls of his feet.

"What's going through my head? What's *not* going through my head? My child is dead, for starters. My wife is out of her mind. My brother-in-law is in a coma, and my crazy father-in-law is missing. Other than that, not much." In a sarcastic tone, he added, "What the fuck do you think?"

"That's about what I figured."

John gave him a look of absolute disgust, before storming out the kitchen door. Dane stayed behind but kept an eye on him. John's life had been flushed down the toilet and not much either one of them could do about it. Still, he didn't want John to do anything stupid.

Dane decided he'd check on Peppe's cabin again. Maybe he could get John to walk that way too. "Let's see if Peppe came back."

John raised his hands in surrender. "Fine, let's go check on the crazy bastard. Then I want to go back to the hospital. See how Tasha is."

Dane nodded. He didn't think there'd be any change but didn't want to mention that. Temper was better than depression. Some seriously hard questions would need to be addressed soon though.

Together they strode over to Peppe's cabin. The door was closed.

John pushed open the door. Dane stayed well back, until the interior had freshened slightly with the open door.

"Peppe? Are you in here?"

There was no answer.

John called out as he entered, "It's empty. Doesn't look like he's been here recently either."

Dane stood by the entrance. "Can you tell if anything is missing? Like could he have come home for supplies and then taken off again?"

"What supplies? The guy doesn't have much."

"Not having much usually means that the little bit you do have is important."

John shook his head and walked back out, pushing Dane outside ahead of him. He closed the door behind them and stood staring out across the land. "Dane, what the hell have I done so wrong in my life that this is happening to me?"

Dane's heart ached. "I don't think you did anything. Your wife has a delicate mind, and recent events may have been too much."

John bowed his head. "I guess that's the easiest way to put it."

They wandered the acreage. Dane didn't want to say the wrong thing but wanted John to talk or he would button up again. John spoke before Dane had to push the issue.

"She's been so weird since her pregnancy, and then that damn grave business started. She'd been her normal sunny self before that. Sure, she had bad days and was grouchy a couple times, but nothing like this. She didn't like gaining weight and blowing up like a balloon, but she adored the baby. She acted as I would have expected. But you've seen her yourself this last month. There was something really wrong there."

"I figured it was the pregnancy and the grave business."

John sighed. "So did I. For a while I wondered if her superstitious beliefs were right—about opening the grave being an omen of bad things to come. Only I'm not superstitious. She is. She asked her priestess for help several times. And when the team arrived, and she knew that everything was going ahead, that's when she started going downhill. Faster."

Dane shook his head at the word *priestess*. Instead of speaking, he stomped on his prejudice. John needed Dane's support, not his questions.

John stood silent, thinking. "I'm afraid she might have done something that accidentally caused the death of the baby." He spun around to face his brother, obviously upset. "I don't *want* to think that, but I can't help but wonder."

"Whoa. Stop right there. You just said she loved the baby." He reached out and shook his brother's shoulders. "Right?"

Relief lit up John's face. "Yes. She was happy, ... was looking forward to the baby's arrival."

"Here's what I'm thinking. She knew that something was wrong inside. She couldn't handle it and probably started blaming everything on the mortuary team opening the grave."

John asked hopefully, "Do you think that could be it?"

Gently Dane said, "Makes sense to me."

John blinked several times. "Thanks. I hope you're right."

Chapter 18

JADE AND MEG didn't waste any time at the hotel. More worried than she wanted to be, Jade changed into jeans and the light work boots she used at the grave site. She scrounged up stuff to take with her for a longer wait, stuffing her pockets with snacks. Filling a couple water bottles finished the job.

She grabbed her laptop. Who knew how long they might need to wait? She might as well make good use of the time.

At the site, Meg went to check on the reefer truck, while Jade walked over to the lab trailer, unlocked it and went in. Half expecting to see something wrong, she searched the trailer carefully, then shrugged. All appeared normal. Same as it had last night before she left.

Meg joined her a few minutes later. "Dane just drove in."

Jade blinked. A slow smile spread across her face. "Nice."

Meg grinned. "Really?" She snickered, as she started to leave. "Don't be too long primping."

Shaking her head, Jade walked outside. Dane was the perfect distraction for the long wait ahead of them. He walked toward her, his stride strong and effortless. But fatigue worried away at his face, and, instead of his normal confident smile, his mouth had a grim set that looked like it had taken root. John wasn't the only one suffering. Jade's heart went out to Dane.

"Hey. Don't you look like shit?" Meg never did hold back.

He grimaced, yet never slowed his forward motion. "Tough times."

Jade walked down the steps and watched as his face warmed. Especially nice was the smile that chased away most of the worry lines.

Opening his arms, he waited for her to get within grabbing distance, then snagged her close and hugged her tightly. "I need this," he murmured against her ear.

She squeezed him back too. "So do I."

He pulled away slightly. "No news on Dr. Mike?"

She shook her head, mortified to find tears threatening. She sniffled and turned to Meg to have the taller woman speak for her. "Meg?" she asked, her voice thick.

"We found the SUV, unlocked, yet still full of all the equipment—at a bluff on the other side of this." Meg wafted her hand in the direction of the hills behind them. "Three of our team have started to walk through from the point where the SUV was found. They're hiking toward us right now."

Dane's frown came lightning quick. "Why would he walk this way if the SUV was there and fully functional?"

"Yeah. That's one of those questions we don't have answers for. He could have fallen and hurt himself. Broken bones, head wound, … all are possible reasons why he didn't return to the vehicle. The guys didn't want to sit and do nothing, and we know head wounds are tricky. If Dr. Mike tried to start the SUV and couldn't, he might have figured he was stranded, and this was the fastest way home." She shrugged. "We don't know much but couldn't leave this option unexplored. The police are checking with the leasing company to retrace the SUV's route. Maybe that will shine a little light on the mystery."

Dane nodded. "Let's hope so."

The three studied the hill. "Stephen seems to think it was perfectly normal for Dr. Mike to have done the hike to see how difficult it might be, in consideration of the rest of us."

"Is he a hiker or something?"

"A GPS buff, outdoorsman, hiker, mountain climber. Yeah, he's very active."

Dane pursed his lips. "When did they leave and how long are they expecting to be?"

Checking her watch, Meg said, "They left over an hour ago, and we're hoping to see or hear from them in another hour or two."

Jade walked around the two of them and studied the hillside. "No sign of them yet."

Dane added, "They'll be lucky to make it in that time frame. John and I have both been over that rise—a couple times, in fact."

Jade spun to look at him. "Really?"

He nodded. "There are several big caves where an injured person could hole up overnight."

"Is it a tough hike?" Jade felt immeasurably lighter, now that she knew there was shelter of a sort. "Maybe we should check those out ourselves. The guys don't know about them."

Walking around, Dane pointed to a small rise. "That path comes out just behind the grave site—and Peppe's cabin, for that matter. Long ago, it was a common path from town to town, and, when there was heavy flooding, people took the hill paths."

Meg wondered, "What are the chances that Peppe and Dr. Mike are in the same place? If Dr. Mike found an injured Peppe ..."

"Why don't we go see?" Jade studied the path in front of them. "We can go up to the top and still keep an eye open for the men. The caves need to be checked out, and the men don't know to look for them."

The two waited, as Jade locked up the lab, before they walked up to the grave site together. Dane took them along the tree line, pointing out Peppe's cabin in the trees.

Jade shaded her eyes from the sun, as she studied the area. "It's nice to see the trees here. I hadn't realized, but Haiti's got a huge issue in that area."

"When Peppe was growing up, this was a flourishing farm. Full of fruit trees, and they even grew coffee for a while. They were one of the first in this area to have running water and electricity. Now the property is past its prime."

"Why are there so few trees in Haiti?" Meg asked.

"So many were cut down for firewood. It's actually a huge issue. Many groups are involved in tree planting here."

"Firewood for cooking. Right. That's another issue here, along with the lack of electricity and running water in most areas."

"Exactly. John says there hadn't been any money to sink into the property for a long time—but they tried different things. Peppe's wife worked, and that kept them floating. They put in the electricity when the hospital went in. Once she was gone, ... well, it really fell down."

Dane kept to the left of the rock pile, and they suddenly arrived at a path that wound its way up the hill. "Here it is. If they find the path and come this way, they shouldn't run into any trouble." Dane took the lead. "I wonder if Peppe is up there. He's at home in this terrain. He wouldn't think twice before going over that hill."

A horrible thought slipped into Jade's mind. "Dane, I hate to ask this, ... but is Peppe dangerous? Like, if he came upon Dr. Mike, would he hurt him?"

Meg's soft gasp told Jade that she'd just followed her train of thought. Dane on the other hand stared at her in confusion. "I don't think so, but I don't really know."

Jade swallowed. "I know it's probably just my crazy imagination again, but we also found out that Susan, the other female team member, had an intruder in her hotel room last night. While we were out, I think."

Dane's brows pulled together. "Did she recognize him?"

"No," Meg piped up. "She could barely make him out in the shadows. She did have the lock checked, and there was no sign of a break-in."

He pulled out his cell phone. "I can't say I'm surprised. This economy has been struggling to recover. Crime is up. That you haven't had any other problems before now is what's surprising. I'll tell John what we're doing."

Jade continued up the hill, Meg right behind her. Dane caught up before they'd gone any distance. "John says he'll give us five hours to locate Dr. Mike, and then we're to call him back. Otherwise he'll call the same officers you spoke with." He grinned at the two women. "At least I get a chance to take you sightseeing. Maybe another time we can do another outing for fun?"

Meg smiled. "Sounds great. We haven't done anything like this since arriving."

"We went shopping," protested Jade.

"Sure we did—once. Since then you won't go back. Not after Magrim scared you. You believe her now, don't you? There's been nothing except bad things happening since she spoke to us."

"Too many." Jade shivered. "Thanks for that reminder."

"True. Maybe we should talk to her again. She might foresee a better future for you now."

Jade made a face, saying, "It would be hard to make it any worse."

They'd been walking the whole time they'd been talking and now started up the incline. Dry needles crunched under their boots. They moved at a steady pace. The dust rose with each step, and the bushes on either side of the path gave off an odd aroma when disturbed.

It wasn't a steep incline. Just enough that Jade needed to focus on her pace and her breathing. She hadn't done anything remotely exerting in the last year, and she didn't want to slow the others down or be left to drag up the rear. She took a sip of water and kept an ear to the conversation.

Meg and Dane were discussing Seattle, of all things.

"Any idea how long you'll be here?" he asked Jade.

"I think about six more weeks." Jade shrugged. "Maybe longer."

Meg piped up. "What about you, Dane? How long are you stay-ing here?"

"A week ago, I would have said a couple more months. Now with the mess of John's family situation, I don't know."

That sobered the conversation.

"Any news about Tasha?" Meg asked.

After slugging back a hefty drink of water, Dane shook his head. "John's tormenting himself over this. He knows she'd been bothered by something for a while. He put it down to the reopening of the grave. She increased her production of those little dolls and the tourist stuff she makes and sells. He thought she was trying to keep her mind off what we were doing and to make extra money before the baby arrived."

He wiped his brow before continuing. "John says he can't re-member when he last felt the baby move. Tasha hasn't been sleeping well. So John moved to the couch. Before then, he used to sleep with his hands wrapped around her belly and could feel the baby turning around, like it was doing yoga."

"Is he blaming himself?" Jade wouldn't fault him if he did. She'd probably feel the same way, if she were in his position.

"Oh, yeah. He's worried that he missed something. Something that—if he'd seen it in time—would have saved them both."

"That's normal. He'll move past it eventually, and, when he does, he'll start the healing process." Meg's tone was gentle, yet professional.

The group continued to climb as they talked. Jade listened most-ly. It was easier to climb that way.

Meg continued. "John's healing may take a bit. There's no change in Tasha's condition, and Emile has slipped again. I don't know that he'll survive. If Tasha does recover, they won't tell her about the baby right away, for fear she won't handle the news well and could retreat inside herself again."

Dane strode forward confidently, unaffected by the strenuous climb. "Honestly, I don't know how John is handling this. It's got to be tough. I know it would be tough on me."

Meg nodded, sadness and compassion blending in her features.

Jade didn't know how Meg could deal with people's problems, not to this extent, not all the time. Jade couldn't do it. "She'll get over losing the baby. I know that sounds harsh, and it's way worse in that she was so far along in her pregnancy. However, in time, women do recover."

At least she had. And now, seeing Tasha lose her baby, Jade realized time had helped her. It's not as if she'd ever forget, but the pain had receded, softened. She'd moved on. "They have to grieve though. If they don't, it's harder to recover."

Meg suggested, "That's often the problem. They don't go through the grieving process. Life stops for them."

Jade agreed. She knew all about that. "I wonder how much of Tasha's condition is genetic, considering her father."

"It's too early to know. First the doctors have to get her physically healthy. Hopefully her mental and emotional states will start to stabilize and strengthen, as her body starts to heal."

Dane turned and asked, "And if it doesn't? What's there for her?"

"If she remains in a catatonic state," Meg explained, "they'll try different treatments, as they attempt to bring her around. If nothing works, she'll have to be institutionalized."

Jade shook her head. *Not nice.* John would go from being a proud papa-to-be, with a beautiful young wife, surrounded by family, to being the only one left alive and sane. Not good. Hadn't Dane said something about John struggling after losing his wife years ago? Tough to go through that again.

Jade wiped her forehead on her T-shirt. It was another gorgeous day in paradise, and that meant the sun was intense right now. She hoped it would ease, as they crested the next hill. She wished for more shaded spots to take a break from the direct sunlight.

Meg seemed oblivious to the scenery. "I'm sorry for John. There's no easy answer. It's a waiting game."

"And, with everyone gone," Dane explained, "John doesn't feel like it's his home anymore. It was Tasha's and Emile's home. They grew up in that house. Without them there, John says he feels like an interloper."

They came upon a series of rocks, obviously walked on over the ages to the point that they were almost stairs cut into the hillside. Dane led, Meg came next, and Jade walked the last of the line. She turned to look back. "Hey. You can see the grave site from here."

Meg joined her and stared over the open expanse of valley. With the blue sky, sunshine, and a gentle breeze, it was almost perfect. "It's beautiful, not such a bad place to be buried."

"From the sounds of it, most of the bodies will be going back in there too. Susan said that they had so few people coming to look for remains of lost loved ones that she didn't know why they were running the clinic."

Jade didn't know how she felt about that.

"I imagine most people know their loved ones are here and are happy to leave them." Meg smiled. "It's a beautiful resting spot."

"*Hmm.*"

They carried on for another twenty minutes and stopped for another breather and to enjoy the view. Jade couldn't get enough of the valley scenery. It was truly beautiful. The air was cleaner, fresher, the higher they climbed. She took several deep breaths, enjoying the easing of the tension on her shoulders as she did. "Shouldn't we have found them by now?"

"Not yet. Another hour maybe?"

"Why don't we call them? Maybe they're right around the corner," Jade suggested.

Meg pulled out her cell phone from her pocket and called Bruce. The three of them stopped and waited. "It's ringing, but he's not answering."

"Then send a text," Jade suggested. "That often works if you can't get through. Could be the hill interfering with the signal too."

With a shake of her head, Meg quickly tapped out a message. They kept walking upward. "Dane, where are the caves?"

"We should see the first one in ten or fifteen minutes. A couple of them are quite big."

"I suppose travelers would have been glad to have them too." Jade didn't think much of the idea though. All she could think of was that predators hid out in scary dark places.

They rounded a corner and came to a stop. Dane pointed off to the right. "Look partway up that hill. Do you see the cave?"

Meg nodded.

"Is this the first one?" Jade studied the black crevasse in the wall, slightly off to the left. "It's a little hard to see, unless you already know it's there."

"Approaching from this side, it is. There are more just ahead."

Meg and Jade looked at each other, then over at the cave.

"I'll check this one out. Just in case." True to his word, he climbed to the opening in a few easy steps. He stared into it for a moment, before disappearing into the yawning mouth. He reappeared within minutes to half step and slide his way back down to them. "Nothing in there. It's small and empty."

"Good. Let's check the next one."

Five minutes later, they approached the gaping black mouth of the second cave.

Jade couldn't say why they all fell quiet. But they did.

DANE STUDIED THE large opening in the side of the hill. John had shown him the caves because they wanted to see if they'd sustained damage in the quake. To rule out that anyone had sought shelter in them. There'd been nothing unusual in any of them back then.

The path appeared well traveled. Any number of locals could come through here. Just because Emile and Tasha considered this their backyard didn't mean it was.

With a glance toward the two women, Dane started toward the second cave. They stayed behind. Maybe it was due to their nervousness, but he approached warily. Large boulders sat piled high off to one side of the dark entrance, as if from a cave-in. The opening was smaller than it looked. Bending over slightly, he peered in, until his eyes adjusted to the darkness, then he navigated to a spot farther in.

Inside, he straightened slightly and surveyed the small open space that narrowed almost to a point at the back. The cave appeared empty. Large boulders dotted the floor, and the light was dim, but there was enough that he could see, as he walked all the way to the back, to ensure it was empty. He understood that the women were looking for Dr. Mike, but Dane hadn't forgotten that Peppe could have taken up residence anywhere here or been injured and lying wounded or dead inside. However, with Dr. Mike, Dane assumed the doctor would be closer to the entrance, if he were here, in the event help came along.

Not so in the case of the missing Peppe. Dane had the utmost respect for the medical profession, yet, when it came to mental instability, they often didn't have any answers. Look at Tasha. He gave the inside one more cursory glance.

"Dane? Is anything in there?"

He headed back to the sunlight. "No, it's empty."

"Nothing in the back?" Meg asked, frowning.

"Not that I saw. And, yes, I walked right to the back."

Jade stepped forward carefully. "I think I'd like to check it out. I've never really been in a cave like this."

Dane stepped aside, as Jade bent down and walked past him. He followed.

She glanced around and walked to the far back. "It really goes deep, doesn't it?" She peered into the darkness. "Did you say there was a third cave? We've checked two. Might as well take a look at the last one."

"Sure, it's only a minute or so away. Come on."

He led the way back out to where Meg was enjoying the sunshine.

"Jade wants to see the last cave. It's actually the biggest."

Meg brightened. "I'd like to see it too. This is a great hike."

Jade smiled slightly. "It would be, except, *where are the guys?*"

Meg glanced down at her watch. "Trust a little more. I'm sure they'll be here soon."

Jade sighed. "Let's hope so."

Dane, who had continued along the path, turned back. "Ladies? Will we check out the last one or not?"

The two women raced to catch up.

Chapter 19

J ADE STARED AT the massive black hole and shuddered. That cave might look good to some people. Not to her. Nothing was comforting about it. In fact, the shivers going down her back told her the opposite. "I so don't like the look of this place."

She felt Dane's curious gaze. He reached out and grabbed her hand. She stared down at their entwined fingers and smiled weakly. "Thanks. Let's go in, then come back outside. I think I've had enough."

"Done," he said easily. "You don't have to come in with me, if you don't want to."

"No, I don't, but I will. Then I'll know there isn't anything to be afraid of inside."

Dane smiled and tugged her closer. She didn't mind. It was nice to have a strong protective male around. For that matter Meg was walking pretty darn close to them both.

At the entrance, they paused for a long moment, allowing their eyes to adjust, then walked around the stack of boulders protecting the entrance. Inside, the cave showed signs of heavy use over the ages— not so much recent activity. A fire pit was close to the mouth of the cave, only no wood or coals were in the area. There were ledges and large flat rocks though. Jade pictured people spending hours here, talking.

At the back of the cave, where the blackness was so thick you couldn't see two feet in front of you, were more boulders. Dropping Dane's hand, Jade headed to the back, toward all the boulders. No reason for anyone to be back here. She just needed to make sure.

She wandered around, stubbing her toes on rocks in the dark and scraping her hands, as she clambered over the bigger ones in her search. She'd just about given up, when she heard the faintest of sounds. "Did you guys hear anything?"

Meg called from the entrance, "No. Nothing."

"Dane? Did you?"

"I'm not sure." He navigated toward her.

Jade thought the sound had come from her left. She climbed carefully, so as to not twist an ankle in the treacherous debris lying up against the walls. A soft moan sounded. She gasped with excitement. "I think I hear someone. Dane, come here."

She moved carefully, struggling to make out what she'd heard. The noise had definitely come from somewhere off to the left and in a little farther. The walls slanted sharply and were heaped with rocks along the bottom. The darkness was cloying. She scrambled over a boulder and came to a halt.

"Dr. Mike!"

"WHAT?" SHOCKED JOY lit Meg's voice.

Dane reached Jade first; Meg came tearing back to join them. "Is it him? Really?"

"I think so. It's hard to see."

"Hang on. Let me move some of this." Dane bent and cleared a space so he could crouch down. Meg and Jade kneeled down beside Dr. Mike, who lay in a crumpled ball. Dane ran through his mental checklist of first aid training, even as Meg checked the unconscious man's head. Dane leaned across the prone man, tracing down his arms to his hands that were tucked behind his back. He came to a stop. Please not. "Shit."

"What?' He felt both women stare at him. About all he could see were the whites of their eyes.

"Christ." His mind raced, even as he reached for his old Swiss army knife.

"Dane, you're scaring us."

"And you need to be scared. He's been tied up."

Shocked silence, then gasps of horror were followed by tears. "Tied up, as in someone brought him here and left him to die?"

"We don't know that. Someone obviously left him here, but they might be coming back." He opened the knife and hesitated. "I wish we'd thought to bring a bigger flashlight. I can't see what I'm cutting by this phone one."

"Let's move him out into the sun and then cut him loose."

He studied the path ahead of them. "I need to clear a few of these rocks. Then we should pick him up and carry him out."

"We'll help you." Meg and Jade started moving more rocks to clear a path. Five minutes later, Dane scooped up the injured man, wincing at the unconscious man's groans, and carried him out into the sun.

JADE HOVERED LIKE a mother hen with a long-lost chick, as Dane gently laid Dr. Mike on the ground. More rocks than dirt and so little shade as not to count, but the sunlight would be warm and welcome to the injured man. Dane cut the bonds around Dr. Mike's wrists. Dr. Mike's arms fell apart as if boneless, and a soft pained groan erupted from the man. Meg grabbed one of his arms and rubbed with short hard strokes. Jade snatched up the second arm, and together they massaged life back into them. Dane worked on Dr. Mike's legs. She didn't know how long he'd been lying in there, but getting the circulation running properly through those limbs had to hurt.

Meg checked Dr. Mike over thoroughly. She found dried blood at the back and side of his head, but not very much. She pointed it out; both Jade and Dane peered at it and shrugged. It didn't look that bad. Meg continued to check Dr. Mike over. "Right ankle is puffy, and he has just the one head injury that I can see. The rest of him appears to be fine. Unless he has internal injuries."

With those words, Dr. Mike blinked several times and tried to open his eyes in the bright sunlight. "Hi," he said in a raspy voice.

That prompted Jade to reach for her water bottle, and, with Dane's help, they hefted Dr. Mike up slightly. Jade held his head steady in the crook of her arm. "Dr. Mike, try to drink some water." She poured the water gently into Dr. Mike's mouth. Just a little to begin with, moistening the inside of his mouth first. Then she poured in a little more.

He swallowed greedily. Taking in more, sip by sip, until he could drink fully.

"That's better," Jade said.

Dr. Mike sighed, then smiled gently. "So glad you found me."

"So are we."

He made an effort to raise his head, then gave up. "I don't feel so good. It seems like forever that I was in there."

"Overnight most likely. The thing is, you're off the beaten track a fair bit." Meg continued, hoping to get him to answer some questions. "We found the SUV and had no idea where you'd gotten to. Or how.

Can you tell us what happened?"

He winced, took a deep breath, and lunged to a sitting position. A surprised look washed over his face. The color drained from his cheeks, his eyes rolled into the back of his head. With a weird squeak he crumpled back to the ground.

Jade cried out.

Meg leaned over Dr. Mike. "His pulse is slow and steady. We need to get him home." Meg stood and spun around suddenly. "Did you hear something?"

Jade turned to look at her. She searched the surrounding rocks and shrubs. "No. What did you hear?"

"Voices."

Dane took several steps toward the main path. "I'll check it out."

Staying on her knees beside Dr. Mike, Jade called out, "Be careful. Don't forget, Dr. Mike didn't tie himself up."

Dane nodded and loped off.

The two women waited several long minutes. Dr. Mike moaned again.

Jade turned to scan the area for Dane. "Still no sign of him. We'll give him a couple more minutes."

Meg glanced at her, a wry look on her face. "Yeah, and then what?"

"Give him another few minutes?" Jade shrugged, shifting to stretch her legs out. "I don't know. I can't say I'm comfortable up here alone like this. Who the hell broke into Susan's room? Could it have been the same person who did this to Dr. Mike?" She glanced down at the injured man. "We have to get Dr. Mike down the mountain somehow. He's our first priority. Will your phone work up here?"

"Oh." Meg pulled it out and called Dane's number. "Dane? Where are you?"

He laughed, his voice easily loud enough for Jade to hear. "I'm coming around the side now."

Meg ended the call and turned to look up at the rocks, where Dane just appeared. She laughed. "There he is and look who's with him."

Hope leaped in her heart. Jade spun around. She stood so she could see better. It was true. "Oh, thank God." Jade waved exuberantly. Dane headed in their direction, with Stephen, Wilson, and Bruce walking beside him.

All four men waved back.

When they reached the women, Stephen gave Jade a hearty hug.

"Hi. What a surprise to see you here. And, thank God, you found Dr. Mike. Dane told us all about it."

Jade laughed happily, as the three men gathered around Dr. Mike, pelting Meg with questions. Bruce dropped to the ground beside Dr. Mike, checking him over. Jade joined Dane a little way off to the side and watched the reunion. "Thanks. Where did you find them?"

A grin split his face. "They were walking toward us on the path. I couldn't help running into them."

"Well, I'm grateful everyone is here. We need to get Dr. Mike to the hospital—and now." She looked around uneasily.

"You're really not comfortable up here, are you?"

Jade couldn't help the shiver that slid down her spine. "Back home I did a lot of day trips. Here—with all the weird stuff going on—not so much. Besides, whoever tied him up could come back."

Despite her worry, she smiled at the laughing group in front of them. They really hadn't expected to find Dr. Mike on this adventure. She felt the relief in their overexuberance. But it wasn't over yet. "Any ideas how to get Dr. Mike down?"

"We could call for help, except we're a little short on clearings for a chopper to land. No stretcher here, and it could be hard to make something like that out of the little bit of materials we have available. So …"

"Oh. I just might have an answer." Stephen plunked down his backpack and pulled out a roll stretcher. "Can we make this work?"

Jade stared. "Why would you carry that in your backpack?"

His boyish grin burst out. "The handle broke, so I took it to the hotel to fix in the evenings. The thing is, this one doesn't have a spine board. If he's severely injured, we might cause more damage this way."

Meg studied it. "Have you fixed the handle?"

He grinned. "More or less."

"We already moved him once. … I suggest we try it. Our options aren't great otherwise."

Silently, working in unison and using their years of experience, they stabilized Dr. Mike's head and neck and shifted him onto the modified stretcher.

Bruce motioned to Dane. Both men took up their positions at either end of the stretcher and picked it up carefully. Dane called back over his shoulder to the women, "So are you coming, or will we wait for you back home?"

Jade shook her head, grabbed the empty water bottles lying

around, and ran to catch up. Together with Meg, they slipped past the three men to take the front position. Stephen and Wilson stepped in behind. Close enough to talk and far enough away to not be in each other's way, they managed the path for close to an hour—at which point they stopped for a short break.

They rested a bit, as shadows lengthened. After a few minutes Bruce called for an ambulance to meet them at the lab. Bruce stood. "Ready? Let's go."

Stephen and Wilson protested that it was their turn to help carry Dr. Mike. Dane and Bruce vetoed the switch, citing the differences in height between the other men as a reason to continue as they began.

They started off slower this time. Jade led the way, with Meg following. Jade's heart lightened when the grave site came into view below. She didn't know how the men were holding up. The two carrying Dr. Mike were doing at least twice the work of everyone else, but they refused the many offers to switch off. At least, Jade thought, going down was easier than hiking up the incline.

Finally they made it to the grave site.

She stopped and wiped her brow. Dr. Mike still hadn't regained consciousness. "Thank God, that might have been a bad trip for him, if he were awake," she said to Meg. "Am I glad this day is almost done."

After that, things moved quickly. The ambulance was waiting at the lab trailers. Dr. Mike was taken away. The others piled into the SUVs and drove out in a procession. Dane turned off at John's house, while the others took a direct route to the hospital.

Dr. Mike was quickly admitted into the ER, but they were told it might be some time before they received news of his condition.

While waiting, Jade decided to wander over to see Tasha. She didn't really want to see her, yet felt compelled to check on her and Emile. She couldn't find their rooms. Heading to the nurses' station, she stopped to ask about Tasha. A friendly young nurse sat at the computer, her smile a gentle welcome.

"She's been moved to a different ward for assessment."

Jade's face froze. She expected that would happen, only she hadn't thought such a move would be made for another week or so. "Right. Is it possible to get an update on her brother, Emile? I was part of the team that brought them both in."

The young nurse's face brightened. She flashed her a white smile. "Oh. Now I know who you are." Then her face fell; she lowered her voice. "Emile didn't make it. He passed away late this morning."

Jade bowed her head, as her heart ached for the family. Poor Dane. Poor John. And then she began to worry about Dr. Mike. Emile hadn't looked that bad when they found him, but he got worse fast, and now he was dead. Could nothing go right for them? "Damn. I'd hoped he'd pull through."

"I think everyone did. I went to school with him, way back when. And we were optimistic here. He started to pull out of it, but, like any of these head wounds, you can't count on that." The nurse smiled sadly, her eyes huge wells of emotion. "Once he started to slip, he fell all the way down."

Jade shuddered. "I am so sorry. Has Tasha been told?"

The nurse took one look around and lowered her head. "It wouldn't do any good. She's not aware of anything. Can't talk and isn't responding to treatment at this point."

Pain filled Jade's mind. "Poor John. He lost his child, his brother-in-law, and his wife. ... Hopefully time will help, and Tasha will come home someday."

The nurse shook her head. "Miracles do happen, but I can't say that I've seen one this bad pull out of it."

"What's her husband to do then?" Jade couldn't help herself from asking, even though she knew there was no answer.

The nurse lifted her face and stared, her gaze somber, wise—and directed right into Jade's eyes. "There's only one thing he can do—start over. This family is gone."

DANE STOOD IN front of the kitchen door to John and Tasha's house. He really didn't want to go inside. Physical exhaustion pulled at him, the kind he hadn't experienced since his football-playing days. Carrying Dr. Mike down the hill had been hard work.

Now he had to deal with John.

He poked his head into the kitchen. "John? I'm back. I'll wash up. See you in a few minutes." Closing the door, he headed to his small cabin for a quick wash and clean clothes. His shoulders ached.

Damn.

He wanted to go home. He needed to stay—but he didn't want to be here anymore.

Except for Jade. If she stayed, then he wanted to stay for a little while longer, for her. It could take that long to settle his affairs here anyway. And then he wanted to return to his old life—in Seattle. His house, his comforts. His home.

But he didn't want to return to it empty. Again his thoughts jumped to Jade. He was determined to explore a relationship with her. And if it worked out …

He was almost done here. He was only here for his brother. He knew it; his brother knew it, and neither one voiced it. He'd stay as long as John needed him. An idea flitted around in his head. Maybe he could convince John to return to Seattle with him? At this point in time, he couldn't see John leaving Tasha. However, if there was no improvement over the next month, then maybe …

John had some hard decisions ahead. Dane frowned. How would this play out? John couldn't make the easy decisions. How could he make the really difficult ones?

And had anyone seen Peppe? Or was he still missing?

What the hell will we do about that if he is?

And what had happened to Dr. Mike? Dane hoped he'd be fine, hoped he'd regain consciousness soon. The injuries hadn't looked too severe. Then look at Emile's; that hadn't looked bad either. That one really bothered him.

As did the thought of someone breaking into the hotel rooms. Who and why would someone want to tie up Dr. Mike, then abandon him in a cave? Was someone targeting the team? Or was some *crazy* out there, wandering around and attacking people, and the hotel break-in was an isolated incident? Given the poverty here, that was most likely.

That the attack on Dr. Mike could have been done by Emile or Peppe hadn't passed Dane by. That Emile had been injured and in the hospital looked bad, pointed to his guilt, because no one came back for Dr. Mike. Maybe his attacker had been Emile. That certainly reinforced that he was likely the culprit. Dane just couldn't imagine why Emile would do something like this though, and Dane didn't know how to broach that possibility with John either.

Something had shifted. Dane didn't get it. His life had been calm and quiet before the mortuary team arrived. Now it was almost as if the grave being opened had poisoned everything and everyone. But surely that wasn't possible—was it?

Chapter 20

HUNGRY, TIRED, AND now showered, all team members arrived for dinner on time. Except Bruce, who'd stayed at the hospital with Dr. Mike.

Jade walked in, as the first plates came out of the kitchen. Her stomach growled as the smells of delicious food reached her nose. She groaned and grabbed her chair. "Oh, Lord, thank you for this food. I am so hungry."

"When are you *not* hungry?" Stephen grinned and passed her the first bowl. "Everyone has taken some of this dish, so help yourself."

She grabbed the bowl. *Fish.* She took several large pieces and motioned for the next dish to be passed her way. Finally, with much joking, all of them ended up with full plates.

"By the way, I sent an email to Tony, updating him on Dr. Mike's rescue and current condition." Meg chuckled at the horrified looks shot her way. "Maybe now we won't have to worry about training Dr. Mike's replacement."

Everyone groaned. "That's not funny."

Meg piped up. "Speaking of which, Tony wants us to increase our productivity."

Outrage rippled through the room.

"Increase?" Stephen barely managed to get the word out through his stuffed mouth.

Forking up another bite, Meg said, "He's hoping we can reduce our time here by a week or two."

"Really?" Jade didn't think that would be possible, ... unless the right DNA results came back soon.

Susan, looking better after a long nap, asked, "What's the rush?"

Meg shrugged. "I don't know. He didn't say."

Just then Bruce walked in. A chorus of questions filled the air. Holding up his hand, he ticked off on his fingers, as he shared information. "Dr. Mike is fine. Has a sprained ankle. They're keeping him overnight for observation. They aren't expecting any problems. He did regain consciousness but was asleep again by the time I was allowed in to speak to him. ... So, no, we don't know what happened to him. He did say Emile's and Peppe's names."

Jade stared at him. "I don't know what possible motive either of them would have to hurt Dr. Mike, and, now that Emile's dead, we might never know. Depends if we can get any answers from his father."

Bruce filled his plate, then answered further questions as he ate. He pushed his empty plate off to one side and faced the group. "And there is one other thing we need to discuss."

Jade knew what it was. She'd been waiting for it. She refilled her plate, stuck her tongue out at Stephen for laughing at her, and waited for Bruce to speak.

"I stopped in at the police station to update them on Dr. Mike. They weren't thrilled obviously. However, the authorities have agreed to look into the skeletons with the chains ..."

"Yeah!" Cheers erupted around the table.

Jade waited. This still didn't feel like a cheering moment. She studied Bruce's face. "But?"

"Only if we do the processing and turn everything over to them."

She put down her fork. "We already agreed that we'd help out in our own free time to be certain that happened." She frowned and looked at Meg and Stephen for affirmation. "Or was I wrong?"

"No, that's correct."

She turned back to Bruce, "So what's the problem?"

"The problem is that Tony doesn't want us doing the work, doesn't want the company name associated in any way with this mess. He also doesn't want any of the remains to be handed over to them, not until we have found the remains we're looking for and have removed them."

"You mean, he's afraid that, if a crime has been committed, then it would reflect badly on the company or interfere with our ability to complete the job?" Jade picked up her fork again and continued to eat. *How typical.*

Bruce sighed. "He's worried that, even if we do locate our target family members, the authorities here won't release the remains we want to ship to the States. That's a possibility. And I can't fault Tony for his logic. We've gotten slightly off on a tangent, and he's just trying to rein us back in."

"Except we had no idea what we'd find in that grave."

Bruce picked up his coffee cup. "No, of course not. Our loyalty has to remain with Tony. Yet I can't walk away from those other victims either."

"There's only so much we can do." Meg sipped her coffee. "We've taken loads of pictures, and we've dug up the remains and processed them to the extent we're able."

Stephen nodded. "So then there is no big deal. We can turn over our findings, and the remains in question, to the authorities and carry on."

A strange look crossed Bruce's face.

Jade caught it and wondered. Then the missing piece clicked. "You mean, that might work, unless one of those women with the chains, like the most recent one, happens to be the adult female we're looking for?"

DANE PUSHED OPEN the kitchen door and wandered inside. "John? You in here?" He walked through the kitchen and into the living room, in case his brother left him a note. He kept his gaze off the creepy dolls. Why the hell hadn't his brother taken that shit down?

"John?" He poked his head inside the only bedroom in the tiny house.

What the hell? The bedroom was a mess. Incense bowls filled the top of the dresser and more little creepy dolls covered the nightstand. He didn't know what had gone through Tasha's mind these last few days and weeks, but it looked as if the slide had been in progress for a while.

John worried him now. How could all this have gone unnoticed, and why didn't he do something about this? Then he remembered his brother's inability to make decisions ...

Where the hell was he? Dane pulled out his phone and called him yet again. Was this the fifth time? Maybe John had gone into town to see Tasha? Then why the hell wasn't he answering the phone?

"Hello."

Dane ran a tired hand over his damp hair at the weary sound of his brother's voice. "John! I've been looking for you. Trying to reach you."

Sounding like he'd hit the last of his reserves, John said, "Emile didn't make it."

Dane closed his eyes briefly. *Shit.* "I heard. I'm sorry. I'd hoped he'd pull through."

"Yeah, ... well, he died this morning, before noon. I came down as soon as I got the message." A yawn, came through the phone. "Ah, hell, Dane. Life pretty much sucks right now."

Dane agreed, yet stayed quiet, not wanting to depress his brother any further. Wincing against the answer to come, Dane asked hesitantly, "And Tasha? Any change there?"

"No improvement. They've moved her to the psych ward."

"What? Already? Surely she hasn't improved physically enough for that move, has she?"

"I don't know. Something about needing round-the-clock care and no beds. The psych ward isn't all that thrilled to have her either. I don't know where she belongs. I want her home with me, only she doesn't see me, hear me. ... She doesn't seem to know I'm even there."

"Aw, hell." Dane couldn't think of anything else to say. "I'm sorry, man."

"Yeah. Me too. The thing is, no one can tell me if she's improving, will improve, or could take a long slide down. She's my wife. For better or for worse. And never did I consider this could happen." He sighed. "And I didn't mean that in a bad way. She's my wife. I love her. I want her home, where she belongs. I know she lost the baby, and that'll be hard on her, ... on us, but we can make more babies." His voice caught on a sob. "I can't live without her. I don't want to."

"You can if you have to. I know this is hard. There has been enough hurt and suffering. I don't want to lose you too."

"I'm not dying. Nor am I suicidal. I do wonder why God hates me so much though."

Dane winced and let his brother ramble. "I don't think He hates you."

"He sure as hell doesn't love me."

In an effort to change the subject, Dane asked, "When are you coming home?"

"Soon. I'm just driving around. I had to get out for a bit."

"Understood. Give yourself time."

"So why is it that I don't feel as I have any time?" Bitterness slipped across the phone line.

Dane frowned. He didn't like the way this was going. "Have you heard or seen anything of Peppe?"

"No. I don't know where the old bugger has gone. Don't care much at this point either." Then moments of silence filled the phone.

What could Dane say?

"I know I'm being a bit of a bastard, yet I can't help it," John continued. "I'll pick up something for dinner and come home. Will you be there?"

"Yeah, I'm beat. Been hiking all day, looking for one of Jade's coworkers. Make it dinner for three. I'm starved."

"On my way."

Dane hung up and smiled. "Now that sounds better." He stood in the middle of the living room, talking to himself, uncertain what to do. Tasha's stuff filled the house. He couldn't begin to get inside Tasha's head; even worse, he now understood her mind had broken. His brother would be back in about fifteen minutes. What could he do to help John? The poor guy had been sleeping on the couch for months now. Not that they'd spoken about it. Should he clean out the bedroom for his brother? Maybe through that process he'd find a clue to help them understand her behavior.

Not bloody likely.

The smelly bedroom made his skin crawl.

He turned on the overhead light and winced. The darkness had hidden the extent of the mess. There wasn't a spot on the floor to be seen. He couldn't believe she owned that many clothes. She'd only worn a couple outfits.

He returned to the kitchen and grabbed several garbage bags. Then he walked out to his truck and put on his work gloves. Taking a deep breath, he started bagging the mess on the floor. There was no easy way to do it, so he just picked them up and shoved it all into the first bag, until it was full. Then grabbed a second one. The third one he stuffed with bedding. He hauled the bags to the patio. Returning to the room, he grabbed a broom, opened a window and finished cleaning. He hadn't found anything but filth.

He stopped beside the first of two small tables on either side of the bed—each had a drawer. Dane was tempted to open it. But this was his brother's bedroom. He shouldn't be poking his nose anywhere here. He tried but couldn't turn away.

Shit. Shit. Okay. Just one quick look. The first table was almost empty. On top were a small clock and a lamp. Nothing else. The other one had to be Tasha's, and it was different. The drawer was full of small bags of herbs, maybe potions of some sort. Or drugs? He winced. That might explain her behavior. Not that he was an expert. It wouldn't explain the loss of the baby, but then, like the doctor had said, sometimes losses like that just happened.

Did John need to know the details? The whys? Would it be easier? Help him with his recovery?

Headlights shone through the living room window. John was home.

Great. Would he appreciate what Dane had done or be devastated by the intrusion? Only time would tell.

He walked outside to meet his brother.

HE STOOD IN his son's cabin—originally built decades ago for the foreman on the farm, then for guests as a way to make extra money, before his son grew into a man. Emile had moved in when Tasha had gotten herself married.

And Emile wasn't here. He hadn't come home.

The ambulance had taken him, and the night had swallowed him.

Peppe ran a shaky hand through his thinning hair. His world consisted of slices of memories that, even when pieced together, made no sense. He'd been in the main house several times since the ambulance had taken away his kids. There'd been no sign of them since. No sign of Tasha. No sign of Emile.

Instead the interloper had moved in. John's brother. He'd cleaned out Tasha's stuff—bags full left on the patio, like garbage. Her things weren't garbage. His little girl wasn't garbage—not like some women.

Someone would pay for this. And soon.

He didn't see John being responsible. He'd always been good to Tasha. To Emile. To him. Not that he'd seen John much. Still, he'd been here for a while now.

John's brother on the other hand ... and that group he hung around with? Peppe shook his head. At the mass grave, he'd seen Dane sniffing around that little blonde who worked at the trailers.

Someone had to pay for this intrusion into their lives and their homes. This was his place. He wanted his son and daughter back. Maybe he could force them to bring the kids home? *Hmm.* The brother? The grave team? He smiled grimly. Or one of the women who were connected to both?

Perfect.

Chapter 21

MORNING CAME TOO early. Jade groaned and rolled over to bury her face in the pillow. She did not want to be awake this early on a Sunday. Weekends were supposed to be for fun and rest. ... Still, they'd found Dr. Mike, and the word was, his condition was improving.

She smiled into the pillow. Today was a whole new day. Sitting up, she grinned at the sunshine peeking through her curtains. Good, another nice day. A day to stay home, kick around, and take it easy. Maybe hit the beach, like she'd promised herself. She'd had enough drama for a lifetime.

Her hotel phone rang. She picked it up. Her brother, Duncan, calling. A happy sigh wafted through her. It was so nice to hear from him. "Hey. What's happening?"

"That's why I called. How are things over there?"

She filled him on the last few days and wasn't surprised at his exclamations.

"Holy crap. Are you nuts! You were supposed to go over there to recover, ... to get back to normal. Not to experience more stress."

She kicked back her covers and leaned against her headboard. "You're right, and I'd be happy to have missed this. But today, after finding Dr. Mike last night, things are looking much better."

"Well, is everything else okay now?"

She told him about Tony's visit and the progress on the site, then remembered to ask him about his life back in Seattle. After they said their goodbyes, Jade got up and took a shower.

Breakfast was a quiet and calm affair, in that she was alone in the dining room. She ordered a big meal and took it to the outside patio to sit in the sunshine. It was still early, and the sun already had enough heat that she chose to sit by the palm trees in a shaded spot. She took her time and relaxed. She was going nowhere today.

A sleepy Meg stumbled out onto the patio to join her.

"I didn't expect to see you here so early." Jade smirked at the disgruntled look on Meg's face.

Meg yawned widely. "I don't want to be here either. I want to be in bed, sleeping. As that's apparently not an option, here I am." Meg carefully put her cup on the table. "If there were any justice, we'd recoup all those lost hours of worrying by sleeping late." Meg pulled a chair over and sat down. "My face feels like sandpaper was scraped over it while I slept."

"I have some nice cream in my room, if you'd like to try some." Jade reached for her last piece of toast and spread jam over it. "Have you ordered your breakfast yet?"

"Yes. I'm just having French toast." She crossed her arms on the table and rested her head on them. With her eyes closed she looked ready to drop back off to sleep.

Jade brightened. "I forgot about that option. I could use some too."

Meg lifted her head and snorted. "Are you nuts? You just ate."

Jade shrugged. "I burned a lot of calories yesterday. Can't afford to lose any more weight."

Cindy, the one waitress who worked on weekends, refilled their coffee cups. Jade ordered another round of French toast, while Meg snickered, perking up enough to butter her toast, then poured on the syrup. Coffee and food seemed to revive her.

By the time Jade's second breakfast arrived, Stephen and Wilson had joined them. Everyone looked tired and worn out, but they smiled broadly, and bright eyes abounded. Yesterday had turned out for the best for their team. In the bright sunshine of the morning, it was easy to see the world in a more positive light.

When Dr. Mike hobbled in, bright but a little worn around the edges, with Bruce behind him, everyone cheered. Jade jumped up and held out a chair for the doctor. She snagged his crutches and leaned them against the palm tree behind her. "How are you?"

He smiled and hopped the last step to the table. "I'm fine. I'm so happy to be back here."

Bruce dropped onto a chair too. "After a great night, the doctors were happy to release him early this morning. We even snuck in a quick stop to update the police. Wait until you all hear his story." He stared at Jade's plate. "I hope you left some for others."

With a cheeky grin in his direction, Jade forked up a large piece of French toast and popped it in her mouth. "I did. Cindy will be happy to bring you a plate too."

"So what happened? Who tied you up and left you there?" Wilson picked up his coffee and took a sip.

Even Jade put down her fork and turned to watch the mixed emotions pass across Dr. Mike's face. "What?" she prompted.

Dr. Mike rubbed his temple. "I just feel a little foolish, that's all. I had locked up the lab, and, on the spur of the moment, I decided to check out this trail. It was right around the corner, nice and close. What could go wrong? I wasn't planning on climbing it. I just wanted to see if it was something we could all do." He sighed, took a sip of tea, then put his cup down and continued. "I parked, got out, locked the SUV, and went to the base of the path. ... The next thing I know, I'm on the ground, my hands tied up, and this old guy is trying to wake me up."

Gasps lit up the room.

He winced. "Now I know it was Peppe. He had a wild look in his eyes, and he smelled something terrible. At the time, I tried to reason with him, then tried to offer him something, anything to let me go. He hardly talked. That guy, for all his lack of size, was on a mission."

He glanced around the room, a wry look on his face. "I know. How could a small crazy old man go up against me? I've got fifty pounds on him, am younger and stronger." He stared down at his teacup, remnants of memories chasing across his face. "Yeah, I'm feeling pretty stupid today."

Silence hit the table.

Bruce smacked him on the shoulder lightly. "Don't be. You might be younger and stronger. However, you aren't insane, and you were out for a hike. You weren't looking for an ambush."

Dr. Mike gave him a half smile. "I tried to fight him, and he whacked me over the head again." He shrugged. "I decided to wait for a better chance. He forced me to walk up the mountain. When it got dark, he still knew where and how to walk. I didn't. Just after we'd topped the rise, I made it a little farther, then fell on the rocks."

He motioned to his crutches. "I couldn't walk anymore. He actually helped me get up and into the cave." Dr. Mike shifted uncomfortably. "I heard voices and hobbled forward enough to see Emile and Peppe having an all-out argument. Emile saw me and my tied hands. I thought he'd help me. Instead he took off down the mountain, screaming at his father something fierce." He shook his head. "Peppe took off after him. Not sure what that was all about."

"We found Emile on the rocks by the grave site. He appeared to have fallen and hit his head. He died in the hospital yesterday."

"Oh, Lord," Dr. Mike whispered, shock rippling across his face. "I'd hoped he'd gone to get help."

"He might have been coming for help when he fell." Meg smiled gently at him.

Jade, speaking in a hushed voice, had another suggestion. "Or Peppe might have caught up to him and attacked him."

Silence filled the room once again.

Everyone sat back.

"Unbelievable. If we hadn't found you ..." Stephen left the rest unsaid.

Dr. Mike grimaced. "Thanks for pointing that out."

Jade reached over and kissed the older man on the cheek. "Except we did find you, so all is good."

Stephen raised his eyebrows. "Except for Peppe. He's still out there, loose. What possible reason could he have had to kidnap Dr. Mike?"

Putting down his cup of fresh coffee, Dr. Mike said, "He kept mumbling about a doctor. As if he or someone he knew needed a doctor. I don't know for sure, but I wonder if he thought I could help Tasha?"

"Oh, wow." And Jade could almost believe that. Especially for someone in Peppe's mental state. "That almost makes sense."

"It would mean he knew that Tasha was in trouble." Everyone turned to stare at Dr. Mike, then at each other.

Stephen snorted. "Anyone would know that. You only needed to look at her to know something was wrong. Jesus, I almost admire him if that's why he did it. At least he was trying to do something for his daughter."

That brought murmurs of agreement from the others.

"Anyone know if there'll be a funeral for Emile?" Meg asked.

Jade shook her head, before answering, "No idea. I doubt Dane and John have it all figured out yet either."

"Yeah, you're not kidding. Is the chaos over?" Bruce asked. "Obviously we'll have to be careful, as long as Peppe is still wandering around. But now that the police are looking for him, we might soon have an end to that problem too. I'll call Dane, after I get a bite to eat. We should be the ones to tell him what happened. He can decide the best way to tell John."

Jade winced. That wouldn't be much fun. Dane wouldn't be impressed with the idea of Peppe being responsible for Dr. Mike's disappearance. He'd feel guilty. He shouldn't because he'd wanted the authorities called in to help find the old man in the first place.

Bruce changed the subject. "We should be getting the next lot of DNA results back soon too. Seems like we've spent a lot of time here, and yet we're still just getting started. I don't feel that we're even close to halfway. What's it been? ... A month now?"

The discussion turned to the job in progress.

Jade settled back, content to listen to everyone else work things out. There was a sense of calm in her heart. She knew John had to be going through a bad time right now, and she felt sorry about his family. Still, she was beyond relieved to have things approaching normal in her world.

Now if they could just stay out of trouble for the rest of their Haitian work term ...

MONDAY DAWNED BRIGHT and clear. Everyone showed up in good spirits, ready to make major inroads on their work—as if the long Friday night and draining Saturday had never happened. Of course a relaxing Sunday had helped to revive everyone's energy levels.

Dr. Mike had chosen to work in the lab trailer. His ankle rested on a second stool, and he worked on charts, while Jade worked on the skeletons. Stephen and Wilson worked up at the grave site. Both men sported decent tans after weeks of outdoor work.

Susan, in good health again, had gone into town with Bruce to attend the clinic. There'd been a lot of discussion about closing it, if no one showed.

The end result was to give it a couple more weeks and then reassess. So far they'd only had a half-dozen people turn up. None of those wanted or could afford to have their relatives buried elsewhere. They just wanted to locate their family members, to find closure as to where and what had happened to them—nothing more. Even though Tony had contacted the media outlets throughout Haiti, to broadcast the offer, the response from the local families had been disappointing.

Jade bustled around her two new cases. She had an adolescent male and a young adult female on her morning docket. With Dr. Mike doing the charts, they could proceed that much faster.

Before long, they were finished. "I'll go grab Stephen. We'll switch these two for two more."

Dr. Mike nodded, but his focus remained fixed on the screens in front of him.

Jade smiled at his intensity, then headed out. While walking up the path, she heard the men's shovels banging away on the rocks. She wished Dane would drive up, even though it was Monday, and she knew he had his own business to take care of.

He'd been at the back of her mind all morning. How was he holding up?

They'd talked several times on Sunday but hadn't managed to squeeze in more than a few minutes of togetherness. Again she wished she had her own cell phone here. She could send him a text to just say hi and to let him know she was thinking of him. She'd put buying a phone at the top of her list of things to do.

"Hey." She smiled at the two dust-covered men. "Can I get one of you to come help move bags for me? I'm done with the first two and could use two more."

"That was fast." Stephen put down his shovel. "I'll help."

"I might as well too." Wilson joined them. "We'll do the switch for you. How's Dr. Mike holding up?"

"He appears to be fine. Having him help out in the lab is speeding things up."

The men quickly exchanged the bags, leaving Jade and Dr. Mike alone again.

"Jade? Any updates on Peppe from Dane?"

"Haven't heard anything." Jade picked up her camera again. "Then I haven't spoken to Dane today."

"I'm sure the authorities would let us know if they found Peppe anyway."

"Good thing." She replaced the camera on her table and picked up her pen and clipboard and wrote down a few notes. She removed a solid gold band from a finger barely holding together. She checked for an inscription, then laid it on a white board and picked up her camera again. "I wonder how John is holding up," she added, as an afterthought.

Dr. Mike pointed out another consideration. "And I'm wondering if Peppe understood the significance of the ambulance taking away both of his kids, with only John and Dane there since. Who knows how much he saw or understood? If he realizes the truth, no way to know how he'll react now. He could blame us. He could blame John or even Dane. They are on his property. And his family is gone. Or he might not even comprehend what's happened."

A heavy silence filled the small room, as they worked.

"Any idea when his wife passed away?" Dr. Mike asked.

"I don't think I ever heard. He's probably done a slow decline since then." Jade looked at him.

"*Hmm.*"

"What are you thinking?"

"Someone mentioned his wife dying about ten years ago. Just looking to confirm. That's within my time estimate of how long the two oldest skeletons have been in the grave. Eight to twelve years is my informed guess at this point."

Jade straightened, a dawning understanding filtering in. "The timeframe puts Peppe as a potential suspect, doesn't it? If his wife died anywhere around then, it could have set him on that path?"

He studied the chart in his hand. "I will admit my thinking is colored by Peppe trying to drag me over the mountain, ... but the proximity, the timing, the means? ... It all fits. He could have caught any young woman and dragged her over that hill into his cabin and who would have known? Of course motive is still an issue."

Jade put down her camera slowly. It was either that or drop it. "Does anyone twisted enough to imprison women need a motive? Seriously. That's a horrible thought."

"Don't worry about it. Probably nothing to it. It was just the coincidence of being a prisoner myself for that short time period that brought it to mind." He pushed up his glasses. "Then again any one of these bodies could have been buried somewhere else, then brought here as a better hiding place. Mixed in with all the others, no one would know. Even the dirt layer could have been added in between. Enough to hide the new arrivals before the loader came back with the next load. It's not as if any security was here at the time of the big earthquake."

"And wrapped in sheets, the chains wouldn't have been visible anyway."

Dr. Mike sighed. "No one cared. This grave was the solution to their major problem. Imagine the chaos at the time. We've found bodies that had been wrapped in sheets, plastic, some taped shut, and others just tossed."

The image he'd painted turned her stomach. "So what you're really saying is that there is little means to find the truth." She spun around in the direction of the reefer truck. "Do you think the kidnapper was in the grave himself?"

"Could be."

She winced as she glanced down at the adult male on her table. "Or even here?"

He grinned. "Absolutely. The thing is, we may never know. We can turn over the evidence to the authorities but—"

"It will be up to them to follow up on it."

Dr. Mike nodded. "I don't think a few more dead bodies in a mass grave will bother them much."

"These women were murdered, weren't they?"

"Yes. The first one we found could have been a captive at the time and killed by the earthquake. Or the kidnapper might have decided it was time to get rid of her."

"And had a perfect grave ready-made for him. Nice. *Not.*"

"And Peppe could also have walked across his property and thrown her in, between tractor trips."

They stared at each other.

"Just sayin'," said Dr. Mike.

So that's how he'd worked his way around to thinking John's Haitian family could be involved? Jade pondered the information. "Which also makes Emile a suspect, based on that thinking. Physically stronger, also in close proximity, also devastated by the loss of his mother? And with Emile dead and Peppe and Tasha off their rockers—chances are good we'll never know."

Straightening his back, Dr. Mike grimaced. "Exactly. The only thing we can do is our job. And hope that, even if the authorities here don't do anything, that a higher power will."

Jade hated that some creep could have been kidnapping and killing women, possibly for years, without paying the price for their crimes.

She slammed down her clipboard and glared at Dr. Mike. A higher power nothing; she wanted justice. "I'm hoping the bastard's already dead. And that it wasn't an easy death. Pinned down and dying without water and food, … for days in a deserted empty house. … Now that sounds about right."

"Exactly." Dr. Mike smiled. "I'm not all about sugar and spice, you know."

AT THE END of the day, Jade really wanted to stop in and to see Dane on the way home. She did not want to see John though. She'd stayed later at the lab, hoping Dane might show up—only he hadn't. On top of that, the trailer was hot, and she was tired. She sighed.

"Okay, what gives, Miss Lovelorn?" Meg's perky voice showed

she was back to normal, after the difficult weekend.

Jade wiped her forehead, reaching again for her water bottle. "*Huh*? What? Oh, nothing."

"Nothing? That's like the fifth heavy sigh in the last ten minutes. Call the man, for heaven's sake."

"Call? *Nah*. He's busy." She took a long drink and recapped her bottle, then stared out the open door. Dust swirled outside in the breeze. Too bad it wasn't swirling inside the trailer, exchanging the old air that sat in here from the weekend with fresh air.

"You're supposed to be working too, but apparently this isn't half as interesting as wondering what Dane's up to."

Jade turned back to Meg and gave a small laugh. "That obvious?"

"Hell yeah. Just be happy the men aren't around," Meg teased. "They'd be hassling you constantly."

She gave a mock shudder. "Nasty. Okay, I'll stop."

Meg straightened from the close-up examination of a leg. "Why don't you just call him? You're an adult, not a teenager."

"So why do I feel like a schoolgirl again?"

With a delighted grin, Meg walked over and nudged Jade's shoulder. "Be the one to make the first move. Call him."

Feeling like an idiot, yet unable to stop herself, she dialed Dane's number. It rang once, then twice.

"Dane, this is Jade." With a half smile at Meg, Jade walked out into the afternoon sun to speak more freely. "I'm just calling to say hi and to see how you're holding up. How's John doing?"

"I'm fine. And I'm glad you called." His heavy sigh came through the line. "John's adjusting. He's already concerned about Tasha and now with this Peppe business ..." Dane groaned painfully. "I don't know what to do for him. His repair business closed after the last earthquake, just before you arrived, but apparently it had been failing for a while. He rented a storefront a few months ago in an effort to get more customers but never even got set up before the smaller more recent earthquake. I've been helping him along financially, but he's proud, and it's awkward. Now, with Emile's funeral and Tasha's long-term care issues, I just don't know."

The sun's rays beat down. The big rocks around the trailers seemed to soak up the heat and radiate it outward. Shadows of light and dark played over the burial ground. Jade wandered from one splotch of sunshine to another. It was a beautiful afternoon. "So what now?" she asked.

"Bury Emile. Wait for word on Tasha. And I don't know what

John wants to do about the baby."

"Oh dear. I never thought of that. A child born alive is buried when they die. I don't know what would happen in this case." That decision might rest with the parents, but she didn't know. Also, in this case, the mother wasn't capable of making any decision. "John has to sort through that. It was his child."

"A daughter." Dane's voice thinned slightly. "The nurse at the front desk told me, in private."

Jade winced. That made it real. She'd never known her own child's sex. "Does John know that?"

"I imagine so. We've never spoken of it."

Jade wanted to cheer him up. "Dr. Mike is doing much better. He's back at work. This last weekend has changed the atmosphere. We like the idea of working harder and going home earlier."

He sighed heavily. "Yeah, I have to admit that going home is looking pretty-damn good from my perspective too. I just can't leave John like this."

"Is that place his?"

"No, it's Peppe's and then Emile's and Tasha's."

"Except, with Emile gone, it will be Tasha's, and, as long as she's incapacitated, it's still John's place. … Right? Meaning, he still has a home?"

"Oh, yes. Look. I'm just about ready to leave off work for the day. Are you at the hotel or at the lab?"

"I'm still at the lab. We're almost ready to go home now. Meg is locking up." Meg did just that and then walked over to the reefer and checked the thermostat. She turned to face Jade, the SUV keys dangling in her hand, waiting for the call to finish.

"Are we still on for dinner on Friday?" Dane asked. "And coffee anytime between now and then would be great."

"Sounds perfect." Smiling, she ended the call and hopped into the SUV, feeling like a schoolgirl again. "Dinner is definite for Friday."

"About time."

PEPPE HAD KEPT watch all week. Waiting. He had a place outside his house where he could keep an eye on everyone's comings and goings. Right now he was more interested in the lab trailer.

He'd waited, but she hadn't been left alone. It's as if she knew. And maybe she did.

Instincts had been bred out of most people—unless they were hunters like him. Peppe huddled deeper into the hollow. He'd kept an eye on the two houses, waiting for his kids. They hadn't come home. He didn't know where they were. He didn't know how to find them.

John might tell him. ... And John might just laugh in his face and call him crazy.

Maybe he was crazy. Peppe couldn't remember anything, not in a straight line. The days were mixed up. His wife's face swam through his mind. He thought he'd seen her yesterday, but, when he'd spoken to her, she was gone again.

Maybe he was crazy.

But he had kids. *Emile and Tasha. Emile and Tasha.* He kept the mantra going over and over again. He had to believe they'd come home.

If they didn't, then what? This one was Tasha's house, but John and his brother lived there now. That wasn't right. It was still Peppe's house.

They'd taken over. John was even driving *his* truck. At least Peppe thought it was his truck. Except he didn't remember the last time he'd driven. He'd driven his wife to work sometimes. He remembered that. Then again, he remembered the farm full of healthy green trees and fruit pickers working the place too. Was that last year? He studied the dead trees, the cut-off stumps, and the dead grass.

Couldn't have been.

He wiped his hand over his face. So many memories. So much time gone. All he wanted was to join his wife, but he had something to do first.

John's truck—his truck—drove into the yard and parked outside the main house.

Right. Now he remembered.

He turned his attention back to the lab trailer.

Chapter 22

FRIDAY DAWNED BRIGHT and clear. Jade couldn't be happier. She'd been focused and dedicated to getting the job done. The week had passed quickly. She'd spoken with Dane several times, and he'd delivered coffee two mornings in a row. She'd come to love those little surprises. He kissed her when he saw her. He kissed her when he left her. She was coming to love those gestures too. She was coming to care for Dane—at least a little bit.

Okay, more than a little.

Emile had been buried in the family tomb on Wednesday. The team had been told on Thursday.

She hadn't had a chance to call Dane all day, as the pace had picked up, and, with Dr. Mike's help, they'd accomplished the workload of two days' worth just today. Now, walking into the lobby of the hotel with Meg at her side, Jade was looking forward to a hot shower and dressing up.

"In a hurry, I see." Meg grinned. "Finally, it's Friday!"

"Finally. We're going out on the water." Jade bounced, as she raced to the stairs.

"Oh, I am so jealous!" Meg's astonishment-turned-envy made Jade perk up.

"What do I wear sailing?" Mentally she ran through her minimal wardrobe. She'd done no shopping here, other than in that first week, and clothes for dating hadn't been on her list of priorities then.

"Good question." Meg stared at Jade. "Pants maybe? When is he coming?"

Jade smiled; that's what she'd been thinking. "Five-ish. So in an hour."

Meg glanced at her watch. "You mean, in fifteen minutes."

"Oh my God. No. That can't be." Jade grabbed Meg's watch and checked for herself. "Oh no. I'm so dead." She bolted up the remaining stairs to her room. Where had the last hour gone? She would have sworn she still had time. She glanced through her limited wardrobe. She really didn't have much choice. It would have to be layers. First she needed the fastest shower possible. Then she dressed in cotton pants, a T-shirt, with a sweater and sandals. It might be warm out now, but there could be a wind out on the water. She'd freeze within an hour, if she didn't have something to cover up with. Her sweater would have to do.

She grabbed her purse and raced to the hotel's front door. Even as she stood here and caught her breath, Dane drove up.

"Perfect. Hop in."

Jade opened the passenger door of the truck and waved goodbye to Bruce, driving up in the SUV. Dane honked as they left the drive and moved onto the main road.

She glanced at him. Damn he looked good. "Are you doing okay?"

He took his gaze off the road to send her a quizzical look. "Yes. I'm fine." He refocused on the road. After a moment he looked at her again. "Don't I look fine?"

She studied his profile. This man always looked good. In a light teasing voice, she said, "Fishing for compliments?"

"Hell no." He grinned. "I don't have to fish normally."

It was her turn to grin. "No, I bet you don't."

He reached across and caught her hand, squeezing gently. "Hey, I'm not a womanizer or anything like that."

"Good. I don't do those." She'd said it flippantly, then realized how he might take it. She stared out the side window, feeling the heat climb up her throat.

His gaze burned once and then twice. She refused to meet it. Damn her quick tongue.

"I'm really enjoying our time together. We've known each other what? ... A month now? I'm serious about seeing you when we're back home."

She flushed, smiled brilliantly at him, yet responded shyly, "I'm serious too."

They drove in companionable silence for several miles. Jade sat up, realizing they were heading toward the water. "This town is so pretty. I never saw anything this nice when I was here last time. The architecture, the palm trees, the blue water ..." She sighed happily, as they drove along the streets.

He pointed to a large marina she hadn't seen before. "Our boat is down here. I've booked a dinner tour. This sailing company was recommended by someone who works for me. This couple will take us out on the harbor and serve a full dinner, while we get to enjoy the scenery." He drove the truck into a small lot and parked.

She smiled with delight. "What a great idea."

Laughing and holding hands, they ran the length of the big dock. The yacht was huge. White with golden trim, The Painted Lady was proudly proclaimed on the bow. It gleamed chrome and steel and quietly stated money—and class. At the ramp, they were greeted by the owners, a native Haitian husband-and-wife team, sporting big smiles and friendly faces. As soon as Dane and Jade boarded, they were offered a choice of wine or coffee. Jade suggested coffee first and wine a bit later.

Dane grinned. "She needs her caffeine fix."

Up on the top deck was a large couch in a brilliant white that almost blinded her in the sun. It was perfect. They had the space all to themselves, with their hosts staying below to give them privacy. Jade leaned back and sniffed the salty air. "Oh, wow. Now this is nice."

"Happy?" He wandered the small space looking at the activity going on around them, as they slowly motored into the bay.

"Oh, yeah. It's a great way to end the week." She slumped lower and tilted her face to let the warm sun and the cool breeze waft across her face. It had been a long week. "I can't believe how much I needed this."

"Now here's something to make it even better." Grace, the woman who'd initially greeted them, arrived with coffee, topped with whipping cream and cinnamon, in big Spanish mugs.

"Thank you." Jade almost swooned at the rich coffee aroma hitting her nose. "I could take this every day."

"Then we'll have to find time to repeat this."

She settled back to enjoy the ride. Jade didn't know anything about boats, and this one was huge. They had perfect service. Small sailboats sauntered by with their cheeky brightly colored sails. The odd powerboat bounced across the water. The coastline drifted by. Jade just drifted.

She asked Dane a ton of questions about Haiti and couldn't believe that he seemed to have most of the answers. When he couldn't answer a couple, he went and asked their hosts. Several times, Grace came up the stairs to ask if they wanted the tourist spiel for different attractions.

Both of them said yes and stood, while she pointed out the various highlights, as they cruised slowly through the water.

The magic continued with the delivery of the promised red wine, followed by a dinner of fresh fish. Jade had no idea what kind, but it was wrapped in large green leaves and baked on coals in a brazier. Bowls of rice and veggies went with it. The smells were heavenly, the taste divine. The longer they cruised, the lower the sun slipped. Deep oranges and pinks blanketed the evening in a peaceful, intimate cover. Replete, and caught up in the enchantment of the evening, Jade settled back onto the couch, with another glass of red wine, while Grace efficiently cleared their table.

Dane sat down beside her. He lifted one arm, and she slid over to cuddle closer. A wonderful meal, gorgeous scenery, company that made her heart lift—it was magical.

Hours later, the cruise returned to port. Not ready for the evening to end, they stood and watched the lights flash on the rippling water. "We'll do this again. I'm glad you enjoyed yourself."

"I more than enjoyed tonight. It was perfect."

Dane slung his arm over her shoulders. "It's only eleven. Bedtime? Or sit by the water?"

"Oh, let's sit by the water. I don't want the night to end."

"*Hmm.*" Dane, his arm still wrapped around her shoulders, tugged her in the direction of a large circular dock, with benches all around. They walked past many other couples. At the end, they sat on a small bench they had all to themselves.

"So much to be said for moonlight on the water." She smiled, laughing lightly at the waves smacking up against the docks all around them. The moonlight danced on the ripples. "There's no visible current, or not much of one, yet the water is so alive."

"Lots of activity going on here, just on a smaller scale than Port-au-Prince.'"

Her voice sobered. "Now that wasn't my favorite place."

He caught her hand in his, squeezing it gently. "I can imagine. We'll fix that one of these days."

"Is it obvious that my experiences there still haunt me?" She watched an expression flit across his face. It was hard to get a clear look in the dim light.

"No, not really," he said slowly. "However, I also know what I've seen and heard from John, and he barely speaks of it."

"I think everyone who was here was affected, changed by the experience. My ex-fiancé wanted the old me back, and she was gone." Said so simply, it was the first time Jade realized how true it was. Her life had changed at that point. "He wasn't able to handle it."

Dane lifted her hand to drop a kiss on the back of it. "I'm sorry for you. It must have been traumatizing. I still wish John would talk about his experiences. I think it would help him."

"And here I thought men didn't like to talk."

A wry smile slipped out. "Maybe. This is different. He's holding in so much, and I can't help but think that all that emotion needs an outlet. It's as if he's two different people—the one he keeps locked up and the one he lets the world see."

She could understand that. "I needed to be alone, yet, at the same time, I needed support. And it was tough for Duncan to recognize that fine line. It was all about balance." She gazed up at Dane, concerned by the darkness in his warm gaze. He cared about his brother so much. "Does John have friends, other family members who would understand? Has he bonded with any of Tasha's family?"

"No. He only tolerated Peppe and Emile."

"Too bad. He has to be feeling isolated, lonely even. He's lucky to have you." She studied the moonlight. "It's beautiful out, ... an incredibly romantic setting, and we're discussing problems."

He laughed, caught her hand in his left hand, so he could drape his right arm around her shoulders. "So what would you like to talk about?"

She cuddled in closer and laughed lightly. "You. Tell me about the rest of your family. What's your life like in Seattle? How old are you? How come you're not married with the requisite two-and-a-half kids?"

Laughing, he filled in the details of his life. She listened, enthralled. Jade turned slightly to watch a small cruiser move smoothly through the water. Its cheerful lights shone and danced on its bow, reflected on the dark water. "This area is very beautiful."

"Not as beautiful as you."

Jade shivered unexpectedly. Was it from the evening air? The magic of the moment? Or his unexpected flattery and the obvious sincerity behind it? He really thought she was beautiful.

Dane hugged her tighter. Jade leaned her head against his cotton shirt. She loved the ripple of muscles and the steady beat of his heart. Something was so very sexy about a man who could take control—and not abuse it. *Someone like Dane.*

She would like to see where this relationship would go.

Starting with tonight.

He'd said she could set the pace.

"Are you okay?"

Tilting her head back, she murmured, "Just thinking about how much I like being with you."

His arms tightened around her, and he cuddled her close. "Good. I'm very glad to hear that. I miss this."

Tilting her head so she could look up at him, she studied the warm look in his eyes. "The closeness? The hugs? Or the hopeful prelude to so much more?"

A rumble of laughter rolled through his chest. "All three?"

She giggled, her mind taking that next leap.

Was she ready? Did she still want to wait? She'd lost most of this last year. She hadn't expected her recuperation to take so long. But it had. She didn't want to lose any opportunity to regain a full and happy life. Now that she was back to the land of the living, she wanted to live. Before it was too late.

Look at Tasha and Emile. Both young, and both had lost everything. Look at John. He'd suffered so much.

And then there was Dane …

She wanted to celebrate what was building between them. Revel in the fact that her body was reawakening, her heart reopening, her emotions rejoicing because these feelings coursed through her.

Dane gently grasped her chin between his fingers, tilting her head so he could see her face, a puzzled look on his face. "Heavy thoughts?"

"No," she murmured, "Light thoughts. Thoughts of joy, peace, satisfaction." She lifted her face to his, sighing against his lips. "Definitely of satisfaction."

His eyes suddenly widened in understanding. She felt a shudder ripple through his body. "What are you saying? Be very clear here." His eyes darkened to almost black. His lips brushed gently across her lips. Once. Twice. Waiting.

Jade smiled, held his head firmly, and kissed him. Heat seared between them, as she laid the hottest kiss she'd ever laid on a man. She burned through her own reserves and burned through his in a greedy all-consuming lust-filled kiss that left them both gasping. "Sleep with me tonight?" she murmured against his lips.

He groaned, his lips feathering across her cheek to whisper against her ear. Shivers raced down her spine, as his husky voice said, "I'll stay, … but … we won't sleep."

He turned his head and sealed his promise with his lips.

THERE WAS A sense of urgency now. Dane grabbed her hand, and they ran, laughing, all the way to the truck. She'd jumped into the passenger side, but Dane dragged her across the seat to sit snugged up against him. She could damn-near drive the truck herself, she sat so close. And it was perfect.

She cuddled closer, her hand on his thigh.

He covered her hand with his much bigger one. "Happy?"

She heard the tinge of worry that had crept into his voice. "Very."

Her hand was squeezed tight, then he relaxed. "Good. 'Cause it would be better if you back out now—not later …"

In the darkness of the truck, with only the headlights for illumination, the air had a sultry mysteriousness to it. Jade was loving this. The last thing on her mind was to retreat. "I'm not backing out. I'm wishing you'd drive a little faster."

He gave a shout of laughter and hit the gas.

The trip back to the hotel was fast and furious, steeped in sensuality and promise that Jade swore she'd never felt before. She wanted Dane something fierce.

They arrived in the hotel parking lot ten minutes later. Most of the lights were off—given the hour, almost everyone should have gone to bed. Jade didn't want to meet anyone on their way up to her room, not because the relationship was a secret; she just didn't want the intrusion. She was selfish. There was magic in the air. She wanted to keep it to herself—and Dane.

At her hotel room, she unlocked the door and walked over to close the curtains. Twisting back, she dropped her key and purse on the small dresser and turned to face him. It suddenly struck her how unbelievably far she'd come this past month. With much of that distance due to this man. Oh, she would agree that returning to Haiti had been the best thing she could have done for herself, but mostly because it had brought Dane into her life.

He stood in the middle of the room, studying her, a slight frown furrowing his forehead. Waiting. She smiled, slowly, sensually. "I won't change my mind."

That wicked grin of his flashed, and he opened his arms.

She walked into them. They closed tightly around her. "Thank you," she said, tilting her head back, so she could see him.

Surprise lit his heated gaze, his eyes dark and intense, … waiting.

She loved that about him. Loved the patience. Loved the control. As much as she might not think she was ready to love, she understood she was already at least halfway there. "Thank you for showing me there can be a bright future. For showing me that not all men are the same. For showing me that being in a relationship again is possible."

He dropped a light kiss on her forehead. Patient. Caring. Understanding. "And are you sure you're ready?"

"I wasn't—until I met you." Her hands stroked his chest, reveling in the smooth expanse of muscles rippling under her touch. She slipped her hands down his arms and around his back as she rejoiced in the sense of rightness. She really wanted this time together.

He seemed more concerned about making sure she was okay with tonight.

Leaning back slightly, she whispered, "I'm pretty sure, when you promised we wouldn't sleep tonight, talking wasn't what you had in mind." That wicked grin flashed again, and he laughed. She tugged his face down and kissed him. Hard.

He groaned. His arms tightened, and then he stole the kiss away. Trailing his lips across her cheeks, he nuzzled her ear, his hot breath sending tingles down her spine, warming her insides. His words, though, lit them on fire. "Oh, we'll talk. Later."

Then, full of powerful and possessive lust, he kissed her.

And she stopped thinking altogether.

Heat flashed between them. Dane's kisses lit her senses. Nothing else was in this moment but him, this passion, this heat that threatened to consume her. His hands were everywhere, stroking, caressing, soothing, as they explored her back, her belly, and slowly, ever-so-slowly, they inched higher. He teased her, stroking below her bra strap, sliding along the top of the lace edge covering her breasts. She twisted, caught in a mindless haze of passion, desperate to have his hands where she needed them.

Finally he stroked upward, cupping her breasts. She moaned as her insides melted and her breasts swelled in joy. Shudders rippled down her spine.

For a moment he paused, pulled back slightly. Sliding his hands under her shirt, he lifted it up and over her head. Her world tilted slightly as he swooped her up and over to the bed, laying her down on the covers. She kicked off her sandals, unhooked her bra. *Whoosh.* ... Her cotton pants hit the floor.

She bounced to her knees, wearing only her panties. She reached for the bottom of his shirt, trying to pull it up his chest and over his head. He took the job from her, tossing his shirt to the floor. She barely noticed, her fingers were so busy with the snap on his jeans. She couldn't undo it. Frantic, she slipped her fingers eagerly inside.

He groaned a half laugh, tugging her fingers free. "Just a minute." He kicked off his shoes, then stripped off the rest of his clothes in what seemed like one motion. Such a wonderful expanse of sun-kissed skin and muscle was before her that she didn't know where to start. Her fingers spread across his chest, exploring, learning, loving him.

She followed the triangle of chest hair down to his navel, where his erection prodded her hands. Unable to resist touching him, she stroked him, her fingers circling and sliding down the long length of him. Then back up. He moaned. She bent her head on impulse and kissed the very tip. He gasped and flipped her onto her back.

"There's only so much of that I can take right now," he whispered. Holding her gaze, he captured her wrists and tugged them above her head in a gentle grip.

Her gaze widened. He lowered his head. He stroked and caressed and nuzzled the smooth skin on the side of her neck, the delicate undersides of her plump, swollen breasts. She ached with wanting—twisted and moaned with need. It had been so long since she'd been held. So long since she'd been loved like this.

No. It had *never* been like this.

Tugging her hands free, she caressed his shoulders and back, loving the small catches of breath she heard from the back of his throat. He raised his head and dropped a deep, drugging kiss on her lips, their tongues dancing deliciously. He trailed his mouth downward, leaving a pathway of heated kisses to her breasts.

Mindless, she arched her back, and he obliged, taking first one nipple, then the other, deep inside. His hand slid across her belly and down to the juncture of her thighs to explore her dewy curls. She parted her thighs for him, opening for his touch. Wanting him. His wicked fingers stroked and caressed, teased and tormented, until she surged wildly against him, twisting, searching for satisfaction and surcease.

"Dane," she whispered, reveling in her body's response, in the heat coursing through her. "Please."

His magical fingers found her sensitive bud, and her hips bucked. She cried out, "Dane, now."

Moving up and over her, he bent and shifted her thighs slightly wider, settling himself closer. Resting on one arm, that hand buried in her hair, his other arm slid under her hips to hold her still. He sat at the center of her. Waiting.

Reaching up, she pulled him down to her, raining fiery kisses wherever her lips could reach. He tightened his grip on her hair, tugging her toward him, and sealed their lips in a kiss that promised and delivered ... everything. And plunged deep into the heart of her.

She cried out. Her legs wrapped tighter around him. It wasn't enough. She needed more.

He settled on top, his kiss gentle, waiting for her to adjust to the invasion, to his size. "Are you okay?" he whispered against her lips, the strain of holding back obvious in the corded tendons on his neck and face.

Wiggling her hips, she purred against his lips, "Better than okay."

He dropped his forehead to rest on hers, staring deep into her eyes, and he started to move. Slowly, at first, almost experimentally. Then he picked up speed, plunging harder and deeper than ever before, driving them closer to the edge. She cried out with each thrust, wanting, striving, needing more. Dropping one hand between them, he touched the tiny nub in her curls, and that did it, just that one stroke of his finger and she soared free, crying out as the explosion overwhelmed her.

She barely heard his shout of release, and her body flew apart a second time, as he emptied himself into her.

Exhausted, he collapsed, rolled quickly to one side, and tucked her up close against him.

She curled into him, happier than she could ever remember. Sated, feeling a peacefulness she hadn't expected, she dozed off to sleep.

Chapter 23

THE NEXT DAY Jade sat out on the garden patio, a coffee in hand. She loved the brilliant green of the palms. Dane had left a couple hours earlier. She couldn't stop smiling. He hadn't quite kept his promise but came damn close. They'd napped, made love, talked and laughed and made love again ... and again.

She should be exhausted. Instead she felt invigorated, full of energy—and very content. She smirked. Maybe *very satisfied* was a better way to describe it.

"Wow. So what has put that look on your face?" Meg and Bruce walked over to join her.

"What?" Jade tried to rearrange her features, but thoughts of Dane filled her heart to bursting. Keeping those feelings inside just didn't work so well. And no way she'd hide their relationship for long. She grinned. "Dane is hot, isn't he?"

Meg giggled.

Bruce rolled his eyes. "Shall I go away? Leave you two together for this girl talk?"

Jade laughed. "No need. Nothing to discuss."

"That's not what it looks like from here." Meg sat down in the chair next to Jade.

"True enough." Bruce ordered coffee.

As they sat in the sunshine, Dane's truck drove into the parking lot. Jade's heart lightened. It was hard to know how to greet him in front of the others. Part of her wanted to race over and kiss him, and another part of her wanted to flatten him on the ground and have her way with him right here and now—again.

Then he came into view, but Dane wasn't alone. A very unhappy-looking John was at his heels.

Standing, she pulled over a couple chairs and ordered two more coffees.

Bruce rose and shook John's hand. "Good to see you. Sorry

you've had such a bad couple weeks. Any news on Peppe's whereabouts?"

John grimaced and sat down. "Thanks. It's been rough. No news. I've checked his place a couple times. I'm sure he's returned and left again, but he's sly, coming and going in the night. He left a box full of papers open on the kitchen table. Papers I'd never seen before."

Dane gazed at Jade, gave her an intimate smile, then winked at her. She gave him a quick wink back, hiding her grin from the others, while her insides melted. Now, at least, her nerves could settle down. She tuned into the conversation.

John continued. "A family tree was atop the papers. Peppe and his wife, Anne, were first cousins. I don't know if that even makes a difference, but I passed the information on to Tasha's doctors."

That bombshell took a bit to settle in.

"So then Tasha's mental instability could be a direct result of faulty genetics?" Jade shook her head slightly. Why don't people consider the results of their actions? "What about Emile? Was he fine?"

"As far as I could see," John replied. "We'll never know how he might have developed over time."

Dr. Mike frowned. "In Tasha's case, it could be a contributing factor. That's something for the doctors to determine."

Staring almost bitterly at each person in the group, one by one, John nodded. "I guess so."

Jade winced. "I just hate that it's turning out this way."

Bruce leaned back. "We all do." He picked up his coffee and had a sip. "Sometimes things happen, and we can do nothing but accept and move on."

"Some things we won't ever know or understand." John stood, leaving his coffee untouched. "It was nice to see you all again. I'll be at the hospital." He turned to Dane. "Are you coming with me?"

Dane stood too, smiled goodbye at everyone, and turned to leave—stopping beside Jade. He bent and gave her a quick hug, dropping a brief kiss on her lips. "I'll stop by a little later."

Her cheeks warmed. Not trusting herself to speak, she smiled her goodbye.

The rest of the group had knowing smiles on their faces but stayed quiet—thankfully.

JADE TOOK THE rest of the day off. She relaxed, did laundry, did her hair. In short, she just lazed around and did nothing work related. She couldn't remember the last day she'd taken for herself. She called Duncan, but her brother wasn't home. Restless, she realized she had a whole Saturday afternoon stretching ahead of her. ... She'd start with a stroll.

She walked out the front door of the hotel and took a deep breath of the humid air outside.

Keeping to one direction, enjoying the flavors of Jacmel, she found herself in a small center, where vendors hawked their wares. She avoided the crowds surrounding one noisy vendor, selling food Jade didn't recognize. As she went around that, she almost walked into another person. Flustered, she apologized and tried to get out of the way.

Her arm was grabbed.

She jerked back instinctively, spinning to see who had grabbed her.

Magrim.

Dressed in a loose multicolored blouse, with dozens of equally colorful beaded necklaces wrapped around her neck, Magrim jingled loudly, as she tightened her grip on Jade's arm. Her black eyes stared up at Jade. "What you believe is wrong. Only the truth can set you free. You are in great danger, until you find the truth."

Jerking free, Jade swallowed hard. She closed her eyes briefly and fought the urge to run all the way back to the hotel. But, if Magrim knew something about what was going on, then Jade wanted to know it too. "Magrim, what is the truth?"

"Evil spirits dwell in those close to you. Save yourself, before it is too late." Magrim sat on a vendor's chair, going quiet and still.

Jade stepped away, cast another look Magrim's way, then bolted for the hotel. Her panic gave her feet extra speed, as she dodged the crowds, ran across the roads, not daring to slow down or to look behind. She only wanted the safety of her hotel room. And Dane. She wanted Dane.

She entered the hotel, sweat running down her back, gasping for breath. She ran into the team's office and found Meg. "Oh, thank God." She slapped her purse down on her desk, collapsed into the closest chair, and spilled out the sorry mess.

Meg gasped, then said, "That's nuts. Danger still? Evil spirits in those closest to you? Surely all that bad stuff is over?" Meg could only stare at her, shaking her head. "I know there's no science to it. I know that, and yet I'm still freaked by what she told you."

"I hear you. Why can't she tell me stuff like, *You'll meet a tall, dark, and handsome man?*" Jade frowned. "Isn't that what they're supposed to say?"

"Yeah, except Dane isn't dark." Meg smiled broadly and shook her head.

"True enough." Jade ran her fingers through her hair. "Christ, she scared me."

"Can you ignore what she said?" Meg suggested, a frown forming, as she studied Jade's face.

"I'd love to," Jade muttered. "But, since I told you what she said, aren't you already considering the handful of people we've met since being here?"

"Considering what? Wondering if they're evil? What is evil anyway?" Meg exclaimed, raising her hands in the air.

"I don't know. I don't want to know." Shuddering, Jade sank lower in her chair.

Reaching out a gentle hand, Meg patted Jade's arm. "I'm sorry. I agree the trip has been fraught with weird accidents and happenings. However, don't let our imaginations take the place of common sense."

Jade released a big sigh. "Right. Got that. Ignore Magrim."

"Jade …"

She spun around, startled at the unexpected voice. "Dane. Hi." Standing up, she headed toward him. When he opened his arms, she ran right into them.

A grin lit up his face. Then he became more serious and stepped back to study her. "Nice welcome, but what's wrong? You look like you just ran a marathon."

"I'm fine." She shook her head. "Just a little weirded out. That's all."

At his puzzled look, she explained about the woman and her prophecy. When she finished, the *nasty* bubbling up in her eased back down again. Anything to do with Magrim set her nerves on edge.

He frowned. "Let's go find her, ask for more information."

Jade stepped back, shaking her head violently. "No. No way. You can go. I'm staying here. I don't want anything to do with her."

Dane glanced over at Meg. "Are you game?"

With a raised eyebrow, Meg stood, a pensive smile on her face. "Actually I would kinda like to go."

Jade gave a mock shudder. "You two are nuts. Feel free. Not me. No way. I'll sit right here and have a coffee." She nodded, liking that idea better and better. "Where it's safe."

Meg studied her curiously. "Have you forgotten? She said the evil is close to you."

"Gee, thanks." Jade turned around, hating the clarification. "So maybe, according to her, I'm not so safe, ... but I feel safe, and that has to count for something."

Meg gave her a quick hug. "That it does. Dane and I'll walk over, talk to her, and walk back. We'll be maybe twenty minutes. You okay for that long? Which direction?"

"Oh yes. I'm just fine. Shoo, ... run along." She used hand motions to push them out the door. "I went that way." She pointed to the street across from the hotel. "No turns and about five minutes straight forward. ... That's where I found the vendors. Go. Get this foolishness over with, and come back safe and sound." She waved them away. "Hurry up. Go."

Meg and Dane laughed in astonishment. "Are you sure you won't come with us? Maybe you should. See her for what she really is?"

"Nope. I'm good right here. I'll go sit outside in that chair right there." She pointed to a deep cushioned lounge chair in the shade out on the patio. "That's where I'll be when you come back. Sitting there, enjoying my coffee and my day." To prove her point, Jade picked up her purse and walked out with them. She headed to the chair and plonked down, waving goodbye with a big smile.

Dane shook his head, then followed Meg through the small gate. Jade sat and watched them leave. Dane turned back to look at her, before heading off.

She smiled. God, he looked devastating, close up or in the distance. She sighed happily, but waved him on when he hesitated. He'd be back soon enough, and they could spend time together then.

With a wave, he turned and hurried to catch up to Meg.

As soon as they disappeared, Jade dropped her smile. Her face hurt from trying to put on a good show. She wasn't smiling inside. In fact, Magrim had terrified Jade this time. She hated to be so susceptible to the crone's words, but some scary shit was going on. She knew the others thought she was foolish. She didn't care what they thought—she was too busy being scared.

"IS SHE ALWAYS like this?" Dane asked Meg, as he caught up with her. Meg could move. Those long legs of hers easily matched his stride. He preferred walking with Jade though, and he missed her already. He'd stopped in at the hotel, hoping to spirit her to the beach for the afternoon.

Then she'd told him about Magrim. Best to get to the bottom of this business and ease her mind. Truthfully he found Jade's behavior kind of cute. She was such a contradiction of science and belief. Look at the difficult job she did identifying dead bodies and how efficiently she did that. Yet she was also freaked out by an old woman's words. Surely her scientific background would allow her to throw off such words as nonsense? Anyway, the fact it didn't made Jade even more interesting and appealing … and brought out his *knight in shining armor* instincts to rescue and to protect.

Meg's voice pulled him out of his reverie. "To a certain extent. Jade is blessed with a strong imagination. Anytime we have a scenario to puzzle through, she comes up with the more morbid conclusions. Take the first earthquake victim—that was a little different. Jade is sure that person was living as a captive, was a sex slave or something along those lines, … and that she was murdered. Jade might be right. … Then again she might not be."

Odd. Dane didn't understand how Jade had come up with that hypothesis in the first place. "I'm sure lots of people suffered major injuries from this disaster. Why would she think anything of that particular victim?"

Meg leaned closer, dropping her voice to a whisper. "That would be because of the chains around the woman's ankle. Something we're trying to keep quiet."

Dane came to a halt. "Chains? Around the ankle of a skeleton? In the mass grave? Are you serious? That's enough to spark anyone's imagination."

"I know, right?" Meg halted beside him. They'd almost reached the busy street corner. A park stretched across one side, while vendors fought for customers and space on the other.

Dane shook his head. *Chains.* "Did anyone ask John about them?"

"No, but we've spoken to the authorities. They want more evidence before they worry about another body in a mass grave. They're short-staffed and have too many other problems right now. Actually I think they'd like to see us walk away from this, just disappear for good. I know the medical problems they're dealing with are brutal, what with cholera and tetanus … and more. Plus the crime rate has spiked too. They don't want to deal with old unsolved crimes right now. For all anyone knows these women *liked* to wear steel anklets."

Her tone made Dane look over at her sharper. "Did you say, *women*? How many?"

"Three, so far."

Dane whistled. "Jesus. No wonder Jade is freaked out. I can ask John if he knows anything about it. He helped move the bodies. If he saw something, I'm sure he'd tell me." Dane couldn't let go of that idea, as he followed Meg through the crowd. He phoned John. "Hey. I'm talking with one the team members, and they found something odd in the grave. They found a body with chains on the ankles. Did you see anything like that when you buried these people?"

Meg dodged around several groups of people, standing and talking. Dane tried to keep her bright blue skirt in sight, as she moved ahead of him. "What was that? Sorry I'm on the street corner, and I can hardly hear you for the vendors hawking their wares. What?"

"Not likely," John yelled.

Dane laughed. "I didn't think so. That's not something you'd forget."

He picked up the pace to catch up and saw Meg stop and talk to an old woman. *Magrim.* "Okay, I'll talk to you later. I'm meeting Jade at the hotel in ten or fifteen minutes, I'm hoping to spirit her away to play with me this afternoon. Don't know when I'll be home." He put away his phone and hurried to hear Meg's conversation.

"She's not talking. Doesn't even respond. I don't know if she's asleep or what." Meg stared down at the old woman in confusion. "I don't want to disturb her."

"Did you call her name?" At the sound of Dane's voice, Magrim reacted violently. She surged to her feet, her necklaces rattling with the sudden movement, her eyes blind. "Danger. You must be careful. It's all around you."

"What the … ?" Dane stared down at her. No wonder Jade had freaked out. This was beyond his experience too, only he was long past the point of letting a pathetic old woman scare the crap out of him.

"Specifics please, Magrim. You scared a friend of mine today. I'd like to know what danger you see around me."

"Little blonde. She's in trouble. Death reaches for her even now."

Shivers slid down his spine. "*What?* Why are you saying this?" His voice rose, hardened.

A small restraining hand squeezed his forearm. "Easy," Meg whispered.

Dane glared down at the old woman. "She terrorized Jade with her warnings. Why and for what? If there's a specific danger, then she needs to say what it is."

"Chains. More chains. So many chains. To bind, to hold, to keep forever." Magrim cackled, like the nutty witch she was.

Dane threw off Meg's hand. "Let's go. She's nuts."

"Tasha, Emile, and Peppe. Tasha, Emile, and Peppe." Magrim continued to parrot the names in a singsong voice.

"Do you know them?"

Magrim dipped her head, setting the necklaces rattling. "Family. Family."

"Oh, *great*. You're related? You're all nuts."

"Careful, Dane." Meg turned back to Magrim. "Is Peppe okay?"

Magrim turned her blind eyes in her direction. "Peppe is dead. Peppe is dead. Emile is dead. Emile is dead."

Dane sucked in his breath. Meg pressed the point. "And Tasha?"

"Tasha is dead. Tasha is dead."

"What?" Meg gasped in horror.

"Don't listen to her. That's what she wants. Just forget about her." He glared at the gathering crowd.

"Dane, that's a horrible thing to say." Meg glared at him.

He raised his hands at that. "Fine. Whatever. However, Tasha isn't dead. We visited her this morning, for Christ's sake."

Chapter 24

D ANE AND MEG hashed the issue over all the way back to the hotel. Meg suggested, "Magrim might be picking up on Tasha's withdrawal from the world."

Dane snorted. "All she's doing is repeating herself. She's a fraud."

They stopped to let the traffic go by before crossing the road. Meg hopped up onto the curb on the other side. They walked at a fast clip back to the hotel. "I don't know how you can be so sure. She did mention chains, and that was just freaky."

"Coincidence. She hasn't said anything helpful. If she'd given names, places, times—then maybe. Instead there's nothing except conjecture and fearmongering. She lives off scaring people. Like Jade."

"The locals believe in her. At least according to the hotel manager, Magrim's held in high regard." Meg related the conversation they'd had around the dinner table with the manager, after Jade's first encounter with Magrim.

"That's good marketing." Something he understood and could appreciate.

"What's good about it?"

"It's a business to her. And her strategy works. You paid her, didn't you?" Dane opened the small gate at the side entrance and waited for Meg to walk through. "I saw you slip her some money. If you believe she can tell you something that no one else can, then you'll pay her for more."

"I have to admit that she kind of shook me up."

"See? That makes for a good business. Magrim just gets to repeat the same information over and over again." What she'd just said proved his point, didn't it?

Meg tried a different tack to get him to at least consider the possibility of Magrim's prophecy. "I'm a doctor and a scientist, but even I can't deny the possibility of Magrim's abilities. The more we learn about our brains and our bodies, the more we realize we don't know everything. We don't have scientific answers for all aspects of our knowledge or experience."

Dane wasn't having any of it. Bruce overheard them and came out to see what all the ruckus was about. They told him about Jade and then their visit with Magrim.

Bruce shook his head. "I don't play around with that stuff. I'm a scientist and shouldn't have any problem shooting it down—but, because I don't understand it, I like to leave the topic well enough alone." Lively intelligence gleamed in his eyes as he spoke, reminding Dane how much brainpower the team had tapped.

The three arrived at the patio, still wrangling.

"Jade's got quite the imagination, so I can see how Magrim might freak her out a little." Bruce pulled up a chair and sat down. "Speaking of which, where is she? What did she do, go get another cup of coffee? Or another breakfast?" They laughed.

Jade's lounge chair was there—she wasn't. Dane turned slowly, looking for Jade. Meg pulled up a chair and sat down.

Dane frowned and looked around, then sat down on the edge of a chair. "We left her right here, when we went to talk to Magrim. Jade said she'd stay here and wait for us."

"I haven't seen her. I was in the office working for the last couple hours. She never came in there."

Meg stood hurriedly. "This was twenty minutes ago. I'll go check her room." She bolted.

Dane watched her go.

"You don't appear to put much stock in the witch woman's words." Bruce propped one leg on his knee and studied Dane.

With a heavy sigh, Dane rubbed the back of his neck, continuing to scan for Jade. "Hard to when there's nothing concrete. I hate to give credence to nebulous warnings." He sighed heavily, finally acknowledging that inside he was starting to wonder. "I'd feel better if Jade were standing in front of me right now."

"That's the scientist's perspective. Give me something to prove, and, if I can go prove it, then I'll consider it. For the strong of faith, they believe that, if your faith is strong, you don't need any proof. For them, asking for proof is doubting your faith."

"Convenient," Dane said, shaking his head.

Bruce grinned. "Isn't it?"

Meg came running out the side door. "She's not there. I asked Susan. She hasn't seen her in the last half hour either."

"Damn." Dane shifted in his seat, and his foot caught on the table leg and then kicked something. Looking underneath, his heart froze. He snagged a small black leather bag and tossed it on the table. "Please tell me that isn't Jade's."

JADE ROLLED OVER, a slight moan escaping. A rumble under her ear irritated her. It sounded so close and yet so far away. She groaned and tried to curl up into a ball and go back to sleep. Yet she didn't think she'd really been asleep. More like adrift on floating clouds. Except she wasn't floating in a sunny space. Everything was gray. Gray light, gray clouds. She would have shaken her head in dismay, only the thought of doing that stopped her.

It would hurt.

She knew that ... somehow.

She couldn't seem to reason out an explanation of how or why.

She noted a mustiness to the air—oils, metals? She almost moaned but caught it before it slipped out. It was important not to make a sound.

But she didn't know why.

Tired, confused, and sore, she slipped deeper into the clouds and slept.

MEG STARED AT the bag, shock, worry, and horror mingling to twist her features. "That is hers." She bent to look under the table, as if thinking she'd find Jade huddled under there.

"And it's been here since we sat down." Dane stared at it, a sense of unease growing in the pit of his stomach. "Shit."

"What?" Bruce studied their faces. "So she left her purse out here. What's the big deal about that?"

"Maybe nothing—maybe everything." Meg and Dane stared at each other. "Except it doesn't feel like nothing, ... does it, Dane?"

He shook his head, his mind racing. "If she's not here, not in the hotel, where would she be?"

"Nowhere without her purse." Meg was adamant on that point. "She never goes anywhere without it."

Bruce pursed his lips and considered the issue. "You're thinking something's happened to her?"

"She promised to sit and wait here for us. We weren't gone twenty minutes." Meg glanced over at Dane for confirmation. "And all this on the heels of Magrim's warnings."

Dane tilted his head and nodded. "Yeah, maybe I can see why you believe we should be a little worried. There have been enough strange things going on." He couldn't help the fear knotting his stomach. Where the hell was she?

"If she's gone, did she go willingly?" Bruce questioned. "Or did trouble come her way?"

Meg nudged the purse. "She wouldn't have gone anywhere without her purse. She takes it out in the field, for God's sake. Something is wrong."

Bruce whistled softly. "Seriously? Are we thinking she's been kidnapped?" He shook his head. "Do we call the authorities *again*?"

"Let's search first," Dane stated. "Start with the hotel. Ask everyone if they've seen her in the last half hour and if they saw anyone else around, other than your team, staff, and the other guests. Are there any other guests in the hotel right now?" Dane asked, standing up, his unease twisting into panic.

"There aren't. The last group cleared out earlier today." Bruce stood too. "I'll start with the kitchen staff and then the manager. Too bad no security cameras are in this place."

"I'll walk through the front door and see if anyone is there or in the offices. I'll find the guys too. See if any of them know where Jade is." Meg hurried inside.

Dane looked around and spoke to the empty patio. "And I'll walk around here and see if I can find anything else." He headed to the parking lot first. If Jade had been snatched, her kidnapper would have had a vehicle. Would anyone just drive in here and snatch her—and that fast—without someone noticing? Could they have walked right up to her on the patio and forced her into a vehicle?

He spun around to study where he'd last seen her. If she'd been taken from under the palm tree, tucked away in the shade like that, it was quite possible that no one noticed. And then he remembered Magrim's words to Jade. Something about *Evil spirits dwell in those close to you. Save yourself before it is too late.*

He spun around and came to a dead stop. The team had gathered inside. He could see them standing and talking. All of them were here and accounted for. Except for Jade. Had one of them convinced Jade to go to their rooms and knocked her unconscious? Not likely, and why would they? They worked with her day in and day out. There'd been better times to snatch her. Like when she worked alone at the lab.

Money for security had been approved but only just. They still had to hire someone.

He realized they were standing in a group, staring at him. He walked inside to join them. "Did you find her?"

Meg shook her head. "No." Grim understanding showed on her face. "I guess you didn't either?"

"No." His heart raced inside. He could hardly think straight. Panic built, as he was no longer able to ignore what his mind and heart had been screaming at him for the last ten minutes.

"She's gone."

JADE WOKE SLOWLY, as if from a deep, dark sleep. She yawned and tried to slip back under but the surface was hard. And she was cold. Pulling into a tighter ball, she willed herself back to sleep. But couldn't get there. She shifted onto her back, wincing at the aches and pains of lying too long in one position. Her head pounded, like a steady sledgehammer going off inside.

Her eyes popped open. A basement ceiling stared back at her. A dirty basement ceiling. More like a root cellar ceiling. She frowned, yet even that movement made her head hurt. She groaned softly, even as other aches and pains slowly entered her awareness. Hell, most of her hurt—and what didn't had gone numb. She struggled to sit up, then looked around. She was sitting on a concrete floor.

That explained some of her aches and pains. There were no windows. No lights. Just an all-encompassing gloominess. She could see, just not very far or very clearly.

Reaching up, she rubbed her temples and tried to swallow. Her fingers came away sticky, with a little blood.

Her throat felt like cotton had been stuffed inside and had sucked all the moisture out, making it impossible to swallow. She tried anyway, wishing for water. It took several minutes in the dim light for her eyes to adjust. There was nothing—no cupboards, no furniture, What the hell? An odd noise sounded in the distance. With her head too woozy to think, she lay down on the floor, trying to let the bits of information roll around, hoping to come up with answers.

Ten minutes later, all she had was a headache.

She sat up again and rolled onto her hands and knees, then stood slowly, anticipating the rush of blood—and pain—to her head. Once standing, she closed her eyes and breathed deeply for several long minutes, before she stood steady. The same odd noises popped in and out of her consciousness. As did cold and chills. Her feet were almost numb, as were her legs. She couldn't sort everything out.

"I don't know what happened, but something's sapped all my energy and strength. ... Just standing is a major accomplishment," she murmured out loud.

Feeling comforted by the sound of her own voice, she took one faltering step. Then another. She had to stop and breathe deeply before trying a third. "Hello? Is anyone there?"

She stepped forward again and came up short. The same odd sound had grown louder. Her leg couldn't move any farther. She turned around. The odd sound fell into place. So did the odd chill on her ankle.

Lifting her leg, she pulled up her jeans. She couldn't think; her mind was blank with shock. Then understanding slapped her up the side of her brain. Wrapped around her ankle was a manacle. A chain extended from that to the concrete wall behind her.

A chain, so similar—too similar—to the ones she'd seen on the dead women from the grave.

Like them, Jade had become a prisoner.

WHILE BRUCE CALLED the same officers who had helped during Dr. Mike's disappearance, the team assembled in the office to compare information. Dane sat back and closed his eyes. His throat closed.

Damn it.

Impatience and the need for action seized his gut. His instincts said to find her before it was too late. What the hell could have happened? The hotel was a public area, but they'd had few guests this past week. Still, any stranger could have walked in and out without attracting too much attention. But not with Jade, ... unless she knew him and went willingly. "Could her disappearance be related to the grave site?" he asked the group.

Everyone stopped and stared at him. "What do you mean?" asked Stephen.

"Have you had anyone angry or complaining about the grave being opened?"

Meg glanced at her team, then back at Dane. "To be honest, the lack of any reaction from the locals is what surprised us. I know everyone is still reeling from the earthquake, the flooding, the cholera, the tetanus, ... but instead of concern about the work we're doing at the mass grave, there's almost an air of apathy. Like they can't deal with much more."

Dr. Mike spoke up. "Their lack of interest and caring suggests we should only remove the remains if they meet our search criteria and should leave the others be. Not test the others at all. So few family members have come forward at our free clinic. ... And, with the pressure from Tony too, putting all our efforts focused in the lab trailers, we'd be done that much faster."

"Have you turned anyone away? Anyone approach you about disturbing the spirits? Anyone give you any kind of suspicious or unsettling reaction? What about more break-ins?"

Dr. Mike glanced from one face to the next, then turned to stare at Dane. "There's been one minor one at the clinic, but nothing was taken. There's been no more here at the hotel that we know of. And, as much as I hate to say it, the only one particularly bothered by our work here was Tasha, your sister-in-law."

"*Great*. Well, she's not capable of kidnapping Jade." He pulled out his phone. "As far as I know, she is safe and sound at the hospital."

"Did you ever check with John to see if anything new was heard about Tasha?" Meg asked. "I'm thinking about what Magrim said."

He grimaced. "Right. She said Tasha was dead."

"What?" Stephen leaned forward. "Did she die?"

"I don't believe so." Dane let Meg tell the others about Magrim's prophecy, while he dialed John. "John? What's the matter? You don't sound very good."

"I just called the hospital. Tasha passed away during her nap, just after you and I left her. I've been wandering around town in a daze ever since."

Dane closed his eyes and slumped against the wall. His brother just couldn't catch a break. "Shit. I am sorry, John. I didn't see that one coming."

"Neither did I. Now I have no reason to stay, do I? Except for Peppe, my entire Haitian family has been wiped out," he said bitterly. Dane walked away from the others. "I'm sorry, John. I know how much you were looking forward to the baby and having Tasha back to normal."

John's unsteady voice was hard to decipher. "Instead I have another funeral to arrange. I wonder if the baby can go in the coffin with her. I think she'd like that."

Dane's heart broke. "I'm sure that can be arranged."

Silence filled the phone.

"What did you call about?"

Dane straightened. "We're looking for one of the team members—Jade, the tiny blonde. I wondered if you'd seen her?"

"Seen her? No. Why would you think I had?" John's voice was devoid of curiosity. Devoid of anything for that matter.

Dane winced. "Sorry for bothering you. When I called, I knew it was a long shot, but I'm desperate to find her. I left her for a few minutes, and, when I came back, she was gone."

"I don't know why you'd be calling me. It's not as if I know her."

Dane clenched the phone tighter at the petulant sound in his brother's voice. "I'm calling everyone. Keep an eye out for her, will you please? By the way, did you ever find Peppe?"

"No. No idea where he is. He might be dead too. Lord knows everyone else is," John said, his voice gloomy and without energy.

Damn. His brother had been through so much. "I'm not. I've been here for you all along. I can't bring them back. I wish I could, but that's just not possible."

"Yeah. I know. But I would like to know why your life is so easy and clean ... and why mine is just plain fucked-up."

The phone went *click*.

Dane stared down at his cell and groaned softly. He didn't know how to get John through this. It had been hard last time. This would be much worse.

"Dane?"

He spun around to find the group staring at him. "Hey. Sorry. Tasha passed away earlier today, right after John and I visited her."

Meg gasped, her hand going to her throat. "So Magrim was right? At least about Tasha. Although we don't know about Peppe. ... Is he still missing?"

"Apparently." He stared down at his phone. "John's in a bad way."

"Of course he is." Wilson stared at him. "He lost his wife and unborn child."

"That would be tough on anyone." Bruce winced, exchanging glances with Dr. Mike.

"And worse when it happens twice." Dane sighed. "He lost his first wife in a car accident. John didn't know she was pregnant, until the doctor told him afterward."

Shocked silence filled the room.

Dane frowned. He studied the uncomfortable look on Dr. Mike's face. Bruce cleared his throat, before adding, "Twice? That's an awful coincidence."

"What do you mean?" Dane asked.

"The chances of that happening twice in one man's life are pretty slim."

Stephen and Wilson slid sideways glances to the other two scientists. "Right, Dr. Mike?" Stephen asked.

Dr. Mike and Bruce were having a silent conversation. As if coming to an agreement, Dr. Mike nodded. "It's not impossible. Some people seem to be plagued by bad luck. If there had been a police investigation in the first incident, the second would definitely warrant a closer look. Particularly if anything else were in John's history. However, both deaths were unrelated and came about by different methods, so it *could* be very bad luck."

It took a moment for Dane to digest what he was really saying. "No. Oh no." He shook his head violently. "Don't even think that. *There. Is. No. Way.*"

Silence filled the room.

Dane added, "Besides, maybe Tasha caused her own death, accidentally or intentionally." Filled with anger, he stood with his hands on his hips, his phone still in his hand.

Meg spoke up. "I don't see Tasha having done something. She's been catatonic since she went into the hospital. Did John say how she died?"

Dane stared at her, trying to sort out how everything had suddenly twisted upside down. Finally he said, "I didn't ask. John didn't volunteer."

The others exchanged sober looks.

Dane could feel an insidious doubt twisting in the back of his mind. No. It wasn't possible. Not John. "Better you consider the missing Peppe. I don't know when I last saw him, but, in his mental condition, he could have killed Tasha too. *Not John.* John wanted his family. He lived for them. Besides, we're jumping to conclusions here. For all we know, Tasha died from complications of the surgery." He pulled out his cell phone. "We can call and find out for sure."

Bruce interjected, "They won't have definitive results from an autopsy yet."

"Easy, Dane," Dr. Mike added. "We're not accusing John of anything. Honestly the prime issue is to find Jade."

Meg cleared her throat. The others turned to stare at her. "I know this won't be popular, but honestly we don't have too many people to consider. So we have to look at everyone, including ourselves." She took a deep breath. "Plus John. Is there any reason that John may have wanted to talk to Jade? Would he have taken her for coffee? Anything?"

Anger twisted inside Dane. Meg was actually suggesting his brother might have had something to do with Jade's disappearance. Red filled his mind. "There is no way. Don't take the suspicion from one bad scenario and make it fit another. John didn't kill either of his wives. Nor did he 'take' Jade anywhere. He hasn't seen her. I just asked him." He stood up, barely holding back the anger threatening to explode. "I will start looking farther afield."

"Didn't Magrim also say Peppe was dead?" Meg repeated.

"I don't give a rat's ass what that old bitch said." Bitter, angry, confused, and—dare he admit it?—slightly afraid, he headed toward the parking lot.

"Dane," Meg called out.

He stopped short and turned back. "What?"

"Be careful."

He shot them all a look of disbelief and walked away.

JADE HAD SCRUNCHED up to keep warm. Her mind raced from idea to idea ... and always slammed into the same blank wall. Her ankle was truly locked in a manacle, and the chain was truly bolted to the wall. She wasn't going anywhere, and she didn't know where she was. Except that she figured it was a basement, with no windows or doors and just the one set of stairs. The mustiness seemed to be growing stronger. ... Maybe something dead was down here.

The reality of her situation added to the chill in the place and sent shivers down her small frame. Cold and hungry, she waited for her captor. Surely he'd come back soon?

Her mind kept returning to the poor victims from the grave. She had no doubt she was in their shoes right now. She just didn't understand why.

Or how?

She had no recollection of being snatched or the journey to this place. The only clue was the dried blood in her hair and that damn booming headache. Her eyes focused farther into the dim space. ... Something was in the far corner, hidden by the dark, and didn't move. Some lumber leaned against the wall; something else was stacked on the floor. Once again she regretted not having a cell phone.

Why her? Had someone looked for her specifically? Or had it been a crime of opportunity? Was her imprisonment related to the excavation of the grave site? Her stomach heaved. She might never get out. She might end up in a nameless grave, like the other women. Unmarked and unknown. Duncan would go mad. He'd blame himself for talking her into coming to Haiti for the second time.

She buried her head in her arms.

She didn't want to die.

She'd just returned to the land of the living.

Chapter 25

MEG SAID, "I'M presuming that's not the way to gain Dane's cooperation."

"Do we really think that John may have killed Tasha?" Stephen shook his head. "That's crazy."

"Better ask Dr. Mike that question." Meg turned to look at Dr. Mike.

"It's a possibility. A probability? Who can say?" Dr. Mike cleared his throat. "We don't know the details on his first wife and know almost nothing about Tasha's death yet."

Bruce joined in. "I will say that the only time I've come across something like this, it was exactly that. Two pregnant wives unexpectedly dying. I agree. It sounds suspicious but without further details …"

"Even if John did do something to his wife," Stephen's voice rose slightly, "what does that have to do with Jade? Isn't that an entirely different issue?"

Dr. Mike spoke again. "Maybe. Maybe not. Dane appears reliable. Responsible. What's going on with John? I can't say I like the little bit that I saw, but that's just my opinion."

Meg stepped in. "Yes. Jade said something about him having had a bad time of it before these deaths. That he struggled in his relationship with his wife … and that his business was failing."

Dr. Mike glanced over at Bruce. "That just reinforces the profile. Failed business, failed marriage. Rather than look at himself, it's easier to blame the wife. Blame leads to the solution. Get rid of the wife. Get rid of the problem."

Stephen leaned back. "That's cold, man."

Dr. Mike's face twisted. "Murder usually is. And I've seen way too much of it."

"Why would he get rid of the baby too? It's his child. Are there no parental feelings?" Meg gave a delicate shudder.

Dr. Mike shook his head. "Again, not if the baby has been pinpointed as the cause of a problem."

Wilson jumped in. "And what if he had nothing to do with the baby's death but blamed Tasha for the death of his baby?"

"Even if he did, what does that have to do with Jade? Let's focus on her and leave the dead for later." Meg stood and paced the area nervously. "We have to find her."

"Do we want to try talking to John? Call in the authorities?" Wilson asked. "You said, wait until we searched. Well, we have. Now what?"

"Not to mention, this is only sheer conjecture," Stephen said, groaning. "I think Jade's imagination is getting to all of us."

"Well, she came up that damn hill to find me. I can't go to bed tonight until we find her." Dr. Mike glared at his crutches. "However, I am a little handicapped. I can stay here and run command central, or I can be a passenger, as we drive around looking. Two pairs of eyes are better than one."

"Was she so unnerved at that old lady's words that she might go for a walk? Go to the beach maybe? If so, someone should drive around that area, check out her familiar haunts, her places to walk … on the off chance of finding her. Do we know if a vehicle is missing? Oh, right. Bruce, you checked that, didn't you?"

Bruce agreed. "They're all here."

"Magrim said Jade should not trust those close to her …"

Wilson snorted. "So what? We're supposed to look at each other with suspicion?"

Meg shook her head. "No. That's not what I meant. I'm wondering if we can trust Dane? And does John count as someone close to her—because of his connection to Dane?"

"How about this? We assume they're both psychotic killers." Wilson stood. "I can't just sit here. I'll walk toward Magrim's booth and the little park. Otherwise, everyone stay together and keep in contact. Enough people have gone missing."

Susan stood next to Meg. "We're coming too."

Bruce pushed back his chair. "I'll loop back through the hotel again. Talk to the staff. Maybe she's showed up since we checked with them." He disappeared into the main building, leaving the other two men alone.

ALONE IN HIS truck, Dane pounded the steering wheel. No way John would survive an accusation like this. He'd been through enough already. It would destroy him. Like it had last time.

Last time?

"Dear God." From the back of his mind, came one old memory he'd forgotten about. With good reason. John's high-school girlfriend, Melia. She'd gone missing years ago. Was it important? Or would it just throw unnecessary suspicion in the wrong direction? Dane needed Jade back, not wasting time doing a useless search in the wrong direction.

His stomach clenched with bubbling acid. Did the story of Melia's disappearance have any bearing on today's? John's teenage sweetheart had run away several times during high school. So, when she took off for good, no one thought anything of it. Dane didn't know where or when ... *or if* ... she'd ever surfaced. She might have. He hadn't kept in touch with anyone from back then. No one he could call and ask.

If he could find out she was fine, then he could forget about any connection to John's wives. And clearing that away would help John's case, letting Dane focus on Jade's disappearance, without John distracting him.

Then again, Dane just might know someone who could give him the answer he needed. *His foreman back in Seattle.* He pulled off to the side of the road, took a look around, hoping to see Jade walking toward him, as he dialed the Seattle number. He waited impatiently for the call to get picked up.

"Thomas? Hey, yeah, it's Dane. I have an odd non-work-related question. Do you remember Mark Coombes? From high school? Do you remember if his kid sister ever surfaced? Remember? She ran away again just before graduation?"

Thomas, his curiosity leaching through the phone lines, asked, "What's that about Mark's sister? Why are you asking me? I don't know. Ask your brother, John. He was closest to her."

"Was he? I couldn't remember." Except he did remember that much. Dane leaned his head back and closed his eyes. He swallowed hard. "I missed a lot of that year. I was in my second year of college back then."

"Yeah, we both were. Her brother, Mark, had a hard time back then. Melia was forever saying how she hated her life. So, when she went missing that last time, everyone took it as normal behavior. Only she didn't come home. I was pretty hot for her back then. Unfortunately she only had eyes for John."

Thomas spoke in reminiscent tones, without any understanding of the turmoil twisting through Dane. He cleared his throat. "I thought they'd broken up before then?"

"They broke up and got together again constantly. It's hard to remember anymore. Like I said, talk to John. He was the last one to see her before she disappeared."

Dane's gut clenched. "Okay, I will. Everything there all right?" Christ he hoped so. His life here had just drained to the sewer level.

"Yeah, everything's fine. I need you to go over that bid for the Stortex job. Any chance you'll get that done today?"

Hell no. "I'll see what I can do. I might be coming home sooner than I'd planned."

Thomas cheered. "That's great news. We need you here. I know long distance is fine for a while, but I'm not you, buddy."

And Dane knew he needed to go home, not just for his company but for himself. But not until he'd found Jade and had helped his brother get his life together. "I hear you. I'll call in a couple days."

"Do that. Don't forget to put that bid together."

"Will do." Dane rang off. He dropped his head back and closed his eyes again, letting Thomas's words repeat in his mind. His stomach wanted to heave, as he considered a possibility he could no longer ignore. *Oh, God.*

Had John done something to the women he'd loved? Even worse, could he have done something to Jade—the woman Dane loved?

"I DON'T WANT to just sit here, waiting until the authorities arrive. What can we do?" Dr. Mike studied the area where Jade had been sitting.

Stephen nodded. "If she were sitting here, she would have been taken out the back way." He pointed behind him. "That's the most direct route. With the road right there, someone could easily have snatched her and stuffed her in a vehicle."

Stephen got up and walked around while Dr. Mike watched. A short hedge separated the hotel's property from the side street, but it was easy to step over. "It would have been too damn easy. Especially if he was already parked here."

Stephen stood where the vehicle could have parked and in ten steps reached where Jade had sat. He made a motion with his arm, demonstrating a simple choke hold, bent down, tossed an imaginary Jade over his shoulder and hopped over the hedge. "Simple."

With a decisive nod, Dr. Mike said, "Less than one minute. Walk up behind her, pick her up, and walk out. Done."

Frowning, Stephen added, "And no one would have seen her abduction, unless they were sitting right here."

"No windows face this direction, no glass doors, nothing."

The two men smiled grimly. "That's what happened. I can just see it," Dr. Mike stated.

Stephen added, "Particularly if he'd watched Meg and Dane walk away. He'd have known he had that window of time."

"I'm sorry to say that I agree. So much strange shit is going on with John and his family that John comes to mind automatically. But he wouldn't have known Jade was here. Or that she was alone. It could just as easily have been an abduction by a stranger. And those are the worst to solve."

Casting a narrow eye around the road and parking lot, Stephen grimaced. "Maybe Peppe is behind this? He's conveniently gone missing."

Shifting his crutches to the other side, Dr. Mike hobbled to his feet. "We only have to look at what Peppe did to me to realize what he's capable of. He could have snatched Jade. He could also have snatched those manacled women we found in the grave. Hell, maybe Emile was even in on it."

"Now that's stretching it." Stephen stared at Dr. Mike, doubt clouding his voice.

Anger colored Dr. Mike's voice. "Is it? Some asshole kept those women chained up. Who had opportunity? Look at where they live. No one would ever hear a woman scream out there."

Stephen stared at him. "That's ugly."

"True, but that doesn't mean it's wrong."

DANE HAD ALREADY checked all the side streets close by when he pulled up right in front of the hotel. His heart was heavy. This time everyone raced to meet him before he'd even hopped out. He slammed the door and hurried in their direction. From the looks on their faces, they hadn't found her.

"Dane? Did you find her?"

He shook his head, as he joined them.

"The others have just returned after looking everywhere for her."
Dr. Mike pointed toward the three team members racing toward them
from the other side of the hotel. "Any luck?" he called out.

"No. Nothing." The three arrived, gasping for breath. "Do you
have any news? Please tell us you have news," Meg asked, worry
creasing her face.

Bruce walked out from the hotel. As everyone turned to him, he
shook his head.

Hope died from everyone's faces.

Dane opened his mouth again, then closed it for a second to
gather his thoughts. "Except, ... well, I don't know if this has anything
to do with what's going on. I wanted to confirm something that
happened a long time ago, so I phoned a friend of mine. Now this
isn't for sure, but ..."

"Spit it out, Dane. We don't have time." Bruce frowned at Dane.

"I've been considering what you said about John. When he was in
high school, he had this girlfriend, who ran away from her home
several times. She always came back. The last time was six weeks before
her high school graduation. As far as I can determine, she's never been
seen since."

Meg gasped, the color leeching from her face. Susan reached out
and grabbed her hand, then asked, "She's still missing?"

"Yes. I just talked to my foreman in Seattle. He was a friend of
the family. It may be that John had nothing to do with her disappearance but ..."

"He had motive and opportunity." Bruce pondered the information. "What did the police say?"

"The police put her down as a missing person. Apparently John
was the last person to see her alive."

Dr. Mike leaned forward. "Don't tell me. They'd had a fight, and
she ran away without him, breaking his heart."

Dane stared at him. "Something like that, yeah."

Bruce stood. "Let's go."

"Go where?" Dane looked over at the others in confusion. What
did they know that he didn't?"

"To John's place."

Whoa. "What?" Dane asked. "On the basis of Melia having gone
missing years ago? There's a chance this is all a coincidence." But even
he had trouble believing that now.

Wilson's angry voice sliced through Dane's protestations. "You
said his other wife died too. ... Maybe he's killing Jade right now."

The color bleached from Dane's face.

Meg gasped.

Bruce walked to the parking lot. "Let's not go overboard. However, if I can consider this guy killed a girlfriend and then his two wives—I have to consider he's gone after Jade too."

Stephen, impatiently jingling the keys to one of the SUVs, stood by the closest vehicle, waiting. He asked, "Maybe, but why target Jade?"

Dane's face turned from white to red as a growing fear burned the shock away. "*If* he's done this, and it's a fucking big *if*, then he's lost everything. He might, in his anger, and considering his mental state, want to strike out at me. He said something that surprised me earlier. Essentially he wanted to know why his life was shit and mine so charmed."

The others stared at him.

"Typical siblings," suggested Meg hopefully.

"Stepsiblings," he corrected. "My mother married John's father, and he came along as part of the package deal."

Dr. Mike and Bruce exchanged grim looks. "Greed and envy could be motive for snatching Jade. Not well-thought-out though, if that's what he's doing."

Stephen opened up the SUV doors. "He's not thinking. He's reacting—to his anger and fear. He'll lash out in the same way he has in the past."

Meg groaned. "I feel for him, after what's happened to his life. I can understand the anger, but to do something like this to his brother ... and Jade?"

Bruce hopped into the front passenger seat. "And we need to find her before he has a chance to release some of his anger ... on her."

THE TRIP TO John's house was completed in silence. Meg sat in the passenger seat, as Dane drove there. The SUV full of team members followed Dane's truck.

Dane's mind churned with the mess in his head. It was hard enough to consider the girlfriend-wife thing, but to take that one step further and to contemplate John abducting Jade was another thing altogether.

He didn't want to believe any of it. This was his little brother. The kid brother he'd adored, had helped, and had been there for all these years. And now Dane was wondering if this same man could have done what these professionals suggested. And, if John had done these things, how well had Dane known him? Really known him? Dane understood anger—any man did. He didn't understand lashing out and hurting others while in a temper. There were other ways to let off steam than hurting the people you loved.

Yet John had changed. Had become someone Dane had trouble understanding.

The property looked deserted, as they drove into the yard. There was no sign of John's truck. Maybe he was still in town. But, if he were in town, that meant he could have been at their hotel when Jade went missing. He swore under his breath and closed his eyes briefly.

"Did you say something?" Meg turned to face him.

"No. Just hoping this mess turns out better than it's looking like it will at the moment."

"Right. Dane, I have to ask. Who said Peppe was not in his right mind?"

He glanced over at her in surprise. "I don't know. I didn't need to be told. I could see it for myself. Why?"

"I'm just trying to sort out the behavior, that's all. And what about Tasha?"

"When I first met her, she was fairly happy and seemed like any other eager mother-to-be. At the end? No. She wasn't normal at the end. And no way you can blame that on my brother."

"I'm not trying to," she said gently. "I'm trying to understand, to sort through the possibilities."

He parked and turned off the engine. Stephen parked beside them.

Dane gave her a hard look. "This is my brother. Remember that when you look at those possibilities."

Chapter 26

D ANE WALKED PAST the small picket fence he'd once considered cute. Not any longer. Now it looked run down and unloved. Everything in his life had taken on a dark tinge. He headed to the kitchen door and didn't wait for the others to follow. They would.

He could already hear Meg running behind him, and the vehicle doors opening and closing as the others hopped out to catch up.

He strode through the kitchen. No sign of John. He headed for the master bedroom and found it undisturbed from the day he'd cleaned it out. John hadn't moved back in. Frowning, he made a quick loop through the rest of the house. "He's not here."

The others stood in the middle of the kitchen, faces blank.

Dane shrugged. "He could be anywhere. Let's check the other cabins. There are three of them. I'll check mine first." He bolted out the door and ran to his place.

Flinging open the door, he strode into the small cabin. Nothing had been disturbed. At least at first glance, that appeared to be the case. He walked through the space and headed back out to the front.

Everyone stood on the small porch or just inside the door, waiting for his verdict.

"Empty."

He led the way to Emile's cabin. They passed several outbuildings. Old sheds, storage rooms, and working buildings from years past, when this place had been a thriving farm. They checked every one.

No sign of John. Nothing.

Lots of rusted equipment and wooden boxes filled the spaces, but mostly they were full of junk.

Arriving at a clearing, Dane pointed out Emile's cabin. "I don't know if anyone's been in here since Emile died."

"Not likely, considering only John and Peppe were left." Bruce strode beside him. "He had enough on his plate without worrying about minor things like that."

Dane shot him a sideways look. "Still think he could have done what you think he might have done?"

Bruce was quick to answer. "Yes."

"Kidnapping doesn't fit John's pattern. Jade wasn't his girlfriend. She's mine. She's not pregnant, as far as I know."

Trying to maintain the pace as Dane's long legs ate up the distance, Bruce explained, "I wasn't thinking of that pattern as much as it could possibly be his way to get rid of a problem in his life. Once something starts to go wrong, he's faced with failure. Rather than accepting that a relationship or a business has come to an end, it sounds like he's getting rid of the cause of his failure—blaming something or someone else, so to speak. And by removing it from his life, he doesn't have to face it."

"Failure?" Dane shook his head. "That's a bit harsh."

"There's no way of knowing. Killers don't think like we do. Although most of the time these people have had a tough upbringing—child abuse, that sort of thing. According to you, you two were always close. You had a good childhood."

"More or less."

"So what could have gone wrong for John? What could have started him on this path?"

Dane looked at him in confusion, very conscious of the others listening in with interest. "Wrong?" He stopped and reared back slightly. "Nothing was wrong. Unless you mean our parents' deaths? My dad passed when I was an infant. John's mom died when he was in kindergarten. Our parents married several years later. We were all close, until they died on a European holiday in John's second-to-last year of high school."

Bruce was quiet for a moment. "Their deaths could have initially triggered his actions." Taking a deep breath, he added, "And it's quite possible that being forced to confront death on a large scale, like the mass grave here, may have triggered his behavior again. Made him reassess where he was in life and what he really wanted."

Dane shot him a look of disbelief, not wanting to consider the possibility. He turned and pointed to a cabin in the distance. "That's Emile's."

Their pace picked up. At the steps, the others stopped and waited for Dane. He unlatched the door, wrinkled up his nose, and flung the door wide open. "God, it's stale in here."

"Not being cleaned and aired out will do that."

"I suppose." Dane headed in. The cabin had an identical layout to his—was maybe a little larger. Clothes were tossed onto the backs of the furniture, shoes forgotten on the floor.

Dane shook his head and strode into the bedroom.

Empty. But then, what had they expected? It's not as if Jade would be sitting there, waiting for them.

"It's empty. Only Peppe's place is left." Dane pointed toward the heaviest treed area of the property. "Let's check it fast, then, … hell, I don't know what we'll do after that."

"One thing at a time." Bruce turned to survey the treed acreage. "Talk about privacy. Dane, where *is* Peppe's place? I can't see anything."

He pointed. "Through those trees. Peppe's place is the original homestead. Peppe built the main house for his wife." Dane raced off in that direction, while still explaining, a sense of urgency dogging his heels.

The cabin was set among the trees. Older, more worn, the front door hung crooked … and stood open. "The cabin should be burned because of the state it's in." Bruce backed away, his hand wafting the air in front of his face. "God, that is rank."

"No kidding."

Dane glanced over to see Stephen and Wilson hold their noses as they tried to breathe. A quick glance at Meg showed a similar reaction. He climbed the few steps and entered. The others stayed well back.

The cabin looked the same as he remembered from his last visit. In fact, it looked exactly the same. The same clothes and brown stains on the floor. The smell could have been just the decomposing food though. He bent and peered closer at the stains on the floor. They were old. He kicked them with his boots. Very old.

He searched the small cabin, his mind wanting to panic. A part of him would be happy to accept all kinds of theories, if they led to finding Jade. Instead they'd hit a dead end. He rejoined the team. "It's empty too."

"Really? I thought for sure we'd find Jade here, somewhere." Meg peered into the room behind him.

Stephen shook his head. "Why here? She could be anywhere."

"I hope not. It'll be impossible to find her then." Bruce backed up several paces to stare around the side of the house, as if looking for an outbuilding.

Dane watched him, and finally something went *click*. "Goddamn it." Dane said suddenly. Something he should have thought of earlier fell into place. He hopped off the porch and headed around the corner of the house. The others followed. The old outhouse stood in the back, the door open.

"What?" The others stared at him, following blindly, confusion on their faces. "Dane, what are you doing?"

"There should be a root cellar here someplace." He shook his head at his own stupidity, as he circled the small building. "John mentioned something about Peppe having done a lot of renovations to this old place. I remember asking to see it when I first arrived, but John said it wasn't his place. Said he was too busy fixing up his store. Another place he wouldn't show me."

"What's that about John's business?" Bruce asked loud enough that everyone trying to catch up could hear.

Dane spun around to explain. "He was working from home, then decided a storefront in town would be better. He leased a place before that recent small earthquake and lost everything. Then last week he told me that everything was gone. He was bankrupt and couldn't bear to tell Tasha." He looked around. The root cellar should be here somewhere. It's the only thing that made sense.

"Dane, is there a building left standing that was John's business?" Bruce called out, his sharp voice finally penetrating Dane's focus.

"Not much of one. I finally drove by there today, but I couldn't see that he'd done anything. I kept asking to see it, offering to help. I'm in the construction business after all," Dane said in confusion. "Only he kept saying he was working on it, and that it wasn't ready to show me yet."

"As in, he kept giving you an excuse to keep you away?" Bruce's sharp voice made Dane stop and turn to face them.

"Yes, I guess so, ... but why?"

"More failure?"

"Dane, where is this building? Might he have stashed Jade in it?"

"It's not structurally sound. Half of one side is cracked and caved in. I didn't stop to look beyond that. There's been so much going on."

"Is there a downstairs? Or a part of the structure that is safe? A place where he might keep her?"

Dane's face shut down. "I don't know." He stopped in front of a blue tarp. "This has to be what I want." He leaned down to pull back the tarp. "I figured there had to be an old root cellar down here." An old rusted padlock secured the large wooden doors.

"Someone give me a hand with this." He looked around for something to smash it with and spied a large rock.

Bruce leaned down and yanked on the lock. "This sucker isn't moving."

"Hell, yes it is. Move back." Dane crashed the heavy rock down on it.

The padlock held, but the old wood splintered in every direction.

JADE TRIED FOR the thousandth time to get her foot free of the manacle. Her blood ran warm down her bare foot. She just couldn't get her heel through the small hole. Desperate for escape, she considered breaking her bones if that would do the job—then discarded that idea. She studied the pin mechanism and the new lock that held the manacle closed. She'd studied the ones on the women's ankles in her lab but not to figure out how to open them. Neither did she have any tools or rocks available to do the job.

She collapsed on the ground. Tears once again welled up in her eyes. She wiped them away. She couldn't function if she let her fear take over. It took anger to beat the fear into the ground. And anger had been a little scarce recently.

Then she thought she heard something above.

Her heart stopped. *Friend or foe?* Then again, what friend of Jade's would know where to look? It had to be her captor.

Panic rose. She pounded it down again. *Think, damn it. You've got a brain. Use it.*

A heavy *thud* above her head had her studying the ceiling. Her muscles tensed. She could hardly breathe.

"Oh God, please. Someone help me," she whispered, as she heard noises at the back of the building. "Please let this be someone looking for me."

She closed her eyes and prayed.

MEG STEPPED BACK. "You guys can go look. I'm staying up here, in the sunshine, where the world doesn't look so dark and creepy."

"That works." Bruce pulled apart the wood fragments and tossed them out of the way to reveal old cement steps, going down into the cellar.

Dane led the way. "Jade, are you here?"

Silence. Stretching out a hand, he was amazed to find a light switch. The small room flooded with opaque light from a single bulb hanging from a cord in the middle of the room.

"Holy shit!"

The other men clambered down the steps behind him and gasped in shock.

Bruce, his voice grim and sad, said, "Well, I guess we know what happened to those manacled women now."

The small room had a bed with blankets, a small dresser with an old-fashioned pitcher and bowl for water. A few blankets and clothing of some kind were tossed on the bed. The other corner of the room had a bucket with a toilet seat resting on top. The structural support standing in the middle of the room was decorated with the one thing that made Dane's blood run cold.

Chains. Chains with manacles on the end, open and loose, hung down from the nails.

"Oh, my God. So it *was* Peppe who kidnapped the women? Holy shit," Stephen muttered.

Dane's stomach sank, and his mind roiled. "*This* is fucking nuts."

"I've been telling you that, man," Stephen said. "This is beyond crazy. We've got a crazy old man kidnapping, abusing, killing young women, and I'm scared to think of how many he took or how long he kept them. Then he tossed their bodies in the mass grave because … what? … It was convenient?"

Bruce, his voice haunted by what was in front of him, said, "Depending on how many women, he might have had several graves. Maybe the earthquake unearthed one? Maybe the mass grave was accidentally put on top? Or maybe he had to move the bodies from their original resting place because it opened with the earthquake, and the mass grave was a perfect opportunity. I don't think Peppe's health or strength is what it used to be. The quake and mass grave would have provided an easy answer. Particularly if he still had one prisoner locked in here at the time of the quake."

Bruce walked to the dresser and using a towel tossed on top, he opened the first drawer then the second. "We need to get the police out here. There are purses, pictures, clothing, even jewelry. Maybe these things can help identify his victims."

Stephen stood in the middle of the room, staring at the center support beam, careful to not touch anything, as he studied the chains. "These are covered in blood."

"No surprise there."

Dane walked over to the center support beam. His voice caught, before he rasped out, "There are names and dates scratched into this pole."

The other two men came to look and found even more than a dated tally. Pleas for help scratched into the wood made Dane turn away, his eyes closing in pain and disbelief.

Grimly Bruce said, "Good, this information will help us identify the victims and provide answers for their families."

"Yeah, except we don't know where this asshole is," Stephen added. "He's still on the loose, and here we are, so focused on John, that we've lost sight of Peppe. For all we know he planned to kidnap Jade from the beginning."

"Christ." Dane sighed, feeling as if he'd just been given a huge reprieve. "This just gets better and better. So my brother is innocent, and Peppe is a killer? Did Emile know? Did he help his father? Did Tasha? Is that why no one could bear to look after him? Why they didn't dare hire a local woman to look after him? In case he killed more women or in case someone found out what he'd done? As that would bring everything back onto them?"

Stephen snorted. "This place gives me the creeps."

Dane smiled, relief washing through him as he realized something major. "At least this proves my brother's innocence. We need to get the police out here right now."

Stephen, shaking his head, took one last look around the cellar. "I'll wait here for the authorities. You go check in with the others, and you might as well check out John's shop. Peppe could just as easily have stashed Jade there. Especially if it's close to the hotel."

Bruce turned to go. "Wilson is waiting outside with Meg. He started retching when he saw this room. We'll leave the three of you here to wait. I don't need to remind you not to touch anything. If you find anything else, contact Dr. Mike and Susan back at the hotel. Call and fill them in. Dane and I will go straight to the shop." Bruce had his phone out and was climbing the steps to call the police from outside.

"And, if you hear anything or see anything, call me on my cell." Dane wrote down his number on a receipt he found in his wallet and handed it over to Stephen. "We have no idea where Peppe is, so be careful. I don't know what the old man might have in his arsenal. He got these women here somehow."

Dane drove into town in a much more positive mental state than he'd left it. Surely his brother was innocent of all the suggested crimes.

And Dane desperately needed to find Jade. To know she was okay and to hold her again. There was so much ugliness here. He couldn't wait to go back to Seattle now.

When this was over, he'd convince his brother to come home with him. That was the best answer. Put this all behind him and start again. Dane could give him a job, a place to live, help him get back on his feet.

Bruce called Dr. Mike with an update that had Dr. Mike gasping with outrage. He told Bruce there'd been no sign of John or of Jade. Fifteen minutes after Bruce had finished his call, Dane pulled into the back of the shop, which he'd only ever driven past before. It looked the same. He reached into the glove box of his truck and pulled out a small clipboard. He rifled through several sheets of paper to find the one he was looking for. "This is it—726 Main Road."

Bruce stared at the broken door numbers on the entrance. "Well, let's go check it out. I really don't want to find any more nasty horrors, like what we just found."

"I just want to find Jade—safe and sound."

The men approached carefully. It was late afternoon now, but still, people walked the sidewalks, and vehicles moved quickly along the street. An ordinary day.

But not for him. For Dane it was as if time had stopped. If Jade were here, it would devastate him. But even then, it didn't mean John was to blame. And, if Jade weren't here, he'd be even more upset and concerned for her. He needed to find her. Fast.

"This wall is cracked enough to enter." Dane shook his head. Why the hell hadn't he come here earlier and checked up on his brother? The back wall wasn't just cracked. It was half gone. Shrugging, Dane stepped through carefully and followed the dirty pathway to a small door. He opened it. Dirty footprints led down the stairs.

Bruce stepped up behind him. "What is it?" he whispered. Dane motioned to the tracks. Bruce grimaced. "Are we thinking he's down there?"

The two men exchanged looks. Dane knew that if someone were still down there, they had the advantage. Then again, Dane didn't have an option. He slipped down the first couple risers as quietly as he could.

He bent down to peer around the corner.

"Oh my God."

JADE'S HEART CLOGGED her throat.

Even as she watched, a large square of light appeared, highlighting stairs in the far corner.

Her muscles tensed. She could hardly breathe. She didn't know whether she should try to make it look as if were sleeping or to sit casually and wait.

That she would finally find out who was behind her kidnapping almost scared her more than not knowing.

Her heart beat so hard that she could barely think. Work boots like Dane's appeared, followed by jean-clad legs. Long and lean. She gulped and shoved her fist into her mouth to stop the whimpers forming in the back of her throat. *It couldn't be. Please not.*

Then a familiar face came into view. Jade stared in disbelief and horror.

It was.

Chapter 27

D ANE RACED TO her side. "Jesus, Jade. Thank God, we found you."

"Jade?" At the sight of Bruce's worried face, Jade burst into tears. Dane wrapped her in his arms. "I'm so sorry. It'll be fine now. I promise. It's over."

She couldn't stop crying. "Thank you for finding me. I can't get free." She kicked her leg out to show them the chain. "I've been so scared. I was afraid he'd come back. Then I was terrified he wouldn't come back, and I'd die here forgotten and alone."

"Never forgotten, sweetheart. We're here. You'll be fine now." Dane gave her a big hug, then stepped back. She reached for him again, scared he'd leave her alone. He grabbed her hands. "Bruce, come hold her. I need to find something to knock that manacle off."

Bruce stepped forward and wrapped his arms around her. He held her close. "I just called the authorities again. I expect they'll escort us all to the airport after this and wait until we get on the plane to confirm that we leave."

Dane shook his head. "I can't say I'd blame them. Now what the hell can I use to get that damn thing off her leg?"

She pointed to the far corner. "A mess of stuff is over there. You might find something to use."

Dane headed to the corner.

"Damn it, Jade. What the hell happened?" Bruce gave her a quick shake. "We were so worried about you."

She sniffled slightly, touching the side of her head, still tender but no longer bleeding. "I was sitting at the table, waiting for Dane and Meg to come back, when the lights went out. I woke up here. With this." She pointed to her foot again. "What *is* this place? Where are we?"

"We're still in town. It's been about five hours since you went missing. Oh, and you wouldn't believe what we found out."

She slid her arm through his, unable to let go of him. They both watched as Dane bent down to check something, then stood again. He returned quickly, with an odd assortment of tools in his hand.

"Dane, what's over there?"

He shot Bruce a hard look. "I'll work on this lock. Bruce, why don't you go see? Maybe you can identify it."

Curious, Jade watched as Bruce hurried to the far end, where he became lost in the shadows. She could barely see him, as he stopped and stared, before dropping to the floor. "What is it, Dane?"

He sighed and stopped fiddling with the lock to look up at her. "It's not what, as much as whom."

"Oh, God." Jade's stomach threatened to heave. *Was* a person over there? *Dead?* Dane hadn't said so, but she hadn't heard a word the whole time she'd been here.

"He'll need to add an ambulance to the fleet on its way." Dane shook his head. "I never thought to call. All I wanted was to get this damn manacle off you." He struggled to break the manacle while Jade watched, willing him to hurry.

The longer it took, the more she started to panic. They had to get away. Fast.

A hoarse, hard voice sliced through their concentration. "Well, well. Look who finally came to visit. Checking up on me, big brother?"

Dane froze. He closed his eyes briefly, his face contorting in disgust. And pain. Jade gasped and huddled in a ball in front of Dane, who was between her and her kidnapper. She couldn't believe it. She didn't want to believe it. Poor Dane. She tried to peer around Dane to be sure. "Dane? Is that *John?*"

Slowly opening his eyes to look into hers, he whispered, "Yeah. I'm so sorry. I'd hoped to get you safely away before your kidnapper returned. Looks like he found us first."

"Stand up, *step*brother."

Jade couldn't see John's face, but his voice conveyed no sign of the weak, ineffectual man she'd believed him to be.

Sighing, Dane dropped the tools and slowly stood. Turning to face John, he motioned at the gun in John's hand and casually said, "What's going on, John? I don't get it. Explanation, please?"

"You never did have the brains everyone gave you credit for. To the world, you were always the first, the best, the biggest. God, I hated that. You were always trying to steal the limelight. And here I find you, trying to steal my new girl."

Dane shook his head. "*Your* girl? You actually kidnapped Jade? Are you crazy?"

John smiled.

Jade peered around Dane. *Oh God.* That look on John's face. So empty, so lacking in anything recognizable. She reached for the tools Dane had dropped and worked frantically on the lock.

"No," John said softly. "I'm not crazy. I didn't figure you'd find Jade so fast."

"I have to admit I had some help from friends."

"That damn team. They're the reason everything's wrong. Then again, they also offered the perfect avenue to bring about a much-needed change."

"Change? Is that what you call the destruction of your family?"

"I didn't touch Emile. Peppe fought with him and knocked him down. The two of them had a whopper of a fight about the doctor he was trying to bring in behind my back to look after Tasha. Peppe was just getting his own back. Emile had already washed his hands of the old man. His death just finished off Tasha, but that had nothing to do with me." He smirked. "Except for the pillow over her mouth and nose."

"What about your high school girlfriend, Melia? Did you do her in?" Dane's voice held a plea that Jade had trouble understanding.

Her gaze shifted from one brother to the other. *Who the hell was Melia?*

Shock sat heavy on John's face. "Wow, you have been doing your homework, haven't you?" He smiled, a gesture that shot ice rippling through Jade.

God, whoever Melia was, Jade was sure that the poor woman had died at John's hands.

"And your first wife, Elise? Did you kill her too?"

"That stupid bitch. She thought she could leave me. She asked for a divorce of all things. Then she didn't even tell me that she was pregnant. Doubt it was mine anyway. Besides, she deserved what she got."

Jade switched her gaze to Dane's face, watching myriad emotions wash over him. His fists clenched, then relaxed. These people Dane mentioned had been people he'd known. People who had been part of his life too.

Anger and disbelief fired up Dane's voice. "And Tasha—had she wanted a divorce as well? Or did you think the baby wasn't yours? Is that what you do? Get rid of women when you don't want them anymore?"

"No. You should give me a medal for Tasha. Now that lady was a bitch. Especially toward the end. And I didn't kill the baby. She lost that all on her own. You can't lay that one on me."

Jade could listen no longer. "She lost it, or you helped her lose it?" Bitterness flowed from her voice. She didn't even try to hold back. This innocent-looking man had caused so much pain and suffering. She stared down at the chain in her hand. So much misery. "Did you kidnap and abuse those poor women under Tasha's nose too?"

Dane shook his head at her, but she didn't understand why.

John chuckled, a hard, nasty sound that made her shudder. "You're as stupid as Tasha was. I wasn't even here then. At least not for all of them." He relaxed slightly, rocking back on his heels. "I didn't kidnap those women. That was Peppe. I had no idea he could be so ingenious. No idea all that time I was stuck with Tasha that he was out scouting new victims. It still pisses me off that he thought of it first. That he'd been doing it for years."

He waved the gun around. "I only found out when I was burying those fucking bodies. Talk about a turning point in my life. Emile brought a woman over and threw her on top of the pile, thinking I wouldn't notice. I might not have, except for the goddamn manacle. They didn't even take the thing off her in death.

"Peppe has a mess of them, hanging in a busted-down shed. They are seriously old. We'll probably find his whole damn family were either slaves or slavers at one time themselves." He grinned a nasty smirk that made Jade wince. "I confronted Emile at the mass grave, and he told me about Peppe—that Peppe hadn't been strong enough to get rid of the body on his own, so he'd had to do it for him."

John laughed, a cold sound that sent shards of ice down Jade's back. "The women were Peppe's slaves. They looked after his every need. Emile wouldn't have anything to do with his father after that. Little wuss. And Tasha could never look him in the eye again. She lived in terror of him being found out."

"Emile even built a mess of crosses with inscriptions for the poor women. Said he didn't know how many his dad had killed, but it had to stop." John laughed again.

The sound crawled inside Jade's skin, like ants to an open wound. She'd bet anything Emile had been the one to write the inscription For All Those Who Have Gone Before.

In memory of his father's victims. How sad.

"Although, the way I see it, you owe me. I'm pretty sure Emile changed his mind about things. That he was looking to snatch one of the team members for himself." John sniggered. "Oh, he never said anything directly, but you could tell that something was bugging him. I bet the idea wouldn't leave him alone. It's not as if he had a wife." John continued, his voice brutally cold and confident. "I'd seen what Peppe had built too. Had a little talk with him myself. Scared the pants off him. He was pretty easy to control from then on, until the dementia really started. Who knew what he might have said."

John motioned behind him. "I don't have to worry anymore. That crazy Peppe was stalking Jade too. I took care of that." He shrugged. "He just cemented my decision to kidnap her. Now I have the perfect place to pick up where he left off."

"You mean, Peppe's little dungeon in the root cellar? Well, the police are there right now."

John's face mottled as rage filled him. "Fucking assholes. That's where I would take *her*. It's a perfect hidey-hole."

Jade gasped. That *had* been his intention. She refocused on the manacle's lock. She tried to keep one ear on the conversation, while she had one eye on that damn gun and the other eye on her ankle and lock. She couldn't see Bruce, but he had to know what was going on. What was he doing? And thank God that John hadn't noticed Bruce.

"The cellar's a crime scene now." Dane's hard voice left no doubts.

John's color receded, as he considered the problem. "I'll keep her here then. When they're done, I'll put it back in order." He shrugged. "No problem." He sneered and studied his older brother. "I'd planned on taking you out eventually, but I wanted you to suffer first. That's why I took Jade. I hadn't planned on it. But you were so happy. So delighted at the unexpected turn in your life.

"Yet mine was shit, and, once again, you were coming out with the gold. No point in you having all that money—or her—when it could all be mine. Poor timing though to kill you so soon after the other deaths." He brightened. "Unless I can make it look like you killed them."

Click. Jade stilled in shock. Dane shifted to stand in front of her, giving her more cover. She slipped her hand into Dane's and stood beside him, finally with the manacle unlocked but still in place.

Dane's hand latched onto hers. He tucked her farther behind him.

"*Aww.* Isn't that so cute?"

Jade cringed at the mockery in John's voice. She leaned her head against Dane's broad back. Her breath caught. They needed a distraction. ... Something to give Dane and Bruce an advantage. Dane couldn't outrun a bullet. But John would have a hard time fighting them both off.

"Shut up. Why did you have to pick on Jade anyway? Surely you knew I wouldn't rest until I found her?" He tensed. Jade recognized his change in stance, just not the reason for it. She peeked around his shoulder. He squeezed her hand tightly, then released it. She accepted the warning and took a second, more cautious look.

Bruce stood in the shadows, a large chunk of broken wood in his hand.

"And you'd have suffered for it every day." John grinned.

"You hate me so much? Why? I don't understand. I gave so much to you. Helped you out so many times. I was always there for you. Always." Jade stroked Dane's back, offering him that support at least. He sounded so disbelieving, so heartbroken. So hurt.

"And that's because, in your mind, I always needed your assistance. My big brother bailing me out again. Pathetic. I don't need you to *fix* me. Or to make my problems disappear."

Bruce approached, the block of wood ready.

"You're the one who asked me to stay here. To help you rebuild."

"Yeah, I needed more money. And time to figure a way out. Money buys anything here." He lifted the gun higher as an example. "Your life has been too damn easy. Besides, having you here made it so much easier for me to do what I needed to do. After all, that's the way I always am around you anyway. You're the big man. The good man. I'm the weak younger brother. And because of that, you made the perfect alibi too. Bet you told everyone, *My brother, John, would never hurt anyone. Life has been hard on him, but he's a good man.*"

Jade buried her face against Dane's shoulder. Oh God, Dane had said almost that exact same thing to her. She didn't want to see what was coming next.

Dane, his voice weary and sad, said, "You could have asked. I'd have given you what you needed."

"Yes, and I would have accepted and hated you even—"

A heavy *thump* cut off his words, as John bent over and gasped. "God damned son of a bitch."

Jade stuffed her fist to her mouth to stop the scream from escaping as Dane headed for his brother. John came up in a lunge and decked Bruce. Bruce's head snapped to one side, and he went down— hard. John spun around as if realizing the window he'd opened.

Too late.

Dane sprang across the last few feet, hitting his brother in the chest. They both went down in a flurry of arms and legs, as they fought for control. The gun skittered across the floor. Jade kicked free of the manacle and raced after the gun, keeping a wary eye on the two men.

She picked up the gun and pointed it at the men. Only Dane was sitting on his brother, one hand at his throat, the other, fisted, wailing into John's face.

Bruce groaned. Jade raced over and bent down to him. "Easy, Bruce. John hit you hard."

He opened his eyes, took a moment to register what had happened, then came off the ground with fire in his eyes.

Jade turned to see Dane land one last blow to John's jaw. John slumped to the ground.

It was over.

"Damn it," Bruce bellowed. "I wanted to get a good one in."

Dane sat back on his heels, still straddling his brother, now gasping for air. "Sorry, I gave it to him for you. And Jade. And Tasha. And Elise. And Melia." He glared down at John, as he stood up. Taking a step away, he added, "So many lives lost. So many more ruined."

Dane turned to look at Jade. He opened his arms. She raced to bury her face against his chest and squeezed him tight. Dane held her close against his heart. Fearing it wasn't over, she peered around Dane's shoulder at John's crumpled body. John wasn't moving.

Sirens whistled from far away. Bruce bent down to check on John's pulse. "He's alive."

"Too bad. What an asshole." Jade reared back to look up into Dane's eyes. "I'm sorry, Dane. I'm not feeling very generous toward your brother at the moment."

He tucked her close against him. "Neither am I. Neither am I."

She turned to face Bruce. "Bruce, who or what is back there?"

He looked at her confusion. She pointed in the back corner. He dropped the wood to the floor, before running his fingers through his short hair. "I think it's Peppe."

The color drained from her face. "Oh, God!"

Bruce smiled sadly. "Looks like John was on a house-cleaning mission."

Jade shuddered and burrowed deeper into Dane's arms. "Thank God, it's over—before he got around to you."

Chapter 28

Three Weeks Later

AT THE SOUND of the truck arriving, Jade walked out of the lab trailer, a big smile on her face. *Dane.* She checked the time on her new cell phone, a gift from the team. *He's on time.* She laughed and waved.

"You two are almost too much, you know that?" Meg stood at Jade's shoulder, shaking her head.

Jade laughed, enjoying the great friendships she'd developed with the team. They'd become like a real family, with bonds that wouldn't break. "Great, isn't it?"

"I'm jealous," Meg admitted. "We've only got about two weeks left. And I miss my Pete. Maybe I should have him fly over for a hot weekend too."

Dane exited the truck, a grin on his face, as he walked toward them. "I heard that. Take him on a cruise. That's where we're headed, as soon as you guys are done here. I can't wait."

"You need the break," Jade murmured, walking into his arms. "How was the meeting?"

"Good and bad. I barely recognized John. These last three weeks haven't been easy on him." He sighed, the rumble rolling up from deep down. "The extradition process is going ahead." He dropped his head to rest against the top of Jade's. "I spoke to one lawyer who said the U.S. wants to try him for the murders of Melia and Elise. Plus they will go through John's history to see if there could be other victims."

Jade closed her eyes at the pain in his voice. What a mess the last few weeks had been. Dane had had it the hardest. She still had nightmares, only they were less disturbing. Dane had them too. Although she hadn't let him know that she'd watched him twist in torment while he slept. "I'm sorry," she said.

He tightened his arms, then released her, keeping one around her shoulders, as he smiled at Meg. "How's it going here?"

Meg smiled. "It's great. We've found the mother and daughter we've been looking for. The DNA results came in today for them. Just waiting for the father's DNA to match up. Then those three can go home, where they belong."

"Wow." Dane smiled down at Jade. "That's excellent. I guess that means you'll relax a little when Duncan gets here next week?"

She laughed. "Maybe."

When Duncan had heard the story of her kidnapping, he'd freaked on the phone and had wanted to come over right away. It had taken a lot to convince him to hold off. Now his visit would be a joy. She couldn't wait to see him.

Jade leaned away a little. "Also, the police have a tentative ID on two of the prisoner women from the grave. But, as in John's case, it's important to find all of Peppe's victims. To find them, identify them, and bring them home."

Tony had pitched a fit over identifying Peppe's victims, but he underestimated the wealthy business owner who had been horrified and had quickly offered financial support to see the job done right.

Thank heavens.

"Home and family is important. So is friendship. And love." Dane's smile turned intimate, Jade's insides now mush.

This trip had done so much for her. For all its horrors and violence, the job here had brought about many good things. She was being held by one of them. She'd survived. Not only survived but thrived.

In fact, by now, she was pretty sure she could get through anything.

That's what she called progress.

USA *TODAY* BESTSELLING AUTHOR

DALE MAYER

HAUNTED
BY
DEATH

BOOK TWO OF BY DEATH SERIES

Chapter 1

T HE CLOUDS SWEPT across the sky, whipped by a blustery northern wind. The sun was high, shining brightly over the lake and shore. It was a perfect summer's day at the lake. Not far from the water's edge, where multiple brightly colored tents sprawled, Chad Ingram followed his buddies up the beach for a short hike. Bruce and Josh, his best friends, were in charge of today's adventure. The girls had elected to stay behind.

This was their last camping trip of the summer, before college started next week. The long-standing group of three young males and their three girlfriends had made the most of the summer weather to get out and to enjoy their time together. This weekend, Tim and Bruce's cousins—Anto and Pero, who'd moved to the US a couple years ago—had joined them.

Chad liked them both, and Pero was easy to get along with. However, his broody brother, Anto, was, by contrast, hard work. But so long as he was on his best behavior, he fit into the group just fine. Some of the group had worked full-time for the summer, others only part-time, and one of their number was doing summer school. Making time together had been a challenge.

And they all knew it was the end of an era. And that making time for each other was important. Next week, each would start on the pathway of whatever future they'd chosen. This weekend was a last chance to let loose before life intruded. Good thing too. Futures were serious business.

Josh had organized this day hike, which was intended to be a fun couple of hours, exploring this side of the lake. With only T-shirts, shorts, and runners, they weren't equipped to do more. Chad liked to do at least one hiking trip a day when they were out. Not going too far and not putting out too much effort, just a break from the beach and swimming and beer drinking. Well, maybe not that last one, as several of them usually carried an open can of beer with them.

This was their second trip to the popular northern area of Washington State. They'd camped at the other side of this same lake earlier in the summer, close to where several members of Bruce's extended-family had cabins. That trip had been such a blast that they all wanted to come back and check out the opposite side of the lake, the less popular side. Where they'd first camped out were hundreds of cabins up and down the lakeshore. That area was open and sunny, with lovely sandy beaches. All of which made it a big attraction for kids and families.

This time the group wanted a different experience. They wanted seclusion, isolation, privacy, and a chance to enjoy their last bit of freedom, without having to follow curfews and noise restrictions.

And, from the looks of the tightly grown forest and steep incline on parts of the hill behind them, they had it.

The group took off up the hill in good spirits. Chad walked last in line, smiling at his friends' antics up ahead. Their laughter preceded them, filling the dense woods, even as the sun fought to reach into the old growth and the tightly grouped stick trees on the left. The air was filled with a heavy pine-scented atmosphere. Although the walk up the hill on the left side had started out easily, it hit the way-too-much-work-to-be-bothered-with category very quickly. Besides, they hadn't brought enough beer to fortify themselves for that much effort.

"Hey, Chadwickie, what's taking you so long?" Josh yelled back from up ahead. He'd been leading the group of males for the last ten minutes but had stopped to see what was holding up his friend.

"I gotta take a piss," Chad called out. "That beer is running right through me."

"Weakling! Jesus, you really can't hold your liquor, can you?" Raucous laughter filled the air.

"Ha, ha. I can hold it that way just fine. I wasn't the one slobbering all over the girls last night, like you and Bruce were."

Chad—or Chadwickie, as his buddies liked to call him to rile him—stepped farther into the dense woods and slightly off the path, then opened his fly. Immediately a bright stream hit the mossy ground and ferns in front of him. He tilted his head back and sighed with relief, enhanced by the mild buzz going on in his head. Life was good.

"Aren't you done already?" called back one of his friends, probably Bruce. "It's almost time to go back to the girls. You're taking so long."

"When you gotta go, you gotta go," Chad murmured quietly, with a contented sigh. He could hear his friends moving farther away, but they were still within hearing distance.

The stream went on and on. Finally he tucked himself back inside and zipped up his khaki shorts. He turned to look for his buddies. No one was in sight.

Shit.

"Hey, Josh? Bruce?" He spun around. "Where the hell are you guys? Anto? Tim?"

There was not a sound, not a whisper of laugher or a crackle of leaves. Nothing. Crap. Where were they?

"Pero?"

Just then, the sun went behind a cloud, and the air around him darkened, adding a sinister overtone to his growing fear. Crackling noises off to the left had him bolting to the right. "Hey, guys!"

Nothing.

Laughter from the way ahead wove through the air. He ran toward it. Tripping over roots and piling through bushes, Chad chased after his friends. They would hide from him for hours—or for as long as they were having fun—if he didn't find them first. They were all jokesters, him included.

But going for a two-hour hike as part of the group was one thing; getting left behind and lost was another thing altogether. *That* was not something Chad wanted. The group had been making hiking and camping trips for the last year. They had been a blast. But they'd all been on fields or beaches in open terrain, where it was easy to see the surrounding area, easy to pinpoint landmarks to avoid getting lost. Never had they been in woods like this, but, of course, that had been the attraction this time around.

Open spaces were fine; beaches were good—great even. This place was eerie in a good way. Kinda like ghost stories around a campfire, a creepy kind of good.

Besides, he knew his buddies, and he trusted them. This was all in fun. He'd take his hit now and dish out more to the others later.

Just to the guys though. The girls didn't prank like the guys did. And he should know. One was an ex-girlfriend and the other? She was the love of his life. There had been a little occasional camping with both his ex and his current girlfriend, but he hadn't gone out with Cia since last Halloween. He'd hooked up with Megan—or Megs as they often called her—in February. She was special. He'd had several girlfriends already, but she had been the first one to touch him inside and to make herself right at home with him. She belonged with him. He loved that connection, that specialness of knowing he'd found the right partner.

His friends thought he was nuts and were always pointing out other chicks and telling him to test drive a few more models before he made a decision. The thing was, he'd already done that. Cia had been one of the worst ones. And his friends just didn't get it about Megs. There was no decision to be made. It had been done for him. He couldn't explain this to someone who'd never experienced such a feeling, but Megs was his, and he was hers. End of discussion.

Chest heaving, he stopped his headlong rush and caught his breath, while he searched the hillside for his friends. Still no sign of the others. Shit. How far ahead could they be? The incline now looked to be a half-mile deep. He checked his watch. *Jesus*. They'd been gone forty-five minutes already. Given that they were close to the time of returning anyway, the others may have circled back toward the lake already.

And that was a damn good idea. They'd always said, if someone got separated from the rest, they were to return to base. Chad should have done that right off. They could be anywhere by now. He didn't want them to send out a search party looking for him. His friends would never let him live that one down. If it weren't for the steep incline, he'd be seriously worried, but the lake had to be down somewhere at the bottom, so how lost could he be?

Still, he'd go back to the girls, while he could still find his way and before he'd take the chance of getting really lost out here.

A flock of birds flew up in a cacophony of sound right behind him. He dashed around a huge tree trunk and slammed up against it, his heart racing in shock. Shit. Somehow a fun afternoon's exploration had stopped being fun. He took a deep breath, hating the nerve-induced adrenaline snaking through his system. A lot of country was out here.

And he was starting to freak himself out.

He'd never been lost or alone in the woods before. Didn't like it much either. Talk about feeling small and unimportant in the vast world of Mother Nature.

"Hey, Josh? Bruce? Very funny, guys. ... *Where* are you? Pero? Anto?"

No answer from any of them. Shit.

He hated this. He couldn't see anything but more brown trees and moss and green bushes in every direction. That wasn't good. His friends were good people, but they were assholes when they pranked each other. Yet Chad had been as guilty as they were.

A branch cracked off to the left. His heart jumped, and he hid behind a tree. He held his breath. *What the hell was that?*

The undergrowth crunched as if someone—something—were walking heavily on it.

All other sounds had stopped.

He swallowed hard and slithered downward to the base of the tree. After a long moment, he peered around the edge of the tree trunk. He couldn't see anyone. Yet he heard a stealthy noise—barely. Branches rustled; leaves slid against each other, and the birds had gone silent, as if they saw something which he couldn't. The noise could have been from an animal. A bear? But he wasn't so sure. It hadn't been his friends. He knew that. They didn't have the skill to move so quietly. They were all elephants.

But hundreds of cabins were here—and likely thousands of people, counting homes, campgrounds, and the park. He waited, still peering from his hiding spot, but he couldn't hear anything else.

Then it hit him. The noise had come from the direction of the lake. From where they'd left the three girls alone.

Alone. … Oh, Megs.

For the first time he realized how stupid they'd been. His heart went into overdrive, and he could barely breathe. Oh shit. Oh shit. *Oh shit!*

Taking a deep breath, he plowed through the brush the way he'd come, around trees, ducking under branches, jumping over fallen logs, and dodging the bushes that reached out to slow his progress. He had to get back. Something was wrong. He knew it. He just didn't know what.

He crossed what seemed like dozens of miles. He wished he knew where his buddies were right now, but it was the thought of the girls that scared him. They should never have been left alone, never.

He broke through the tree line, gasping in pain, his body trembling with panic, sweat coursing down his back and soaking his T-shirt. And, at last, he came to a dead stop.

Megs was there, with Stephanie. The two girls were in the lake, floating on air mattresses about twenty feet from shore, talking and paying no attention to anything but their conversation. Relief washed through him at the sight of Megs's long, lean body stretched out under the sun. He bent over, struggling to breathe.

She was fine.

Even as he watched, she was pointing out something in the sky to Stephanie. He doubted they even knew he was here. Those two had been close friends for years and could talk about nothing for hours. Confused, he straightened slowly and looked around.

The area was peaceful. Normal. And this normality made him feel like an idiot for overreacting.

But where was Cia? She wasn't emotionally close to the other two females. And she wasn't the type to share confidences with other girls. She was all about the guys. And that had made it a little hard with all the relationship-switching that had happened within the group. Cia had been the one to break up with Chad, and a good thing it had been too. It had saved him the job. For all her good points, Cia came with a couple really negative characteristics.

Normally she could always be found sitting to one side, reading one of her never-ending books. He spun around, looking for her, but found no sign of her.

Maybe she was napping, as she'd been tired, complaining of the heat when they'd left.

"Megs," he called out, "where's Cia?"

Megs twisted around, saw him, and gave him a warm smile. "She went to lie down. She has another headache."

Right. Of course she had. Cia got major migraines. He'd never known anyone else to have them before. It had been quite an education, as they completely crippled her at times. Feeling better, he walked to the water's edge and splashed cool water on his face. If anyone realized how completely he'd overreacted, they'd make fun of him for days.

As he straightened up, his face cooler and his heart no longer trying to escape his chest, he realized that the inner disquiet hadn't been fully calmed. Not able to let it go until he was sure, he walked over to Josh and Cia's tent. "Cia? Are you in here?"

He hated to wake her, but he had to know for sure.

The flap was down, so he lifted the corner and peered inside.

Empty.

He straightened up, cupped his hands around his mouth, and called across the water, "She's not here. The tent is empty."

Just then the rest of the guys thundered through the trees, half running, half crashing into each other, all laughing and joking. "There you are." Josh grinned at Chad, as he jogged over to him. "We got into a crazy game of hide-and-seek in the woods. We weren't sure if you were with us or not at that point."

Bruce and Tim approached, gasping for breath but still scrapping over who had arrived first and second.

"I wasn't," Chad snapped, hands on his hips, as he glared at his friends. "And no thanks to you guys. You could have waited for me."

The others grinned, totally digging him being pissed off. He couldn't blame them. If their positions had been reversed, he'd have done the same. No sign of the Novak brothers. Chad spun around to see them—Anto first, coming through the trees; then Pero, much farther down.

Damn. Chad faced the gathering crowd. "I can't find Cia. The girls said she went to lie down and have a nap, but she's not here."

The responses came from all of them at once.

Bruce brushed off the news with a shake of his head. "Stop worrying. She won't be far away."

"Probably grabbed her book and found a shady spot to read."

"Anyone check the outhouse?"

Chad was having none of it. A horrible certainty had filled him. This was seriously bad.

At his insistence and, with the other two girls now back on shore, they spread out to search … everywhere. Grim-faced and sober, they finally regrouped an hour later.

There had been no sign of Cia.

She was gone.

Chapter 2

Seventeen Years Later

THE SUN SHONE through the windshield, warm and soothing after the tumultuous last few months. Meg Pearce stared at the wilderness through the passenger window, as Pete drove down the highway. She didn't remember any of this area. In fact, she'd been lost since leaving the highway. It had been a long time since her last trip here. That one had been so horrible that she'd managed to avoid coming back to the area so far. Only it was Pete's favorite spot ...

And Pete had been insistent this time. As she hadn't told him the real reasons why she hated this area, and, as she'd run out of excuses, what choice was there now? She could explain, but she really didn't want to open up old wounds. She had enough relationship issues to deal with since her brother's death. So, if this helped, then she was all for it.

Where had the time gone?

Listless, she watched the miles speed by—just like the years had. These last months had been hell, months of emotional turmoil, handling of necessities and adjusting to the new status quo, which hadn't left much time for grieving. Worn out now, she was a mere fragment of her old self. She needed this rest and some time away—time to recoup her energy and her passion for living.

All that had disappeared with her brother's death and the changes and challenges that had come with it. Such as parenting his twelve-year-old daughter and dealing with Pete's unhappy reaction to the new situation. Not to mention Janelle's unhappy reaction to her new life. No wonder Meg's normal *oomph* had disappeared. But this was a vacation, and, as she knew already, if her mood sucked, so did Pete's and Janelle's. But if Meg could pull out of it and be cheerful, then she could usually get their moods turned around too.

"Hard to believe something like this exists, so close to civilization," she joked, partly because they were two hours out of Seattle and not that far from the Canadian border.

Janelle sniped, "Who said *this* was close to anything." She glared out the window from the seat behind Pete. "We're in the middle of nowhere," she wailed.

Meg smiled. It was a small thin one, but all she could manage on short notice. The last thing she needed was more of Janelle's histrionics, but, given that technology, which her niece appeared to depend on, worked only sporadically up here, Meg and Pete could be in for a lot more of the same. For herself, Meg was looking forward to being unplugged for a few days—or longer, if she needed to. Not that she'd left her cell phone behind. But that was only for business and safety issues. As for Janelle, one day of being unplugged was one day too long.

And, for Pete, he'd lightened up a lot, once he realized they were actually going on this trip. He'd been here many times over the years. He loved being in the bush, renovating this place, working with his hands. It's what made him so good at the construction work he did. Meg traveled for months as part of her work, making it hard to get time away with Pete. And, when she did, it was never here. *Never here.*

She wasn't looking forward to this trip but had to admit she could already feel some of the tension draining from her shoulders and spine. She took a deep breath of the woodsy air. It was so different from the smog of Seattle and from the wet coastal smell after a rain or the humidity of Haiti. That had been a tough job. It had ended on a good note, but the pain of what she and her team had gone through had been life changing.

Maybe that's why she had had this change of heart. With what she'd survived over in Haiti, followed by the events since her brother's death, surely Meg could deal with a seventeen-year-old ghost now.

She cast a quick glance to the back seat of the double-cab truck, where Janelle was pouting in the corner. These last few months had been hard on Meg, but they had been hell for her niece. Meg's brother's death in a car accident had been the latest of a long string of incidents that had torn Janelle's life apart. The first was her mother's death to disease, followed by relocation to Seattle to be closer to Meg and Janelle's grandparents. Her brother had always thought that Meg would be a good influence on his struggling daughter.

Being uprooted to Seattle—and unloved, as Janelle had put it— she'd been very unimpressed by the move away from her school and friends. She'd had a hard time adapting to her new social situation. And, at the same time, she had been still dealing with the loss of her mother.

Then months after slowly rebuilding a new life in Seattle, her father had been taken from her. Sometimes fate was a bitch.

Pete slowed the truck on the long stretch of empty road. Meg leaned forward, wondering how he could find an overgrown turnoff in this mess of woods and brush. Even Janelle sat up and looked around.

"This is a back way to the cabin. It keeps the nosy neighbors from knowing when I'm here." Pete turned the truck onto a deeply rutted track, overgrown with waist-high grasses. Janelle groaned, as they drove onto yet another road, taking them deeper into the wooded area. It was darker and much cooler here, with tall spindly trees blocking the sun.

Meg knew it would open up soon. Good thing, as the darkness creeped her out.

Damn. Talk about old fears flaring up.

How many times had Pete vacationed here without her? Not that coming here alone had been his fault. She'd been the one gallivanting off with her job. She'd had a bad case of wanderlust all her life that had only been partially slaked after the Haiti trip. At least she hoped it had been. With Janelle now part of the family, Meg couldn't just get up and run off anymore.

Meg hit the button to open her window. Cool air spread through the warm cab. Having slowed down, there was a light breeze, but it was not enough. She wanted to gulp in freshness, innocence, and renewal. All things she so desperately needed to find again.

She leaned back and closed her eyes, willing her adrenals to hold on, hoping peace and quiet were on the way.

"You okay?" Pete asked, concern coloring his voice.

"Fine," she murmured, not opening her eyes. That was another thing on her list—to repair her relationship with Pete. This year it was as if they were brother and sister instead of lovers. Her job, a bone of contention a year ago, had taken second place to Janelle's sudden arrival into their world.

Since the two had bonded by the time her brother had died, keeping Janelle with her and Pete had been the natural option. Meg's only other sibling, Aaron, had moved across the country, while Meg had been in Haiti. That had been tough, as she'd been close to his teenage sons. She'd been happy to take in Janelle and, with the internet and cell phones, Meg had easily enough stayed in touch with Aaron and his sons.

Only Pete hadn't seen Janelle in quite that way. A temporary situation was fine. Long-term? Not so much.

Pete had wanted to start a family a few years back. He'd lost his own father in a car accident, while still a young man. It had been an accident he'd barely survived. Meg had seen the pain some of the injuries still caused him. He should have been able to relate to Janelle's loss, but instead it seemed to remind him of his own loss—and his inability to deal with it ever since.

Meg winced at the reality of the first mention of having a child being almost eight years ago. She'd been dragging her heels, knowing it would curb her trips around the world. Of course that had been part of Pete's *having kids of their own* thing—to keep her at home. Now, with Janelle, Meg had been home more. Only Pete wanted his *own* family. Not broken pieces of Meg's brother's family.

Letting her head roll to the side, Meg stared at the trees, as they slapped against the side of the truck. The ruts in the road were deep, and every bounce brought on a mother of a headache. The bright blue of the lake twinkled invitingly through the trees. It wouldn't warm up for another month, and, with the horrific storms in this area over the last few years, the lake would likely be frigid cold right now.

"We're almost there, aren't we?" Meg asked, hating the fatigue coloring her voice. She glanced over at Pete to find him staring at her with a raised eyebrow.

"Yes, just a few more corners."

A grin flashed as a lighthearted idea swept through her. "Stop the truck. Janelle and I'll walk ahead." A laugh escaped. "We'll probably beat you there."

She didn't give him a chance to argue. She pushed open her door and jumped out of the still-rolling vehicle. She motioned to her niece in the back seat. "Come on, Janelle. Let's take a shortcut. The cabin is up just a little way."

"No, wait," Pete said. "We're almost there." The powerful engine revved, as the front end of the truck dipped into a rut again, the large tires spinning in the air before catching the ground. "Meg, get back here," he shouted. "You don't know where you are going."

"You said it's at the end of the road." She laughed. "How hard could that be?"

Janelle giggled and jumped out, slamming the door shut behind her. She ran ahead, catching up to Meg quickly. Of course she didn't walk like an adult; she bounced, with her jet-black curls flouncing around her shoulders. Meg smiled down at her. She was a beautiful kid. Her mother's Spanish ancestry had given her beautiful creamy skin and midnight-black hair, so different from Meg's own pink skin and brown hair.

"Come on. The road curves up again. We'll cut through the trees and be drinking tea before he even gets there." The two waved at Pete and bolted through the trees on the right. With Pete hollering his protest into the wind, Meg laughed and laughed, chasing Janelle into the stick forest. It felt good to sprint, and the laughter sent delicious feel-good vibes down her spine.

Without much natural light and in crowded conditions, the pines had grown up tall and skinny, forming a tight wall. Meg frowned. She hadn't remembered this much overgrowth.

It had been years, but still …

She could see the road as it turned up ahead, so it wasn't as if they could get lost. The truck labored on behind them. Pete had stopped yelling, and, with the fresh air blowing across her face and rifling through her hair, Meg was already feeling better. And her headache had magically disappeared.

She and Janelle slowed to a stroll, just enjoying the moment together.

"How long are we staying here?" Janelle asked, walking at Meg's side. The running and dodging of trees had put a rosy flush on her young cheeks.

"Just for two nights. We'll head back on the afternoon after that." Meg smiled down at her. She held out her hand, her heart giving a slight bump when Janelle reached out to hold it. While her niece may look like her mother, she acted so much like her father as a kid that it brought both pain and joy to Meg's heart. "It's a chance to get away and a chance to relax."

"Like a spa?" Janelle asked hopefully, looking around uneasily. "Please say yes."

Meg laughed. "Not quite, but it will be fun."

Janelle looked at her doubtfully. "Promise?"

"I promise." She looked down at the trusting soul beside her, Janelle now pointing at something off to the side. A steep hill was up ahead, and, about one-third of the way down, a tree had fallen, now hung up on a ledge. Heavy storms and the spring thaw could do that. Mother Nature still liked to call the shots in her world.

"What's that?" Janelle asked, pointing again to the left.

"Nothing." Meg wrapped her arm around Janelle's shoulders. "Just some downed trees, or rocks—maybe from a small mudslide after a heavy storm."

"No, not that—I mean that shiny white thing over there."

Meg let her gaze travel in the direction Janelle had pointed at, skimming past, hesitated, and zinged back to rest on the round white ball. Her breath caught in her throat. Her mind screamed, *No!* Her muscles tensed, and her gaze hardened.

Then she relaxed. It couldn't be. Not out here. This was just the side effects of her job. She saw bodies everywhere. "It's just a rock," she said reassuringly.

It *had* to be.

No way a body would be out here. Of course her rational mind immediately kicked in and snorted at the thought. Hunters went missing in the woods all the time. A lake was close by, and all kinds of weekend warriors and partiers came up to get away from city life. A body could definitely be here.

One body in particular.

But she so didn't need to see one this weekend. A part of her wanted to tug Janelle away. Maybe come back in another day ... or year, but ... the rest of her knew she couldn't do that. She had to find out what they were looking at. Her conscience wouldn't let her do less. Not to mention she'd spent more than half her lifetime wondering when a particular set of remains would be discovered. That she was once again in the same general area where her friend had gone missing? ... Her insides were shaking. It *couldn't* be.

She dropped Janelle's hand and told her, "Stay here. I'll take a quick look. Just stay here." She took a few steps in the direction of the white thing and glanced back to ensure Janelle remained in place. "I won't be but a second. Besides, if I'm any longer, Pete will win the race." With a big grin, she dashed across the short distance.

"No, don't." Janelle's panicked voice reached out to Meg.

Crap. Meg spun, her gaze darting back to see Janelle, frozen. Janelle, who had done nothing but deal with death for the last year. Janelle, who couldn't sleep and desperately needed this time away. Janelle, who didn't need the specter of death intruding here—because it had intruded enough already. And then she found her niece running toward her, fear clearly etched on her small face. Meg shouted, "Stop!"

Janelle came to a bumbling halt, her face scrunched up, tears forming in her eyes.

"Honey, don't come any closer. You might fall and hurt yourself. Plus this hillside could come down at any moment. I'm coming to you. Stay there."

Janelle sniffled, and Meg knew she had no choice. Since coming to live with Meg, Janelle was terrified of something happening to Meg and that Janelle would be left alone yet again. Taking out her cell phone, Meg quickly noted the GPS location of where she had stood.

"Auntie Meg?"

With one last glance at the rock, still too far away to be seen clearly, she started back to Janelle. "It's nothing."

With a big carefree smile, she grabbed Janelle's hand and ran up toward the road. The cabin had to be close. And she wanted it to be even closer by now. "Let's beat Pete!"

Laughing again and gasping for air, they crashed through the tight brush onto the road just ahead of the truck.

Waving at Pete, they picked up their pace and raced to the cabin.

And beat him.

AN UNEASY TRUCE settled inside Meg—for the moment. She couldn't get that *rock* out of her mind. There'd been something about it. She'd been too close to it to ignore it and yet too far away to have recognized what it was. She was afraid it might be so much more than a rock.

She needed to return and find it to confirm. But how could she, without alerting Janelle? And she'd have to tell Pete, which could be a really bad scenario. She'd have to choose her words carefully and pick her timing even better.

Somehow.

Pete had a hell of a temper, and she didn't want to set it off. She didn't fear him, but Janelle had had enough distress in her young life. Even a healthy debate with Pete these days disturbed her. That girl needed to rest and to heal. That Pete and Meg were having more issues than usual just made it that much harder to keep the atmosphere friendly, open, and supportive.

If only she could take another look. And make sure. Her mind wanted that to be a rock. They didn't need death to intervene here. Not when this trip was all about finding joy in life again. But her heart? … Well, her heart wanted to find her friend. She's been waiting for an answer for so long. What if she'd just found it?

"Earth to Auntie Meg?"

Meg started and then turned to smile at a frowning Janelle, peanut butter sandwich in one hand and an apple in the other. "How can you eat both of those together?"

Janelle grinned a big sticky peanut-buttery grin, then took a big bite out of the apple. Meg shuddered. She picked up an apple for herself and took a big bite.

"What were you thinking about?" Janelle asked, her mouth full.

Automatically Meg said, "Don't talk with food in your mouth." Then she winced, as she heard echoes of her mother's voice. "Sorry. That was instinct."

"Yeah, yeah." Deliberately it seemed, Janelle took an oversized bite and worked her jaws to munch it down to normal-size pieces, so she could swallow them.

Meg had to turn away. Before her brother's death, Janelle ate normal food normally. Now she seemed to delight in eating weird combinations in the most irritating ways. Was it to annoy Meg? Maybe. More likely it was for attention.

It had been a very tough year for them all.

Pete walked inside. "Did you leave anything for me?"

Meg pointed to the large sandwich sitting untouched on a plate. "That's yours."

She walked outside to sit on the top step. It was early in the afternoon, and they had two days ahead of them. Two days to rest. Two days to enjoy the great outdoors. Two days to not work.

Except ... she *had* to go back to that spot.

"Who wants to go fishing this afternoon?" Pete sat down on the step beside her, half of the sandwich in his hand, the other half on a paper plate. The first disappeared in three bites, as Meg watched him. He'd always been a big eater, but being outdoors seemed to amplify this. He picked up the second half and demolished that in a couple bites as well.

"Not me. I'd be playing games on my cell phone, but, oh, you wouldn't let me bring it." Janelle pouted in the doorway behind them. "Of course you and Auntie Meg could go fishing, and I could stay here and play games on *her* cell phone."

"Not going to happen." Meg worked to keep her voice neutral. "We came to get away from all that. Remember?"

"I saw you use your cell phone when we were racing Pete," Janelle accused, her voice disgusted and pointed. "So how come you brought your phone?"

Pete slid a sideways glance at Meg.

Damn. She fumbled for inspiration. "I wanted to take pictures."

"Then how come I can't have my cell phone so I can take pictures?" Janelle jumped over the few steps and strode down the path, muttering, "Unfair."

For all her best intentions, Meg couldn't hold back a heavy sigh.

"Are you sure you want to raise her?" Pete asked, yet again.

"Yes," Meg said firmly. "Besides, no other family member can." And Meg loved her niece.

"She could go to your brother. Or even into foster care." Pete nodded down the pathway. "At the rate she's going, she'll want to go in the system."

"Only because she doesn't know how bad it can be." Meg stood, irritated at Pete's suggestion. She was unwilling to get into another argument on that same issue again. Janelle was her niece, and Meg was happy to have her live with them. In truth, she was delighted. She missed her brother. The grief was a deep ache that never seemed to go away.

And Janelle had already wormed her way into Meg's heart. The months of getting to know her before her brother's death had been a gift. It would have been so much harder to have her come to them as a stranger. This way, the bonds of love and friendship had already been established.

Even if Janelle were lashing out in anger and saying some of the most hurtful things Meg could have imagined a child saying, she knew that Janelle was reacting to the terrible situation and the major change in her life. She understood, even if Pete didn't.

Still, finding herself in the middle of the two of them and the constant warring, the constant role of peacemaker was wearing Meg down.

Not for the first time, she wondered what final toll her brother's death would really take on her own life. She'd thought she'd been through the worst.

Now she was beginning to realize that the turmoil had only just begun.

"WHAT IF I don't want to go fishing?" Janelle asked, her body rigid, glaring at the sun reflecting on the lake water. "I hate boats. I hate the woods. This trip is stupid."

"That's enough." Anger vibrated through Pete's voice, as he snapped at her. "We came here to enjoy ourselves, not put up with more whining from you."

Meg winced and stared up at the sky. She closed her eyes at the soft sniffles from her niece. Janelle went from anger and disgust to tears and heartbreak in a snap these days. Right now, Meg had to admit she'd like a good cry herself.

"Then go without me," cried out Janelle. "I'll stay here."

"No." Pete's voice brooked no argument. "Get in. We're here. The least you can do is go out for an hour and give it a try." Disgust laced his voice, as he gazed down at Janelle. Pete had never been around kids much, and his first foray into them hadn't been easy. Meg was about ready to step in yet again, when Pete added, his voice softer, calmer, "You've never even been in a boat. How can you say you hate it? Come on. Just think of all the stories you can tell your friends when you get home."

Janelle perked up.

Meg closed her eyes on a whispered sigh of relief.

Another situation had been averted.

"Meg, you look tired. Why don't you have a nap, while we go out in the boat?"

Surprised, Meg stared up at Pete. Normally he would never voice such a suggestion. Inside, hope bloomed. An hour alone would be wonderful. She not only needed a break, she needed peace of mind. And that meant returning to the spot she'd marked with her GPS.

Pete stepped closer, whispering, "You know that she behaves differently when it's just her and me. Let me try this. Maybe we can get on a better footing. Just think. We might enjoy the weekend after all." He leaned over and kissed her gently.

Janelle, now with her life jacket on, climbed into the boat; then Pete pushed off. Janelle didn't look back at Meg.

Maybe that was a good thing. Meg was still dealing with Pete's first kiss in over a month.

In fact, it might have been much longer than that. Her heart was breaking, as she watched her partner and niece paddle out to the middle of the water. Just another sign of all that had gone wrong in her life. Maybe, just maybe, they'd hit a point where they could turn that around.

Feeling better than she had all day, she waved at Pete and strode back up the path to the cabin. She retrieved her cell phone and brought up the coordinates of the site she'd entered.

Knowing her time was short, she picked up a light jacket and a couple plastic food bags, wishing she had gloves with her. Hoping to avoid problems, she entered the coordinates of the cabin so she could find her way back. With a last look at the lake, where she could see Pete's and Janelle's heads close together, with rods in their hands, Meg took off into the woods.

The sun was bright and strong when she left the cabin, but, once into the deepest part of the treed area, the sun couldn't penetrate, and coldness ruled there. She closed her jacket and picked up the pace. If things blew up between Pete and Janelle, they could be back in half their allotted time. Meg had no excuse for not resting up. At least, not one she wanted to share with those two.

She checked her cell phone. She had to be damn close. Sure enough, the location should be just off to her left. She glanced around. The area did look familiar but not so familiar that she could have found this spot without having marked it first, as she approached it now from a different direction.

Please let this be a rock. She'd seen too many horrific things in her life to not check it out. Besides, death was her job. She dealt with it every day. But, as the last month had proven, dealing with dead bodies that you didn't know was a whole different process than dealing with the death of a family member. She'd never seen her brother in a morgue or dealt with the process of identifying his bones, like she'd done with bodies in Haiti and in so many other countries.

In those cases, the people had been dead a long time. The hole they'd left in the families was already closed and healed over. In many cases, the families themselves were deceased too.

Meg took several more steps to the left, shifted around a tree, and stopped. Yes. This was the right place. Taking her time to observe the area, she clambered over a fallen tree, feeling her fingers slipping deep into the moss growing over it. This was such a rich and different world from what she was used to.

Long green vegetation hung from branches high overhead. The leaves underneath her feet were spongy, decomposed. She knew the weather had changed over the last few years. What had once been dry and hazardous seventeen years ago had now become moist and musty. Heavy rainfalls and strong tree growth had blocked out the sun and had resulted in the ground becoming more boggy than dry in the lower-lying parts.

Looking up the steep incline behind the area, she could see an old mudslide had taken a corner of the cresting hillside above.

Carefully she worked her way closer to where she'd seen the odd bleached item. Her fingers clenched, making her realize how sweaty and nervous she'd become. *Please don't let this be human remains. Not this weekend.*

So much was at stake. And keeping death away from her personal life was hugely important right now.

She navigated under a low-hanging branch to a small hollow.

There.

She'd found it. Turning around, she checked to ensure she was still alone. She was, but what was it about being out in the middle of nowhere, in a dark and lonely place, to make someone worried that they were being followed? Her rational mind knew she was alone, but her emotions were all over the place.

Giving her head a shake, she surveyed the thick humus around her. Nothing looked askew from what she'd seen on her way over here. Now to double-check that all was good and to get back to the cabin, before the others noticed she'd left.

Still seeing nothing out of the ordinary, she closed the distance between her and the rock in two large steps and then bent down.

Shit.

Rocks didn't have structural sutures. Neither did they have occipital orbs on the front. This one did. It was definitely a skull.

Having almost convinced herself it would be nothing more than a weathered rock, she gulped for air, while her mind automatically cataloged the find.

Skull, small, a vertical forehead and rounded, so it was a female, likely Caucasian. The lower jawbone lay twisted slightly to the side. In spite of the moss and the humus, she noted the teeth were intact. They should get DNA and decent photographs to match dental records. And that's just what she saw on the surface. Tiny bits of material peeped through the dirt. There would be more, lots more.

She stared off into the horizon and swallowed several times. Her initial glimpse said a young adult female lay before her.

She closed her eyes and whispered, "Oh, dear God."

It couldn't be. And yet, … given the moss and the condition of the skull, these remains had been here a long time. But seventeen years long? Possibly.

Surely not, but inside she hoped so. *Please, let this be Cia.*

She pulled out her cell phone to check for reception. She had less than one bar. Like that would do much. Still, she had to try. She quickly grabbed the GPS location from her cell phone and sent it to Chad Ingram at the Seattle police station. Knowing the chance of her message getting through wasn't good, she didn't waste any effort typing a lengthy message.

Her fingers fumbling, she finally managed to get down the words: **Body at location, please come.**

Chapter 3

M EG CAREFULLY MADE her way out of the immediate area, then, unable to help herself, picked up her feet and ran back the way she'd come. Inside, her heart pounded, while, outside, her skin chilled with the breeze, as she raced from the scene behind her.

Damn it.

Why here and why now?

Pete would be so pissed off when he found out. He'd blame her. Last year he wouldn't have. He would have laughed it off and said, *Trust you*. Not this year. He had so many good points, been so accepting for so long, but Janelle's arrival had changed so much.

Or was it Meg who had changed so much? She had to admit that was very possible. She was not the same person she'd been a year ago either. And maybe she wanted different things herself now.

How much difference a year could make …

She reached the cabin, hearing Janelle's excited voice in the distance. Thankfully it was coming from the lake. Meg rushed into the cabin, quickly washed her face, checked her appearance for twigs and moss, and then strolled down to the water's edge.

"Well, don't you look happy?" she said to Janelle, with a big smile. Janelle's face split into a wide happy grin that made Meg's heart squeeze. It had been a long time since she'd seen her so carefree. At least Janelle had had this moment. And maybe Meg could keep her out of the worst of what was to come.

She had to. Janelle had been through enough.

"Did you get a nap?" Pete asked, with a relaxed look on his face.

Obviously the fishing trip had been a resounding success. She shook her head and lied, just a little. "I tried but couldn't, so I went for a walk instead."

He nodded, reached into the boat, and pulled out two still-flapping fish. "And we caught dinner. That makes you the cook."

"Wow!" Meg laughed, enjoying the moment. "I can do that, but you are so cleaning those things, before I take over."

"*Eewww*, clean them? That's gross." Janelle backed up several steps, her face twisting in revulsion.

Laugher rolled across the lake. With Meg's help, Pete pulled the boat alongside the dock and tied up. He handed the tackle box to Janelle, the rods to Meg, and then pulled out his pocketknife. "I'll take care of these now down here. You two can go on up. A cup of coffee would go good right about now."

"Yes, boss." Meg smiled and followed Janelle up to the cabin. The sound of Janelle's excited laughter lifted Meg's sadness. For now, Meg would take what joy she could.

By the time Pete had arrived with the fish nicely cleaned, the coffee was percolating on the stove, and Meg had a salad washed and ready to go.

"Oh, lovely." She turned on the burner, got the pan hot, and added the fish. "Dinner will be soon, so let's set the table and get washed up."

Janelle made a moue, but Meg shook her head. "You smell like the fish you helped catch. So wash with warm water here or go back down to the lake for a dip."

Cringing at the second idea, Janelle came to the sink and scrubbed her hands. "I don't really smell like those fish, do I?" she whispered to Meg.

Holding down the laughter to a minimum, Meg whispered right back, "You smell much better now."

With a beautiful smile, Janelle turned to set the table. Meg stared out at the late afternoon sun, dappling through the trees. Damn it. Why couldn't this perfect family moment be extended for the weekend? Maybe Chad hadn't gotten her message. She brightened. That would be great. The bones had lain there a long time, from what she'd seen. They could remain there another day without harming anyone.

With that happy thought, Meg sat down to dinner.

An hour after dinner, her cell phone beeped. Oh no. She reached for it, wishing she'd put it on Mute.

Call me.

That was it. She glanced up, both Pete and Janelle staring at her disapprovingly.

She offered a small smile. "Sorry, I thought I had it turned off."

"So turn it off now." Janelle frowned, as Meg continued to stare at her. "It's not fair that you have your phone, and I can't have mine."

Meg couldn't resist a small eye roll as she murmured, "Slightly different scenario, kiddo. This is work, not games."

"I thought you told them that you were going away and not to call." Pete's voice was tight, cold.

She sighed. "I did."

"And?" How could his voice, already chilly, become like polar ice with that one word? So smooth and so silky, it sent chills down her back. She groaned lightly. "Please, can we talk about this outside?" She nodded at Janelle, who sat quietly, watching and taking it all in.

He frowned, then relented. "Fine. Janelle, clean off the table. We'll heat up some water to wash dishes when we come back in."

That invoked an immediate response. Meg went through the door before the last of the screeching could be heard. Janelle hadn't had a problem with helping out and doing chores until she'd lost her father. Now gaining any cooperation from her was a challenge.

"That girl needs a stronger hand," Pete said brusquely, as he followed Meg out. "You let her get away with too much."

"I know," Meg admitted, "but, right now, she's got a lot to deal with."

"And rules will help her deal with it effectively." He leaned over the railing at her side. "She'll appreciate you for it later."

"Maybe." Moodily Meg stared at the darkening sky. "For all the beauty here, there is a dark underside to this place." She felt more than saw his sideways look at her.

"That came out of the blue. I think it's time you changed your profession. You are always so depressed and negative these days."

"Well, this time, I have good reason." It was now or never. She wouldn't get a better time. Calmly she collected her thoughts and then explained what she'd seen and how she'd gone back to check and had confirmed what she'd originally suspected.

He just stared at her, the whites of his eyes bright in the dim light. "You can't be serious?"

"Oh, very serious." She watched the emotions rush through his gaze. His features were always more closed than open, stern more than lighthearted. He'd been raised by a father who hadn't spared the punishment and had then died when he was seven. It had molded Pete into a strong but also hard man in his own right. Their decade together hadn't always been easy, but it had been rewarding.

"And what did you do about it?" he asked, his voice knowing and yet flat. As if realizing he'd have to make the best of it.

She winced. "I texted a cop in the Seattle department that I know."

"Texted?" He stared at her.

"Yeah." She held out her cell phone. "The reception is lousy. I was hoping the text would get through better than a call would."

"Was that the text you received over dinner?"

She nodded.

He sighed and looked up at the stars. "Was it really too much to hope you could leave work behind for a couple days?"

Now that wasn't fair. She hadn't planned on finding a skeleton. She hadn't gone looking for it; well, she had, but only to confirm what she'd seen the first time. She opened her mouth to protest, but then slowly closed it. It so wasn't worth it. She waited quietly.

"So is this person coming here? And, if so, when?"

"I don't know. He asked me to call, but there is no reception."

"Good. Then call when you get back home. Give us a chance to work on there still being an *us*."

With that, he turned and walked back inside, leaving her staring after him. Jesus. Were they that close to there not being an *us* anymore? Her throat seized up. She knew they were having major trouble; she just hadn't realized they were that close to the line.

And, if they were, how did she reconcile her own personal ethics with her personal life? And was her work, in this case, a deal breaker?

She should be calling Chad, and, if that didn't work, jumping in the truck and going back to town and raising the cavalry to come and help. But it was dark, and she didn't know the road. So it was foolish to leave at this time of night alone, and she didn't want to ruin her family's weekend. Considering that she had limited communication out here, would it matter if she waited overnight?

The remains had been there for years. Would another day or two make a difference?

"Auntie Meg? Are you coming inside?" Janelle's timid voice squeaked out into the darkness. Hell. Janelle, already dealing with enough right now, had been unsettled by Meg's exchange with Pete.

No. Given the circumstances, it wouldn't be wrong to wait until morning.

CHAD WAITED FOR a response at his desk, a desk he should have left hours ago, but it was hard when a haunting voice from the past contacted him about an event that had directed his path in life. And might solve the mystery he'd spent half his life trying to solve.

Had Meg even made the connection? She *must* have.

But then they'd all worked to forget that terrible night so long ago. Maybe Meg had done a better job than Chad had.

She'd certainly forgotten about him, until now.

He'd tried to forget her but had failed. So he'd tried to honor their history instead. A history that included Cia, who'd disappeared without a trace that afternoon so long ago. A brash young group of kids, who'd gone for a fun weekend trip, had come home a group of ravaged adults, forever changed.

Being older, more responsible, and having had a prior relationship with Cia, Chad had felt connected in a bigger way. He also felt guilty. He should have tried to track whatever he'd heard in the woods that afternoon. That he hadn't had eaten away at him for years. In his nightmares, someone was always spiriting an unconscious Cia through the woods, while Chad had hidden away like a coward.

That guilt sat permanently on his shoulders, breathing with him, as he went about his days, waiting for something, *anything*, to blow the case open.

And now it had.

Going to see Cia's parents back then, and trying to explain, had been the hardest thing he'd ever done. Her parents couldn't handle the loss of their only child. The mother had died of an overdose of prescription drugs not long afterward. And the father? Well, he'd called Chad almost monthly, after finding out Chad had been accepted into the police force, asking if he'd found out anything new. Then he'd had a heart attack a few years back, still not knowing what had happened to his daughter.

Chad didn't want the same sad end for himself. Until now he'd been afraid that that was where he was headed.

How could Meg send him that little bit of information and leave him hanging?

He returned to his computer to dig for more information on the location, on any missing persons, and on Meg herself. He'd kept an eye on her progress over the years. As if unable not to, he'd watched her grow into a stunning woman and a highly respected anthropologist in her field. He'd taken a secret joy in finding out that she'd stayed single, but it wasn't something he wanted to examine closer. He also knew she had a long-term relationship.

What the hell had she been up to lately?

And who else had she told about her find?

MACK PICKED UP his cards and took a look, a pair of kings to start. Not bad, not great, but enough to put him in the game. As he tossed in his ante, his cell phone buzzed.

Damn thing.

"Hey, Mack, you gonna play or talk to the little wife all night?" Frank smirked.

Mack snorted. "Ain't her." No way would she interrupt his poker night, unless the house was burning down, and she'd called everyone else already. "It's probably work."

"You're not on call, are you?" Joe asked, tossing his cards on the table in disgust.

"I'm always on call," Mack growled. "I'm getting out next year."

"Ha, you say that every year," one of the guys said.

Mack was used to the ribbing. The group had been meeting for over a decade now. He knew them better than his own brother at this point. He pulled out his cell phone. His gaze locked on the text message. His mood dropped rapidly. Shit.

He'd known this day would come. He just didn't know about the days after this one. In the beginning, he'd burrowed into this case like a bulldog, determined to prove one of the kids a killer and, therefore, to find the others innocent. But he hadn't been able to. He'd crossed a lot of lines back then and had been slapped back. He shouldn't have been on the case in the first place. He should have handed it off. Only he hadn't been able to. Not when his family had been involved.

But there'd been no answers. No closure—for anyone. For a long time, the worry and frustration had eaten at him. Then, with the passing of the years, it had slipped to the back of his mind. Until now ...

"Is it really possible?" he murmured, shock rippling through his beer gut. A deep sense of inevitability gathered underneath. Could they finally have found her? Cia Barnes's disappearance was one of the most frustrating, perplexing cases of his career and the most personally unnerving.

Chad's message included the coordinates in a link. He clicked it, his lips twisting at the technology Chad had used. It was typical of the younger generation and always made Mack feel like a dinosaur.

His stomach rolled, as he recognized the area. Of course he did. He owned a cabin up there, like a lot of other people he knew.

And he'd spent weeks searching for the missing girl. His nephews, three of them, had been part of that group. Idiots. He stared off into space, doing the math. It had to be close to fifteen years now. Or maybe even more. And every time he'd seen his nephews, he'd been reminded of it. Bruce had been badly affected by Cia's disappearance. The other two had been less so but still disturbed enough. The youngest boy had died in a car accident five years later. He'd always wanted to clear his name. The older one, now mostly alone, had gone quiet, and he'd changed. He had nothing to do with Mack's family anymore.

They'd all been badly affected back then. Lives had changed and not necessarily for the better.

As Mack stared at the map, a sense of certainty, readiness, settled in his gut. Maybe now he could find out the truth and could close a chapter in his own life.

THE NEXT MORNING Meg woke, feeling unrested. An early morning chill had her pulling the covers up to her chin. The old blanket had seen better days, kind of like the cabin. She lay quiet, staring at the open timber frame ceiling over the bed, waiting for the unpleasant memories to slip back into place, hidden away with the pain and the sense of loss she'd experienced so long ago.

Maybe Cia had drowned, and her body had sunk to the bottom of the lake? That had certainly been a popular theory at the time. But the divers couldn't find any sign of her. Then it was a deep mountain lake, spring-fed, and apparently bodies often sank and stayed down. There were other possibilities but never any proof for them.

The guilt was bad, but not knowing was ... the worst. Had Cia wandered off to join the hikers as a last-minute thought? And had she fallen and hurt herself so severely that she'd died? Or had someone forced her into the woods? Meg knew Chad blamed himself, but he hadn't been there at the time. He'd come back to find Cia gone, *but* she'd disappeared while Meg and Stephanie were swimming in the lake. Sure, they'd been deep in a discussion about their respective boyfriends at the time, but surely they would have heard a scream, a struggle, any outcry at all, if there had been one. They'd certainly heard Chad's shout.

But they'd heard nothing from Cia. *That* dark silence had persisted through Meg's nightmares. The boogeyman had nothing on Cia's attacker.

And that just led Meg back around to the situation again. They'd assumed that Cia had been kidnapped, stolen away in broad daylight. But they'd never had any proof. And just because Meg had found a set of remains close to where Cia had gone missing, it did not mean that these were Cia's. But Meg couldn't stop thinking they might be.

It would be a relief if they were. She needed closure on a most difficult time in her life. It was too late for Cia's parents, but others needed to know what had happened. Like the eight who'd survived the weekend. Not just Meg. She hoped that there would finally be answers and not more questions.

"Go back to sleep. Sleeping in late is one of the good things about a vacation." Pete's sleepy voice drifted up from under the covers, where he was buried. The country air held a chill that had her snuggling under and closer to him. Thankfully Janelle still slept.

Then she didn't have Meg's nightmares.

"You can't do anything about it right now, so sleep."

Meg rolled over and tried to do just that. And couldn't. She pretended to sleep. She did need rest, but inside, the tension coiled tighter and tighter.

A storm was breaking in her world. She knew it and couldn't prepare for it. But it was coming regardless.

Then she heard it.

A truck driving up the road toward the cabin. Would it turn in? The main road went on up and past the cabin turnoff.

Beside her, Pete stiffened, and the room chilled instantly. An eerie stillness took over. Her stomach knotted. Please, not yet. Please, not now.

She held her breath, listening, and, sure enough, the engine shifted, and the growl changed, as it slowed down. Even from inside the bedroom, she heard as the truck bounced over the ruts.

Her eyes closed. *Shit.*

Chapter 4

M EG SLIPPED OUT from under the covers, gave a slight shudder at the chill, and dressed quickly. It would take a few minutes for the truck to get to the GPS coordinates. She had no idea how long it would be before the driver would continue the drive to the cabin. If he even knew about this cabin ...

She hadn't called Chad back last night. She'd tried but couldn't get any reception.

Maybe he'd come to check out the location alone.

What she knew for sure was that, if Chad had gotten the message, he'd come. No way he could ignore a body found in this area, any more than she could.

She hoped he didn't ask the one question she didn't have an answer for. *Where had she gotten his phone number?* In truth, she didn't remember the origin, but she'd kept it close for many years. As if waiting for this moment ...

She should have told Pete about this part of her past a long time ago. It would be a little rough doing it now. Yet it was another thing she needed to do. Should have already done so, in fact. So why hadn't she? She mulled it over, as she made coffee. There'd been a lot she hadn't shared with Pete, too much really.

Had she just shoved it deep inside, never wanting to touch such a painful topic again? No one would blame her for that, except Pete. And he'd have a point. Partners shared their feelings, their fears, their lives. She'd traveled so much that, every time she'd returned home, there'd been almost a honeymoon air to their relationship. Then she would pick up and take off again. Why? And was she done with that aspect of her life now? She wanted it to be done with. She wanted that vagabond part of her to be settled enough to stay home and to raise Janelle. And to be happy with that life.

It needed to be, or Janelle would suffer. Meg winced, as another truth hit home. Janelle would suffer—like Pete had suffered.

Moodily she stared out the window. Life had been good to her, but had she been good to life? She hadn't been all that concerned with Pete's feelings every time she packed up and took off. She'd been a willing participant in a job that took her anywhere and everywhere.

Her last job in Haiti was a prime example. She'd gone over to retrieve a man's family, who had been killed in the massive earthquake over a year ago and buried in a mass grave. That job started out simple but said nothing about the horrifying twists that she and her team had experienced in the meantime. Poor Jade and Dane, the two of them had gone through hell, but, like the phoenix, they'd risen stronger and happier than ever.

Meg was jealous. And that was just stupid. She had Pete. They'd been together for years and years. They knew each other inside and out. And that's where she stalled. Because the truth was, she hadn't shared with him that defining moment that had sent her on her path around the world and away from him. So just how honest had she really been? How well did he know her? And if *she* hadn't shared—had he?

So how well did she really know him?

Her interior foundation, that of knowing she had been on the right path with the right person, cracked a little more. She bowed her head, struggling to breathe. Dear God, this hurt.

And it was far from over. This crack was just the top opening up, leading to the crevasse below.

Her life was splitting apart. ... All she could do was grab on to it and try her best to survive. It was now. It was here. It was time.

"Is the coffee ready?" Pete's heavy voice growled from the bedroom. "Sounds like that's the end of the sleep we'll get tonight."

She caught back a sob, rubbed her cheeks, and answered in a somewhat casual voice, "Yes, it's almost done." Walking back to the coffeepot, she heard the bubbles furiously working away inside. She turned off the burner, threw a cup of cold water inside to calm the grounds, waited a moment, and then poured two cups.

Picking hers up, she walked outside to the low-hanging veranda. The cool air bit her cheeks. It was the dead of summer, but, up here— with so many trees blocking the sunlight, adding in the winds, before the heat of the sun hit—it might as well be autumn.

Across the water, the sun had already crested the hills on the other side, but the long, warming fingers hadn't reached her yet. Too bad, she was cold inside and out. A buzz in her pocket had her reaching for her cell phone to read the incoming text.

Where are you?

She stared down at her phone, then out in the direction of the trees where she'd sent him. There really was no option. She quickly answered. **Coming.**

"Are you going to meet them?" Pete's voice spoke from the other side of the screen door. A barrier she couldn't miss.

With a quick nod, she said, "It will be easiest this way and the fastest."

"I'll stay with Janelle."

She turned to give him a thankful smile, didn't detect a response, sighed again, put down her empty cup on the railing, and walked away.

It took ten minutes for Chad's truck to come into view. At least she hoped it was his truck. She'd only caught sight of him a handful of times in the intervening years. They had a lot of history, and it didn't help that she'd loved him for a long time. She'd gone camping that fateful weekend, knowing he was the man for her and knowing that their relationship was strong enough to survive the upcoming college year apart. Knowing, no matter what, they could make it through the worst life could throw at them.

And, as if challenged, Cia had then disappeared, and that disastrous weekend had split them apart almost instantly. And it had kept them apart for years. So much for *forever*. ... So much for *knowing* anything ...

She had to admit to being excited about seeing who he was now. He'd been tall and rangy as a young adult, not yet fully grown into his height. He'd had promise though, and she hadn't been alone in seeing it. Chad had always been popular with the girls. Dark hair, dark eyes, with that whole bad-boy thing going on, he'd been the love of her life—until her life as she had known it had come to an end. They'd never officially broken up, but everything had come to a paralyzing halt.

She'd gone on to college alone. There'd been the odd phone call, the odd unexpected awkward meeting, and the reviews of the case for a few months, then less and less as time had marched on.

Until now.

Her footsteps slowed, as she approached the single vehicle. Was it him?

She took a deep breath, wiped her hands on her jeans, and stepped around the truck.

Only she couldn't see anyone.

She checked the coordinates on her cell phone and realized he'd likely parked and walked from here to the site. She followed.

"Megs?"

It was Chad. That same deep voice she remembered so well, that same old nickname. A surprising warmth washed through her, filling her heart. He'd been such a special friend. She turned slowly and saw him.

"Chad." Her smile was tremulous but real. "And it's Meg now."

He was older now, and more filled out, but still with that same charming grin splitting his face, giving her a glimpse of the young man she'd once known and loved.

In two strides he was at her side. His arms opened. She stepped inside, instinctively loving the way his arms closed tightly around her. For just a moment, she relaxed into his comforting embrace. For just a moment, she let herself slide back in time—and enjoyed the closeness. He squeezed her gently before stepping back, his hands on her upper arms, holding her still, so he could look at her. His gaze warmed, as he stared down at her. "Damn, you look good."

So did he. She couldn't believe the heat churning up her insides. She hadn't had anything to do with him in so long, and yet it was as if they were back at the beginning of that fateful summer, when they'd been so in love.

She opened her mouth to speak, but he snatched her up again and squeezed her tight. When she was freed this time, the words exploded from his mouth. "I couldn't believe it when I saw your text. Nothing like spiking my attention with the one hope I'd lived with all my life." He stopped, then corrected himself, quietly added, "We've *all* lived with."

Tears came unbidden to her eyes. She sniffled slightly. "So true, that nightmare has haunted my days and nights and colored my actions, even when I wasn't aware of it."

He shoved his fists into his jeans pockets. "I hear you." He stared off into the trees, his Adam's apple bobbing up and down several times. "When I think back to all the times, when I wondered, worried, and felt that I could have, should have, done more ..." He ran a hand through his hair. "I just hope this is her."

"No way to tell yet." Meg walked closer to the site. "Did you see it?"

"No. I was just searching the area, taking pictures before entering the scene." He glanced at her. "You're the expert in this field."

Her smile slipped. "I had to do something." She glanced at him.

"Like you."

Their gazes met in understanding, and, on that note, they approached the area cautiously.

Standing on the one side of the moss-covered tree lying in front of them, she pointed out the gleaming white item in the half light. "That's the skull showing."

"And you've checked it?" he called back, as he took several large strides forward and then squatted. "Sorry. Of course you have."

She approached but stayed off to one side. She allowed her gaze to roam the area slowly, as she searched for more bones, clothing, items, ... anything to identify the body and to understand what had happened. The ground was a muted display of greens and browns, and, in the dim light, they blended together, making everything harder to see.

"What can you tell me from the little bit you've seen?"

Taking a deep breath, she verbalized her instant cataloging of the scene. She waited a beat. "You know this is likely to be a crime scene." He shot her a direct look. She nodded. "We're all expecting that Cia died by someone else's hand."

"And yet we don't know for sure that this is her." He studied the ground around the skull, as Meg watched.

What appeared to be years' worth of organic matter decomposing to rich humus hid most of the evidence.

"And it could be a dumping ground or even an accidental death." He straightened. "I've already called help in. A team is on the way."

"Of course you have." She laughed, even while shaking her head. Chad had always been extremely proactive. "Even without seeing the body."

"I didn't need to, as I did my research on you instead."

Her eyebrows shot up. "Really?"

"If you say a body's here, then I'm sure there is." He straightened. "Now tell me that it's Cia, and I'll do everything I can to find the bastard who did this and to hang him from the nearest tree."

Except that he wouldn't. He wanted to. She wanted to. But they were both professionals, and, unfortunately, taking the law into their own hands couldn't happen.

"So tell me. Is it her?" He stood and stared into her eyes, as if willing her to give him the answer he wanted to hear.

"Not so fast," she said in a gentle voice. "I can't identify her just like that." She shrugged. "I can tell you this female is Caucasian and is of the approximate age as Cia was when she vanished, but beyond that ..."

"That's a good start. And it says that it *could* be Cia." He glanced down at the gleaming skull. "Are you sure there's nothing else you can tell me?"

"Well, this girl didn't die from a bullet to her forehead," Meg quipped, recognizing her need to ease a difficult situation with humor. In the distance, she heard the sound of approaching vehicles.

"There is that." He pinned her with a direct look. "Damn, Meg. After all these years, what are the chances?"

"My vote?" Meg thought about location, the length of time the skull had likely laid here, the thickness of the humus. While she knew it was just guesswork at this point in time, there were her instincts, her gut feeling. Abruptly she said, "I think it's her.

His breath whooshed out. In a low voice, he added, "So do I."

CHAD WATCHED MEG leave. He understood she was here with her family. And that felt wrong to him. The last time she'd been here, she'd been with him. But that wasn't the only thing different. Still tall and slim, Meg had revealed a calm maturity now, a sense of going through hell and coming out stronger for it. He'd seen her name mentioned in several articles and always heard her spoken of with respect.

He was proud of her. She'd become a hell of a woman. Then he always knew that she would turn out to be someone special, that she would mature into the promise he'd always seen in her. Cia's disappearance had been difficult, but Meg had gone on to do well regardless.

Chad's life, meanwhile, had been waiting for this moment. And everything else had been put on hold. He'd never married, never had a family. Hadn't done the traveling he'd wanted to or built that log house he'd always planned to build. Everything had been consigned to the category called *later*.

A life interrupted. He sighed and ran a weary hand down his face. Maybe now he could pick up the threads and carry on.

Still staring in the direction where Meg had disappeared, he wondered how she'd been able to pick up her life and to carry on. Instead of it being something he should be happy about, it made him edgy. As if she had no right. And that was just stupid.

Being female, she hadn't come under the same cloud of suspicion

DALE MAYER

as he had. Although being *the replacement girlfriend*, as one cop had called Meg back then, she'd certainly been heavily questioned.

Their relationship hadn't survived Cia's disappearance. None of their relationships had. Six guys and three girls had been in that original group. Three pairs and three spares, and they'd all known each other. All had spent a lot of time together. He'd trusted them. Now he could barely remember the details of their lives.

Yet it felt right having Meg here at this time. Her finding the body had to do with that whole life-interrupted thing.

He heard the sound of a truck in the distance. Good. That should be his team. He wanted to get moving on this scene and to find the answers and, once and for all, put Cia's case to rest. So he could finally get on with the rest of his life.

MEG HATED TO leave Chad and the site, but she wanted to check up on Janelle. Make sure that Pete hadn't gone fishing and left her to wake up on her own.

Besides, Meg couldn't do more at the site now that the team had arrived. Chad had been fully engrossed with taking care of business. She wanted to be a part of that team but hadn't been asked. Better she took care of things here first.

Her empty coffee cup still sat on the railing, where she'd left it. Almost a message. As if it waited for her, just as Pete had done all those years.

Another heavy sigh slipped out. Seemed to be all she did these days. There was so much trauma and so many adjustments. But such was her life right now.

Pete had put up with a lot from her. She could only hope he'd put up with a little more.

She walked inside the cabin and thankfully found both Pete and Janelle sound asleep. She couldn't deny the sense of relief at not being questioned about being gone so long or about bringing her work once again into their home. And there was coffee. Feeling that she'd been given a reprieve, she filled her cup and snuck back outside to enjoy it.

Once settled on the veranda, Chad filled her mind. He looked the same. Older, more mature, harder even, as if he'd seen a lot more of the darker side of life than most people had. Then so had she. They were so much alike; even the paths they'd taken had been along the same lines. What they'd had back then had been so special and so short-lived that she felt like she'd been looking to repeat it ever since—but hadn't found a way of doing it.

She frowned and stared down at her swirling coffee. Life with Pete had been good. It was just different. It didn't matter if it hadn't been the same. Pete was here and now.

Chad and she had gone their own ways a long time ago. It was not as if they had a relationship to go back to, not anymore.

Melancholic and borderline depressed, she couldn't fathom a way forward.

Then she heard the sound of more vehicles. She wondered which anthropological specialist they'd brought in and realized yet another truth. She wanted—no, needed—to be part of that team. She *had* to be involved, to know for sure that no mistakes were being made and that no shortcut had been taken that would stop them from getting to the truth.

And yet she had no right to be involved. She shuddered.

Her cell phone rang. "Hello."

"Are you busy?" Chad's strong voice came through, loud and clear, as if he were standing beside her.

She almost looked to see if he was. "Not more than I was a few moments ago when I left you. Why?"

"I need an anthropologist. The team came without an archaeologist or an anthropologist. They've been trying to find one who is available but aren't having much luck."

"I want to," she answered slowly, knowing he needed a specialist to collect the remains and to work on their identification, "but that might not be a good idea, given our potential connection with the victim."

"But we don't know who the victim is at this point. There are many missing women cases. And your name on this list of consulting experts came up, *and* you're here on the spot. And there is the weather factor, with a storm possibly tonight. We have limited options. If you can give us a hand collecting the remains and the evidence, it would be a great time saver. The longer the remains stay here, the less chance we have of collecting all the evidence. And, once the media find out, more people will be here, digging around ..." He left the rest hanging.

She understood. The media would latch on to the discovery within hours, if not sooner, and then there'd be the curiosity seekers. The team must collect everything before then.

It's what she'd hoped for. The opportunity she hadn't expected to be offered.

"I'm on my way." She disconnected and stood.

"Where are you going?" Janelle's soft voice crept through the screen door. Meg instinctively hunched her shoulders. With yet another sigh, she opened the door, placed her mug on the counter, then hugged her niece. "Some men need my help for a couple hours. It's just down the road. I won't even need to take the truck."

She peered into Janelle's eyes, hoping she understood and was okay with it. But a maturity well beyond her twelve years stared back at her. "You found a body down there, didn't you?"

Meg wanted to lie, wanted to keep death out of the cabin, only it had already crept in. She whispered ever-so-softly, "Yes. I did."

There was no change in Janelle's gaze, but she hung on Meg's every word.

"I will be back as soon as I can. I promise."

"Take me with you."

The plea was so soft and hesitant, it almost broke Meg's heart. She gathered Janelle into her arms. "I can't, honey. That's no place for a child."

Or for a niece who had too much death in her life already.

Janelle pulled back, her body vibrating in outrage. "I'm not a child anymore, Auntie Meg."

"I know." And Janelle had been through so much that she'd grown up more than most other kids her age. "But in the eyes of the law you are." She smiled down, tugging a stray strand of hair off Janelle's face. "I'll be as fast as I can."

Janelle's gaze bored into Meg's, as if by will alone, she could force Meg to return faster. "Promise?"

With a lopsided smile, Meg promised.

"And, if she isn't, we'll go down there and drag her back up here." Pete's smooth voice spoke from the living room behind them. Still tucking his shirt into his jeans, he nodded at Meg, adding in a slightly colder voice, "So be quick, or we'll be the first two of your curious public."

She winced. It was so not the role she wanted Janelle to be in. And she understood Pete's warning. Not liking it, but knowing it was the best she'd get under the circumstances, she dropped a kiss on Janelle's cheeks and headed for the door.

Only as the screen slammed behind her did she note that she hadn't kissed Pete goodbye. Again.

Outside in the fresh air, racing down the path to the work she loved, she could leave behind the anger, the sense of oppression, the uncomfortable changes that life had forced upon her. She loved both Pete and Janelle more than life itself, but that life had become incredibly wearying lately.

She could only hope better times were coming.

And maybe this was just what she needed. Inside, a building excitement took over. What if they'd finally found Cia? Meg could leave that part of her life behind.

And finally get on with her future.

Chapter 5

C HAD AND HIS team were waiting for her.

She nodded to the others, listened to his brief introductions, then went to the truck. They'd brought suits and supplies. She geared up, grabbed her gloves and several tools, and moved carefully to the remains. On the way, she murmured to Chad in passing, "Thanks."

"You're welcome. Figured you would like to be in on this one," he said, with a knowing look in his gaze.

She paused, gave him a quick glance. "In all ways," she said, then bent down and got to work.

The work over the next few hours was painstaking. As she concentrated on the remains, Chad stayed close by but out of her way, while the rest of the team went about mapping the scene, photographing, and marking finds. The bones were scattered and, once located, were marked. Trees had fallen over time in a crisscross pattern, keeping the bones relatively contained.

Meg worked on the torso. Under and surrounding the rib cage, tiny rotten pieces of material poked through the surface debris. As Cia might have been only in a bathing suit at the time of her disappearance, that would also fit. Some materials had decomposed entirely, others only partially. Some had never deteriorated. The lab would determine more. The original color of the material was no longer identifiable, having been stained some kind of deep woodsy color.

All the moss that grew on and around the bones had to be collected and returned to the lab to confirm no evidence was in the foliage. The team had set up commercial lights to assist in the collection process, giving a weird sci-fi glow to the area.

In spite of her best efforts to remain neutral, her heart pounded as she lifted each piece of bone and examined it, looking for answers. The bones had been cleaned by Mother Nature, giving further proof of the length of time the body had been exposed to the elements.

"The remains are scattered. We'll need to search for all the pieces." She glanced around, looking for other markers. Considering the location and the fallen trees, that made sense. There were signs of animal activity, and that was to be expected too. "Both femurs are missing."

"We have a femur over here," called out one of the other techs from beside her. Straightening, Meg winced as she realized how long she'd been bent over in that position. She stretched slightly, gave a slight moan, and then stepped back to hand over the last of the bones she'd tagged to be moved to the truck. There was more to do, but the work was moving quickly. She glanced at her cell phone. Not bad timing; even Pete shouldn't be too upset at her for this.

She made her way over to where the femur lay. Picking it up carefully, she noted the head appeared to have fused. That placed the victim between the ages of eighteen and twenty-four. Cia had been eighteen at the time of her disappearance. Given the length of time, which she could only estimate …

Chad held up a tape measure—their gazes meeting. He quickly measured the length of the femur, while she did the mental calculations. "The victim was right around five feet tall."

A long hard breath shuddered free from Chad. "And Cia was five feet tall—*a hair over*, as she liked to say."

Meg nodded. She closed her eyes. Then straightening her spine, she said, "Let's finish this."

The excavation was time-consuming to do properly. With the evidence of animal activity around the remains, Meg wanted to ensure she had every bone possible. Two more of the ribs lay at her feet off to the right, and a couple pieces of the spine were on top of each other to the left.

The skull was next. She moved it onto a large sheet and examined it carefully. She kept her feet firmly in place to avoid shifting anything, just in case she lost something important. She found no head wounds, no indication of a blow to the head as the cause of her death. There were small animal marks, but the top of the skull was amazingly undamaged. The lower jaw bone, in similar shape, was placed next to the skull. She was happy to see large healthy teeth and even happier to see the molars. Not only could they pull DNA from them for identification but they certainly put the age of the victim within the seventeen to twenty-two range, which was another point in favor of these bones being Cia's remains.

As Meg scooped up the debris from around the head, a smaller white bone caught her eye. She lifted it carefully and held it up, her professional eye immediately understanding that she was holding the hyoid bone.

The breath gushed out of her chest, and, for a moment, she couldn't breathe. It was too early to make a formal cause of death, and she, for all she wanted to be in on the examination of these remains, might not be the one to find the official cause of death. Yet this bone gave her a lead in that direction. It had been fractured.

And it answered one question—in her mind, at least.

Chad leaned closer. "What did you find?"

She looked over at him, her eyes wide, knowing the sheen of tears in them was unmistakable. An eerie silence filled the air. Several of the team walked closer, as if understanding something important was about to happen.

"This victim"—she swallowed back Cia's name—"was strangled." Then she couldn't help herself from whispering, "Cia was murdered."

CHAD STARED AT the small bone in Meg's hands. He swallowed hard. They'd known it. There'd really been no other answer.

But knowing it wasn't the same as proving it. And he knew it was too early for conclusive identification, but, given everything they knew so far, he was sure they'd finally found Cia. And that made his spine freeze. At this moment in time, everything locked down, as he realized what had happened here seventeen years ago.

His gaze fastened on Meg's, knowing that she was thinking the same thing. The sadness in her eyes, the inside knowledge of what Cia had gone through—that same knowledge was streaming through his mind. Strangulation wasn't easy to do effectively. Cia, so tiny and petite, would have fought like a tiger, claws and teeth if she had had to. But, given her size, there wasn't much hope of her throwing off an adult male attacker.

Chad nodded, breaking their locked gazes. "Okay. Let's finish this. Let's take Cia home."

WITH CHAD'S WORDS echoing in her mind, Meg returned to the job at hand, focused and determined to do her part in solving this mystery. Her heart hurt from Cia's pain and the sense of fear that Meg could swear still lingered over the area, so strong and thick, as if she could reach out and touch it. Meg knew it was the memories, the inside knowledge that made this job so much more difficult for her.

But the same inside knowledge also made her the right person to be here—helping to take their friend back home.

The hours went by, as Meg worked on with incredible thoroughness—to the point of overkill. But she refused to let up. She didn't dare miss anything.

As the last of the bones were collected and packed for transporting, she walked back to where she'd found the skull and bent down for one last look. Something glinting below the skeleton suddenly caught her eye.

She crouched lower and carefully scooped up the next layer, including what had caught her eye. It was a necklace. Using her fingers, she gently tried to clean it, but it was as organic looking as the debris around it. It was a small simple heart-shaped pendant. She remembered all the girls wearing them back then. Turning it over, she found something inscribed on the back of the heart.

"What did you find?" Chad dropped down beside her. His breath caught, as he saw what she held in her hand. His voice hoarse, urgent, asked, "Can you read it?"

Using a flashlight, she tried to read the inscription. She could barely make out the words. *Oh God.* Her heart squeezed, and her breath locked deep inside.

Wordlessly she held it up into the light, so he could read it for himself. He whispered reverently, "*For Megs. Love you always.*"

They stared at each other. Pain, fear, and understanding filtered into his gaze.

"Meg, is that yours?"

She swallowed hard, closed her eyes, then opened them to look directly into his worried dark eyes. Then she nodded and whispered, "I think so."

CHAD LET HIS gaze wander over Meg's devastated face. Tears were in her eyes. He hadn't thought about the cost to her personally of taking on this job. He'd been thinking of the cost to her *not* being involved. From what he knew about her, from his research and the articles written on her, she was very exacting in her work. She was a perfectionist that coaxed the most from the evidence. He needed that, both professionally and personally.

And now he'd hit a snag he could never have foreseen.

But first things first; he motioned at Larry to take over the chain of evidence and to document everything that had just happened. With one last glance at the necklace, he nudged Meg into putting it carefully in the bag, where it was sealed and written on for the evidence tracking.

He tugged her to her feet and walked her back out of the circle. "You did your job. Let them finish this up."

"You know my being here is a problem now, don't you?" She stared at him, dazed and unfocused.

Shit.

Who could have prepared for this? The best thing was to follow procedure and to carry on. It's what they all did best. Process the evidence and see where it led them.

And if it led them to the woman standing corpse-like in front of him, then he'd follow it there—and find a way to clear her name. The prosecutor would say Meg had been wearing this necklace when she'd fought with Cia, as she had killed her. The necklace had fallen off during the struggle, unnoticed by Meg at the time.

Chad had no doubt she'd had nothing to do with Cia's disappearance. Stephanie had also backed up Meg's statement that she had never left her sight. In other words, they'd provided each other with alibis. And that could be another problem.

He watched in silence, as the techs continued working the crime scene.

Why would that necklace have been here? After all these years …

"When did you notice it was missing?"

Meg glanced at him, her gaze unfocused, as if churning back through the memories. "I don't know. I don't remember a time that sticks out." She shrugged helplessly. "Who can remember that long ago? I missed a lot of stuff back then. We packed in a hurry, left in chaos."

How true. Back then Chad had been taken to the police station. He didn't even know who'd packed up his stuff. Just that he'd gotten it back at some point in time. It had been hell. She was right. Who could remember?

And it was a small, relatively insignificant item that could have been removed at any time. Before Cia had gone missing or afterward. Cia could even have taken the necklace to wear herself. Either borrowed it, as the girls had often done before, or stolen it from Meg herself. In fact, if Meg had it there at the camping trip, everyone had access to it. But why bother?

Unless Cia had taken it herself ... or someone had wanted to implicate Meg.

And that meant one of their camping group—who else would have known about it? And that was just wrong. He'd sworn that his friends were innocent at the time.

But he was older now and, hopefully, wiser.

He would swear Meg had nothing to do with Cia's disappearance, and Chad knew he hadn't. That left six others. Could he, in good conscience, *still* say they were all innocent?

It had been so much easier back then to band together and to choose to believe in a stranger abduction. Chad knew now that those were the hardest kinds of abductions to deal with. Strangers who picked random victims for weird reasons that lurked in their minds. This made it hard to track them and even harder to find a pattern in their behavior, making them almost impossible to catch.

With nothing surfacing in the case over the years, the stranger abduction theory had seemed more and more likely. But was it?

Did the necklace even change anything? Or just confirm that someone had it in their possession. Hell, for that matter, Meg could have lost it while they were all out searching for Cia. "Could she have borrowed the necklace from you?"

Meg frowned, her head tilting to the side, as she considered the concept. "It's possible. We shared clothes and jewelry and make-up all the time. I'm not even sure why I would have had it with me that weekend. Josh gave it to me."

"Josh? Then Cia wouldn't wear it, would she? She was going out with Josh at that point."

"I know. But she'd been bugging him for jewelry, so maybe wearing it was to put pressure on him. As if saying, *See? I know you bought this for Meg. Prove you love me more by buying me something better.*"

"And of course the last line, with the overtones of *See? I know you loved her more than me. This just proves it. You didn't give me a necklace.*" He couldn't quite keep the bitterness out of his voice. Cia had been a lot of things—fun, pretty, smart—but she'd been conniving to boot. She wanted things, expensive things, all the time.

"It's not an expensive piece, just a trinket really. I kept it because Josh gave it to me." She kicked the dirt at her feet.

Chad felt his heart start. "You weren't upset when you broke up with Josh, were you?"

She gazed at him, blinked, then finally understood. "Oh no, I wasn't. It was not good for either of us. Yet he was my first serious boyfriend. I wanted to honor that time in my life, and so I kept it. And obviously I didn't care that much because I can't remember losing it or even being aware of losing it."

That sounded like the Megs he knew. And his mind immediately wondered if she'd done anything to honor their relationship?

And, once that thought entered his mind, he couldn't let it go. They'd been more-than-good together. It had been the best relationship he'd ever had. He'd had several since then, but they hadn't been the same. They hadn't been Meg. How sad was that?

And why was that?

He hated that instinctive answer in his head, in his heart. Because his was a life interrupted, to be continued, so to speak. It was way down the road, waiting for when Cia came home.

As he stared around at the organized chaos working to claim Cia, he wondered what that meant for him, … for Meg, … for them … now.

MEG RETRACED HER steps to the cabin, walking slowly, carefully, afraid a misstep would send her world listing again. It felt as if it mattered where she placed her feet. Somewhere along the line she'd gone off the track of the life pathway she'd expected to be on. It had taken a hard right, and she'd forgotten to stay on course.

Now she felt suspended, weak, hurt, and injured in ways she couldn't understand. Her thoughts and emotions were left hanging.

Chad had to follow the evidence, and he would. She knew that. It was also the right thing to do.

The necklace had been a shock. It *was* hers. At least she thought it was. The inscription stated her name. And she had no reason to believe another Megs was in the vicinity. Or another Megan, for that matter. She'd been Megan all through school, but her friends had called her Megs. A nickname her mother had abhorred. So, of course, Meg had encouraged its use.

After Cia's disappearance, Meg knew there was no going back to Megan or Megs. That was a time of schoolgirls and innocence.

She'd lost that.

Then there was the whole guilt thing. Her adult mind knew she hadn't done anything wrong, but a part of her was stuck in teenage mode from that time and couldn't shake off the guilt. She'd been there. On the spot. At the time, she and Stephanie had been deep in gossip. So involved that Meg hadn't seen Cia go to her tent or even leave for a walk. Meg certainly hadn't noticed Cia being carried away.

That was the worst thing. How could someone disappear right from under their noses without anyone noticing?

She approached the cabin silently, wishing her heart wasn't so empty and her head wasn't so full.

No sounds came from the cabin. It would be good if Pete had taken Janelle fishing to get her mind off what Meg was doing. Maybe she should have lied to Janelle, but the child was old enough to understand what Meg did for a career.

She opened the cabin door and entered. The place was empty. Sighing, she snagged an apple from the cooler and returned to the veranda and followed it around to the other side of the house. She could see out onto the lake, but the boat was nowhere in sight. She walked to the lakeshore and still saw no sign of the boat. Good. Maybe they'd enjoy their trip and come back happy.

Happy was something *she* hadn't felt in a long time.

She strolled down to the end of the dock, enjoying the way the water lapped at the edge of the wood. Once at the end, she surveyed the lake, looking to see her family.

Only there was no sign of them.

Unable to stop the jittery feeling inside, she walked farther along the beach, climbing over rocks and ducking under low-lying branches. She could try texting Pete, but he'd been the first to suggest they leave all electronics behind this weekend. So chances were good he'd been the first to ditch his. He hated the damn thing anyway. Not much of a sacrifice for him.

For her on the other hand, … yeah, she loved all electronics and made no excuses. She used as much up-to-date technology for her work as she could, used cloud-based storage for everything all the time and always stayed connected, both professionally and personally.

She was a creature of today's world. Pete was a bit out of the loop in today's technological world. Janelle had been born in this era and didn't understand that the tech hadn't always been here. In fact, she complained when the internet was slow, when her songs wouldn't download fast, when her pages wouldn't load immediately.

Meg chuckled. Janelle was a child of the instant-gratification generation. Meg could only wonder what the next few generations would be like.

With perfect timing, her cell phone rang. Glancing around guiltily, Meg answered it. "Hello, Chad."

"Are you okay?"

She had to stop and think before answering slowly. "I can't say that I am fine, but I am holding."

"Good." The obvious relief in his voice warmed her. "I was worried about you. Finding that necklace really threw you."

"Didn't it throw you?" she asked quietly, only a tiny bit of bitterness leaking through. "Didn't you, for one moment, wonder if it had come off in a struggle that ended Cia's life and that I hadn't known about the loss at the time?" Even as the words burst loose from her, something inside her recognized the hard ball of fear that she'd never quite managed to let go of. Instead she'd kept it stuffed down deep inside. And now there was no holding it back. Torrential waves of emotions rolled over her, making her bend over, gasping for breath, trying hard to hold back the contents of her stomach.

It was the fear that she would be found guilty of something she *hadn't* done. She'd been so afraid that somehow someone would find her guilty.

"No." The response blasted through the phone, instinctive, reactive, righteous. "I definitely did not think that. You, more than anyone else, should know what I went through that weekend. I *know* you had nothing to do with it."

She had gone through so much hell back then that she thought she would never sleep again. She knew she hadn't done this horrible thing. She also knew Chad hadn't. But they'd always worried they'd go to jail for a crime they hadn't committed, as so many other people had.

Still, his natural response, the absolute belief in his voice, was a soothing balm to her raw emotions. A slight bitterness continued to leach through her soul nevertheless—albeit now at a slower rate. "But your knowing won't stop the cops from looking at me sideways and from digging deep into my life to see if they can find a way to pin this on me."

"I'm a cop. Remember?" Chad took a deep breath. "I know this is tough. It's tough for all of us. And ... I will admit that it'll get worse, before we can solve the case and put it away forever."

Meg added, "You shouldn't even be working this case. Your bosses won't let you. You know that, right?" Meg wiped her dry eyes. There should be tears; they were inside her soul, just not ready to fall yet. "It's stupid. I have wanted to find her for so long. I have needed closure on that part of my life, ... and, now that it's here, now that we might have found some answers, ... I don't want to go there. I'm afraid this is a Pandora's box, and I'll regret ever having opened it."

"Don't say that. We didn't do anything to her, but we've been punished, and have been punishing ourselves, as if we had. This is our chance to get at the truth. We owe it to ourselves. And we owe it to Cia. She didn't deserve whatever happened to her." The force and conviction in his voice had Meg straightening her body and running her hands through her hair.

"I know. I have to believe this is for the best, but it's hard." She sighed and admitted, "I've felt so alone all these years. Finding her brought everything slamming back."

"You are not alone. You have your family. Don't isolate yourself. Share this with them."

She stared out over the lake and wondered about that. In fairness to Pete, he hadn't been given entrance to that part of her life. She'd shoved her history into the same damn hole as the rest of the mess. "Pete doesn't know."

Silence.

She winced, understanding the myriad questions her statement must bring up. She was being forced to examine a few of them herself. Why hadn't she shared? And, if she couldn't share before, why, after ten years, couldn't she share now? And was it Pete? Or was it her? And the big question—what would she do about it going forward?

"I'm sorry."

That surprised her. She frowned. "Why?"

"Because this is too big for you to hold inside. You need someone to hold you, even just for a moment. Troubles shared are easier troubles to bear."

"And do *you* have someone to share this with and to hold you at night?" This time the silence was awkward, uncomfortable. She bowed her head and pinched the bridge of her nose. "I'm sorry," she said softly. "I had no right to ask that."

"It's fine." But, when he spoke again, it obviously wasn't fine. "I have had several relationships since you, but none of them strong enough to last. And, like you, none of them were close enough to share this with."

"We've always been alone, haven't we? Always waiting, always isolated." Now there was no holding back the tears in her eyes. Tears for the lives impacted on and destroyed by Cia's disappearance. When he didn't answer, her anger flared at him, at herself, and at the situation. She snapped, "Haven't we?"

The slow, deep exhale whispered through the phone, mingled with and supported his soft answer. "Yes."

Chapter 6

M EG DIDN'T KNOW how long she been sitting on the end of the dock. She should have been making something to eat. Or, if she was lucky, Pete would have caught more fish for her to cook. Truly she didn't care either way.

Her mind was fixated on the necklace. What she had deliberately withheld from Chad was now a nasty, festering suspicion inside her. For all Cia's good qualities, the fact remained that she had some not-so-nice qualities as well. For Meg, it was wrong to say bad things about dead people, but there it was. And Cia had always been jealous of Meg and of what Meg had had.

It wouldn't be the first time Cia had *borrowed* something of Meg's. Also it would have twisted the knife into Josh, something else Cia had liked to do.

Not for the first time, Meg realized that, had Cia lived, Meg would not have stayed friends with her. They hadn't been good friends even then. They'd been part of the same group. And that was different. There'd been an air of finality to that last summer. Meg had known that they were going their separate ways, once college had started. She couldn't even remember each person's plans. Theirs had probably changed too. Meg had planned on becoming a dentist. She laughed at that now.

Chad had planned on becoming an engineer, along with one of his best friends, Josh. So much had changed …

The soothing sound of splashing water brought her attention back to the lake. Pete and Janelle. At last. … As she glanced at her cell phone to check the time, she realized she'd only been waiting a half hour. Not bad at all. As she watched them come closer, she realized Janelle appeared to be dozing, her head resting on her arm, the other trailing in the water. Pete, in front, was rowing smoothly and steadily. This was his favorite type of relaxation.

He was lucky to indulge as often as he could. The cabin had been his uncle's, and he'd left it to Pete in his will. There'd been such a wealth of satisfaction on his face, when the property had been signed over to him. The timing had been such that Meg had been on the verge of leaving on yet another job. Then Pete had left too, his truck loaded with tools and supplies, to make the modifications to the place he'd always wanted to be done.

She waved at him as they came closer. He nodded but was silent. The soft dip and pull of the oar in the water continued at a steady pace for a few moments, until he brought the boat alongside the dock. Meg grabbed the bow and held it steady, while Pete turned around and noticed Janelle. "Hard to believe she's still asleep. She's been out for a good hour."

"She must have had a bad night," Meg said quietly, reaching for the rope and tying up the boat. Pete worked his way to where Janelle lay and gently picked her up. The boat rocked, but Pete held steady until it stabilized. In four strides, he was up on the dock. Grabbing the tackle box, Meg then followed the pair up to the cabin.

Her phone rang before she'd taken a dozen steps. It was Chad yet again. With a cautious glance at Pete's back, she answered softly, "Hello."

"I'm heading back into town. I'll call you when I get the paperwork sorted out."

She knew what he meant. His choice of anthropologist hadn't turned out to be the best one, now that her necklace had been found with the remains. "Fine, we'll be here for another night. Then we'll head home tomorrow afternoon."

The door slammed closed in front of her. Damn. "Or maybe we won't. I don't know yet. I haven't had a chance to talk to Pete."

"I wouldn't leave it too long," Chad warned.

"I know."

"Anyway, I'll speak to my boss, but, considering you did the excavation, it should be you doing the examination. I know there are some issues, but are you willing to follow through, if I can make it happen?"

"Yes." And that's what she had wanted. What the protocol was for this sort of situation in Seattle, she didn't know. A case-by-case basis, she would assume. "You didn't have to ask."

"You're not heading off for distant parts right way, are you?"

Not anymore. But he didn't know about her brother's death and the other changes in her life. "No. I will be home. I'm trying to figure out my own career at the moment."

"Good. I'll get back to you."

A warm smile bloomed inside her at his reassurance. "Thank you."

"Don't thank me. Help me to catch this asshole. He's ruined everyone's lives for long enough. It's time we ruined his."

CHAD HOPPED INTO his truck and prepped for the long trip back. He was hungry and tired, yet excitement, ... eagerness, had lit a fire in his achy muscles and had kept his brain moving. The techs weren't done yet and probably wouldn't be for another few hours. Before heading back to town, he wanted to drive around and take pictures, catch the lay of the land. He'd already downloaded maps of the region on his GPS but wanted to see for himself what cabins were here and how far away they were from each other.

He'd come here time and time again, looking for Cia, searching for any evidence that could shed light on her disappearance. It was an obsession at first, then a hobby. Over the years, the trips had gotten farther apart. He hadn't been here for five years. But that didn't stop him from downloading the latest images of the area every time Google Earth updated them. He had topographical maps, aerial maps, and satellite photos. His original folder had become a zippered briefcase heavy with data.

He'd done some research on the owners of the cabins seventeen years ago, and then, when he'd been able to access the databases once he was in law enforcement, he'd gone deeper.

But he had found nothing useful.

He knew it was too early to confirm the remains as Cia's, but there were good grounds for assuming they were. He'd spent an hour taking pictures and then marking off a grid, noting where the three pairs and three spares had their tents set up all those years ago. Definitely they were within walking distance, but not the *carrying a person* walking distance. Not unless that person was in awesome shape and bloody strong. That was another reason to let Meg off the hook. Back then, she'd been called gangly. She'd grown into her height and had filled out some. She could probably have lifted Cia—tiny doll-like Cia. But Chad doubted that Meg could have carried Cia that far.

No, this had all the markings of a male aggressor. He winced. He knew all too well what often happened to women in those situations. He could only hope that Cia's end had been mercifully swift.

He'd noticed Meg's enforced calm, as she'd gone through the process of collecting the remains. It had been that strong silence that had him watching her carefully. This was difficult for her. For him too. But she'd maintained a professional demeanor the whole time. Until she'd found the hyoid bone—and then her necklace.

Chances were good that Cia had been strangled to death, given the current evidence. And that was a downright personal way to kill someone. Was it someone who'd known her? It was that question that kept bringing him back to the group of friends who'd gone camping so long ago.

Sure, she could have wandered off on her own.

But she hadn't strangled herself.

THE CABIN WAS largely silent as Meg entered. Waves of disapproval emanated from Pete. *Geesh*, what a surprise. *Not.* Janelle sat up on the old couch, yawning. "Auntie Meg?"

"Yes, honey, I'm here."

Janelle gave her a tired smile. "Good. I wondered how much longer you would be."

Meg laughed lightly. "And imagine my surprise when I came back to find you both out enjoying the sun, fishing on the lake."

Janelle brightened. "You were home before us then? I wanted to wait for you, but Pete said no, that we couldn't spend our whole lives waiting on you to walk away from work."

Her childlike delivery did nothing to impact the overtone in Pete's words. The message was so typical of Pete. She refused to glance at him. She dropped a kiss on the top of Janelle's head. "I'm glad you went fishing. Was it fun?"

Janelle shook her head. "There were no fish," she complained. "And it was hot. I got really tired."

"And you had a nap, all of which is good." Meg straightened up. "I guess that means I need to find something for dinner, seeing as how you guys didn't catch anything, *huh*?"

Janelle grinned. "I want grilled cheese."

"Really? We're out here camping, and you want a grilled cheese?" It had to be Janelle's favorite meal. And it was so not high on the healthy food list. Then sometimes one needed to toss the list in the garbage. And this weekend, the list probably should be burned.

"Pete, what about you?"

"We brought hamburgers. We can't keep raw meat past today, so it's hamburgers, regardless of what anyone wants." On that categorical note, he walked over to the cooler and pulled out the sealed and dripping bag from the ice. He slapped it on the counter and proceeded to make patties.

An awkward silence followed. Meg glanced over at Janelle, who was biting her lip nervously. Meg wanted to run away and hide. When did a person hit overload, and when did it all become too much?

She didn't dare hit that point. Janelle needed her. And Meg didn't think she'd ever been needed before. Her parents were almost past child-rearing age when she'd been born, and, while they had done their duty by her, their relationship had been an independent one. It still was. Meg called them on special occasions, but they'd moved to a warmer, drier climate a long time ago. And now their cool relationship had chilled even further. She'd just always assumed it would improve, but it hadn't.

With a reassuring smile, she turned to help Pete get out the rest of the fixings for the burgers. Pete walked outside to light the barbecue. She watched him with sadness in her heart.

"Auntie Meg?" Janelle came up beside her to stare out the window at Pete. "Why do you stay with him?"

Her breath caught in her throat. She tried to smile but failed. Still to her, honesty *was* the best policy, so she answered Janelle's question, "We're just going through a bad patch right now."

"Really?" Janelle picked at a piece of lettuce. "I don't remember ever seeing a 'good' patch."

Meg looked at her sideways. "This last month has been tough for all of us."

"You weren't happy before Dad died either. He always wondered why you felt you had to settle for this, when you could have found someone to love instead."

"He didn't say that to you, did he?"

"Not to me, but to Grandma on the phone. I overheard him."

That hurt. It was also all too possible. Darren had been closer to her parents. Then he'd been a lot older. Did they really believe she didn't love Pete? Surely not. Pete and she had been together a long time. They had gone through a lot to get here. He loved her, even if he didn't show it. And she loved him. But lots of relationships went through a cooling-off period.

She didn't want to think it was any more than that, but Janelle wasn't ready to let it go.

"You guys don't hug. He never kisses you. You don't hold hands. I thought people in love did all that."

People in love? Were they that different from people who loved each other? Meg was stumped for an answer. She tried a different tactic. "Some people are more demonstrative. Other couples are happy to touch less." She shrugged. "I guess Pete and I are in second group." There was a long silence. Meg looked up from the tomato she was cutting. "What?"

"You always hug and kiss me," Janelle noted.

So true, but Meg didn't want to make the obvious connection. She knew there were problems with her relationship with Pete, but she didn't want them pointed out by anyone, much less by her too-observant niece.

Thankfully Pete came in then to say the burgers were ready.

Dinner was a quiet affair. Janelle could barely eat; her eyes drooped with fatigue. Meg eyed her carefully. The fresh air would have made her tired, but it should also have made her hungry. She didn't eat enough as it was now.

But then Meg was having trouble getting down her own burger. Finally she managed to finish it. She cleaned up the dishes quickly and suggested a walk, but the others declined. Janelle grabbed a book and went to her bed. Meg suspected few pages would get turned before Janelle crashed for the night. Maybe sleeping the weekend away was a good thing to do at this time. Then again, it was hard to know what was best.

Pete headed back outside to clean up and to pack up the barbecue. Meg took a seat on the veranda, as she waited for the kettle to boil for some tea.

"So are we leaving in the morning?" He stood, hands on his hips, glaring at her.

She glanced over at him in surprise. "Why? I thought the plan was to leave in the afternoon."

"We were, until you found another excuse to work. Don't you have to go deal with the remains?" The cool tone of his voice spoke of suppressed curiosity.

"Not necessarily." She relaxed back into her chair. "There are other qualified people back in Seattle. They just couldn't get someone to come out here today."

"And why did it have to be today? Surely tomorrow would have been soon enough. You found the body yesterday."

She sighed. "True. Having reported it, the media would likely hear, and then any number of strangers could come traipsing through the area. That's the worst thing to have at a crime scene." She pointed at the cloudy sky. "Also, the weather is set to change. No one wants to lose the evidence."

"Crime scene? Evidence?" His voice rose sharply. "How do you know a crime has been committed?"

"We don't." She tried to reassure him. "It's just that we treat each scene as if it were and hope the evidence proves it wasn't. This person could have died a natural death." She didn't of course, but it wasn't Meg's place to say so.

"Could you tell the sex?"

"Of course. The remains are those of a young woman."

The silence was oppressive. He gave a harsh bark. "She hardly died of natural causes then, did she?" He got up and walked to the far end of the veranda. "Odds are she was murdered. Then you already knew that, didn't you?"

She closed her eyes. Her professional and personal lives were once again butting up against each other. Since when had it started doing this? It never used to be an issue. And since Janelle's arrival in their home, Pete knew Meg wouldn't ever be leaving again. So why was there this continual discord?

"What, no answer? You, whom the experts call on for answers, have nothing to say now?"

Inside, her stomach sank. He was in a rare mood. And she didn't need any more emotional storms right now. But almost as if he realized he could push even harder and take a bigger cut out of her heart, he pushed deeper. "Oh, right. It's confidential. You can't tell me."

"Yes," she murmured quietly. "It's a police matter now, but that's not the point. I only collected the remains. Tests have to be done in order to determine the cause of death."

"Bullshit," he roared. "You'd know. Within minutes of seeing her body, you'd have known if Mother Nature had taken her or if she'd died by her own hand or someone else's hands."

"Lots of times, yes, I know, but sometimes I truly do not know. There are no one-answer-fits-all-scenarios here."

He snorted, disgust and old anger filling his dark features.

Meg watched him warily. She wasn't comfortable with this man she lived with anymore. Where was the man she fell in love with? Or even a year ago? That man was calm, funny, accepting. This one seemed to do nothing but pick away at small things in bitterness and anger.

Without warning, his fist lashed out and slammed into the railing post. She winced as blood flew from his ripped knuckles. She jumped to her feet and started toward him, but he turned and held out his other hand. "Don't come any closer. This is your fault."

She gasped. "My fault? That you were an idiot and punched the wood?"

Oh shit. At the word *idiot*, he locked down and became shadowed, as if icing up. His gaze turned almost black. "I. Am. Not. An. Idiot."

"I didn't mean it that way," she said, hastily backing down. She took a deep breath. "I'm sorry. I guess we're all touchy right now."

He stared at her, with no give in his expression.

She didn't know how to cross the impasse dividing them. He was so on edge right now, anything could set him off.

And that she didn't need. She'd seen more than her share of what happened to women when they came too close to a man's wrath.

She turned and quietly walked back inside. Closing the screen door softly behind her, she left him alone to his righteous anger. She paused at the doorway and looked back at him, searching the growing darkness, hoping to see some softening. When there was none, she realized they'd crossed yet another invisible line.

One she wasn't sure could ever be crossed back over again.

HE STARED DOWN at his cell phone. Jacob, the owner of the café, had called. Said there were a mess of cops at the lake. And an old set of remains had been found.

Interesting …

He smiled, a cold smile of anticipation.

Wait until Stephanie heard. She might have tried to change herself, but some characteristics were too ingrained for that.

Not that the location was a guarantee of finding what they were all hoping for. It might reveal Cia's remains. Then it might not.

Now that everyone, most likely everyone anyway, knew, what would they do next?

Chad and Megs would race around and try and solve the case. Of course. They were two do-gooders with brains and vengeance on their minds.

Stephanie would huddle and quake and shake and hope that Cia had died of natural causes. But she knew inside that this wouldn't be the case. Had she ever voiced the reason for her own breakdown? Did she even know it? Or was that inner fear, that inner knowing, that had destroyed her all these years?

She was so weak. She loved all the excesses, and they loved her. Her emotional state had been evidenced years ago. Unlike him, for he'd planned that weekend. Not that events had turned out the way he'd intended.

So many people in this world let life just happen. Randomly. These people were the victims of circumstances, the pawns of the world. Others, those like him, were the chess players, moving things around cunningly to suit their own needs. They planned ahead and took care of what needed to happen, in order to achieve their own ends.

They were the rulers of this stupid world of peons.

People like Megs and Chad were the enforcers of this said world. And that was such a joke. They might have turned into enforcers. Back then though, they were just victims, other victims of his actions.

People like Stephanie were the garbage in the street. He could have taken care of her a long time ago. But enforcers needed someone to enforce. The Stephanies of the world were perfect. They needed people. And people need to be needed.

Just think of Stephanie's life and how many people had been needed over the years to keep her alive and functioning. There were all the cops who had arrested her for drugs, prostitution, and petty theft, if that's what shoplifting was called in the mug books. Then there were the counselors, the ministers—how many different religions had she joined, trying to save herself? And the doctors, nurses, and emergency workers helping to save her life after overdosing or taking a bad hit of drugs.

And that was only in the first few years ...

He shook his head. These people needed Stephanie. People like her gave them all a sense of purpose. Stephanie, in fact, gave them a reason to go to work each day and to earn a paycheck.

As for Stephanie herself, she should feel good about herself. Look at all the busyness she was creating. Instead of being depressed, she should be cheering. Of course, being depressed was good for business too. It meant more rounds of doctors, therapists, and drugs, prescription ones this time. So easy to get hooked on those, wasn't it?

Now, with a new set of remains to fuss over, he'd bet she was a real basket case.

He smirked.

He hoped they all were.

Chapter 7

MEG WALKED INSIDE. It was still early, but the sun had gone down, adding to the darkness caused by the overgrowth of trees. She was tired from her restless night and emotional day, but she knew sleep couldn't be further away. She curled up in the one single chair in the living room and stared out over the water. She couldn't stop thinking about the necklace and that last day so long ago. And the conversation that went on over and over again in her head.

"Did Cia tell you?" Stephanie asked. "She's slept with four of the guys here, and she is planning on doing the next one this weekend. The last one of the group she turned down. You know how she likes to do the chasing."

"No way." Meg listened to Stephanie's litany of complaints against Cia. Meg's mind was buzzing, as she tried to figure out who Cia had slept with. Chad, for sure. After all, they'd gone out for months, although that had been a while ago, so ... "Who else has she slept with?" Meg asked.

"Ha, you don't know, do you?" Stephanie laughed and laughed. "What is Chad like in bed? I've often thought about it. He's really cute."

Meg grinned. "Chad and sex are like chocolate and peanut butter—they naturally go great together.

"That's what I figured." Stephanie giggled. "And Cia said something similar."

"She did?" Meg turned to her friend, outraged. She looked back to the shore, where Cia sat on the beach, looking like the perfect model that she was. All that perfect creamy skin was getting sun-kissed. She wouldn't burn. Instead lucky Cia would end with a lovely golden glow. Everything she touched was perfect.

Megs—tall, with long wavy brown hair—would never look perfect. "So who is she planning to seduce this weekend? And does Josh know?"

"Oh, I doubt it." Stephanie giggled. "He'd kill her if he did."

Such prophetic words.

Even after seventeen years, Meg had remembered them. She'd known Josh well back then. She'd gone out with him for a couple months herself, but she hadn't gone to bed with him.

It hadn't felt right. She hadn't had the same instant need she had had with Chad.

Had Josh known about Cia's plans? Had the man she'd selected known what she was up to? Maybe she was testing the waters.

Meg couldn't even think of who it could be. There was Chad, Josh, and Stephanie's boyfriend, Bruce, who was also one of Chad's best friends. Those two had been together for years. And Bruce's cousins, Anto and Pero Novak. It was the first time they'd come camping with them. Both were dark and intense looking. All the girls had giggled over their good looks.

But not Megs, she'd barely noticed them. She'd only had eyes for Chad. Other than these people, the only other person there that weekend had been Tim. She'd thought he might be gay, but he'd never mentioned it. She'd wondered about him, as he'd studied the brothers as much as the girls had.

She hadn't spoken to or seen Tim since that weekend. She thought she'd heard something about him living overseas for many years.

Meg rubbed her eyes, wishing the memories would leave her alone.

But she couldn't stop thinking about Cia's conquest ... and the one guy she'd turned down.

In the background, she heard Pete come in and go to the bedroom, probably for the night. For herself, she didn't even want to join him. However, if she didn't, there'd be a bigger fight tomorrow. She could sleep out here, but ...

The door slammed behind her. She turned around in surprise. Then she heard the truck start up.

Shit.

Where was Pete going?

And more important—was he coming back?

CHAD WELCOMED THE city lights. He was hungry and tired and pissed. He'd gotten nowhere with his phone calls to locate another anthropologist. Seemed as if everyone was out of town or didn't want to make a decision. And a decision needed to be made.

He'd driven for hours around the area where they'd found Cia, renewing his memory of the layout, noting the cabins, old and new. The popular lake had developed into quite a summer destination. And he had learned nothing new. Of course he hadn't. But they had the remains. With any luck, they'd find evidence that would point to her killer. And he had no doubt Meg's findings would prove out. She was highly respected in her field, and, on this case, more likely than on any other in her career, she would want to find the truth.

And so did he.

His phone rang. A favorite restaurant was just around the corner. He pulled into the parking lot and checked the number. It was Stephanie's.

Needing food before tackling that phone call, he entered the restaurant and ordered himself a big steak and baked potato. Alone, tired, and caught between edgy excitement and energy-sucking frustration, he stared moodily at his cell phone. The GPS coordinates Meg had sent showed clearly on his phone. This was it. He knew it. But he couldn't *know* it for sure, not until the lab went over everything and found something he could work with. Then again, he knew about the necklace. Could it be Meg's own necklace? Was there any chance that Cia would have made another one just like it to piss off Josh? She hadn't been the nicest of females, and, when she wanted something, she went after it like a cobra.

Josh would have been helpless against her wiles. He'd been lovestruck from the beginning and could barely do anything but stare at her all the time. It had been a big joke back then. But everyone knew he would cheerfully give Cia anything she had wanted. But that honeymoon phase hadn't lasted. Toward the end of their summer, Josh had asked for advice about how to break up with Cia. He wanted to start college as a free man. He was also afraid that Cia had been cheating on him.

Breaking up was easy. No reason to kill her to end the relationship.

Another call came in. "Is it her?" Stephanie's harsh voice cut through the phone, reminding Chad that more than just his life had been affected by Cia's disappearance. Other people needed closure too.

"I can't confirm it until the tests come back, but, given the age of the victim, the proximity to the location, and a few other determining factors," he paused, then finally said it, "I think so."

"Holy Christ." Stephanie cleared her voice. "After all this time."

"Yes. Finally."

After a solemn pause, she asked almost diffidently, "Could you tell how she died?"

"Not officially." He knew that wouldn't go over well. Stephanie's life had spiraled out of control after that fateful weekend. She never did go to college, and a cycle of booze and deadbeat relationships had followed. Somewhere in the last few years, she'd straightened out. She now worked at a grocery store and had been in a relationship for longer than a year, although that had recently broken up.

"And unofficially?"

"Unofficially she didn't likely die by natural causes. However," he stressed, "we don't know much yet."

She took a deep breath. "We knew it had to be, but I'd hoped, so hoped, that she'd just gone for a walk and had gotten lost."

"And yet we had how many people out there looking for her?"

"But we never found her back then, and now her remains are found in relatively the same location?" Stephanie asked, "So how come we didn't find her back then?"

"That's just one of the burning questions we need to answer."

"Someone really killed her?" Stephanie's voice thickened, and she swallowed hard. "Was ... was it one of us?"

Just then his waitress arrived, bearing his plate of food. What had seemed like a great idea when he'd pulled into the parking lot, now looked like sawdust before him. He closed his eyes and sagged against the back of his seat. "I hope not."

"We'll have to go over it all again, won't we?"

Her voice was so plaintive, so despondent, it made him ache inside. That was one question he could give a definitive answer to. Only she wouldn't like the answer. "Yes, we are."

"AUNTIE MEG?" JANELLE'S voice called through the darkness. Meg startled. She'd been sitting in the same chair for hours, waiting for Pete to come back. And he hadn't. And he might not.

That would be fun.

She reached Janelle's side and sat down on the edge of her bed. "What's the matter, sweetheart?"

Janelle's tears flowed. "I miss Daddy."

Oh Lord. Meg's heart hurt. She laid down beside her niece and gathered her into her arms. "I'm so sorry. I miss him too."

And the floodgates burst. Janelle burrowed deep into Meg's arms, and all she could do was to hold on tight—a pillar in a storm of emotions that asked questions and raged at the unfairness of life, yet offered no answers. The storm seemed to last for hours, and, for the first time that evening, Meg was grateful that Pete wasn't here.

He didn't have much patience with Janelle's emotional bouts. Meg locked down inside and rarely indulged in tears.

Janelle was a whole different case. Meg dropped several kisses on the girl's temple and held her close. Her own tears weren't far off. He'd been her brother, and she missed him too. They hadn't been super close, and she was sorry for that. He'd been a stalwart supporter. He'd been there for her all those years ago, and she needed to be there for his daughter now.

Poor Janelle, she'd lost so much. And there was no guarantee that life hadn't finished ruining things for her yet either.

As Meg knew only too well, fate had the power to piss their lives right down the drain, again and again.

Finally Janelle sobbed her grief and misery out, with only the occasional hiccough coming through. After another long few moments, Meg pulled back slightly to look down on Janelle's tear-stained face.

Janelle had fallen asleep.

Meg hated to disturb her. In fact, she hated to move, period. A night sharing the bed would be a good answer. She wouldn't have to face Pete when he returned, and Janelle wouldn't have to be alone tonight.

She moved to reach for a folded quilt at the end of bed.

Janelle cried out, her arms instinctively tightening. Her actions squeezed Meg's heart even further.

"It's all right, honey. I'm here."

"Don't go," Janelle whispered, her eyes closed, sleep just a breath away.

Meg managed to tug the quilt over her shoulders. She settled down deeper into the bed, nudging Janelle back slightly so there was room for the both of them. "I won't. I'll stay here all night."

"Promise?" The little voice was muffled further by the quilt pulled so high, but Meg heard it, and the pressure on her heart squeezed even tighter. Janelle was precious, scared, and she needed her.

Meg could do no less than be there for her. In a soft voice, hugging the little girl close, her own heart overwhelmed with love, she whispered in Janelle's ear, "I promise."

INTERESTING. ... SO they did find Cia's body. That gave him pause. Had he left anything behind? He'd racked his brain over it for a full hour but couldn't think of anything that he hadn't thought of before. There could be a hair or two, but they'd camped together over the weekend, so a hair wouldn't be definitive evidence in this cold case. Besides, there would likely be the girls' hair there as well. Those girls shared clothes, hairbrushes, and jewelry.

So why not men?

He smiled. The police had taken long enough. And, if Cia's remains hadn't been found accidentally, she could have lain there for another twenty years.

Still, this way was more fun.

So long as the cops didn't figure this out too soon. ... And, speaking of cops, it was interesting that Chad had given up engineering to go into law enforcement. What a waste. Chad had some serious brainpower. He'd have made a fine engineer.

Megs had become an anthropologist. Who'd have thought she was smart enough for that? And then Stephanie, ... that she'd turned out to be a drugged-up whore was no surprise. She'd been man-hungry since way back when.

The other guys had changed their plans for their futures too.

It made him feel good. Powerful even.

He'd done something that had made everyone reevaluate their lives.

That was good—great, in fact.

Without Cia's disappearance, they'd have continued on in their meaningless ways. He'd made them stop and think and do something better with their lives.

His actions had given them purpose.

Really they should be thanking him.

Chapter 8

MEG WOKE WITH a start. She lay still, almost frozen in place. Her mind raced to orient herself; after years of traveling, it was instinctive. She was in the cabin but not in her bed. Then she heard a sound, a snuffle.

Janelle.

The stiffness slid from her shoulders and spine, and she relaxed into the mattress and groaned. Her body ached everywhere. Janelle's body had sprawled from top to bottom and from one side to the other during the night, with Meg trying to take up the least amount of space on the edge. No wonder she hurt.

A noise outside had her looking toward the window. Trees swayed on the other side of the glass, a long branch stroking the pane with each brush. The clouds looked gray and crowded.

Still, it was light out. And that meant morning. Considering her evening and night, she'd take that as a good sign. And then she remembered.

Had Pete returned? Or had he left them stranded in his cabin?

She hoped not. But it wasn't the end of the world if he had. She could hitch a ride, if any of the techs were still working, and, if not, well, she'd call someone for a ride. Unbidden, Chad instantly came to mind. He would never leave two females stranded.

Ever.

She snuck out of bed, careful to keep the covers over Janelle. For all that it was technically summer, a chill filled the air and a bite of ice hit the floor. She hadn't planned on sleeping fully dressed, but there were definite advantages to it now.

Walking quietly out to the kitchen, she put on coffee, her answer to the world's ills. Then she walked out to the veranda and saw the truck.

Relief washed through her. He'd come back for them. Thank God for that.

Using her cell phone, she checked the time. It was only 6:30 a.m., her normal waking time and hours ahead of Janelle's. She smiled at the reminder of Janelle's horrified protests at being woken before ten. Noon was more her style.

She checked on Pete and found his bed empty. Her breath sucked in hard. He was an early riser, but she hadn't heard him or was that what had woken her this morning?

She stepped out onto the veranda and gasped at the cool air. There was no sign of him. Maybe he'd gone fishing. She strolled down to the water's edge.

The boat was there, but Pete wasn't.

Slightly disconcerted, she walked back to the cabin, not wanting Janelle to wake up alone.

The inside of the cabin was quiet and calm. She poured herself a coffee and checked her cell phone. She had a little bit of reception but not much. It was too early to call Chad, and she hadn't kept in touch with the others from that long-ago weekend. In fact, she'd gone out of her way to distance herself from them.

Now she felt the pull to reconnect. They would understand and would be going through the same emotions and issues she was. And they'd also be looking for answers.

She looked at her contact list. She had only Chad's number. As she stared at the small unit, a text came in. Talk about synchronicity. It was Stephanie. How the hell had she found Meg?

Did you hear? They may have found Cia.

That was all, but it was enough. Knowing the news would get out soon enough, Meg responded. **Yes. I found her.**

Oh God. Are you okay?

And, just like that, the years dropped away, and Meg reconnected with her old friend. The texts came back and forth, hard and fast, as they caught up. Meg hated learning about the bald truth of Stephanie's life, as she offered it up in pieces, but Meg so understood. She had buried herself in work and had tried to focus forward, whereas Stephanie had buried herself in illegal stuff and had wallowed in her past.

They'd both been haunted by that one weekend. Anger rose, sharp and cutting. Anger at the person who'd so carelessly tossed away beautiful Cia. Anger at the same person who'd destroyed so many lives and so many hopes and dreams.

They'd been forced to live with something no one should have to.

The relatively unknown group of survivors who felt guilty for *not* being the victim of violence was phenomenally large. Many clung to a support group because those were the people who understood. So many more avoided the support groups because they couldn't talk about their own experiences and didn't want to remember and rehash the same events over and over.

Meg had avoided the groups. Stephanie had just recently joined a group.

It was a case of each to their own.

"Auntie Meg?" Janelle stood sleepily in the open doorway, rubbing her eyes. "What time is it?"

"Wow. It's almost eight o'clock." Being up this early was unusual for Janelle, but she'd slept in the boat yesterday and had gone to bed early last night. "Aren't you up early?"

"When are we leaving?"

"Good question," Meg said lightly. "Pete has gone for a walk. We can ask him when he returns."

With that, Janelle turned around and went back to bed.

If only Meg's life were so easy.

Pete walked through the front door a few moments later, a lighter, calmer Peter. Meg smiled brightly at him, so happy to see the return of the old Pete she knew and loved. "Hi. Did you have a good walk?"

He nodded. "I thought, given the circumstances, we should probably head back early. I went to the roadhouse in Wistery last night. Apparently the locals have already heard, and they've been talking to the media."

"Shit." And yet life went on. People would always talk, and the media would always listen. "Well, let's hope the techs are done with the crime scene."

"I just walked the area, and it seems like they are, at least initially."

"Ah. Yeah, I wanted one last look, before I leave too."

"Go now," he urged. "I'll grab a coffee and start packing up."

Feeling much better, Meg tossed him a grateful smile and ran.

CHAD LOGGED ON to his computer at work. He'd already called the lab and had his ass reamed out for pushing. He could wait like every other detective was doing.

He understood, but he didn't like it. Still, he had lots he could do. This wasn't technically a cold case. It was Daniel's case, but Chad had always thought of it as Mack's case. Then it had almost finished Mack's career. He'd caught it when it was fresh but hadn't disclosed that three of the suspects were close relatives. Daniel had taken it over, and Mack had been disciplined and almost kicked off the force. Seventeen years had dimmed the events for everyone, but those involved. Mack had kept on Daniel about the case over the years. And so had Chad.

Good thing the three of them had come to terms with this years ago—uneasy terms, but cordial, at least in public. Mack's heavy hand had made the young Chad into a man, but he'd become a detective on his own. Badge in hand, he'd stopped by Mack's desk and showed it to him. Mack had smiled and slapped him on the shoulder. "I knew you'd make it."

Those words had helped bury some of the animosity between them. Chad had felt like a loser for a long time. Hell, the same damn feelings of insecurity had even threatened to overwhelm him at times. He should have gone after that person in the woods. That he hadn't had haunted him every day. And now, maybe he could do something about it.

Finding Cia's remains would break the case wide open.

He'd asked Stephanie to keep quiet for the moment but realized he'd asked a lot of her. He'd given her Meg's phone number, suggesting she call her. The two had been close once.

He'd already contacted Josh and Bruce. He'd stayed in touch with both of them since that fateful trip. Hadn't seen much of either of them in over a decade, but, with phones and texts now, staying in touch was easy.

Now he thought about contacting all the others from that weekend, only this time it would be in an official capacity. He wanted to go over their old statements first. And then see if they would change them this time. The years could do funny things to the mind. Forgetting was normal, but sometimes the stuff that popped out of people's mouths was the truth that they hadn't wanted to express before, out of concern for both the dead and the living.

MEG WALKED SWIFTLY through the trees. She couldn't believe the change in Pete's mood, but she was grateful for it but also surprised. A little sprinkling rain had started.

The rain made walking under the tree canopy a wet experience, as the rain slid off the trees and soaked her. She didn't need her GPS to find the right location. The pathway was imprinted on her brain. And the yellow tape let her know when she'd hit the right area and also made her steps falter.

The surge of mixed emotions made it difficult to continue. She stared at the stark reality, with a deep, dark stillness inside. Yet also an overwhelming sense of relief. They'd found her finally. They could now bring Cia home.

Meg had almost given up hope.

And to think she'd been the one to find her. So close to their camping spot, and yet just far enough, deep enough in the woods that Cia had been missed all these years.

Rain dripped on Meg's cheeks. She swiped the moisture away and realized it wasn't rain at all. Tears had formed in the corner of her eyes and had poured down her face. Oh, dear God, poor Cia. What had happened to her friend? And had it happened right away or had the poor girl been held captive for a while? Please not that. Much better to think she'd gotten into a fight that had gone bad.

But to think that, after all this time, her friend had lain here all alone, waiting to be found.

Meg's shoulders shook, and she started to sob. For years she'd kept that pain stuffed down deep inside. Now, alone, she could let it all out.

She collapsed onto a log outside of the taped area and let her emotions pour out. This wasn't why she'd come here one last time, but, now here, it seemed like the only thing she could do.

She needed to honor her friend. And she needed to say hello after all this time. And most of all, she needed to say goodbye.

Now Cia could go to her family and be buried with them. And, although this final send-off could happen now, closing the door forever would have to wait until they'd caught the bastard who'd done this to her.

It was time.

THE DRIVE HOME was slow, the rain pounding harder with every mile. Just driving through the slick ruts had Meg clenching her teeth and wondering if they should have stayed until the weather had changed again and the roads had dried up. She couldn't imagine being stuck in the cabin with a weeklong bout of this weather. Yet it could be days before it cleared. Besides, she needed to be back in Seattle.

As for Cia's remains, she hoped that Chad had worked some magic, but, either way, she'd follow the progress of the case through him.

She could get on with other aspects of her life. After her emotional outpouring at the site, the walk home had left her feeling cleaner and more renewed than she'd felt in a long time.

And that allowed her to see the next step in her life. She had to get Janelle back on track, but more than that, Meg needed to get her relationship with Pete back on track again too. Or, and she winced at the thought, she needed to change the track. As much as it might hurt to contemplate this, Janelle was now part of her life, and the two of them were a package deal. If Pete, who had said for years that he had wanted a family, couldn't deal with it, then so be it.

Having been away from home so much, she'd always considered the condo as being primarily his, although they had both picked out where they would live together years ago. He'd chosen the furniture, while she'd been gone one time; he'd painted the walls another time.

And, if they were splitting—again came that pang to her heart—then where would she go? What options did she have? Her brother had left her some money, and there was his house. She'd put it on the market recently, not knowing what else to do with it. The small brownstone was not someplace Pete would live.

But what if Pete were no longer part of the equation?

All this hinged on whether Pete was prepared to take on Janelle. If he were, then maybe they should look at moving to a new location anyway.

The more she thought about it, the better she liked the idea.

She turned to mention the idea to Pete and realized how tired he looked. She said, "I'm looking forward to going home."

He swiveled his head to look at her. "You mean, to get back to work, don't you?"

"I don't have a job right now, remember?"

"Aren't you going to be handling the remains that you found?" he scoffed. "Of course you are!"

Damn. He was pissed again.

She stayed quiet. With any luck he would calm down before too long and could be back to normal by the time they were home. Thank God Janelle was asleep. It seemed like it was all she'd done this weekend.

Maybe it had been a good thing, given Pete's disposition. The hot and cold reactions were wearying.

They were heading for a major storm, and she wasn't looking forward to it. In all her years with him, he'd been reasonable and easy to talk to. Now he was cold and distant, alternating between angry and angrier.

Not quite true, he had had moments like the one this morning when he had reminded her of the man he used to be. It was Janelle's permanent presence that seemed to have finished him off.

Or maybe Meg had been the one to hit the wall. Certainly this weekend she had. Her emotions were all over the place, and anger simmered just below the surface. She realized how much she hated these confrontations, and the more regular they were, the more she hated them.

Change had to happen, and it was looking more and more like today might be the day it would.

HE WANTED ANSWERS. Answers about what they had found and what test results they were getting done and how would he get those.

He could ask Stephanie, but would she know anything? Not likely. And Megs? Well, she wouldn't likely give him the time of day.

So Chad was the best option, unless old Mack was still alive and kicking. He'd always been good for a beer and some chatter. Not that he'd give anything away, but he'd be a place to start.

Not his choice of victims and such a pain to dispose of afterward.

But he needed to stay on top of the news somehow. With Cia's remains now come to light, what were the chances that a few of those loose ends that he'd discounted as not mattering all those years ago might just matter now?

After all these years?

Surely not.

Something needed to happen, and finding Cia's remains definitely counted as something happening.

He gazed down at the long history of his life and wondered at the juncture in that history and the direction it had led him in ever after. Did he regret the impact of his decision so long ago? No, not really. Sure, his life had turned out differently than he'd planned.

But planning as a teen was like throwing popcorn in the wind and seeing where the pieces would land. He'd done something similar, then chosen from among the pieces he'd liked.

Now, some of those pieces had hooks and might be coming back to snag him.

Or maybe not …

He'd gotten very adept at being the predator and not the prey.

Chapter 9

M EG FELT THE thunderclouds building within minutes of being home. She needed Pete to hold off, until she could find something or somewhere for Janelle to hang out, so she didn't witness the explosion. Hell, Meg didn't want to witness it either. Yet she knew it was the only way to clear the air—one way or the other. At the moment, the *other* was starting to sound damn good.

Luckily Janelle came running to the kitchen, while Meg was wiping out the cooler. "Can I go to Linette's place, please?"

Janelle was almost dancing in place. Meg already knew the homework had been done, and it was perfect timing, as far as she was concerned. "Absolutely but home at five o'clock, please. And make sure you have your cell phone turned on and no leaving Linette's place."

With a big grin, Janelle took off. Linette lived in the same condo complex, making for easy access between the girls. Linette was a regular visitor and a nice girl. Also, she was a good student in school, which, if Meg were lucky, might rub off on Janelle.

Meg heard Pete yell, "Don't sl—"

Slam.

Meg let out her pent-up breath slowly. Not a good start.

"Damn that kid," Pete snarled. "She has to stop slamming the door." He walked in with his arms full from unloading the truck. "And she has to start cleaning up her own mess."

"She'll learn." Meg busied herself with drying the cooler. She didn't know how to open up the subject.

"Will she? When?" He snorted. "I could be dead first."

Meg winced. "She's not that bad."

"Says you. She's nothing but work."

Now that wasn't fair. "Not true. We're just not used to having kids around. We have to learn to get along too."

"No, I fucking don't." He slammed his load of cups and jackets, and a half-eaten apple, onto the table. "I didn't sign up for this."

Here it was, ready or not. She took a deep breath, grabbed the edges of her frayed control and said, "Then maybe we need to talk about that."

"Talk about what? That it's her or me?" He pointed a finger at the closed front door, through which Janelle had just disappeared. "Oh, I get the message all right. It's her all the way apparently." His voice clipped through the message with military precision and left her gasping from the cutting words. "We were fine until she arrived in our home."

She couldn't hold back. "So let's talk about whether you still want me if she comes as part of the package."

Now it was out in the open.

He stopped, stared at her, the muscle in his jaw pulsing. Fire burned in his gaze, but not a fire that warmed her or made her feel welcome. There was something cold, empty, and final in his eyes.

Forever final.

She hated that this was it. He hadn't said it, but she knew.

His mouth opened, and she caught her breath, waiting, half hoping for a rescue and a change in direction, but knowing it wasn't to be. And she wasn't sure she wanted one. Not at this point.

Then his jaw snapped closed, and he turned around very carefully and stalked into the master bedroom. She heard him opening closets and drawers. She swallowed and closed her eyes. Dare she follow him and push the issue? With her rock-solid foundation having turned to quicksand, she didn't know where she stood. And she needed to.

Instinct told her to leave him alone. Her gut said run. Her heart was beyond speech; it had swelled to the point of bursting from the sense of this achy loss inside.

Closing the cooler lid carefully, she placed it on the table and stared at the items Pete had dumped in a pile. Some of it hers, some of it Janelle's, and none of it mattered. Still, everything needed to be cleaned up. He'd always hated a mess.

She should leave. Go and pack an overnight bag for her and Janelle. Pick Janelle up at her friend's and go to a hotel for the night—or for the week. A half sob escaped. She didn't know what to do.

With a heavy sigh, she rubbed her face with both hands, hating the pressure in her chest and the indecision of what to do, yet knowing she had to do something.

And then he did it instead.

"I'm going away for a day or two." He stood cold and implacable in front of her, with an old scuffed hockey bag in his hand. Fully packed, he didn't look like he'd be home anytime soon. And from the edge to his voice, and the jut of his jaw, it was clear he didn't plan on explaining himself either.

She nodded slowly, holding back the tears that wanted to pour out but instead standing dry-eyed in front of him, as relief warred with the pain of his leaving. "That might be a good idea." She wanted to say more. She needed to say more. They both did.

Yet neither spoke.

He nodded and walked out, without a backward glance. He closed the door so very quietly and the very gentleness of this gesture added to the finality of his actions.

At least this time she was no longer at the cabin without transportation. She could thank him for that much. She had a roof over her head, a bed for the night, and a place to keep Janelle that wasn't a cold impersonal hotel. And her car was outside—her brother's car. She hadn't bothered buying one, as she'd been traveling for so much of the time.

Then none of it mattered now. Her life was splintering around her, and the relief at finding Cia's remains had been replaced with a feeling of regret. And inevitability.

She put her head down on her arms and burst into tears again.

CHAD'S PHONE RANG. He glanced at the time; it was four p.m. He picked it up off his office desk and answered.

"Detective Mack Monroe here. I hear you've found a breakthrough in our old case."

With a smile, Chad leaned back in his chair. "Hey, Mack, how are you doing? Did you get my text?"

"I did. And I'll be doing much better when you tell me what I want to know." Gruff, brusque, and a loner, Mack was a bulldog, following a lead until he found the answers he needed. Then he stood by the case, until he had caught the asshole who had got on the wrong side of his file. He just didn't care about those who got in his way or those he might damage through this process.

"We might have found the remains of Cia Barnes."

"About damn time." Mack coughed several times. "Give. I want the details. All of them."

With a short eye roll, Chad told him what he knew. What he'd already told Daniel.

Silence fell when he was done. Chad could almost see Mack thinking things over. "Who'd have thought it would take that long for her to be found?"

"I know. It's been a long time. I'm just hoping that we can close this one now."

"I bet you are. You didn't like being on the opposite side of my interviewing skills, did you?"

"No," Chad answered emphatically, hating the reminder of how Mack had taken the guilt-ridden young Chad and pounded him into the ground, looking for a confession. He'd felt like a lowlife, and Mack's constant hounding had been brutal. It had changed Chad forever. Even now he had a hard time forgiving Mack for that. And Mack didn't give a damn. The real problem was that Chad had felt Mack's suspicious gaze turned his way more than once in the ensuing years, as the case hung between them. Even though Mack had almost gotten kicked off the force himself in the process, he'd never let Chad forget.

Still, Chad was a man now and a damn good detective. He understood the lengths they were forced to go through sometimes in pursuit of a resolution to a case. But he'd never been the bastard Mack had been. He'd also come to understand it was Mack's fear for his nephews that had driven his behavior. Fear was a powerful motivator.

For that reason alone, Chad had to admit to being suspicious of Mack. He'd been at his cabin that weekend and close enough to have killed Cia himself. Only Chad hadn't found that out until after Mack had pushed the innocence out of him forever—good thing too, or Chad might have pushed back …

"I'm still having trouble processing that Megan Pearce found the body. She just 'happened' to trip over it, *huh*?"

"Yes." Chad hated to see the suspicion rest on Meg's shoulders, but he knew that it was normal at this stage. Everyone and everything would be reexamined. Like it or not, their lives would be put under a microscope again, and that included his own life.

"So where do we start?" Chad would have deferred to Mack even if he hadn't been the original detective on the case back then. Some men just commanded that type of response.

"It's time to bring everything back up and take a fresh look. I'll talk to Daniel. Plus, I want to talk to the labs. Wish I'd seen the site myself."

"I did contact you, but you never answered," Chad reminded

him.

"Yeah, I know. It was my poker night." He coughed a harsh, raspy sound that made Chad wince.

"You still haven't quite given up on smoking yet, have you?"

"Hell no." Mack coughed again. "And you still haven't stopped nagging. Just like my wife."

"Yeah, I can't imagine why she hasn't stopped," Chad joked. "Maybe it's because she doesn't want to be alone in her old age."

"Sure she does. She'll hate having me underfoot all the time." He paused. "So what aren't you telling me?"

Chad sighed. "I was waiting for you to stop choking. Under the body we found a necklace. It's hard to make out the inscription after all this time, but it appears to say, *To Megs, with love.*

"Megs?"

"Yes. Megan—Megs. It was Meg Pearce's nickname." Chad stared across his desk at the far wall. "Obviously Meg couldn't have strangled someone and wouldn't then have left her own necklace behind."

"Unless she didn't know it had gone missing. It could have come off without her noticing in a girl fight." His voice hardened. "Strangled?"

"That's what Meg's preliminary observation says."

"What a big coincidence for Megan. Not only does she find the body but she was one of the suspects at the time of Cia's disappearance. And, the icing on the cake, she finds her own necklace with the remains."

"I know. Strange, isn't it?"

"Yeah, I think so." That same laconic voice that had caused Chad so many nightmares when he'd been interviewed rang through the phone. Chad let out his breath slowly, as he formulated his thoughts. It wasn't just Meg that Mack was asking about. It was also about whether Chad believed in Meg and, if so, why. "I was there when she found the necklace. She was surprised and horrified."

"She could be playing to both scenarios," Mack said in a noncommittal voice.

"True enough, but she was also completely distraught over finding the bones."

"Again, she could be playing to both scenarios."

"Maybe, but she didn't do it," Chad said, tired of this. "I know that for sure."

"Right. So, now here's the next question." Mack paused, and

Chad braced himself. Mack was always good for shock value. "Are you still in love with her?"

Ah, there it was. The one question he'd avoided since receiving that text message. How did he feel about her now? She'd been the love of his life, until their lives had blown up. Lack of trust, horror at the unimaginable, not knowing how to cope, all of those factors and more had played a part in her breaking up with him. If they'd had more time together, or a stronger, longer-lasting foundation before life had blown up, they might have made it.

However, at the time, everyone had scattered. Chad had gone morose and angry, until he'd finally turned it around. He had realized that Mack and the rest of the cops didn't have any answers for him, and Chad would have to find them for himself. He just hadn't expected it to take seventeen years.

He'd always figured when they found out the truth, he could go to her and tell her that she was free, he was free, and that it was time to move on—together. Only the years had gone by, and he hadn't found any answers either.

"And the telltale silence." Mack laughed so hard that he started coughing. "You still care."

"I don't know what I feel," he admitted quietly. "I've barely seen her since that weekend."

"And that means nothing, as you well know. Your life together stopped—waiting for you to solve the crime."

"Only she went on with her life." And he knew it wasn't fair, but there was a smidgeon of jealousy, almost anger, underneath his acceptance. Of course he wouldn't have wanted her to be alone for all these years. She was a beautiful person. She deserved to be happy. No, he wouldn't wish that on anyone.

"And so did you."

Chad startled at Mack's dry comment. "Yes, but not quite the way she did."

"What? So you're mad she made a better go of doing without you than you did doing without her?"

That sounded so wrong when put like that. Juvenile. "Stupid, *huh*?"

"Ya think? Sounds like perfect timing now. Don't waste this opportunity."

"I thought you said she might be our perp?" Chad hated that about Mack. He always twisted things around and forced Chad to look at life in a different way.

"I said she might be. You're the one who is so gung ho that she's innocent." Mack's derisive tone sent Chad's back up.

"She *is* innocent."

"Good. I'm still trying to figure out why the hell you aren't at my desk, so we can haul all the evidence back out and take another look." And he rang off.

Chad shook his head and stared at his dead phone. Typical Mack. And yet different. There was a hint of excitement in Mack's voice. And that was good.

Maybe this time they could find the answers they both needed.

WOW. AND DOUBLE wow. Megs and Chad back together again. Well, not together-together, but still close together. Who would have thought this could happen? Then he hadn't foreseen this happening at all. Life was like that for him. He looked forward but only a day or two at a time. Certainly not seventeen years down the road. What a waste. Life was for living, not worrying about what might happen too far down the road to see.

He shook his head. What a joke.

Still, this was an interesting turn of events. Not one that required action on his part. He was happy to observe and to see where it led. To see what Chad did and to see what Megs did.

She was the center to all this anyway. At the time, he'd been dumbfounded, waiting for the fumbling idiot police to lock in to the truth—and lock him up for the rest of his life. Then, after realizing they'd missed it altogether, he'd found it as funny as hell.

Everyone had focused on Cia, as if to say that this whole mess revolved around her. She would have liked that. They'd missed the salient points and, therefore, had missed the center of the whole issue. From a point way off to the left, the authorities had fumbled around blindly. Of course they had never found anything. What was there to find? Well, Cia of course, but she was nothing but a whiney whore anyway.

No. No one had thought to look closer at Meg back then.

He smiled. Well, they would now, wouldn't they?

Chapter 10

JANELLE BARRELED INTO the kitchen and skidded to a stop. "Auntie Meg? What's wrong?"

Meg frowned, trying to pull her thoughts back to the moment. "Why do you think something is wrong?"

Walking toward her slowly, Janelle appeared to search Meg's face. "You're baking. Mom only baked when she was upset."

And what did one say to that? When would Meg stop feeling like she was stepping on ghosts? Meg stared down at the batch of brownies, ready to pour into the pan. She instinctively headed to chocolate when she was upset, and baking brownies had seemed like a good answer.

Now … not so much.

"I'm sorry, honey. I was craving chocolate."

She watched as Janelle took several slow steps forward, her face a mixture of confusion and hope. "So, you are okay?"

She had to laugh. "I'm much better now. Just seeing you puts a smile on my face."

A beautiful smile lit up Janelle's face. And Meg realized how little time she'd taken to say something nice. God, she sucked as a mother. Her brother should've chosen better.

"Auntie Meg?" Uncertainty threaded through Janelle's voice. "Now something else is wrong."

Meg schooled her features, hating that Janelle was so sensitive. "No. Honey, I was just realizing how poor a job I've been doing, looking after you." Meg walked closer and enfolded her in a gentle hug. "This is such a learning curve for me. I'm sorry, but you need to have patience with me."

Janelle's arms crept around Meg's back, and then she hung on tight. Tears came to Meg's eyes, and she cuddled her. Such love was here. And Pete wanted nothing to do with it.

How sad.

"Where is Pete?" Janelle pulled back slightly to look up at Meg.

"Is he here?"

"No." Meg gave her a bright but shaky smile. "He's gone for a day or two."

It took a moment, then Janelle's face brightened. "Really?" She stepped away. "That is great."

"It is?" Meg asked curiously. "Don't you like Pete?"

A shadow whispered across Janelle's face, as she danced away from Meg. "He's okay."

"But only okay?" Meg pressed gently. Did Janelle really not like Pete? And if not, why not? Maybe separating would be a good idea, if only for Janelle's sake.

Janelle's dancing slowed, and she stared down at the floor.

Meg caught her breath. "Janelle, can you tell me what you don't like?"

She caught a glimpse of Janelle's uncertain look, before she hid her face behind her hair. Meg took a step closer. "Janelle, please tell me. It's important."

Her niece stilled, her shoulders hunched. Inside, Meg's stomach clenched. "Honey?"

So soft and gently, Meg had to lean closer to hear Janelle say, "He scares me."

"When he's angry?" Meg asked gently.

Janelle nodded and then added, "And he's always angry."

Meg wrapped an arm around the girl's shoulders. How could you explain that the anger was because he didn't want her? She couldn't say that. It would devastate her. "He's going through a lot right now. That's why he's left. To rest and relax and to sort some stuff out."

There was silence, and then Janelle whispered, "Is it wrong to hope he doesn't come back?"

The breath gusted out of Meg's chest. Here was another difficult question. "No. It's not wrong. Let's just hope that, if he does come back, he comes back happy and wanting to be here." She wasn't ready to share her own plans, not until she had arrangements in place. Too many questions and no answers would only increase Janelle's insecurities. Better to wait until tomorrow. "In the meantime, I have some decisions to make. Just know that you will be with me no matter what. Okay?"

Janelle smiled. "Okay."

"Now, how about I get these brownies in the oven, so we can have one after dinner?"

And now Janelle beamed.

For the first time in months, Meg enjoyed the evening with Janelle. There were no tantrums, no whining, and no sign of tears. All because Pete had left.

Later that evening, after Janelle had gone to bed, Meg knew a corner had been turned.

Pete may have chosen a few days away, but that time and distance had also given Meg the clarity to see what she needed to do.

She wanted to move out—before Pete came back. Even if it was only a temporary move, she could see tonight just how much improved Janelle was, without being in that constant negative atmosphere.

But moving out wasn't so simple. She had a house to go to, so that was a gift. But she'd have to contact the real estate agent and pull it off the market, at least for the moment. It was only a few miles away, so Janelle could at least stay at the same school.

Only Meg would have to deal with Janelle's emotional state, if she moved her back into her old home, the home where she'd lived with her father. Meg probably should never have removed her in the first place. At the time, it seemed that staying with all those memories wouldn't be a good idea.

She set about making plans.

The more those plans formulated in her mind, the clearer her understanding became. The emotions settled inside.

This was the right thing to do.

With a notepad, she started on a list: pack up, contact the Realtor, grocery shop for the house.

The house would be clean in the sense that it was good enough for house buyers to come by and look, but she'd have to change out the bedding. Janelle hadn't brought much with her to the condo, just a couple suitcases. The rest was in the fully furnished house that Meg had pushed off as a problem to solve into some distant future, like when the house was sold. Instead this was looking like a godsend.

She studied her bedroom. She'd never been a clothes horse and being ready to travel at the drop of a phone call hadn't given her much time to accrue much. What she did have was boxes of treasures she'd brought home from her travels. They were in storage until she and Pete could buy a bigger house. They were well past that point now. Meg had a healthy bank account, and, although she needed to sort out her professional future in town, she had the qualifications, experience, and the references to find something, somewhere, to make her happy.

After Janelle's school year finished, they could talk about changing locations. Maybe by then, Janelle would have settled in.

Either way, they would start a new life together.

LATE THAT NIGHT, Chad walked into his bedroom, turning on the television, as he headed toward the shower. He stripped down, dumping his clothes in the hamper, before stepping under the hot water. The water sluiced down his back, easing the tension that he'd been unable to get rid of all day. He needed answers.

Hell, he'd needed answers for a long time …

He stayed under the water for a few minutes longer and then shut off the soothing heat. Drying quickly, he wrapped the towel around his hips and headed back to his bedroom.

He made it to the doorway of his bedroom and stopped short.

"Breaking news tonight. There may finally be a break in the Cia Barnes case. A set of female remains has been found in the area where she disappeared seventeen years ago—"

"Shit."

"We'll have more of this latest news in a few minutes from our own Mike Clifford, who is outside the apartment of Stephanie Thornton. She was one of the girls who was camping with Cia on that fateful weekend when Cia went missing."

"God damn it. Not Stephanie. She can't handle this." He reached for his phone and called her. Stephanie had been through so much. She didn't handle stress well.

Or anything else, for that matter.

He texted her immediately. **Don't go outside. Don't answer the door. Media. The news is out.**

After sending the message, he tried to call her again.

Still no answer. He tried several more times, as he stood in front of the television and half watched the news coverage. The reporter was going on about the mess that had happened, but so far there was no sign of Stephanie showing up. They didn't appear to be saying anything they hadn't said dozens of times already over the years.

Thank God.

If they found out about that damn necklace, that would be seriously bad for the case, bad for everyone, and really bad for Meg.

The public would convict her in a heartbeat.

STEPHANIE WHIMPERED. SHE tucked deeper into her closet, hating the lights from outside that flashed into her ground-floor bedroom, with the headlights and camera crews outside.

Damn it. Bruce should be here with her and protecting her from them.

She wanted to go back to the way things had been before, when Bruce had still been her best friend and lover. She'd tried to resume a normal life after Cia, but their relationship hadn't been strong enough to handle her slide into alcohol. When she'd added the drugs, Bruce had walked.

She'd gone on an all-out bender then. She'd woken up years later, hating who she was and what she'd become. She'd hated Bruce for giving up on her.

She couldn't do this again, not alone anyway.

It had damn-near killed her last time, and at least then she'd had Bruce. She should have been the one to die, not Cia. It would have been so much easier than this long, slow torture. Tears burned in the back of her eyes. She'd shed so many over the years that they never fell anymore.

She'd used drugs, alcohol, and men to dull the pain, to hide the fear, hoping that one of them would finish her off. Instead she'd survived. It had been two years since she'd made the decision to live, to forget, to move on, and to acknowledge that she'd suffered enough. Two years of feeling like maybe life was worth living. Two years of thinking she could do this. Two years since dumping the bad habits—*all* of them.

And she had finally started talking to Bruce again. It was only texting so far, but that door had been opened. For that she was grateful.

And then they had found Cia, and everything had come rushing back: the pain, the terror, the endless nightmares, the *what ifs*, the constant looking over her shoulder. She didn't even know what she was looking for. She just had that incessant sense of being watched.

A cry escaped before she could suppress it by shoving the bottom of her shirt into her mouth. Shudders racked her body. She tightened her grip on her knees and rocked back and forth.

Now—as if those years recovering from the trauma had never happened—she couldn't stop looking over her shoulder again. She remembered the sly looks, accusing stares, uncomfortable silences. The cops had been bad, and the whispering from friends and family had been even worse. But the media? ... They had been horrible.

And now the media had found out about Cia's remains.

And worse—the media had found *her*.

MEG COLLAPSED ON the bed, exhausted from too much thinking. She was exhausted too from the turmoil in her head. This was way too much stress. She pulled a blanket over her legs. Sleep couldn't be further away.

Just then her cell phone rang.

Chad said, "Cia's case was on the eleven o'clock news."

"So it's started." She took a deep breath. "They haven't found me yet."

"They found Stephanie." Chad's voice lit up the room. "She thinks she's being watched, and she's getting hang-up phone calls." He took a deep breath, exhaling noisily. "Lots of them."

Meg winced at that last bit. She asked cautiously, "Watched? Like stalker type watching?"

"Yes, to the first question." He sounded distracted. "And although it could be nothing, she's pretty scared right now."

"Has she seen anyone following her?" Meg sat up, brushing her hair back over her head, hating the thought.

"No." He cleared his throat. "That's part of the problem. Since Cia's remains have been found, Stephanie's become very emotional. She went off the rails when Cia first disappeared. You may not have seen it, as you left for college as soon as you could. I don't know what you know about her history through the years, but she lived pretty rough for a while."

Meg had been under such emotional stress for so long that she had no trouble relating to Stephanie's problems—or her method of handling them. She murmured, "I'd heard."

"Yeah, well, it's hard to tell at this point if this is something serious or not. I figured I'd better check and see if you'd had any similar problems."

"No." Thank God, but then she had to wonder if she would have even noticed with everything else going on in her life.

"I'm not trying to panic you." Chad's voice soothed her nerves. "Obviously you both need to take extra precautions right now."

She pulled her knees up to her chest and tightened the blanket. "Great, just what I don't need right now."

"Why?" He backed up. "What's wrong?"

"Pete's not here right now." She waited a moment and then said quietly, "He's moved out temporarily."

He sighed. "I'm sorry."

Inexplicably her eyes burned, as she fought back the tears. She mumbled, "Thanks."

"Does that mean you're alone?"

"I have my twelve-year-old niece here."

"And you have a safe, secure place, right? Locks, alarms, and a security system?"

"Yes. At least, I think it's decent." She thought about it. "However, as we know, there's always a way to get in." Moodily she played with the fringe on the blanket, hating the thought, the necessity of having to reexamine the issue. "Are you expecting trouble?"

"No, but we have to consider that finding Cia may have blown something wide open." His voice sharpened. "And this may have alerted her killer."

Meg caught her breath. "Are you thinking Steph's hang-up caller was Cia's killer?" She shook her head. "That doesn't make any sense. This guy kills a girl, and then, seventeen years later, he's stalking another one? It's more likely the media checking to see if she's at home."

"How do we know that Cia wasn't stalked in the first place? There were other campers at the lake and another campground on the other side." He added thoughtfully, "Not to mention the dozens of cabin owners there over that weekend."

"It's possible, I suppose." Thoughts twisted in Meg's head. "Is there any reason for Stephanie to be nervous now?"

"What do you mean?" Chad asked curiously. "You mean, nervous about Cia's death? That would only be if she had something to do with it. And we ruled her out a long time ago."

"Maybe she knows something? Or is protecting someone?" Meg sighed. "Sorry, I'm grasping at straws, trying to reach for an explanation, the same as I have done for the last seventeen years." She stared across her bedroom, wishing Pete was there. At least she wouldn't have to worry so much about an intruder. "I know Stephanie didn't have anything to do with Cia's death. I was there with her the whole time."

"The *whole* time?"

"Yes, except for my trip to the outhouse. Yet Stephanie was in the same place where I'd left her. She wouldn't have had time to kill Cia and to move her."

Silence.

Meg chewed on her bottom lip. "Chad? What are you thinking?"

"I'm just wondering at the concept of more than one killer. It's not something we'd—I'd—given much thought to before."

"Two people working together killed her?" Meg fell silent as she thought about it. "That's pretty awful to contemplate. I kept myself sane all these years by convincing myself that it *had* to be someone I didn't know who killed her."

"If that's the case, why did you walk—no, run—away from all of us?" he asked, a hint of accusation in his voice.

She let her breath out slowly, carefully. "Because I couldn't be sure of anyone anymore." And that hurt her to admit—even to herself.

"Even me?" The tone of voice was right, but the barest hesitation, that diffident note made her realize what her absence had done to him. She'd hurt him badly. In the process, she'd hurt herself. Her fear had torn them apart and had destroyed the special relationship they'd had together. And she'd never meant to do that.

"No," she whispered, the tears that were never far from the surface now rolled down her cheeks. "Not you. Not then and not now." She sniffled.

"Then why?" he cried out, his voice cracking from emotion. "I tried to call, but you were never home, and you never called me back. I stopped by, and either your dad or your brother wouldn't let me in." He swallowed hard, the sound clear through the phone lines. "Finally your dad told me to let it alone and that you were trying to rebuild your life and that I should do the same." He cleared his throat. "I wanted to hate you. I tried to, … but I couldn't."

She hadn't known about the visits. However, the calls were on her. She'd run from the devastation of that weekend, from the horror of the investigation, from the reality that life was no longer nice. Or fun. Most of all, she'd run from the realization that bad things did happen to good people, and sometimes there was no escape.

"I'm so sorry. I just couldn't handle anything more." And she was sorry. For so much. She didn't even know how to explain it, but she tried. "The police were looking at me because Cia was your ex. They were looking at you and suggesting to me that you'd killed her and how well did I know you? I just didn't know what to think. They made me so confused. I had no idea what was going on, and I just ran and went to college and never looked back."

"Never?"

She winced. "I tried not to. I thought that if I could just keep moving forward, then I wouldn't have to face that time in my life again."

"And you are okay with that?"

There was disbelief, curiosity, and a hint of derision in his voice. She deserved it but didn't like it. However, he deserved an answer. "I tried to be. But it always felt …"

"Unfinished?"

"Yes." She gave a wry laugh. "To be expected, I suppose. Maybe now that will go away too."

"I'm not sure I want it to go away."

His voice was so faint that she wasn't sure she had heard him correctly. Her breath caught in her throat. "Pardon?"

"I said, I'm not sure I want it all to go away." And this time there was no doubting the strength of his voice.

Only she wasn't sure exactly what he meant. Stumped, she said nothing.

"No response?" he asked wryly.

"I'm not sure what you are saying." She tried to keep her voice light. "Care to clarify?"

"I'm saying I don't want to be relegated to your history. I don't want to be part of your life that goes away." He paused, sucked in his breath, and then let the rest of his words pour out. "I know this isn't the best time. I know you're dealing with a potential breakup. I guess I just want you to know that I'm here." He paused for a long moment, then added thoughtfully, "In fact, … I always have been."

And he hung up.

"WAY TO GO, Chad." He stared down at his cell phone and groaned. "Smooth, really smooth."

He hadn't meant to say that. Any of it, but the words had slipped out before he could call them back.

And now he didn't know what to do.

Hanging up like that was also stupid. Teenage stuff. And, in a small way, he almost felt that way. As if finding Cia's remains had sent them all tumbling back in time to that frozen part of their lives and to the emotions from back then. Insecurity, betrayal, horror, and … anger.

Meg was the one part of his history that he was hoping to reconnect with. In his head, they hadn't broken up—they were on hold, until Cia's disappearance had been resolved. And how arrogant was that?

Very. And he didn't care. He had to put it out there.

But his timing sucked.

Meg was dealing with a difficult breakup of her own. Good timing for him, in that she was breaking up, but really bad timing in that she needed … time. And although her relationship was on the rocks, that didn't mean it was over, though he could hope.

A text came in. Stephanie. He read the single-word message.

Help.

Shit.

MEG WALKED TO the window again and stared out into the black of night.

Emotions rolled through her. Could Chad have really been holding a torch for her after all these years? What had he said? Something about not wanting to be kept in the past? She pondered the years gone by. Would she ever contemplate returning to her childhood sweetheart? And so fast? Surely that wasn't smart.

She groaned and stretched out on the bed.

Why had he said that *now*?

Talk about bad timing. But her traitorous heart said, *Think of it as a second chance. A chance to correct your course—to get back onto the path you had planned on taking with him.*

But she knew there was no going back. Not to a time of innocence.

But he's not asking you to go back. He's asking you to meet up with him again. The diverged roads were curving back to each other and, once again, becoming as one.

God, how appealing was that?

Visions flashed across her mind of Chad's smiling face, as he had held her tenderly in his arms, the gentle look in his gaze, when she had woken to find him staring down at her, as if she were the most precious gift. The joy of holding hands and being together, fitting together like they were meant to be. And they *were* meant to be. They had spent hours making plans and sharing hopes and dreams. They were going to be together forever.

Forever had lasted one summer.

Then she'd left and had never even said goodbye.

Sitting here in the lonely darkness, Meg realized that *she'd* avoided meeting him, seeing him, because then she could avoid having to do just that—saying goodbye. That way, the door stayed open … just in case.

Now that future was here. And one door in her world was closing. Was she ready to walk through the other? So soon?

Yeah, talk about shitty timing.

TIMING WAS EVERYTHING.

And before the cops learned anything new, he had to find out what they knew now. Just in case he needed to take care of loose ends.

Stephanie was the weakest and easiest link. He would have thought that the years of substance abuse would have taken care of her eons ago but apparently not. How could her body have survived all these years?

It had been interesting, watching her suffer, but even that joy had waned. And now it was too dangerous. He'd loved the grateful sound in her voice when he'd called her to talk. To invite her for coffee.

She'd been so happy to connect again. She was so pathetic.

God, he loved it.

He waited outside the coffee shop, nursing his drink. He'd chosen a remote spot with very little traffic. He had gone in as part of a crowd and had walked straight out with his cup. Just in case there were cameras, he'd kept his face down and his hat on. He didn't want to avoid anything. But neither did he want to be memorable. Not that anyone was looking for him … yet.

Stephanie was driving. He'd chosen a place just too far away for her to walk and not convenient for her to take a bus. He wanted her vehicle. It was much easier to travel that way. He had a pair of stolen plates in his bag. It would be easy to switch them around, and no one would be looking at the car-plate combination.

Only she was late.

Typical female—wants to meet but can't be bothered to show up on time. It was bullshit. He allowed a little of his loathing to leach through. Females were bitches. In heat when they thought it would get them something and conniving mouthpieces when they didn't get it.

A small dark blue compact drove into the parking lot.

About time.

He put a big smile on his face and waved.

Chapter 11

C HAD RACED TO Stephanie's apartment. She hadn't answered her phone since he'd received her last text for help. The older cement building had been around longer than she had, but no graffiti was on the walls, and the hallway was clean. Not that Chad spent any time checking.

She had a ground-floor apartment, and the glass doors to her small patio were closed. Inside, he knocked on her door.

No answer.

He pounded again. "Stephanie. It's Chad. Open up." He put his head against the door and listened. No sound came from inside. "Stephanie!"

The door on the left opened. A tiny head appeared. Bright eyes under an almost pink scalp, with a ghost of white hair, peered out. "Are you looking for Stephanie? There's nothing wrong, is there?"

Chad walked over to the frail but hopefully nosy neighbor. He pulled out his badge. Her eyes lit up at the sight of it. "I'm looking for her. Have you seen her tonight?"

The head bobbed. "Oh yes, she went out with a friend."

Finally a break. "Did you get a good look at him?"

This time the woman shook her head. "No, I didn't. She told me about him, as she was leaving to meet him." The birdlike woman frowned. "I can't remember exactly what she said." She pointed to her watch. "I remember the time though, because I was waiting to watch my show." She beamed up at him. "It was just before eight o'clock."

"And she didn't say anything about where they were going or what they were doing?"

The wispy cloud of white hair about her head bounced. "Oh no, but she was so excited. She was real bubbly, like a young girl again."

Chad nodded. He glanced back at Stephanie's apartment. "I'm afraid she might be in trouble."

"Oh dear, I haven't seen her come home yet, but sometimes she doesn't, you know," she said almost apologetically. Chad could see the woman being accepting of Stephanie's old lifestyle. As Chad studied the paper-thin skin, he couldn't help but see the decades of rough living she herself had experienced.

"Damn." He glanced back at Stephanie's closed door. What to do now?

"I can see if she's home. Just in case I missed her." The woman pulled her keys from the pocket of her oversized sweater. Then locking her door, she walked across to Stephanie's. "I come over all the time to spend time with Chester."

"Chester?"

"Yes, her big tomcat. He's a baby, gets really cranky after too long alone."

Didn't they all? Chad quickly checked his phone. No more texts. *Damn, Stephanie, where are you?* The little old lady already had the door open and had gone in before he could stop her.

"Wait." He was too late. He raced behind her. He stopped in the open living area and gave the place the once-over. Not much had changed since his last visit. The place held few furnishings, and what was there were old and faded. Still, the place was spotless and showed no sign of a disturbance. He smiled to see it so clean. It matched the new Stephanie. She'd cleaned up her act both inside and out. Now, if only he could find her alive and well.

Walking through the one-bedroom apartment, he found Stephanie's neighbor sitting on the double bed, stroking a very large gray cat. The cat appeared undisturbed at Chad's presence.

"What are you looking for?" the neighbor asked curiously, her gaze following his every move.

"Anything that might tell me who she went out with and where they might have gone."

"Oh, I don't think you'll find anything," the woman replied in that chirpy little bird voice.

He spun around. "And why is that?"

She beamed. "Stephanie said it was a secret."

MEG COULDN'T SLEEP. She wandered around the apartment, a cup of herb tea in her hand. Their bags were half packed and possessions half sorted. She couldn't focus. Her mind spun endlessly from Cia to Pete to the media to the mess of her life.

It was too early to call in a few favors to find out what evidence had been pulled from all the material she'd sent back. She should be the anthropologist who examined the remains. She'd collected them. She wanted to be the one to examine them. She'd been in at the beginning; she needed to be there at the end. And yet she could understand the naysayers. Authority thrived on red tape, rules, and creating hell for people. She knew that. Still …

Chad would share what he could, if only to get her professional opinion on the case. That might have to be enough.

It was also too early to contact the people she needed to in regard to the move to the house. And too early to call her friends and talk it over with them. Then who would she call? She'd deliberately kept people at a distance over the years. They couldn't hurt you that way.

She was tempted to call Jade. Of anyone, she'd understand. And she'd offer constructive suggestions. Jade was nothing if not practical. That she had Dane at her side just rounded out Jade's world perfectly.

Once again, Meg walked to the stack of bags on the floor. She couldn't stop feeling that Pete could be back soon. He'd said days, but … it could be just overnight. Or he could be back within a few hours even. Confrontations were not her thing. Look at her history—she always ran when things got tough, except with Pete. Then she might have hung on too long.

And why did she think that might have had something to do with cutting out too quickly on Chad?

She collapsed on the living room couch, not liking the look she'd taken into her character. She hadn't meant to run all those years ago, but it didn't change the fact that that was exactly what she'd done.

Maybe Chad wouldn't want anything to do with her when he got to know the new Meg. She wasn't Megan or Megs anymore.

All those years when Pete had been okay with her absences, she'd been overjoyed that he had been so accepting. But why had he been so accepting? Surely that wasn't normal. Shouldn't he have wanted to spend more time with her?

Jade could be away from Dane the odd time, but she would never choose to be separated. Meg had damn near run at every chance she'd been offered.

And here she was—running away again.

She stared at the bedroom door, then at the heaped bed that she had no hope of getting into tonight. And she needed to finish packing, so she could get them moved, while Janelle was at school.

What she didn't take, she had to be prepared to leave behind. So she'd been tossing stuff out as she sorted. And that had created another problem, as memories overwhelmed her. They also highlighted that Pete was not the same person she'd originally fallen in love with, and she didn't like the new person in the way she'd loved the old one.

Then her mind swung to consider the old Chad and the new version.

That she didn't know who Chad had become was another disturbing thought. That she was even considering Chad in that light again bothered her. She'd never been unfaithful. She'd never even been tempted. And while thinking of him in that light wasn't crossing the line, there was a sense of having done *Chad* wrong by having a relationship with Pete.

And how did that work?

It didn't. It was stupid.

But it's how she was beginning to feel. And to right that wrong from so long time ago, she had to level the field again. Good thing she'd already decided to move out and to leave Pete.

Her inner voice piped up. *Except you haven't yet made the final decision that your relationship with Pete is over. You have come to that point but have shied away from making that final decision.*

But inside you have.

And you have to go with your gut.

"Auntie Meg? What's the matter?"

She spun around to find Janelle rubbing her eyes and looking ready to cry.

"I'm sorry. Did I wake you?" She walked over, glancing at the clock in the living room at the same time. It was past two in the morning. "Let's get you back to bed. It's a school night, and you need sleep."

"I *was* asleep, but something woke me up." Her voice wavered.

Meg tried not to wince. Janelle had had such horrible nightmares when she'd first arrived. "More nightmares?"

She nodded.

Meg needed to keep Janelle from seeing her overly-heaped bed, as this so wasn't the right time for explanations. Meg wrapped an arm around her niece's shoulders and gently tugged her back toward her room.

"Come on. Let's get you back to bed. I'll stay with you, until you fall asleep again."

Besides, Meg knew sleep was beyond her tonight. She cuddled up to Janelle, waiting until she fell back asleep.

CHAD STOOD ONCE again in Stephanie's apartment. He had posted a bulletin on her vehicle and plates, and her description had been sent out to all divisions. He ran a hand through his hair. His stomach was knotted, and his nerves churned.

He'd done what he could do—and, as was so often the case, it wasn't enough.

Three hours had passed since he'd received her text—three hours of frantically searching her old haunts, knocking on doors, and sending out alerts.

So far, nothing. No sign of Stephanie or her vehicle.

Gloves on, he started going through her apartment. Closets, drawers, and all surfaces were checked for notes, address books, diaries, something to show who she'd gone out with. And it had come up empty. He walked into her bedroom again and started dissecting her bed. He found a notebook under her bed. He picked it up and flipped through it.

It appeared to be meandering thoughts, disjointed in time, with no dates or names. He tried to make sense of it all and skimmed over several pages of writing but found the rest of the book empty. As the book was covered with a thick layer of dust, none of it appeared to be recent. He dropped it on the bed and went to the night table. The drawer was stuffed with books—romance novels, if the covers were anything to go by. At the bottom at the back was a small jeweler's box. He tugged it out and studied it. The velvet box was old, burgundy in color, some spots worn right through the nap. He opened it up to find two small necklaces, with a single silver heart pendant.

He lifted one and turned on the lamp to see it better. The silver heart looked familiar, so he turned it over to see a simple inscription. *To Stephanie, with love.*

The words alone made him sit up and take notice. That had been the same wording on the necklace they'd found with Cia's remains. Only in that case, the necklace had had Meg's name on it. Same style, same look. It would take the techs to match it any closer than that.

But it somehow followed ... that the same boyfriend gave the girls this gift?

And that might mean Josh. Again. Stephanie had gone out with him before hooking up with Bruce.

He closed his eyes. His best friend back then had been everyone's friend. And the girls had loved him, *all* the girls. All the time there'd been a lot of envious looks directed his way as he switched his partners on a regular basis back in school, but, at the same time, he was solid. And even though he had had a lot of girls, he was with only one at a time. He never cheated. And he didn't need to—they all just lined up for their turn.

That also meant he had no reason to kill any of them.

He'd been smitten with Cia in the beginning, but that had worn off quickly. He'd known they were done, and Cia was eyeing her next boyfriend. Josh hadn't cared. He'd also had other interests and had planned to break up her with after the camping weekend and before starting college.

Did Josh have it in him to kill? Accidentally maybe. Premeditatedly? No. Chad would bet his life on it.

Instinctively he wanted to say Josh had had nothing to do with Cia's disappearance. But was that fair? He needed to take a new look at everyone. That's what Mack had said too.

They would start fresh. Go over everything with a magnifying glass and tweezers, if necessary.

This time they would find the truth. And, if Josh had killed Cia, then Josh's ass would get nailed.

Chad closed his eyes.

He hoped it wasn't his best friend.

MEG WORKED THROUGH the night. She collapsed at two a.m. and woke up at five a.m., and then she carried on. She had the bulk of her belongings sorted and bagged—a stack she was taking and a stack that she wasn't. Then finally, just before time to wake up Janelle for school, Meg remade the bed, took one last slow look at the bedroom that held so many loving memories. They'd warmed her for so many long cold nights. And now there was nothing but icy sadness.

Fatigue had taken over. She swayed, overcome with pain and grief.

Then she heard Janelle get up and go to the bathroom.

Meg poured steel into her back and pushed back the hot ball in her throat to be dealt with at another time, yet again.

One of these days that space inside would explode from the pressure—but not today.

Today was big. And the knot in her stomach was a fear that ate away at her insides. She was afraid, now that she'd started, that she wouldn't get out in time, before Pete came back.

With one last glance around, she closed the door on her past and turned to face a sleepy Janelle—her future. And, for the next hour, Meg could do what needed to be done.

She could get through this.

"Good morning, sleepyhead. How are you feeling?"

With Janelle promising to get dressed quickly, Meg headed to the kitchen to make breakfast.

Janelle left on time, and the moment the door closed behind her, Meg kicked into high gear. She lugged her bags to her car and stowed them in the trunk. When that couldn't hold any more, she filled the back seat. It took several trips to get these loaded. In the front passenger seat, she loaded the bags she was giving away to charity.

Puffing with exertion, she raced back upstairs, feeling as if she were running out of time, her nerves jangling every time she heard a truck or saw a tall man. In Janelle's room she stopped to take stock. The place was relatively neat, but Janelle still had dirty laundry, school stuff, and some other items that she'd chosen to take to Meg's. And they all needed to be packed up and returned to her old house.

For just a moment, Meg wondered if she was doing the right thing. Maybe they should move to a neutral setting.

But, no, she didn't have time. If Janelle didn't like being back at her old home, then it would only be temporary. But she had to go now.

It took another hour and six more trips before Meg took a final look at Janelle's room, then at the rest of the apartment.

She took the stairs on the last trip and walked to her stuffed car. She'd go to the closest Goodwill store and get rid of those items first.

Unlocking her car, she opened the door. A voice called out from behind her.

"There she is. Megan Pearce."

She spun around only to see a TV crew, racing toward her. The cameras were a dead giveaway. "Shit."

She hopped in, locked the door, and turned on her engine.

"Wait! We just want to talk to you."

Just as the reporter reached her car, Meg peeled out of the lot. So much for privacy. Damn good thing she was moving out. In her rearview mirror, she watched the crew climb into their van in an attempt to follow her, which was so not going to happen.

She took several corners in an effort to lose them and took the long way to run her errands.

The last thing she needed was to talk to the media. They'd made her life hell once. She wasn't signing up for a second round, if she could help it.

But how long would it be before they tracked her down at her new location?

STEPHANIE TREMBLED. SHE lifted a hand and watched as her whole arm shook. Her chest rose and fell in short gasps. It felt as if she'd been running for hours. She'd been on the run before, but she'd forgotten the adrenaline rush or the pain as the shock wore off.

If it wore off …

Damn, she was scared. She kept her eyes closed, knowing that the whites of her eyes would shine in the dark of the night.

The problem was that she didn't know what she was running from. She should have met Bruce for coffee. Now she figured she'd taken a wrong turn in life again. And that she was being followed.

But by whom?

She slipped around the dingy corner into a back alley she knew all too well. No one could find her here. She was in the world that she'd struggled so hard to get out of again.

But right now it was a perfect place to blend in and to hide away.

She had to stay safe. She didn't know who had killed Cia, but she knew it had to be one of those guys she'd camped with. She couldn't trust any of them.

Not now.

And she wanted to live. For the first time in a long time, she *wanted* to live.

Chapter 12

MEG SCRUBBED HER face, then put on heavier makeup than normal—but she was deluding herself that she'd camouflaged her exhaustion—then walked out of her brother's house. Her muscles ached and her back was telling her that she'd done too much. Yet what were the options? The bags had to be unloaded and unpacked and the cleaning had to be done. The house had been empty for months. And there wasn't any coffee. She needed to shop for food and a few basics.

The lab came first.

She drove her brother's car to the Forensic Support Services lab and parked in the staff parking lot. She'd been a consultant out of this office off and on for many years. She could only hope her earlier phone call had brought the results she'd hoped for.

Inside, she identified herself and strode down to Stacy Carter's office, a forensic pathologist. Of the same age, the two had been friends for years. Professional colleagues at first but that had quickly morphed to mutual respect and a developing friendship. A friendship she'd called on this morning.

Stacy looked up, a warm smile breaking across her face. "There she is. Meg, who can't take a weekend away without tripping over a body."

Meg smiled wanly. "Too true and you're not the first to bring up that point."

"Pete, *huh*?"

Meg winced. "Yeah, it was the last straw for him."

Stacy's chocolate-brown eyes widened in shock, and the smile fell away. "Oh, no, I am so sorry." She stood and walked around her desk to look Meg in the eye. "You two have been together a long time. Maybe you can work this out."

"Maybe." Meg shrugged. "Yet I may not want to anymore." She stared around the office, not certain she was ready to talk about it, but she didn't have too many people she could share this with. Stacy was

346

one of them, so she took a deep breath and explained about everything that had happened since Darren's death and Janelle's arrival in her world.

When she was done, Stacy reached out and gave her a hug. "I'm so sorry. You've had a rough couple months. But you are doing the right thing. Janelle needs you. Obviously Pete doesn't."

Meg gave a half laugh. "That's one way of putting it. Thanks."

"And these remains you found, you believe them to be of your old friend?"

Meg, relieved to be onto other issues, nodded. "All of the evidence points in that direction. Obviously DNA tests will need to be done to confirm it, but the victim is the right age, height, and in the right location."

"And the necklace?" Stacy was always a direct person. Meg appreciated it. It was so much easier to deal with.

"I think it's mine."

"Hence my role?" At Meg's nod, Stacy added, "Okay. I'll do the examination. You'll observe. The process will be videotaped, with audio to ensure you aren't touching the bones or compromising the evidence. Yes, that's overkill."

Meg laughed. "In our business, nothing is overkill."

Stacy smiled. "How true. But, if this goes to court, we both have to testify."

It was such a pleasure to work with a professional. "Exactly."

Stacy led the way to the lab. "Now, let's go see if we can help your friend."

CHAD WALKED INTO one of the many empty rooms at the station. He felt like shit. There'd been no sign of Stephanie. He didn't even know which places she haunted, and neither did her neighbor. Stephanie hadn't contacted Chad and hadn't shown up for work.

He'd called her friends, but no one had heard from her. On the off chance, he'd texted Bruce but hadn't heard back from him. For all intents and purposes, she'd disappeared.

If it hadn't been for her last cry for help, he hated to say, he would likely be considering she'd disappeared with her druggie friends for a few days.

But maybe that *was* her cry for help. Maybe she'd been hoping that he'd stop her before she spiraled out of control again and went back to her old ways.

But what if this disappearance wasn't her return to bad habits? What if it was connected to Cia's disappearance? The timing was suspicious, coincidental, and convenient.

With that thought uppermost in his mind, he headed for the room Daniel had booked for this process. He stood in the doorway. Daniel should be here already but apparently wasn't yet. The room wasn't empty though. Boxes had been stacked two high at the one end of the table.

He couldn't contain his excitement as he strode closer. It had been hard moving from being a suspect in a disappearance to a cop and now a detective in his own right. Especially with Cia's disappearance always hanging over his head. From Chad's point of view, this find had been a long time coming.

Finally they could catch the asshole who had killed Cia.

"Figured you would show up early." Mack walked in, hitching up his pants. He carried a chipped coffee mug filled with coffee in one hand and a stack of files in the other. "Just not this early. Daniel isn't even here yet."

"I'm not that early," Chad protested, then grinned sheepishly. "And so what if I am?" He shoved a hand through his hair. "Any news on Stephanie?"

Mack shook his head and dumped his files on the table at the opposite end of the table to the boxes. "No, but her disappearance might have nothing to do with Cia's case. Stephanie's disappeared into the streets many times before. If she's relapsed, then that's on her, not on you." He looked up and studied Chad. "Are you sure you're ready for this?"

"Are you? I've been ready for seventeen years, and there's no way to know about Stephanie," Chad snapped, then reined back his impatience. "But, if her disappearance is related, … I want to find the bastard and her, … fast."

"Yep, me too. But, for me, this is just one of many cases I'd like answers to."

"Yeah, but it's the only one that happened in your backyard."

Silence.

Chad looked up, caught Mack's narrowed-eyed gaze, and grinned. "Do you really think I don't know who owns each and every one of those cabins?" He added smoothly, "Besides, you're Bruce's uncle, not to mention Anto's and Pero's uncle as well."

Mack dropped his gaze to his folders, a thick frown forming on his pug face.

Chad studied him. "I know that you shouldn't have been on the case back then. I know about you almost getting kicked off the force over it all. Does that bug you?"

"No. You just surprised me, that's all." He shuffled through the folders. "Now, if you're done, maybe we can get to work. Daniel should be here any minute."

Chad filed that reaction in the back of his mind and turned to the top box. He moved it down beside the first and opened the lid. Instantly all thoughts of Mack's cabin flew out of his head. This was the gold mine of evidence laid out before him.

Finally. Now he could get the answers he'd always been looking for.

Maybe he'd be in time to save Stephanie. Inside, he doubted it. He hated to think of it, but he was afraid it was already too late.

MACK WATCHED CHAD burrow into boxes, like a child who'd found lost treasure. Chad had lost a lot back then, his innocence being at the top of that long list.

Mack had been so sure that Chad had killed Cia Barnes. And Mack had had no doubt that Cia was dead. Years of experience said the odds were not in that young girl's favor. Those same odds also said it was one of those six young men from the camping trip who'd killed her.

And three of them were from his own damn family. That had been tough. His other family members called him, day in and day out, crying and screaming for him to do something. And he had a big family. They'd nagged him endlessly. Over the years, the case had ended up being the one taboo subject at any family gatherings. It was as if, by ignoring it, the three men would be innocent.

Sure, Mack had seventeen fewer years on the force back then, but he'd been sharp, and he'd understood the vagaries of human nature even then. Chad had headed the suspect list. Mack admitted to having leaned on him pretty hard, hoping for a confession in order to clear his nephews. Instead Chad had held up, and Cia's case had remained unsolved—and a permanent worry to eat away at Mack.

But Chad had gone from a shocked, scared innocent to a bitter realist and an even more scared man.

Mack had seen the change before his eyes. The memory saddened him. At the time, he'd been glad of it. He'd wanted the smart ass to grow up and to see the pain he'd caused Cia's family and friends and to feel the full force of the law and to be scared and to need to feel the heavy hand of punishment. Mack had done a lot wrong back then. Almost ruined his career over the choices he'd made. However, he'd done it to try to prove his nephews innocent.

Then one day, Chad had walked into the station with his own badge.

Now Mack grudgingly admitted he *might* have misjudged the guy. The young kid had grown into a solid young man. But ... leopards didn't change their spots, and killers never forgot what they had done, no matter how long it was between kills. That meant this kid was *not* off the hook.

And this was very suspicious timing for Stephanie to go missing. If she had panicked about the remains that had been found, she had had an interesting way of reacting. Stephanie was a drug addict, who, if she'd ever known anything incriminating, had either forgotten about it or had lost the credibility to prove it a long time ago.

Also interesting was that the only person who thought she was missing was Chad, and Mack only had his word on her disappearance. Something he would have to point out to Daniel.

But Mack had seen people act in a lot of ways. So far as he was concerned, while Chad was looking through the evidence for suspects, Mack would take another look at *him*.

MEG WAITED OUTSIDE the school grounds for Janelle to walk out. She'd texted her already, saying that she'd pick her up.

Now, seated in the car, with the heat pounding down on her and after the fullness of her day, Meg just wanted to close her eyes. Exhaustion had nothing on her. She wanted nothing more than to go home and sleep.

And that so wasn't an option.

She had to face Janelle first.

"Auntie Meg? Are you sleeping?"

She laughed at Janelle. "Get in the car, silly. I admit I'm tired, but I'm not sleeping."

"Sure looks like it to me," Janelle muttered. "Can we go home, please?"

Uh-oh. Meg cast her niece a quick look, then turned on the engine. She drove to the house, wondering how long it would take.

Two blocks apparently.

"Auntie Meg? I thought we were going home."

Meg changed lanes and took the next left. A couple moments later, she pulled into her brother's driveway and drove into the garage. She turned off the engine, twisted in her seat, and turned to look at Janelle.

In a calm, quiet voice, she said, "We are home."

Janelle's eyes widened uncomprehendingly. She frowned. "What do you mean?"

With a buoyant smile, Meg unlocked the door and got out. She waited for Janelle to grab her backpack and join her. She closed the garage door with the button at the side of the interior door. Then she unlocked the door to the house. She returned to the car and opened the trunk, and started unloading the grocery bags she'd stashed in the back. When she walked into the kitchen, Janelle stood in the center of the kitchen, staring at her.

"A little help, please." Meg gasped as one of the bags started to slip. Janelle jumped forward and grabbed it before it fell. "Start putting away stuff, and I'll go get the rest."

It took ten minutes before the groceries were unloaded and put away. Janelle grabbed an apple and a spoonful of peanut butter—and again stood in the middle of the room, right in front of Meg. "Now what's going on?"

Blowing a strand of hair off her face, Meg smiled. "I would have thought that was obvious by now. We'll live here from now on." She studied Janelle's face, looking for some inkling of a reaction. "If that's okay with you?"

Janelle was quiet, as she munched on her snack. "It's fine by me. Why?"

Meg wanted to prevaricate, but that wasn't the best way to move forward. "I have thought a lot about my relationship with Pete and decided that the best thing would be some time apart."

Instead of the happy reaction she'd expected, Janelle frowned. "Have you broken up with him?"

"Not yet. He went away for a few days to consider our relationship, and I decided that I wanted to be gone before he came back."

"And will he be mad at us?" Janelle asked, her eyes narrowed, her voice cautious.

"I'm not sure." Meg smiled. "Maybe he'll be relieved."

"Did you leave him a note or something, so he knows where we are?" Janelle's voice rose in fear.

Meg tilted her head. "You are concerned about him?"

At that, Janelle dropped her gaze to her apple.

Meg caught her breath. "No. You're worried about him being angry?"

Janelle lifted her face slowly, uncertainty shining in her beautiful eyes. Then she gave a faint nod.

Right. That fear factor again. "Ah, honey, Pete might get angry sometimes, but he's not dangerous." She hoped. Meg walked over and wrapped her arms around her niece in a comforting hug. "Not to worry. I'll speak with him about our future soon. But, as the condo is Pete's, I felt this was the best interim home we could have, as long as it doesn't bother you."

Janelle glanced around. "No. It won't. Dad and I didn't live here very long anyway." She spun around. "It's bigger than the condo, and I can have my old room back. It still has some of my stuff in it."

"Right. I've brought everything—at least, I hope I have everything—from the condo. Go on up and take a look. Set about organizing your stuff, and I'll start dinner."

At that, Janelle took off.

Meg sagged against the kitchen counter and dropped her head backward, before slowly rotating it to ease the knots building up all day. Why had she thought this step would be a hugely difficult deal? It had been easy.

She'd expected endless questions, and instead there'd been essentially nothing. That didn't mean the questions weren't still coming, but, for now, conflict had been averted.

She still had a few more loose ends to tie up, like the security system needed a second look, but that could be tomorrow's job.

Tonight they'd be fine. Besides, no one knew where they were anyway.

STEPHANIE WOKE UP alone, cold, and scared. The sun was up, reaching into the back alley. God, she was still alive.

She wasn't sure she deserved to be. And she wasn't sure she wanted to be. The place reeked with vomit and urine ... and something else she didn't want to think about. But this is what she had to deal with. She straightened, hating the pain in her back, the agony of an empty belly yet again. She didn't dare go home, but that's where she wanted to be.

And damn her for being such a fool as to lose her cell phone. She couldn't even remember where her car was at this point or even where she was in relation to it, for that matter.

God, Stephanie, you're such a loser.

Then she remembered being followed. And ducking out of sight and then running for her life. Had she shaken him off?

Or was he on the street waiting for her. *Shit!*

Chapter 13

C HAD LEFT THE office late, frustrated and depressed.
With Daniel, they'd opened the boxes, gone through all the evidence and every statement, and then set up a new board with position locators, indicating where everyone had been at the time of Cia's disappearance. Then they set up a timeline of events.

It had been a futile exercise. He'd bet the new material they'd worked up would be exactly the same as what he had at home. He was counting on it. Yet he would spend the evening checking it out. He'd taken copies of what he could photocopy and had taken pictures of the rest.

The answers had to be here.

Somewhere.

Once at his apartment, he cleared off his dining room table and unloaded the work he'd brought home. Then, with the same precision he'd used at the office, he reopened and set up the case files he'd kept at home.

He had just sat down to work when his phone rang. *Josh.*

"Who killed her?" Josh began without preamble, a hard edge to his voice. When Chad didn't answer fast enough, Josh's voice rose. "Damn it, Chad, who fucking killed her?"

"Easy, Josh. I don't know who killed her." He cleared his throat, knowing Josh needed answers as badly as he did. "It's too early to say yet. We don't know anything at this stage."

"Damn it."

There was a dark silence, then Josh growled. "Is it her? At least tell me that."

That much Chad could give him. "We think so. Right height, age, location. However, DNA will be weeks before confirming. They are looking for dental records to compare." He waited.

"How could we *not* have found her?" The pain in Josh's voice made Chad wince. "We searched for days."

"I don't know about you, but I went back several weekends, hoping to find her—or something that would explain what had happened to her."

"So did I, over several weekends as well. I couldn't forget about her. Who could? Damn it. When I heard the news, I knew it had to be her."

"Me too. Meg found her, you know."

"Meg who?"

"Megan. Megs. She goes by Meg now. She's an anthropologist. Has a mess of degrees. Like a lot of us, she switched her name to one the media didn't know so well. She went on with her life and became someone."

Josh gave a harsh laugh. "Glad someone did. I sure as hell didn't."

"That's not true, Josh. You might not be an engineer, but you're doing something you love."

"Surveying for a company that is given contracts *by* engineers is not the future I had envisioned for myself. We were both planning on engineering, but …"

Chad didn't want to get into that discussion. Too many years had passed to worry about a change in career paths now. "It's also not doing drugs and curled up in a back alley somewhere."

"Stephanie is a great way to put my life in perspective." Josh sighed. "I wished I'd done things differently though."

"Don't we all?"

"Do you? Do you wish you hadn't gone into law enforcement? You've spent every day trying to hunt down the killer."

"I know, and, since we found Cia's remains, I'd like to think we have a chance now to find out what happened. So that—"

"So that we can get on with the rest of our lives? Oh, don't worry. I've thought the same thing. But what future? We've lived with this hanging over our heads for so long. I didn't do it. You didn't do it— but we might as well have because of how we've let it affect our lives. It's been criminal, that's what it is. Yet we aren't criminals."

"No, we aren't." Chad tried to ease the conversation down a notch, but Josh was just gearing up.

"But that's how we've been treated. Since then, I feel like I'm always being watched. That, if I don't pay a parking ticket as soon as I get it, I'll go to jail for life. It's as if I slipped through on that one transgression, and now the law is looking for another way to nail my hide and to throw me in jail, as if that's where I should have been all this time."

"He—"

"Do you realize that if we'd been convicted of accidentally killing Cia, we'd be out by now?" He snorted. "Instead we did nothing, but got a life sentence anyway."

"Stephanie is missing," Chad finally managed to say. There was no easy way to say it.

Silence.

"Missing—how?"

"That's just it. I don't know. She sent me a text asking for help. Just the one word. *Help.* Nothing else and nothing since. She's not at home and hasn't been home since then. No one has seen her since she left in secret to meet a 'friend.'"

"Shit. You think something has happened to her?"

"I don't know." Chad stared out the window. "Yet I'm afraid something might have."

"She could just be meeting her dealer. After quitting her drug-taking, any meeting with him makes him a 'secret' now. Had you found out, you'd be pissed at her, same for anyone else in her circle. She always was a drama queen."

"And a nervy one. I know. However, I can't get the timing out of my head."

"That Cia's remains have been found and that Stephanie has gone missing? You don't think she had anything to do with Cia's death, do you?"

"No, I don't—or Meg, for that matter. But what if Stephanie didn't tell all the truth back then? What if she knows something, or what if the killer thinks she knows something?"

Josh laughed. "That's your cop's instincts getting to you. Chances are, she's shacked up with someone, and her cell phone battery has died. How many times over the years has she called you to get her a place to sleep at night? Help with getting her out of jail? Help with finding her rehab assistance? She has even called you to help her rent an apartment because she had no references. She'd only rented the flop-by-the-hour ones before then."

"I remember." Talk about memories that Chad would not like to resurrect. "She had no one else."

"Hell, of course she didn't. Even Bruce finally had enough, and she had him on speed dial for years. He's still sweet on her, but he still walked away. Hell, we all walked away, once we realized she was on a downward slide and looking to take everyone down with her."

"And I walked away too." Chad groaned softly, hating the rush of painful memories.

"Hey, man, don't hold yourself to blame for that. At some point there is no helping those who won't help themselves, at least not if they aren't interested."

"I know." Chad stared at the wall, with all the case information. "She's been doing so much better these last few years. I'd like to think she's turned a corner. She's called several times since the word got out."

"She'll have it rough if the media finds her." Josh sighed. "That would send her into hiding."

There was silence. Chad had nothing to add. Josh was right.

"Funny about Megs, though."

"Meg," Chad corrected automatically. "What's funny?"

"Look at what she does for a living, and then she's the one who finds the remains." He snorted. "Almost like it was meant to be."

"Merely a coincidence."

"I thought you didn't believe in those."

"It was Meg's first time back in the area since that weekend. She was staying at one of the cabins down a way. It was a fluke she even found the remains. While she'd be better prepared than most people at finding them, it still hit her hard, when she put the facts together."

"Yeah, I imagine. How is she doing?" Josh's voice changed, deepened, making Chad wonder if he still carried any lingering emotions for Meg. "I presume you've talked to her since?"

"Yes, I have, and she's holding. She's good people."

"I know. She always was."

There was that odd twinge in his friend's voice. "You aren't still hung up on her, are you? I thought you got over her a long time ago." *Like before she started going out with me*, but Chad didn't say that last bit. There was no point.

"I did get over her. I was just wondering what she's like now. Look at how Stephanie turned out. It seems like Meg went in the opposite direction. She chose something so focused and so demanding that it's like she has to be in control, ready in case of a repeat event."

"That's because she blames herself. If she'd only kept a closer eye on Cia, she would have known what had happened to her, that kind of stuff."

"No one could keep an eye on that girl. I always wondered if she'd crept off on her own to meet someone. She was my girl, but I knew it was over. She was already looking for her next mark. In a way, I was too. It was more so for my ego than anything else." He gave a self-deprecating laugh. "Now I'm used to getting dumped."

Chad sighed. "Oh no, did Kim leave?"

"Sure did. The minute the news hit the wire and the phone calls started, she bailed, saying she hadn't signed up to live with a murder suspect."

Shit. "I'm sorry, man." If anyone had been dogged by the bad press, it had been Josh. Another prime suspect from that weekend because, when things got rough with his relationships, the cops always brought up the fact that a prior girlfriend had disappeared. And then the women usually left after that.

"Anto was the lucky one, dying like that. A head-on collision and, *boom*, no more suspicion, no more threats or lingering doubts from supposed family and friends."

"Yeah, except that he's dead."

"And safely out of everyone's suspicious eyes. I don't know about you, but dying was the easy way out. Staying alive and dealing with this shit has not been fun."

Depression had always been an issue for Josh, ever since that weekend. Now every time he came up against another hurdle, he seemed to drop down further and further. So far, he'd always managed to pull up again, and, maybe this time, they could solve Cia's case, and that would stop the vicious cycle. They all needed a break from their pasts, Josh more than most.

Then there was Stephanie.

Chad was afraid it was all too much for Stephanie. She might never survive this—regardless of her reason for disappearing. He wasn't sure he could help her anymore, not if she'd gone off the deep end yet again.

MEG WAITED UNTIL Janelle went to sleep, a chatterbox right up to the end, before slowly walking back to her new bedroom. She sat on the bed and stared around. She'd put away her clothes and had stored as much of the other stuff as she could in the bottom of the closet. She kinda felt like she had deserted Pete.

And that felt wrong, but she was too tired to change it now; maybe on the weekend.

She collapsed on the bed with her arms above her head and tried to relax. Today could have been so much worse. Thankfully it had gone relatively smoothly. At the lab, she'd observed so intently that

Stacy had laughed at her a couple times, saying it felt like she was back under examination by her toughest profs.

Meg hadn't meant to be that intense, but sometimes she didn't dare have anything go wrong—or have anything important get missed.

And nothing had been. Sadly not much to see. Meg was convinced they'd found Cia, but outside of cause of death being confirmed, Stacy had found nothing new. She'd pulled DNA that would be tested against that of Cia's father, but, after having gone through the bones and having the rest of the soil sifted and looked at for evidence, they hadn't found anything new. That hadn't made Meg happy, but it was what she'd expected.

She wanted to tell Chad. However, for many reasons, she shouldn't call. She groaned and reached for her phone. She had just as many reasons *to* call. Besides, it would be nice to connect. She had been feeling a little disconnected all day, and she'd expected to hear from Pete by now. That meant he was staying away longer than planned or had come home and had found her gone and hadn't come after her.

He would likely know where she'd gone. It's not as if she had any number of places to go to. This choice made sense, but he might not see it that way. And did she care if he hadn't come after her? No. She would be relieved when that final conversation was over. Until then, she was waiting. And that was uncomfortable.

First things first; she dialed Chad's number, trying to ignore the fact that she'd called Chad instead of Pete.

"Meg, I heard you were busy today?"

That surprised her. "Did Stacy call you?"

"No, Daniel and Mack spoke with her."

"Oh, *Mack*." Damn, just hearing that man's name was enough to send the willies down her spine. "I thought he got kicked off the case."

"Yeah, it's technically Daniel's case, but you know that Mack won't ever stay out of it."

"Oh, yeah, I remember him—built like a crushed cement truck and with an attitude to match."

He started laughing. "That sounds like him, but I've come to respect the work he does."

"Bet that wasn't easy." She thought it might have been damn difficult. "He was an asshole to us."

"Yeah, but then he figured one of us had killed Cia."

"I suppose. Still doesn't make him a nice guy." She remembered how terrified she'd been of the detective. The hard look in his eyes had given her nightmares for months.

"Well, not sure he is now either, but he's good at what he does."

"Except that he couldn't find Cia's killer either."

"True. First, did you find anything on the bones? I tried calling several times today, but your phone went to voice mail." He gave a short laugh. "And I drove past your place today. The media were all over there."

"Yes, I barely avoided them this morning. I haven't been back there since." She groaned. "I should have mentioned it before, as the damn media could make it look like I skipped town." Quickly she filled him in on her night and day. Toward the end, she yawned, then yawned again. "Sorry. I'm exhausted."

"With good reason. Sounds like you need a good night's sleep."

"Or two or three. I just wanted to see if you had anything new." She hated the hopeful note in her voice, but, damn it, one of them should have found something.

"Nothing. We're going back to the beginning and taking a fresh look at everything. We will have to come around and speak with everyone again."

"Oh, *fun.*"

"I know. It's not what we want either. I have other cases to work on too, and this is Daniel's case, not mine. So expect a call from him soon."

"Thanks for that positive note." She didn't want to speak to anyone again. "I so don't want to remember the details from back then."

"We have your statement but expect to be questioned to see if you want to change or add anything."

"There isn't anything," she said tiredly. "I gave as clear an accounting as I could back then. Nothing has changed in my head, just that I am seventeen years older, wiser, and more cynical."

"Aren't we all?" He paused. "Have you eaten?"

She smiled and ran a hand through her hair. "Yes, I have Janelle to maintain some semblance of normality for. I really don't want her affected by this."

"You know she will be. As much as we'd like to avoid it, the families are always affected."

"I know. Doesn't mean I like it. She knows I found a set of remains, but she doesn't know anything about whose remains they may be or how they are connected to me."

"You might want to tell her. It's not a good thing for her to find out from someone else."

"I know." She considered the issue but didn't like any of the options. "Damn."

"Sorry. I'm going to contact the others."

"*Ugh*. That's a tough job. How is Pero doing? Last I heard, he was recovering from a car accident that killed his brother, Anto. But that was like eleven, twelve years ago. Pero was okay but ... his brother? ... Yuck."

"He was a good friend. I didn't realize you didn't like him."

"I liked Pero. None of us girls liked Anto. And I never told you because he *was* your friend." She smiled at the memories. "He was important to you, and you were important to me. So I put up with him."

"I never knew."

"No," she reminisced. "Lots of things you didn't know."

He laughed. "No way," he scoffed. Then he paused for a long moment, before asking curiously, "Like what?"

She laughed. "Oh, I don't know. Lots of things. We were so young and intense. I was scared to screw it all up, but I did anyway."

Damn. Meg closed her eyes. She shouldn't have said that. Waves of emotional exhaustion hit her in never-ending painful ebbs and flows. It was the only reason she'd said that. It wouldn't have slipped out otherwise. But it had, and now she had to deal with it.

"What? No. That's not true. You were perfect, always."

"So not true," she whispered. "I was horrible, just horrible, back then."

"What are you talking about?" His voice deepened. "You were never horrible. It's not in you."

She stifled back the tears, hating the weakness threatening to overtake her. She should never have called him. Her throat was clogged, and she couldn't get the words out. She swallowed several times, but that hot ball in her throat refused to budge.

"Is this to do with Cia?" His voice broke through her pain.

"Yes," she replied. "You know that, when she disappeared, we were gossiping about her? *About* her. That's like how horrible we were. ... She was dying, and we, ... well, we were sniggering about her."

Just the memory burned hot and hateful in her head. God, she hated how she had acted back then.

"Christ, Meg, you were barely eighteen. Everyone gossiped. And everyone gossiped about Cia. Jesus, she got around." He sighed. "If nothing had happened to her, that would never have been an issue, but, because something did, it put a spotlight on each of our behaviors at the time." He groaned. "Remember what I did? I almost went out of my mind, knowing she'd died because I'd been a coward, too chicken shit to find out what that noise was."

"No, that's not true," Meg cried out, shocked out of her self-pity. "You could have been killed yourself."

"And maybe I could have stopped it before anyone got hurt." He gave a harsh, short laugh. "Instead I've spent every day wondering *what if …*"

"Like the rest of us. We all wondered if our actions could have changed the outcome, and, of course, there is no way to know."

"Exactly. … This has ruined all our lives, but we can't let it control us forever."

"Like Stephanie." Meg sighed. "I feel so sorry for her. I should have stayed in touch, but I just couldn't handle it."

"Yeah, we got that. I stayed in touch early on, but I was struggling too. Then, by the time she hit the streets, even though I tried for years, I couldn't help her anymore. She contacted me a few years ago, saying she'd cleaned up her act, asking for help."

"What kind of help?"

"To get some counseling, help her find a place to live, that kind of thing."

"You've been a good friend to her." The sound that came through Chad's end of the phone made her wince.

"Not good enough. She's missing right now, and I've done all I can do, but there's still no sign of her."

"Shit." Her reaction was as much for the worry and frustration in his voice as for the fact that Stephanie was missing.

"Exactly." He sighed. "Everyone is assuming she's taken another dive into the drug scene to forget."

Meg sat up and crossed her legs. She ran a hand through her hair. "Has she done this since cleaning up?"

"Unfortunately, yes." He added, "Once after losing a job. It was a slip-up but not a bad one."

She winced. "Some events are enough to shake even the most stable of us."

He gave a short laugh. "And no one would consider her stable."

"No." So true but they'd been good friends at one time, and Meg wished Stephanie had had an easier time of it. "Well, I hope she shows up soon. Otherwise …"

"Yeah, I know." He cleared his throat. "Enough of Stephanie for now. With the media out hunting up anyone connected to Cia's disappearance, I suggest you keep a low profile for the next week, while we work on the case."

"Will do." She stood and walked to her window, where she peeked out from the side. "The street looks clear. They haven't found me yet."

"Good. Let's keep it that way." His voice deepened. "I wouldn't want anything to happen to you."

She sighed. "You know the timing really sucks, don't you?"

"I know." His voice lightened so much she could almost see his smile in her mind, "I'm just letting you know your options."

"Really?" She laughed. "Is that what you call it?"

"No pressure," he stated firmly. "I'm here if you need me or if and when you are ready to see if we have anything worth rekindling."

She both loved and hated the shiver of delight slipping down her spine at his words. He'd always had that effect on her.

After saying good night, she murmured a few moments later, "What a concept." Maybe that's why she'd gone for Pete. Stable, solid, and comfortable Pete. He'd never take her camping and have someone get murdered. No, but he had taken her to his cabin, where she'd found a body.

Maybe she was destined to live a life that always touched on crime. Certainly she could have focused on that with her work, but she'd chosen a more humanitarian way to use her education and skills. Yes, crime was often involved, but she'd spent so much time working on old, oftentimes large cases that the crimes, for all their horror, were distant and, therefore, easier to deal with.

Opening a mass grave to identify bodies from an earthquake was much less personal than identifying Cia's body found in a lonely faraway place in the woods. The mass grave in Haiti had had an additional creepy criminal aspect to it, but that had been a one-in-a-million-lifetimes' chance of occurrence.

She'd gone through enough horror back then. And she'd never told anyone at the time about her own history with Cia. It wasn't something she wanted to share. It was something she *couldn't* share.

Tuesday Morning

CHAD WAS STILL trying to gulp coffee before shooting out the door on the way to work, when Daniel called. "I'm calling them all in, including you."

"Shit. A little warning and a little time for them to arrange their lives would have been nice." He threw back the rest of his coffee, then called Meg.

"Good morning."

Her voice, warm and welcoming, brought a smile instantly to his face. Then he realized she'd lose both when she realized what he needed.

"What's up?" Her voice had cooled. "Chad?"

"Sorry, just giving you a heads-up. Daniel called. He wants everyone in the office today for questioning."

"Really?" She gave a choked laugh. "Well, I can make it, but I wouldn't be so sure about the others. Let's see. Anto and Cia are dead, and Stephanie is missing. Besides you and me, that doesn't leave many. Josh, Pero, Tim, and who? Bruce, right?"

"Right, only Josh, Bruce, and you live in town. Tim is in Europe, and I have no idea about Pero. I haven't heard from him or about him for over a decade."

"I'll go straight there. Let's get this over with." And she hung up.

Damn. Chad knew it was asking a bit much without warning, but he'd hoped for a better reaction than that.

He grabbed his keys and drove to work. At the station, he was surprised to find Mack waiting with Daniel. Chad asked, "Did you reach everyone?"

"I will," Daniel said. "No worries there."

At his tone of voice, Chad spun and looked at him. "What's going on? What have you found out?"

"Stephanie is now officially a missing person. I went to her place. Found this." Mack tossed a small evidence bag on the table.

Chad walked over and checked it out. "Right, it's similar to the one found with Cia's remains."

"Right. And according to Stephanie's statement, she was Bruce's girlfriend at the time. But she has the same type of necklace as the one we found with Cia's remains."

"True enough. But she also went out with Josh earlier. In fact, the guys all bought them, as they were all the rage. What one girl had, the next must have or something better. As they were all friends, it was easier to just buy the same. So either Bruce or Josh could have bought it for her."

Daniel, shoving his long sleeves up his arms, asked, "Are you sure?"

"Look. A lot of friends were in our group. Some came on one weekend but couldn't go on the next. But, within that group, a lot of the couples changed and paired up with others. In fact, the more I've thought about it, it was only a couple hours' drive away, so anyone could have known of our camping plans and taken advantage of Cia being alone."

Mack just stared at him. Derision was clear in his gaze. "You got to take off those rose-colored glasses, boyo. One of you six males killed Cia, mark my words. There wasn't another friend making the drive out there just to pick her off. Neither was it a stranger or a random killing. No." He stabbed a finger at the files in front of him. "It was someone in your group."

Chad glared at the files under Mack's thumb. "I damn well hope not."

"Both of you calm down," Daniel snapped. "And if you can't be impartial about this, then I don't want you anywhere near me or the case, until I find the bastard."

"I *am* impartial." Chad wanted to note that Mack was not being impartial, but that wouldn't help his case. In fact, Daniel could shut out Chad. But that wouldn't help anyone. Mack only wanted to clear his nephews. Chad wanted to clear *all* of them …

"Just because I don't want it to be a friend doesn't mean I'm not going to follow the evidence." He picked up the bag with Stephanie's necklace in it. "This is hardly evidence. It just proves that Cia and Stephanie may have had the same boyfriend."

"Not Cia. Meg. That necklace had her name on it."

"And that could mean nothing." Chad explained, "Cia wasn't the nicest or easiest girl to be friends with. She might have borrowed the damn thing, or she might have stolen it. I can almost guarantee that she wore it to bug Josh. He'd bought it for Meg but hadn't bought Cia one. She'd wear it just to push him into buying her one."

"And then he killed her in a fit of temper?"

"Josh? Hell, no. He didn't, doesn't, have much of a temper. Although, given the years this mess has put us through, I'd have to say he's likely to have developed one. I called him this morning, and he was already trying to dodge the media."

"Good. Let's hope he's pissed enough to say something incriminating."

"Whatever."

"I don't want you in on the interviews."

Chad knew that was coming. "Fine, but I'd like to listen in."

Daniel stood and towered over the portly Mack. He seemed to consider that and then nodded. "Fine. Just let me know if you catch anything. Megan is waiting, so Mack will start. Maybe seeing him again after all this time will jog something loose."

Oh, shit. That was so not likely.

Chad followed Daniel and Mack out the door. It would be a hell of a day. And it had only just begun.

STEPHANIE STARTLED AT the noise.

"There you are, Stephanie. What's the matter?" The man laughed, his voice coldly amused. "Remember me?"

Christ. Stephanie bolted for the far end of the street, dashed into another alleyway and came up against a blocked exit. Her heart pounded, as her instincts screamed at her to run.

She didn't recognize the man or his voice. But, God, she knew the fear.

"There's nowhere to run." The man came closer.

She spun around, searching for a way out, when she felt something prick her arm.

How had he gotten so close, so fast?

"That wasn't so bad, was it?" His voice stretched and receded, as the walls in front of Stephanie twisted and warped into a weird shape. She fell against one wall, her body sliding to the ground.

"Have a nice trip. And this time, please die."

Chapter 14

M EG SAT IN the small room and waited. She didn't flinch or fidget. She'd been here before. She wasn't a scared young girl anymore, and she hadn't done anything wrong. She worked on the side of the law now herself. Mack might try his scare tactics, but Meg was no fool. She'd already contacted her lawyer and had a brief conversation with him.

He'd offered to come in, but Meg didn't want to take that step yet.

She wanted to help the police. She wanted Cia's killer to be caught, and Meg damn-well wanted her life back.

She checked her cell phone for what had to be the tenth time in the last half hour. Still no contact from Pete. As much as she wanted a peaceful end to their relationship, she couldn't help but worry. She hoped he was all right.

The door opened to let Mack in. "Are you late for something, Miss Pearce?"

Meg looked up. "No, I'm not."

His gaze drilled into hers. She stared back, quietly, calmly.

"Good. I'd like to have you tell me again what happened on that day Cia went missing."

"And correlate it to my old statement?" At Mack's nod, Meg said, "I can't add anything. However, to the best of memory, this is what I remember." And she launched into her story. Thank heavens she'd clarified that point with her lawyer. How accountable could one be for discrepancies between two statements on the same event taken seventeen years apart? Not much apparently. Given gaps in memories and time passing, she could remember only so much. When she was done, Mack handed her a copy of her old statement. She read it with interest. And found it to be the same. "Well, nice to know age hasn't affected my memory that badly. Yet," she added, with a small smile.

"And now we come to this necklace." Mack tossed a small bag at her.

She picked it up, expecting to see the same necklace she'd excavated at the site. Instead inside was a shiny newish-looking one in the same style. She turned it over and read the inscription and laughed. "Typical of Josh. He never could figure out what to get people for presents."

"Josh?"

"Stephanie's old boyfriend, I think after me and before Cia, yet before Stephanie hooked up with Bruce." She gave him a crooked smile. "But who could remember? Back then, it was musical boyfriends."

"For you?" Mack's gaze, dark and intent, studied her carefully.

"Not really. I went out with Josh for a couple months. Then about six to eight months later, I started going out with Chad." She shrugged. "That was it for me."

"And what about Cia?"

Meg tilted her head. "Again, it's hard to remember. She'd gone out with Chad before me, but months earlier. Then she went out with Josh at the same time I was going out with Chad. I think she'd been out with Bruce a few times as well. As for the others Cia may have dated, I don't know."

"And Stephanie?"

Meg winced. "That I am not sure of. She was going out with Bruce and had gone out with Josh for a short while. Who else? Honestly, I don't know."

"Did she ever talk about her boyfriends?"

Meg thought it was an odd question to ask now, but given that Stephanie wasn't here to answer questions herself, maybe not. "All the time. It was typical girl talk."

"Did she mention anyone else?"

"What do you mean, anyone else? Any other boyfriends? Wannabe boyfriends? I don't understand."

"Cia's remains were found, and, right away, Stephanie goes missing. Is it too far a stretch to believe that maybe the same male did something to both of them?"

"I wouldn't like to think so." Meg felt her heart sink. "That would be horrible."

"But you are not a fool. So who else did Stephanie mention?"

With a sigh, Meg slouched back into her chair and cast her mind backward. "Stephanie loved keeping track of other people's relationships."

"But you didn't?"

"No." She smiled lightly. "I had my own, and I was really happy with it."

"If you were so happy, why did you break up with him?"

There was no mockery in his voice, but his tone was too even. Too ... something. ... She couldn't figure out what it was. "I guess you had to be there to understand."

His gaze narrowed, darkened. "Try me."

She stared back calmly. "No."

His eyebrows shot up. "Really?"

"It has nothing to do with the case." She added carefully, her tone even and controlled, "Our break-up happened after the crime and in no way impacted what happened beforehand."

"For all I know, you two were in on Cia's murder together. After your unholy pact, you couldn't love each other, knowing what you'd done together and split. You've hardly spoken since." He smiled. "Have you?"

"No, we haven't." She'd be damned if she'd give him more than was required.

Just then the door opened, and Chad walked in. Meg stared at him. She didn't smile. This scenario was awkward enough without any sign of friendship—or the signs of anything more—showing through.

With a hard look, Mack nodded to him. "Did you have something to add?"

"Meg, you said that Stephanie and you had been gossiping while out in the water. Was anything in that conversation indicative of who Cia might have moved on to next? Or who she *wouldn't* move on to?"

Meg frowned, trying to remember. "I remember some of it. Although I'm sure I brought this up back then. Stephanie had been talking about who Cia had slept with and who she hadn't. Stephanie never did tell me the names though. She did say Cia had slept with four of the guys who were on the camping trip and was planning on sleeping with a fifth that weekend."

Mack leaned forward. "That weekend?"

Chad shook his head. "Couldn't be, she was sleeping with Josh on that trip. She was sleeping in his tent."

"I know. That's what I'd been trying to figure out when you called out to us." She shrugged. "I never did get the name from Stephanie. I also don't know if Stephanie was telling the truth. She loved to stretch the truth and loved to gossip." She stopped and forced herself to correct her words. "We all did, but Stephanie thrived on it."

Mack stepped in. "You're sure you have no idea who Cia had planned to sleep with?"

Meg shook her head. "No, none at all." She shrugged. "Considering who was there, there weren't that many choices."

"Already sleeping with Josh, had been sleeping with Chad here ..." Shuffling papers, Mack asked, "Don't know about Bruce, so that leaves Pero, Anto, and Tim. Was there time for Cia to disappear to meet up with this mystery date?"

Chad stared at Meg. She stared back. Chad shook his head, saying, "I don't know. I wouldn't have thought so."

"I don't know for sure." Meg lifted her shoulders. "And we never saw Cia after she went into the tent."

"*If* she went to the tent ..."

"Right." She switched her gaze back from Mack to Chad. "And if she didn't, she could have walked off. We'd always considered that she might have run after you guys to join the hike. I hadn't considered she might have been having a tryst." Even that old-fashioned word seemed wrong. She tried to look at it from a different perspective and then shook her head. "No, I can't see it happening."

"And of course she didn't," Mack said, "because someone killed her. Most likely, she was meeting a man or someone pissed at her, who'd found out about the meeting."

"Josh?" Chad snorted. "It wouldn't have been him. He didn't care. He was breaking up with her anyway. Even Stephanie and I knew that. You could see it was over."

"*Over* is one thing." Mack tossed down his pencil and sprawled back, stretching his legs out in front of him. "Having someone stepping out behind your back with a buddy is another thing."

"True, but it does happen. I can't see Josh being so angry that he'd kill her over it. And if he had, where is the other male in the picture? Had he come upon them afterward? And then killed her? Because, if he'd come up on them earlier, he would have seen them and said something."

"Not if both were involved."

Both Chad and Meg frowned at Mack.

"What?" Meg asked cautiously.

"What if Josh came upon the two of them, got angry, and Cia was killed in the fight."

"And then both of the men made a pact of silence?" Chad asked, studying Mack. "It could shake out that way. We've certainly seen similar cases, but not with Josh."

Mack turned on him. "Oh, and why not? Because he's a good guy? Because he's your friend? Because of what?"

"Because he's too honest." Meg couldn't stay quiet. She knew how awkward this was for Chad, as well as for her. Yet she doubted that Josh was guilty. "Besides, the second man is hardly going to cover for the murderer, certainly not in the long-term. He'd done nothing wrong, so why should he?"

"Bullshit. Cia's death might have been accidental, a crime of passion so to speak, happening while hot tempers raged. But what about afterward? Panic would have ensued. Then cold reason would have taken over. If Cia's current boyfriend and her new love interest were both there, they would have both assumed they'd be held responsible. Or one could convince the other they wouldn't go down for this alone."

Chad frowned, and Meg could almost see him considering the issue. "We wondered if there were two of them," Chad admitted, "but I hadn't considered Stephanie and someone else."

"Stephanie? Why her? How? I don't understand." And Meg didn't. How had they gone from Josh to Stephanie? Nothing made sense. She hadn't once seriously considered that Cia had gone to meet someone. It had been one of the many suggestions tossed around at the time, but it had so lacked in reasoning that it had been dropped.

Over the years, the idea had popped up from time to time but was then dropped again. Watching the men pull out the idea and turn it over and over yet again made her nervous. It was one thing to consider one of her friends as a murderer but *two* of them? ... *That* was hard to believe.

"On the other hand," Mack suggested, "Stephanie might have known something or might have been helping someone. She was easily manipulated and easily coerced. And, if she had known something, she would have been too scared to tell."

"Or too scared of getting someone else into trouble," Meg noted, easily seeing that aspect. "I suppose that would also help explain her decline into drugs and all."

"How is that?" Mack stared at her.

"It's just that, if she were hiding something, she'd feel guilty and would need to handle that guilt somehow. The easiest way would be to try to forget, and how does one do that? Substance abuse is the most common way."

"By the same token, I'd expect some long-term reaction from Josh, if he'd been involved." Chad explained further, "Definitely anger is there, but moreover the damage to his life because of this event. There's no guilt. No sadness. Nothing to indicate he's hiding anything."

"This, after seventeen years, is to be expected." Meg sighed. "Think about it. After all these years of keeping this information hidden, it would feel normal. It would feel natural. There might be an underlying tension that permeates everything, and that tension may snap at some point, but not unless something jars it."

"But having found Cia's remains—that is a pretty big jarring." Mack added, "Our killer has to be worried."

"Josh isn't showing any sign of that."

Mack snorted. "Why would he? He doesn't know we are close."

"Are you close? Do you have anything to pin this on Josh?" Meg shook her head. "If you couldn't pin it on him seventeen years ago, nothing was on the body that could do that now either."

"Not true. Now we know the cause of death and the location of the body in relation to the rest of you at the time."

"And what about the necklace?"

"A necklace I suspect Cia *borrowed*," Meg said, "but who could say after all this time."

"When did you notice it missing?" Mack asked.

"I *never* noticed. At least I don't remember ever noticing it had gone missing. It wasn't an important piece for me. And, after that weekend, we all packed in a rush, and our emotions were everywhere. If I'd noticed it missing then, I would have just assumed it had been lost in the chaos of the investigation."

"That's no help."

She stood. "No. I wasn't much help then, and I can't add anything now."

"Except for the gossip on Cia's lovers."

"True, if the gossip was the truth." Meg nodded. "Now, if we could find Stephanie, maybe we could ask her."

"What about the other males? Do you know much about them?"

"I was less with them than anyone else. Chad"—she looked over at him—"you would know more about the guys than I would." She walked to the door. "I knew Bruce and Josh, but I had only met Pero and Anto a couple times before that weekend, outside of passing them in the school hallways. As for Tim, I can't even remember his face." She shrugged. "I know some were related, but I can't remember now who was related to whom."

"Bruce was a cousin to the brothers. Their family had come over from Croatia, when they were little. I think Bruce's mother was their aunt," Chad said and nodded sideways to Mack.

"And Bruce's family had a cabin on the other side of the lake, right?" Meg asked, not quite understanding Chad's head motion. "Where we camped that first time?"

Chad nodded.

"I want to go back." The words ripped out of her throat so fast that she didn't realize what she had said.

Chad snapped, "No."

"I need to." She stared at him calmly. As she thought about it, she realized she *really* did want to go back. She wanted a chance to explore and to look for anything that might give them some answers. She knew it was too late, but she couldn't get it out of her mind that maybe, ... just maybe, she'd find something else. "If we now know where she was found, and I know where I was and where Stephanie was, we can walk the route and time the distance from one spot to the next. It will help sort out who could have been where. And maybe catch someone in a lie."

"No. We were all in the woods together—and lost most of the time. We can't pinpoint their location like that."

Mack looked over at him. "Except you gave us a pretty clear map of where you heard the other person. If we take your statement as fact, that rules the three of you out, therefore we need to plot out where everyone else was at the time."

"And we could do it on a map, but it would be easier if we went there and measured it out," Meg repeated.

"We did that last time, and it didn't help," Chad added slowly, as if thinking this through, "but there are better tools available to us now."

Meg checked her cell phone. "I've got to go. If you drive out there, let me know. I want to come. I can help." She nodded to Mack and Chad. "The sooner we figure this out, the sooner we can find out who did this. At the moment, I'm seriously thinking it must have been Anto."

"Why?"

She groaned. "Because he gave me the creeps back then." She stared at Chad. "And I'm going back up there."

"You're not going alone." Chad's voice brooked no argument.

She smiled gently. "Good. I don't really want to go alone. Janelle has a sleepover at her friend's house tonight. So my window to travel is now." And she walked out. She had almost made it to the front door, when Chad came running up behind her.

"Wait up."

She stepped through the door to the top step, before turning. "What's up?"

"I'll go home to grab some equipment, copies of everyone's statements, and a map. Then I'll swing by and pick you up." He headed back inside, without giving her a chance to respond.

Meg made it home in record time. She packed a light bag, made a quick call to Deirdre, Linette's mother, and explained that Meg wouldn't be at home but available by cell phone. "We'll try to get back tonight, but just in case …"

Making sure she had everything she thought she would need, she packed extra gloves and a large flashlight. She wanted to hike to the top of the mudslide, as she had been able to last time. Remembering the heavy rain, she grabbed a warm jacket and put on hiking boots. She realized Pete might have gone to his cabin. It was his place to hole up. She didn't want to intrude or to get involved in an argument. It was bad timing, or, as the old saying went, worse timing.

A sound outside had her grabbing her keys and cell phone, lifting her bag and letting herself out of the house.

Chad waited for her in the same truck she'd seen at the excavation site. Good. At least it would make the trip. He hadn't mentioned staying anywhere overnight. Hopefully it wouldn't be required, but she'd packed just in case.

And didn't that thought make her heart race. Knowing how Chad felt about her made her both uneasy and, yeah, … excited about the coming night. She'd spent a lot of nights with him, but sleep was the one thing they'd never managed to do. But then young love and the heated nights had been all about exploring their passion and expressing their love. It was something she'd never experienced since.

"Ready?" he asked.

She looked at him, wondering if a hidden meaning was in that question, then realized it didn't matter, even if there was. The answer would still be the same.

Clipping the seat belt firmly in place, she settled back and said, with a smile, "Yes, I'm ready."

CHAD TOOK THE highway on-ramp and pulled smoothly into traffic. They had a long drive ahead of them, but he enjoyed driving. He hadn't mentioned staying overnight anywhere because Meg had enough to deal with.

"I've been thinking about Stephanie," she said.

"What about her?" He took his eyes off the road long enough to search her features. There'd been a note of … he didn't know what, something hesitant, maybe even fearful. "Are you worried about her?"

"Of course. Even if she's gone back to her old ways, it would still be bad news. Anyone who makes it out of that dark hole has made a huge change in their lives. Sliding back into it again, though …"

"It's hard to know in her case. It isn't the first time, but she's been clean and sober for a long time now."

"She sounded so normal when I last spoke to her. That conversation made me more aware of who she is today and how disappearing doesn't seem normal for her."

"Oh, it's normal. It's just that you didn't see much of Stephanie before reconnecting. So your view is slightly twisted."

"Meaning, if I'd known her these past years, I wouldn't be surprised by her actions?" She settled back into her seat. "I wonder if that's true."

She went as if to speak once more. He waited. When she remained silent, he asked, "What?"

"I guess I just wondered if you were still looking for her?"

He frowned. "Constantly—I was out last night, driving around her favorite haunts. I've been asking her old employers and friends, but there's no sign of her."

"But that just reinforces what I mean. If she'd gone back to the bottle or drugs, she'd be visible. She might have gone away inside, but physically she'd be somewhere. Right now, it's as if she's just disappeared from the face of the earth. That takes more skill than she has."

"Skill?" he asked. "Are you suggesting someone might have helped her to disappear?" It did fit that she might have wanted to run away. "Honestly I hadn't considered that."

"Either willingly or unwillingly, I just don't think she knows how to drop so completely off the grid on her own. And whoever is helping her could be friend or foe. No way to know yet."

"It won't likely be family. She cut ties with them years ago, and then they reciprocated when she ended up on the streets."

"But that could have changed in the years after she cleaned up her act."

"True." He pondered the issue. "She has no credit cards and hated bank cards because she used to steal them from other people. She used cash only."

"But did she have money to plan ahead? I understood she was pretty much living from paycheck to paycheck. One paycheck alone won't get her too far."

"And she got paid every Friday. Five days at minimum wage buys a bus ticket across the country and not much more."

"Exactly."

He glanced at her again. "Who would help her?"

Meg shrugged. "I have no idea. I don't know who her friends are."

"She was supposed to be meeting a friend in secret, according to her neighbor."

"And did she have a bag of belongings with her?"

"No." And that's why he hadn't considered that she may have left for a few days. But then, why tell the neighbor about the secret meeting? Was it to throw someone off the scent, and, if that were the case, why the cry for help? Maybe it was because she'd changed her mind about it.

"Then ..." Meg dropped her head on the back of the seat. "Hell, I don't know. Unless this guy, not that we know it's a guy, but this person, whoever, would be the last person to have seen her."

"Precisely."

"Damn. That could be anyone who doesn't want the police to call on them. It doesn't mean they were looking to hurt her. They could be helping or they could be—"

"Her drug dealer." He sighed. "Sorry. I didn't mean that to come out as harsh as it did." He opened the window slightly to bring in fresh air. "I'm just frustrated. I've done as much as I can, and still it's not enough."

Her tone weary, Meg said, "Is it ever?"

"Sometimes."

Silence filled the cab of the truck. Chad knew the odds of finding Stephanie were good. Given her history, she just might not be in decent shape when they found her. Finally he said, "I have to believe this time it will be enough."

He glanced over to see her reaction and realized her head had fallen against the passenger door. He glanced at the road, then back over at Meg, but her chest rose and fell in a steady, relaxed manner. She'd fallen asleep.

MEG CAME AWAKE slowly. The steady movement of the truck rolling down the highway had lulled her into a comfortable, relaxed state. The truck engine soothed her soul. She'd needed her nap. It seemed like her nerves were just waiting for the rest of her body to follow through.

She yawned and rolled her head toward Chad.

"How are you feeling now?"

She smiled. "Better. I've been running on empty for a long time."

"Not healthy." He smiled to cut the criticism in his words.

"I know, but sometimes it's unavoidable." She straightened to look around. "Where are we?"

"We're coming into Wistery. I thought we could stop for a break and pick up some coffee and maybe a bite to eat."

"Food sounds good. Coffee sounds even better." The long stretch of countryside had gradually morphed to the odd house here and there. She saw the sign for Wistery next. "Good. It's just a few minutes down the road."

"The roadhouse is right here." Chad slowed the truck and went around a series of hairpin turns and, as he pulled out on the other side, she saw the sign.

"Stan's Roadhouse?"

"We stopped here that camping weekend and picked up treats."

"Really?" She glanced at him in amazement. "Are you sure? I don't remember that at all."

"Not much I don't remember from back then." He pulled the truck to a stop in front of the café and turned off the engine. "Ready?"

Still stunned at what he had remembered over what she'd forgotten, she nodded. "Let's go."

Inside, the air was cool, and the restaurant empty. "I guess they don't get much business."

"It's early yet. The lunch crowd won't be here for a bit."

She glanced at the clock on the wall. It was just after eleven a.m. "We made good time."

"Good. We have lots of work to do. We probably should have held off and left early tomorrow."

"Too late now." She smiled and walked up to the front counter.

"I'll grab this." Chad stepped up beside her. "My treat." He studied the menu for a moment, then ordered a couple large sandwiches to-go and an extra large coffee. Then he turned to her. "What do you want?"

"Not that much," she murmured. "I eat like a normal person, but the sandwiches sound good."

With a smirk, Chad doubled his order and then snagged a couple wrapped muffins and coffee cake slices at the counter. He walked over to the cooler and pulled out four bottles of water to add to the order.

"We didn't come well prepared, did we?" She eyed the stack at the counter. "Then I wouldn't have packed for four days anyway."

"This is just for today. We will be working. That means keeping up our strength." With a big grin, he unpacked a muffin and took a large bite. "I missed breakfast."

She shook her head and made a trip to the ladies' room. On her way back, she noticed a couple people walking inside. She didn't know them but knew the town enjoyed both the benefits and the detriments of summer residences. She wondered if the business struggled to stay afloat in the winter. Summer would be fine, but as for the rest of the year? She wasn't so sure.

Glancing around, she saw Chad paying for the lunch. She watched while he finished, picked up their bags, and joined her at the door. "Ready?"

She laughed as she pushed the door open to step outside. "Seems like you've been asking me that a lot lately."

He grinned. "And I'll continue to ask."

At the truck, she took the bags from him and waited while he unlocked the doors. Hearing something, she turned around, gave the parking lot a wide sweeping glance. The place appeared empty. Shrugging, she placed the bags on the seat and went to climb in, when she saw something out of the corner of her eye. She turned and looked at the big window in the front.

Someone stood there, watching her.

Shit.

Pete.

"MEG? IS THERE a problem?"

Meg, startled, turned back to Chad. "No. No, there isn't."

He studied her. She made no move to get into the truck. In fact, she turned to stare back at the restaurant. Chad leaned over, so he could see what she was looking at. A few people were seated at the front tables, but they appeared to be in conversation among themselves and not concerned with Meg.

"Meg?"

"Oh, sorry." She gave a sheepish smile and clambered in. Slamming the door closed, she took one last look at the window and sighed.

"Did you see someone?"

"I thought so," she admitted, "but he wasn't there when I looked the second time."

"He?"

Her breath gusted free in a heavy *whoosh*. "I thought I saw Pete."

"Your boyfriend?"

"Ex-boyfriend," she corrected. "I have moved out."

"Does he know that?"

"I don't know," she admitted. "He hadn't returned home by the time I left, and I have yet to hear from him."

"Would he have come out here?"

"Definitely. He loves his cabin, comes every opportunity he can."

"Then it could be him." Chad thought about that, as he drove the truck back onto the highway. "Will that be a problem?"

She glanced his way, her face troubled. "I hope not."

He raised his eyebrows at that. "Good thing you didn't come alone then."

"I don't think he'd be a problem. Pete has never been violent."

"Good." Chad picked up speed, so they were going at just over the limit and thought about what she'd said.

And what she hadn't said.

WITH ANY LUCK, Stephanie would take a bad trip into hell and stay there. It might take a while. He should have stayed and finished the job.

But, this way, it was all on Stephanie's head. She'd be yet another overdose and yet another dead junkie—no big deal.

Stephanie's friends would sigh and would whisper about how hard it had been to kick the habit, and, after a respectful few moments, they'd take a trip themselves.

After all, it was hard to go straight in life.

And he needed to move on. Get more loose threads tied up.

Getting caught after all these years was so not on the agenda.

Chapter 15

MEG TOOK A large bite of the half sandwich in her hand. She'd avoided talking about Pete, but that didn't in any way stop her mind from twisting about him. Would he understand she'd come here for work? Even if she wasn't getting paid, she was helping to solve Cia's case. But then he didn't know about Cia because she hadn't told him about her.

He did know about the grave though.

She stared down at the sandwich. Ham and cheese heaped with vegetables. And it tasted like cardboard. She dropped her hands and leaned her head back, wishing she hadn't seen him. Now she couldn't stop thinking about him and what had been and all that it could have been.

The warmth oozing from Chad made her feel bad, yet good. In fact, right now her emotions were all over the place.

"How's the sandwich?"

"It's good. I'm just tired."

"Eat up. It will ease back the fatigue." Chad drove with one hand. The other held the sandwich he had partly scarfed in a few bites. He'd already eaten a full sandwich. Meg looked down at her uneaten half of one and realized he was right.

She took another bite and chewed slowly.

"Are you scared of him?"

She shook her head, swallowed, and answered, "No. I just haven't cleared things up with him. It feels awkward. We're not together, and we're not apart. It's over, but I haven't told him."

"You haven't spoken to him at all?"

The disapproval in Chad's voice made her realize the situation from a man's perspective. "No. I left before he returned. I really felt it was over when he walked out, that he knew it and that I knew it and that he was giving me time to get out."

"But?"

"But, because we haven't had that final conversation, it feels incomplete."

"Do you know when he's due home?"

"No. Normally he'd text me, call me, ... something, but this time there's been nothing. Which I guess is reasonable if we have just broken up." She stared moodily out the window, as she finished her sandwich. "Then I never contacted him either."

"Maybe you should."

"I was just thinking that, but I doubt he'll answer." She brushed her hands off, scrunched up the sandwich wrapper, and stuffed it back into the to-go bag. She grabbed her phone and texted Pete. **Where are you?**

She waited. Nothing.

"No answer. He comes out here to get away. Hates his cell phone at the best of times." She couldn't believe the relief she felt. It had been a shock to think she'd spied Pete at the restaurant. And the fear of a confrontation had kept her on edge, worrying.

She was back at Pete's favorite place with Chad but without Pete. How would he react? It was not as if she'd planned this, but Pete wouldn't know that. She didn't want him thinking she'd broken off with him to start up with a new guy—or worse, having been engaged in an affair while still with him.

She was still mulling things over, when Chad slowed the truck. She sat up and surveyed her surroundings. "This isn't the same place."

"No. I wanted to go into the park from the side of the lake and take a look around first."

She barely remembered where they'd first camped, except it had been pretty. Another ten minutes of driving through the trees, then the tree line opened up to show the lake sparkling in front of them. In spite of her worries, a happy sigh escaped. "Regardless of the circumstances, it's a pretty spot for Cia to have lain all these many years."

He glanced over at her in surprise. "That's a nice way to look at it."

Chad parked the truck, and they both hopped out. The campground road went farther around the lake. From where she stood, Meg could see dozens of camping spots had already been taken. A large grassy area was up ahead with picnic tables and the occasional barbecue stand.

She shook her head and laughed. "I barely recognize the campground. It looks so different."

"They've done a lot of work over the years. The trees have grown.

Another dozen or two cabins have been built over there." He pointed to the left. "Most of those cabins weren't there back then." He turned around and nudged her to pivot too. "Most of the ones behind us are new too."

"Wow. This place sure is popular. I was afraid the roadhouse couldn't make a living all the way out here, but loads of people are here." Rows upon rows of summer homes and houses stood tall in front of her.

"Let's go to the water's edge." He took her arm. "I want to show you something."

They walked down the path side by side; Meg couldn't believe how developed the area had become on this side. She would never have recognized it. And, from Pete's side of the lake, this couldn't be seen from either the deck or the cabin. She had no idea any of this existed. Janelle would love it here.

"I also brought maps of the area—from seventeen years ago and now."

"That's smart." She walked to where the water lapped the rocks. "What did you want to show me?"

He pointed to the left. "The road continues on around that end of the lake and goes up the hill on the far side. If you follow the line all the way over there ..." He moved his arm in the direction they were talking about. Now she was looking straight across the lake.

"There's the campsite we stayed at last time. And you found the remains over to the right, ... by that darker clump of trees."

She shook her head at the short distance. "It was so close to the camping spot?" It had seemed much farther at the crime scene.

"Close enough for it to have been one of us, but, if you see the cabins along the road there"—he pointed—"it's also well within the distance of anyone who'd been at the cabins at the time."

"But how many of those cabins were there back then?"

"About three-quarters of them, and the ones that were there were empty that weekend ... supposedly." He stared at her. "As far as we could tell at the time, we were alone over there."

"But that spot is within easy reach by anyone on this side too. In fact, we were clearly visible to anyone on this side of the lake."

"Correct."

"It's not even, what? ... One-quarter mile across? A good swimmer could swim it, but a power boat could cross in no time at all."

"We would have heard power boats. And we did. We heard several of them. Remember, some people were out waterskiing that day?

Besides, anyone could have driven around the lake, parked, and traveled the last bit on foot."

"True. And … we saw canoes and kayaks, as well. There were a lot of people at the lake then. It was the end of summer."

"Exactly, so what are the chances that all those cabins on the far side and at the end were not occupied?"

"If many on this side were, then odds are that many over there should have been too."

"Well, at least some of them. Instead, according to the police report, *all* the cabins were unoccupied."

She stared at him, back at the long stretch of cabins, and then said slowly, "That doesn't seem right."

"It doesn't, does it? Only I haven't found anyone who'd seen residents at the cabins."

She tried to think back. "I can't remember myself. Were there lights on?"

"I have pictures from back then. I should dig them back out and see what shots we took at the time. Maybe there were night shots."

"There were!" She turned to him. "Remember? We were taking pictures of the campfire and our tents?"

He nodded. "I'll have a look when I get home." He glanced sideways at her. "What about you? Do you have pictures?"

"Maybe—I gave the film to the detectives at the time." She stared at him. "I have no idea what happened to it."

He narrowed his eyes. "They developed mine to get a look at the pictures."

"And did you get all the pictures back?" She studied the cabins, now brimming with life on the left. "Too bad it was before the digital age. We'd have so much more information available to us today."

Hearing the sounds of trucks pulling into the lot, she glanced back and asked, "What now?"

"I have some help. We'll measure everything we can and time it. Then map things and compare them to the statements we have from everyone who was there, as well as from those at the cabins."

"That's what we came for, but I'm grateful to see a crew to help."

"No way we'd get it all done in time." He started back up the path. "Let's get started."

With one last glance toward the cheerful, sunny shores, she followed behind him to find the crew unloading the equipment. Some people she recognized, and some she didn't.

As the teams were setting up, she stared out across the water, wondering how Cia's remains could have stayed undetected for so long. The site was steep and rough, dark and thickly populated with trees. The cabins weren't close, but they were accessible.

Just not *easily* accessible, but *someone* had known about the remains. And she was determined to find out who it had been.

CHAD SPLIT THE techs into teams. He left one group at the campsite to start surveying and took the other over toward the old campsite with Meg.

He parked roughly in the same spot as he had years ago. Then he explained the plan to the team.

He handed the maps and pins over to Meg. He followed behind her—with the laptop and the rest of the supplies—to the nearest picnic table. Meg already had the map spread out and pinned in place and was leaning over it, studying it carefully.

He gingerly unloaded his armful and leaned over beside her. "Find anything interesting?"

She murmured, without raising her head, "The whole thing is interesting, considering we have inside knowledge. How long does it take the killer to meet Cia, kill her, and stash her so she'd never be found?"

"Or perhaps stash her temporarily, then come back and move her."

She screwed up her face at the thought. "Kill her, hide her body, then come back later and move it? That wouldn't be fun."

She stabbed a finger on the map at the point where the closest cabins were located. "Unless, desperate to hide the body, he may have taken a chance on an empty cabin."

Chad took a deep breath. "That's all too possible."

MEG STUDIED THE closest cabins. "Weren't they all checked out thoroughly back then?"

"They checked out what they could. According to the records, a thorough search of all the premises was made."

"And they didn't find her. Either because she wasn't there, or she was so well hidden, or someone was protecting our killer, or the cabin owner was the killer." She straightened up to walk around the picnic table. "So we have to go back to the owners."

Chad murmured, "I wasn't sure whether you remembered or not."

"Remembered what?" She continued to study the map.

"That Mack is Bruce's, Pero's, and Anto's uncle. And he owns a cabin here."

Shock hit her first, then disbelief, then a slow burning anger. She raised her head slowly to study Chad's closed face. "Really? Now I know why he was such a hard-ass to us back then. He was trying to prove his family innocent by making us guilty." She stared out at the water, hating the bitter memories and the fear that his name could still bring up in her. "That bastard."

She shook her head. "And although he seemed nicer this time, I can't say I trust him." She frowned. "I don't know that I trust many people anymore."

"Except for me, you mean." He grinned, as she gave him her narrow-eyed look. "Just keeping it out there …"

"Are you ready to go back to the site?" Needing to get away from the subject of Mack, she raised her eyebrows, looked at her boots, and added, "If so, let's go."

With that, he left one of the crew at the campground and led the way to the crime scene. It took them a good twenty minutes to reach it. Meg noticed Chad seemed to be timing their walk and making notes as they went along. It made sense.

She just couldn't imagine any of the kids they'd camped with having the brains to make and carry out an elaborate murder scheme. More likely Cia's death had been an accident. And it was just dumb luck that her body had stayed hidden for so long.

They continued to walk on in silence. Then Chad stopped abruptly. She stepped up beside him. "What do you see?"

"Nothing. No signs are left that we were here at all."

She studied the layout and frowned. "Any of the locals could have ripped down the tape, and tourists could have taken it as a souvenir. You know it happens all the time."

"*Hmm.*"

She approached the area surrounded by fallen trees and stopped to take a closer look. She knew the techs had searched for hours, and she trusted that they'd done their jobs, but that didn't make it easier to believe nothing more was to be found. They needed evidence that would point them in the right direction.

"Are you okay?"

"Yeah, I just wished we had found more."

"Always. But we could tear up this whole side of the lake and still find nothing." With a grim look he pointed. "I want to go up there. I want to see for myself."

CHAD STUDIED THE hillside, as he climbed up the steep bank. A huge fallen tree hung on a small ledge, almost at the top of the precipitous hill. It would have been a challenge to have carried a body up here. Chad didn't remember the ridge from before. But, if Cia had planned to meet her killer here, that would have made it easier. However, it would have been difficult to imagine anyone carrying her up here. And Cia hated hiking. So she must have had a hell of a reason to make this trek. With a final scramble, he reached the crest and climbed to the solid top. He offered a hand to help Meg up the last bit. She'd barely broken a sweat. He loved that she had stayed fit all these years. "There's the campsite." Chad pointed it out for her.

She crouched to peer through the branches of the surrounding trees. "Years ago it would have been much easier to see."

"Yet we wouldn't have seen anyone up here from down there." He pulled out his phone and texted John, the tech who was working the campsite. From where they stood, he saw John read the text, then study the hillside, where they stood. His phone buzzed. "John wants us to move around to confirm if he can see us."

They shifted around and watched. John's features weren't clear, but they could identify him. Yet he couldn't see them.

"That answers that question. We're completely hidden."

"And we would likely have been hidden on this hilltop back then as well." Meg stepped to the other side and pointed to the cabins below and to something else as well. "Look. Is that a pathway?"

"Shit." He moved behind her and searched for where it started. "It also connects to a well-worn path down below. Come on." He led the way to where two paths joined up.

"How come we didn't see it before?" she asked, behind him.

"It's the angle. It's completely covered with leaves and branches. If you didn't know it was here, no way you'd accidentally stumble across it. Plus we were looking up. It's hard to see, unless someone is walking on it."

They slid down the last bit and landed on the path they'd seen. They stopped to look back the way they'd come. Scrambling down the hillside left a dark gouge in the earth, but leaves were already drifting down to hide their tracks.

"Let's go." Chad led the way up the new path that veered uphill to the right of where they were.

"This place is full of trails."

"I suppose that's no surprise, given the years, the population, and the summer influx of tourists."

"But this isn't the most hospitable location for hiking." She caught her breath, as she crested the rise to stand beside him. "Or maybe it is. This is gorgeous."

The whole lake had opened up in front of them. Between the trees, the blue water twinkled and shone happily. They could see clear across it.

"Obviously more than a few local people would know about this spot," Meg said.

He smiled at her grimly. "It's time to canvass the locals again."

"Go for it. I'm staying here for a bit," she retorted, staring at the beautiful vista. With the sun barely reaching through the trees, the air was heavily scented with pine. A gust of wind blew toward them, lifting the leaves and dropping even more.

"I'm not leaving you alone up here."

MEG TURNED TO look at him in surprise. "Why?"

"For several reasons, but the one I'll go with is that a murderer is still walking around free, who is probably aware of what we are doing here right now."

She wrinkled up her face. "Nice thought. *Not.*"

He smiled. "Is there anything else you want to look at while we're up here?"

"Lots." And there was. "I think this whole place needs to be explored. A dozen bodies could be here. How do we know Cia was the only victim?" She turned to look at him and raised an eyebrow. "Or had you already considered that?"

"Considered and dismissed." He shrugged. "At least until any evidence comes up that points us in that direction."

"Including Cia—until now." She studied his face. "They had some bad storms a while back, didn't they?"

He snorted. "Are you kidding? The weather patterns today versus the weather patterns of seventeen years ago? No comparison. I don't know whether it's because of global warming or what, but this area has been hit with a lot of storms. As you said, a few bad ones came through a couple months ago."

Meg now ignored him. Cia's remains must have slid down from where they'd first climbed. That small ledge up ahead wasn't a large space, but it was big enough. And that fallen tree could hide many things. She pointed to the one area in question. "I want to go back over there."

He never questioned her reasoning, just returned where they had started. It was a rougher climb getting back up. For every step she took, she slid back, as her feet tried to dig into the hillside to grab hold. The slippery leaves made her boots slide more than climb. Finally they made it the top, and, with her chest heaving, Meg gasped for air. "That wasn't much fun."

"No. The ground is still wet from the rain."

She walked a few steps back from the edge, afraid it might all go. "It would take someone in good shape to climb up here."

"Maybe and maybe not." Chad pulled a folded map from his pocket. He studied it for a moment, then pointed to a spot. "Look. This road goes farther up. It should pass somewhere nearby." He turned to look up the slope, then pointed. "Somewhere up there. And it's much easier to come down a slope like this, than go up one."

Why hadn't she considered that? It was much easier to see their position on a map than from within the heavy tree growth. "So they could dump the body easily enough." She kicked the heavy leaves at her feet. "And, in this ground, it would be easy to bury the body."

"If they cared to …"

"True enough." Some killers never buried their victims, either wanting nothing to do with them once dumped or enjoying the sight of their handiwork again and again. Turning a professional eye on the scene, she studied the ledge and the hill above it. "You can see where some of the dirt and soil have eroded. That tree falling would have caused a mess of damage too."

"This area was searched when we found Cia's remains. No one found anything."

The ledge was close to fifteen feet across and almost completely buried under this massive tree that must have come down in a storm. The tree had fallen with the trunk downhill, hanging off the ledge. Large roots had dug into the soft dirt, keeping the tree in a weird hanging balance. The heavy branches lay uphill and across this ridge, but, in the process, they appeared to have knocked away a large portion of the original ledge. Hence, the mudslide that sent Cia's remains down the hill.

Meg looked at the tree, seeing more dirt and leaves already layered on top of it. "Look." She pointed down to where one of Chad's team stood at the site of Cia's remains. The tech was planting a large pole in the ground to use for measuring distances. "After a couple years in that lower position, this mudslide has become almost natural looking. It's completely covered in leaves and deadfall now. That tree didn't come down this year. It must have been down for at least a year—if not two to three years ago. I'm sure an expert can confirm."

"And the locals might add something."

She walked to the far side and looked over the edge.

Chad grabbed her arm. "Careful."

Standing beside her, he pointed to John, now walking around the campground, cell phone in his hand, talking into it. "The campsite is still easy to pinpoint."

Meg turned her back and tried to peer on the other side of the tree. It was huge. With a backward glance at Chad—still facing the lake and talking to his team—she slowly climbed on top of the tree trunk. Once up, she balanced and walked several steps forward to where the branches were thickest at the top of the downed tree. She crouched down and peered between the bark and tree limbs crisscrossing everywhere. She couldn't tell for the darkness and the dirt if anything valuable were in there to find or not.

"See something?"

"Can't tell. It's hard to see," she called back.

"Here's a flashlight if that helps." He hopped up onto the log behind her.

And Meg felt it move. "Shit."

"Whoa. I'm off." He jumped down. "Careful, that's not very stable." He moved around slightly to come up on the side. "See if you can reach it." He held out the flashlight for her. She shook her head. "Just toss it."

He gently lofted it into the air, and she snatched it safely. "Got it."

"Good, take a quick look, then get off in a hurry. We don't want the whole thing going down."

She turned on the flashlight and faced it into the shadows. Had the techs searched this closely? There—more sticks, more leaves, more dirt. She cast the long halo of light over and around the space, making sure she got a good look.

Then she stopped. Her heart raced. She could just make out something jammed under the branches. She caught her breath. Something white. Something round. Something dead.

Shit.

Another skull.

Chapter 16

MEG LISTENED TO the discussion with half an ear. She knew what she'd found; she just couldn't reconcile it with being related to Cia's murder. Had she been killed by a stranger after all? And by a serial killer, no less? Had he been here, dumping a previous victim, seen Cia on the beach, and snatched her?

Meg's mind spun, even as plans were being put into motion around her. It had been hours since they'd first discovered the second body. Hours of phone calls and plans being made, maps pulled out and looked at, and people talking. And yet more talking.

She knew the next steps were incredibly important. They needed to excavate that entire ledge, down to where she'd found Cia's remains. No way to know what else might have gone down in the mudslide. She'd only seen the one skull up there, so exactly how many would they find? The ledge was big enough for dozens.

What she did know was that this was a whole different issue now. More than one set of remains changed the nature of the killer. And the profiles of the victims all came into question. And who had had access to this location?

So often, bodies were dumped where no one ever found them. Hence, killers made deals with the police to give up their victims' locations.

She sighed heavily, hating the ache in her heart that seemed to permeate her whole body. She'd be sore tomorrow. And that sandwich she hadn't cared about eating on the drive in was long gone. She would need to find more food soon and some coffee too.

They were waiting for chainsaws and the men to operate them. The tree needed to be removed carefully, so as not to disturb the remains caught in its branches. The tree was big and old and would be taken out section by section.

A cup of hot liquid was shoved into her hands. She stared at it in surprise, then with dawning delight. Coffee! "Thank you," she murmured, blowing steam upward to bathe her tired eyes.

"Are you cold?" Chad asked, sitting down at the picnic table beside her.

"No, I'm fine." She smiled reassuringly at him. "Just a little overwhelmed."

"With good reason."

"It changes everything and nothing. I can't help but wonder if that weekend created a serial killer out of one of our friends or if a serial killer found a conveniently close victim."

"Too early to tell. You'll make yourself crazy thinking about it right now." He took a sip from the hot cup in his hand. "The men should be here soon. I'll take them up to the scene and have them start sectioning off the tree from the bottom."

"I'm coming." She stood.

"Why not stay here and rest?"

She shook her head. "No, I need to be there. It'll take hours, so let's get started." Determined to do her part, she walked in line behind the techs leading the three men with three saws. "Or maybe it won't take that long."

BUT IT DID.

Not only was there little room for anyone to stand on that ledge, but no one could work at the area Meg had marked off to search for bone remnants and other evidence, not until the tree was dismantled and carried out of the way.

She and Chad stood at the second ledge and watched the work in progress. Chad had already photographed the area several times and appeared to be intent on cataloging every step of the process.

She couldn't blame him. These pictures would be valuable.

"Could this place be visible from the aerial photographs?"

"No, I've gone over the old aerial photographs many times. Once Google Earth is updated, I will get those updates and compare them to the older versions. The tree growth is just too thick in here for the satellite to be of much help."

One of the men had finished cutting the lower half of the tree into long slices, and the other two men were cutting each into removable pieces. Then the other guy moved higher up and cut off another segment.

"Once he has that piece out of the way, we'd be better off removing branches or parts of branches." She motioned to where the larger branches on the ledge dominated. "He'll be an hour doing that easily."

"I doubt it." Chad smiled. "Maybe twenty minutes, tops."

And Chad was right.

Impatiently Meg waited until the last section had been cleared enough for her to stand in, then led the way back to the remains. She studied the branch pattern, looking to open up the space, while not disturbing anything below. The man operating the chainsaw had had the same idea. He started removing the branches on top first, and, with Chad's help, lifted them clear, and laid them to one side.

They did that for the next four big branches, then the chainsaw guy separated branches from the trunk and began chewing into the wood, until all that was left was the top ten to fifteen feet of the tree and its branches propping up the main trunk. Systematically, with both Meg and Chad helping, they removed the last of the branches from the ledge.

When the final smaller branches were removed, Meg pulled out her camera and took some pictures. Not a lot to see at this point, just the leaves from the fallen tree and the dirt the branches had snagged to pull down on top of them. She stepped back and studied the area.

"Are you good to go?" Chad asked.

"I need my tools and gloves." And so much more, she thought, but didn't say it. He knew what she needed. They'd been here before. She turned to smile at him, but he'd taken off down the hill. She watched until he made it to the truck and grabbed her bag. He started back up.

Hearing a sound, she turned around with a smile. Her gaze landed on the main man who'd operated the chainsaw. She nodded to him. "Thanks for the help and for being so careful …"

He wore a hard hat and earmuffs, with a full shield protecting his face. Even so, she recognized something about him.

He grimaced, pulled off his hard hat and nodded to her. "You're welcome, Meg."

She gasped in astonishment.

"Pete!"

CHAD WAS ALMOST to the path where he'd stood with Meg earlier when he heard her cry out. He searched the cliff edge in panic, but she still stood where he'd left her. And she appeared fine—but maybe not so fine after all. She was stiff, and, although she was talking to the man in front of her, she wasn't smiling. Chad couldn't hear the conversation, but just something about her demeanor worried him.

And had she said *Pete*? Was he her boyfriend? That wouldn't be good. But his appearance wasn't totally unexpected. Chad wished he'd been there to see Pete's reaction. And to meet him. Who was this man who had held Meg's love for over a decade? It would be interesting to know him.

With his arms full, Chad hoofed his way back up the hill on the path. At the path junction, he scrambled up to the ledge and almost lost his load.

"Easy. Let me help." Meg reached out and half unloaded her gear. "I should have come and helped you."

"Not needed. I managed just fine." He straightened and caught his breath. Pete wasn't here. "Where did our chainsaw operator go?"

Meg winced. "Home. It was Pete. He got a call asking him to come and lend a hand here."

"Pete?" He studied her face. It was normal. Not stressed, upset or angry. "Are you two okay?"

She shrugged. "He didn't have much to say, just a hello."

"And that's it?" He didn't know what to say. "Isn't that a little odd, considering you've moved out?"

"Yeah, well, I told him that I'd moved out for a few days to think too." She smiled grimly. "Maybe I should have said more, but it was really not the place."

"How did he respond?"

She smiled. "He nodded and said he understood. He also said that he was sorry about the mess I found here and that it was a sad business."

"Yeah, isn't that the truth."

He watched as Meg turned her attention to the scene in front of them, effectively killing off the conversation.

MEG DIDN'T WANT to discuss the totally awkward meeting with Pete. He looked good. Happy and at peace.

She couldn't ask for more. The one thing seeing him again had done for her was that it had helped her realize the truth—that it was over. She had had a few pangs of sadness, a twinge of grief, regrets for what had been, but, at the same time, she no longer felt that pull.

What they'd had before had died a slow death this last year. Although they were both to blame, her maybe more than him, there was no sense of guilt.

An era had passed. As for her, she was just grateful this meeting had been in private. He'd seemed to understand. He'd been friendly, and she couldn't ask for more at this point.

Now she had something else to focus on, and she could park Pete where he belonged—in her past. She walked carefully to the area which had been marked off. She stood and studied the ground, looking for a place to start. Then she got down to work, clearing away the bits of branches and searching the layers underneath. A skull was up on the left, against the hillside, and a femur tip sat on the right. It had yet to be determined if they were from the same body. She suspected that, as she dug into this mess, likely to be more than one body here. A tap on her shoulder had her turning to face Chad. "What?"

He pointed to the left, several feet in front of the skull. Covered by leaves and small sticks, easy to miss because of the full eye sockets, was yet another skull.

Sadness crept through her tired frame. "Damn."

"It's what you expected though, isn't it?"

She nodded, her gaze moving slowly across the surface and back to the hillside. Her gaze zipped past and then back again. There was a jaw bone, still partially attached to another skull. "There's number three."

"I wonder how many we'll find before we're done."

"Too many. Let's get at it."

STEPHANIE SMILED AT the gruesome clown face in front of her. Weird. ... Then a lot of things in her life were weird. Tonight was the most bizarre. One minute she'd been rushing into a coffee shop, and the next thing her head hurt, and she was here. In Clownsville ...

She peered through the darkness, trying to sort out the strange images from the truth. If she hadn't known better, she might have thought she'd taken a bad acid trip. Unfortunately she'd experienced more of those than she cared to remember. Was this another one? It had to be; nothing else made sense.

Her head lolled to one side. She tried to straighten it. Only she had no strength to keep it up. Breathing was about all she could do.

And sleep. She was good at that part.

And forgetting.

She'd spent a lifetime trying to forget her life. For the most part, she'd done well, … maybe too well.

Her eyes fell shut. She tried to open them again but couldn't.

Her stomach heaved, and wild crazy colors zinged through her mind. Her surroundings spun and twisted. As for her stomach? God, her stomach …

She curled into a tight ball and buried her face in her hands.

Please, let this be over *soon*.

Chapter 17

M EG STRAIGHTENED SLOWLY, almost crying out as the twinge in her back struck again. Damn, it had been a long night. And it was still ongoing. She stopped to look around. Eerie shadows from the big lights filled the small space, as teams in white worked quietly away in the darkness.

It was a scene out of a horror movie—or her life. How many times had she been in a similar scenario before? There'd been almost too many times to count them.

This excavation had been going on for hours. So far, five skulls and multiple sets of bones had been collected. What bothered her was that these bones, all skeletonized, were old. As in no fresh body had been placed here for at least ten years. Had the space filled up, and the killer moved on? But, if so, where to?

Or had he stopped killing? If so, why? Anto came to mind. Death was a hell of an excuse.

So far, she'd found only young female skeletons. That didn't mean there weren't children or males in here though. Putting the bones together would be a fun puzzle. And that also meant that the jumble of bones that they had assembled earlier—from what they had thought of as Cia's remains—could, in fact, be from some of these skeletons. That might explain the missing bones. Of course animal activity would too.

"How are you holding up?" Chad joined her, a thermos in his hand.

"Is that coffee? And, if it is, how come you have some, and I don't?"

"I'm sharing it with you." He smiled at her, but his gaze was searching, as he studied her face.

"I'm fine," she said brusquely. "Or I will be when you catch this bastard."

He poured coffee into the thermos cup and held it out for her.

"Working on it. Can you tell whether these victims died before or after Cia?"

She shook her head. "Given the level of decomposition, I can't tell here. I may never tell you what you want to know with any level of accuracy. Within a couple years, it is difficult. If we can ID some of the women, find out when they went missing, we'll get some time frame to work with. I doubt any of them have been here much longer than fifteen years, but I can't say for sure."

"Do you want to take a break and sit in the truck and warm up?"

Holding the thermos cup to her lips, she tried a sip of the hot brew. It slipped down her throat, easing some of the dryness that had set in the last few hours. "Thank you," she whispered, before taking another sip.

"You're welcome. Are you sure you don't need a break? Food and drink are coming for everyone. Should be here in minutes."

She brightened at the idea of food. "That would be good."

A shout beside her had her spinning around in time to watch yet another corner of the ledge collapse and slide down the slope. The team working below easily moved out in time, but the layer filled in the space, forcing them to clear it away to get below it. A light rain had started meanwhile; *so not* what they needed right now.

"We need to hurry. It's degrading fast."

"I know." He nudged her toward the path. "A truck has just come in. That will have the food. Let's catch a few minutes. We're two too many up here as it is right now."

In that, he was correct. With a wary eye on the unstable edge, she handed him the empty thermos cup before carefully making her way down to the ever-widening path below. A light flashed on in front of her. "Thanks."

"Hey, it's late, and we're tired. Let's not have anything else happen."

She passed several other team members going up. One held a huge cookie in his hand. She eyed it hungrily. "Hope you left me some of those."

The tech laughed. "Only if you get there fast."

At the truck, a circle of people stood, eating. Meg walked closer, when a large hand landed on her shoulder and directed her to the picnic table that held a couple open spots. "Sit. I'll grab food."

Too tired to argue, she sat down and gently massaged her neck. She stared out at the lake. The moonlight was playing tag with the gently rolling waves. It would have been beautiful, except for the surreal look to the campsite, full of vehicles and white-suited personnel.

They'd found a dump site. As depressing as that reality was, it was also hugely positive. Hopefully they could identify these victims and bring them home to their families. That would make it all worthwhile. Then hopefully they would find the killer through what he'd left behind. ... That thought made her want to rush back to the scene. They would have yards of dirt and humus to sift through, looking for small bones and evidence. Some they would never recover. It just wasn't possible. However, some of the evidence that they would find should surprise even the killer.

And that was the good part.

She already knew a lot about him. He despised women, tossed them away like garbage, after using them as he wanted to. He picked young Caucasian women, between the ages of sixteen and twenty-six, and she might even narrow that down in the lab. He was physically fit and likely middle-aged at this point, but she wouldn't count on it. It seemed that the killers were getting younger and younger, and this one had been killing for fifteen years already. It wasn't out of the range of possibility for their killer to be her age, give or take a few years.

Most likely he was too smart, and, for him, people as a whole were a big joke. Yet he was stupid. Look where and how he'd left the bodies. Right above a popular camping spot. He hadn't even bothered doing a decent job of burying them. So far, they'd found blankets and plastic at the site. From the dirt on top, he might even have collapsed part of the hill above on top of the bodies. He must have figured the bodies would never be found, or, if they were, who cared? It's not as if the cops would ever find *him*.

Well, she sent a silent message out to the killer. *You're wrong there. We will get you. And it'll be soon.*

CHAD, AFTER MAKING sure Meg was safely ensconced with food and drink, headed back to his truck. Mack hadn't shown up, and Chad was pretty damn sure this wasn't his poker night. That he wasn't here said a lot. And Chad didn't like it at all. Daniel was on his way though.

Chad dialed Mack again. The phone went straight to voice mail. "Mack, where are you?" And he hung up the phone. Sure, Mack could be anywhere, but anything to do with this case and missing people sent up alarms. No one was likely to suspect a cop, but that didn't mean a cop wasn't part of the bad team. Chad paused. Was he thinking Mack had had something to do with this, either personally or by association? No, surely not? But then what would exclude him? He had a cabin on the lake. He had access to the files and could have doctored anything he wanted to at any time.

What about motivation? There was none. That was the problem. Many males were the right age group, healthy enough or strong enough to commit this type of crime, but they must have a reason to do what they did.

Mack had no reason to be involved, unless he was protecting someone—like his nephews.

Shit.

That wasn't enough to look at him as the killer. Yet it was enough to wonder if there wasn't a connection that needed to be looked at closer.

A call from the campsite caught his attention.

It was Meg.

MEG WATCHED, AS Chad loped over. He raised a brow at her. "What's up?"

"They found something." She frowned up at him. "They want both of us up there."

"Let's go," he said immediately. "Let me grab a bottle of water to take with me."

She nodded, polishing off the last of her apple. She picked up her garbage and tossed it into the can and turned to climb back up the hill. At the base, she stopped and looked up. She glanced off to the hillside, thrown in darkness in comparison to the lit-up area. She swore the trees were closer together, as if protectively watching over those they'd hidden for so long.

Stupid. But it made her feel better to think Mother Nature had been an active caretaker all these years. This was no longer just about Cia. It had become so much more.

As she stood waiting for Chad to join her, she realized that she was waiting partly because going up that hill one more time looked like too much effort. She dropped her head forward and massaged the back of her neck.

"Tired?"

"Of course." She smiled a little grimly at him. "Then we all are. Let's get this done."

Once again at the path to the ledge, one of the techs called Chad over. "We've found another skull and a necklace."

"Shit. That makes six women."

"Seven," Meg corrected. "Cia."

He stopped and looked at her. "Do you still think it's her, when we now have six more young women? We made the preliminary identification based on location, age at death, her approximate height, age ..."

"And the necklace," added Meg. "Let's not forget that."

"That's the other reason why we called you up." Another tech, a woman this time, walked over and held up a bag. "This last victim had this on her."

The bag held a small silver necklace.

Meg gasped. "It's almost the same."

Chad took the bag and held it up to the light. He shifted it so he could see the small heart-shaped pendant on the necklace. "It is the same. The question is ..."

The tech spoke up, "It's got an inscription on it."

"Oh no," Meg whispered. "Please not."

Chad handed her the bag. "Hold it." He pulled on a pair of gloves, then opened the bag. He poured the contents into his palm and held up the small heart-shaped piece.

His voice soft and deadly, he read, "To Megs, with love."

Meg cried out softly.

ANGER LIKE CHAD hadn't felt in years flashed into existence at the pain he saw in Meg's eyes. There was no longer any doubt this nightmare had gotten so much bigger. But the impact on her? ... That too had grown proportionally larger and much more damaging. "It's not your fault," he said more harshly than he had intended, but, even as he watched, her eyes in the early morning light appeared to be great big orbs of pain. Haunted by memories. Haunted by unanswered questions. *Haunted by Death.*

Chad carefully poured the chain and its devastating message back into the evidence bag and handed it over to the tech. "Take good care of this."

"Not to worry," she said. "I'll put it with the others."

Meg, still at his side, froze, her gasp hard and terrified. "Others?"

Chad put an arm around Meg's stiff shoulders, willing her to keep it together. He understood what she was going through. "Yes, we've found four already."

"Exactly the same?"

"Yeah, they all appear to be."

Meg started shaking. The techs had returned to the section where she'd been working.

With no one watching, Chad tugged Meg into his arms and hugged her, tight and hard. "Hold it together. If you want to be in on this, I need to know you can handle it—whatever 'it' may be."

She stiffened and stepped back. She nodded, her eyes still dark and haunted, but she took several deep breaths. "I'll be fine. Thanks for the reminder."

"I know more than anyone what this means. We need to understand everything, so we can nail the bastard."

Grim-faced, she nodded. "I'm with you there. Let's fry his ass."

INTERESTING STUFF. ... They'd found the dump site.

He pondered what difference that would make. Not even two hours' drive from Seattle meant millions of people were close enough to be considered suspects. None of the locals would be stupid enough to have a dump site in their backyard, so to speak.

He checked his cell phone yet again. Still no official news.

That was good. The longer they took, the better for him. Besides, they wouldn't find everything. He sat back in his truck and smiled at the thought of all those busy bees at work, cleaning up his mess, trying to analyze his motives and to sort out his victims.

Again, all these people should be happy. He had given them jobs and had kept them employed. Kept their paychecks rolling in, so they could get drunk on the weekends. He turned his attention to other factors. Stephanie. *What should he do about her—if anything? Cia had told him that Stephanie knew. But, if she did, why hadn't she said something years ago? Or had Cia lied to him all these years?*

And he hadn't stayed free all these years by being stupid. No, Stephanie would have to go but not in the same way as his girls. He laughed, the sound reverberating inside the truck. She just needed to die—the same way as she'd lived.

Pathetically.

Chapter 18

F INISHING HER PART of the job wasn't fast or easy, but, by the time the early morning sun's rays came through the trees, Meg knew it was time to go home. She didn't need to stay as long as she had, but knowing that more victims could be here had kept her searching—just in case.

They'd found six new female victims—six women to bring home, potentially giving six families some closure. And Cia—if it was Cia. In her heart, Meg still believed it, but here were other victims to consider now.

The one thing she hadn't mentioned was, in contrast to Cia's petite stature, two of the other victims were tall, easily over five foot eight, and two others were close. That was directly opposite to Cia. Had that been on purpose? Or was it because there had been a lack of choice in victims, or was it not a factor at all?

Seven victims, so far. How many more would they find before this was done? She stood at the edge of the ledge and stared toward where the highway curved above them through the trees. Techs and cops had been working, searching the highway area since the light had first broken through; so far, little else had been found. A woman's shoe, or what was left of it, and an old rotten blanket. Both had been bagged and tagged.

They might belong to the victims or the killer. Or to no one related to these deaths.

They really were in a guessing game.

Chad stepped up beside her again. He'd been the Saint Bernard of watchdogs tonight, always seeming to be there, just in case he was needed. She didn't remember him being so solicitous but, then again, look at the situation.

The sense of being looked after was new and different. She'd been with Pete for years, but she couldn't remember such concern. Maybe it was because she'd always been so independent before, boldly tearing around corners of the world that most people wouldn't dare tread and doing a job most people wouldn't want anything to do with. She'd come and gone and had known Pete would be there when she got back. He was always happy to see her on her return, but she never saw that same concern that Chad had shown her these last few days.

Then she'd been knocked off her emotional feet a while ago. Maybe she looked like she needed looking after now.

Also … she kind of liked it.

"Home time," he said, a weary smile on his face. "We'll get you back, so you can sleep. The remains will be waiting for you in the morning." He gave a short laugh. "Make that tomorrow morning."

Good. She nodded and, too tired to speak, helped collect the gear she'd used, now to take down the hill for the last time. Still, she didn't want Chad leaving if it was just to take her home. She could grab a nap in the truck, if that were the case. Better they do what needed to be done than leave. "Are you done here?" she asked. "Because, if not, I can grab a couple hours in the truck and save you the long drive back again."

"Not happening. I'll be back tomorrow and likely the next day. We have doors to knock on for starters." He motioned around her. "However, we have men on it."

"Right. Surely the neighbors must have seen or heard something." She stumbled over a tree root and would have sprawled face-first but for Chad's restraining arm. "Thanks."

"Easy on this next bit." He explained, "We've done so much climbing, we've packed the area down, but that's brought the roots up."

"I'd like to do a trip through here later, when I can see better." She gave him a wan smile. "And when I'm not so tired."

"That's possible. First, some rest."

"Amen to that." With him supporting her, he led her to the truck, then unloaded her armful into the back. "I have to go speak with the others. Get in. I'll be just a minute."

She nodded and struggled into the cab. It was just as cold inside, but being even this much closer to going home helped.

Leaning her head back, she closed her eyes and let some of the stress roll off her shoulders. Even though she'd seen similar scenes before, they never failed to hit her hard.

Those poor women and poor Cia. She'd never had a chance.

At the same time, the likelihood of the killer being one of her old friends was minimal—until you factored in the necklaces. Necklaces she'd been trying hard to forget. The implications were too horrific, too nasty to let sit quietly in her psyche. She'd been involved in lots of serial killings and knew that most of the killers had personal issues with one of the victims, usually the first one. Whether the victim was a stand-in for someone they couldn't kill or was the real target of the killer's rage, it was personal and usually about an emotionally charged relationship.

Her eyes drifted closed. Maybe after a nap, she could convince Chad to take her right to the labs. By the time they reached Seattle, Stacy was likely to be starting her day. Meg would help. This was no longer a simple job.

She sighed heavily and let the drowsiness take her deeper.

Her last thought as she went under was that not many people had used her nickname, *Megs*. She'd been Megan in school and only Megs to her close friends back then. Only a few came in that category. It was someone from way back then.

Someone who had hated her.

Someone who had killed her by proxy, … over and over again.

Seven times over.

CHAD WALKED BACK to the truck with John, one of the other team members, at his side talking. "We need to take another load back. Maybe you should drive one of the vans and let the doc drive the truck."

"I'll ask. I know she's pretty tired though."

"Yeah, it's been a long night for all of us."

"And we're not done."

John snorted. "We could be at this for days." He spun around to look back at the site. "Just look at that place."

Chad pivoted to stare at the stripped hillside, crawling with workers. "I know, depressing."

"And in a way, smart."

"Why's that?"

"It's dangerous enough to keep people away. Animals have been at the bones but not in a big way. He's used something to cover up the smell somewhat, but nothing hides the smell of decomposing bodies. It's high up, so the smell didn't stay down low. Up there, the breeze is more likely to take the odors upwind. Accessible from the highway above and yet still walkable from below, if he wanted access."

John's tone was normal, but the admiration made Chad's stomach heave. He searched John's face carefully. In this game, the killer could be anyone. And given that killers often returned to the scene of the crime and could be found in all sectors of life, law enforcement had had their share of bad eggs too.

John turned, caught Chad's gaze, and laughed. "Hey, it's okay. I'm doing a research paper on serial killers. That's why there's the interest."

Chad chuckled. "Good thing. I was about to check your history."

"I'm not old enough for these killings. Not unless I started in elementary school." John grinned. "Yet this guy has stayed hidden for a long time, so he's got some balls."

"And that's an assumption you can't make ever." Mack, grizzled and growling, walked toward the two of them. "This guy could be behind bars right now for another dump site of bones we've already found and prosecuted him for."

Chad stared at the rumpled detective. When the hell had he shown up? And where'd he come from? "About time you showed up. What's the matter? Holiday hours for you or something?"

"I'm here. Damn middle of the night, you know?"

"Yep. Been here all the night myself." Chad nodded toward the hillside behind Mack. "Found six sets of remains."

"All killed a long time ago." Mack snorted in disgust. "The killer could be married and have kids by now."

"And this could be one of twenty dump sites for his victims," John said enthusiastically. "Who knows how many he's killed."

Both Mack and Chad stared at the tech. He grinned and shrugged. "Hey, this is a great case."

Mack turned his back on John. "And you're taking off already?" he asked Chad.

"Been here a long time. Meg's finished, so I'm taking her back. I'll grab a couple hours, then return."

Mack spat on the ground and nodded. "Sounds good. I'll head over and get up-to-date on the case." He turned and walked away.

Chad murmured, "I bet you will."

"You two got a problem with this case? A little territorial dispute, by any chance?" John asked.

Hating that he'd let anything show, particularly with someone who had so much interest in the case, Chad shook his head. "Nope. This is Daniel's case. The original missing person's case was Mack's from a long time ago."

"And now?"

Chad walked over to his truck. "Now it's bigger."

MEG WOKE UP, as the truck door opened. She straightened up, her brain—slow to realize she'd been asleep—was slow to click into their location. She didn't recognize where they were.

"I'm going in to get some coffee. Do you want one?"

She blinked at Chad a couple times, trying to shake the sleep from her eyes. "Yes, please."

He smiled and shut the door, walking toward the café at the truck stop. She pulled out her cell phone and checked the time. It was almost seven in the morning. Wow. If they were lucky, she could go straight to the labs. Not that she'd had anywhere near-enough sleep to function at an optimum level. Still, she didn't want to miss anything.

She hopped out of the truck and went into the shop to use the washroom. Giving her face a quick scrub, she returned to the restaurant, feeling better. Chad was in the process of paying for the drinks. She walked over, realized she was hungry again. Stepping up behind Chad, she ordered half-a-dozen muffins to take with them.

"Good idea. Hope several of those are for me."

Tossing him a cheeky look, she shook her head. "Maybe, after I'm done."

He scoffed. "You won't even eat one."

She chuckled. "We'll see."

Back in the truck, he drove back onto the highway. She opened the bag and handed him a muffin. She took a bite of hers. "*Hmm*. It's still warm."

"Good. Nights like this, we'll take our comforts where we can."

"And the sustenance as well. The nap helped a lot. I was thinking you could drop me off at the lab. I could get started with Stacy."

"Nope. You are going home. Maybe after a few hours of sleep and a hot shower, you can reevaluate where your energy level is at. Then decide. Not what's in your best interests but what's in the best interests of the case."

"Damn." He was right. She polished off her muffin, took a sip of her hot coffee, and said, "I'll text Stacy. Update her on what's happening." She brought out her cell phone. **Stacy, need help and need to help. We found six more victims and four more necklaces. Same inscription.**

She waited a long minute and then sent a second text. **Please help me.**

CHAD WATCHED HER in concern. He took a sip of his coffee and glanced her way. She was starting to show the wear and tear around the edges. He felt like a damn mother hen.

The necklaces had changed everything.

Finding the old dump site had opened up the field again to other serial killers, including those already incarcerated. It was one thing to consider a friend who had killed by accident or in a passionate rage. It was quite another to consider that he'd carried on killing. And, if he had, why had he stopped?

"Anto again," he whispered, under his breath. Could it be? He'd been a great guy most of the time. Moody but solid. Chad groaned. Or not. The killer could have just changed his dump site. And considering Canada was so close, he could have just crossed the border to a new life.

"I was thinking about Anto too." She sighed and stared out the window. "Nice to have spent half my life wondering if my friends are killers. *Not.*"

"I hear you. Anto could have been the killer, and that would explain the victims in relatively the same time period. And why the killing stopped. If we can ID the bodies, all female, and find one who went missing after Anto's deadly accident, then it would rule him out."

"Yeah, none of us girls liked Anto."

"And here I thought all of you were swooning over the brothers' accents."

Meg smiled at the silly memories his words brought to mind. "There were some. But, of the two, Anto was the scary one. Something was just off about him. Even Cia didn't like him." Meg shrugged. "Not that we ever knew much about either of them."

"I had several classes with Anto. He was not quite two years older than his brother but behind a year. So he played catch-up, taking some extra courses in my year, even though he had enough credits to graduate."

She frowned. "I wonder if that's the one guy Cia turned down."

Chad took his gaze off the road briefly. "How would that play out with the necklaces?"

Meg stared at him, seeing through the tunnel of time so long ago. Answering slowly, she said, "I never really knew him. I only met him through the group, and I was always with you." What she didn't add was that she'd had eyes for no one but Chad. She'd been so lost in love that she'd not even noticed other men. "When did he die?"

"Five years roughly after Cia went missing, I believe. I'll have to check my notes."

"Five years and seven victims in that time? That's possible," Meg said.

Chad nodded. "But remember. The killer might not have stopped killing. He could have just moved."

"True enough. We should check the surrounding areas," Meg added thoughtfully. "Who knows what we might find."

"A couple cadaver dog teams are coming out. They'll do a sweep of the area. The next dump site could be a state over."

"And then there could be no more."

"Let's hope so." He glanced over at her. Her head was back, her eyes closed. Reaching to his dashboard, he put on the country radio station and kept the volume low. With any luck, she'd sleep the rest of the way home.

"It has to be one of us." She turned her head toward him, her eyes bare slits. "You know that. And he hates me."

Not much Chad could do but acknowledge the truth. "I know. Every time he killed one of the girls, he was killing you."

"So …"

"It'll most likely be one of our friends." He pounded the steering wheel in frustration. "But those girls didn't die *because* of you."

"Really?" She narrowed her gaze at him. "It's me who this asshole is killing in his head. It's not just Cia on my shoulders now. All seven young women have lost their lives because of me."

"No," he snapped. "This is on him, not on you. You are not responsible for the horrible things people do because of their emotional issues. Maybe Cia's death could have been a crime of passion—the one that started all this—but the others? No way."

He gently clasped her fingers and gave them a squeeze. "You have to keep this in perspective. Otherwise this, more than anything you've gone through so far, will destroy you." He took his eyes off the road for a long moment. "And that we can't have. There are people who need you. Janelle needs you. I need you."

Her fingers tightened on his, making him smile.

There, he'd said it again. Just in case she hadn't gotten the message so far. That she hadn't responded didn't matter. She had to be mixed up and confused. It could be a long time before she was ready to try another relationship. Chad had to be patient. After all, he'd already waited seventeen years. What were a few more months?

"Thank you," she whispered, the utter weariness in her voice making him wince. At his questioning look, she added, as her eyes drifted closed, "For being there."

JUST LIKE OLD times. Chad and Megs are together. That pissed him right off. Then everything pissed him off these days.

That dump site, for one. Who'd have thought that spot would get found?

On the one hand, he was ready for those remains to be found and dealt with. As long as they were dealing with the part that didn't involve him.

On the other hand, he wanted to keep his secret. And maybe go back to his little hobby. With a difference. He'd spent a lot of time building his little hideaway. Just in case.

He'd be really pissed if they found that.

Chapter 19

MEG DRAGGED HER sore, aching body into her house, as Chad unloaded her bags.

"Shower, then to bed. A couple hours' sleep, and you'll be as good as new." Chad took the bags to the bottom of the stairs and looked around the kitchen. "This is nice."

"It was my brother's house. It seemed like a good idea, when I needed a place to move in to."

He nodded. "Sorry about your brother. I don't remember him well, but I recall that he was always a happy guy."

That made her smile. "So true. Darren always saw the sunshine in life."

"You have a lot of that too."

She shook her head vehemently and then put a hand to her temple at the pounding from the movement. "No. I might have when I was younger, but it's been a long time. I would have said I was *balanced* now, but I realize a lot of that is a front. I was waiting for closure to move on with my life."

"It's happening." He turned to leave. "I'm heading out."

She trailed behind him, all too aware that he had to be as tired as she was, if not more so. She'd managed to sleep on the way home. "You're not going back to the site right away, are you?"

"I'll go home and sleep for a couple hours, then drive back." He stepped out onto the front porch. "Will you be okay?"

She smiled. "I'll be fine. I admit I want to rush to the lab, and I'm jealous you are going back out there. I need to take another look around, but I'm also needed in the lab." She glanced at her watch. "Janelle will be home this afternoon too. So shower, sleep, then lab and family."

"Good. I'll check in on you in a few hours." With a final wave, he walked out the front door. She watched until his truck drove down the block and turned the corner. Then, with a wide yawn, she headed upstairs for a hot shower, wanting nothing more than to collapse in bed.

HOURS LATER CHAD stopped by his office to check his email and phone messages. There was a message from Josh.

He dialed the number on his office's landline and waited for Josh to answer. While waiting, he checked his cell. Unfortunately nothing new on Stephanie.

And neither was Josh answering.

Then he tried Bruce. He might or might not be in town, but Chad wanted to connect in some way. They usually talked every couple weeks.

When he'd left the office yesterday, Daniel was supposed to contact the remaining four males from the original camping trip. Had he? And, if he had, did he learn anything new?

Josh should have come in for the interview yesterday. And that was probably what the calls were about. Chad called Stacy, but she wasn't answering her phone. Then why would she? She'd be in the lab, working on the evidence that had been shipped in.

His phone rang. Mack.

"Are you coming back?"

"Yes, just catching up with things at the office. What's going on there?"

"Lots of legwork still to be done. The techs have finished and are packing up. The weather is getting ready to start pissing down again."

"Not good. We've been hampered by bad weather since we found the first set of remains."

"True enough."

"Did you talk to Josh yesterday?" Chad asked abruptly.

"Yep, I did."

He volunteered nothing further. "And the other three?"

"Couldn't get a hold of Bruce, and Tim is in Switzerland. He'll call me tomorrow."

"Okay."

Mack said abruptly, "You know that it's one of you."

There was the dig Chad had been half expecting. "It's not me and not Meg, nor Stephanie. Anto is dead, so that leaves four males."

"*I* can count." Mack's voice was cool, hard. "And there are still five males."

Shit. "Are you back on that track again?" Chad snapped, his anger flaring to life. "I've spent my life trying to solve this case. For the last time, *I did not kill Cia.*"

Silence came first. "Yeah, I hear you." This time Mack's tone had lightened.

Chad closed his eyes and tried to pull back the hot rage. It was an old accusation that, no matter what, he couldn't escape from the suspicion of being involved. Wrong place at the wrong time—it had just ruined his life. "So, what about Pero?" He kept his tone neutral.

"I'm still trying to track him down. No one has heard from him in years."

The disgust in Mack's voice made Chad smile. Being family, Mack had a better chance of getting in touch with Pero. From what Chad understood, the Novak brothers hadn't been all that friendly with Bruce's extended family, as it were.

"I've left a message with family members."

"Right." As if that would work. As the less well-known of the group, he and his brother had come under suspicion as much as the others. Then the car accident that had taken his brother and father had sent Pero to hell and back physically. The last thing he would want would be to go back to that painful time in his life and talk with the cops again.

Hell, anyone could understand that.

"I'll call him," Chad offered.

"You do that, but I want to be there when you talk to him. Bring him in and let me know when." His voice hardened, as he added, "Got it?"

"Got it." Chad ended the call, getting some small satisfaction from the childish move. He walked to his board and checked his notes on Pero's contact information. He dialed and waited. Nothing.

No one had heard from Pero in years. Not since the accident. Several had gone to see him at the hospital, but he'd been in bad shape. His recovery had apparently taken years.

Chad had visited him around the same time, but Pero didn't want company. He'd been angry and grieving and hurting in a big way. Broken pelvis, shattered face from going through the windshield, and that had been just for a start. Pero had also lost the rest of his immediate family in that accident. His mother had died years earlier.

After that, they'd lost track of each other. Like the rest of the group, no one wanted to stay in contact. It was uncomfortable yet addictive at the same time. No one else knew what they'd been through. No one else understood. The connection was something they wanted, yet, at the same time, they didn't want, as it was a reminder of a horrible time in their lives.

So some, like Meg, ran as far away as they could get; and others, like Stephanie, couldn't get away. No matter how far or how much they struggled, the same issue always kept bringing them back—to this.

MEG WOKE UP achy and tired. She'd slept for hours—hours when dead bodies and dead friends ran screaming through her mind. Waking up to a film of sweat on her skin and a pounding heart hadn't been nice.

She sat up slowly, hating the bone-deep weariness. Just that little movement brought tears to her eyes. She couldn't imagine how she'd feel by bedtime tonight. Moving carefully, she stepped into a hot shower and let the water run over her sore muscles. She only had three hours until Janelle was out of school. She'd hoped for more, but she'd slept the time away.

Feeling more refreshed, she dressed quickly and decided to forgo coffee. She'd pick one up on the way to the lab. However, she needed food. The last of the muffins had been left in Chad's truck. She hoped he was enjoying them. Her stomach growled. She opened the fridge, removed the cheese. She cut herself a decent slice and then chose an apple to go with it.

Within minutes, she was driving to the lab to meet Stacy. Her visitor's pass got her through to Stacy's office, which, of course, was empty. Under the same circumstances, Meg would be in the lab too. And Stacy was just like her. A spare lab coat hung on the back door of the lab. She put it on and stepped into Stacy's domain.

"About time you showed up." Stacy's cheerful voice called out from the far side of the room. "What is this, summer holiday hours?"

Meg laughed. "I could use a holiday, so if you're offering …"

"Ha, I'm planning a trip to Belize in the fall, if you want to come along." Stacy was involved in a six-way puzzle of bones, as she laid out the skeletons. "Come. Give me a hand. I'll be all day putting these pieces together."

"It's quite a mess, isn't it?"

"Yeah, to say the least. It's so much easier if you find one skeleton at a time." Stacy walked over to the fourth table in the row of six and laid down a femur, below a broken pelvis.

"You've done well so far." Meg joined Stacy to study the various partial sets of skeletons laid out on the tables and felt overwhelmed with sadness. "This is really terrible."

"They always are. Don't just stand there." Stacy nodded toward the bags and boxes on the table. "Get busy."

MACK STUDIED THE map that Chad had left behind at the site. It was an aerial shot, showing the lots of each place on the lake. Chad had marked out the exact location of both evidence sites in relation to the highway and the lake. Then, with careful penmanship, he had drawn in the name of each owner with the letters T or O beside them. He frowned.

What kind of code was that?

The techs were busy packing up. Men were out, going from door to door, knocking on all the cabins. Finding out what anyone had heard or seen, if anything.

He doubted anyone had. It was a long time ago.

Glancing around, he noted a line of cabins on the right that he wanted to check out himself. Walking around the chaos, he headed in the direction of the first cabin. He remembered that sucker going up years ago. He'd been young, just in grade school. But his grandpappy and his pappy knew the family doing the building. Back then, everyone knew each other. Everyone helped each other.

This cabin had been built by a lot of hands, and it was one of the earlier ones, before the place became fashionable.

Mack walked up the long pathway to the first cabin and knocked on the old wooden door.

As he looked back at the long line of years behind him, he realized that last thing still hadn't changed.

Everyone still helped each other out.

Sometimes they had to.

Chapter 20

C HAD ARRIVED AT the campsite to find it virtually empty. The techs had gone, and, although he could see Mack's truck, he saw no sign of the man. He opened his phone and called him. And heard a phone go off a few feet away.

"I'm right behind you," Mack growled. "You should try looking first."

Chad rolled his eyes and, disconnecting his phone, turned to face the grizzled detective a couple feet behind him. Mack appeared to be in a royal mood. "Where are we at?"

"Nowhere, as usual. No one saw anything. No one heard anything. No one knows anything."

Chad shook his head. Why wasn't he surprised? It was so typical of people. Everyone kept to themselves. "Have you contacted everyone?"

"Everyone who's here. At least a good couple dozen cabins are empty."

"Give me the address of those not here, and I'll track down the owners and call them."

"*Nah*, I'll do it. I know most of them anyway."

"Maybe it's better that I do it. More official."

"They aren't murderers here," he snarled. "It's the dumb kids who like to visit that raise hell around here."

Chad glared at him. "We didn't raise any hell. We were quiet. Just out to have a nice weekend trip before the end of summer."

Mack didn't say anything, but his lip curled down.

Chad tried to be reasonable. "Look. I know you consider this your backyard and blame us for bringing this mess to your doorstep, but we came here because of Bruce. Remember? Your nephew?"

"I know who Bruce is. And that was the first trip you guys made here. But the curfew was too early for you, the place too crowded, so you headed to the far side of the lake next time, where you could cause some trouble."

"For the last time, we didn't cause any trouble."

"There was booze, and you were all underage, a girl went missing, now turns up murdered. What do you call that?"

Chad had heard it over and over again from so many people, and it always pissed him off. There was no presumption of innocence for those living under the shadow of having gotten away with murder. That was a joke. He'd lived with that shadow for seventeen years.

He wanted out from under it. And he wanted Mack to get the hell off his back.

"And let's not forget that you were at your cabin that weekend, and, for all I know, you decided to walk on over and take out a young girl for yourself," he snapped, his voice harsh, cold. "Pretty easy to make the evidence disappear when it's your case, isn't it?" As Mack's face darkened, Chad added, "How did it become your case anyway?"

"Because I was here, when you idiots lost her." He scowled. "Someone had to take control after you punk-ass kids trampled the place."

Chad snorted. "Right. And how come your search parties never found her body when it was here the whole time?"

"And can you confirm that? For all you know, she was held captive somewhere for a week or two, then killed. Unless your 'professional' can prove otherwise, and I wouldn't trust her word anyway."

"Hey, knock it off." Daniel joined them. "They can probably hear you two fighting on the other side of the lake, for Christ's sake."

Chad glared at the two of them. Daniel was Mack's age and had been around just as long—if not longer. Daniel was good people, but the older set tended to stick together.

"Whatever. Just make sure that those addresses of the ones you checked go down in the file, or you can bet your ass I'll be walking around and disturbing each and every one here to find out who you missed and why." Chad strode past them, his irritation and anger vibrating through him. Christ, would this never end?

"Hey, wait up." Daniel ran behind him. "Take it easy, will you?"

"Why, so you can rag on me too?" Chad unlocked his truck door and opened it. The frame was jerked out of his hand.

"Calm the fuck down. You are not driving in a temper, and, although Mack usually has that effect on people he works with, you should be used to it."

Chad glared at him, hating to hear the sense in the words. He struggled for control, when he just wanted to drive away and to tear up the pavement. But that was suicide.

"Fine, I'll calm down. But Mack is done accusing me with his sly digs. If he's got proof of my involvement, then he better pony up, or I'll be heading to the captain myself. Mack couldn't nail this on me seventeen years ago when I was a scared kid, and he can't now. I'm not a kid anymore, and I'll be God dammed before he ruins my life any more than he already has. He's a fucking asshole, and the evidence points to him just as much as it does to anyone else. And you can bet I'll be taking that to the captain too."

Out of nowhere, Mack appeared, fury flashing on his bulldog of a face.

And he charged.

MEG CHECKED HER cell phone. "I have to run. Janelle is out of school now."

"And you're back at her old house?" Stacy made a shooing motion with her hands. "Go. Just come back tomorrow." She smiled and returned to the work in progress.

Meg said, "Thanks. I'll be here bright and early."

She was already texting Janelle, as she took off her lab coat and grabbed her purse from the locker, where she'd placed it earlier. She could have stayed longer. Janelle wouldn't want to be coddled, but the fact remained they were still uneasy with their new living arrangements. She would just as soon help make the adjustment easier. Janelle would also be happy to hear that Meg had spoken to Pete—at least, a little.

Janelle hadn't responded by the time Meg made her way to her car. The traffic was surprisingly light. Still tired, she drove home carefully, grateful when she pulled into the garage and shut off the engine. She grabbed her purse and cell phone and unlocked her door. Inside she checked her phone again. Still no message from her niece. Glancing at the clock, she realized it was still a few minutes early. Meg could have driven to the school and picked her up.

A big yawn escaped her. She needed more sleep, but it would ruin the night ahead if she tried to nap now. She'd go to bed at the same time as Janelle.

First, some food. She rummaged in the fridge and pulled out the fixings for a sandwich. She didn't know what Janelle had had for lunch, but chances were, she'd be hungry when she got in.

By the time she had two sandwiches, sitting and waiting, Janelle still hadn't texted. Meg picked up her phone and called. Her niece would either be staying late because of homework or was walking home. Hopefully she could improve her marks now. Teachers hated it when the kids' cell phones went off, but it was after school now, so Janelle shouldn't get into trouble.

The phone rang and rang. Irritated, Meg canceled the call. Had Janelle left her phone at school, or was she in detention?

Her stomach growled. Meg put on the teakettle and sat down to eat her sandwich, with her eye on the clock. Every ten minutes, she called but still got no answer. By the time she'd finished eating, she was dialing the school and had managed to catch the principal, before he left for the day. "Hi, Meg, glad to hear from you. Janelle is doing much better these last few months." Meg winced. Janelle might have been doing better a few months ago—but this last month with Pete? So not. "Good, I'm glad to hear that."

"Yes, I'm really happy for her," he said in a chatty voice. "She's had a tough year, but she's handling it well."

"I've been waiting for her to come home this afternoon. She's not answering her phone. Have you seen her?"

"No. Not this afternoon." His voice deepened. "I'm in the main office. Let me check the book." There were sounds of papers being turned. "Oh, here she is. It says she signed out twenty minutes early."

"She signed out?" Meg's throat closed. With great difficulty she swallowed and asked, "Are you saying that she left with someone?"

"Yes," he hastened to assure her. "I can't read the signature though."

"Oh God."

"You didn't know?" His voice sharpened. "Who could she have left with?"

"I don't know." Think, damn it, *think*. "She had a sleepover yesterday. Did Linette sign out as well? Maybe they were under the impression that it was to be for two days."

"It must be something like that." His voice lightened. "I'm looking through the names, but it doesn't look like it. No sign of Linette having signed out."

Meg turned all business. "I need to see that signature. Stay there. I'm five minutes away."

"But—"

She hung up, lunged for her purse and keys, and ran. She was close to twice her stated time, but he stood in the office, waiting for her.

"Here it is." He pulled a book toward her, open with a page of signatures. He stabbed at one signature.

She studied it. And realized it wasn't legible or familiar.

"Have you contacted her friends? That would be my first thought."

Meg held up her cell phone. "I'm dialing as we speak."

"Linette, hi, it's Meg, Janelle's aunt. Is she there with you?"

"No, she said you were picking her up early."

Meg's heart sank. She raised a trembling hand to her forehead. Working to keep her voice calm, she asked, "How did she know that?"

Silence. Then Linette said in a timid voice, "I don't know. I thought she got a text, but I don't know for sure."

There was a fumbling sound, and then she heard Linette call out, "Mom, can you talk to Janelle's mom?"

Then an adult voice came on the phone. Deirdre said, "Meg, what's the matter?"

"Janelle didn't come home. There's an unreadable signature signing her out early from school."

"Unreadable?" Deidre asked cautiously. "You don't recognize it?"

Meg choked back a sob. "No. I don't."

"Can you think of anyone who might have taken her from school? An uncle? A grandparent? And there's no reason to think it has to be a male. Is there an aunt or a best friend who could have planned a surprise?"

Meg's mind raced, as she tried to come up with a logical reason for someone, anyone, to have gone anywhere with Janelle.

Deidre asked tentatively, "Meg, what about Pete?"

"I thought of that," Meg said steadily, and she had. "It's not his signature."

Another silence.

"Is there any reason why he'd try to hide his signature?"

"No, there'd be no need to. He's been in her life for a long time. There'd be no reason to try and hide it." Meg thought for a long moment, then blurted out, "She isn't answering her cell phone."

"That's okay. The girls were playing games on their cell phones all last evening, and they almost ran down their phone batteries. Janelle forgot to bring her charger last night."

"Damn." Meg cast a worried look at the principal, who stood nearby, waiting to help. "Okay, if she calls, let me know."

"I will. And let us know when you find her."

"You bet." Meg hung up the phone and studied the signature again. There was no hesitation in the penmanship. Whoever had been using that signature had been doing it that way for a long time.

She lifted the book and handed it to the principal. "May I get a photocopy of this page? Of the signature? Please."

"Sure. That, I can do." Happy to have a constructive way to help, he warmed up the machine and quickly printed off a copy for her. "Let me know what else I can do."

She nodded. "I will."

"What will you do?"

"Call the police."

And she dialed Chad's number.

CHAD TOSSED MACK back several feet and surged forward to lift him off the ground and throw him back farther. His phone rang in his pocket. He ignored it, fury still riding him hard, as he glared at Mack scrambling to his feet. Daniel stepped between them. "God damn it, Mack. What the hell are you doing?"

Mack lowered his head, as if to plow forward again, bloodlust in his eyes. Daniel stepped toward him. "Back off. You're both on duty. So knock it off."

Keeping a wary eye on Mack, Chad stepped back a little and rolled his shoulders to ease the tension. As much as he'd like to pound Mack to the ground himself, it wouldn't help. And one of them needed to keep their cool.

He'd had enough of Mack's goading.

Mack glared at his old friend, and then his gaze settled on Chad. His face turned fierce, and, for a moment, it was as if time stood still, as they waited for Mack to choose his next move.

Chad watched his muscles tense.

Then Mack eased back slightly, and the dangerous moment passed.

As Chad watched, Mack turned and walked away.

Daniel took a deep breath, then muttered, "Stubborn bastard."

He spun all the way around to face Chad. "Why did you goad him?"

"Because I've had enough. For seventeen long years, I've listened to his accusations. I've had a gutful."

Daniel studied him for a long moment, then grimaced. "And maybe you should have done this a long time ago. But stay away from him now, until he cools off."

Chad said, "I'm going back to town. Better we work on different angles of this case."

Daniel nodded and walked away.

Chad hopped into his truck and headed back the way he'd come. He never should have left the damn city. Better he work the computer side of this investigation. Mack was okay on a computer, but he wasn't the best. Chad, on the other hand, knew he was good.

With any luck he'd be home in just over an hour, and the need to get back pulled on him. He slammed his foot on the gas. It wasn't until he hit the city limits and was only a few minutes from the office that he remembered the phone call. He blamed the confrontation with Mack for that.

He pulled out his phone and checked his message.

"Shit."

MEG DROVE HOME slowly, following the path Janelle would most likely have taken, if she were going home. Meg searched every block, every crosswalk, and even waited outside a small corner store, until she was sure there was no sign of her niece. All the while, she waited for Chad to get back to her.

Inside, her stomach acid churned her guts to sewage. Everything had knotted in fear.

Where was she?

Meg couldn't handle it if something had happened to Janelle.

Meg had lost so much already. Immediately she was assailed by guilt. She should be thinking of poor Janelle. She had to be scared, terrified.

"Please. Whoever you are, please look after my niece. Please don't hurt her," she whispered, and her whispers became prayers that she barely recognized.

She pulled into the garage, her hands shaking so much she could hardly put the car in Park. As she exited the car, she realized Janelle might have come home in the meantime or left a message on the home phone. She ran inside. "Janelle, are you here?"

The kitchen was empty. Meg ran through the main floor, then upstairs. "Janelle? Janelle!"

No answer. The house was empty.

She ran down the stairs to the landline and hit the button. There were no messages. Not one.

"Damn it, Janelle, where are you?" she wailed. Back in the kitchen she stared down at the sandwich she'd made earlier for Janelle. Meg's phone rang, and she snatched it from her pocket, hoping for a call from Janelle.

"Oh thank God. Chad, Janelle's not here. She was signed out from school twenty minutes early. She got a text, at least according to one of her friends, who said I was picking her up early." She gasped out the words so fast, she couldn't catch her breath. Finally she took several deep breaths to calm down.

"Take it easy. We'll find her. I'm sorry I didn't get this earlier. I'm almost back in the office now and just walking down the hallway. Did anyone see her leave the building?"

"I don't believe so, without canvassing a school full of kids to find out. The school secretary had to leave early, so the principal was doing double duty and wouldn't have been watching. He said he hadn't seen her this afternoon."

"Have you tried her phone?"

"Yes, but she's not answering it. More than that, she was at her friend's house for a sleepover, and she forgot her charger."

"So she can't call. Her phone is likely dead now or will be soon."

"Yes. I spoke to her friend's mother, and both girls ran their phones down last night."

"Okay, so I know you've been thinking about this, but who would know she's there? And who would be comfortable enough with a school setting to understand that they'd have to sign the child out?"

"I don't know, but anyone familiar with the school or any school. It's pretty standard procedure in this day and age, I imagine."

"*Hmm.* I need a recent picture and some basic description. I'll get an Amber Alert out immediately."

"Right." She hated this, but it was a necessity. She quickly gave him a physical description as her laptop turned on. "I'm powering up the laptop to find a digital photo to email to you."

"Good. And, when you've done that, sit down and make a list of all the adults you know in town who know about Janelle and where she goes to school."

"Right. That might take a while."

"Not really. You've been pretty focused on rebuilding a life with Janelle. So the list can't be all that long."

"Am I including even the real estate agent?" Meg had a document up on her laptop and was trying to add in the people whom she knew. And who knew about Janelle. She put down Pete and Deidre, Linette's mother. And Sam, Linette's father. Who else?

"Did the Realtor know about Janelle?"

"Sure, I contacted her about not selling the house so we could move back inside." And that had been what—two days ago?

"Then she goes on the list." His tone was brisk. "Did you get the laptop up?"

"Yeah," She tucked the phone into her shoulder and created the email, attached a decent picture of Janelle and sent it off. "It's on the way. Oh, here's another one. I'll send that too."

"Good. Now work on the list."

"Right." She pulled out a chair and sat down. "I can't just create this in a minute, you know?"

She added her Realtor to the list.

"That's fine. The email is here." His voice turned gentle. "She's stunning."

Tears filled her eyes. "Yes, she is." She sniffled. "She's got her mother's dark Spanish good looks. There's no resemblance to me or her father—until you get to know her. She's her father in her stubborn personality."

"And the second picture?" His voice changed, cooled. "When was that one from?"

"That was this last weekend with Pete. They went fishing." She studied the picture on her laptop. "She was so excited about catching the fish. She threw up such a stink at going in the first place. Now look at her."

"And the man?"

She raised an eyebrow. "That's Pete."

Silence.

Damn, she was hearing that a lot lately. "I guess you never met him."

"Oh, I think maybe I did."

She sat back, only just now catching the weird tone in his voice. "Oh, at the second dump site of course. He was one of the guys with the chainsaws. Sorry, I'm just really distracted."

"Sure, I saw him there, but he was in full gear, and I never met him. He left before I arrived." He took a deep breath. "I believe, and I could be wrong because it's been so long ago, and he was in bad shape then, but, Jesus,... *no*, I have to be wrong."

"What are you talking about? Pete has lived with me for close to over ten years. Of course, it's possible for you to have met him before. I'm sorry I didn't introduce you."

"No. You don't understand. Hell, I don't either, but I swear he looks like Pero."

STEPHANIE STUMBLED THROUGH the weird door in her world. She knew she was dying. She wasn't happy about it but had gotten past the point of caring.

Except about Bruce—he would be her regret. She loved the big idiot and always had. And they'd been star-crossed lovers since Cia.

Damn that woman anyway. Her getting herself killed had messed up Stephanie's life. She should have been married to Bruce and have two perfect kids.

Now that wouldn't happen.

There was no one to save Stephanie. There never was.

A noise outside her mind caught her attention. With great difficulty, she rolled her head sideways, letting it hit the cement on the other side. She had to try. "Help," she said, but the words came out in a barest of croaks. She tried again. "Help …"

"Hello?" Then came sounds of running feet and a strangled yell, as someone dropped to her side.

"Stephanie, hang on," Bruce said. His face had never looked so good. She didn't know what he was doing here, especially in this ghetto of an alley.

"I was following you, hoping you wouldn't go to your dealer. Then I lost you." His gentle hand cupped her cheek. "Now I've found you again. Please, don't do this anymore."

Tears trickled from her burning eyes. "Bruce, I …"

"*Shush*, don't try to talk. I'm getting help." He was busy punching numbers on his cell phone.

She smiled. Look at that. This time, there *was* someone to help. "Bruce, I didn't do this."

"What?" he exclaimed. "Then who did?"

But the cloud of consciousness moved over her, and she passed out.

Chapter 21

MEG REARED BACK. "What?" she asked cautiously, studying the picture she sent him. "Pero, as in Anto's brother?"

He cleared his throat. "This is the only picture I have seen of Pete. Do you have some older ones?" Meg's gaze zeroed in on the wall, where she'd hung a picture of her and Pete from their first year together, from back in happier times. She kept it there more to remember Cia now than as a reminder of Pete. "I have lots, but I have to find them. Most are on the computer. Hold on."

"I didn't mean to shock you."

"Well, you did," she snapped. "And so what if he is? It's not as if I'd seen him for years, and I hadn't known him back then, as it were." But it *did* matter. She knew it did, and inside her heart raced. She so didn't need more shocks right now.

Her fingers were busy clicking through her laptop folders, selecting and attaching pictures to send. "I'm sending more pictures."

"And it might have something to do with Janelle's disappearance. You say it wasn't Pete's signature. Was it a man's handwriting?"

"How would I know?" she snapped, hating the suspicion. "I saw him yesterday. Remember? He was helping us clear away that downed tree, one of the guys with chainsaws."

"I remember. I also remember that we made it back in lots of time and so could he."

"But why? There's no logical explanation for why he'd have taken Janelle, particularly in secret. He doesn't even like her!" she finished, her voice rising to a shrill tone at the end.

"He doesn't?" There was a heavy pause, as Chad digested that news. "How could he not? She's just a child. And she's hurting."

"Yeah, well, he doesn't. Or maybe it's the whole situation he doesn't like. Years ago he wanted a family, but later admitted it was more to keep me at home. While my brother was alive, Pete and Janelle got along famously. They used to do movie-and-popcorn nights, and I swear they were more about popcorn fights than anything." Her voice thickened at the happy memories. "Then my brother died, and Janelle's stay became permanent, and everything changed."

"Sometimes, when a situation is forced on people, it takes time for them to adapt."

"Yeah, well, he didn't adapt well," she said shortly. "Maybe if we'd lasted, he might have, but I wasn't prepared to put Janelle through more trauma and abandonment."

She closed all the folders on her desktop. Her mind raced through the possibilities of where Janelle could be, as well as Pete and Janelle's turbulent relationship. Then she realized he wasn't speaking. "Chad?"

"I'm here."

He might be there, but his voice was aged, weary. As if he'd seen too much in life. "And?"

She stared at the series of pictures she'd sent him. They were memories of happier days. Sadness filled her. She scrubbed her eyes with her sleeve. She hated feeling out of control and so emotionally done. But, since her brother's death, life had been one roller coaster after another of pain. She needed life to come a halt. She needed things to work out for once. She needed Janelle home, safe and sound. "What are you thinking?" she asked Chad.

"I'm thinking that Pete is a dead ringer for or actually is Pero."

She shook her head. "No, he'd have told me."

"Why?"

"Because …" She didn't have an answer. They'd shared so little. If they'd known each other back then, wouldn't he have said something? Hell, she'd walked away from them all because she wanted nothing more to do with anyone from that time period. They all had in some ways. So maybe he had to. Maybe he hadn't recognized her?

Chad spoke again. "He was in that car accident. It damaged his shoulders. He used to stand so tall and straight. But then, after the accident, he lost his take on the world, as well as his happy attitude."

At a weak attempt to diffuse the tension, she joked, "At least he was the nicer brother."

"Yeah, he was decent."

"He is decent."

"His hair was jet-black back then."

She remembered that. "Why would it be black now but without that strong jet-black look?"

"Probably because of the accident. He was in the hospital for months." Chad added thoughtfully, "Was he heavily scarred?"

"No. He had some, probably more than a lot of people, but not all over." She tried to cast her mind back, but years of conversations were hard to remember. "I did ask him once about them, and he said something about being in an accident. But he never elaborated."

"Does Pete have any family?"

"His dad died in a car accident and he had an uncle who passed away a few years back. Pete inherited the cabin from him."

"Ah."

A wealth of subtle information filled his tone that she didn't like. "What does that have to do with anything?"

"The brothers were related to Bruce. Remember? They were all cousins. And we were at the lake because Bruce knew about the place, as he and his family owned several cabins there."

And now she *did* remember. Bile rose up the back of her throat. Blindly she walked to the sink, where she filled a glass with water. She took several sips, trying to ease back the nausea.

Either Pete or Pero—it didn't make a difference. And, if she kept telling herself that, she might believe it. Somehow if he were Pero, it was a betrayal. Yet she just didn't understand how.

"That would be pretty sad, considering I spent the last ten years trying to stay a long way away from anyone associated with that part of my life." She gave a half snort. "Not nice to think I'd hooked up with one of the main players and never knew it."

"And maybe he didn't either."

But Chad's tone of voice said he didn't believe it.

"That's quite possible. You changed the form of your name."

They both said together, "So did he …"

"Have you got the photo still up where Pete and Janelle are fishing?"

She clicked several times to bring up the picture in question. "Yeah. What about it?"

"The look in Pete's eyes …"

Her breath caught back a sob. "What are you talking about?" She bent to study the look in his eye and then relaxed. She'd seen that look often lately. It was directed at her—almost as if he hated her. "Yeah, he's not been real happy lately, especially with me."

More silence came.

"As I look at that picture, I realize just how unhappy he is." Meg rubbed her forehead, wondering what she was missing. "Look. I know I'm tired and not functioning on all brain cells at the moment, but you have to spell this out for me. What are you seeing that I'm not?"

"You are the one who took the picture, correct?"

"Yes," she snapped impatiently.

"So, … he's not looking at you."

Oh God.

CHAD KNEW THAT look in Pete's eyes. There was more than anger in that gaze. There was hate. Pete hated Meg's niece. The missing Janelle.

"Was anyone else around when you took that photo?" he asked casually, already knowing the answer but needing her to confirm it. He was already searching his database for Pero's details. What had Mack said about not getting a hold of him?

If they assumed Pero and Pete were the same man, did Mack know this? Or did he only know Pero, not that he was living with Meg as Pete? Could someone hide in plain sight for over a decade? Not that Pero was hiding—he had just avoided his family. It's not as if he was doing anything illegal. But, according to Meg, Pete came to the cabin a lot. According to Mack, he barely saw his nephew, yet both had cabins at the same lake.

And a lot of nastiness was going on at that lake.

"No." Meg was breathing heavy. She said suddenly, "I'll call you back."

Chad stared down at his dead phone and slowly laid it on his desk. Poor Meg, this was not an awareness everyone could handle. She was better prepared than most, but it was different when your family was in danger.

Family. He sat back and considered that. Family threaded through this whole mess. Was Pero the one who'd killed Cia? The Pero Chad had known years ago hadn't seemed like that type of guy. He'd been real popular with the girls, real popular with everyone, in fact. It was his brother who had been morose, broody even, and not as friendly or open.

That Anto had died so young had been so sad and such a waste.

After his accident Pero had been bitter and angry and seriously depressed. He'd resembled his brother a lot during his recovery. Then Chad had lost track of him.

Maybe that's why Meg had gravitated to him, even if she hadn't known. Not that they knew now. Honestly Pero's face had been shattered in the accident. He didn't look like he used to. The surgeons hadn't gone in and put his face back together. They'd left things to heal on their own, as was common in some cases. But nothing had healed like before.

He wasn't disfigured; he was just ... different looking. And, in all fairness to Meg, he was just different enough to make Chad himself question if he really was Pero.

And just because he might have hooked up with Meg and had a cabin at the same lake where Cia had gone missing didn't make him guilty. Any more than Mack was guilty for having been at his cabin that weekend either.

And wanting it to be so didn't make it so.

He needed to connect with Bruce. Maybe he could identify Pero from this picture. They were cousins after all. But he knew Bruce had had little to do with his family now, especially Mack.

Chad walked over to his wall, where he had the case photos up and notes to look at the timeline. He'd only had a chance to put down yesterday that they'd found the other bodies. But, according to Meg, they would all have been deceased close to the same time as Cia—within a few years. And that *within a few years* was frustrating. Until they had identifications on these women, there was no way to narrow that down. This left both Anto and Pero/Pete as viable suspects.

So, in theory, Pero could have killed those women, and then been incapacitated, and that would have stopped the killing spree. He would have hooked up with Meg soon after his recovery and could have turned over a new leaf as Pete. A happy relationship might have been enough to keep him from returning to his murderous ways.

Maybe ...

He ran a search on Pete and got the make and model of his truck, then sent out a regional BOLO alert. Better to be safe. ... He added Janelle's picture and a basic description of both Pete and Janelle.

Next he ran a search for missing women in the age that Meg had stated, from two years before Cia's death to five years afterward. He ran it for the whole state. That would give him a place from which to start.

Within minutes he'd found thirteen hits. He bent to read the details.

MEG VERY CAREFULLY set her phone on the kitchen table. Then taking a deep, controlled breath, she screamed. And screamed, then screamed again, as fear and anger burned hot like a poker into her heart. The sound went on and on, and she couldn't stop it.

Shuddering in the aftermath, her mind still frozen and lost, her rage still bubbling, she finally calmed enough to catch her breath and to swallow the sobs, until they only rippled down her spine, instead of quaking through her.

She couldn't stand the thought of Pete hating Janelle with the level of viciousness that Meg had seen in his eyes in that photo.

What kind of man hated a child? With her arms wrapped around her belly, she rocked in place, trying to get through the horror to where she could deal with the reality on the other side. Janelle had been living with them for six months. Had Pete felt like that before then? Or was it recent?

She cast her mind back carefully, going from weekend to weekend, month to month, wondering and worrying if she'd left them alone. Was that why Janelle was so afraid of him? Did she know how Pete felt? She must have known subconsciously at least. Had he said anything to her? Threatened her? Hurt her?

Even if Pete had let his guard down in this photo, that didn't mean he'd kidnapped Janelle from school. But he was the one person who Janelle would have left with. She wouldn't know not to. She would have assumed that Pete and Meg were friendly, maybe even back together again. Who knew what story Pete might have told her.

He could have even said he was taking her to meet Meg.

And he might be innocent.

God, this was making her nuts.

There was one thing though. If he'd taken Janelle, and that was a big *if*, then Meg had one advantage. She knew Pete like no one else did. And that was always the key to hunting predators; getting inside their minds and thinking like them.

Where would he have gone?

To the cabin of course. She closed her eyes and realized how much of her life revolved around that damn lake. She reached for the phone.

"Chad. If Pete has taken Janelle, he'd take her to his cabin." She took a deep breath. "I'm driving up there to look."

"Whoa. You're not thinking straight. And you're not in any shape to drive. I have men still up there. I'll contact them and have them keep a look out for Pete and Janelle." He took a deep breath. "Give me a moment to get a hold of them, and I'll call you right back."

"Wait. I need to do something. How can I help?"

"By doing what you do best." He added, "I'm sending you some files."

And he hung up.

CHAD THOUGHT ABOUT calling Mack and realized Mack wouldn't likely take his call. With any luck, Daniel was still there. He was one of Mack's cronies but appeared to be a straight shooter.

"Chad, what's up? Are you still hanging around, or did you head back to town?"

"No, I drove back. Probably should've stayed, given this latest development."

"Oh, what's up?"

"A child is missing. The Amber Alert has gone out, but we have reason to believe she might be at the lake." Chad proceeded to bring him up to speed on what he knew. "Pete's cabin is on the same side as the crime scene but down farther. Mack should know which one, if he's still there."

"Yeah, he is." Daniel cleared his throat. "I'll see if I can track him down to help."

"Good. A door-to-door search is ideal. The girl is twelve years old and is only four foot six and maybe seventy pounds. Long black hair and very pretty, a china doll sort of look. I have pictures. I'm sending them to your email now."

"Good."

"There's also a picture of Pete. He's a long-time summer resident, and he was one of the men who helped out with cutting up that tree on-site."

"In that case, I can call the guy who hired him. If we can confirm he's been here all day. No way he ran all the way back to Seattle to snatch a little girl."

"Any confirmation either way would help out a lot."

"Right, I'm on it."

"There is one more issue." And he proceeded to explain the Pero/Pete mess and their connection to the case and … to Mack.

MEG WONDERED WHAT Chad was talking about, when an email came in with photos.

She read the short note. He'd found thirteen cases of missing women who fit the general profile of those missing in a ten-year period, with the day Cia had gone missing in the middle. She opened the first one, and her mind stalled.

She studied the photo, the shakes starting all over again.

This so couldn't be.

But, as she read the case number, she noted the name. Brenda Durnet.

She picked up her phone, then realized she needed to be at Chad's office for this. This would be a long night, and she didn't want to be alone, especially not now. She grabbed her purse and laptop, sent him a quick text, telling him to expect her, and ran out the door. The traffic had picked up unfortunately. It took her close to twenty minutes to cross town. She was more frustrated than anxious by the time she arrived. Her mind was locked on the one image she'd looked at. She should have taken the time to check out the others but had wanted to see Chad first. Maybe they could look at them together to both deal with the shocks she knew were coming.

Damn it. She really didn't want to be alone right now.

She walked into the station, phone out to call him, but he was waiting for her.

"Meg, are you okay?" he asked, his concern rolling over her in warm waves.

She shook her head. "No, I'm really not." She took a deep breath. "Anything on Janelle?"

"No, not yet. Come on back to my office," he said, wrapping an arm around her shoulders. "Do you want a hot drink? A coffee? A hot chocolate?"

"Maybe later," she murmured, hating her weakness. Now that she was here, that weakness just wanted to invade her body. She hated relying on anyone. For years she'd stood on her own two feet, and now she felt like she had none to stand on.

"Come. Sit down." He led her to the spare chair in his office; at least, she presumed that it was his space. He disappeared. "I'm just getting you a hot drink," he called back.

"Fine." She opened her laptop and turned it on. By the time he returned with two cups of steaming liquid, she had the laptop up and running. He placed a hot cup down beside her.

"So I spoke with Daniel, and they are doing a door-to-door search, looking for Janelle and Pete. He'll talk to Mack and show him Pete's picture. As his uncle, he should be able to identify him." He paused. "Let's find that much out for sure."

Meg just nodded. The theories had been coming in fast, but they were still just theories. They needed facts. And that was something she might have. "You sent me some photos."

"Is that why you came running down here? You could have stayed home. I'd have stopped off at the end of the shift and brought you up-to-date anyway."

"Yeah, well, I can't just stand around waiting for news, so I went to work." She turned the laptop around, the first picture loaded up for him to see. "Remember this photo?"

He pulled his chair around the corner of his desk beside her and sat down. He studied the picture and nodded. "Sure, it's one of the case files I pulled. Why? Do you recognize her?"

"Yes. And you should too."

His gaze flew up to lock on hers. "Why?" He studied the picture again. "And I don't."

"You went to school with her. So did I."

"No way."

He strode to his computer and tapped lightly on his keyboard. "I'm bringing up her file."

"Do that. Her name is Brenda Durnet. I was in her English class."

"How can you remember anyone from school?" He shook his head. "I certainly can't."

"Think nerd. Chess club, student leadership, et cetera. And the reason I remember her is my brother was sweet on her for a while."

Chad raised a brow. "And so someone else we know is missing. That's sad again."

"Yes, but it's also good. She's one of the girls we just found."

That relaxed gaze locked down and hardened instantly. "What?"

"See the teeth pattern?" Meg stared down at the smile and the very crooked teeth on the bottom jaw. "That is damn-near identical to the last skull we found."

Chad stared so hard at Meg that she could almost hear the spinning of his brain cells, as he processed the information and the implications.

"Do you have her dental records on file?" she asked.

He checked the file. "Yes. They were added in. And they are digital." He frowned. "We're lucky there. With lots of these old files, we'd be digging around in the storage units for something like that otherwise."

"Send the X-rays to Stacy and ask her to match it. She'll know which one."

With a nod, he tapped on the keys.

She waited, staring down at her old school friend. They hadn't been close, but they'd been friendly. Brenda was the type to be friendly to everyone all the time. Well, someone hadn't been so friendly back to her.

"Done."

And her breath whooshed out, surprising her. She hadn't realized she'd been holding it in. "Good. That's one."

"You're that certain."

"Yes. The teeth caught my interest. I spent quite a bit of time studying that jaw bone."

"Okay, what about the others?"

"I honestly haven't looked. I came here instead."

"Good. Have a drink of that hot chocolate. It will make you feel better." He rolled his chair closer. "Now, let's go over these other photos together, and maybe we'll get lucky with another one."

Meg would have nodded, but she was busy sipping greedily away at her hot chocolate. It had been years since she'd had any. It wasn't great as far as hot chocolate went, but, for the shocks she'd been dealt lately, it was warm and soothing. When the cup was half empty, she replaced it on the desk and turned her attention to the photos.

She brought up the second one. Both studied the blonde, and Meg said, "I don't remember ever seeing her. And there's nothing distinctive about her that's catching my eye."

"Next."

They went through several more, when one photo jarred Meg out of her comfort zone—yet again.

She tapped the screen with a long nail. "I know her."

"You do?" Chad leaned closer to study the pretty young woman. She must have been in her early twenties. I've never seen her." He got up and went to his computer. "Her name is …"

"Cynthia. She was my old neighbor. Moved away, … oh, maybe nine, ten years ago."

"Was last seen leaving her condo just over ten years ago. She never showed up for work on Monday morning. No one knows her whereabouts from that Friday after work through the weekend." He studied Meg's face. "How do you know her?"

"She lived in the condo beside us. Well, I hadn't moved in yet, as I was still dating Pete, but I'd met her a couple times, coming and going. She seemed really nice. She moved out a couple months after I moved in."

When he didn't say anything, she looked up. At the look in his eyes, she was filled with dread. "What are you thinking?"

He pursed his lips. "I'm thinking it all comes back to the same person—you, and, therefore, maybe ... Pete."

MACK SAW DANIEL before he saw him.

"There you are." Daniel called to Mack. "I've been looking all over for you. We've got a problem, and I need your help."

"What's up?" Mack might not be at his best—in fact, he was still pissed—but Daniel was good people, and, if he said there was a problem, then there was a problem.

"Missing child and the guy who might have taken her was helping us at the crime scene and has a cabin on the lake."

"Shit." Mack's stomach knotted. "Explain."

Daniel launched into the explanation he'd been given. "That's all Chad had. He's hoping we can go door-to-door and find either or both. Or at least confirm that Pete was here all day and couldn't have made it to Seattle and back again."

"Sounds as if Meg just had a tiff with him. It's probably nothing."

"Oh, I don't think so. According to Chad the two of them split this last weekend, and Meg and her niece moved out. You know how that goes. I say, we find this Pete and find out for sure." Daniel hesitated, and then launched into the rest of Chad's message. "Chad says there's some confusion about whether this Pete could be your nephew Pero."

Mack's face froze, and his gaze turned glacial.

Damn. Daniel tried to bring up Pete's picture. "It's not showing up very well." He held it out for Mack to see.

His gut twisted. Mack stared at the piss-poor image. "Who can say anything about *that* picture? It's so damn small. Besides, I haven't seen my nephew in years—a lot of years at that."

"Yeah, it's hard to see anything."

The expression on his old friend's face never changed. Daniel took a deep breath and forged on. "Chad also said you might know which cabin is his."

Daniel had turned to look at the cabins that Chad had mentioned.

Clearing his voice, Mack said, "Yeah, Pero's cabin is that old one over there."

"Good. Let's go. That little girl is quite a looker. Sure hate to see anything happen to her." He brought up the photo from his email. "Look at her."

Mack glanced down and was surprised to see a beautiful child staring out at him. "That's Meg's niece? Never would have thought it. No family resemblance there."

"No, apparently she takes after her mother, who died quite a few years back. Then her father was killed in a car accident, and she moved in with Meg and Pete."

"Maybe Pete just wanted to spend some time with her, explain that the relationship has changed and that they'd still be seeing each other." Daniel glanced at him, not commenting on the Pero/Pete issue thankfully.

"Maybe, but you and I both know a lot of other reasons for some guy to be picking up a beauty like this. And most of those beauties aren't quite so pretty by the time these assholes are done with them."

"Let's hope this is all a false alarm." But, inside his gut, Mack had a pretty good idea that things were not quite as innocent as he'd like them to be.

"I've already called a Jim Sutton." Daniel added, "He's the guy who hired Pete for the chainsaw work. Said Pete's well-known in the area for lending a hand. He hasn't seen him all day; thought he'd headed into town this morning."

Mack nodded, feeling a push of inevitability. Damn. Some things fate just insisted on controlling. "Let's go see if he's home."

Chapter 22

M EG WAS TIRED by the time they got through all the files that Chad had found. And underneath all the activity was an insidious fear, as she waited for news about Janelle.

Every time the phone rang, her heart jumped, and her stomach wanted to heave. She wanted to go to the cabin and find Pete. She'd texted him several times and had tried calling, but he never answered. She wanted to ask him herself.

To pass the time constructively, she had Brenda's file open in front of her. And Cynthia Wood's sat beside her. Both women had gone missing abruptly—just as if they dropped off the face of the earth. Neither had had a steady boyfriend; one friend thought Brenda had one, but, if she did, Brenda hadn't shared any details about him.

As for Pete's old neighbor, Cynthia, she'd dumped her boyfriend months before. The police had looked at him closely but ended up taking him off the suspect list.

Meg had little to go on with Cynthia's case. With Brenda, X-rays showed she had broken her left femur as a child and had two cracked ribs from a fall off a horse as a teenager. Those breaks would be fundamental to her identification, and all the information was immediately dispatched to Stacy, as she would find out if one of the skeletons had similar injuries. Meg hoped so.

Seven women were in the morgue, one most likely Cia, and Meg had thirteen missing persons case files, counting Cia. So many families would be watching and waiting by the phone, hoping for news of their loved ones. Six families would be disappointed, unless the police could find another dump site. But how many women would one man kill?

She flipped through the thirteen cases; the two women she had recognized were brunettes, like Cia and Meg herself. They were both young, like Cia, although Pete's neighbor was a couple years older. Of the other women, only four were similar. Two of the women she discarded from the group were overweight and didn't fit the pattern.

One was quite a bit older, and another was into a lifestyle that was rough and also didn't fit the pattern. No, as she studied the women, she realized she'd picked out her particular six to match the bones in the morgue. And she could only hope that Cia matched the first set.

"We haven't discussed one other issue."

Meg checked the time on her cell phone for the zillionth time in the last hour. "And what's that?"

"The necklaces."

"They found four, yet six victims—not counting Cia and her necklace. Maybe we missed a couple, or they could still show up."

Chad added, "You're thinking that the killer had a half dozen or more made up and made his victims wear them?"

"Yeah, that's the most disgusting thing I could imagine, considering they have my name on them." Meg hated to think someone had so much anger toward her that these women had paid the price for it.

"It's unlikely that we'll track down whoever bought the necklaces, but I'm hoping the person who did the inscriptions might still be around."

"Jorgensen's Jewelers." The name just blew out of her mouth. "That's where Josh bought mine."

"Excellent. Let's see if they are still around."

"They are." She smiled. "We walked in there a few years back. Pete bought me some earrings for my birthday."

Chad was already on the computer. "Found them." He picked up the phone. "I wonder if they still do inscriptions." He checked the time. "They closed down a few years ago. Damn."

"Doesn't that figure." She swallowed. "Your teammates haven't checked in yet."

Just then his phone rang. "Oh, good. It's Daniel."

"DANIEL, WHAT DID you find?" Chad asked.

"Nothing as yet. Mack can't tell from the picture if that's Pero—says he hasn't seen him in forever. But we went to Pete's cabin, which was empty, and Mack says it's Pero's cabin. He inherited it when his brother died. Mack searched inside, but no sign of Pete or the girl." He added, "A door-to-door search is underway, and we've got a couple people looking to track down Pete. Everyone we've spoken to says that he's been here all day."

"But you haven't been able to confirm it?"

"No. No one can say when they saw him or where. I'll give you a call in a bit."

"Thanks." Chad hung up and turned to face Meg. The crestfallen look on her face tugged at him, as he watched her clench her fists.

"They haven't found her, have they?"

He watched her lower lip tremble, then firm, as he answered, "No. Daniel has spoken to a couple people who believe they've seen Pete today at the lake but can't say when or where for sure." He took a deep breath. "Pete's cabin is the same cabin as Mack's brother left to his nephew, Pero."

She stood still, a frown wrinkling her forehead. "Really?" At his nod, she shrugged. "So maybe he is Pero."

And that was it. Chad stood. "It's a waiting game now. Yet we also need to keep up our strength. Do you want to go out and grab some food or shall I order pizza in?"

"Pizza," she said so quickly that he raised a brow.

"I don't want to leave," she said. "Just in case …"

He nodded. "I'll go put in an order. Back in a moment."

She nodded. "I want to see where these women were living at their last-known residences."

SHE WALKED OVER to the map of the state of Washington on the wall and found a map of Seattle nearby on the table. Grabbing a few pins, she posted the second map up on the wall beside the first. Then, using the files, she placed a blue pin where Brenda had lived, then a second one for where Cynthia had lived. Approximately thirty condos were at that address. That alone offered many potential suspects. Walking back to the files, Meg picked up her next four choices for the remains she'd found and took a different-colored pin and placed one at each last-known residence. She also took a red pin and placed it at Cia's address.

Then she stepped back. The cluster was close together—except for one. Cia's.

What did that mean?

Shaking her head, she retrieved the pages on the other seven girls from the missing persons' case files Chad had found, and, choosing white pins for them, marked their residences as well.

She'd just finished, when Chad walked back in. From the look on his face, he didn't have any good news.

"No pizza?" she asked lightly. "It took you long enough."

He managed a smile. "Sorry, it will take twenty minutes."

"Ah." She placed the last pin and stepped back several feet to study the change.

"What have you found?" He stood beside her. "Is there a meaning to the colors?"

"White are those missing women I have no idea about." And, true enough, if there was a pattern to the white pins' locations, she couldn't see it. "The red pin is for Cia. Blue is for the two women I'm fairly sure of. The yellow pins are for the four women that I picked out from the files you gave me, as potential matches for the other four sets of remains."

She turned to glance at him, noting the surprise on his face. "What? You told me to do what I do best."

"And apparently you did." He pointed out the blue and yellow pins with one white pin. "These are very close together."

"Yes, but this map isn't the best. One of just this neighborhood would help us take a closer look." She motioned to the white pins that were sprawled across the city. "These can't be ruled out, but they aren't so likely."

"Interesting that you picked four yellows and three are in close proximity to the right area, and this one isn't. You're almost eerily accurate. How the hell do you do it?" Chad's phone rang. "Hi, Stacy. I thought you were long gone for the day."

"No, working late, it's almost the norm these days. Tell Meg that she is right about Brenda Durnet. That's a positive ID on our first one."

Chad turned to Meg. "Stacy says that's a yes on Brenda."

"Oh, Stacy is still working?" She held out her hand for Chad's phone. "Hey, Stacy, that's great. I have another one for you. Cynthia Wood." Meg looked at Chad. "We sent the information a while ago and …" She walked back over to the stack of four, removed the one located out of the hot spot, and read off the names of the other three missing women.

"Wow, that's fast," Stacy said. "Let's see what we have to make the ID with. We may need a family member's DNA."

"Hopefully it won't be necessary, if we can grab dental records."

"I'm on it," Chad said from behind her.

Meg turned and realized she'd walked to the end of the room to stand in front of the map again.

"Good," Stacy replied. "I think we might have dental records for one of these. I remember her case. Her parents come in regularly, bringing bits and pieces. We've called them once over a potential match, but it didn't turn out to be their daughter. I'll have to check." Stacy hung up without saying goodbye.

Meg laughed, as she handed the phone back to Chad. "She's as bad as I am."

"Yes, she is. And that's a good thing." He was busy clicking away on his keyboard.

Meg assumed he was helping Stacy on the case material.

"Interesting."

"What?"

"Just a second." He wrote something down on a scratch pad, then clicked again, then wrote something else. She waited, staring at the pins. So many victims and these were just the brunettes. So sad.

"Okay. Here we go." He got up and walked around his desk, with a notepad in hand. "Here is everyone's home address from the camping trip." He stopped opened a drawer and pulled out black pins. "Let's add this to the grid and see what we have."

Chad put in his, then Josh's and Bruce's addresses. Meg grabbed two more and put them on Stephanie's address, then Cia's.

They all went to the same school, so it made sense that they would be living close together. On the map, the pins made a strong visual effect. Once Chad had finished with the last ones, he stepped back and handed her a pin. "Now put in your old home."

With an inner tension radiating through her, and yet another glance at the clock, hoping for some news on Janelle, she took a black pin, found her old family home, and pinned it.

Hers was right in the middle of the cluster. She stared at it, wondering what it meant.

Then he defined it. "It all centers on you."

MEG STARED BLINDLY out of the window. Chad's office overlooked the parking lot. Rain filled the sky, while tears filled her heart. *It all centers on you.*

These were hard words to hear and to bear. The necklaces had already said she was involved in a big way, but seeing it visually on the map …

She couldn't get the image of her home in the middle of the dots. She spun around, and picked up another black pin and placed it at the second place she'd lived at, then placed a third at Pete's condo, where she'd been living over the last decade.

If anything, that put her even more in the center. She hadn't realized how close to home she'd stayed. As she looked at it, how close to Cia. She'd instinctively stayed close to the problem and, it seemed, may have subconsciously chosen a boyfriend from the same group. If Pete was Pero, that is.

Would Pete have remembered her? She hadn't changed much—at least she hadn't been through a severe car accident. But, as she hadn't known him back then, it followed that he hadn't known her either, surely …

So they were two strangers who had a past connection which neither had remembered.

That theory worked for her but maybe only because she wanted it to work.

The worry, the tension coiling tighter inside, left her wanting to pace the room—or to hit something. For the first time in years she felt the need to run, to run as hard and as fast as she could and to wear out this pulsing fear.

"Are you okay?"

She spun around to face him and opened her mouth to blast him, when a voice at the doorway said, "Chad, the pizza is here."

She closed her eyes and waited for the voice of reason to cool down her temper enough to speak calmly. Chad walked past her, and a strong warm hand landed on her shoulder for a gentle squeeze.

She focused on her deep breathing, trying to regain control. Then the aroma of pepperoni pizza filled the air, and tears filled her eyes. God, he'd remembered. She hated all pizza but one, … pepperoni.

And just like that, memories once again flooded her psyche. Evenings spent sitting on his parents' deck, cuddling, while watching the rain, pizza and popcorn beside them. Early morning after a night of heavy lovemaking, swimming in the early dawn, their bodies still heated from their passion so recently spent.

God, *those* had been the days.

She wanted them back.

That sense of freedom, of knowing you owned the world and your life would go the way you had planned it. The rash arrogance of believing the world was theirs to do with as they wished.

How wrong could she have been? She bowed her head. She wanted to feel young again, to feel loved, and to feel vibrant and full of life again. She had to think about all the years with Pete. Why had he stayed with her? Sure, they'd been good together, comfortable together, like a well-worn pair of shoes. You hated to get rid of them because you knew how hard it was to break in a new pair, even though you knew the old pair were bad for you. In the same way, she had stayed with Pete—he just wasn't bad enough to get rid of ... yet.

And how sad was that?

Her relationship with Pete had slipped into the *old shoe* category, comfy but just not exciting. It had taken her brother's death to make the changes she'd been unwilling to make before.

She bowed her head. *Janelle*. Dear God, please let her be safe.

CHAD SET DOWN the hot pizza on an open spot on his desk. He went to say something lighthearted to help her get over this, when he saw her shoulders shake. Damn.

He walked up behind her, making sure she'd heard him, wrapped his arms around her shoulders, and tugged her backward against his chest to squeeze her gently. "Easy, sweetheart."

She caught back a sob, but her shoulders continued to shake.

"*Shush*. Easy." Chad turned her around gently and wrapped her into a gentle hug. She snuggled in closer and burrowed her face against his chest and bawled.

He held her close and waited out the storm, loving the feel of her in his arms again. Yet her inherent strength had taken on a new fragility that scared him. She'd had so many shocks. She had held it all together, almost in a cold way. Several of the guys had made comments about her demeanor. But Chad knew the real reason for the coolness. Control. Meg was all about control because so much of her life had gone out of control and had stayed that way.

He rubbed her back gently, easing the tension from her spine. But no one could keep this much emotion locked down for so long. This release was good for her and for him. He rested his head on her cheek and held her close. A part of him wanted this moment to never end, and another wanted it to stop immediately, so that she wouldn't be in pain anymore.

Finally her tears stopped flowing, and her sobs quieted to the occasional hiccough.

"Feeling better?"

She leaned back slightly and gave him a watery smile. "Yes, thank you. And I'm slightly embarrassed."

Reluctantly he let her step back. He brushed her hair off her face, then leaned in and kissed her on the forehead. "Don't be. You had to release this tension. You've been under horrible pressure for days."

"Make that weeks, months even." She stepped back, wiping her eyes gently. "Ever since my brother's death."

"And today has just finished it."

She sniffled, tears welling up again at the reminder. She took a big gasping breath and asked, "Any news?"

He shook his head. "Not yet. But we will find her."

To take her mind off her missing niece, he said, "Let's eat, while we have a moment. When the calls start coming in, it'll become bedlam."

Her eyes brightened at the thought of calls coming in with news. She walked over to the pizza box and opened it and smiled. "How could you remember?" She picked up the biggest slice and took a bite.

"How could I forget? Or forget that you always took the biggest piece?"

She laughed. "That's because I eat so little. It's slightly fairer this way."

"Yep, the same twisted logic as the old Megs."

That brought real humor and wonderful memories to her mind. "Oh, I do remember those many arguments."

"Good. I hope you remember the many great times of making up as well." He smiled, pouring as much heat into his gaze as he could. She *had* to remember. They'd been thunder and lightning together, different, unique, but perfect—a matched set. As they should always be.

She lifted her gaze and caught his. Her eyes widened, and she almost gasped. Pink flushed across her cheeks, and he'd never seen anything more charming or sexy. God, how he wanted her, yet this was so not the time or the place. Yet he wanted it to be. He wanted to tear off her clothes and take her on his desk, like he'd done once in his home so long ago.

He swallowed. Then he swallowed again. He clenched his fists.

She took a step closer, her pizza forgotten in her hand. She swayed toward him.

"Damn," he whispered hoarsely. "I really suck at timing."

Her lips tilted. "You never used to have a problem in that area before."

He closed his eyes, willing them to another world, where he could take her in his arms and remind her of what they'd had. What they could have again.

When he opened his eyes again, she stood before him, with a warm, loving smile on her lips. "As we can't feed one appetite, then I suggest we feed another one." With a smirk, she popped the pizza to his lips.

"Definitely not the same thing," he mumbled, his mouth full of hot deliciousness.

"Later," she said, with a sexy twinkle in her eyes. "Much later ..."

And his heart swelled at her words. "Is that a promise?"

She laughed and shoved the pizza into his mouth. "We'll take it slowly and see."

"Not too slow," he mumbled around his mouthful, then swallowed. "You've got until the weekend."

Chapter 23

MEG GASPED IN shocked laughter. How typical of Chad. "I don't think so. That is so *not* going slow."

"Get used to it. I've given you fair warning." He eyed her pizza slice.

She leaned in to search his gaze but moved her pizza farther out of his reach. "You're not serious?"

He grinned, walked to the desk to snag a piece of pizza of his own. "I am so serious." He took a big bite. "We have a lot of time to make up for."

She gazed at him, her heart racing in shock and excitement. Chad had always been like this. Taking charge, been commanding, and then so very caring.

"That gives us this week to wrap up our history and get started on our future."

And then his phone rang.

She raced over, excitement and fear rippling through her. *Please let it be good news.*

Chad answered, his gaze zeroing in on Meg's face, all the fun dropping from his expression. "What? Really? Yes. Thank you. We'll be there in"—he checked his cell phone for the time—"twenty minutes." He disconnected but held up a hand to stop her.

"What? What is it?" Inside her stomach was jumping in panic. "Please."

"It's not Janelle."

Her stomach bottomed out like a cement pillar in the ocean. "Then what is it?"

"It's Stephanie. She's in Emergency."

"Oh God."

"They're working on her right now. They said we could see her in twenty minutes or so."

"Good. Let's eat first and then go."

THE HOSPITAL SCREAMED chaos as they entered. Meg stood at the front entranceway, hating having to even enter. Dozens of people had to be in there. Chad tugged her close, wrapping an arm around her shoulders. "There's been a major pileup on the highway." He motioned through the crowd. "Let's go this way."

She followed blindly, hating the smell of fear and sorrow, panic and pain. God, one never forgot it. Her brother's accident had paralyzed her, and, in a small way, she'd blamed the hospital. It had been so difficult to deal with the shock of his death, the harried nurses, the forms to fill out. Where was the person to hold her and to tell her it would be all okay?

Oh, wait, that had been her job for Janelle, who had been at school. Meg had tried to get her to the hospital in time for her to say goodbye to her father. They hadn't made it.

If only they'd been called just that little bit earlier, if only the traffic had been just a little bit lighter, ... only God hadn't been so generous that night.

Chad reached a hand back and grabbed hers, tugging her up behind him. "She's up here." He led her to a long hallway that was almost graveyard quiet in comparison to the waiting room they'd just passed through.

Meg could walk beside him now.

"Has she woken up?" Meg asked.

"She hadn't when I called before leaving. She has been stabilized though."

"Good. I'd hate to see her finally succeed in killing herself, now that we're close to solving this hell."

He stopped at a large room with double doors. He peered into the window. "She's in here."

Meg looked in and saw rows of beds on either side of the room, green curtains partially concealing the occupants. Yeah, it was a typical hospital ward. He pushed open the door and walked to the right bed. Stephanie lay quiet, asleep. Her breathing was calm and stable. A man sat beside the bedside. A man she didn't recognize.

"She's so pale," Chad said.

Meg's attention was drawn to Stephanie. She walked closer.

"But she's alive," said the other man.

That voice. Meg lifted her head to study Stephanie's visitor. Then she recognized him. "Bruce?"

He stared at her blankly, and then a smile broke across his worried features. "Megan? Megs?"

She smiled. "It's Meg these days." She studied his features. He'd been such a fun-loving guy back then. He and Stephanie had had big plans. Then, they all had.

Chad smacked Bruce on the shoulder. "Everyone's been trying to reach you. Where the hell have you been?"

Bruce snorted. "Trying to save Stephanie."

Meg turned her attention back to her old friend, prone on the bed. In fact, she looked as white as the sheets around her. And her neck looked uncomfortably swollen. Tubes ran in and out of her arms, and that stillness to her had Meg wondering if she wasn't still standing with one foot in her grave.

"She won't wake up tonight," Bruce said.

"What happened?"

"God only knows. She was supposed to meet me for coffee, but she called it off. Said she was going to meet someone else. I was pissed. Then I got a text from her—all garbled and making no sense. Something about being scared." He sighed. "I'd followed her to see who she was meeting. Only she drove into a parking lot and sat there and waited for a long time, then took off. She drove downtown, parked, and started walking. I followed. Then she went really freaky and ran away."

"Jesus," Chad said. "Any idea who she'd planned to meet?"

Bruce shook his head. "After she ran away, I spent hours trying to find her. When I did, this is the shape she was in."

"She found her dealer then, I guess," Chad said, staring down at Stephanie.

"I don't know that she did. I asked her to stop doing this to herself, and she said she didn't do it." He frowned down at the silent woman. "Then she passed out. She hasn't been awake since."

"What?" Chad exclaimed. "She didn't do this to herself?"

Bruce stared at him. "No. She didn't."

"Then who the hell did?"

A SHORT WHILE later, back out in the parking lot, Chad wrapped an arm around Meg's shoulders, wanting to tuck her in his damn pocket and keep her safe, but that was so not possible.

"No news on Janelle?" Meg asked in a subdued tone.

He winced, pulled out his phone to check, even though he'd just checked a few moments ago. "No. Not yet."

The barest of shivers rippled down her back.

"Are you cold?" he asked.

"No. Scared. Bordering on panicked. I want her back, safe and sound."

"If Pete has taken her, do you think he'd hurt her?"

She lowered her head, her hair hiding her expression. Speaking slowly, thoughtfully, she said, "I wouldn't think so. But the Pete I know is not the killer we are hunting. If they are the same person, then obviously the answer is"—she took a deep breath—"yes."

On cue, Chad's phone rang.

Meg stiffened, she turned to face him, hope ... and fear warring across her face.

MEG DIDN'T DARE breathe. Please. Please. *Please, let this be good news.*

Chad said, "Really? Where?"

He glanced at his watch. "We can be there in just under an hour and a half." His gaze locked on Meg's, a question in his eyes.

"Yes," she said. "Have they found Janelle?"

He shook his head. "Just Pete's truck. And it's been hidden away."

"Wait." Her heart plummeted. "What if he doesn't have her? We can't leave here and find out someone else has taken her."

Chad hung up. "Do you want to stay here then?"

"No!" She closed her eyes and took a deep breath. "I just wish it wasn't so far away."

"Everyone is out looking for her, but, if there is any chance that Pete has taken her, we need to find him. His truck was found in the bush, a few miles from the campsite."

She gasped; her skin flushed with an iciness she knew wouldn't leave, not until she had Janelle back in her arms.

"What?" He grabbed her shoulders. "Do you know of another place he'd have stashed her?"

"Not really," she whispered, her mind racing. "He hunts and has spoken of having blinds at various places." She shook her head. "But why would he be a few miles into the bush?" Shudders racked her body. "I can't stop thinking about the dump site."

"Think about this logically." He stared at the sky for a long moment and then glanced back at her. "Whoever took her was someone she knew well enough to leave with. That someone must have known where she was at the time, and, even more important, ... that particular someone must have known they could sign her out of school and not raise any suspicions in doing so." His gaze, caring and somber, rested on her. "What does your gut say?"

At his words, her gut clenched so tightly, she was left gasping. "When you put it that way ..." God, what a betrayal. Still, she had to get the word out. "*Pete.*"

"Exactly."

Chapter 24

THEY MADE IT faster than they had expected, with Chad stretching the speed limit to get there quickly. But, for Meg, sitting in the passenger seat, her knuckles gripped white, it wasn't fast enough.

According to Daniel, the vehicle had been parked, not run off the road. It didn't appear to be damaged in any way. Apparently the owner of the truck stop café knew of a couple of Pete's spots and had driven around to check. He'd been trying to prove that Pete hadn't done anything wrong.

The same owner had also said he'd never seen a kid in Pete's care.

Then Janelle hadn't been with Pete all that long, and, according to Meg, he'd never been alone with her. And he'd never taken her on a trip out of town. And, if he had her now, she could have been unconscious and hidden, where no one could have seen her.

Not that Chad would mention any of those suggestions.

Meg sat motionless beside him. Too quiet. He knew what thoughts were running through her head. He couldn't imagine the feelings, but he'd been with victims' families enough to know this would be one of the most horrible scenarios he could imagine.

He wanted to say something comforting but couldn't think of anything to say.

So he said nothing.

His phone rang again. He had it in his holder on the dash. He pushed the Talk button. "Hello."

"Chad, Daniel again." Daniel took a deep breath. "We're not sure from when, but there is a child's sweater in the back of the truck."

Meg gasped; she stared at Chad, her eyes huge.

"What color?" he asked.

"It's a deep purple, with a turquoise trim on the sleeves."

Meg nodded, her eyes closed. "That's Janelle's."

Chad hated this, but he needed to ask. "Meg, Janelle was at the cabin on the weekend. Did you drive up in Pete's truck?"

"Yes."

"Did Janelle have that sweater with her at that time?"

Her eyes widened in understanding. "Oh, I'm not sure."

"We need you to be sure." He cast another glance in her direction. "Think. She must have had some kind of warm clothing with her?"

"Sure. We all did. The mornings are brutal, and there is no central heat in his place. It's on his To Do list."

"And was that sweater one of those items she'd have taken?"

Meg sat back and took a deep breath. "Give me a moment. I'll go through it in my mind."

Chad said, "Daniel, I'll call you back."

"Good enough."

The silence was long and thick, as Chad waited for Meg to go through the events in her mind.

"I can't place it that weekend," she whispered. "I can't focus. I'm so scared."

"I know you are, honey. Stay focused. Did she have that sweater on this morning?"

She turned to look at him. "I don't know. She was at the sleepover."

"Then call the mother and ask." He waited patiently, as Meg dialed her niece's friend's house and asked.

"Right. I know Linette loved the color of that sweater. Purple is always a hit, isn't it? Thanks, I'll pass this on to the police." She hung up the phone. "According to Deirdre, Janelle had the sweater in her backpack. She wasn't wearing it this morning, but it was in her bag, when she walked out the door." She leaned back and closed her eyes. "And therefore—"

"If it had been left in the truck from last weekend at the cabin, she couldn't have had it with her this morning." He added, his voice grim, "Now we have something concrete to go by. And Pete has just moved up the suspect list."

MEG NEVER SAID another word, as they raced toward Pete's truck. Her mind flit from shock to shock, and she couldn't bring the churning washing machine of emotions back under control. She could barely breathe. But passing out in Chad's truck was not an option.

She sensed his glances coming her way, and she knew he was worried. But, if Janelle were hurt—or worse, dead—nothing he could do about it, for her or for Janelle. And Meg was likely to get up and run—a long, long way away.

She didn't dare think about Janelle being hurt. She'd been picked up at 2:30 p.m. Pete had had her for over four hours.

Her mind refused to think about all the things a man could do to a child in that time period. Meg had to try and stay focused.

She had to be strong for Janelle's sake.

That little girl needed her. Now more than ever.

They turned one last corner, barely noticing the GPS on Chad's truck flashing the final destination. Dozens of vehicles had pulled up behind Pete's vehicle, and, sure enough, it was his truck. She would have recognized it anywhere.

"Will you be okay?" Chad asked, as he pulled up behind the cop car on the shoulder and turned off the engine.

"Find her. Kill him. Then I'll be okay," she snarled and bolted from the truck.

"Hey, wait up." With Chad racing behind, Meg dashed toward the truck and the group of men standing there.

Snagging her arm, Chad snapped, "Meg, easy."

She froze in place and realized she'd almost blundered ahead and compromised the scene. That scared her more than anything. She had to be smart. As smart as, even smarter than, Pete.

Chad gripped her shoulder, and whispered, "If you are not in control, you will have to leave. This isn't me saying this. It's the men here handling the case, who will order you to be taken back to the station."

She took a deep breath, froze all her emotions, like she'd learned to do a long time ago, and nodded. "Got it." She walked forward carefully, aware they'd attracted the group's attention. "And thanks."

She should have brought gloves. As if reading her mind, Chad handed her a pair from a box sitting on the ground. Blue gloves. She smiled at the color. She'd used similar ones on her last job. Just the reminder of her own professional history helped steady her. She could do this. *She could do this.* "Anything useful inside?" she asked casually.

The first man motioned to the sweater displayed on a rock. "That."

Chad spoke from behind her. "What do you have so far?"

"The suspect has been hunting in those woods for a lot of years. Apparently he has favorite spots. We're assuming he has the little girl with him. To that end, we have two dog teams coming in."

"Dogs are good," Chad said. "I presume his cabin has been thoroughly checked."

"Yes, it has."

That voice sounded familiar. She turned to face it. *Mack.* She nodded. "Good. And search parties?" She opened the truck door, stood up on the running board, and peered inside.

"We know what we're doing. Too bad you're forced back here. It's not exactly your favorite place."

She froze. Then, very slowly, she turned to look back at the man who'd terrified her so long ago. Her voice biting, she said, "No, it's not. But it is yours, I believe."

His face turned a ruddy red. A second man at his side tugged Mack out of the way.

"Easy tiger," murmured Chad, stationing himself beside her protectively.

The second man spoke up. "Hey, Chad."

"Daniel."

Meg assessed the man who'd called Chad on the phone about the sweater. She gave him a five-second assessment and realized he was a different type of fish than Mack.

His gaze was steady and clear, with intelligence gleaming through its depths.

"Is it hers?" he asked her.

Meg nodded. "Yes, it is."

"You didn't even examine it, so how could you know?" he asked gently.

"I sewed the turquoise trim on it," she said quietly, staring directly at Daniel. She needed someone besides Chad on her team. She had no idea how far Mack's influence had spread.

As proof went, it was hard to beat. Daniel studied her, his eyes narrowed, his gaze intent. Then he nodded, and Meg knew she'd passed some kind of test.

She turned back to peruse the inside of Pete's truck. It looked the same as last time, except for a take-out bag from the café. She handed them off to Chad. "Did anyone see Janelle in the truck when he bought this?"

"I'll ask." Chad took the bag from her. "The techs will be here in a few minutes."

She nodded. "I know, but we have no time to waste. I just can't see him forcing Janelle out in the woods here."

The men were silent, no one wanting to voice the other options.

She sighed. "Most likely he has convinced her another cabin was through here, or either she was unconscious or ..." She set her lips together, refusing to say the last option.

"Do we know what's on the other side of these trees?" Chad asked.

"The lake, ... *duh*." It was Mack again.

As Meg was about to blister him, she caught sight of Chad's face. Right. Let him deal with the asshole. She turned and ignored the harsh words. Daniel's voice rose in the melee, but she was more concerned about the small notebook on the footwall of the passenger side.

Leaning forward, she plucked it up and pulled it open. It was Janelle's. She used it to keep track of her homework, a necessary step for the less-than-stellar student. She made it to the last page and read Janelle's note. *Leaving early. Yay! Pete is picking me up. Boo. We're meeting Meg. Yay! We're going to the cabin again. Boo! I get to miss school. Double yay!*

Silently she held out the book to Chad, so thankful she'd ended up coming. Janelle was here somewhere. "That answers that question."

He took it from her, read it, then read it aloud for the others to hear. "So we know he picked her up from school and brought her out here. From the sweater, we know she got into his truck. The question is, where has he taken her and why?"

"There are lots of places on the lake." This came from a man in the back. "Too many options."

Meg spoke to him. "Do you know other places on the lake where Pete might be hanging out? Maybe other cabins owned by relatives? Or friends?"

"Pete's a bit of a loner, but he often goes fishing with some of the locals. Their cabins aren't too far from here."

"Is there a path through here at all?" Chad asked. "Any reason for him to have parked here?"

"Pete likes to hunt wild mushrooms. He's got spots all over the place," said the same man at the back of the group.

Chad looked at Meg for confirmation.

She felt like an idiot, but she shook her head. She hadn't known. She also didn't think he'd ever eaten any he'd picked. "Does anyone know if it's mushroom season?" she asked. "And, if so, what kind of mushrooms?"

There was a scramble, as men pulled out phones and moved slightly away to hear.

Daniel walked closer. "We've already followed this direction to the lake, and we didn't see or hear anything."

Meg stared at the woods in front of her. "How far is it to the lake?"

"A few hundred yards, maybe a bit more."

She nodded. "How about a fishing dock?"

"One. It looks like there used to be a cabin a long time ago, with the dock still there, but it's rickety."

"Pete has a boat up at his cabin."

Daniel shook his head. "No boat when we were there." He turned and talked to someone beside him. "Bill is taking another run up to the cabin to double-check."

"Not alone," Chad said. "If Pete's gone there from here, he's looking for privacy. Doesn't want anyone to know that he's there or that he has a passenger." Chad studied the trees. "The truck is pulled far enough off the road for a purpose."

"And that's about the only reason to do it this way." Daniel studied the truck. "So no one would know."

Meg did another quick search inside the truck and came up empty. "I can't see anything else here."

"Good. The techs had just arrived. They'll do a once-over, then tow it back to town."

She nodded and jumped down. Walking around the front of the truck, she studied the trees and the ground, searching for the pathway. The dogs should have been out here already. Yet she knew that, if they didn't live in the vicinity, it could take precious time.

Time Janelle didn't have. Would Pete keep her at the cabin? No one knew about him. But he was always planning ahead, always thinking down the road. She couldn't help but think he'd have a secondary place to take Janelle.

Another cabin? He'd been ecstatic when he got this one. He wasn't flush. He did well doing construction work, but it wasn't making him rich, and these cabins weren't cheap. So then what? He could build what he wanted. He had the know-how and the strength. However, he couldn't be obvious about it.

"Has he done any repairs on cabins around here? Is he known to help his neighbors out at all?" She turned to ask Daniel. "And, no, I don't know. The first time I was here with him at his cabin was this last weekend."

Daniel nodded. "He's been known to help others. Several neighbors have commented on that. He helped put a roof on one house and separated a basement into a suite. That type of thing."

"What about building a safe space in someone's cabin?" she asked calmly, thinking of all the empty summer homes. Who'd know?

"And how could he do that? The owners are obviously going to notice." Daniel snorted. "Not to mention having a girl screaming in their basement."

"Unless they don't live there," Chad said quietly. "And Pete might know some of the absentee owners. He might have done some work on their places."

"Pero did and more." Mack stepped forward, his ruddy face working furiously. "He's a caretaker for one of the Williamsons. Jackie Williamson is out of Germany. He owns the summer place at the far end. I'd heard a long time ago that Pero had been keeping an eye on it. The owner hasn't been here for years." He added, his eyebrows beetling together, "If not for decades."

Chad looked at him, wanting a definitive answer. "And would that be Pete or Pero?"

Mack's face chilled. "I guess we'll have to see, won't we? *I* don't know Pete."

MEG WATCHED FROM inside Chad's truck. With Mack on board, the men scattered in organized chaos. The techs were here to deal with the truck, as she waited for Chad, who was lining up last-minute details. She wanted to be first on the scene at the Williamsons' cabin, but, at the same time, she was terrified of what she'd find.

Chad opened the truck door and hopped in. "Sorry for the delay. We have to do this right."

Meg was glad she wasn't in law enforcement. She'd bust down every door in her way, if it meant finding Janelle. And to hell with the law. "Are the other men going to continue to search here?"

"And at Pete's cabin. Don't worry. Daniel is coordinating all the efforts. He's good at it. If she's here, we'll find her."

Meg leaned back against the bench seat, hating the constant tension that lived under her skin. That sense of being coiled so tight that she'd break if she heard the wrong thing. Fear was under that tension and also a rage like she'd never felt before, that lifted the fear higher and higher to the surface. A rage that would demand answers, if someone had hurt Janelle.

She'd been angry before, but she'd never felt *this* emotion before.

That it sat just under her skin was scary because she knew the casing keeping it contained was fragile and so incapable of holding it back if it decided to blow.

And she didn't know what she'd do if it did. She knew now, after feeling that rage, that if she had to, she could kill. That she was no better than any of the other animals Chad had spent his life trying to lock away.

The only difference between her and them was that thin protective shell.

And what would happen if she could no longer control it?

CHAD CAST A concerned look at Meg. She had a look on her face that he'd never seen before. Not on her face. But he understood it. He'd seen it before on parents who'd found out about atrocities committed on their children. Under the horror was a rage so horrific it had to be experienced to be understood. And it had always scared the parents. The emotions were so rare and so shocking when they flushed through the system that few people knew how to handle them. Hence, crimes of passion were committed.

And Meg looked to be dealing with her own right now.

"Are you okay?" he asked gently.

She shook her head. "Not really."

He sighed. He knew exactly what was going on. "You can't do it, you know?"

She made no attempt to misunderstand. "Yes, I can."

He stayed quiet for a long moment, wondering how to reach her and how to diffuse that rage.

"And what about Janelle? She's lost everyone already. Does she have to lose you too? Just so you get your revenge?"

"It's not about revenge."

Her voice, so cold and clipped, made him wince. "I've seen parents say the same thing over and over again. The problem is that killing Pete won't change anything he's done. It will only make you feel better—for that one moment in time—only for that. Then, there is the rest of your life."

"How could he?" she cried out, her voice breaking. She rounded on Chad. "She's so little. So fragile. How could anyone want to hurt her? She's done nothing to him."

"It's not about what she's done. It's about this person being ill."

"That's an excuse. We coddle these people and smack their hands, telling them they did a bad thing. These assholes say they are sorry, do a year or two in jail, and then get out on good behavior. Where is the justice in that?"

"For some it's not much, but it's the system we have. It's what we can do. And you know he won't get just a year or two. We'll build this case so he's not going anywhere for a long time."

She laughed.

A broken sound that shattered his heart. God, she'd been through so much already. And the night wasn't over yet.

"You don't know that. Look at how broken our justice system is. Killers walk all the time. Rapists rarely get caught, and so many others aren't even given a decent sentence."

"And many killers never see freedom again. Thousands of rapists are taken off the street every day, and so many more are paying the price for their actions." He reached over and grabbed her hand. "You have to believe in the good. In the right. You can't focus on all the wrong in the world. We've been hit with the shitty side of life, but it could have been so much worse. Cia paid the ultimate price from that trip so long ago, but we've been paying too, every single day, and it's tainted everything in our world. We have to let it go. We have to move on."

"Can you?" she whispered.

He pulled the truck over and parked it beside several other trucks. "We're here." He squeezed her hand. "To answer your question, yes, I can. And so can you."

"No, Chad. I don't think I can." She looked him in the eye, her voice cool. "Not until I have Janelle back, safe and sound." She turned to scramble out of the truck. "Only then will I move forward and leave this all behind."

Chapter 25

MACK WAS SPEAKING with four other men when they arrived. Meg opened the truck door and hopped out. They'd parked at the neighbor's house and now stood at the edge of the Williamsons' property—just out of sight. She studied the location carefully. This lot was larger and more secluded than the ones they had passed on the way in. Large mature trees offered shade, and a huge cedar hedge ran down either side of the property. In other words, there was total privacy.

Then she turned to face the cabin. Maybe *summer palace* was a better description. It was huge. And anyone looking at it would assume it held expensive items worth stealing.

No sounds came from inside. No banging, talking, no music or sounds of activity. It looked empty. And she so hoped it wasn't.

If Janelle were in there, she'd be kicking up a ruckus—if she were able to.

Meg walked over to Chad, who was deep in conversation with the others. He reached out and pulled her closer, letting her into the discussion. "We're going to split up and go in from the two entrances. I want you to stay here."

She stiffened. "No—"

"Yes," he said firmly. "I want you to stay here to see if anyone flees from the house, while we go in." He shot her a warning look. "Do not go after him or her. Do you understand?"

Damn. Still, she nodded quickly. And he was right. If they all went inside, someone could flee the place, and they wouldn't know. He continued to search her face, as if remembering their earlier conversation.

Thankfully that rage had dissipated between then and now. As much as she wanted this asshole dead, she wanted Janelle home, safe and sound first. "I'm fine."

He gave one short nod, then went back to making plans. Within minutes, the group had broken up and headed toward the house.

After a strong hug and a gentle kiss to her forehead, Chad followed them.

Meg took a deep breath, whispered a silent prayer to the God she'd hoped was there but had lost faith in a long time ago, and slipped to the hedge, so she could do her part.

The five men scattered, trying to cover all the doors on the main floor in the house.

The cry came from the far side. "Police, open up."

One cop on this side tested the door. Finding it locked, he backed up, then rammed forward. The door popped open, and he fell inside.

An eerie silence surrounded the house. She could no longer see anyone. And that disturbed her more than anything else. It was as if she was alone in a bizarre science-fiction film—only the plot made it a horror movie instead. She bit her bottom lip, worrying and hoping she'd see them soon.

More shouts came from inside, but they sounded like the men speaking to each other.

Shit. Her nerves were knotting her inside. She rubbed her sweaty palms on her jeans. Where was Janelle? She had to be here. Her heart raced, then slowed. She didn't know where else to look.

"Meg!"

She looked up. Chad was in an upstairs bedroom, his hands cupped around his mouth, getting ready to call her again.

She ran, "What?"

"You can come in. We're searching the house, but it appears empty."

Shit.

CHAD LOOKED OUT the window and watched as Meg raced forward, then went back to his room-by-room search. "Anything?" he called out to the team in general.

"No, except someone has been here recently. And food's in the fridge."

Interesting. The owners hadn't been here in years, so who was using it? Squatters? Or Pete? Chad finished checking out the closet and then ducked down to search under the bed. Nothing.

In the hallway, he heard Meg racing up the stairs. "Are you sure?" she called out.

"We're going room by room," said Chad. "This bedroom is empty."

Meg turned to the closet closest to her and opened it, full-on shelves but no Janelle. He watched Meg for a moment to confirm that she'd be okay. Not only was she okay but she pulled a small flashlight out of her pocket and searched the top of the closet for an opening. Disappointed, she faced him. "We'll have to find the attic too."

He nodded. "And we will." He walked into the next bedroom and repeated the process. By the time he'd completed a thorough search, he found Meg standing anxiously at the doorway.

"Next level," she said and bolted down the stairs. He raced after her. Downstairs, all the men were moving through the house in organized efficiency.

They only had the basement left.

Finally the team raced down the stairs. Meg could hardly breathe, and her side ached fiercely, but that was nothing to the massive disappointment that clutched at her heart and squeezed it when she realized the basement was just a big open room.

"Nothing," she whispered, tears gathering in the corner of her eyes, her heart breaking slowly, piece by piece. "Nothing's here."

"Hold on. Let's take a closer look." He walked to the wall closest to him and tapped. The others spread out and did the same, but all the walls appeared to be made of solid concrete. And that's what she had expected.

She walked behind the stairs and searched. Nothing was here. She wanted to crawl away and hide, be someplace alone, and let her tears pour out. Instead this horrible tension gripped her tight and made her want to scream.

The shakes started at her shoulders, and, by the time they'd hit her hips, she couldn't stop them. She stood in place and waited for the men to finish.

"Hey, over here."

Meg spun around. Two men, Daniel and someone she thought was called John, were at the far side, heads together.

Everyone ran toward them. Meg, walking very carefully, too scared to hope, and yet desperate for good news, was on their heels.

"A crack is in the wall here."

"It's wood. Painted with cement-like paint to blend in.'

"Looks like he painted the whole foundation here in the same paint."

"Let's get it open."

"Can't see a handle."

Meg closed her eyes, willing them to hurry. "Why not just bust the thing down?" she whispered, praying for patience.

"Because they don't want to hurt anyone inside," Chad murmured at her side. "They've got it now. Hold on."

She gasped for another breath and held it, as the door popped open, almost spilling the men inside. A shout went up.

"She's here."

And pandemonium ensued.

MEG GASPED IN joy. The relief was so great she could hardly draw another breath. Oh, *thank God*. She reached the open door and bolted through it. And came to a dead stop.

A single bed was in the corner of a long narrow room and a rough-plumbed bathroom at the other. The men crowded around the still form in the center of the bed. Meg walked closer, as if in running she'd lose control. She struggled to keep her composure. They'd found Janelle—but had they been in time?

Janelle lay fully dressed in her purple jeans and T-shirt, her runners still on. Meg choked back a gasp, her hand jumping up to cover her mouth—and the scream wanting to escape it.

Chad stepped toward Meg. "Easy. She's just unconscious."

"Just?" Meg took a long gasping breath, dropped her clenched hands, and slowly stepped up to the side of the bed. Daniel was checking Janelle's vitals. "That doesn't look like a normal unconsciousness."

"She's been drugged." Chad wrapped an arm around Meg's shoulders. "There are needle marks on her arms."

"Oh God." She covered her mouth with both hands and stared at him with wide eyes. "Poor Janelle."

"Yes … and lucky Janelle." He squeezed Meg's shoulders and tugged her in closer for a long moment. "We found her. And she's safe. She doesn't appear to have been physically hurt. We got to her in time." He let out a huge breath. "Take a deep breath. She's safe. We made it. And an ambulance is on the way."

"Thank God." She let out a shaky breath and nodded. "Right. Thank you."

"Don't thank me. It was a group effort."

Meg sat down on the edge of the bed, as the men made room for her. Gently she picked up Janelle's limp hand and held it tenderly in her own. Even in that position, she saw the round reddened mark on the inside of Janelle's elbow. Her eyes wandered to Janelle's pale face. Her normal porcelain skin looked waxy; her hair was tousled and knotted.

"The ambulance has been called." Daniel straightened up. "She doesn't have any other visible trauma, so I'm presuming at this point she's been drugged and is still under. If we're lucky, she'll stay that way until we get her to the hospital, where she can be more thoroughly checked over."

Meg closed her eyes at that. They were talking rape. The doctors would need to be sure she hadn't been, and, if she had a rape kit, it would be done. God. That was hard enough to explain to a traumatized adult, but to a child? … Meg could only hope the drugs were ones that weren't going to hurt her, beyond keeping her subdued.

Impossible to think of Pete knowing about such things.

As if he'd read her mind, Chad asked, "Meg, does Pete have any experience with drugs? Would he know how to give them to someone?"

She hated to not know. She forced her mind to think back. "I can't imagine how." Then something twigged. "He's done some work on large animals and helped with horses. Maybe he would have had some experience through that."

"Who with?" Daniel had a notepad opened.

She shrugged. "I'm not sure of the names. He spent a spring helping someone around here do some work. About forty, fifty miles away maybe."

"Good enough, that can't be too hard to confirm." Daniel snapped shut his notebook and walked away.

"How are you holding up?" Chad asked.

"Fine." She gave him a watery smile. "More than fine." She lifted Janelle's hands. "We'll both be great. Now."

"We have to find Pete before he leaves the state," Chad said, his tone dark. "If he escapes this area, he could restart somewhere else."

"And who knows what else he's done here," she said, her gaze on Janelle. "But Cia could have been with Pete … or Anto. They were brothers. And both could have been involved."

"That's possible." Chad nodded. "Lots to sort out yet."

"But the biggest panic is over." Meg pressed Janelle's hand against her cheek, so grateful to know she was safe. They had a long road ahead of them. And that was okay.

For the first time in hours, she knew they would have a road to travel.

CHAD WATCHED THE ambulance pull away, with Meg sitting at Janelle's side. He hated to be separated from them, but they had an all-out manhunt going on here.

And for all he knew, Pete could have gone back to Seattle by now.

And that had Chad calling for security for Janelle and Meg from the minute they arrived at the hospital.

"Are you ready, Chad?" Daniel called over to him. "We're splitting up the grid and calling in the local law. Roadblocks are up."

"Pete could be driving anything at this point or"—Chad turned to study the terrain around them—"he could have crossed over to Canada from here already."

"Yep, if he's smart, he's long gone, but, if he's still here, then we'll find him."

"I'm wondering if Janelle is safe in the ambulance," Chad said, staring down the empty road.

"At this point, I doubt he'd go after her again. More likely he's cut and run."

Chad agreed, but, if Pete was also their serial killer, he had a lot of history here, and he might not be so ready to let it go.

Daniel was speaking again. "We have a team coming to go over this room. Lock down the case tight, so this asshole can't wiggle loose."

"Right." Chad turned back to Daniel. "We can get prints from here and match them to Cia's case. We all voluntarily offered our prints way back when. His should be on file."

"Good. That would be one step crossed off."

"Let's get to it. It'll be a long night. Again."

MEG HAD TO sit opposite Janelle in the ambulance. She stared down at the little girl, alternating between wishing she'd wake up and wishing she'd sleep through the next couple hours. The red spot on her arm, where they'd assumed she'd been injected, looked angry. Her breathing was raspy, having gone from deep comatose to uneven and ragged.

The paramedic was keeping a close eye on Janelle and on the machines monitoring her vital signs. She was doing poorly, and Meg didn't need to be a medical professional to know that.

She sat back and closed her eyes, finding herself wishing she had religious beliefs to help her through this time. She'd only ever had herself. She'd been close to her brother Darren. He'd been a huge help to her years ago, knowing many of the people she'd gone camping with. He'd been a couple years older than her, close to Pero's age. In fact, he and Pero had been friends—until Pero's accident. Meg hadn't kept track; she just remembered the odd bits and pieces of conversation she'd heard.

And ... she sat back. Her brother had met Pete. He'd never mentioned anything about thinking Pete reminded him of anyone. And her brother definitely would have done so. Even Mack was Pero's family, and, although he was still waffling, considering where and how they'd found Janelle, he'd finally been forced to admit they might be one and the same man.

She noticed a road sign as they went by. They'd be at the hospital within minutes. She was surprised when, all of a sudden, the sirens went on and the vehicle sped through the lights ahead. She turned to look at Janelle, but the paramedic was leaning over her, right in front of Meg, blocking her view.

Shit. Was something wrong?

The ambulance peeled to a stop. The doors were flung open, and Janelle's stretcher was wheeled out, disappearing into the depths of the hospital. Meg got out slowly. They were at the same hospital as Stephanie. God, how many hours ago had that been? She glanced down at her cell phone to check the time. It was past midnight.

She stared up at the starry sky, with a full moon enhancing their brightness. Add the artificial lights from the hospital, and it was practically evening out here. She walked into the hospital, stopping for one last look out into the balmy night.

Easy for Pete to see in this light.

And easy too, for the cops to hunt their prey.

Chapter 26

M EG LOOKED UP from the chair she'd been sitting in for hours. *Chad*. With a gasp, she rushed over to him and threw herself into his open arms. "I wondered when you'd get here."

He swung her into a tight embrace. She snuggled deeper, laying her cheek against his heart. It felt so right to be here. His arms tightened, and then released her. Reluctantly she stepped back to look up into his tired face.

And knew he didn't have good news. "He's still out there, isn't he?"

"Yes, the search is ongoing. The roadblocks are up ..." He shrugged. "We're doing what we can."

"He's smart. If he wants to leave the country, he will."

"Not likely at this point. We've alerted the airports and border patrol."

There wasn't any point in saying more. The hunt was on. If Pete had made it out, he had made it out. Little anyone could do that wasn't already being done.

"How is Janelle?" Chad asked.

"It was pretty dicey there for a while. She seems to have had a bad time with the drugs. The doctors say she's stable now, but she'll be out of it for a long time."

"Good. Then come home with me. We both need showers and some sleep. We'll come back after a rest and check up on her."

Meg stared at Janelle, undecided.

"You can't take care of her if you aren't in any reasonable shape."

That was hard to argue with. Finally she nodded. "A shower sounds good."

He wrapped an arm around her shoulders and tugged her toward the front doors of the hospital. "I've already set it up for the hospital to call us if there's any change in her condition. Or if there's news on the manhunt."

"Are the others still out there?"

Chad snorted. "We have teams all over the place."

They were in his truck and on the way home, when she realized he was taking her home to his place.

And that was just where she wanted to be.

He pulled the truck up into the driveway of a small bungalow of cedar and glass, and she loved it immediately. "This is beautiful," she said, a yawn catching her sideways.

"Thanks. Come on in. Let's get you cleaned up and settled for whatever is left of the night." He unlocked the front door and stepped in.

Meg trailed behind. She wanted nothing more than a quick shower and a bed.

He led her to a small bedroom, stopping at a closet, pulling out several towels. "Here's your room and towels and a washcloth. You have a bathroom in your room, so you should have all you need."

Except you, her mind screamed. And she'd have laughed out loud if she could have. Of all the nights she didn't have any energy for relationships, tonight was it. She smiled good night, walked inside, and closed the door. He never said a word, just headed on down to his own room presumably.

The hot water was breathtakingly soothing. If only she had some nightclothes to wear. She searched the room and found some T-shirts in the dresser. She pulled one on, letting it drop past her hips. As it was long enough to double as a sleep shirt, she crawled into bed. Turning out the lights, she then fell into a deep sleep.

CHAD SCRUBBED THE grime out of his hair. It looked like he'd been crawling through the brush and dirt for days, not hours. He'd been glad to make it back home. Swinging by the hospital had been instinctive. He knew Meg would still be there, watching over Janelle. He would be too in the same situation.

It was, in fact, what he was doing with Meg right now. Watching over her. He wished she was in his bed, but it was too early for that. Besides, he'd said he'd give her until the weekend. And he had meant it.

But it was damn hard.

He just wanted to hold her close. Could he? Would she be upset if she woke up to find him sleeping beside her?

Or was that pushing the line?

Deciding he'd better not push the issue, he went to his own bed and turned out the lights. But he wasn't able to sleep, as the unsolved issues on the case kept his mind churning through the information. All the possibilities ... There were just too many of them. He lay here for a full hour, trying to go to sleep, then gave up. Just as he turned his light on and reached for a book to read, he heard it.

Meg. Crying.

Shit. Talk about something guaranteed to break his heart.

He got out of bed slowly, pulled on a pair of boxers, and walked to his door. Should he go to her? He didn't want to intrude if she needed privacy, but he hated to see anyone in pain—Meg, most of all. Calling himself all kinds of a fool, he walked over to Meg's door and knocked lightly. No response.

He stood undecided, then rapped again, a little harder.

The door opened under his hand. He peered around the corner. She lay still, her breathing broken by sobs. She was crying in her sleep.

His heart melted. She'd been through so much and had remained so strong for Janelle's sake. But who was being strong for her?

Knowing it was beyond him to walk away, he gave in. Walking over to the empty side of the bed, he crawled under the covers. Settling in, he tugged Meg into his arms. Instantly her sobs eased. She snuggled in deeper, took a long broken breath, and slept on.

Holding her close, he slipped off to sleep right afterward.

MEG WOKE UP, tangled in the covers and incredibly hot. She threw back the covers and lay half asleep, as her body cooled down. It was summer, but normally she didn't wake up this way. Then she heard it. Breathing. She twisted around to look and found Chad, asleep in her bed.

She glanced around the room, reorienting herself. Here she was in Chad's house, in his spare bedroom, and in his spare bed, her bed for the night.

And his too apparently. Yet it felt so right. As she lay here, she realized how well he'd aged. In the past, she used to watch him as he slept. She had always woken up before him. It used to make him mad. She would just laugh. But here they were again, together, as if all those seventeen years hadn't happened.

This was where she belonged. Why had she ever left? When had the doubts become bigger than the knowing that they were right together?

Mack was likely to blame for that. Then again, he'd only shown up the cracks in the relationship; and she'd been the one to turn it into a rift. It was as if she'd been waiting all this time to come back home.

And he'd been here, arms open, welcoming her back. Luckily he wasn't married with a family of his own. None of her camping group had managed a *normal* life like that either.

They had all wanted it, but none had achieved it.

"What are you thinking?" he murmured beside her, his voice sleepy, sexy.

"That this feels like a homecoming." She twisted around again so she could look into his eyes. Eyes that were now open and so very welcoming.

He smiled a slow, slumber-filled smile that sent her pulse tattooing against her chest.

"That's because it is. It's taken you a long time to find your way back to me."

She stared at him, realizing it was time to shine a light on another long-held and discarded truth. She whispered, "You were supposed to come after me."

He leaned on his elbow to look at her in dismayed shock. "Shit." He dropped his forehead gently onto hers. "I didn't know. I thought you wanted to leave us all behind."

"I was confused. Scared. And I wanted you and needed you. But, at the same time, I couldn't stay here. So I left," she whispered, knowing it was the time to bare the truth. They'd already lost so much time. "I ran as far and as fast as I could. But I was hoping ... that you'd come after me."

"And I would have—if I'd thought there was any chance that I was welcome." He closed his eyes. "When I think of all those lost years ..." He hugged her close, rocking her gently, as a warm silence filled the room.

"Thank you," she whispered.

He lifted his head, his gaze narrowed thoughtfully as he looked at her. "For what?"

"For waiting for *me*." She pushed herself up onto her elbow, then leaned over and kissed him.

Meg couldn't believe how swiftly the years slipped away. It seemed so natural, so right, to be in bed with Chad. She deepened the kiss and sighed with pleasure, as his hands stroked up her arms, ...

gentle, accepting, loving.

She broke the kiss and dropped her forehead to rest against his.

"You're welcome," he whispered, the warmth of his breath floating soothingly against her cheek. "I'm just so glad it's finally our time." He reached up and captured her lips for a second loving kiss. She smiled against his lips. "You said you'd give me until the weekend."

He lowered his head and closed his eyes. "I did, didn't I? Foolish me."

"Of course I didn't say how long I'd give you," she whispered teasingly.

His eyes flew open. He stared at her hopefully. "No, you didn't. And I'm a fast learner. I don't need until the weekend to adjust."

"Are you sure?" She dropped gentle little kisses on his nose, his cheekbones, his chin. "I wouldn't want to rush you or to take advantage of the situation."

He swallowed hard. "You wouldn't? No, of course you wouldn't."

She smiled and dropped kisses down his neck to his broad shoulders. His fingers strolled her shoulders, always staying in contact, but compliant to her wishes.

"Not if you aren't ready to take this step," she murmured, stroking her tongue across his collarbone. "I'd hate to push you."

"It might be hard, but I think I'll be fine." He gasped as her tongue dipped into the hollow of his neck. "It will be a challenge, but I'm up for it."

She stilled, and then she smoothed her hand slowly down his chest to his belly, loving the way his muscles rippled under her touch. She curled her fingers gently into the thick V of hair that disappeared below the boxers. *Boxers.* They were new. Then so was her sleep shirt. She slid down the bed to allow herself more access, moving the blankets down, trailing her lips across his chest to his nipple. "Are you sure?"

Her finger danced along the edge of the boxers, then slipping under the soft material and feeling Chad's breath catch in his throat, he released it in a gust, as she removed her fingers.

"I'm sure," he gasped.

"*Hmm.* Maybe I should check it out further." She nipped at his nipple; his fingers clenched her arms. She did it again. Then again.

Shivers rippled down his skin. "Witch," he muttered thickly.

She chuckled. She rose up on one elbow, so she could see his face. "I could stop." She toyed with the waistband on his boxers. Then she stroked down the surface of the material, loving the way it jumped under her fingers. "I'd hate for you to feel pressured."

"Oh, I'm feeling the pressure all right."

She wrapped her fingers around the long length of him and squeezed gently.

He groaned—a loud, guttural sound of relief and pain. "God, you're killing me."

She smiled lovingly. "So not. But I am having fun."

"Good. Then I want to play too."

She found herself suddenly flipped over on her back, Chad resting between her sprawled legs and holding himself just above her. He stared down at her, an odd look in his gaze.

She tilted her head slightly. "What?"

He smiled sheepishly. "Have you any idea how long I have waited for this?" The longing in his voice, his need, brought tears to her eyes.

"I'm so sorry."

He placed his fingers over her lips. "*Shush*. Don't be. I always knew you'd come back. I'm just so grateful that it has finally happened."

She sniffled, his words warming the lonely corners in her heart, making her aware of just how empty her life had been.

"Don't." He dropped gentle kisses on her cheeks, trailing down to her ears. Shivers slipped across her skin, which chilled, then heated, under his ministrations. "None of it matters. I loved you back then, and I've loved you every day since."

Now the tears ran in a gentle, slow stream. God, those words, … the love in his voice … And she'd walked away from him and had suffered every day since. And here he was, forgiving her, wanting her, and—so, so precious—*loving her*.

After all she'd done.

"Stop. Please stop crying, Megs." And the use of his old nickname made her smile through the tears.

He lowered his head and took her lips in a deep, drugging kiss, full of memories and renewal. It was so familiar and yet so different that her senses swelled in response. She tugged him down, loving the weight of his body on hers, loving the emotional connection of his words, but needing as well the physical blending of their bodies.

His kiss deepened, as he slid his tongue inside her mouth to tango with her own. She wrapped her legs around his hips, hating the material still between them. Then felt his hand slide up between them, smoothing into her waist and up over her ribs. She shifted restlessly, waiting, wanting so much more.

But he didn't give it to her. His hand stayed just below, so teasingly close to her breast, yet out of touch. She smiled against his lips and dug her claws into his back.

He stiffened and cupped her breast. She moaned, arching at the exquisite feeling. It had been so long. His touch was so new and so needed.

"More?"

"So much more," she whispered. "I want it all."

He leaned back, a slightly worried look in his eyes.

"Stop trying to do the right thing," she whispered. "And love me."

That opened the firestorm, and, when he lowered his head this time, there was no hesitation. No doubt. He drove his tongue inside her mouth, as he plunged his hips deeper into the hollow between her legs.

She arched higher and rotated her hips slightly. He still had on his boxers, and those needed to go. She hooked her thumbs into the waistband and tugged them downward. He shifted to the side, reached down, and slipped them off. He kicked the tangled bedding to the floor.

When he turned back to her, she'd lifted the T-shirt over her head.

His eyes gleamed in the early morning light, as he stared down at her, lowering her to her back again. One hand cupped her breast, and he leaned over and suckled the nipple deep into his mouth. She cried out, cradling his head, as her body pulsed with heat. He shifted to the other breast, giving it more attention, loving the tip, and brushing the early morning growth of beard so gently across the pouting nub.

"Oh," she cried out again, the slight pain of his stubble instantly soothed by the moist heat of his mouth. She reached for him, wanting, needing to touch him.

"I don't think I can let you go this time," he murmured. "I've wanted you for so long."

Shifting slightly, he slipped his hand between their slick bodies and drove his fingers into her moist curls. She lifted her hips, then shuddered helplessly, as he found the pulsing nub.

"Please, let the first time be both of us together," she cried out, as need and heat twisted inside. She was already so close. "I don't want to fly solo—come with me."

He rose higher, hooked her leg up over his hip, and, with him sitting at her entrance, he leaned over and whispered, "Together."

And he drove home.

She cried out, as emotions and sensations surged through her. He withdrew slightly and then drove in again. She rose to meet every thrust, as she shifted, taking him yet deeper.

Tension twisted higher and higher.

She cried out, "Chad."

"I'm here. You're safe."

And her world exploded.

Dimly in the background, she heard him groan, as he followed her into oblivion, and collapsed softly beside her.

PETE STARED INTO *the shadows of the bedroom, rage coiling inside.*

She'd gone to him, to Chad. He'd seen her work with him at the site. Had noted that caring attitude that went far beyond their being professional colleagues. And had watched them from outside the house, when they'd found Janelle. The noise of their cheers was painful to his hopes and dreams. He'd stayed behind, until Chad had left, and had followed him back to town and straight to the hospital. Pete hadn't had time to decide his next actions, when the two had come out and had gotten into Chad's truck. He'd followed them.

To here. To this.

He couldn't believe it of Meg.

He didn't want to believe it of her.

Hadn't ten, almost eleven years with him pushed Chad into the category called history? To never be revisited? Apparently not.

Chad had coaxed her back into his bed—so easily—just like he had done when they were teens.

Pete had watched, hating that Meg had never looked at him, had never even seen him. She'd been friendly, but then she was friendly to everyone. He was nothing special.

It had always been Chad.

When Pete had finally managed to woo her into his bed, and into his life, after years of trying, he'd done everything he could to make the relationship work. She hadn't recognized him, and that was good. He'd worked hard to keep it that way. He'd never complained about her trips away—and some of them had been for months on end. He'd never complained about her inability to commit to a more permanent relationship. He understood she was still affected by that camping trip. So he'd never brought it up. That he'd been the cause of it all had never bothered him. It had caused the rift between her and Chad, and that had been a wonderful side benefit.

Now, as if all those years with him hadn't mattered, she'd fallen right back into Chad's arms, as if she'd never left him.

Bitch.

Whore.

And yet still he loved her.

This was Janelle's fault. She'd driven a wedge between them. She'd turned Meg away from him. He'd been just about to take care of that little problem, when he realized he'd been found out. He wanted to blame Janelle but figured he could place the blame at Chad's feet for that. Losing Janelle would have sent Meg back into Pete's arms.

But instead Chad had saved Janelle, and Meg had fallen into his bed.

Or had it happened before?

When had she turned to Chad? She hadn't had time with that Janelle bitch living with them. Christ, that kid had taken all Meg's attention and all her love.

He hated that little slut-in-the-making.

He would have gotten his revenge on her too—if it hadn't been for that bastard Chad.

Now look at the two of them. Cozy as anything.

Like hell. Rage—too long submerged—rose to the surface, clear, hot, and cutting.

He walked to the truck he'd used earlier for working the site. Chainsaws were still in the back of it.

And gas.

He opened the lid to the gas cans.

Chapter 27

M EG WOKE TO a sensation of rosy warmth, snuggled deep into Chad's arms. Janelle was safe. Meg was back with Chad, and it was even better than before—but then there was Pete. Yet, as Chad had said, "The police are on to him."

She smiled, loving the strong male scent.

Her nose wrinkled at something else.

Smoke?

Jesus. She bolted upright. "Fire!"

Flames were licking up the window side of the bedroom. That crackling sound of a good flame was just getting a stronghold on the wood. The air was filling with smoke.

"Chad, wake up." She gave him a hard shove, already reaching for her phone to call 9-1-1.

"What the fuck?" Chad bolted from bed and into his boxers and disappeared, making her realize she would be running out of the house nude in a moment. She threw the T-shirt back on and her jeans, grabbed her purse and her shoes, slipping them on as she ran. Thick smoke filled the room so badly that she could hardly see.

"Let's go." He was dressed, his truck keys in his hand. He grabbed her hand and raced to the front of the house.

Then she started to cough.

He shoved her to her knees. "Crawl to the garage. The flames are all around us. Go, go, *go.*"

Still coughing, her shirt pulled up over her mouth, she crawled on all fours behind him. By the time they had reached the garage, all she could hear was the roaring fire and the sounds of sirens—too far away to save them.

She hoped Chad had a plan.

The garage door was locked, but he managed to reach up and get it unlocked, and tugged it open. Through the gray smoke, she watched him motion her through the door, as a bit of fresh air came out from the garage. She coughed and gasped, struggling to make the short distance, but couldn't catch her breath. Then she didn't have to.

She was picked up and shoved in the front seat of the truck.

The whole garage was in flames around them.

He ran around to the other side, hopped in and fired up the truck. He didn't even wait to open the garage door, he put the truck in Reverse and blasted through it and out onto the street. Wood shattered, sending chunks onto the windshield. Her window automatically opened, and she gasped and coughed in fresh air.

Pulling the truck off to one side, he parked and turned off the engine. He coughed several times. "Are you okay?"

Tears ran from his reddened eyes, but the look of fury on his face had her answering quickly. "I'm fine, but smoke inhalation is not the best way to wake up."

He grinned, reached over, and kissed her hard. "Good. Let's go. I want the paramedics to check you out."

She went to speak and ended up coughing again. He exited the truck and came around to her side and opened the door. At last, she heard the sirens round the corner. An ambulance stopped in the middle of the road. Chad led her, still coughing, to the driver.

"Look after her." And he disappeared to speak with the firemen.

Meg let herself be led to the back, where she was given oxygen. After a bad coughing spell, she could finally breathe.

"Was anyone else in the house?" the paramedic asked.

"Just Chad and me." She closed her eyes and worked on breathing. Now that she was safe, the shakes were starting. She was pushed gently onto the bench inside the ambulance. A blanket was wrapped around her shoulders. She sank deeper into its folds, whispering, "Thank you."

"No problem. Stay here and rest."

Chad appeared in front of her. "Meg?"

She smiled at him. She lowered the oxygen mask. "I'm fine."

"It was arson."

"Yeah, I got that." In fact, she also thought she knew who it was who had done it. "Pete?"

Chad nodded. "He'd be my first choice. I gather he wasn't real happy about you breaking up with him."

"He would have been more upset if he had seen us in bed." She shrugged. "It was over a long time ago. Just waiting for the ink to dry, so to speak."

Chad glared at his house, well past saving now.

She followed her gaze, realizing belatedly what he'd lost personally. "I'm sorry."

He glanced down at her. "So am I, but this is not your fault."

That was debatable, but she didn't have the energy. "Is Janelle safe?"

He pulled out his phone. "I had security on her all night. As I haven't gotten a call, I'm presuming all is well, but I'll check."

She hadn't known. "Thank you."

He moved away slightly to talk. She stared at the mess around her. The fire trucks, the ambulance, the cops, the neighbors, everyone watching. She just wanted to hide away until all this was over.

Her gaze wandered, her mind lost on the chaos. She caught sight of something, her mind slow to compute just what, when Chad stepped in front of her.

"Janelle is fine," he said, with a big smile. "She's awake."

She blinked and got it, then said, "Don't look around. Pete is in the crowd, behind you to the left."

Chad froze. "Are you sure?" he asked hoarsely. He had his cell phone out. At her nod, he texted someone. "Men are moving into position." He looked up at her. "Get ready. All hell is going to break loose soon."

His cell phone beeped. "Is he still there?" he asked Meg.

She didn't want to look and alert Pete but knew it would be impossible not to. "He's on the move, going behind you now."

"Stay put."

And just then someone in the crowd screamed. Chad spun and ran, and it looked as if the crowd had scattered. Meg hunched lower, trying to sort through the chaos. Her gaze darted left, then right, frantically searching for Pete and Chad. There they were, in the distance. She watched Pete dart between several people, then dash behind a car, with Chad hot on his trail.

Several other cops converged on the same spot. Shouts rang out, and then the crowd dispersed. She watched the cops split and disappear and realized Pete must have slipped through. *Damn.* She needed him to answer for Janelle. She didn't know if he was also responsible for Cia and the other victims as well, but this had to stop.

The crowd grew in volume again and then receded. Her nerves were shot. She couldn't watch anymore. She shuffled backward to lean against the side of the ambulance bench and closed her eyes. Her eyes still burned, and the tearing had slowed down, but her throat swore it had been rubbed with sandpaper. Not to mention the smell. Smoke coated everything, and that nasty burning smell permeated the air around them.

She wanted all this to go away and everything to return to normal. She needed Pete caught and safely put away behind bars. God, how did he keep evading the cops?

"Meg."

And there he was, right in front of her, a baseball cap on his head, tugged low, hiding his features. He hopped inside the ambulance to sit beside her, slamming and locking the doors behind him.

She shifted, the movement, bringing on yet another coughing fit. He patted her on the back, even as she tried to evade his touch. His hand slipped up to her neck and squeezed gently. She turned on him. "Hello, Pete. Or should I say Pero?"

She tried to stay calm and interested, when all she wanted was to claw his eyes out. The men had to be not far away. Pete wasn't a damn ghost. Surely someone had seen him. Surely someone would come. She slipped her cell phone to one side, hitting the Redial button to call Chad. She coughed hard, not having to fake it, to cover her actions.

Surprise lit his features. "Figured that out, did you?"

"Somewhere around the time you kidnapped Janelle." The pain of that betrayal caused her to cry out, "Why did you hurt her?"

"That bitch. She's the reason our relationship was in trouble. After your brother died, it's like you became this milksop nanny. Anything Janelle wanted, Janelle got. We didn't have a relationship anymore. I tried to give you space, … anything to make it work." He shook his head. "Then you found that damn skull, and I knew it was the end."

"I'm sorry." She took a deep breath, surprised to realize that, after all this, she really was sorry. "At the time, I was hurting from losing my brother and knew Janelle was hurting too. It was natural to turn to her for comfort and to give comfort to her."

"*Right.*"

His tone was so derisive that she wondered how he'd kept his emotions in check all those months. Stalling for time, she asked him just that.

"Easy. I spent our entire relationship waiting for you to get off standby and into the game. But no matter how patient I was, how understanding, you never engaged in the relationship."

She gasped. "That's not fair." God, where was Chad?

"Yes. It is. I hated that you loved Chad all those years ago. When we got together, I figured it was finally *my* time. Instead all I got was the shell he left behind."

In spite of everything, she felt a pang for all his pain and some guilt for her actions. It was all such a waste. She'd been hurting everyone, when she had tried so hard to avoid doing just that. And also to avoid being hurt herself again. Pete didn't deserve her apology, not after all he'd done. But maybe an apology would help appease his anger. "I'm sorry." She whispered, "I never realized."

"No, of course you didn't. You weren't aware of anything. You stayed locked inside and never came out. A coward."

Stung, she fired back. "Is that why you killed Cia? Did she spurn you too?"

He laughed. "That bitch did the opposite. She was free for the taking. Anytime, anywhere."

"No, that's not true," Meg said. "Cia didn't want Anto. She hated him."

"Ha." But his tone of voice changed, got colder, nastier. "She did not hate him."

She stared at him. God, the look on his face. … She didn't recognize him. And his reaction was so … off. What was going on? She said slowly, "Cia loved Cia. Your brother terrified her. Hell, he terrified me."

And then Pete smiled; a creepy smile that seemed to start in his eyes and then to twist him into someone else. Shivers slipped down her spine, and instinctively she tried to shuffle farther away from him, but he had her pinned against the corner.

"And yet you've been sleeping with him for the last ten years."

She stared at him in horror. And then she got it. *Finally.*

Bile rose up the back of her throat, and she vomited over the edge of the stretcher in the ambulance.

And he laughed and laughed; a maniacal sound of sheer enjoyment that had her heaving a second time.

"You and your high-and-mighty attitude. Chad this and Chad that. Cia was the same, only it was Pero this and Pero that. Well, I knocked that out of the bitch fast, when she realized I was the one meeting her in the woods and not my brother."

"You killed her?" She gasped, hating the shocks that were continuously sending her off balance. She could hardly think. She desperately wanted Chad to come; surely he could hear the conversation.

He shrugged. "I was going to take what she'd been offering around so freely, but, when she saw me, she pulled the offer." He smiled coldly. "As if I was going to accept that. I just clamped my hands around her throat and squeezed. She died so easily. I didn't think it would be that simple." He smiled in reminiscence. "I raced to the cabin and stashed her in there, until the hoopla went away. I'd just got my license that summer and had wheels to borrow. Came up a few days later and buried her up top."

Meg, her stomach still heaving, shuddered. She had to keep him talking. Give Chad time. "And what about the others?"

"It's addictive, you know?" His tone was now conversational and thoughtful. "And did you notice they all looked like you?"

She hadn't thought they looked anything like her. "And the necklaces?"

"I wanted them to wear it. Cia had yours on. The bitch. But, after her, I was afraid it wouldn't be the same anymore. So I had them made to allow me to pretend, ... at least for a little while."

And her stomach heaved again. "Oh God. You kept them alive?"

"Not for very long. I hate tantrums and tears." He shrugged. "I kept them at the cabin. My uncle never knew. Neither did Uncle Mack. I did wonder though, so I laid enough doubt that it was probably his precious Bruce," he added thoughtfully. "Then the accident happened. Recovery was hard. There was the grief over my brother, whom I loved. Then I hooked up with you, and I realized that stage of my life was over. It had been all about you. You were my love, my reason. I didn't need those girls anymore. After all, my dream had come true," he mocked. "Until Janelle arrived ..."

"How could you kill those women?" she whispered, feeling really odd, her thoughts foggy, distant. "Are there more?"

"No, but I'd planned for more. I went to a lot of trouble to build that room at the Williamsons' house. It was an easy solution for Janelle and any future others. Only, when I got her there, I realized I didn't want her. There was only one woman for me. You were mine for almost eleven years. I'm not willing to let you go. And if I can't have you ..."

His voice changed. Softened. And that was just wrong. She tried to see into his eyes. Only she couldn't focus. "What have you done?"

And when? When he'd first arrived and squeezed her neck? Could he have done something to her then? So fast?

Her vision started to waver.

"Pressure syringes are the greatest invention and so easy to get a hold of," Pete said, tugging her into his arms. "I have you again. No one can take you away from me. Ever. It's a perfect ending."

Black spots appeared in her eyes. She heard shouts from the

crowd outside the ambulance. "Why?"

He sighed happily content. "Because you are mine. *Forever.*"

No. It couldn't be.

"Meg. I love you. I always have." And Pete slumped over her, his weight pressing down heavily on her shoulders.

She tried to scream. Tried to call for help. But her voice didn't work.

Her vision wavered—the world around her blurring.

Then she blacked out.

CHAD SAT AT Meg's bedside, her hand cradled in his. He'd damn-near been paralyzed by fear when he'd finally realized what he was hearing on his cell phone. He'd raced to the ambulance, unable to contact anyone else because he couldn't break the connection of Meg's call to him.

The panic run to the ambulance and the even faster race to the hospital had been heart-stopping.

The doctors had done everything they could, but Pete had injected himself with a massive dose, and he hadn't made it.

Good thing. Chad would have killed him if he hadn't.

And he didn't want to spend the next ten years behind bars, not when he could spend them with Meg instead.

Now if only she'd wake up. The doctors appeared confident that she would. They'd done everything possible and appeared satisfied with her condition.

Only there was so much they didn't know.

Then that went with this bizarre case too. So many strings to tie up. The paperwork involved would be days, weeks, in the making. Mack had been with him, as they tried to open the doors. The two had heard most of Pete's no make that Anto's confession on the cell phone. If, ... when, ... Meg woke up, she'd fill in the blanks hopefully.

The fingerprints from the truck had verified Anto's identity. He'd taken his brother's spot after the accident and had started a new life soon afterward with Meg. To the best of anyone's knowledge at this stage, he'd never killed again. But they had a lot more evidence to go through before anyone was comfortable making that statement with any certainty. The secret room was being printed now. Hopefully they'd get a better idea of who'd been forced in there—if, indeed, anyone.

Mack had been horrified. He'd stayed behind to clean up the mess of what was left of Chad's house. They would need to talk. Eventually.

Right now, Chad had no plans to leave Meg's side. Daniel had already come by and had dropped off Chad's laptop, which he'd forgotten in his truck overnight.

His case board, his years of notes, clippings, maps—everything else at home—gone. Maybe that was for the best at this point. They now knew who'd killed Cia and the other girls. Now Chad could move on.

Still, he'd loved his home. But not as much as he loved Meg.

And Meg loved Janelle. He'd taken a quick trip to see Janelle, who'd burst into tears at the news about her aunt. He'd been quick to reassure her that the doctors had said Meg would pull through, but Janelle had been desperate to see for herself. And, if Meg didn't surface soon, he might go get Janelle and bring her here. That little girl had been through enough, and, if seeing Meg would make her feel better, then he was all for it.

When he'd told her about Anto, Janelle had gone really quiet. Then she'd said, "Good. Maybe I can sleep at night again."

He'd wanted to ask more, but she'd rolled over and closed her eyes.

He'd taken a long look at the beautiful girl and had returned to Meg, his heart heavy, knowing what Anto had intended. Janelle must have known something was wrong, if she couldn't sleep at night. Thank God, Meg had gotten wise and had moved them out in time.

And he'd heard from Bruce. Stephanie had woken up. She was still groggy about the turn of events that had landed her on death's door, but she did confirm that she'd planned to meet Pete or Pero, as she knew him, for coffee. Then she had changed her mind and had run. Bruce was sticking pretty close to her side, especially now that he knew she'd most likely not been going back to her dealer.

Chad wished them well. Maybe, with Cia's case solved, they could all move on together.

Now, if only Meg would wake up.

Then a soft voice whispered, "Hey."

He glanced around. The room was empty. He looked at Meg, and she smiled at him, a frail small one but a smile nevertheless. His breath gusted free, and he gave her a brilliant smile in response. "Oh, Lord, is it good to hear your voice. You scared me."

"Scared myself," she murmured, her smile tremulous and hopeful. "Pete? God it's hard to say Anto."

"He didn't make it. He gave himself a large dose of whatever drug he was using."

Tears collected at the corners of her eyes. He didn't know if from relief or regret, but, knowing her compassionate heart, probably a bit of both.

"The doctors worked on you for a long time." He grinned sheepishly, lifting her hand to kiss her knuckles. "They said you'd pull through, but I wasn't so sure."

She squeezed his hand. "I'm here. Can't say I feel very good though."

"To be expected." He leaned over and kissed her cheek, needing to be closer. If he had his way, he'd lie down beside her and tug her into his arms. Instead he said, "I don't think the doctors would recommend anyone racing out of a burning house, then being drugged to the point of death."

She smirked. "You forgot about being ravished first."

He chuckled, loving her bright spirit after all she'd been through. "There is that."

Her gaze widened, as something else hit her. "Janelle?"

Ah, he wondered when she'd remember. At least now he knew her brain was alert and firing properly. "Awake," he said quickly, "and wants to see you."

Meg smiled. "Good." Meg looked around the room, as if searching for her clothing to make a run for it. "When can we get out of here and go home?"

He patted her hand. "Not happening. You're not going anywhere until the doctors clear you. They went through a lot to keep you alive."

"Oh." Her head dropped back onto the pillow. "So not likely today?"

"I wouldn't think so." He leaned over and kissed her gently. "You need to recuperate from this week from hell."

"In bed preferably." She winked. "Join me?"

"Oh, gross!"

The words from the doorway had them both turning to see Janelle walking independently, but holding on to a nurse's arm.

"Janelle!" Meg struggled to sit up, only to collapse back, her arms wide open.

Janelle raced to the bed, where Chad scooped her up and laid her down beside Meg. The two females wrapped their arms around each other and burst into tears. Chad stepped back toward the doorway to give them some privacy and to keep watch. The nurse stepped out into the hallway.

Mack approached from the other direction. "How is Meg?"

"Alive," Chad said, his voice cool. "And she appears to be fine." Chad turned to nod at the two females cuddling on the bed.

"Good, good." Mack stared at the happy reunion. "It will be a long road ahead for the little one."

"And for Meg." Chad forced himself not to add, *No thanks to you.*

"For all of us, in a way," Mack mumbled under his breath. "What a shitty trip."

Chad heard and understood Mack was talking about the journey from Cia's death to now. "You going to be okay?"

Mack stared at him in surprise. Then gave a curt nod. "Yeah. With that asshole no longer able to play games with my head, I'll be fine." After another long moment of silence, he sighed heavily. "I'm sorry."

It was Chad's turn to stare at Mack in surprise. Then he nodded. "Apology accepted."

Mack turned and walked away, his shoulders bowed. Chad watched him. Mack would have to live with his actions over the past too. None were criminal, but they wouldn't make him shine either. Then that was his problem. Chad had enough of his own to deal with now.

He turned back to find both Meg and Janelle smiling at him. He snorted. "All right. What are you two up to? With those looks in your eyes, I'm sure it's trouble."

Meg laughed. "So not. Besides, we were just having some girl talk about you."

And damn if he didn't feel some heat climb his throat.

Janelle giggled a delightfully free sound that had Meg tugging her back into a rocking hug. They looked so enchanting that Chad wished he could join them. He paused in thought, as he stared at the two females, who were now such a huge part of his life.

Then he figured he might as well start as he meant to go in life.

In two strides, he arrived at the side of the bed. Ignoring their laughing protests, he snagged them both into a big bear hug.

With Janelle's laughter ringing in his ears, and Meg's loving gaze locked on his, Chad knew he'd never been so lucky.

Life was good again. *Finally.*

USA TODAY BESTSELLING AUTHOR

DALE MAYER

CHILLED

— BY —

DEATH

BOOK THREE OF BY DEATH SERIES

Chapter 1

Three Years Ago

S TACY CARTER SLID across the fresh white powder to come to a rest on the top of the small rise. She smiled up at the stunning blue sky and tall evergreen trees dusted in white.

It was a gorgeous day at Blackcomb Ski Resort in BC. A place she and her brother and their friends considered their home away from home. Their winter and summer play home was close enough to Seattle to make it an easy drive and far enough away to make it a change.

They were staying at her brother's friend's cabin, one they'd come to many times over the years. It was perfect. The day. The mountains. The situation.

Her best friends—they were like sisters really—Francine and Janice were up ahead. Or they should be. They'd been boarding.

However, Stacy hadn't been feeling well and had been in town all morning. Feeling better, she'd come out to meet them at the top of Gorman's Peak. It was a well-known run that could take one farther into the backcountry, and, yes, out-of-bounds if they wanted to—and her friends often wanted to. Stacy wasn't like that. She hated breaking the rules. But so many of the others loved to ski and to board the pure, untouched runs down the backside. They'd been doing it for years, and conforming to the new rules and regulations was difficult. And not appreciated in many cases. Areas that her friends had played in for years were carefully watched now.

Many of the tougher runs had been closed all week due to avalanche hazards. Although that disappointed several of her friends, Stacy didn't mind. She'd been skiing this resort since forever. There were lots of runs to keep her interest.

Then she was calmer, more relaxed, when compared to the other two women. They were the play-hard-and-love-harder variety.

Stacy was much gentler. More safety conscious and much more

laid-back. She would have been happy to grab a coffee and to sit at the top of the run to just enjoy the moment. She worked hard at her job and preferred to relax when on vacation. Life was about balance.

Her two friends were both dashing raise-a-little-hell modern women. Stacy had never understood just what drew the three of them together, but something had, and it worked. They were opposites who complemented each other. They'd been friends for close to a decade. They'd changed over the years that they had known each other, with Stacy becoming more laid-back over time, whereas her friends had gotten wilder, becoming even more daredevilish.

The men loved it. Loved them.

Stacy had watched in bemusement, as Janice ate up a lifetime quota of men before she was twenty-nine. With her long black hair, a slightly olive tint to her skin, and massive brown eyes with long lashes and pouty lips, all on top of long and lean physical perfection, yeah, she could have any man anytime. And she did. Often. She also never let her heart get involved.

Francine was a slightly curvier and shorter version, but just as much of a go-getter. She'd been following in Janice's tracks since forever. Not quite as good as Janice in boarding, or with men, but Francine never seemed to care. She was content to take second place. However, she'd never slide to third. No, that was always Stacy's spot.

Not that Stacy cared. She'd always felt slightly out of sync with the other two, but they all loved each other.

It was all good.

Her phone beeped.

She pulled it from her pocket and smiled. *Janice.* She read the text, and her smile fell away.

Damn it. Janice wanted to end the day with a splash on the long back trail and cut to the cabin at the right time. Only that run was out-of-bounds. According to the text, the two would meet Stacy in a few moments.

She quickly texted a reply. **Back runs closed due to avalanche hazard.**

And waited.

She didn't have to wait long. The next text read **Phooey.**

That was it. Stacy stared down at it, chewing on her bottom lip, and wondered. Out loud, she murmured, "Phooey what, Janice? As in phooey that's too bad, or phooey like that'll matter?"

Stacy shifted positions, so she could see her friends ride up the lifts. They'd be about ten minutes, if there wasn't much of a line at the bottom.

She sat back to relax.

Francine texted her next, asking where she was. She answered. Then deciding it was better to ask than worry, she texted Janice and asked, **Which run do you want to take down? The face looks great.**

She knew her attempt to convince Janice to go down the sheer drop in the front of the mountain wouldn't likely work if she was set on going down the back to the bowl, but the face would be perfect. Usually no one was there, leaving them lots of space to take jumps, to weave through the trees, or to just cut a narrow strip, racing to the bottom.

Her phone beeped again. *Janice.* **I want to take Gopher Run to the bowl.**

Damn it. **The bowl is closed too.** The bowl was an inbounds area—as long as the weather cooperated. When it didn't, it was a closed area. Like everything connected to the resort and winter sports, safety was paramount. They had a great medical center here, and the search and rescue teams were second to none. Thankfully Stacy hadn't had any reason to use either.

She studied the chairs swinging in the gentle breeze, as the lifts toiled upward, carrying the many groups of happy winter enthusiasts.

"Stacy!"

Stacy turned in the direction of the yell, then smiled at Janice and Francine and waved.

Hearing her name again, she caught sight of her brother and two of his friends, who were also her coworkers, Mark and Stevie, several chairs below the women. "Hey," she yelled back.

Within five minutes, they all stood in a group at the top of the runs, just out of the way of the others getting off the lift.

"We're going for another run. See you in the cabin in an hour or so." With a big wave and lots of hoots and laughter, the three men jumped over the steepest part of the face.

Stacy grinned at their antics. They were all incredibly skilled and a joy to watch. "Awesome! We'll follow." With a big grin still on her face, Stacy turned her skis, planning to follow the guys off the top edge. "Come on, women. Let's go." She slid forward slightly, then twisted to make sure Janice and Francine were following.

They weren't.

Shit.

Awkwardly Stacy flipped her skis around, now facing the direction where the women stood, and Stacy struggled back the short distance to where she'd left them.

And reached only their trails, from where they'd plunged over the back of the mountain to the bowl. "Damn it, Janice. Why don't you ever listen?" she cried out to the vast white expanse in front of her. "That whole area is a bad deal right now."

Then Janice had always done as she pleased. Stacy wished she'd said more in her texts. Had she made it clear how dangerous the area was? It was closed. Avalanche warnings. Surely that spoke volumes about the snow conditions. She studied the pristine area in front of her, looking for their tracks. The women were already halfway down.

"Fine, then I'll catch you on the upside again." Although, as frustrated as she was right now, maybe she'd just head toward the cabin. She was in perfect alignment to cut across to a run that would take her back there.

She hated to see them do this. They were always taking unnecessary risks.

Like wild birds that had to be free to do their own thing.

Sure, Stacy had more understanding of the risks than most people, given her job. So many ended up on her table at the morgue because they made the wrong decision.

Given her experience with accidents and death, was it any wonder she worried about them?

Decision made.

She pushed off and glided along the ridge. She could see the women a long way down the slope. They should be turning right to head to the bowl and connect to several other runs lower down to bring them back around to the bottom of the chair lift they'd just gotten off of. Stacy debated waiting for the two to make their way back up again but decided she had already spent a lot of her time waiting for them.

She carried on for a few more feet, when she glanced down at the women, she saw them cut to the left.

Into the out-of-bounds area. And away from the chair that would bring them back up to where Stacy was. Would they turn left lower down and head toward the cabin? There was a run that cut off and would take them back home.

Her heart damn-near clogged up her throat, as she watched their devil-may-care attitude, while they raced across the mountain face and started the beautiful long zigzag pattern. "Damn it, Janice. Why do you always have to push it?"

She wanted to turn away and to ski her own path down to the

cabin, but she couldn't tear her gaze away from the two women. They were incredible boarders, so graceful they looked like birds floating in the sky, crossing the mountainscape below.

As Stacy watched, she thought she heard something. A muted, deep booming sound. And a gentle rumble. She glanced around, but no one else was close by, and those farther away were busy laughing with their own friends. Several groups came off the lift and never stopped, skiing right on down again.

She glanced back at her girlfriends. Her gaze struggled to catch sight of them racing far below. They should be wrapping around the mountain to the left to catch the run toward the cabin. Only they were still going straight down the mountain.

And then Stacy saw the reason for the rumble.

One of the hard crusted overhangs of snow at the top of the peak had finally let go of its tenuous hold on the rock and had pounded onto the snow below. The impact started the massive sheet of snow to shift in a slow-motion slide that picked up speed the lower it went.

Within seconds, an avalanche raced downhill.

Down to her friends.

"Janice, move it!" Stacy screamed, her hands cupped around her mouth, but they couldn't hear her. Of course they couldn't. No way her voice could be heard over the noise of the destruction racing toward them.

Neither could she stop screaming at them to move faster.

The women needed to turn left. Now. And, once again, they had to take it to the limit and go down even farther. Finally they started the curve to the left, away from the cliff edge ahead of them.

"Jesus."

Stacy could only watch in terror as the two women suddenly noticed what was bearing down on them. Both women crouched down and raced as fast as they could out of the oncoming path of the avalanche.

"Faster," Stacy screamed. "Faster."

And faster it was.

The avalanche picked up speed …

And picked up the two women …

And tossed them into the white snowy melee.

As Stacy stood in horror and watched, the massive wall of snow and women slipped off the rock edge and out of her sight.

Forever.

Chapter 2

Three Years Later

S TACY STARED AT her brother and repeated, "You want me to go back? To Blackcomb Mountain? Tomorrow?" She shook her head, her long blond hair flying wildly around her head. "No way."

"Yes," George said to her. "It's time."

"It doesn't matter if it's time. I can't go." In a quiet voice, she added instinctively, "I'm not ready."

And yet … she stared across the restaurant, almost blind to the steady stream of customers walking through the popular place. He'd pointed out a truth that Stacy had come to realize lately.

It *was* time. She shuddered. But that didn't mean she was ready to face the grief, … the loss she'd been through. Or face the place where it had all happened. Yet she knew she would remain crippled until she did. "I'd rather go where it's warmer," she muttered.

"You might, but, since you won't go on any vacation at all, that won't happen either." Calm, direct, and gentle, George leaned forward earnestly. "Look. You don't even have to do any skiing. Bring some books and hang out in the cabin. Enjoy the break. Face a few memories and move on. This isn't an all-out crazy sports event. It'll be a gentle go-at-your-own-pace kind of thing. Yes, it's the same cabin, so there will be a few ghosts. Face them." He grinned, adding, "Then grab your camera and do what you do best. Well, besides, dead people …"

Trust him to get her to crack a smile. "Yeah, I do those all the time, so why would I want to go back and see more—at least in my head?"

"I think *because* you deal with bodies and *because* you can't find your friends—to have their bodies to care for, a funeral to arrange—it makes it that much harder for you to find closure."

Very insightful of him. She played with her coffee spoon, turning it over and over again in her hand. "I hadn't considered that." True.

She saw death like most people never had a chance to. She was a forensic pathologist, after all. Bodies were her stock in trade. But the bodies on her table were strangers. Not her best friends. It was different when the losses were personal.

"We're cooking the food ourselves—"

"Ha," she broke in teasingly. "Now I know why you want me to come. You want me to be the chief cook and bottle washer."

"No," George protested, but not much heat filled his word. "If you wanted to do it, that would be great, but, no, we are all expected to do our parts."

"*Uh-huh.* Sure." She didn't necessarily believe him, but finding out this tidbit made her feel better about going. She wouldn't be expected to ski every day, like the others. She was an experienced skier and an intermediate snowboarder, but her first love during winter was her camera. The thought tugged at her, going back to some of those indescribably beautiful days with the brilliant icy scenes. She had been getting into it with her earlier travels, and that had stopped as her trips had stopped.

At the same time, she'd turned away from many aspects of her life. It was a move that had surprised many. She had retreated within—from everyone and everything. To heal. To adjust to the new reality of her life. It had changed her. When she'd recently picked up her camera again, she'd done so quietly. Privately. Before, she would have considered herself open and friendly. Now she kept to herself and shared little, even with those closest to her.

Her brother had called her secretive and had considered it part of her depression. Maybe he was right. Yet he didn't know about all the issues—good and bad—in her world.

Life used to be simple. Then, when she was wide open and enjoying her day, fate took scissors and cut away the very steps she was standing on. As if to say, *Comfortable, are you? Well then ...* Snip, snip, snip. *How about now?*

She wiped those thoughts from her mind and forced a smile at George's hopeful look. She'd dealt with a lot of her issues. Most of them anyway. She just hadn't shared how far she'd come with him. And that was too bad. He was still worried about her. In many ways, his concern was justified, but it wasn't any longer. She was almost philosophical now.

Life was a bitch, and then you died. Sometimes you died earlier than planned. She'd seen a lot of death. Sometimes it was comforting. Everyone came to the same end. Just the routes people took were different.

It was time to let him know how well she was doing.

"If I can come and go at my own pace, do a couple day trips on nice sunny days, stay home when I want to be alone"—she chuckled at his rolling eyes and his bright, happy grin—"then I'll come. I'll help with the food, but I won't be responsible for all of it."

"No worries. I meant it when I said we're all pitching in." He stood and tossed money on the table to cover their bills. "Besides, Royce is a damn good cook."

With that bombshell, George walked to the front door, as if to leave.

"Hey, you can't just say, *Royce is a good cook*, and walk away," she called out, racing over to stand in front of him. "You didn't say he was coming."

George raised his not-so-innocent gaze in a wide-eyed look of surprise and said, "Oh, didn't I? Well, he's part of the group. He always comes. Not to worry. We're just looking to get away for a week, you know? Just a chance to relax and to hang out."

She glared at him.

"Besides, what difference does it make if he does come?" He gave her a knowing grin. "You don't even like him."

For the life of her, she couldn't hold back the wince or the flood of memories that took over her psyche. She'd known Royce since forever, as he was her brother's best friend. But the hardest part of that history was the carnal knowledge she'd kept to herself. And, wow, had that been good. And hot. And so damn addictive that she'd walked away, afraid she could never let him go. He wasn't long-term material. Certainly not marriageable material, likely not monogamous—whereas she couldn't be anything but. But being with him had made her wonder for a little while if she could do it his way, ... which was not likely, given what little they had.

A wild, crazy, all-out sexual weekend.

A weekend she'd loved. And hated. Because it had changed her. She'd gone to him hurt, in need. She'd taken everything he'd had to give and had wanted more. So much more that she'd been terrified.

And he'd been unaffected.

How fair was that?

Then she'd been grieving. She'd needed to reaffirm life. She'd needed to reaffirm that she wasn't alone. She'd needed to reaffirm that she had a reason to get up in the morning. A reason that didn't involve dealing with loss.

For the duration of that weekend, he'd given her what she need-ed. That she'd gotten so much more was a shock she hadn't liked. But she'd been a big girl. And she'd known Royce, a bad boy, would never make a partner for life. He'd done the rounds. Even with Janice and Francine. Then that was hard to blame him for, considering the women's own dating habits. Besides, how many wild animals mated for life? They made for a hot, unforgettable mating session, but after that? They were best left to go their own way.

She'd seen him a time or two since then in Seattle. From a dis-tance.

She hadn't spoken to him. Or been in the same room with him. She'd been too afraid. The sparks between them were obvious. And she was essentially private. At least now that she'd locked down her emotions.

That way was easier to deal with the blows that life dealt her.

And she had dealt with them. It just hadn't been easy. There was one she was still working on.

Guilt.

Being a survivor sucked in many ways. She'd had nightmares for months and still wasn't sure why her friends had to die that day. She knew she wasn't responsible, but she couldn't help but think she hadn't done enough to stop her friends from going down that side of the mountain. Surely there'd been more Stacy could have done.

Maybe this trip would help release her from that heavy burden.

She watched her brother race out of the restaurant. He'd just set her up, darn him. She made a face at his retreating back, then shrugged. He was right. It was time. And, at least this way, it would be easier. She wouldn't be alone. She'd be hanging out with people who understood her and what she was going through.

She wondered if several of the guys from work would be invited, Mark and Stevie in particular. They'd been part of her brother's group for a long time. Rock climbing, snowboarding, hiking—their life was a big party. Stacy had been involved in the group for a long time, at least when her girlfriends had still been alive. They'd been party animals too. Maybe because everyone around Stacy was so extreme, she'd been the opposite. Quiet. Calm. Careful.

Now she was even more so.

Loss did that to someone.

Considering she hadn't planned this trip, she wouldn't mention it to her coworkers, not until she heard back from her brother. Maybe the group was full up. Maybe there was no room for Mark and Stevie to join in this time. A group would often run eight to ten people, cabin capacity. Maybe a couple more, but too many were a hardship to plan meals and activities and to keep track of where everyone was.

Given the hour, she didn't waste any time in getting back to her office. She had no shortage of work ahead of her. It had been great to spend some time with her brother. He was a bit of an oddball himself. He didn't do ... anything. Yet he did everything. Though he had a degree in economics, he'd made it big-time doing sports action videos. He was now working for a large camera company, running around the world, taking videos of crazy stunts. He had a large group of buddies who set up crazy bungee jumps and skydiving formations. He and his buddies loved it.

She had to admit it sounded like a pretty fun way to get through the day. At least while George was young and in his prime. Maybe later he'd find something less dangerous. She couldn't help worry about him. Especially now. They'd lost their parents a long time ago. George had been old enough to live on his own, but Stacy had gone to live with her aunt and uncle. She and George had stayed close. But losing her parents young had made her afraid something would happen to her beloved brother. For that reason, he usually didn't share the details of some of the crazier stunts he was involved in. Thank heavens. She had enough nightmares to keep her awake at night.

Although outdoorsy, she wasn't much of an extreme sports fan. She wasn't into adrenaline. Too hard on the system. And she hated major shocks. Her brother thrived on them. He and his friends played punk-ass jokes on each other all the time. To her, they were horrible, but the group of guys he hung with thought they were hilarious. And, true enough, he played just as many on his friends as they did on him.

You had to be one of them to understand.

The double doors to her lab opened automatically, as she stepped on the entrance mat. She strode through and brought out her security card, sliding it down the key lock and heading inside to the morgue. When working with the dead, she liked to think she'd learned to appreciate life a little bit.

"Enjoy your lunch?" Mark asked, doing wheelies on his computer chair, when she walked through the lab. Some martial arts schedule was up on his monitor, like that was allowed. And likely why he had it up there. He was quite a pro himself and taught on the side.

"Yeah," she said, grinning at his antics. He was the same age as her but acted a dozen years younger. Then so did her brother. Maybe that's why she got on so well with Mark and Stevie. However, she preferred Mark more as a friend than a coworker, since he didn't necessarily have the same work ethic, preferring to skip out early to meet the guys for the next adventure in progress. Still, he was good people, and that counted. "I had lunch with George."

"Really?" He grabbed the desk to stop his wild ride. He stared up at her, shoving his long hair back off his face. "And?"

She raised an eyebrow at him. So he did know. She had wondered. Chances were good both men—or rather, overgrown boys—she worked with would be going on this weeklong fun adventure. She paused, considering that. How much of a real break would it be, if she went with guys she worked with?

Not by a stretch could she use that as an excuse to get out of this trip. No, she was going. ... If she had a few last-minute qualms, well, that was to be expected. Besides, both men loved these trips and were huge board fanatics. They were also search and rescue volunteers. They deserved their fun on the slopes, like anyone else.

"He wants me to go on this ski trip to the cabin," she tossed over her shoulder, as she carried on down the hallway to her office. "You know. ... Go back and face my memories. A great idea in theory, but ..."

"Wait, he did?"

"Yes." She grinned as she heard his footsteps. She knew he couldn't leave it alone.

"Well"—Mark popped his head around the corner—"what did you say?"

She waited a beat, then looked up at him, still smiling. "I said yes."

GEORGE WALKED QUICKLY away from his sister. He needed to get as far away as soon as he could, before she changed her mind. He half expected his phone to go off so she could do just that.

He walked with purpose. The sooner he could escape the crowd, the faster he could call his buddy. Royce owed him a beer for this one. George had hoped Stacy could be persuaded to come with them, but Royce had bet she wasn't even close.

George didn't understand what had happened between those two. Yet somehow the relationship had gone from the two of them being friendly, with lots of teasing and joking, to a cold silence. It was uncomfortable being in the same room with them. That was the only thing that bothered him about the two of them being together on this trip. Everyone was coming for a vacation—not to partake in a cold war.

He gave the street a quick look, then dashed across to the small park on the other side. He walked to the park bench, sat, and called his best friend. "Royce, you need to find a way to make peace with Stacy before this ski trip happens. I don't want the week ruined with you two fighting."

"What are you talking about?" Royce joked. "It's not like Stacy will go. Besides, should that miracle happen, you'll see. Nothing's wrong between us."

"Bullshit. You've been pushing for this as much as I have, and God knows Stacy needs to get back out there, but there must be peace between the two of you, *before* we go."

"I promise. If she actually says yes, then I will make a point of speaking with her."

The mocking note in Royce's voice brought a savage grin to George's face. He was so going to enjoy the next few moments.

"Then you'd better get ready to face that because"—he paused for dramatic effect, savoring the moment and his victory—"Stacy said yes!"

"SHE SAID WHAT?" Royce sat back in his home office computer chair and stared blankly at a wall across from him. He didn't dare breathe. He waited, hoping George would repeat his words.

"She said yes."

The breath gushed out of him, and he closed his eyes. *Oh thank God.* He collected his thoughts quickly. George would razz him endlessly, if he understood how rattled the call had made Royce. "Good for you for getting her to finally agree."

"Yeah, I'm hoping she won't back out. She needs this," George agreed.

"She's still so pale," Royce said. "She hasn't fully recovered from that bout of flu a few months ago."

"That's because she didn't take the time to recover." George scowled. "Instead she worked herself to the bone."

Royce nodded. "That completes our numbers then. Three women and five men to start and two more, one of each, coming for the weekend." He stared across his tiny apartment. "I still can't believe she's coming."

"I did have to promise that she could come and just read a book by the fire. Pick a day trip or two to do a couple runs, as she wishes. Along with not having total kitchen duty."

"Good. She needs the rest. We all might take a day or two off and follow her lead. The weather is calling for cold and sunny, but that doesn't mean it won't change in an instant."

"I'm just damn happy she's coming."

"Me too." George rang off, leaving Royce staring at the phone in his hand, only one thought uppermost on his mind. Stacy was coming. He had one week to redeem himself. One week to show her that he deserved another chance.

He groaned. Why had he promised to fix the issue between Stacy and him *before* the weeklong vacation? And in such a manner that she didn't cancel out on the trip? That would be a disaster for everyone involved.

But especially for him.

He knew George didn't understand the problem Royce had with George's sister, and it wasn't exactly something Royce could share. And he had to do something quick, since they were leaving tomorrow. Feeling caught between a rock and a hard place, he realized one thing.

He'd better not screw this up. Or else.

Chapter 3

S TACY'S AFTERNOON GAVE her plenty of reason to regret her decision. Sure enough, Mark and Stevie were both going. They'd both been in and out of her office so many times that afternoon that she was ready to scream.

They were so excited she was coming.

She was already sorry she'd said yes.

Still, she felt both chagrin and relief at having agreed. She couldn't stay hidden forever. Besides, she didn't have the heart to cancel on George now. He would be so disappointed—and especially in her. Although she'd cancel on Royce in a heartbeat.

She finally managed to close her office door and to get some work done. By the time she made it home at the end of the day, she was tired and irritable and still pissed. She'd worked herself back into thinking she should cancel the trip, but she felt locked in to her decision.

She unlocked her apartment door, walked inside, and threw her coat and purse on the counter. Her home phone rang, as she wandered into the kitchen. She picked it up. "Hello?"

There was silence on the other end of the phone.

She hung up. The call only pissed her off more. The caller was lucky. If he'd responded and tried to sell her something, she would most likely have given him an earful. She opened her fridge door and sighed. She hadn't gone shopping yet. The last thing she wanted was takeout. But, if she wanted to eat—and she needed to—that looked to be the best option. She didn't want to do too much shopping, as she was leaving soon. She planned on some major resting time, trying to regain some of her lost pizzazz for life.

She stood in her kitchen and stared out the window.

The afternoon was cool and the sun still high, but it was cloudy. Kind of like her mood. Then she remembered the fish and chips on the boardwalk. Now that was a hell of a good idea. And the run there would be good for her. She'd been slacking off on her running lately. Time to pick it up. She was fit but always tired. That bout of pneumonia had damn-near killed her. She'd told George it had been the flu, as he would have worried all the more if he'd known the truth.

From the sheer number of times he'd called to check up on her, maybe he had known.

It only took a quick couple moments to get changed and to tie up her hair. Then she was out the door and running to the boardwalk. Ten minutes later, she found her rhythm. She stretched out her legs, the longer strides eating up the miles. She smiled as she breathed in deep fresh-air-hogging breaths.

It felt good. She ran a couple times a week, but she should do it more often to reduce her stress levels.

Light traffic was on the roads around her, but, with the evening soon upon them, most people were looking to get home. A breeze picked up, making her smile. She ran into the light wind, loving the cool feel on her face and chest.

She watched the birds swoop and dip, as they played in the wind, still hopeful for handouts from the people walking by. Sure enough, an old woman sat on one of the many benches and threw out chunks of bread. The birds were loving it. Stacy laughed, as several fought in the air, and both lost the tidbit to a third bird. Up ahead was the fish-and-chips van. She waved at him, as she jogged by. "I'll catch you on the way back."

"How long will you be?" he called out.

"Fifteen."

"I'll have it ready."

She laughed and waved back at him and kept on running. She'd try to make it faster. She rounded the corner and picked up her pace. She raced around the loop and started running back the way she'd come. After another few moments, she slowed her pace again, until she was just walking. The breeze picked up, and she waved her arms around to cool down and to loosen her limbs. Before she knew it, the smell of fresh fish and chips wafted toward her.

The vendor was waiting for her. "Here it is. Two pieces and a large order of fries."

"Do I look like I need a large order?" she joked, handing the man her money.

"No money required. The guy planning on helping you with those fries already took care of it."

She glanced up at the vendor, startled. He motioned behind her.

She turned, tray in hand, and froze. Damn it.

Royce.

Well, there was no help for it. She smiled at the cook, so he knew she was okay and walked over to sit across from the man she'd done her best to avoid for the last couple years. It was all she could do to act cool and composed, when she couldn't stop staring. She wanted to eat him up—he looked so good. Dark wind-blown hair. A snug-fitting sports jacket over jeans that loved his body almost as much as she did. Then that had been part of the problem. The chemistry between them was combustible. Always had been. When she'd been a teen, she'd had no end of wild fantasies about this man.

Then she'd grown up.

"Why?" she asked coolly.

"I figured, if we could get past some of the awkwardness, it would make for a nicer week for everyone."

She picked up a fry and dipped it in the ketchup before biting down. "Awkwardness?" she asked him straight out.

"Is there none?" One corner of his mouth tilted upward. "No? If not, that's great."

She blinked, not sure what to say. "I'm good. Sorry you aren't."

Royce leaned back and stared at her. "So you'll be that way?"

She lowered her lashes. Inside, her stomach churned. Lord, she hadn't expected this. "Be like what?"

"Whatever." He snorted and stood. "I guess we're good then."

And he walked away.

Shit. She stared down at her fish and chips, which had lost their appeal. She felt sick. "Wait," she called out.

He slowed his steps but didn't stop.

"Royce," she called out. "I'm sorry." She hated saying that. Yet he'd caught her by surprise, triggering her defenses.

He continued to walk away.

ROYCE TOOK TWO more steps before coming to a jarring stop. "Damn it."

He wasn't going to do this. The cold war was supposed to stop. That meant he had to stop this behavior too. Besides, he'd promised George. Shit. He stood, his back to her, his hands on his hips, hating this.

"I said I was sorry," she repeated, and her small voice made him feel worse.

He spun around and looked at her, sitting there, her plate of food untouched and going cold. At the motion to the side, Royce noted the cook, encouraging him, gesturing for him to retake his seat and to work this out.

Royce felt like an idiot standing here. He walked back. "I'll sit and talk, as long as we *talk*." After her gaze slid away from his, he sat down and added, "And you eat. You're even skinnier now." Even as he said it, he winced. The reference to their history was like shining a spotlight on the big white elephant standing between them.

Still, it had the desired effect, as she picked up a piece of fish and took a bite. She closed her eyes in sheer joy. "Oh, I forgot how good this is."

"All that fat and carbs, you mean?" he asked in a humorous voice, trying to ignore the tightening sensation in his groin at the sheer sensuality in her voice over the simple pleasure of fast food. "You've always been such a health nut."

She shook her head. "Not really, but, in my line of work, nothing like seeing clogged arteries and abdominal fat choking the life out of people to remind me that I could make better food choices."

"Absolutely. But there is a time to make choices for other reasons." He motioned to the meal in front of her. "Like right now."

She polished off the first piece of fish and picked up the second.

The cook showed up and gave her a takeout container full of hot fries and removed the cold ones. "Now you eat. I cook. You eat. That's the way it's supposed to work." Then he returned with an extra piece of fish. "Here. You need one more." Then he disappeared again, leaving them alone.

Royce grinned at the surprise on her face. "See? I'm not the only one who thinks you are too skinny."

She rolled her eyes at him but dug in.

He let her eat, wanting to confirm she got a good meal down. She'd probably only had a few pieces of rabbit food and a yogurt or some such thing for lunch.

When she finally slowed down enough to breathe, she let out a happy sigh. "This is marvelous."

"He does a great job."

She nodded, popped a fry in her mouth, and chewed. Then, out of the blue, she said, "Maybe I should cancel after all. Be easier."

"Oh no. You're not using me as an excuse to get out of this."

She narrowed her eyes at him. "I said yes, didn't I?"

"Sure you did, but second thoughts and all that ..." He grinned. "I'm sure your mind was reaching for excuses the minute your brother walked out of the restaurant." With a knowing eye, he watched the color rush across her cheeks. "I thought so."

"Whatever." She shrugged. "I'm still looking for ways to get out of it. Of course I regret saying I'd go. But George has been working on me since forever. So I finally gave in." She lifted her gaze to him. "Besides, maybe it'll be fine."

"That's the attitude. You can do this."

He hadn't meant to sound patronizing, but obviously she thought he did, as he could see her temper building in those incredibly blue eyes. She'd been the best thing to happen to him, and he hadn't a clue—not until she'd blown out of his life as fast as she'd blown in. She'd been a butterfly before, living life large.

Until that damned avalanche.

Then she'd gone quiet and dark. She'd been in so much pain, so needy that weekend, that he'd had no choice but to be everything she needed. The depths of emotions she'd pulled from him had surprised him as well. He'd always been a lighthearted *love 'em and leave 'em* type of guy.

She'd had a profound effect on him that weekend. Made him want something different for his future. Something he thought might be obtainable, after being with her.

And he'd changed. For the better.

He'd planned to show her that he'd turned over a new leaf, but she'd shut him out of her life. Completely. Now he hoped that his long wait was over. That she'd finally worked through whatever demons terrorized her. He understood to a certain extent. He'd gone a little crazy with his own demons, after he realized he couldn't get around her locked doors. He'd played on an extreme edge of life, sports, drinking, driving race cars ... Taking chances he wouldn't normally take. George had pulled him to one side and had asked what the hell had happened that gave him such a death wish.

Now he wished he hadn't said anything to him. In truth, all he'd said was one word, but it was enough. *Stacy.*

George had worked to keep them apart after that.

Now this week was coming.

Royce knew Stacy could handle it. She'd treat him like she treated everyone these days.

She'd just freeze him out.

He didn't want that. He'd been on the receiving end of her

moods already. Now it was time for that deep freeze to warm up—and hopefully let him back in.

After all, that was where he belonged.

INTERESTING. HE STOOD off to one side, trying to stay out of the wind that had suddenly come down with a cutting edge to it. Pedestrians moved around him, as they headed home.

He couldn't remember ever seeing either Stacy or Royce in this part of town. And never together. So what was going on? He almost felt left out. At that, he laughed. Of course he was left out. They didn't know he was here.

And, if they did know, would it make a difference? It was hard to say.

Likely they'd ignore him, as they always did.

Or rather like she'd always ignored him before. Somehow he appeared to be invisible to all women. Until he stopped them in their tracks.

Then they had no choice but to see who he really was.

He smiled. And, if the pedestrians took a close look and scuttled past at top speed, all the better. He preferred his insular existence.

It made it easier to carry out his hobby—his buddy called it art—*but one no one ever seemed to appreciate the skills required.*

Especially not the women who played key roles in the final pieces— forever.

Chapter 4

S TACY FELT LIKE shit. She hadn't meant to start off on the wrong foot. In fact, she'd pushed off the thought of seeing Royce, like a dose of medicine to be taken with a screwed-up face and loud complaining. That he'd caught her off guard with his unexpected presence said much about how he'd affected her already.

"Truce," she said seriously. "I don't know why you get my back up. I know we have a history, but we've both moved on. So no reason we can't be friends." She caught a downward movement of the corner of his mouth and quickly amended, "Or at least cordial enemies." She looked at him hopefully.

He just gave her a flat stare.

"Fine." She threw up her hands. "What do you want from me?"

"Cordial enemies would be at the bottom of the list. Friends would be dragging along down there too." He glared at her and stood. "As to what I really want, I'll leave that to you to figure out. It shouldn't take a smarty pants like you too long."

And he walked away.

Her mouth opened, but no words came out. She watched him leave. Who else could drop a bomb like that and walk away unscathed? He'd scored a direct hit, and she knew she would feel the bruising for days. Not to mention worry on his words.

Had he meant what she thought he'd meant? No, surely not.

She stood and threw away her last few fries in the garbage. The wind had picked up again, giving it a snarky bite, as it brushed past her cheeks. She strolled home, her mind working on what he'd said and on what he deliberately hadn't said. Even an imbecile could work it out. He didn't want to be enemies and neither did he want to be tossed into the friend zone. That left the closer-than-friend arena, and she didn't want to go there.

But heated memories prodded her.

It had been a horrific phase in her life. He'd been there for her, but they'd been animals. Taking what they needed, giving back, but, as it was such a blur, she wasn't sure she'd acquitted herself well in that department. She'd been so lost. Yet, through it all, he'd been there, an anchor in her world.

She'd appreciated it. Yet she couldn't stay. She'd seen a future with him that she couldn't have. Because of who he was. Because of who she was.

Did she really want to open that door again? He'd been the hottest lover she'd ever known. However, sex was no basis for a relationship. Maybe he just wanted an affair. She frowned. She didn't do those, and that's all he did.

Or was she just hoping that's what he wanted?

One thing she did know. She hadn't had a serious relationship since losing her girlfriends. It hurt to lose those you loved. And, damn, she'd loved those two. Everyone had called the three of them a matched set.

Since then, she'd dated a few odd times but hadn't taken any to bed—except Royce. And he would be the last one she would want a relationship with. With his hobbies and extreme sports, not to mention his part-time job photographing these extreme sports, there was a good chance she'd lose him too. Although she knew he was working on a completely different career path, she had to wonder how much of that would stick or would that adrenaline always call to him?

No, that was enough. She would find a nice staid accountant and settle down eventually. A crazy live-life-on-the-edge kind of guy was not the type of man she was looking for.

However, since they were leaving tomorrow for a weeklong vacation, sharing a cabin, she must find a way to get along with him.

For everyone's sake.

REALLY? STACY WAS coming? Finally, after all these years. A dream come true. Something he'd worked for, toiled over, waited anxiously for—and now it was happening. He wasn't sure whether he should be screaming for joy or remorse.

He knew she was ready for this.

Hell, he was ready for this.

But did she realize how important this trip would be?

Chapter 5

T HE MORNING OF the trip came too early. They weren't leaving until almost noon, as the journey was only a couple hours long, but crossing the border could hold them up. They also had to grocery shop on the other side, before driving the last hour to the cabin.

Stacy was still trying to gather the necessities of life, remembering at the last moment that her brother had said to bring extra thermals. George had all the sporting gear and equipment. She just needed to bring enough clothing and cold-weather gear for the week. And books. She was looking forward to a few hours of skiing but found that sitting in front of the fire, a book in hand, with the nice rich aroma of a pot of stew simmering beside her, was just as appealing. And maybe spending time with her camera.

Books. Damn, she hadn't packed any books. She raced back to her room and snatched two mysteries she'd picked up last week. She couldn't wait to dive into them. While trying to stuff them into her already-full bag, the doorbell rang. "Shit." She ran out of her bedroom and pulled the front door open, not even looking at her brother. "I'm almost ready. Just need another couple minutes."

"Not a problem. We've got a little leeway."

Royce's voice stopped her, and she turned. "Where's George?"

"Downstairs, reshuffling gear to make room for your bag." He surveyed the room. "Have you got much more?"

She ran back into her bedroom, checked her list, and realized she had it all. "No, I think I'm done. It's just this bag." She picked it up and groaned. "Damn it. When did this get so heavy?"

"Since we're not flying, weight doesn't matter."

"It does if I have to lug it very far on the other end." She carried it to the front door and dropped it, then took one last look around, while she pulled on her coat. "Okay, I'm good to go."

He picked up the bag easily with one hand and walked out ahead of her.

She locked the door, a pang of fear zinging through her as she did so. This was her first trip away since that avalanche had ripped apart her life.

She could do this. She had done this many times before. *Remember, Stacy. You leave home every day before you go to work.*

But, in the past three years, she'd never left her home overnight. She'd never risked it. She'd lost so much on the last trip that she hadn't been able to.

Not until now.

What if this time, *she* never came home?

As she got into the back seat of the Land Rover her brother favored, Stacy noted Royce had taken the passenger seat up front. Good, it was crowded enough with six of them traveling in this rig, without having to deal with Royce sitting next to her. They still had to pick up Geoffrey. Thankfully Stevie was traveling with Mark in his truck, and they were taking much of the other gear and provisions. They'd stop at a store on the other side of the border for fresh produce for the week.

Stacy smiled at Kathleen, George's current girlfriend, one who'd actually lasted longer than six months. "Good morning, Kathleen."

Kathleen grinned at her. "Can't believe you're here. This will be great."

"I hope so, especially after George hollered so much about me coming." She leaned forward to see another woman on the other side of Kathleen. "Hi, I'm Stacy, and George is my obnoxious brother," she said, by way of an explanation.

"I'm Yvonne," the tall redhead said, with a big smile.

The other two women laughed, while George protested the insult from the driver's seat.

"Who else is coming, George?" Stacy asked.

"You already know about Geoffrey, Stevie, and Mark, plus Kevin and Christine are last-minute additions, but they won't arrive until the end of the week."

"Really?" Stacy asked in delight. "That's great. I haven't seen Geoffrey in such a long time."

"Actually I think he's coming because you are coming," George said, with a big grin. "I've been trying to get him to come along with us forever. He's boarded this region several times a year but rarely with us, and the last time was quite a while ago. We're picking him up on the way out of town."

"He's also a spelunker, isn't he?" Kathleen asked. "This area is hugely popular for ice caves too."

"Yeah, Geoffrey's first love is caves. Some in this area never thaw. There was talk of opening up a few of them to the public in a touristy kind of way."

That elicited groans from everyone in the vehicle. "That would be horrible," Yvonne said. "If people want to see those caves, they should do it the hard way."

Stacy withheld her comments. She understood both sides. Tourists brought in big bucks to the smaller communities that generally surrounded the wilderness areas, but, at the same time, that type of tourism brought other problems with it. It needed to be managed carefully, so as to not damage the delicate balance of the ecosystem. However, she knew better than to get into a discussion with raised tempers on both sides of the debate.

Feeling eyes on her, she looked up to see Royce staring at her in the rearview mirror. She remembered he'd been on her side on some of those discussions. And his warm gaze invited her to share in those memories.

She flushed and turned her gaze out the window.

What the hell was she doing here? And why did she suddenly feel like she'd made the right decision in coming?

GEORGE KEPT A wary eye on his sister. He loved her dearly, but, like any siblings, they'd done their share of fighting. Both artistic and active, they'd had their problems, but they'd stayed close regardless. She was the brain. He was a jock. Somehow they'd still found enough common ground—maybe just sibling love—to work through all the problems. When her friends had disappeared in that avalanche, she'd gone a little crazy. He'd tried to help. So had the police. Hell, she'd badgered them hourly, then daily, for news, leads, any tidbit to help her sleep at night.

When there'd been nothing to report, she'd died a little bit inside. As time went on, instead of picking up the pieces and getting on with her life, she'd pulled inside—a turtle-like shell growing on her back—in a state of waiting. As if she knew the answers would come. Eventually. And, until then, she couldn't get on with her life.

It had been beyond sad. Depressing and debilitating for everyone around her.

Then something had changed. Now George realized it was due to Royce. Too bad George didn't know what had gone on between them, but Stacy had suddenly turned a corner. She'd started to return to life. More reserved. More afraid. More damaged. But alive and living once again.

For that, he was grateful to Royce.

Stacy was still tottering on the edge. At this point, she could go either way. That's why this week was so important. George didn't want anything to set her back. That she'd come was already a wonderful surprise. He'd been expecting her to cancel every hour since she'd agreed. But she'd stuck it out, and here she was. Now it was just as important that she have a great week. Deal with a few ghosts and move on even more. He'd do everything he could to make that happen.

His sister was special. The work she did was difficult and yet so important for everyone else. And no one was there to make her feel special. To hold her when her world collapsed. He'd hoped Royce would be the man to take that place but apparently not. Royce had always remained in the background, keeping a watchful eye on George's sister.

George sneaked a quick glance at Royce, sitting in the passenger seat beside him. He was busy staring out the window. George looked back at this sister in the rearview mirror and smiled.

Maybe more was there than George thought. She stared at Royce like she didn't know what to do with him. But her gaze was intense. Interested.

That was always a good sign.

Seeing that, George felt much better. He barely hid his grin. It could be a great week after all.

AN HOUR LATER, Royce knew he shouldn't have come. Damn. Behind him, he heard Stacy's laughing response to Geoffrey's teasing comment. Those two had been getting along famously since Geoffrey had joined them not far out of town. Who knew she'd actually tease and play like she was doing right now? And why not with Royce? He held back a shudder, as he suddenly realized that he had no idea whether Stacy had a boyfriend or not. The atmosphere between her and Geoffrey said not. But she was lighter, more playful. So maybe she was open to the concept.

Still, that just pissed him off. He wanted her to be open to a relationship with him. No. One. Else.

"Hey, Royce, what are you frowning at so heavily? Jeez, you look ready to kill someone." Geoffrey called out, his comical tone eliciting laughter all around.

Except from Royce. "Nope, just thinking about life."

"Wow, that's deep, man. Sounds like your last girlfriend ditched you. Sorry. I know how much you loved her."

Again, that overly mocking solicitous voice brought on more laughter and pissed Royce right off. He'd broken it off months ago, and it had been casual at best. Another attempt on his part to fill his life with companionship. What could he say? He'd been lonely. In a casual voice, he said, "Not a biggie."

"That's all right. Lots more where she came from," Stacy said coolly. "Right, Royce?"

Royce turned to look back at her, caught something hard in her gaze, and felt a pain deep inside. But he'd be damned if he'd show it. He snorted and joked, "There always is." As she turned away, a curl to her lip, he repeated, "There always is."

Chapter 6

THE TWO VEHICLES stopped on the other side of the border for gas and coffee. Stacy had missed breakfast, so she loaded up on muffins to sustain her, until they arrived at the cabin. She ignored the teasing and munched happily away, watching the miles go by. She'd forgotten how beautiful the journey was. They would start climbing up the mountain roads soon. The Land Rover would make it to the cabin just fine. If there'd been other vehicles in and out lately, it would be even easier. The plan was to meet up with the other vehicle at the lunch stop on the other side of the border, then stay convoy-style, in case one or the other got into trouble. With the border crossing and shopping involved, the trip ended up being a longer drive but one well worth the effort. It had been three years since she'd been here. As she looked out at the icy mountains ahead of them, she realized it had been too long. It was desolate. Cold. And incredibly beautiful.

By the time they arrived at the cabin, it was late afternoon, and the evening sky had settled like a cold dark blanket on the region. Being in the mountains, once the sun went down, the night settled in early. If it weren't for the powerful headlights of the Rover leading the way and the expert knowledge of her brother, Stacy didn't think they'd have found the driveway. As this was also a popular climbing area, there had been signposts, but, with the drifting snow and the thick soupy darkness, they'd been hard to see.

George parked in front and left his headlights on, until Royce opened the cabin door and ascertained that it was empty and available for them. They'd booked it for the week, although a few might stay just for the weekend. It was owned by one of George's friends and made available to the group at large for a pittance. They'd all made good use of the owner's generosity over the years.

The cabin had an emergency generator in the back. As the women worked to unload gear, the men set about bringing light and heat to the cabin.

Within minutes, a huge fire blazed in the big heater stove, and a pot of water was put on top for making hot drinks, while the hot water tank was turned on. Food would be needed soon, but, for the moment, everyone was just overjoyed to be here. Stacy wandered through the cabin and chose to claim her bed up in the loft. It would be the warmest place, and she was no fool. This might be a vacation, but there'd be more icicles and thermal underwear here than bikinis and tropical drinks.

She dumped her bag in the loft next to one of the beds, each topped by a thin mattress, and went downstairs to claim a down-filled sleeping bag from the stack her brother and Royce had supplied. They were used as bedcovers.

"Stacy, where are you setting up?" George asked.

"In the loft, if that's all right."

There were a few calls and nods of agreement, as that freed up several private bedrooms within the cabin. She noted that George and Kathleen took one of them, and the two guys she worked with took another—with double bunks on both walls, as did the other bedroom.

Only a few other choices remained for sleeping. Royce had yet to pick one.

And neither had Yvonne or Geoffrey.

GEORGE LAUGHED AT his sister's choice. "Hey, Stacy, how come you have to hide away upstairs, like that?"

"Ha," she said. "I just wanted to make sure you and Kathleen managed to grab a private room for yourselves. And not sure if other couples were happening"—she grinned—"like Stevie and Mark, I'm just being nice."

Everyone cracked up in laughter, as Stevie turned on her. "Hey, it's not like that," he protested, but it was an old joke among the group, as these two guys had been best friends since forever. "There are other beds in our room, if you want to bunk with us."

Stacy laughed and shook her head. "I'm good. Besides, another couple is joining us, so they will need a place to sleep too. Just think. The lot of you can have a foursome!"

A pillow hit her in the chest, as Mark tossed one at her. "That's all right. Go ahead. Hide upstairs. We know when you don't want to spend time with us."

She threw the pillow at Stevie. "I just know where the warmest spot in the house is."

"True enough." Stevie smirked, adding, "But, if you slept with us, you'd be even warmer."

The other males in the group raised their hands. "No problem, you can sleep with me."

"You don't want to sleep with them. I'll keep you warm."

Stacy snickered. "Like that'll happen."

"Hey, what's wrong with us?" Stevie protested in an injured tone.

With an eye roll, Stacy muttered, "Too much to count."

The pillow hit her in the face, amid a howl of laughter.

LOOK AT QUEEN Stacy. Always apart. Always in her perfect little bubble. Not touching anyone. So untouchable. The perfect ice princess.

He narrowed his gaze.

If that was the way she wanted to be treated …

He barely held back the unholy grin threatening to break loose. Not that anyone else would understand. Well, one would. The talk continued around him. He shifted slightly, so he could keep her in his view, as he considered the issue. He'd thought about it before and had discarded it as not possible. Too much trouble. But his years of experience had helped. He might pull it off now. Especially since she was here.

Of course someone else wanted her too. That could be troublesome.

"Hey, Stacy, your turn to make popcorn," George said, nudging his sister. "Come on, lazybones, get up."

"Hey, I'm tired too," she protested, but she got up and headed to the kitchen good-naturedly.

An interesting proposition, he thought, as he watched her stroll forward. No doubt his hobby had become almost too easy. He must up the ante to keep the game interesting.

And it was, but now that something harder, more challenging had come up, his other prey seemed paltry. He wanted to be ready for more. But was he?

Still, this was Stacy. He'd have to fight to get her for himself. An interesting twist to an already challenging concept.

Then again, it was the fear of being caught that gave him the thrill.

Of course he could do it, if he chose to. He just had to figure out how. And when.

ROYCE SLID DOWN on his corner of the couch and closed his eyes. He was also tired. He'd barely slept last night. He hoped he would tonight. Yvonne had put her bag in his room though. In a separate bed, thank God. He had no idea if it was a random choice or she was just looking for a place to call her own. Either way, she'd sleep only two feet from him. When he'd seen her bag there, he'd turned to look around, and, sure enough, he'd seen Stacy peering over the loft railings, staring right into his room.

She'd been pissed.

Damn right. He hoped it choked her. And immediately he felt like a heel. He hated feeling this way. Wanting to walk away from someone who obviously didn't want to want him but was angry that she still did.

How could she not want what they'd had together? It had been the best thing in his life. To think he'd been alone feeling that way made it so much worse. He wanted her to be just as involved. To want what they'd had.

He hadn't been able to throw it away. How could she?

Royce tried to ignore Stacy's tired steps to the kitchen to make popcorn for this group. Then couldn't. She'd been outside a lot today and was still recovering from a long illness. Damn it. Frustrated and angry, he hopped to his feet and strode into the kitchen. He ignored the smirks and smiles he knew were evident behind his back. They could laugh. They had no idea what he'd been through—was going through.

A lovesick man who would do anything to get Stacy back in his life again.

All he could do was hope she'd see their relationship in a different light and give him a second chance. And, because he cared, he wouldn't let her work herself to death like this. She should be in bed. Not making popcorn for these goofs.

He stopped at the doorway and opened his mouth to say something—he had no idea what—when he realized she just stood there, head down, shoulders slumped. Eyes closed. Shit. He stepped forward, and, in a voice too low and too harsh for his liking, he snapped, "What's wrong?"

In a sudden jolt, her eyes flew open, and she spun around. She shook her head hard, her hair flying around her shoulders, maybe to clear the sleep that was obviously clouding her brain, and said, "Nothing. I'm just tired."

"*Just?*" He took the few steps to bring him to her side. He reached out and grabbed her shoulders. "Of course you're tired. Go sit down. I'll make this." He turned her in the direction of the others and gave her a gentle push.

He studied the table in front of him, where the cast-iron handheld popper was filled with popcorn but didn't have the butter out or ready to melt. He measured it quickly and dumped it into the popper.

"No," she said, turning back to the table. "I'll be fine."

"You're not fine," he said in a low voice. "Why won't you let me help you?"

The popcorn popper was held tight in her fist, as she turned away, but her gaze lingered on his. He thought she wouldn't answer for a long moment, but then she opened her mouth. He bent his head to hear what she said, his gaze trying to read her gently moving lips. Her voice had been so soft that he wondered if he'd heard her correctly.

She walked back into the main room to pop the corn on the big fireplace. But her words rippled through his mind in wonder and almost broke his heart.

He thought, hoped, she'd said, "Because it hurts too much."

Chapter 7

STACY FORGOT HOW high energy this group of friends was. They worked hard, and they played hard. Such was their life. She watched the men tease the women and bug the other guys. She was in a category altogether different. She knew them all, with the exception of Yvonne, and had been friends forever with some of them. That she worked with two of them, not all the time and not all day, made for an odd relationship there too. Then there was Royce and that bit of history and Geoffrey with their long-term friendship. At one point he'd asked her out, but she'd refused, realizing she liked him as a good friend only. He was a great guy, and she was more than happy to have him along.

And, unlike many of the others here, he wasn't an adrenaline junkie.

Safety was always her prime concern. Even more so now after what had happened to her best friends.

She cozied up by the fire, grateful for the moment. Her brother had brought a huge pasta dish to heat up on the big heater stove for tonight, but it was taking its time warming up. So was the cabin. The conversation went around in a mix of laughter and arguments. The others were already planning their trips out tomorrow. She was still thinking a book by the fire was the right answer.

Royce plunked down beside her. "Are you going out tomorrow?"

She studied his face, aware that the conversation had died down around them. "I'm not sure. What are the plans?"

"Two groups," he said. "One is heading to the runs beside the waterfall. The other is going to the snowboard park."

"*Hmm.* High winds, freezing cold air, or my camera in the sunshine." She grinned. "I'll go with the sunshine."

There were exclamations at that one.

"I'm good with a camera," George said, "but she's gifted."

That drew a snort from her. "Not likely. Look at the stuff you take pictures of. You have to be gifted to do that."

"And then look at your images. They are surreal. Like you see something no one else can," George countered.

"Hey, I didn't know you were *both* photographers," Kathleen said. "Really? How come I haven't seen any of your work, Stacy?"

Stacy curled her lips but stayed quiet.

"You have," George said. "You just didn't know they were hers."

A surprised pause stopped everyone, as they turned en masse to look from him to her.

She groaned. "It's no secret. I made a little bit of a name for myself way back when, that's all."

"And what name is that?" Royce asked, his gaze narrow, searching.

She shrugged, uncomfortable with having the spotlight turned her way.

Her brother answered. "You guys have the privilege of being in the presence of Eternal."

A shocked silence filled the room. Stacy wanted to laugh. She didn't know whether the name was bringing that reaction or the fact that they didn't know the name.

It was no big deal. She'd been doing photography since she was in her teens. She had stopped for a long while, after losing her friends. She'd been lost herself back then. After her weekend with Royce, she'd picked it up again. That was when she'd started working on her new project—Faces of Nature.

"Really?" Stevie asked in shock. "And you didn't tell us? We've ranted and raved to you over so many of those photographs over the years. And you never said anything."

"I thought Eternal was dead," Kathleen said, with surprise.

Geoffrey walked to stand in front of Stacy. "Seriously?"

She shrugged. "It's no big deal."

"It's a very big deal." He snorted. Then he stopped, as if considering her words. "You know, in hindsight, that makes a lot of sense. You went through a lot of phases. I remember that series of ice-climbing photos you took. The images in the ice that you managed to capture that even those of us who'd been there with you couldn't see."

"Well, I for one haven't ever seen your work," Yvonne said in a tight voice to go with her tight smile. She tossed her long red hair.

"I didn't expect anyone to. I haven't done much work lately." That was a lie. She'd done a lot recently but under a different name. Another pseudonym. She looked at her work as an artist looked at his.

Some of it she hated, and some of it she loved. And some of it she loved but was unsure how anyone else could.

So she'd started a new name. It's not that she'd been a different person, but this new work was different for her. She hadn't shared that name with anyone.

Yvonne popped up and said, "I really like Rebirth's work."

Managing to keep her face bland, inside Stacy jolted at hearing her second name mentioned.

"I don't know that one." Royce made an odd sound. "And what's with the artists putting up their work under these abstract names?"

"I can't answer for everyone," Stacy said, "but, for me, it was about the photos in that series."

Everyone looked at her, confused. She laughed.

Her brother said, "I hadn't thought of that. You're signing by the series."

"On the back is my real signature," she added, with a smile. "In your case, George, you don't own your photographs. You work for the company, who gets the rights to all your work, so it's not an issue."

He nodded thoughtfully. "At the moment. Who knows where I'll be down the road? I hadn't thought about the individualism with my work."

She didn't add that she'd been in a strange space when she'd started doing her professional signature series that way. In truth, they weren't signatures. They were titles. But as there was more than one photograph in the series, the name had stuck. The world loved different. It added mystery to her work.

Considering this was the first time Stevie and the rest were hearing about her work and seeing the slightly injured looks on their faces, she realized that their relationship would be changing again too. Maybe it was time. And maybe that was the real reason for coming on this weeklong adventure. She needed fresh inspiration.

It would center on letting go.

She needed to open up the narrow scope of her world. Her girlfriends were gone. She wasn't responsible for what had happened to them. She couldn't hide away on the off chance that something might happen to her. And, if fate intervened, making it her time, then she needed to come to terms with that. Still, it was time to move forward. Time to move on. Time to say goodbye. Somehow.

She'd been looking for months for some new inspiration. She'd been working on a massive urban portfolio of her local area for some months now. She hadn't shown anyone but the gallery owner. He'd immediately booked her for a showing under her Rebirth name. She knew that, at the release of this next set of photos, the world would understand some part of who she was.

Now she needed to heal the other areas of her life, and coming here was part of that.

She settled back comfortably. For the first time, she felt that spark of need, that spark of creation in her soul. She'd find her inspiration here.

She knew she would.

All she had to do was recognize who or what that was.

Then do everything she could to learn how it ticked.

ROYCE WATCHED GEORGE and his sister interact. Not only was affection and sibling love there, but there was no professional jealousy. At least none that he could see. George was fanatical about his work. Always had been.

Yet his stuff was all action.

George, as if realizing Royce was out of the loop, came over, his phone out in front of him, and he clicked on something, then held it out for Royce to see. In a quiet voice, he said, "This is one she did several years back."

Royce shot him a quick look, then glanced at the image. It was a flower, dying from the outside in. As if in pain, the leaves were curling in on itself.

"Kind of depressing," he muttered. He had to consider that a few years ago meant three. If ever someone had been affected by the loss of her friends, Stacy would be the poster child.

"Look closer."

Frowning, Royce studied the photo. And startled. It was a huge aster type flower, the tips brown and dying, almost hanging like rotten teeth. Yet juxtaposed to those teeth was a series of tiny buds reaching up toward the brown tips as if ready to feed off them. And, sure enough, a single drop of dew hung down, giving the life force to the little ones that they might grow strong. The aster in death was reaching out a hand and helping, offering the gift of life.

Royce stared, hating that he'd read so much into the picture. Surely that wasn't what she'd meant to show. He glanced over at Stacy, speaking quietly with Geoffrey, then let his gaze slide from one person to the next, then on to the next. Finally he came back to his best friend.

"Do you see it?" George asked quietly. "Or tell me what do you see?"

"I see the old and dying reaching out and nurturing the young."

Stevie walked past just then and leaned over and saw the image. "Oh, that one. God, those teeth give me the chills." And he walked away.

"Some people only ever see the teeth."

"I saw those first," Royce said. "Then saw them more as umbrellas but also directing the gift of water to the buds below."

Stevie walked back. "Yeah, you could see that. Or you could take the teeth concept one step deeper and realize those buds are feeding off the mother plant's decaying flesh." With that, he sauntered away, a beer in hand.

Royce stared down at the image. "Not a nice thought."

"It's why her work's so popular. People see different things with every one of her pictures. Are they innocent and spiritual or dark and devious?"

Royce shot his gaze back over to Stacy. As if sensing his look, she turned to stare at him. He dropped his gaze back to the image and recalled the disturbing interpretation Stevie had mentioned. "Have you ever asked her?" Royce asked George.

"No," George said, putting away his phone. "Not sure I want to know the answer."

WELL, HE DID. He'd been listening in quietly, studying the pictures with interest but from the sidelines. Stacy was a photographer? Like what the fuck? He hadn't pegged her for the artist type. As his daddy would say, she was all book smart and life stupid.

Now he found out she has a hobby. Not just any hobby but one of his hobbies. Well, one he was working on developing. It kind of went along with his other hobby. As he sat here, contemplating the implications, he started to burn inside. Like, how dare she?

If, and that was a big if, she was the artist known as Eternal, then she was considered a leader in her field. One with a perspective like none other. Touted as a fresh look on life.

What bullshit.

She was like every other bitch he'd met on these trips. Only, in Stacy's case, she was too good for anyone—not just him. She wanted to be the queen and have everyone dote on her. Well, he had plans. Plans for her. To put her in her place, like she had him all these years.

She would see the results of her actions then. It might be years late, but revenge was best served cold.

And he would make sure she was damn cold.

A shudder rippled down his spine. Goddammit. He clenched his jaw so hard that he swore he heard his teeth grinding.

He glanced down at his hands. A tremor was already starting. He shifted, tucking them out of sight. No one could know.

No one could suspect.

Or else he'd have to ramp up his agenda. And make Stacy pay—now.

Chapter 8

THE NEXT MORNING, Stacy woke up cold and sore. She had no explanation for the aches. Maybe from the long drive yesterday? Maybe the extra heavy running workout schedule she'd put herself through this last week? As she rolled over, a groan slipped out. Well, there was that answer. She'd earned those aches from sleeping on this uncomfortable bed last night. Maybe she should take another look at her choice of sleeping quarters. Although all the beds were probably topped by the same thin mattresses. After a day out on the snow, she would sleep regardless. She'd gone to bed before the others and had felt self-conscious doing so. She opened her eyes to study the large loft. Was she alone here? Was she so lucky?

It appeared to be so. For some reason, instead of cheering her up, she felt let down. As if finding out no one had wanted to share her space was deliberate. Silly. Everyone was in groups already. And plenty of bedrooms were downstairs. So why would anyone come up here?

And, if she felt a pang of upset over the concept of Royce having paired up with someone else, then she'd stomp on it. She and Royce weren't an item. Never had been, not when the relationship could be measured in a matter of hours and days, not weeks.

Besides, she'd chosen the warmest place in the house. If that didn't seem to matter to the others, well, it did to her. She'd been out of the loop with this winter playtime, and she was feeling the cold big time. If the fire wasn't lit and coffee not bubbling, she so wasn't getting out of bed.

Of course several in the group were likely to be cuddling up with someone special. That would keep anyone warm. She halted on the image of Royce and Yvonne.

He could do what he wanted.

Hopefully the others had stayed up late drinking. That would mean no early risers.

She smiled and curled up again. She could actually see her breath.

And she'd come why?

She closed her eyes again, breathing the cold air deep inside. Wafting upward was the smoke of a fire and the smell of coffee, all combined with the rustling movement from down below. Sliding forward, she looked through the railings to see who was awake.

And damn if her heart didn't jump for joy. Royce. His open sleeping bag was in front of the fire, where he'd obviously slept. Dressed in just long johns, he was poking at the fire, willing it to burst into flame. A pot of coffee sat on the stove. It wouldn't be ready for a while yet, but at least the process had been started. A coffeemaker was here somewhere, but coffee made this way had a special flavor.

She leaned over farther, wanting to confirm that he had slept alone.

He had.

Instantly she felt terrible. Plenty of room up here in the loft. She would have shared. Damn it. Then again, as she studied his bedroll down by the fire, why should she? Likely his had been much warmer than hers, and it was pretty damn smart of him too. Although, as she'd gone to bed early, that place would hardly have done her any good.

"You could come down and warm up," Royce called up softly, not turning around.

She waited, wondering if he was talking to her. When he twisted slightly to stare up at her, she wanted to pull back, like a little kid. Instead she stared down at him casually. "Is it warm enough to venture down?"

He grinned. "If it isn't, you sure won't want to go outdoors."

"Not sure I am anyway." She yawned. "Let me know when the coffee is done."

"Ha. You're not the boss here, sis," George called up from the closest bedroom. "It's first come, first serve on that pot."

"And I'm here on the spot," Royce called back. "Good luck getting any."

There was a mad scramble from all the rooms, as the men left their beds and raced to the pot. In various states of heavy winter underwear, the gang huddled around the heater stove and watched the coffee boil.

"You're all nuts," she called down, sinking lower into her sleeping bag.

"Ha. Look who's out here in the middle of nowhere with us," George called up.

"Don't remind me," she muttered.

"I heard that."

She ignored him. But tucked inside her warm bag, she smiled. Life was good. She lay back peacefully, enjoying the novelty of her surroundings. Below her, the conversation between the groups floated up. Everyone discussed the day ahead. She was thinking that what she was doing was the perfect activity. She yawned. How had she become so worn out? Maybe it was the constant overtime and the heavy workouts. She'd filled her time so she didn't have to think. And now that she had nothing to do, no reason to get up, it was hard to do anything but doze off again.

"Hey, sleepyhead."

The voice woke her from her daydreams. She rolled over to find George standing over her, a mug of coffee in his hand. "Sorry, I guess I fell asleep again."

"You need it," he said, his voice serious. "You're exhausted." He squatted beside her and lowered the cup to the floor beside her head. "I don't think you even see how bad you've gotten. You're completely worn out." He plunked his butt on the floor. "You are working yourself to the bone."

"I'm not that bad," she protested, rising up on one elbow.

Stevie called up from below, "Yes, you are. You're the first one into work and the last one to leave."

Mark added, "And you usually come in on weekends."

"Not to mention," George said, "what are you running now, 5K and 10K?"

"Both," she said. "It depends on the day of the week and how I'm feeling." She smiled and lay back down. "I'm in bed now. I might just stay here today." At the frown forming on his face, she added quickly, "Maybe go out for a couple runs, when it warms up outside."

"Ha." He laughed. "I bet you're still in bed when I return."

"Hey." She kicked him through the sleeping bag. It was a faint effort and hurt her more than him. "That's not fair."

"We'll see." He grinned. "You were always hard to get out of bed."

"What? When I was six?"

"Maybe." He stood, a big smirk on his face. "Stevie and Mark and I are heading out to do a quick check on the snow conditions. Then we can make plans."

"No breakfast?" she asked, not moving and having no intention of moving anytime soon. "Make sure you load the fire to keep it going."

"Maybe you should work on breakfast." He headed to the stairs and called back, "We'll be back in just over an hour. And we'll be hungry."

She groaned. "Listen to you, giving orders already."

"Always, sis. You're the boss at work. I'm the boss here."

No arguing that. She lay on her back and listened with half an ear, as the group discussed the array of runs offered. They wanted to do as much as possible over the next week. She had no such ambition. As it stood now, going downstairs was about all she could manage. She sipped her coffee and relaxed. The more she relaxed, the more she realized how long it had been since she'd let her guard down. The last few years had been very stressful. Too stressful. She'd seen herself how bad she'd gotten. The nights she hadn't been able to sleep. She'd worked herself until she collapsed to the floor, then picked herself up and did it all over again. She hadn't really noticed, until she'd been flattened by pneumonia.

What she hadn't realized was that others had noticed.

Of course one was her brother. If anyone would notice, it would be him. Or maybe not. She worked with Stevie and Mark. They'd seen her day after day, as they worked in the lab. She'd been promoted just after her friends had died. As a way to avoid being overwhelmed with grief, she'd worked her ass off. Staying late, coming in early. She'd picked up extra duties and had kept her own. She still did.

Then she'd spent a weekend with Royce and, after that, had done everything she could to forget him.

Instead of just missing lunch, she'd also skimped on breakfast, and, when she got home, she often crashed before eating a decent dinner.

The end was a foregone conclusion.

She'd caught herself before completely collapsing. She'd actually gone to a doctor, something she rarely did but knew she couldn't put it off anymore, before she got any worse. If she couldn't work, she didn't think she would have survived.

The doctor had been horrified when she'd seen Stacy. Immediately she had been heavily dosed with vitamins and minerals, put on heavy antibiotics, and weighed and measured, so she could check her progress.

That had been her epiphany.

A massive wake-up call.

She'd only realized as she'd stood on the scale in the doctor's office how dire the situation had gotten. She'd been a hair over 105 pounds. At five foot nine, that meant she was a skin-covered skeleton. And she'd seen more than her fair share of those. The mirror showed her starkly how much she'd let herself fall. How she was only a step away from death. She could just imagine her coworkers performing an autopsy on her young bag of bones and wondering what the hell had happened to her.

The doctor had also ordered her to a psychiatrist for a mental health checkup. Stacy had been just scared enough that she'd gone. It had been difficult to convince the good psychiatrist that she wasn't suicidal or bulimic or anorexic. As she'd tried to explain, she'd seen the decline herself. Her actions were that of a woman trying to forget. To remove herself from the world that had become too painful.

Just not in a suicidal sort of way.

But the psychiatrist hadn't been so easily convinced. Indeed, she'd seen him for over three months, before she realized he'd helped and that her emotions *had* stabilized. If nothing else, she understood what she'd done. And how she'd gotten to this point. With his help, she had picked herself up, made a promise to take better care of herself, and to rejoice in the life she'd been so quick to underappreciate.

It had taken six months to add a layer of flesh under her skin and another six months to get the rounded look back on her face.

Still, it had scared her. It had also shown her how weak she'd become. And how greatly she'd been affected by the loss of those she'd loved.

She'd vowed to never let that happen again.

Only she'd fallen sick again a couple months ago—a relapse—minor, yet scary when she considered how slow her recovery had been. In some ways, still was.

She'd brought her physical health back as far as she could but understood that it was sitting on a delicate balance. And so was her emotional state.

"Are you coming down here or staying up there all day?"

She startled. She'd been so lost in her own musings that she hadn't even realized where she was. Or who she was with. She sat up and looked over the railing.

"Oh, so you are awake." Royce stood in front of the heater stove. "Are you coming down? Or"—his voice deepened—"are you scared to be alone with me?"

"Alone?" she asked. She bounded to her feet and leaned over the railing. Sure enough, no one was down there. "Is everyone else asleep?"

He shook his head. "They're gone." His grin flashed. "George came back and checked on you, but you'd dozed off—again."

"I'll be down in a few minutes." she cried out, unaccountably flustered. She hadn't meant to sleep again.

"Don't worry about it," Royce called up. "Get dressed and come down for a fresh cup of coffee though."

"I'll be right there." She dressed quickly, picked up the cup still full of cold coffee, and carried it down the stairs. He stood in front of the stove, holding the coffeepot, when she made her way around him. She dumped the cold coffee and rinsed out her cup and returned to where he stood, her cup held out in front of her.

He filled it.

"I'm surprised I slept so much," she said, with a smile.

"It goes with the territory. Coming out in the cold like this often tires someone out. Especially someone who isn't used to it."

"I do remember. It's been a while though."

"Three years by any chance?"

She knew he was asking if she'd been skiing since the avalanche. "Not since then," she said. "Everything was before then."

He didn't agree. "Not everything."

That deep dark voice rolled through her, bringing back memories better left forgotten. She glanced at him sideways from under her lashes, but she stayed quiet, not sure what to say. After a little silence, she asked, "When will they be back? I was supposed to have breakfast ready for them."

That brought a healthy laugh from him. "In that case, let's get them something to eat. They're likely to be here in about fifteen to twenty minutes."

He walked over to the coolers of food and opened them. He found what he was looking for in the second cooler and hauled out sausages and eggs. He nodded to one of the boxes on the side. "Several loaves of French bread are over there. And crumpets."

"Oh, now that sounds good." She pulled out the crumpets and one loaf of bread, then spied the wire toaster rack, where she could clamp the bread in between the racks and hold it over a fire. She turned to glance at the open fireplace. "Toast would be good."

"Absolutely. Have a piece now," he suggested. "I'll put a pan of sausages on the stove, and we'll do a big mess of eggs as well."

She quickly cut several slices of French bread and sat in front of the fireplace, making toast. The others might not be here on time, and that was okay with her. She'd eat it all with the appetite she'd worked up.

"I hope you plan on sharing that."

"If they get home in time."

"I'll have a slice, please."

And, with that, they slid into the easy camaraderie they'd had years ago.

THAT HAD HAPPENED easier than expected. Royce hadn't been sure when she'd first come down, but, after a few awkward sideways glances and a weird buffer of space between them, she seemed to settle down with being alone with him.

Good.

He wanted a lot more, but, hell, he'd take baby steps, if that's all he could get right now.

She was so damn skinny still. He wanted to feed her several meals before the others returned. As he watched, she broke off a piece of toast and popped it into her mouth, closing her eyes at the taste.

Christ. She was 100 percent into everything she did. It was damn irritating when she turned that concentration into ignoring him, but, when she'd turned it on him that weekend? ... Well, she'd blown every other relationship out of his reality, and he finally found what he'd been missing all his life.

Her.

Now she was here. He wondered, should he bring up their history? Say something about their future—not that they had one together, but, if things went well, they could have something to work toward. He hated the gauche feeling of being a teenager again. Worrying about what to say. Worrying about every nuance on her face when she looked at him. Worrying about making the correct interpretation from everything she said.

But they were alone.

So it was a good time to talk. To ask what he'd done that had sent her in hiding and that, whatever it was, he wished he'd known. Because he was damn sorry about it.

He opened his mouth and said, "I'm so—"

And heard sounds of the crew laughing outside.

Stacy shot him a disconcerted look. "Did you say something?"

"No." He shook his head. "At least nothing important."

Chapter 9

THE GROUP WAS loud and raucous when they came in the front door, bringing freezing cold air and lots of laughter with them. Now in the boot room, George stomped the snow from his feet and took off his boots. Going through an interior door, he stepped into the main room of the cabin and announced, "It's a gorgeous day out there. We will have some awesome runs today."

Royce grinned. "Glad to hear that. Did you go up Robber's Trail or over to Sycamous Trail?"

"Both—well, almost both. We went to the base of Robber's Trail, then took Green Trail to Sycamous. Both were great." He walked over to the fireplace and held out his hands. He was joined by the others, all huddling around the flames.

"Something smells great," Stevie said, his head tilting up for a bigger sniff. "Toast." He sniffed again. "Stacy, did you make breakfast?"

She shot him a look at the disbelief in his voice. "I do cook, you know? But Royce did most of the work." She turned around and grabbed the platter of toast she'd made and held it out. "However, I did make these."

"Yes," he crowed. "Toasted on an open fire."

"That's the best kind."

"Hey, pass it over here."

Within seconds, the platter had been reduced to several of the smallest pieces. She grinned and placed it on the small coffee table.

"Stacy?"

She turned around. Royce motioned her toward him. "I'm serving. Can I get you to deliver?"

And, with that, she had a plate for everyone. Some of them stood in front of the fire, others sat on the couch, and several took their plates to the small dining table.

George motioned to Stacy with his fork. "Where's yours?"

"Ha, I ate first." If she hadn't been looking at him, she'd have missed the narrow-eyed look he tossed at Royce. As she turned away from him, she also caught Royce's nod in response. Really? She wondered about making an issue of it but decided that it was just her brother ensuring she was looking after herself. He would need to see for himself that she was okay.

She couldn't blame him for worrying. If their positions were reversed, she'd do the same thing.

She loved him.

He loved her.

That's what caring was all about.

While the others ate, she and Royce washed the dishes in companionable silence. She put on a second pot of coffee, while the group discussed where they were going. Given it was just day one, several people were determined to make the most of their time. Others were more concerned about overdoing it on the first day.

She knew she'd be asked about her plans soon. She had no idea but heard one group talk of the runs by the frozen waterfall. That was where she wanted to go. With the blue sky and sun, she'd be sure to get some amazing photos.

She walked up to her loft room and dug around for her gear. She put on different socks, her thermals, and her outer layer. That was the easy decision. Now what did she want to take for camera equipment? She pored over her lenses. She didn't want to pack anything unnecessary. However, any camera buff would be in the same boat—they would want to take it all with them. Just in case.

In the end, she cut her choice down to the basics, then headed back downstairs. She caught George's surprised look. She shrugged. "I thought I'd come and see what the light is like."

"Three groups are going out right now," Royce stated, his gaze penetrating. "Where are you planning to go?"

"To the waterfalls," she said lightly. "Unless anyone objects?"

"Glad to hear you're coming," Stevie said, a big smile on his face. "Make sure you catch my good side."

That brought the insults flying, as they teased him. Stacy just smiled and sat down to put on her ski boots. The others were in various states of dress, as they all got ready to go back out. George sat beside Stacy, and she asked him, "Anyone staying here to keep the fire going?"

George shook his head. "No, it will hold fine."

She smiled. "I'll only be out for a few hours."

"Good. Don't overdo it."

"I won't."

"When you're ready," Royce said, "someone will come back with you."

"No need," she said smoothly. "I'm an old hand at this. Remember?"

"Safety first, remember?" Royce repeated. "I'll be making sure you get there and back." His tone brooked no argument. If anything, he shot her a hard look, as if to remind her who was the boss. Then he grabbed his jacket and walked out.

She made a face. And here she'd thought she'd just have her big brother worrying about her. Still, this wasn't a small resort. It was dense with hundreds of runs, and people were often only found missing when, hours later, they didn't show up. Often no one could say exactly where to look. After the avalanche that had ripped apart this group's lives, they had adopted a few rules. *Never alone. Always let someone know where they would be at all times. Do not do anything stupid.*

ROYCE STOOD ON the closed-in porch dubbed the boot room and breathed deeply. The bite of the cold helped stabilize his mood. It had been a great morning, with just the two of them. Friendly. Companionable even. As if the years of silence between them had never been. He paused to reconsider. It was as if the years *including that weekend* had never existed. He'd been friends with George since Stacy had been in pigtails. He wasn't sure exactly when it happened, but somewhere along the way he started to care for her more than he should for his best friend's kid sister. George hadn't been the one to warn him off. Stacy's father had. And in no uncertain terms. Stacy was going on to university and getting a real education. She didn't need a bad-boy jock giving her the eye.

He'd hated that meeting. But he'd respected the man. And the lecture. He'd backed off and had stayed well back. He'd stepped forward, after she lost her friends, and she'd had these massive walls up, keeping him firmly on the other side. He'd given her space. Then about three months afterward, when he'd tried again, he had been rebuffed in no uncertain terms.

It had surprised the hell out of him when she'd come to him many months later, but he was no fool, and, from the first touch, they'd gone up in flames.

And, damn it, if immediately afterward, she hadn't given him the deep freeze of all deep freezes. He'd backed off, giving her space, thinking to come back in a few months. It hadn't worked out that way. She'd shut and locked that door.

She'd stayed behind that icy wall ever since. He'd hoped she'd drop it one day, but he hadn't waited. He'd gone on with his life. Somewhat.

He had no idea when she would ever warm up enough to let someone join her in her icy prison. Even better, to let her heart open up and let that icy exterior melt forever.

God, he hoped he was there when it happened.

"You okay?" George stood beside him, reading his reactions.

George knew Royce well. And knew how he felt about Stacy. How he'd always felt about her. He shrugged. "I'm fine. It's just weird."

"Yeah, it would be. I'm hoping it's all good."

Shit. This was his garbage. Not George's. "It's all good. It's great to see her here." He grabbed his board. "Now if only we can get her through the week."

He glanced over at Stacy, as she joined the rest of them, satisfaction rippling through him as he watched her settle in. All through the drive yesterday, she'd been an outsider. Although sitting in the vehicle *with* them, she hadn't been one *of* them. Even last night, she'd been uncomfortable with George bringing up her photography. Particularly the controversial ones. Her Eternal series.

Her room choice for sleeping had also been indicative of how she felt. She'd chosen the loft. Maybe for the reason she had voiced, but also so she didn't have to share a room with anyone, again keeping herself separate.

Yet more than one bed was up there. However, no door for privacy. He'd planned to go up to the loft with her, needing to be close. Not too close, but close enough to keep an eye on her. So she would know she wasn't alone. He'd actually hoped that she'd be waiting and watching to see if he shared a room with Yvonne. Instead, by the time everyone had crashed—well after she'd gone to bed—she'd been sound asleep.

He should know. He'd crept upstairs, intent on putting his bedroll up there as well.

Instead he'd decided, since she was sleeping so well, that he'd stay down by the fire and let her have her space.

That might have been the right thing to do, as she'd slept soundly. He'd shushed the second group as they headed to their bedrooms, to avoid waking her. And it had worked. She'd slept though the ruckus.

Now this morning she was comfortably in the middle of the group, as if she'd never been so separate. A little too comfortable with Geoffrey though.

"*Hmm …*" George said in a low voice. "She's not interested in him, you know?"

Heat washed up Royce's neck. Damn. He'd hoped George hadn't noticed. She was always so relaxed, so playful with Stevie and Mark, that Royce couldn't help but wonder about her closer connection to Geoffrey.

"They're just friends."

Royce pulled on his belt and slammed it home, checking his buckles. "I'm sure they are." He knew that; it's just that he didn't want them to become anything more.

"Good." More clicks and snaps sounded as George put on his helmet. "Are you good?"

"Yeah." And Royce was. He always was. Like he and George had discussed, they'd do everything they could to look after Stacy and to see that she enjoyed her first vacation since that fateful time.

Then maybe they could coax her out of her shell again.

BITCH.

That was the nicest thing he could say about her. She'd slipped into place with the group, and damn if he didn't feel like he'd been ousted to make room for her.

Stupid bitch. There, that was better.

Maybe he'd do a series of portraits too. Her face in stupid positions, so that everyone could see her true colors.

The thoughts only festered in his mind. He'd tried to clear them out. And failed.

She was like mold. Insidious and all-encompassing. Everything she touched succumbed to her will.

Like hell.

If anyone was the ruler in that department, he was it.

And she'd learn that lesson soon enough.

Chapter 10

S TACY STOPPED, STABILIZED her breathing, and then climbed up another rise. Ski boots were not made for walking. However, it was an easy climb. Her movements were strong and steady. She'd been more overwhelmed by the extreme beauty of the frozen waterfall than the physical exertion. She'd forgotten the sheer joy of feeling the fresh air fill her lungs and the burn of her muscles, but her heart was full of laughter.

The scenery was spectacular.

She was glad she'd come. She crested the top, and damn if Royce wasn't waiting for her there. She did a quick step and laughed out loud. Life was good. She dropped her skis and clicked her boots in the bindings.

"You aren't as out of shape as I thought you'd be," Stevie crowed at her side, giving her a big hug. Their helmets clanged against each other.

She let him. It went with the day and the scenario. She'd have stomped him if he'd tried that at work.

"You're doing great out here, you know?" He gave her a big grin.

She rolled her eyes at him. "I haven't been that bad."

He gave her a serious look. "Yes, you have."

Startled, she took a closer look and realized from the deep, dark, troubled look in his eyes that he cared, like really cared. And she was touched. "I'm better now."

"*Now*," he muttered. "Finally. It's been a rough couple years, watching you fall apart, then put yourself back together again, as if the new model was made of steel, fortified so you'd never be hurt again."

"Wow, does everyone know about that?" Being a private person, it was disconcerting to think that others knew of her breakdown. "I thought I'd hid it much better."

He rushed to reassure her. "You did a great job, but, for those who knew you and loved you, it was hard to watch." He shrugged sheepishly. "We couldn't help you, besides being friendly and supportive. And hoping you pulled out of it."

She nodded. She tilted her helmet back slightly and rubbed an itch along her forehead. She didn't know what to say. She'd been unaware of so much back then. Now that she was pulling herself back into line, she regretted not knowing. Maybe she wouldn't have fallen into such a downward spiral if she hadn't been alone.

But she had. And here she was today. Realizing she had more friends than ever. "Thanks, Stevie. I hadn't recognized much around me back then. It was a difficult time. Thanks for standing by me."

"Always. We'd tried to get George to do something ..."

She shook her head, a startled laugh coming out. "Good try. George loves me dearly, but he's never been able to force me into doing anything I didn't want to do."

"And yet"—Stevie threw his hand wide, pointing to the wide expanse of frozen beauty all around them—"here you are."

With a shout of laughter, she slugged him lightly on the shoulder. "I hate to disappoint you or to knock George off a pedestal, but I'd already decided it was time to face this. I came because George requested that I come, but, if I hadn't come this time, then I'd have asked to come another time."

At Stevie's look of dismayed astonishment, she laughed again. "At the risk of really ruining your mood, I'd also like to find some new inspiration for my photography." She motioned to their surroundings. "I need to heal myself and get back to living life like I used to."

OH, LOOK AT that. The ice princess deigned to come out and play. He hid his smirk and waved at her. Bitch. He smiled brightly. "Hey, nice you came out." He buckled up his belt. "You're just in time to have some fun."

Then I'll have fun with you later. Whore. After Royce, are you? He watched her smile at the man in question, a burning sensation in his gut. They were all whores. Women. The scourge of the earth.

Royce slugged him on the shoulder. "You're next."

"Ha. Race you to the bottom," he responded. "You'll never beat me."

"You're on."

He put all thoughts of Stacy into the back of his mind, as Royce took off. No way would he let Royce win. "Like hell, prepare to get your ass whupped."

 That started the laughter, the cheers and jeers from everyone around, as they urged the racers on.

 And he laughed. Damn, he was good. He grinned. Soon he'd make sure everyone else knew it too.

Chapter 11

THE REST OF the morning passed in a blur of runs. They skied and boarded and took the lifts to the top. It was fun and bloody cold. Stacy opted out after several runs. She was sore and tired but thrilled to be here.

She pulled to a stop by the frozen waterfall. "Go on," she said, waving her group past. "I'll stay here for a couple runs and rest. See you on the next pass."

And the others whooshed by with hoots and hollers. They'd be gone close to forty minutes, before returning to where she waited.

She laughed, watching them race down in front of her. It was a stunning day. As the silence descended, she tilted her head skyward, letting the warmth of the sun land on her face. She opened her eyes and turned to look up at the frozen waterfall. Such beautiful ice forms. Who said white was white? This was so much more than that.

The sunlight was perfect. It bounced and echoed, a soundless splash of color across the scenery.

And she saw it. That face. A hidden gem of perception. Like when naming one cloud an elephant and another a snail. There. A head, ... mostly a profile, hidden in the crags above her, a play of lights and shadows. Her heart pounded with the excitement of this discovery.

She studied it for a long moment, trying to mark the spots that defined the nose and eyebrows, the chin, so she could find them again from the other side of her viewfinder. The longer she looked, the more intense the spark grew. This was truly special.

She removed her backpack and dove in, searching for her camera. Her hand closed around it, and she sighed with relief. She'd been sure it was in here, but, in the joy of the moment, there was that fear that she'd somehow forgotten it or worse—had lost it. She pulled it out, pulled off the cap, and lifted it all in one movement. The sun was changing. She needed to grab as many shots as she could.

She peered at the ice wall. Where was it? She studied the area, looking for the markers she'd set in her mind. Where? She took several shots anyway, knowing that, just because her mind might not have seen it right now, it didn't mean she wouldn't find the image markers later, when she had prints of the pictures.

There.

She caught sight of the tip of the nose. From that point, she looked back to find the eyebrows and the jaw. Beautiful. Like seriously beautiful. She started clicking, trying to catch it in its entire splendor. As the light changed, she saw several long waving columns of frozen ice rolling down the cliff, like locks of curly hair. Mesmerized, she quickly became lost in her panic to get her shots before the light changed again.

Click.

Click, click.

There. She shifted. *Click. Click. Click.* She could hardly breathe for fear of missing something. As the sun shifted, the rays brought yet another image into focus. Oh God. Stunning.

"So beautiful," she murmured. The icy beauty locked into the mountain was something she'd never seen before. *Ice maiden*, she'd instinctively called her. Frozen in time. So appropriate, given her friends' snowy graves were somewhere here too. Maybe she'd do this series as a memorial. What a wonderful way to say goodbye.

Potential titles for the series just rolled off her lips, as her camera never stopped. She walked closer and then stepped to the right. More shots from the left. At one, she swore the sun had picked up a tear on the woman's frozen features. A big fat dewdrop-shaped ice ball hung delicately on her cheek. "So gorgeous."

"What is?" Royce asked quietly behind her.

She gasped in shock. Lost in her world, she hadn't heard anyone else approach.

He reached out an arm to steady her, for the first time making her aware of her body, now cold and tired. She was swaying on her feet.

"I think it's time you came back to the cabin," he said in a harsh voice.

She frowned and then glanced up at the frozen waterfall to see the clouds had moved in. Her frozen lady was barely visible. Now there was a gloomy, sinister look to her.

And just as powerful. She lifted her camera, lost once again.

"That's enough, Stacy." He reached out and grabbed her elbow, forcing her to turn around. Dragging her gaze from his face, she looked back at the waterfall and noted her frozen lady was asleep once again.

She turned to look down at her pack. Only it wasn't here. Her pack was somehow hundreds of yards away from where he found her. Surprised at the distance, she turned to study the path she'd taken in her need to capture her frozen lady and realized she'd, indeed, walked that far away on her own. The path was churned up from the effects of the warming sun and her movements—the twisting, crouching positions she'd used to take her shots.

Bizarre.

As she put away her camera, a sense of having touched something special filtered through her. If she'd caught what she'd hoped to catch, this could be her best series ever. They were simple, yet stunning. At least she hoped they were. The sky darkened even more. She stood and motioned to the cloud cover. "I thought the weather was supposed to be good all week?"

"That's life in the mountains. Storms blow in and out without warning. At least today was great." He smiled and adjusted her pack on her shoulders, having caught the corner of her coat. He had her skis in his other hand. "Now, back to the cabin."

She went without protest, casting one long last look at the lady sleeping in her frozen home.

With the sun completely obliterated, there was no sign of her at all.

Stacy could only hope she'd caught the image she needed to prove to the others that the ice maiden mirage had ever existed in the first place.

ROYCE HAD BEEN watching her for the last hour. Several times he'd moved in to say something, only to realize what he thought was a break in her concentration was actually just a shift. Not enough for her to be aware of her surroundings either. He'd watched the cliff behind her with worried eyes several times. She hadn't seemed as aware of it as he was. And that bothered him. Hell, everything about her concerned him. She was something else. Her focus was so intense, so complete.

Something about the way she perceived the world around her was so at odds with others. Maybe she had a heightened sense of perception. He didn't know. It was just special. The photography she did was unique. He wished he could see what she saw when she looked at the cliff face. He'd looked plenty of times already and had no idea what had necessitated hundreds of shots. If not thousands of shots. He knew if he saw the final piece, he'd recognize the area, but, until she pointed out what was so special, he wouldn't have seen it first.

Then she'd almost fallen. And not by tripping. From fatigue. She didn't even seem to realize her own limits.

Damn that girl. Had she any idea how tired she was?

He'd moved into position soon afterward. He had mentioned leaving within minutes, but she hadn't even registered he was there. He'd waited another twenty minutes before he'd pushed it again. He doubted she'd even noticed the passage of time.

They skied back to the cabin. It was a gentle slope, but he kept a close eye on her, in case she fell.

It was late afternoon, and, with the heavy cloud cover, the winds had picked up. It was getting ugly quickly. "A storm is moving in fast."

"I see that." She slipped down a path through the trees. The trees were dark and cold. The atmosphere gloomy. Dark. And much colder. The wind was gone, which helped, but the darkness fell faster. He was pissed. They should have left a long time ago. It was his fault. He'd seen her. Had known they should have left earlier, but he'd stayed, so she could take her damn photos. Anything for her.

He was a fool. A lovesick fool.

Chapter 12

S TACY PULLED HER jacket closer around her neck. The chill was bone deep all of a sudden. There'd been no warning of the change of weather. Or, she winced, she'd ignored them. Typical of her.

"Are you okay?" Royce called out to her into the eerie silence of the woods.

"Very." Knowing he might not be able to hear her as they skied down the slope, she gave a little wave.

The woods appeared to be endless. She knew the cabin was likely only ten minutes farther. She pictured the warm fire ahead. That and a hot rum toddy, together with a hot meal, kept her going. She was not normally nervous in the dark or in the woods, but something about the combination of the two ratcheted up the anxiety factor tenfold. She had to admit to being glad Royce was close by. He was a strong, steady man. And, for all the problems she had with him, he was a good man to watch her back.

They wound their way down the slope to the long flat stretch at the bottom. When the path was wide enough for two, Royce shifted up beside her. She hated to say it, but it was a comfort.

He pointed out a small light in the darkness.

Her heart lightened. That should be the cabin. "Are the others back already?"

"They should be."

She shot him a disbelieving look. "No way. They would've passed me on their way back down."

He nodded. "And, while you were busy taking pictures, they probably did another couple runs, then called it quits. Chances are, they've had at least two drinks and have already eaten most of the dinner."

"They'd better not have," she said. "I'm starving." She took a deep breath and winced, as her lungs filled with icy air. She coughed once, then twice. She felt more than saw Royce's hard look. "I'm fine."

"Good. No more sick days for you."

She grinned. "No. I can't afford any more of those." She could, but, such as life was, it was only because she had a great medical plan where she worked that such a thing was possible. She desperately wanted to cough again but tried to hold it back. She plodded on.

Royce clicked on his helmet's headlight.

A broad beam of light lit up the gloomy sky. Relief filled her. And she hated to realize how nervous she'd really been.

A shout across the pasture was heard clearly.

"Someone is out looking for us," she said, with a smile. "I'm sorry. I didn't want to worry anyone. I really had no idea it was so late."

"No worries." At her sidelong glance, he grinned. "It's not your fault." As she hit a bump with one ski and almost fell, he reached out a hand to steady her, then she righted herself. "Besides, I was keeping watch on the time. We're coming home just when we're supposed to."

There came a second shout.

Now a third. A sense of urgency in the voice.

"What's wrong?" But she knew.

"Someone's missing," Royce replied.

They met up with Stevie and George, rushing toward them. "Mark and Geoffrey are missing."

Royce was immediately all business, his cell phone in his hand. "No reception."

Stacy glanced from one to the other. "A search party?"

Stevie nodded. "Yes, but let's get you back to the cabin."

She shook her head. "No. I'm slowing you down. The cabin's in sight. You'll need Royce."

The three men stared at each other. She said impatiently, "Come on. Let's not be foolish. You need to head back up now. Hopefully they just are having equipment troubles or lost track of time or the storm caught them unaware."

Behind her, came a sudden shout.

Everyone turned. It was Mark and Geoffrey. Everyone cheered.

"Oh, thank God," she murmured.

"Well, that's that then," Royce murmured.

As the other two met up with them, Geoffrey grinned. "It was my fault. I wanted to check out another slope. Sorry for the worry."

"No problem. Let's head back."

As one, they trooped toward the warmth of the cabin.

ROYCE WALKED INTO the cabin to cheers and shouts, as those left in the cabin realized everyone was back, safe and sound. The smell of fresh chili filled his nostrils. Good. He was starving. He caught the look on Stacy's face and almost grinned. She looked ready to steal the bowl from George's hands, and George saw it. He held his bowl to the side. "Get your own."

She grinned. "Will do. Just make sure you save me some."

Royce packed away his boots and gear in the boot room. He came back inside, just behind Stacy, her own footsteps faster and perkier now that they were back. The high energy of the group was contagious.

He headed for the chili pot, happy to see a lot was left. He dished up one bowl, only to have it gently removed from his hands. Stacy flashed a grin at him and said, "Thanks."

He could only grin back. At least she was looking better. He scooped a second bowl full and set it down. And damn if Geoffrey didn't pick it up. "Thanks, man." But an odd tone was in his voice.

Surreptitiously Royce studied Geoffrey's face. He had a sour look as he stirred his chili, adding sour cream and cheddar to the top. "What's the matter?" Royce asked.

"Nothing," Geoffrey said, his tone brusque. "At least nothing more than usual." He turned away at the same time Royce turned, and he watched as Geoffrey caught sight of Stacy standing beside her brother.

And damn if that look on Geoffrey's face wasn't a lot closer to hate than just some sour look.

It chilled Royce to the bone.

GEORGE STUDIED THE undercurrents going on around him. Damn it. Stacy was in the middle of it. Again. Kathleen squeezed his hand. He smiled down at her, loving the reminder of her presence at his side. It was not something he was used to. He'd had dozens of girlfriends, and none had left him feeling like half of him was missing when they were gone.

Not since Kathleen. Besides, he'd hoped that having Kathleen and Yvonne along would help Stacy adjust to being here. The group had been doing these trips together for a long time. They were friends. He trusted them all.

It was a great feeling.

As he glanced over at his sister, then at Kathleen, he realized that, right now, his world was complete.

Chapter 13

THE ARGUMENT THAT broke out startled Stacy. She hadn't seen it coming. Hadn't even noticed the undercurrents—until they'd turned into a riptide.

"I was being safe," Geoffrey snapped. "Sorry if I didn't meet your expectations."

George glared at him. "You know the rules as well as any of us. Stick to the timeline. If someone has to go out after you, then you're putting them at risk."

"So no one needs to come after me," snapped Geoffrey. "I'm not an amateur."

"Neither was Andrew Corso. He's still missing. And so is Karl Henderson. They were both experienced skiers."

"Well, they couldn't have been that experienced then, could they?" Geoffrey said impatiently. "Come on. I've been coming to these mountains for over a decade. I've never even had a close call."

Stacy hated the raised voices and the dissension. Not good for anyone. Especially not good for a small group like theirs. "We just don't want anything to happen to you," she said in a gentle voice.

He rolled his eyes at her. "Neither do I want anything to happen to you, Stacy, and we were just behind you."

"True. I got lost in my photography," she admitted, with a small smile.

"And what's Royce's excuse?" Stevie asked, with a laugh. "Did he get lost in you, I wonder?"

Raucous laughter filled the air and eased the tension brought on by the earlier sharp words. Trying to hold the tidal wave of heat washing over her cheeks, Stacy smiled good-naturedly. As she slid a cautious gaze at Royce, hoping he realized Stevie's comment was a shot in the dark, she realized he'd gone silent. Grim.

Shit. See? This was why she wasn't into relationships. They were too much work. She stood and collected the many empty chili bowls. "Thanks so much to whoever made the chili. It was delicious."

"I made it," George said, with a grin.

She laughed. "That's why it was so good—it's my recipe."

"Hey, it's Mom's recipe originally," he protested. "Now it's got my own personal touch, thank you very much."

"Yeah, like what?" she challenged him with a grin, happy to feel the others relaxing. It was the way the evening should be.

"It's got elephant garlic in it instead of the regular stuff," he said quickly.

Kathleen laughed, then added, "And that's because the store was out of the regular stuff. You asked them specifically for the little guys."

He gave her a mocking look to shut up, but the rest of the room had already erupted into laughter.

Stacy carried the bowls into the kitchen and called back, "I'll do the dishes if someone wants to carry that kettle of water in here and pour."

Instantly several people hopped to their feet. She busied herself packing away the rest of the chili into a glass bowl. Chances were good it wouldn't have a chance to get cool before someone would look for seconds. Boiling water splashed into the sink. Instantly soapy bubbles formed.

"Thanks," she said to Stevie.

"No problem. I was hoping there'd be hot water for showers, but it doesn't look like it this time."

She stopped to think about that. They'd had hot showers the last time they were here, but it had to do with the water outside coming in, and the pipes being wrapped around the stovepipe to warm up the water. She turned on the tap, and hot water gushed out. She laughed. "Old habits die hard. I could have just used this hot water."

"Better you didn't." He interpreted her gaze. "There's running water, but, with this many people, no way we could keep the hot water for everyone to shower."

He refilled the kettle and carried it out to the big heater stove. Not only was the steam needed for the air, which would dry out quickly, but this way there'd be hot water for the proverbial teapot. And speaking of hot drinks, she filled the coffeepot and carried it out to heat up as well. Coffee was another staple for her. She'd brought a pound herself, just in case.

Only half listening to the conversation going on around her in the living room, Stacy quickly finished up the dishes. She couldn't help but wonder at the undercurrents of hostility she'd caught earlier. She knew she'd been in a fog for much of the last few years as to what went on within the group, but she'd like to think that, if it had been serious, then someone would have mentioned it to her. She'd definitely pulled the ostrich thing and had buried her head in the sand since losing her friends. Like, why them? She couldn't help asking herself that for the ten millionth time.

Both women were fun-loving and people-loving. They weren't mean or nasty or selfish or stingy. They were wonderful. Why did Stacy deserve to live and not them? She was no better and no nicer than they were.

"Hey, Stacy, what are you thinking about so deeply?"

Startled, she pulled herself back to her surroundings. Now that Stevie had drawn the attention to her, everyone stared at her. She smiled and said, "I just realized that, as I've been out of the loop a fair bit these last couple years, I don't know all of you as well as I'd like to. Some of you I've known for years, and yet others"—she brightened her smile—"I barely know at all."

"Well, you've known me for years," Geoffrey said. "So no mystery there."

"But there is. Whatever happened to ..." Stacy frowned, trying to remember who his last girlfriend was. "Karla?" she hazarded a guess.

The group burst out laughing. Geoffrey gave her a mock solute. "Yeah, as if that's so important. My failed love life. She's gone. As in gone years ago. Something about not liking my lifestyle."

She winced. As she remembered, he'd been very much in love with Karla. "Sorry about that."

He shrugged good-naturedly. "It wouldn't be so bad, except for the way she walked out. She just walked. Took her stuff, and, from one day to the next, she never answered my calls or contacted me again."

"Ouch, that's have to hurt," Mark said. "Don't know why women do that. I had that with my last one—Becky." He groaned. "She was the sweetest little thing, with a wonderful chipmunk-cheek ass."

That brought the room into gales of laughter.

Stacy shook her head. "Somehow I don't think she would have appreciated that comparison."

"Oh, I told her that a time or two," he said, with a big grin.

"And you wonder why she walked?" Kathleen hooted. "Maybe

leave off the comparisons next time."

"*What* next time? He's been on a long dry run since," Geoffrey said.

"Ha, no longer than yours," Mark teased.

Geoffrey winced. "True enough. It was a rough-enough exit that I didn't exactly want to jump back into the relationship arena." His grin widened. "Now I'm just waiting on Stacy here to get back in, so I can scoop her up."

"Like hell," she teased. "I'd bore you to death with my shoptalk."

"Considering you work on dead bodies all day, *boring* is not quite the right word I would have used." Kathleen gave a tiny shudder. "Thanks for being as sparing with the shoptalk as you appear to be."

"You learn early that it has a tendency to kill a dinner conversation." Stacy had tried to be sensitive to other people's feelings in regard to her profession.

"And why would a beautiful girl like you go into such an oddball career, I don't know," Stevie said, shaking his head. "Yet a lot of women are choosing your career."

"Why is that?" Geoffrey asked.

"I always figured because we already deal in the creation of life, so it makes sense to want to be involved with the other end of the spectrum and learn about death."

"But you're an anthropologist, aren't you? As in very old bones?" Kathleen asked.

"I'm the forensic pathologist for Seattle. However, I also have a degree in anthropology, so I consult on a wide variety of cases."

"Death. Murder. Suicide." Kathleen shivered. "That's a rough field to work in."

"Comparatively very few people end up on my table because they've been murdered." She withheld saying that usually the worst ones did. She loved the challenge of the unusual. And, to be honest, she loved outwitting the criminal mind. When she could find pivotal evidence in a murder case, she felt a huge sense of satisfaction. That she had an overlarge caseload of unsolved deaths in her files made her angry and sad at the same time. Still, most of her work was of the more normal variety.

"As we convinced Stacy to get out into nature and away from the death that she lives in, I suggest we change the subject," Royce said.

George picked up his GPS and asked, "Anyone used one of these to chart maps on the mountain?" He held it up. "Mark, weren't you the one showing this to me?"

The room erupted at the new topic.

Stacy sat back and let the group run with it. She knew she tended to make people uncomfortable. She didn't always know how to handle that discomfort, but she seemed to have skirted past it tonight.

She waited a little longer, then excused herself.

She was cold, tired, and just a little sick of being around so many people. She could use a few moments to herself—and a good night's sleep.

ROYCE WATCHED AS Stacy made her way to the bathroom. When she came out, she looked tired. Her slow climb up the stairs seemed to take more effort than he expected. Then the cold would have a huge effect on her. When she disappeared from sight, he turned back to the group and caught Geoffrey glaring at him. Royce lifted an eyebrow. What the hell was his problem? Geoffrey got up and went into the kitchen. Royce watched him, wishing he understood what the hell that had been all about. Out of the corner of his eye, he caught sight of George studying him. He faced him and asked quietly, "Do you know what that was?"

George made a tiny motion of his head toward where Stacy had disappeared to.

Royce settled back into his seat. Damn it. Was Geoffrey sweet on Stacy? Not good. Royce contemplated the issue and realized it really didn't matter. Anyone could be sweet on Stacy—they still wouldn't get her.

She was his. She just refused to admit it.

BITCH. SHE WAS his. She just didn't know it. But she would soon. He glanced around the cabin, feeling the sense of connectedness within the group. The group she'd joined and shouldn't have been allowed to.

She didn't belong.

She shouldn't have come this week.

It had been great without her all these years. Without the reminder of her rejection. But her stupid brother just had to bring her back into the fold.

His gaze switched to Royce and hardened. And so had Royce. With-

out her around, life would be different. It would be back to just them. The way it used to be. The way it was supposed to be.

He was starting to hate all women.

Chapter 14

S TACY WOKE SEVERAL times in the night, cold and achy. Not good. She needed to be careful, to stay warm, and to ensure she didn't get sick again. It had been a long, painful year, one she couldn't repeat. She hadn't thought to be out so long or so late yesterday. She still wasn't so sure how that had happened.

Except, when she got lost in her art, she got *lost* in her art.

Was it a coincidence that Royce was with her then, or had he been keeping an eye on her all afternoon? She rolled over and bit back a moan. Her shoulders and arms throbbed. Damn. She should have thought ahead and taken an anti-inflammatory. Then she would likely wake up loose and moving freely. Possibly still with mild pain but not the feeling of having her muscles locked in place, every movement a hard tug to get them going. And it was cold. Damn cold. She snuggled deeper into her sleeping bag and closed her eyes.

"Hey, sleepyhead. Time to get down here, if you're planning on getting any coffee," Stevie called up to her.

She groaned loud enough for him to hear. "You could deliver," she said, without hope, knowing that would make her the butt of the jokes but not caring. They'd all been drinking heavily last night. She, on the other hand, had gone to bed early. Again.

If she were home, she would have made coffee and brought a tray back to bed with her. No such luxury here. Then she heard a welcome sound. The heavy thumps of footsteps. She smiled, "I hope that means coffee is coming."

"It is coffee, but I also wanted to make sure you're okay this morning," Royce said in a quiet no-nonsense voice.

She rolled over in surprise, the sudden movement causing the pain to flare up, and she barely held back the cry. But his knowing gaze said he'd seen it.

Hating not being in as good a shape as the rest of them here, she stuffed her feelings of insecurity down deep inside. No room for that out here. Good health was paramount for her—not self-esteem issues. Should she fail in keeping herself safe, then the others would be required to step in and to rescue her. She couldn't withstand the guilt. Not again.

She hadn't been responsible for her friends' deaths, but she felt that she was. And that made all the difference. She couldn't help but feel that she should have known what they were planning to do. That she should have done more to warn them about the snow conditions. Warn them about how their behavior had gotten them into trouble before and to play it safe this time.

And maybe she was just overwhelmed with survivor's guilt. She couldn't sort through her feelings, as she couldn't step back. She needed to get closure on their deaths, so she could analyze it better. She couldn't help but feel they were around every corner on that damn mountain, and, if she would just look a little harder, she would find them.

To bring them home.

Royce squatted and placed the steaming mug of coffee beside her bed. He held his other hand out for her. She frowned at the two reddish-brown pills in his palm. "For your muscles."

Her gaze flew up to his, seeing that knowing look in his eyes. She sighed and plucked them from his hand. She swallowed them quickly. Knowing she wasn't acting gracious, she forced out a "Thank you."

"Look at that? It didn't choke you," he sneered, standing back up.

She closed her eyes. This wasn't her. She was generally a polite, easy-to-get-along-with type of person. But something about Royce just got to her. Or maybe it was because, although she was feeling cruddy, she'd like nothing better than to have him lie down beside her and take her in his arms.

"I am thankful," she muttered.

"Just can't show it, can you?" he mocked. But something else was in his tone. Frustration maybe?

Her gaze flew up to his, and damn if heat didn't flare between them.

Her breath caught in the back of her throat. His gaze was an overwhelming warmth that slid through her, warming up all the cold places inside.

She desperately wanted to tear away her focus, but he held her captive. Then, as if he cut a string, he broke eye contact to stare over the loft railing, down at the group below, a muscle in his jaw throbbing out his aggravation.

She shuddered, hating the lassitude inside her, now that he'd given her that magical invisible stroke of his touch. She didn't know how he did it, or what exactly he'd done, but it always felt like a soothing stroke of his hands—only without physical contact. Then she realized that he was as affected as she was. He was having trouble controlling his breathing. It came out in short raspy breaths.

She hated this. This awkwardness between them. "It can't go anywhere, you know? That's the problem."

He stared at her in astonishment. "What are you talking about?"

She flushed. She'd completely misread the situation. Shit. Shit. Shit. She was a complete idiot. "Nothing," she mumbled, sliding down into her sleeping bag and rolling away from him.

Please just leave, she whispered in her head, as she lay still.

"I'm leaving, for the moment," he snapped, "but we'll talk about this again."

"Nothing to talk about," she whispered, mortified.

"Yes, there is. What you just said is garbage. Nothing's stopping us from having a relationship—but you."

And he turned and stomped down the stairs, leaving her stunned into complete silence.

There wasn't?

ROYCE SHOVED HIS sadness and frustration deep inside, as he rejoined the others, but, from the look on George's face, Royce knew he'd failed there. Whatever. He glanced over at Yvonne. She appeared to be deep in discussion with Geoffrey. She'd been sending out signals all last evening that she wasn't averse to spending the week with someone. For a brief moment he'd contemplated it, more to pay back Stacy for all the pain she'd given him and then realized that it likely wouldn't have hurt Stacy in the first place. But he had no wish to find that out for sure.

It was also a step forward that he could never reverse. Not to mention it was hardly fair to Yvonne. She might want a weeklong fling, but that didn't mean she wanted to be used as a pawn in a broken relationship. Who would? Ashamed for even considering the thought, he'd quickly tossed it from his mind.

"Plans for the day?"

Royce listened, while George laid out the day's runs he wanted to hit. He called out to his sister, "Stacy, are you skiing today?"

"I'm coming with the group but bringing my camera," she called down.

George smiled. "Sounds great. Then get that skinny butt of yours down here and eat. We'll be pulling out in thirty."

ANOTHER PERFECT OPPORTUNITY wasted. George needed to shut the hell up. Royce needed to leave Stacy the hell alone. What was wrong with these people? She was nothing. A whore. That was it.

He stomped out to the boot room part of the cabin, where all the gear was stowed. He needed to get his boots on. Not to mention a whole mess of other gear. At least his new gloves were holding up.

Now if only Stacy would leave her camera behind. That would also make his day.

The others would follow soon enough. If he were lucky, one group would follow his lead, and they could get up the mountain early. That's what they were here for, after all.

Something they'd all do well to remember.

Instead of fawning over the bitch.

Making sure she had her coffee when she woke up.

That she had a group to ski with all the time.

What the hell was this? Babysitting?

They were all so damn predictable. And so was she. Always late, always making the others wait for her. Always quiet, so the others spoke up for her. Jesus. Enough already. He opened the door to the outside and smiled. Clear skies and fresh snow. Absolutely the best conditions.

Now if only they could get there before the damn snow melted and winter was over.

Chapter 15

S TACY MADE IT on time. Barely. She'd dressed, raced down to the bathroom, then inhaled breakfast and coffee, before gearing up for the morning outside. She wasn't skiing today, so she wore winter hiking boots. Should make it easier to walk in the snow. That was about all she could plan for right now. At least her body shifted and moved with grace at this point. A few twinges and squeaky joints but essentially she was doing well.

She packed up her travel mug, sorted through her camera lenses, and quickly grabbed a bigger memory card. Last night she hadn't taken a look at how full her storage was. Big mistake. She didn't dare not have enough while she was out there. The last thing she wanted to do was come back because she couldn't take any more images.

Not that she planned on being out for long. She was making dinner for everyone today, since she had agreed to take a turn. She hadn't brought anything preplanned though, so someone needed to give her the menu for the week, so she didn't accidently use up ingredients needed for other meals.

As she strode out the door, she cast a last look behind her at the cabin. She wasn't the last one out. Royce locked the cabin and placed the key on the top of the doorframe. The lock was more to stop the elements from opening the door than to keep anyone out. They'd all been briefed on the location of the key on the first day. Basic safety.

The early morning light hit the side of the cabin, bounced off the window, and split into a wide band. Colors rippled on the rays. It was beautiful. And it almost blinded her. She lifted her hand to shade her gaze from the glare. Like so much light work, a bit of information was helpful. Too much and it was a killer.

"Let's go." Royce walked past her, reminding her that the rest of the group was striding out strongly in two directions. She had to stop and think. Who was she going with today?

"This way." Royce stepped in behind the first group. "We're going back to the same place, but it's relatively easy terrain. Maybe you can find something to photograph there."

"I'm sure I will," she said in subdued tones. It was the first thing she'd said to him after his earlier comment.

"Are you okay?" he asked.

She nodded but stayed silent. In fact, speech would have been difficult. What did she want to say? At the moment, she had no idea. Did he really want to have a relationship with her? As in a real one or just another weekend fling? God, she wished she knew her own mind.

Or maybe she wished she knew her own heart.

Something she hadn't known for a long time.

They continued to hike in companionable silence, when the group stopped. There were shouts ahead. Royce picked up his pace.

"What's up?" she asked, when they reached the other three.

George said, "One of the other group fell into a ravine of some kind."

Immediately their group headed in the direction of the other group. With the sunny day and no cloud cover, the cell phone reception was strong and clear. Good thing. George continued to talk to Mark, as they moved across the plateau to where the second group currently stood.

They'd been heading to a different run that day. No one had been along that path in days. Crossing as they were now was hard going. The leader had to break a path in the deep snow. Stacy was smart enough to stay in the middle of the pack. Of course, Royce pulled up last place to ensure there were no stragglers.

"Was anyone hurt?" Stacy asked.

"No. Not at all. He slid down more than anything."

She nodded. "Good."

George's phone rang again. "Apparently the fault line goes a fair bit in our direction, so approach carefully," George said, after he put away his phone.

He pulled out the long stick he'd found earlier and stabbed the ground with each step. The others held back and waited. In deep snow, anything could be waiting below. Most of this area was popular with skiers and climbers from all over the world, but, like everyone, her group wanted to play where others hadn't gone before. *Figures.* Still, even the popular runs ran into trouble sometimes.

Snow that appeared to be more solid than it was often hid a small gulley.

Up ahead, more shouts could be heard. With the others in front,

Stacy couldn't see who was shouting.

Royce said, "That's them. We're almost there."

Stacy had her camera around her neck. She wanted to break rank and take pictures as they approached but wasn't sure where she was in relation to the fault line they were talking about. So she stayed in place.

George changed direction, stepping into the trail their other group had already made. The walking got a little bit easier yet again.

And suddenly she could see them. Her group spread out, so she could step closer. Sure enough, a bit of the ground had given way, and Stevie appeared to have slid, rather than falling down. He waved up at her. "Hey, Stacy. Glad you came to see."

She laughed. "I'm just wondering why you're still there. With all the help around, I'd have thought you'd be back up on top already."

"Ha. I actually tried to climb up by myself, but the bank keeps coming down."

"Of course." They always did. She stepped back and pulled out her camera. Within seconds, she had Stevie's predicament captured for posterity. Then she took another and another. When Stevie understood what she was doing, he called out a mocking protest. The others all laughed. Stacy kept clicking, as they worked to get Stevie up from the fifteen-foot-deep hole. She made sure to document where it started and stopped, if for no other reason than to mark it on the maps for other people.

A few more depressions were on one side. She carefully followed the light, so she could see the full scope of the depression, faint until she saw it in the shadows, and where it ended. "It stops here," she called out.

"Which means that it likely goes underground for another twenty plus yards. Such is the way of faults," Royce said, as he walked toward her, so he could see the magnitude of the fault line himself. She watched the narrow edge in his gaze, as he studied the ground. She couldn't resist. She pulled out her camera. The look of intensity on his face, the knowledge in his eyes. He knew his stuff. And that sense of authority was damn sexy.

And she sure as hell needed to stop thinking like that.

She stepped back again.

And felt the snow give way.

She cried out in surprise.

And fell.

GEORGE HEARD STACY call out. He spun around to see her disappear from sight. "Stacy!"

The others raced toward her.

Royce held out his arms. "Wait. We don't know how far the fault goes."

George took a cautious step forward. "Stacy, are you okay?"

"Yeah, I am."

The sound of her voice hit Royce so hard that he had to stop his headlong plunge and close his eyes. *Oh thank God*. All business now, he called out, "Are you hurt?"

"No, I'm fine," she called back. "Just pissed at myself."

"No need to be," he called down to her, carefully walking forward and poking the ground with long sticks, making sure it was solid enough to stand on. They stepped forward as a wall and the poking continued. They'd almost reached her when the wall of snow caved in front of them.

And there she was. With the bank down and the crevasse widened, it was easy to see her now. She stood on her own two feet—staring up at them. She studied the space and turned to the left. The group was walking down the path and poking into the ground to make sure it was solid, but they had seemingly opened up the crevasse as far as they could see. They had quickly opened up the space between Stevie and Stacy. Stacy walked toward Stevie with every new step that opened up until she could see him.

She laughed and ran over to give him a big hug. He picked her up and twirled her around, only the ground was full of snow and ice chunks, and they both fell down to the amusement of everyone watching.

It took another twenty minutes before the two of them were standing on solid ground. The group had continued to collapse the snow along the fault line, so it would be visible to others.

"Well now, that was a fun trip, but let's move on," Stevie said.

"Nope. We're not going anywhere," George called out. "Royce, come here, please."

Royce walked closer. "What's up?"

George glanced behind at the others, slowly making their way over. In a low voice, he said, "This." He pointed into the crevasse.

To the boot attached to a man's leg, partially buried under the fresh snow.

ROYCE STARED AT the cowboy boot. "What the hell?"

He skidded down the loose snow and managed to stay on his feet. He walked over and scooped the snow off the body. The way the snow had fallen had buried the top half of the body. "George, you start making the calls."

"Yep, on it."

Royce heard the others talking up top and the sounds of several other people making their way down the slope toward him. He hoped it wasn't Stacy. She had had enough death in her world.

The snow kept sliding down the slope and constantly filled in the space he had cleared. He glared at the snow bank. There really was no help for it. He bent and grabbed the man's ankle and tugged. And it didn't move. Shit.

"I'm here. Hang on," Stevie said. He approached with a tiny shovel. With the two of them, they made short work of spreading the loose snow around the side and out of their way. Before he realized it, they had the bulk of the snow off the man. And he used the word *man* loosely, as the head and face were still buried. Stevie dropped his shovel beside the body and fell to his knees, then carefully brushed the rest off the man's face.

Royce studied the solid marble-looking body and had to wonder. How long had it been here? That didn't change the fact that the dead man didn't look in any way like a winter sports enthusiast. Neither was he dressed for cold weather.

But, if he wasn't either of the missing men he knew about, who was he? Why the hell was he out here in the middle of nowhere?

"I'm here," Stacy said, from behind. "Let me see."

Chapter 16

ROYCE STOOD WITH his hand out, saying, "You shouldn't see this."

Stacy choked back a laugh. "Really? And why is that?"

He groaned and smacked his forehead. "Somehow, for one moment there, I completely forgot who and what you were."

"I didn't," Stevie said, with a grin. He motioned his hand toward the body. "After you."

She rolled her eyes and walked closer to the unexpected gravesite, as others made the necessary phone calls. She'd seen more death than most, but this hadn't been on her plans for the day. Still, death was never on one's plans.

Royce and Stevie had started cutting stairs in a solid slope behind her. It was a faster and more effective answer than using ropes and hauling the dead weight up that way.

Squatting beside the dead man, she studied his features. She didn't recognize him. Thankfully. Young, between his late twenties and late thirties most likely. She studied his posture, the angle of his body, the look on his face. She stood and walked around the young man. Only silence came from the others, as they watched her work.

She hadn't seen too many who came in from a deep freeze like this. The temperatures always played havoc in looking at time of death. She motioned to Stevie to roll over the body. No blood was anywhere. No visible injuries. She checked his fingernails and the tips of his fingers. His eyes. Death had been fast.

Then she pulled up his sleeve as far as the stiff material would go and found raw marks on the guy's wrist. She quickly checked his other wrist. Both showed signs of having been restrained. No blood showed, no broken skin, but the angry redness spoke volumes.

She never said anything to the others. A quick search of his pockets turned up no ID. Curious and curiouser.

"Another climber, do you think?" George asked. "There are a few missing."

"Potentially." She frowned. "But, considering he's not deep enough for the fall to have killed him, no blood shows from an injury, and he was within walking distance to the cabin—why?"

"Drunk?" asked George. "Going for a walk often makes sense at the worst times after a few drinks."

"True enough." She stood back and stared at the man's boots— cowboy boots. "He's certainly not dressed for the weather. Even his footwear is more suitable for a stroll than a winter hike."

She glanced off in the distance, trying to mentally place the road, wondering if he'd had a car accident and had wandered off, looking for assistance. If he'd been in shock, he could easily have gotten lost and disoriented. But this area wasn't well-known, and those who frequented it were better prepared as to what to expect. And where would his vehicle be, if he'd driven here? The police would have reports on abandoned vehicles in the area, but it often took days for such vehicles to be reported in a resort like this—particularly if he'd gone off the road.

She sat back on her haunches, puzzled. For all intents and purposes, at first glance, it appeared as if he had succumbed to the elements. The real question was, what was he doing out here in the first place?

And how did the marks on his wrists relate?

She checked her watch. "The police will still be an hour or two, I suspect."

"Head back to the cabin, and we'll stay here and keep an eye on him," George told her.

She shook her head. "No, I'll stay." She'd seen worse. Had waited in worse conditions. The body was her responsibility now. She would not leave.

The group split up, half choosing to carry on and to get in a few runs, whereas the rest of the group, with the exception of Stevie, headed back to the cabin to wait for the coroner's office.

Stevie pulled his thermos from his pack and offered her a cup.

"Thanks," she said, with a smile.

"I'm surprised everyone left," Stevie said, with a grin. "Royce has become your watchdog. Why don't you give the poor guy a break and go out with the man?"

She let out a startled laugh. "I don't think you're reading the situation correctly," she said, shaking her head.

"I don't think you're seeing the situation for what it is. He's always watching you. As you climb the stairs for the night. As you come down in the morning. As you leave the room." Stevie smirked. "He's got it bad."

"You're exaggerating," she said comfortably, knowing she was being teased.

He hooted. "Like hell I am."

"Really?" She studied him curiously. "He's not that bad surely?"

"Hell yes, he is. And I tell you, Geoffrey does the same. Maybe a little less often."

"Now I know you're having me on."

He shook his head. "No, I'm not. I'm warning you. Those two might come to blows over you."

The seriousness of his tone had her staring open-mouthed at him. "No way." She shook it off and took a sip of the coffee. Standing over a dead body and listening to Stevie's wild talk, she would take comfort where she could.

"Are you okay for a moment here?" Stevie asked. "I saw another depression a little farther over. I just want to make sure it's solid."

"Go for it." She motioned to the stairs. "I'll stand on top and watch, so I can make sure you're safe too."

He laughed. "You know me. I'm always good."

"True enough. But life happens to everyone."

"You're a worrywart now. You didn't use to be. You used to love life. Laugh at life."

"I did." She knew that. "But, after losing our friends, and then getting so sick …" She let her voice trail off.

"I know, but as you just said," Stevie added, almost running up the stairs behind her, "life happens. So why worry?"

"That seems to be the problem now," she muttered. "I can't stop worrying."

"No point in worrying about what you can't control." He grabbed his stick and headed to the other side.

"And the stuff I can control?" she called after him. "What about that?"

"You have to let life happen."

"Maybe," she said in a low voice, "but that doesn't mean I have to like the results."

BY THE TIME the body was removed, questions answered, and photos taken, Stacy had to decide whether to head back to the waterfall or go back to the cabin. She cast a wary eye at the cloudy skies. "Back to the cabin for me."

"Good." Royce, who'd returned with fresh coffee just ahead of the cops, turned to Stevie. "What about you?"

"I'll meet up with the other group and see if I can get in a couple runs."

Stacy started to walk back to the cabin. "Royce, go with Stevie. No way I can get lost now." There was almost a highway back to the cabin. Snowmobiles had taken the body out on a rescue sled. She could still hear the engines droning their way down to the waiting ambulance.

"I still don't think you should go alone," Royce said, coming up behind her. He reached out and grabbed her shoulder to stop her. "Stacy."

"Look. Stevie is likely to run into more trouble than I will. I'm following tracks the whole way back. I'm fine."

He watched her stride away, her body relaxed and moving easily.

Stevie stepped closer beside him. "I'm also fine. You go on with her."

"Ha," Royce said. "She's right. The track to the cabin is easy to follow. Finding the group of boarders for you to join them is a whole different story."

"Nah. I know the runs they're on, and Geoffrey just sent me the GPS coordinates." Stevie smacked him on the shoulder. "I'm good. Go on after her. You know you want to."

At that last part, Royce shot him a dark look, which rolled off Stevie's back.

"Hey, I'm just saying ..."

"Saying what?"

"Saying you're wearing your heart on your sleeve for the world to see."

"Damn it." That was the last thing he wanted to hear. His misery should be private.

"Don't worry about it."

Except George already knew. That meant Kathleen knew. So who else?

He started to turn away, when Stevie added, "Of course, with the competition, I'd watch your back."

Royce stopped and stared at him. "What competition?"

Stevie tossed his pack on his shoulders and headed in the direction of the group. "Geoffrey. That guy is mad about Stacy."

"What?"

"Yeah," Stevie called back. "He watches her almost as much as you do."

NOT BLOODY LIKELY. No one watched her as much as Royce did. Of course he'd kept it from everyone else. That was part of the game. They were all so damn stupid. Simple. They couldn't see the viper in their midst. He laughed out loud, uncaring if they heard him. He'd been doing this for a while now. He was good at it. The others weren't stupid. They were actually very smart. It was just that he was so good that he made them look like fools.

Stacy was the smartest of the lot. Only she'd not been around for a long time, so she would have missed the subtle nuances of the group dynamics over the last few years. It would be interesting if he could fool her as easily as he had the others.

Obviously he still could. But would her multiple degrees make any difference when the chips were down?

He doubted it.

Chapter 17

BACK AT THE cabin, the atmosphere was slightly louder than normal, as those who had elected to return hashed over the identity of the man. And why'd he'd be there of all places.

Stacy knew that too often people did a lot of stupid things for even stupider reasons. There wasn't much that humans did that could surprise her anymore. Of course what they did to each other was often worse.

As she entered, leaving her gear and outer clothing in the boot room, an awkward silence followed, as if they'd been caught gossiping. She smiled at everyone. "Stevie and Royce have gone to meet up with the other group."

Silence.

"I didn't think he'd leave her alone," muttered Yvonne.

Stacy stiffened slightly, pretending to not hear. What she'd heard just confirmed Stevie's earlier words. So it was more than just Stevie who had noticed.

"The coffeepot is full, if you're looking for hot coffee," Kathleen said quietly.

"Thanks." Stacy filled the teakettle and put it on the stove too. She actually would love a mocha but wasn't sure if anyone had brought hot chocolate. She certainly hadn't thought that far ahead.

She realized as she'd stared at the kitchen that she'd planned on doing dinner. "Do we have a menu planned for the week?" she asked.

"Sure do. Today is pasta."

Another awkward silence passed. "And your name was penciled in beside it," Kathleen added.

"If that's okay?" someone else asked awkwardly.

Stacy wondered at the constant treading on eggshells around her. Was she really considered so delicate that she might break down at being asked to make pasta? Really? She knew her name was there. She'd put it there. "I volunteered for tonight," she said lightly.

And damn if there wasn't a perceptible softening of the air. Weird.

She studied the ingredients. "I do wonder about what I have to work with though. I don't want to use up any ingredients that were planned for other meals."

"No worries there," Kathleen said. "We have this sheet here." And she wandered over to Stacy, paper in hand. "It shows what we bought for each meal."

"Oh good. That will certainly make it easier."

"There's no leftover chili from yesterday, I presume," she asked, glancing around the table. "I could use a bite to eat."

There were several guilty looks.

She laughed. "No worries. I'll make a sandwich."

That was one thing she knew they had plenty of. George often scarfed them down as snacks. Bread was a very important food item for her brother. She found a loaf of French bread and decided that would be garlic bread for the spaghetti. Then she started in on the onions and garlic. She was tired, but not wanting to sit with the others or to lie down, she chose instead to make the sauce while she still had the energy.

She'd forgotten how the cold seeped into her bones and zapped away her energy. She'd been out there, standing around and waiting for hours. The others had been better off, as they had gone snowboarding, and the other half had come back into the heat. Grabbing a couple slices of ham and cheese, she made a simple sandwich to eat, as she worked on the sauce. With any luck, it wouldn't take too long, and she might catch a nap before the others came in.

As she worked, she wondered at the lowered voices. Were they trying to have a secret conversation? And, if so, why?

She hated it, but she couldn't help listening in.

"You know he's been crazy about her forever."

"What happened between them?"

"The fact that there was no 'them.'" And the snickers started.

Stacy froze, her head down. Really? Had everyone always known? Although they didn't appear to know about the weekend she'd spent with Royce. Thank heavens. But that he'd been crazy about her? Had she had her head so buried in the sand for these last few years that she had no clue? She tried to think back to what their relationship was like before that weekend. It had been casual. Teasing. She'd never considered him relationship material.

He was a playboy. He made a great toy to play with for a weekend, and that was it.

That he'd been anything but that during their weekend together made no sense.

She'd shoved that discrepancy to the far corners of her mind for a long time. But now the issue rose to consume her thoughts again.

Had Royce cared more than she'd suspected? But if he had—for how long? Had he been just hiding his feelings for her all along? No, surely not. She remembered the long string of women he'd flaunted through those years. He'd been enjoying every moment. That was one reason she'd never taken that walk on the wild side. Then, when she did, he'd been so caring and compassionate; it had been the opposite of what she'd expected. And maybe that's what had thrown her off yet again. As he wasn't the man she'd expected to find in her bed.

But she'd needed him. As she'd never needed anyone before.

What she couldn't understand—even today—was why had she chosen him?

And why had he accepted?

ROYCE STAYED AWAY from the cabin, happy to spend a couple hours on the mountain. He'd chosen to go with Stevie after all. Especially after realizing that following Stacy to the cabin would only confirm everyone's suspicions.

It had been the right decision. He texted George to say they were on the way back. As he confirmed the message was sent, he smiled. At least something was working today.

Stevie stepped up beside him. "Hey, see? That was worth it, wasn't it?"

"It was. Nice to get up there, even if only for a short time."

"We did get a couple hours, but, of course, it went by too damn quick." His stomach grumbled. "And now I feel like I have to eat." He held up his hand, pulled off his glove, and tried to hold it steady.

"Low blood sugar?"

Stevie sighed. "It's getting worse every year."

"And you're looking after it carefully, right?"

Stevie laughed, pulling an energy bar from his pocket. "Absolutely." He held up the bar and took a big bite.

Royce eyed it. "Don't have a second one, do you?"

Stevie drove his empty hand into his pocket and pulled out a second bar. Royce accepted it, with a big smile. He ripped open the package and took a big bite. "Pasta for dinner."

"Great," Stevie said. "I won't have any problem eating my share." He waited a beat, then added. "And yours."

"Ha. I'll be eating mine. I do hope we brought enough food. I'm starved."

"George arranged the food, so hopefully that's not an issue." But he did look a little worried. Stevie was tall and scrawny, with whipcord strength, and performed all sports like the athlete he was. He could climb the most difficult of all climbs like a monkey. He had a great sense of humor and loved women, as Royce used to love women, only Stevie didn't have quite so many options as Royce.

Then Royce had tired of it. Of them. He'd gotten in too deep emotionally over Stacy many years ago and had gone a little crazy for a while, trying to get over her. She'd been too young. She'd been George's little sister.

She hadn't been for him.

He'd bedded every willing woman he could find. The more he did, the more he loathed himself. And the more he hated himself and thought he was not worth Stacy's time, the more he fell into the same damaging cycle, proving his point over and over again. The women rolled through and blurred his mind, as the names and places mixed with the never-ending video of faces.

He looked back on that stage of his life and cringed. He wasn't proud of it. In fact, he was pretty damn ashamed. Still, during those years, Stacy hadn't seemed to give a damn what he did. Although she'd been friendly, she'd never shown any interest in him. In fact, she'd ignored him.

When she'd come to him without warning, he'd figured he'd found heaven. Instead he'd learned what purgatory was. He'd been trying to find his way back home ever since.

In the days, weeks, months afterward, he'd done a lot of self-examination and had seen his life through her eyes, and he'd been ashamed all over again. So he'd straightened up and had tried hard to show her his different side. And she never noticed.

It damn-near broke him.

She was so close and yet so damn far away.

He didn't know how to cross the impasse. He knew it was there. He knew it needed to be crossed. He also knew that Stacy wouldn't even acknowledge that it ever existed.

And, if she didn't know it was there, she wouldn't know to cross it. And he desperately needed her to take those steps across the bridge.

He would be waiting for her at the end of that bridge. Hell, he'd hold her hand and help her across that bridge, if she'd just take the first step.

He needed her to take that step. And to save him.

WOW, NOW THINGS were getting interesting. He'd wanted to laugh when he'd seen the body. Like really? The guy never made it anywhere. Too bad. He would have liked to tell the asshole that his sneaky escape was useless. And that he'd almost made it out alive. But almost *didn't count. The dead guy never knew how close he'd made it to surviving.*

Stupid idiot. Look at the way he was dressed. Besides, it wasn't his fault the guy had taken off at a dead run into the storm. Like, what an idiot.

Still, he almost made it, so he'd award him a few brownie points for that. After all, the guy was dead. He could afford to be generous.

Chapter 18

STACY WOKE IN the middle of the night, chilled, her heart racing in a panic, her nightmare still clinging like wet cobwebs to her brain. She shuddered at the clamminess of her skin. What was that all about? She rarely got nightmares. And didn't appreciate the odd occurrence. There wasn't a sound in the cabin but for the odd crackle of the fire in the big heater. She snuggled lower in the bed, hating the darkness. She wondered if finding the body today had set off her nightmare. Anyone normally would get a nightmare from something like that. But she wasn't just anyone. Bodies were her business.

But something was beyond odd about this one. Her mind had already cataloged the case, even though she wouldn't be the one working on him. She had an urge to send a text message to the coroner, asking about drug tests on the victim. Although they wouldn't be back fast enough to satisfy her.

There was also no guarantee the case would be worked on anytime soon. If the local office was as overworked as Stacy's, the coroner would be overwhelmed. And, not to forget, she wasn't even in her own country.

She closed her eyes, determined to get some more sleep. She needed it. She was feeling the cold more than she had expected. Her body should be snapping back faster than this. That it wasn't made her look for the stressors inhibiting her healing.

Royce was at the top of that list. Then there was the poor man they'd found today. Too many suspicious elements were in that case. Poorly dressed for the weather, missing ID. No sign of where or how he'd gotten there. It could have been a body dump, but why there and when? The police had confirmed no abandoned vehicles reported in the last month. It could be spring before his vehicle was found, after all the snow had melted away.

Had someone else found him and stripped the wallet from the man's pockets?

People did the damnedest things. Especially when stressed. So the man could have quite easily removed everything from his own pockets. As soon as hypothermia set in, confusion was the rule. Victims lost their way, and what seemed to make sense at the time made no sense under normal circumstances.

Nothing was normal about his situation. If there'd been a car close by, then maybe it would make sense, but no roads were anywhere near there, except the one to the cabin.

She yawned.

And that's when she heard it.

A door opening. She grabbed her cell phone and checked the time. It was two in the morning. Who the hell was going outside?

Or were they coming in?

If so, why?

She peered over the edge carefully. Maybe it was monkey business. She could see Yvonne sleeping beside Royce. She slept in her own bedroll but close enough for him to reach out and touch her, if need be.

The person who'd been outside had on a heavy pullover with the hood pulled up. She tried to look outside, but the darkness was absolute. There was a shine from outside due to the snow on the ground, but she had no way of knowing if it was snowing. But it would be cold regardless. She would have likely pulled her hoodie up over her ears too. She shifted cautiously to see his head turning away from her. Shit. Had he seen her? She wasn't doing anything wrong, but it seemed that she was spying, and she didn't want anyone to think that.

Only then did she hear the heavy rasping breath below her. Waiting.

She felt the first stirrings of fear. And she realized that, for all her casual attitude about choosing the warmest place in the house, she'd also chosen the one where she was alone. The most unprotected. And worse, she was trapped here. If someone came up the stairs, she had no place to go to escape. She could scream, but what if they came up while she was asleep?

She'd never know until it was too late.

ROYCE JERKED AWAKE. Shocked into awareness, he sat up and studied the quiet room. Yvonne slept in the bedroll beside him. She was a quiet sleeper, no snoring or restless shifting in the night. Made for an easy bedfellow. At least he thought it was her. With the covers pulled over her head, who could tell? And they'd all been plenty drunk last night, so it could be anyone. These trips were like that.

As he sat in the dark, the chill worked its way into his bones. He wasn't a light sleeper normally, but he'd had a hard time getting to sleep these last few nights, so he had several drinks last night, hoping it would help.

Now a sense of something wrong washed over him. As if he'd missed something important.

There was an odd noise in the main part of the cabin, but it was hard to decipher over the heavy winds beating against the cabin walls. As he lay back down, his ears intent, his mind wondered why it mattered. So what if he'd heard something? People got up in the night all the time. He would often get up to go to the washroom, get a drink, and walk around because he couldn't sleep.

No biggie.

Then he realized it had been the outside door he'd heard. That latch made a loud heavy *thunk* when it shut securely. Someone had gone outside. He sat up again slowly. Walking around outside in the middle of the storm was an easy way to get lost. The group had a general rule of no smoking indoors, so maybe someone had gone out for a smoke. He went through the list of people here, trying to figure out who might have gone out and whether he had to worry about them. He hoped not.

But he never heard the door open again. He waited. And waited. Then he had to consider that what he'd heard was the person coming back in. No way to know until everyone got up in the morning. Determined to put it out of his mind, he rolled over and tried to go back to sleep.

HE LOVED THE night. It was his time. So was winter. The darkness and cold were a perfect marriage for him. He never felt the chill the way other people did, and this resort was his playground—and hunting ground. Maybe he was more reptile than human. He'd long ago understood his nature. Had been a problem accepting it. But after that? ... Well, it was who he was. And what he was—it was pretty damn unique. He'd always wanted to be different.

Interesting that he was that different.

He sat comfortably in the back corner of the cabin. Out of sight of everyone and under the loft.

Where she was.

He watched as Royce slept. He'd been awake earlier but had fallen back into the deep sleep too much alcohol created.

It was great for a temporary buzz, just not so good if you needed to do something—or wanted to do something. But for him, watching the others imbibe too much made for great entertainment. He learned a lot from watching them. Who they really were on the inside. Who they chose to cuddle up with for the night.

It amused him. People were fake. Then so was he, and that just proved his statement. Picking through the layers to find the person inside made for a great hobby. It also allowed him to assess them as potential subjects.

Most failed his examination.

A few excelled, but, for this trip, one person was perfect. He knew her name was up for a special piece already—even if it wasn't his piece—but he wouldn't let her stay as part of that homage. In fact, it might be time to take care of his friend too. He pretended to be an artist for his buddy's sake, but he had no doubts about what he really was. And why he did what he did.

Still, knowing that Stacy was here and available for the taking was something he couldn't let go of. Although, in a way, his friend had a prior claim. She would complete his trio. He'd wanted to finish that one for a long time. So maybe he'd let her be part of that exhibit for a little while. Then move her to his.

He could make a move tonight. Or maybe wait until the end of the week. They were all a little more on edge, after finding Brian today. He wanted to laugh out loud at that one. Talk about perfect timing.

And he hadn't even planned it.

Chapter 19

SPIRITS WERE HIGH the next morning. To Stacy's ear, it was almost artificially high. They'd brushed up against death again yesterday. It was sad and difficult, but everyone knew the risks of their fun-filled sport. And, of course, everyone pushed off the risks, until it was in their face again. Last night they'd had a chance to deal with the gloominess and the sadness, but, after a good night's sleep, everyone looked more rested. Or at least they were trying to look that way.

It didn't appear to have affected her coworkers' moods. Then they had an edge, as they were in a line of work to hers. There was a reverence for life among the three of them. And a very healthy respect for death.

At a distance.

But, over the years, as she had lost various family members and then her two best friends, death then became so upfront and personal. She'd had no idea how to deal with the growing accumulation of her personal losses.

The others had experienced this too. Kathleen had lost a boy-friend to a car accident years ago. George had lost a few friends in a hang gliding accident. He'd grieved for months, then had dealt with it per his usual aplomb. For Stacy, she'd cared so much—or had carried so much guilt—that the loss of her two best friends had stopped much of her ability to function. And losing Janice and Francine seemed to remind Stacy that the bodies on her lab table had grieving family and friends too. That all had made every new one in the morgue even more difficult. Hence, her damn slow-ass recovery.

Royce stepped in front of her, with a big plate of eggs and toast.

"Hey, where did you get that?"

He nodded to the kitchen, his mouth chewing through a large bite of sausage.

"Damn." She really didn't want to miss another meal. She couldn't believe how hungry she was today.

"Are you coming skiing with us?" George asked.

"I'm bringing my camera and will do a little skiing, but I saw something the other day, and I want to see if I can find it again."

He nodded. "We're going in two groups again."

"I'll be in the last one then," she said. "I need food. As I'll be taking pictures, I don't need to race." Skiers and snowboarders alike were notorious for wanting to be the first ones on runs.

"The first group is leaving soon."

"I'll meet up with you in a couple hours," she said, as she filled her plate.

"That works."

There was a flurry of activity, as the first group grabbed their gear. She snuck around behind the stove and headed to an empty seat beside the fire. The first bite was so good that she almost moaned. "Oh, wow, not sure who made breakfast, but these eggs are lovely."

"Royce did."

"Nice job, Royce."

She glanced up to find him walking out to the boot room. Maybe he hadn't heard her. As the door slammed shut, she figured he definitely had. "What's his problem?" she muttered to no one in particular.

Stevie just laughed at her.

She forked up another bite and ignored the rest of them. She hadn't slept well. Maybe that was the cause of her appetite. Or maybe she was just starting to heal. She certainly felt better. Stronger.

"Hey, did you leave anything for the rest of us?" Stevie asked, sitting down beside her.

She shook her head. "Hope not. If I did, it was a mistake."

"Wow, aren't you nice."

She popped a big bite of sausage into her mouth and stood up. "I'm about to get seconds. Did you get any?"

He held up a cup of coffee. "I'll drink this first."

"Your loss."

"Whoa, you weren't kidding about extras, were you? *Geesh*." He bounded to his feet and raced around, until he was ahead of her. He was busy scooping up eggs, when she snagged a piece of toast and returned with a cup of coffee. He sat down beside her. "Did you ever notice the effect of death on the others?" He said it in a low voice, as several other people were still getting dressed in their outerwear.

She nodded. "Just because we're used to it doesn't mean anyone else is."

"It's as if their fear of mortality kicks in. Really weird."

"Everyone likes to think we're invincible. Instead we're an organic system that is way too delicate."

"Soft-shelled with no defense system against Mother Nature," he mumbled around his food. "Such easy prey."

The way he said that last bit had her studying his face with a sharp look. He was right. But it sounded as if a predator looking for easy prey was a great game. Something it wasn't.

"That's a horrible thing to say," Yvonne said, seated on the couch across from them. "I had no idea you considered humans so inferior."

"Not inferior. We have brains, and we can think. Reason. Act. Rationalized action. That's what saved us from extinction," he said.

Yvonne snorted. "Doesn't sound like what you were saying before."

"What?" he asked in an injured tone. "I didn't mean it in a bad way." He caught Stacy's gaze and rolled his eyes. In a low tone, he said, "See what I mean? Add a dead body and everyone has an issue with life and death."

She laughed. "Of course. It just reminds us that we can't escape death."

"Yep, today or tomorrow. Our time will come." In a dark, mocking voice, he added, "The question is, will we die by our own hand, old age, or will someone else help us along the way?"

"GEORGE," ROYCE CALLED out quietly to his friend, walking behind him. "Did you hear anyone leave the cabin in the night?

"Nope." George walked up beside Royce. "What time are we talking?"

"Between two and three."

George shook his head. "I was sound asleep. I had trouble going to sleep, but, once I made it there, I never woke up until this morning."

"I wish. I woke to something weird. Thought I heard someone walking around but couldn't see anyone. I realized it was the outside door I'd heard, at least I thought I'd heard, but again I never could confirm that."

"I wouldn't worry about it. Chances are it was the wind slamming the door closed. You know that outside door is always being left ajar." George shifted his pack to his other shoulder. "Besides, so what if someone was walking about? We've both done that many times ourselves."

"True. I don't know why it bugged me but it did. It seemed ..." Royce thought about it, adding with a foolish grin, "Maybe sinister."

He expected George's laughter, but instead George nodded and said, "I can see that. I thought I heard someone the first night we were here. I didn't understand it at all. Why go out during the night?"

Royce stared at him. "Really? Two of three nights? That's odd."

"Unless someone is going out to have a smoke."

"Then they are keeping that habit a secret, as I don't know anyone here who smokes."

George plodded along, sinking into the deep snow with each step, both working harder than they had to, as the path was really only wide enough for one.

"I'm surprised you haven't mentioned the dead guy we found," George said in a low voice.

"I would have, but someone's always around." Royce glanced around to see Kathleen in a deep conversation with Yvonne over the latest boards. "I'm trying to figure out how the guy got out here."

"I know. If we'd seen any vehicles, it would make more sense. There was a mention of it on the news this morning, but they are withholding the guy's name at this time and haven't released much in the way of details." George glanced back at his girlfriend. "I wish it hadn't happened on this trip. I wanted to get Stacy away from death."

"I hear you. Unfortunately she's a magnet for death."

"Not intentionally."

"She's coming out today, isn't she?" Royce asked, hating that sense of wrongness he'd woken up with and hadn't been able to shake.

"Yes, why?" George asked.

"No reason." He paused, thought about it, then added, "Except something feels off."

"Yeah, glad you said that. I feel the same way." He waved to Kathleen. "Let's keep an especially close eye on the women."

"Definitely. I really don't want this vacation to involve a death again."

George, already walking back to Kathleen, turned, and, with a somber voice, said, "It already does, remember?"

Chapter 20

OUT IN THE sunshine, there was lots of laughter and teasing. Ten minutes into the trip, Stacy stopped, thinking she might have left her camera back in the cabin. She put her pack down and dug through it. After a frantic moment, she found it in the side pocket. "Well, thank heavens for that."

She stood back up again and realized that her group was slightly ahead. She took several pictures of them, loving the casualness of the scene. Friends walking, talking, laughing. Looking forward to the day ahead. She glanced around, as she settled her pack on her shoulders. The place was pristine white. It was beautiful. Clean. So innocent looking. Except for the treachery always underneath.

Speaking of which, … she lifted her camera again. *Click. Click.* Phenomenal icicles hung off the trees to the left. They were huge. And would give someone a severe blow if they came down on top of their head.

She had no illusions when it came to snow and ice conditions. They were here snowboarding and skiing, but there were no guides. No safety guardrails. They were all past that level. They had all helicopter skied and had done other equally demanding sports. They were all fit.

But shit happened.

"Stacy? Come on."

Damn, she'd gotten lost in her camera again.

She watched the group ahead of her stop and point out a snowcat slowly heading down the mountain. She'd heard the resort was opening up new runs on this side of the mountain but hadn't thought to see the equipment actually working on it right now. From that long ski run, they could ski into the village below and hook up with other runs. And that was a damn good idea. Except the snowcat was going down the hill and not up. So not the way she wanted to go.

In fact, right now she wasn't sure she wanted to go anywhere. She waved the other group off to go on ahead; then she found a spot to sit in the sun. She hated to admit it, but she was tired. Maybe this was as far as she would go today. She needed to tell the group her plans, so they wouldn't worry.

Just then her phone rang, Royce wanting to know where she was. Apparently the second group had said she wasn't with them. She turned to study the direction the other group had gone, and, sure enough, they were out of sight already.

She texted back, telling him exactly where she was and that she was in view of the cabin.

Shit.

She laughed at that succinct answer. He had such a mastery of words. **I'm fine. I'll just take a few pictures. Nothing wrong with me sitting here and enjoying life.**

Not alone.

Sigh. **Why not?**

Because I don't like what's going on.

She glanced back at the text to reread it several times. Cautiously she responded, **What is going on?**

There was such a long silence that she wondered if he'd planned on answering her. Then it came back.

I'm afraid that man was murdered.

ROYCE STARED DOWN at his phone, wondering if he should have sent that text. Still, he wanted her to stay safe. The one day that George wanted to keep an extra eye on the women, and Stacy chose this day to be on her own. Like really? Royce was already on the other side of the second mountain. He'd be almost an hour getting back to her.

I'm fine. I'll be careful.

That was so not his point. He loved that she didn't address his comment. Did that mean she agreed? Had considered it? Or thought he was making a big deal out of nothing? And maybe he was, but something was not right.

He carved left and then right. These runs were empty, as they so often were at this time of morning. They weren't the easiest to access and commanded skill to do well. George and Kathleen were closer to town. They'd decided to have lunch at the pub. Royce would have loved to join them but got the impression that they were looking for a few moments of private time.

He wished. Then he brightened. If Stacy was alone, he could get some private time with her. Hell, he could be there in less than an hour. He had to hit the bottom of the run, catch the lift going up the opposite side, come down the seven-mile run, and grab the trail leading to the cabin. He dropped lower and picked up speed.

At the bottom was a coffee shop. He bought two cups and hopped on the first lift up. With his hands full, he couldn't text her that he was coming. And boarding the lift with two hot cups was not the smartest move on his part. He could only hope that the coffee would still be hot by the time he reached her. It was tricky taking the corners he needed to take. A part of him was hoping she had her video camera running as he came around. What a classy shot that would make. He finally hit the homestretch and cut to the right hard and slowed. Ha, he made it.

He straightened up and searched the trees for her. Someone was up ahead on the left. He called out, "Stacy? You there?"

Nothing. He searched the trees and thought he saw someone moving past another pocket of greenery. A red stripe on the jacket. Stacy didn't have any red on hers. At least none that he remembered.

He came to a stop and studied the furtive figure. His hackles rose. Nothing special was wrong. Just nothing spectacularly right. People could be here for any number of reasons, but none good that he could think of. The area was only accessible if the person knew the area well. And that he was doubtful of.

It was off the beaten path.

"Stacy?" He called her name louder again and again. No answer. He slid forward another few feet, his gaze hard. His ears were tuned and his gaze intent on the area he'd last seen that person.

No sign of him.

Anywhere.

Worse, no sign of Stacy either.

Damn it.

Where was she?

IDIOT. SHOW OFF. Lovestruck fool. Did Royce really think it would be that easy? To see him? To understand he was there? To understand what he was doing? So not.

He wouldn't be stupid here—unlike Royce, who held two cold cups of coffee in his hands, searching the woods. Stacy wasn't here. At least not right here.

He thought she had been. He'd tracked her down to this area, but, when he finally picked out the perfect spot to watch her, she was gone. He kinda liked that. He had no problem with a game of hide-and-seek. Predator and prey. Winner and loser.

The outcome was inevitable.

This was fun but not challenging. It was better to drag it out. See the normal reactions change to that inner suspicion of needing to look over her shoulder—of not being sure why but unable to stop checking.

Because, of course, her instincts were there, just not as finely tuned as her ancestors of hundreds of years ago. Obviously Stacy's instincts were better than most, as she'd booked it out of here. Interesting. So where the hell was she?

Royce appeared to be searching for her himself.

Great. Now to see who would find her first.

Chapter 21

D AMN IT. STACY wished Royce would stop yelling long enough to hear her own calls. But she was keeping her voice hushed, whereas he was letting the entire world know she was missing.

Great. If the guy watching her from the crest above her didn't know she'd been down there before, he sure knew now. She didn't know whether that watcher was just an innocent bystander or not. She'd caught him in her camera view several times and had managed to get a couple pictures, but they were a long way away. She doubted there would be enough detail to identify him. But it would prove she hadn't imagined him.

She'd held back texting anyone about it. She didn't want them to think she'd crossed that fine line of paranoia, now being back on the mountain.

But maybe, after this, she shouldn't hold back. Or maybe, after this, it just proved she was nervous over nothing. Something she wouldn't have thought of herself. She wasn't scared to be here. Or of something happening to her. It was more that something might happen to her friends.

She wasn't sure what to say to Royce's earlier comment about the man being murdered. It wasn't for her to confirm. And it was too early to judge. But all the indications pointed to foul play. It was hard to argue away the marks on his wrists. He might not have been murdered, but that didn't mean he hadn't been running for his life to escape something horrible and had succumbed to the elements.

Silence had descended on the area. She peered through the boughs of the big fir tree she'd taken refuge behind to see Royce standing nearby, staring, such a horrible look of loss on his face. And she realized maybe the others were correct. Maybe he really did care.

And damn if that didn't make her feel terrible. She'd been keeping him at a distance. Thinking he'd been mocking her. Playing with her. Treating her like his other relationships. But what if he was trying to show her that he cared?

Trying to let her know she was different.

Or was that just wishful thinking on her part?

There. A shadow shifted on the ridge above them. Movement to the left. Royce spun and stared up behind, where Stacy had seen her stalker earlier. "Hello?" he called out.

No answer. There was a heavy rustling sound, but, if anyone was still up there, they were leaving or were already gone. She stepped out from behind her hiding place. "Royce," she hissed.

He spun back again, relief washing over his face. Followed by instant anger. "What the hell were you doing hiding back there? I almost had a heart attack thinking—"

"*Shh*," she snapped in a harsh whisper. "Someone was sitting up there for a really long time, staring at me. But they were hidden from view. It made me really uncomfortable, so, when I thought I could, I slipped out of sight and waited."

His gaze was intent, searching her face. And, damn, he saw a lot. "He really scared you, *huh*?"

Trying to keep her voice calm and logical, she said, "A couple times these last few days I felt like I was being watched. I never could see anyone though."

"What?" He stared at her in shock, anger still burning bright in his eyes. "And you're just now telling me?"

"When was I supposed to mention it?" she asked in what she thought was a reasonable tone of voice. Apparently he didn't agree.

"Tell me all of it." When she didn't answer fast enough, he snapped, "Now."

Feeling a sense of déjà vu, she said, "It's not much ..." Then gave him the little bit she knew.

"And last night? Were you awoken in the night for any reason?"

"Yes! Were you?"

He nodded. "I thought I heard the outside door open and close."

"Which isn't all that odd or alarming. People go outside sometime in the night."

"I know." He nodded. "That's part of the problem. It could be completely innocent."

"So why are you so worried? It sounds like everyone's imagination is going wild."

"And your stalker today? Was that also your imagination?" He held out a cup of coffee for her. "This is probably cold by now ..."

"That's fine. I could use the caffeine hit." She accepted the cup gratefully, touched by his thoughtfulness. She had no idea how he managed to do it, but the cup was still full and lukewarm.

He took a drink from his cup and made a face.

She grinned at him and took a big drink. "It's not hot, but it's caffeine."

"And the stalker?" he asked, staying persistent.

She raised her free hand. "All right. So maybe that incident wasn't my imagination."

"And, if it wasn't, then likely the other incidents weren't either," he said thoughtfully. "Still, I don't understand who this person is and what they want."

"Neither do I." Of course the clouds moved in and changed the bright sunlight to overcast and cloudy. The cool coffee was also having an effect on her. She shivered. "I think I'll head back to the cabin."

"Then I'm coming with you." He bent down and picked up his board and motioned in front of him. "Shall we?"

She started off in the right direction. "You don't have to come with me, you know?"

He snorted. "We've just finished discussing a stalker is following you …"

"Right. Fair enough." She was happy to have the company.

The trip back was quiet and uneventful. By the time she made it inside, she hated to admit she needed a rest. She would love to lie down, but the cabin was too cold.

"Go sit down, and I'll get the fire going again."

She gave him a grateful smile of thanks and put her stuff away in the loft, grimacing at the mess she'd left in her panic to get down on time. When she returned downstairs, a bright blaze was going. She filled the coffeepot and put it on the heater stove, then went to work, making a few sandwiches for the two of them. That done, she walked through the cabin, poking her head into the different rooms. She wasn't sure what she was looking for, if anything, but she'd seen red on the jacket. If one was here, then she'd like to know. But chances were good the owner of the jacket with the red stripe was wearing it still. It wouldn't be here.

"The guy is still out there most likely."

She turned away from George's bed to look at Royce, standing behind her. "What do you think I was doing?"

He shrugged, but his gaze was shrewd. "You're going from room to room. So you tell me."

With a dark look, she brushed past him. "I was just checking to see if anyone was here or not."

"*Not* is my vote." He followed her back to the kitchen, where she quickly cut the sandwiches, placing them on two plates and handing them to him. "I'll bring the coffee," she said. "Take these over, please."

"Sure. They look great. Thanks."

She didn't respond. It was just a sandwich. As she sat down beside him in front of the fire, he took a bite, studied her, and then asked, "So did you see anything besides red?"

She shook her head. "I only saw a strip of red in the trees. Nothing of his face or other gear."

"If it was here, it wouldn't be on your stalker out there," he said.

"Yeah, unless they whipped home and changed their jacket, then went out again." She smiled grimly. "And came in with the groups, as they arrived home."

He swallowed the bite in his mouth, as if the food were drier than he'd like. "Is that your logical mind at work or is that a really nasty imagination conjuring up horror stories? Are you really suspecting one of us?"

"You forget my line of work."

"That is not a nice thought." He took a huge bite of a sandwich and stared thoughtfully into the fire, as he chewed. "I guess that would be the easy answer, but not the smartest, as there's a good chance he would be seen or his jacket found."

"And the difficult answer?"

"It's a large mountain. Any number of people could have seen you and decided to stalk you."

"And the other incidences?" she asked, before popping the last of her sandwich into her mouth. She stared down at her empty plate, then decided a second would be good and stood.

"Same thing."

"Maybe." She started in the direction of the kitchen. "I'm going to make another sandwich. Do you want more?"

"Yes, please." She started building a second sandwich for both of them, as he leaned against the doorjamb, finishing off the first one. She was just about done when he said, "I wonder."

"Wonder what?" She slapped the tops of the sandwiches, then cut them in half. She took his plate from him and filled it again. She picked up her plate and turned back to him. "Wonder what?"

"You searched the rooms to see if there was a jacket. As in you were looking for something that might have been left behind. Did you happen to consider that we should instead be looking for what might be missing?"

She stopped cold. There was a weird tingling inside her. Her mind cast through all he wasn't saying. "You think someone might have searched the cabin while we were gone?"

"A cabin inhabited by a large group of people here on a vacation? If I were a criminal or someone looking for a quick score, there would be easy money here, wouldn't there?"

His tone had darkened with an ugly overtone. She stayed quiet, thinking about it. "And?" she asked, when he didn't continue.

"And, if I saw a woman I really liked the look of, I'd be tempted to follow her back to where she was staying, so I could learn more about her."

Unbidden, her gaze went to the loft, where she'd dumped her camera bag. And the disarray she hadn't expected to see. She'd been in a rush this morning, but she hadn't been in that much of a rush—or had she? She found the days and mornings blending into each other. She couldn't remember.

"Do you think we should be checking to see if we've been robbed?" she asked in a low voice, studying his face carefully.

"I think I'll be taking a closer look at my stuff. I didn't bring much of value, but there is a different perspective on what that word means to people."

Stacy carefully set down her sandwich, her appetite suddenly gone. "I think I'll go up and check," she murmured. She walked past him to the stairs, feeling his gaze on her every step. Up in the loft, she stopped and looked around first. Her bed appeared to be as she had left it. Nothing was different on it or around it. She wanted to make sure, so she flipped back the covers and then quickly remade it.

Her camera bag was tossed. The contents haphazard on the bed. The lenses were worth a lot of money. Seeing them made her feel better. If their belongings had been searched, surely a thief would have snagged the high-priced lenses.

Next she turned to her bag. She lifted it up to rest on the bed. She slowly removed everything inside, her mind mentally ticking off the items as she did so. Two pairs of jeans, two sets of thermals, seven sets of underwear, and two heavy wool sweaters. She kept on until the bag was empty.

Then she turned to the side pockets. The first was packed with her toiletries. Normal. Everything was there, as far as she could tell. She opened up the other end of the bag and pulled out the few things she'd stuffed in there. Then sat back on her heels. She stared at the pile and wondered if she'd have missed anything. She stood up and flicked on the light switch. And studied the small space.

Several extra bedrolls were available, but she hadn't used any of them, just the one atop her bed. She hadn't even been over there to check any out. But one was disturbed. As if someone had sat on it, maybe. She frowned. To her knowledge, no one had been up here, but ... here was proof that someone had been. Maybe. ... Or maybe it was just her mind becoming overwrought. Damn.

She repacked her things carefully and realized something else. She packed the same way all the time, but that wasn't the way she'd unpacked. Someone had taken her stuff out of her bag and had carefully packed it, just not exactly the same way she had done so. She had to stop and wonder if she'd made the mistake. But she knew herself better than that.

She was a creature of habit. And a neat freak. A condition that had only gotten much worse, since so much in her world had gotten out of control; so she'd locked down on what she could control. She was only just now easing up some of those restrictions she'd put on herself. Coming here was one of them.

She walked back down slowly, her mind wondering at who and why, when she hit the bottom stair and saw Royce standing there, holding out her plate, with the sandwich.

"And?" he asked.

"I can't be sure, but I think someone went through my bag."

He scowled. "Anything missing?"

She shook her head. "I don't think so." She stared into his eyes, her mind racing through the items she brought. Finally she shook her head and repeated, "I don't think so."

ROYCE POLISHED OFF his second sandwich in a few bites. He got up and poked the fire, while she ate slowly. He understood. She was processing. There was a lot of information to sort through.

"You said you thought the man we found had been murdered. Do you have any evidence that points that way?"

He shook his head. "Proof? No."

She nodded, as if she had suspected as much.

He stood. "You must have your suspicions."

"Sure." She grabbed his plate and walked into the kitchen. "The circumstances were beyond odd. The marks on his wrists revealed he'd been tied up recently, and he wasn't dressed for the weather." She sighed. "But he's not on my table, and I can't know for sure." She glanced at him. "Without the details from the autopsy, I'd say Mother Nature killed him—it's just a question whether someone contributed in any way."

"Can you make a professional call and find out?"

She glanced over at him, as he came closer and leaned against the counter. "I was trying to avoid doing that. You know—that need for a vacation?"

"Yeah, *some* vacation." He looked at the fatigue lines on her face. She needed something to brighten her day. And he had just the answer. "Let's go sledding."

She looked at him in shock. "What?"

"I said, let's go sledding. There's a big run not far from here. It's safe and long and a ton of fun."

An odd look entered her eyes. Then she shrugged. "Sure, why not?"

He grinned. "Let's go."

He tugged her toward the doorway. "Get your boots and coat on. I'll grab the magic carpets."

At that last bit, she turned to stare at him, then giggled. "Magic carpets? Really?"

His grin widened. "Really."

Warmly dressed, the two ran out the door. He led the way to the top of the hill he knew well. It led down to the parking lot. At the bottom of the run, they could board the tram up the other side. Then they would have fun on a few of the smaller runs. This area was well-known by the local sledders, and often the tourists joined in on the fun.

And that's exactly what Stacy needed. He was the perfect person to introduce her to a childhood favorite sport.

She was way too serious most of the time, and now she was wary to boot. There might or might not be a stalker, but, for the next few hours, it wouldn't matter. They'd have nothing but a great time.

He hoped.

WHAT THE HELL was Royce carrying—and why? He watched the two race to the top of the hill on the left, and damn if they didn't both get on something small and bright and slide down the long easy slope. From

where he stood, he saw them bouncing and flying through the air, hitting a bank of snow and jumping forward into the suddenly raised cloud. He heard the shrieks of laughter, and something tightened inside him.

How dare they?

He didn't want them having fun like that.

He didn't want them laughing.

He definitely didn't want Royce getting any closer to Stacy.

With a snarl, he sat back on his haunches and stared at the two of them. They were almost at the bottom of the hill now, still laughing and cheering the ride on. Fear, anger, disgust, and so much more roiled through him. He wanted to hit something. Lash out at the two of them.

Make them pay.

And yet … why?

They were having fun—so what? At least if they became closer, they'd hurt that much more when one of them went missing.

He contemplated ruining two lives with one act. His hobby was definitely getting more complicated.

That worked.

As long as they didn't find anything important out there, he was good.

Actually he was great.

Chapter 22

S TACY COULDN'T REMEMBER ever having such fun. She felt like a kid. Like how cool was that? She sat on the sled, Royce's arms around her waist, and raced down hillside after hillside in complete abandon. The way the mountain had set up the sliding area allowed for both skiers and sliders to go up the chair lift, but, at the top, the paths split off, and both wound down in different directions. She had no idea this area was even here. She'd seen other sledders over the years, but being a die-hard skier, she'd relished every moment she had on the mountain, and that meant always with boards strapped to her feet. At least one, if not two.

It was great to switch that up—or down as the case may be. She loved this.

And the attentiveness Royce showered on her, the way he constantly held out his hand to help her up, always an eye out for her care, warmed her inside. She didn't remember ever seeing this side of him before. Surely it had been there but not directed her way. Probably at one of his gazillion girlfriends. And that was the difference. It also made him that much more attractive. She understood the women falling for him.

After all, she had too—once. That didn't mean she was willing to repeat it. But a part of her wanted to.

She shrieked as they hit a large bump, and the snow flew in her face, the icy crystals biting into her skin. Then she laughed. For all the icy wind hitting her, the cold sting of the snow made her feel alive. Revitalized. For this, she thanked Royce. He'd shown her a good time these past few hours.

The sun was going down behind the mountains, casting long shadows on the trees and adding a chill to the day. Still, it had been a fantastic afternoon. Her morning had been good too. She'd gotten decent pictures earlier today.

From this happier position, she had a better perspective. She had some distance from the mess of her belongings and realized there could be any number of reasons why her bags might have been searched—either of the two women might have needed monthly supplies unexpectedly for one. As for the stalker? Maybe it was someone out for a hike, and he'd stopped to take a few pictures. As she had.

And the man they'd found? That had nothing to do with them. He'd had an unlucky death. Until she knew more, she couldn't say what had happened or why, and speculation was dangerous. As she knew all too well. "That was fun." She stood and brushed the snow off her coat.

"Do you want to go again?"

"Do we have time?" She turned to study the chair lift. It was still running, but there was no line. A single boarder stepped onto a chair as their turn came. She studied the clock. "We don't have time. Maybe we can go up one last time, but that's it."

He turned to look at her. "Let's grab this lift. We have to catch the Hummingbird lift to go even higher, then turn toward the cabin."

She frowned up at him. "Can we do that?"

He shrugged. "I have before, but it's a little touchy."

"Ya think?" She grinned. "As long as you know where we're going, let's do it."

He grabbed her hand and raced to the chair. The lift operator was walking around, checking his watch, as if looking to see when he could shut it down. She screamed, "We're here. We're here."

The lift operator waved at her.

She laughed as she ran through the empty path leading to the chair. "Thanks!"

"No problem. You still had a few minutes. This is your last lift though."

"No problem. We need to catch the Hummingbird as well too."

He nodded. "I'll tag them that you two are coming."

"Thanks." She hopped up onto the chair, Royce taking the seat beside her, as the chair scooped them up and carried them uphill. "Glad we made that."

"It's a long hard walk if we hadn't," Royce agreed. "Too bad no coffee is at the top of Hummingbird."

"Oh, I could really use some hot coffee," she exclaimed, "but we could hardly sled home with our hands full of hot drinks."

He laughed. "We'd be wearing the coffees on the first bump."

"True. Besides, the rest of the group will have coffee made."

"Sounds good to me."

The chair rose up to another tower, weighed down by ice and snow. The beauty was incredible, the stark contrast between Mother Nature and the steel structure incredibly strong. She loved it. The trees stood tall under their white snowcaps, and some bowed under the weight of the world beside them. There was no sound but for the steady hum of the steel cable slowly climbing higher and higher.

The higher they climbed, the colder the air and the more biting the wind. She huddled deeper into her jacket, her collar pulled up over her ears. Damn, she'd forgotten this chill. They'd been racing into the wind as they streamed down the mountain, but sitting still like they were now, the cold was treacherous.

Royce reached out and wrapped an arm around her, pulling her close. She nestled in and closed her eyes, letting her breath warm up her face.

She was glad they were heading back. Honestly they should've gone back earlier, but, with the sun up and having so much fun, it had been easy to push away the idea.

Now she wished she'd thought to think ahead.

"You okay?" Royce's warm voice tickled her ear and heated up her neck.

She nodded but stayed quiet.

"Good. We're almost there."

In fact, the chair lift slowed, and the chair swung slightly, as it slowed its ascent. She got ready to jump off and get out of the way before it hit her.

As they landed, he grabbed her hand and raced her over to the sister lift.

Thankfully this one was short. At their landing on the top, she shivered. The wind was bitingly cold. "Wow, this is nasty up here."

He nodded. "Not to worry, we won't be here long." He motioned at a path going down the back. "We need to go down there." She nodded and sat down on the hard plastic. Instead of trying for a big running push, then hopping on, the way he always had before, he just sat down behind her and pushed them forward with his hand. The sled took off but at a slower pace.

It curved to the left, taking them toward the slash in the trees. She was grateful they weren't going at top speed. She couldn't imagine what would happen if they hit a tree.

Then she understood. The trees, although a long distance away, were up a small rise. If she'd been on skis, it wouldn't be noticeable, but on the magic carpet, with much of the momentum already running out, they barely crested it. At the top, he put his boots down and slowed them to a stop. He pointed to the right this time. Down below, a long way away, was the cabin.

"We could walk, or we could slide."

"And how do we stop when we get there?" she asked, worried.

"We'll have to crisscross our way down. A lot of deep snow is on the side of the hill, and that will bring us to a stop, at which point we turn and cross to the other side again."

"Oh, that makes so much sense." She laughed. "Let's slide then."

And that's what they did.

As they neared the cabin, someone from inside must have seen them because, before they came to a stop just in front, the rest of the group had all tumbled out to see them.

"Oh, man, if I'd known you were going sliding, I'd have come too!" complained Stevie.

"I had no plans to throw myself down the mountain on a little piece of plastic," Stacy said, with a laugh. "Boards, yes. Plastic, no."

George reached down and helped her to her feet. "You look like you had a blast."

"I did." She beamed up at him. "We had tons of fun."

She watched him nod at Royce behind her back, thankfulness in that glance. She reached out and hugged her brother. "I'm feeling much better."

"Good."

With his arm wrapped around her, George turned to look up the mountain. His forehead creased. He looked from her to Royce and back again. "You were with Yvonne, right?"

Stacy shook her head. "No, I haven't seen her. Why?"

"She hasn't come back, and no one remembers seeing her since last night. Possibly this morning."

"I saw her this morning," Stacy said, "but she wasn't here when we came back around lunchtime, nor have I seen her since." She turned to Royce and asked, "Have you?"

He shook his head. "She was with us until just before lunch. Then we split up, and I met up with you."

Stevie grabbed his coat and gloves and announced, "Therefore, she's gone missing. And that's not good."

ROYCE CONTACTED SEARCH and rescue and was one of the first to volunteer. They'd been to the resort enough over the years that their assistance had been requested in the past. Now hours later, he was cold and chilled, and bad weather was moving in quickly. All the public venues had been checked, the local runs searched, and her photograph shown to everyone. The initial hope that she'd stopped off at a pub for a beer waned, when all restaurants and pubs were checked, and there was still no sign of her. It was dark. The four of them that had been part of the search and rescue volunteer group drove up to the cabin. Lights blazed inside. Geoffrey had stayed behind with Kathleen and Stacy, in case Yvonne had returned on her own. They'd been in phone contact with each other all evening, but there'd been no sign of her.

Now with the search called off for the night because of encroaching bad weather, everyone was exhausted and somber on the truck ride back to the cabin. It would be a long night for Yvonne, if she were out there in the elements. It was only slightly reassuring that she was an old hand at winter sports.

"I can't believe, after all our efforts to keep the group together, that she's gone missing." George's voice was hard, angry, his grip on the wheel tightening. He couldn't hold back his frustration. He looked like he wanted to punch something.

"She could have picked up a stranger and planned a private evening with someone."

"You'd likely know about that, right?" George asked, staring at Royce. "Wasn't she after you?"

Royce winced. "Not really. I turned her down."

"Really?" Stevie leaned forward. In an aggrieved voice, he added, "Wow. You could have turned her my way."

Royce managed a smile, albeit a poor one. "Wish I could have, buddy."

"Why would you turn her down?" asked Mark.

"Ha." Stevie grinned. "His interests lie elsewhere."

An odd silence followed, as Mark considered the issue. He asked in a pensive voice, "So?"

Reaching the cabin, George parked, while Royce let out a bark of laughter and hopped out of the truck. He walked to the cabin door to find the rest of the group standing just inside the boot room, hope and fear on their faces. He shook his head.

Gasps filled the air, and tears immediately came to Kathleen's eyes. She ran past Royce and threw herself into George's arms.

Stacy walked forward and, in a low voice, asked him, "Nothing at all?"

He shook his head. "No one has seen her." He was so damn tired now. Inside and out. Dispirited, he took off his coat and hung it up on the hook. Then bent over to take off his snow-packed boots. When he straightened, he realized he was the last male in the room, ... and Stacy still stood before him. He could smell the coffee behind her. He glanced at her curiously, wondering why she stood here, almost awkwardly in front. When he went to move around her, she put out an arm to stop him.

He stepped back slightly out of view of the others. "What?" he asked in a low voice.

"This," she said. And stepped forward to hug him.

His arms closed around her. Surprised but delighted, he held her against him. Something he'd wanted to do—and had been doing in a different way—all day. Just knowing she was here, safe, caring to be with him, offering him comfort, ... it mattered. After a long moment, she stepped back, with a smile. "We need to join the others before they come looking for us."

He didn't give a damn if they did. He just wanted her back in his arms. "Stacy?"

She stopped at his voice and looked at him.

"Why?" he asked her.

Her eyebrows shot up. "You looked like you needed it." She turned and left him standing in the boot room.

He *had* needed it. Looking for Yvonne had been difficult. Deaths happened often on a mountain like this. It went with the territory. But he sure didn't want any to happen on his watch. No, he wasn't responsible for Yvonne having gone missing—but it felt like he was. At least partially. He knew they would all feel that way.

And, until they found her, there'd be no answers.

He walked toward his room and stopped at the doorway. Stacy was talking to Kathleen not far away. He called her over. "Stacy, when you took a look into the rooms earlier today, was Yvonne's stuff in here, like this?" He nodded to her bag, dumped upside down on her bed.

Stacy joined him at the doorway. "I don't know. I can't remember. Would she have done that herself?"

Kathleen stepped up and asked, "What's wrong?"

Royce called out to the group in general. "Did any of you notice Yvonne's bag earlier? Was it always dumped upside down like it is now? Did anyone here touch it?"

The others crowded around.

"It looked like that when I saw it."

"No, I didn't touch it."

"I looked in earlier," Kathleen said. "I wondered if she had taken her wallet. If she had money, then she could be in the pub."

"Good thought." Royce walked inside the room and gazed at the items on the bed. "I don't see it here, did you?"

Kathleen brushed forward and joined him. "It didn't look like this before. And her wallet was right here." She flipped the bag back on its proper end and shifted the items on Yvonne's bed. "It *was* here."

"So she might have come back and gotten it?" Royce asked. That would be good news. Maybe she'd been the one who rifled through Stacy's stuff. Or someone altogether different had, and, after finding Yvonne's wallet, had taken it. Shit.

"Stacy and I wondered if someone had searched our belongings today." He turned to the others. "I suggest you all check your own stuff and confirm nothing is missing. I have to pack up Yvonne's stuff for the police. They were supposed to be here tonight, but, given the storm that just moved in, it will likely be in the morning." The others scattered, as he unceremoniously stuffed all of Yvonne's belongings back inside her backpack.

A new face appeared in the doorway.

Royce startled. Shit, he'd forgotten that the other two would be joining them. "Kevin, I know you just got here today. Sorry, man."

Kevin stood awkwardly to the side. "Christine and I got in about an hour ago. I'm sorry about Yvonne. That sucks." He looked around the large cabin. "I left my gear outside in the boot room. Not sure where everyone has bunked down. Is there an empty bed, or do I join whoever is in the loft?"

A tiny gasp came from behind him, and Royce knew instinctively that having Kevin join Stacy up there would not be her choice.

"I'm moving anyway," Royce said, snagging up his gear and putting it all together. He left Yvonne's bed alone. "I'd like to keep her bed for her—just in case."

"Oh, absolutely, but I don't want to chase you away," Kevin protested.

"You're not." Royce grinned. "I've been planning this move all along." And he turned, brushed past a narrow-eyed Stacy, and walked up the stairs to the loft where he casually dropped his gear and returned to the living room and the waiting coffeepot.

She never said a word.

Damn right.

"SOUNDS LIKE A tough week for you guys," Kevin said to the room at large. "I'm sorry to hear that."

The room quieted down even further.

"We've done all we can do for now," Geoffrey said grimly. "Let's hope that Yvonne's tucked away, nice and warm somewhere, enjoying life so much that she never thought to check in."

"I hope so," Stacy said.

"I don't know Yvonne all that well." Kevin glanced over at Stacy, before his gaze continued to Kathleen. "Is she the kind to take off like this?" He settled back, trying to fit into the group that had been together for days already and feeling a bit like an outsider. He knew them all. Had gone on trips with them all, although not very often. And not with all of them in this same group.

"No. I wouldn't think so," Kathleen said, tucked up close to George. "She'd shown interest in Royce, so I would have thought she would work hard to get back to him."

Kevin looked over at Royce and hid his grin. Royce looked decidedly uncomfortable, as the guys chuckled and elbowed each other at his expense.

"Ah, well, maybe she's having dinner with someone who is more appreciative," Stevie said, grinning. He glanced at the kitchen, where Christine and Mark were working hard. "Is there food coming soon?"

"Yep. Be right there," Christine called back.

Someone's stomach growled loudly. Kevin shrugged, as everyone looked at him. "Sorry. Long drive here." He called out to Christine in the kitchen. "I'm surprised you're doing okay, Christine. You drove in with me."

"Ha, I've been snacking while I've been cooking."

"That was smart." He could have gone in and snacked too but felt odd with all the other males out searching for the missing woman. Thankfully it looked like dinner was just about ready.

"And food is here," Christine said, coming out with a huge cookie sheet full of nacho chips covered in ground beef and onions, topped with cheese, alongside big piles of guacamole and sour cream.

"Oh, yum."

"Yay, food."

Mark came up from behind with a second tray. Both trays were placed equidistant on the table, and, as soon as their hands were gone, the crowd dug in.

Christine and Mark came back with several bottles of wine and a third tray of more nachos.

After that, it was chaos. Kevin was glad he'd come in right now.

The only thing that bothered him was their ability to forget the missing woman. He could almost understand.

But, if he were missing, he'd sure be hoping they'd be looking for him all night.

THEY WERE ALL fools. If they were really friends, they'd have gone looking for Yvonne, even if the search had been called off until first light.

Idiots. They still had no clue. Of course that's how he wanted it, but it would be so much fun to add an element of suspense to this mess. But he wouldn't give himself away. This was too much fun to cut short.

Besides, he had worked hard. If he was the only one to appreciate his skills, then so be it.

Too bad though, he'd love to have someone show some appreciation.

He studied Stacy. Maybe if he kept her alive long enough, maybe she'd come to understand.

Maybe she'd see him for who he really was. Finally.

Chapter 23

THE EVENING WAS subdued, as everyone kept expecting the phone to ring or a vehicle to come up to the door and Yvonne to walk inside. It never happened. There was no word from her or about her. Neither did she come home. Stacy, already in her PJs, sat curled in the armchair all evening, sipping her wine. She'd hoped this wouldn't be a sleepless night, but, given the circumstances … When the wind picked up outside, screaming through the cabin, howling as it pounded on the door several times, she jumped, thinking it was Yvonne, trying to open the door against the wind.

Royce leaned over and patted her hand. "It's just the wind."

"I know." She gave him a small smile. "I just keep hoping it's her."

"We all are."

Stacy nodded. The long day was having an effect on her. Not to mention the warm fire and the several glasses of wine she'd had to help her relax. She couldn't get over the thought of Yvonne, injured, lying in the snow somewhere, wondering if she'd make it through the night. And damn if it didn't bring back all the old fears of her friends being buried alive in that damn avalanche. She hadn't slept for months after the accident, always waking up from the nightmare of seeing her friends waiting for rescue—a rescue that never came.

She stood slowly, feeling her muscles seize up. She gently stepped around the many legs stretched out in front of the fire.

"Are you heading to bed, Stacy?" George asked quietly.

She nodded. "That sledding wore me out today. I was laughing and screaming so much, my throat is feeling a little rough."

He frowned. "That's not good. Your immune system is already shot."

She would have hugged him if she could reach him, but he appeared to be cradling Kathleen in his arms, as she snored gently. "She needs to go to bed too," Stacy said, nodding toward Kathleen.

"I'm thinking we all do." Royce stood up. "I'm beat."

"Yeah, me too." Stevie rose as well. "Good night, all."

Stacy called out to him, as he started toward the bathroom. "Good night, Stevie. You worked hard today. You need some sleep."

"Ha, I work hard every day," he replied, but his words were slurred. His eyes dropped, and damn if he didn't sway in place. As Stacy watched in alarm, Royce walked over and led him down the hall to his room.

"Almost there." At the doorway, Royce gave him a gentle push. "Go lie down."

Stevie went like an obedient puppy.

Stacy stood on the bottom of the stairs and felt her heart melt a little. Royce had done just the right thing. Stevie was a big kid, but he'd had a tough day. To know Royce could take care of others like he did also said a lot about who he was on the inside.

And she found she liked that inside man more and more.

After brushing her teeth, the same lassitude that had overtaken Stevie filled her bones. Then he'd had more wine than she had. Chances were good the alcohol was stripping the energy from her bones.

Just moving up the stairs made her feel like she'd gained one hundred pounds. As she crested over the top step, Royce pounded up the stairs after her.

"Are you okay, Stacy?" he asked. "You are starting to scare me."

"I'm fine," she muttered, not even trying to hold back a yawn. "Just did too much today." She stumbled over to her bed, crawled in and pulled the covers up to her chin.

"Stacy?"

His voice sounded strange. "*Hmm*?" she mumbled, so grateful to be in her bed at this moment. It was cold, but her skin was colder, so even that little bit felt wonderful. She slowly relaxed.

"Stacy," Royce snapped sharply. "Look at me."

"Can't."

"Yes, you can."

He shook her shoulders hard, her head snapping back and forth.

"Ouch. Stop that. It hurts."

"Good. Open your eyes."

"No, go away." She wanted to be pissed, but there was no heat in her voice. She tried again. "Leave me alone. I just want to sleep."

"That's what I'm afraid of." Royce lowered his head. "Think, Stacy. You are too sleepy. Too tired. This isn't normal for you."

She struggled to think from behind the black fog in her mind. "No, been sick. Did too much."

"Maybe, but, if you'd open your eyes, you would see how dilated your pupils are."

Silly. "I've been drinking," she mumbled, trying and failing to open them. "'Course they're dilated."

Her eyelids were roughly opened, and a light flashed.

She wanted to cry out but couldn't. She sagged against him, heard the heartfelt "Shit" coming out of his mouth—then knew no more.

SHIT, SHIT, *SHIT*. Royce cradled Stacy's limp body in his arms for a long moment. He laid her back down on the bed and stared at her precious face. Stevie had been just as tired. Then he remembered Kathleen. He leaned over the railing and stared down into the darkness. The only light was coming from the fire. The flames flickered and danced, as if appreciating an audience—finally.

Royce raced down the stairs. George snored on the couch; Kathleen snored gently in his lap.

He raced to Stevie's room to find Mark already out cold, just like the others.

"Kevin?" He pushed open the door. The heavy rhythmic noise coming from Kevin's chest said much about the depth of his slumber. Christine slept in a tight ball above him in the bunk beds. Geoffrey snored loudly on the opposite set of bunks. They'd all helped kill several bottles of wine tonight.

Royce spun around and ran back to George. He lifted Kathleen and carried her to George's bed, then came back and shook George's shoulder hard. When that got no reaction but a disjointed movement of his head, Royce hauled back and smacked him across the face. George groaned. Royce repeated it.

George groaned again. "Wha—"

Royce smacked him a third time.

George's eyes popped open, and he glared at Royce. "You'd better have a hell of a reason for doing that."

"Everyone's been drugged."

George's eyes widened. His gaze was unfocused, but Royce could see the wheels attempting to turn behind them.

"What?" he choked out, as he tried to stand. Royce grabbed his arm and pulled him to his feet. He stood, swayed, and fell back down again. He looked around, then back at Royce. "Kathleen? Stacy?"

"They're both out of it. They're in their beds."

The relief in George's gaze made Royce realize just how much George cared for Kathleen. Like Royce, George had had many relationships in his active life. He loved women. And women loved George. But Kathleen appeared to be his sweet spot.

Royce was happy for his friend. Now if only Royce could get Stacy back in his life, he'd be happy for both of them.

"Help me up," George ordered, a little more grit in his voice than before. Royce hefted him back to his feet. "To the boot room," he ordered. "Maybe the cold will knock some sense back into my brain."

With Royce keeping a steady hand on his friend's arm, he led him out to the anteroom, where the gear and outerwear were stored. The bite of cold air hit their faces. "Take a few deep breaths," Royce said.

George walked back and forth in the small space, as he focused on getting fresh air into his system and clearing his head.

Then he turned and faced Royce.

"What the fuck is going on?"

RAGE SAT IN George's gut and festered. He stared down at Kathleen, seeing the drug-induced coma for himself. "I want to call the police. Right now. Have them sort this out."

Royce had already collected the wineglasses and empty bottles in a box for the police. Hopefully they'd test it all and find the drugs used. George wasn't showing too much reaction at this point, which was a damn good thing. Then again, he was a big guy and wasn't much of a wine drinker. But how else had the drugs gotten into their systems if not through the wine? It was the only thing everyone had shared—except for Royce. He'd just had soda pop in his glass. It could have easily looked like wine, particularly in the evening light.

He tasted wine in his glass at one point, as a bottle had been emptied, and another opened. Used to it, as often the others tried to trick him into drinking it, he'd just gotten up quietly and dumped it. Casting his mind back, he tried to remember who had opened the bottles. They needed to know that in order to determine if they'd been tampered with. And it was likely too late for that, given everyone's comatose state.

Royce spun. "Jesus. You're fine, but what about Kathleen? She's really tiny."

"I checked. She's definitely drugged, but, when I shook her, I did get a response." He glared at Royce. "I won't be smacking her around."

"I wouldn't either." Royce smacked him on the shoulder. "Just you."

"Next time, go a little lighter," George snapped.

As they walked into the kitchen and stared from the doorway, George wondered out loud, his voice hard. "Is it one of us?"

Silence.

He looked over at Royce to see his jaw muscle flickering in a staccato tempo. "What?"

"I'm wondering if it's related to Yvonne."

"Her disappearance? Or are you thinking she did this and booked it?" George laughed, his voice harsh. "How badly did you let her down? Would she have done this in revenge?"

Royce shook his head. "Honestly, not bad at all. I thought, at the time, she'd been joking the way she had said that it would be warmer for both of us if she joined me in my bed." He laughed ruefully. "She laughed. I laughed. I didn't think anything about it."

"And it might not be anything. It's hard to say at this point." George ran his hands down his face, as if that would help shake the last of the cobwebs from his brain. He wanted to hit something so badly. That someone had done this was unbelievable, but to all of them at the same time? Disgusting. Why had no one seen anything? Then he realized they might have, but he wouldn't know until they woke up.

"Who had access to the cabin today?" Royce asked.

"You mean, who didn't have access?" George responded. He walked into the main room of the cabin, crossing to the kitchen sink. He reached for a glass and turned on the tap. Water poured. He filled the glass and took a long drink. It felt good. His throat was parched. Dry. He emptied the glass, then refilled it for Royce. "Were you drugged?" George asked.

"Not really." But he stayed quiet, thoughtful.

"What does that mean?"

Royce turned to face him. "I hate wine," he said. "There was wine in my glass at one point in the evening. I tasted it, realized what it was, and dumped it down the sink. I refilled the glass with pop and sipped that all evening. But there was an odd taste to it."

"So you're thinking the wine was drugged, and some of it either stayed in your mouth after that one sip or in your glass because you didn't wash it clean?" He considered the several bottles of wine that had flowed freely. They'd each brought several, so they weren't all from the same store. "They must have been tampered with here."

"With all of us getting up and pouring drinks, it could have been anyone." Royce's voice hardened. "I've been trying to think of how it could be anyone other than one of us, and I can't."

"Anyone could have come in during the afternoon," George reminded him. "You yourself saw the rooms. Our belongings had been searched."

"But not just anyone could have known which bottles would be used or likely have had time to tamper with them, while they were still sealed." He stared at George, grim lines at the corner of his mouth. "This is no longer a random break-in."

"Shit."

Chapter 24

T HE LIGHT HURT her eyes. Stacy slammed them shut and moaned. It shouldn't be like that. She tried to sort out where she was. And remembered. She was at the cabin. They'd been boarding and sledding. Then she remembered. *Yvonne.*

She bolted upright and gasped, both hands rushing to support her head. She fell back before the sledgehammer in her head succeeded in getting out. "What the hell?" she whispered. "How much did I drink?"

"Stacy?"

Suddenly Royce was there. His hand was gentle, soothing on her forehead. "You'll need a bit of time. Take it easy and just rest in place for a moment."

"What happened?" she tried to enunciate clearly, but her tongue felt swollen and awkward. Something was wrong.

"A hell of a hangover," Royce said.

But no laughter was in his voice. He sounded worried. She opened her eyes a slit and peered under her lashes. "I've had hangovers. This is not a hangover." She closed her eyes and took several deep breaths. "My stomach doesn't feel very good."

"Nope, and no one else's does either."

At that, she stilled. "Bad wine?"

"That's one way to look at it."

"We were drugged," she said softly. Her eyes flew open. "Was everyone affected?"

"I was the least," he said. "I did have a sip, then dumped it."

"Right." Now that her brain was waking up, she remembered how he hated wine. He drank most alcoholic drinks but not that. "But someone tried?"

He was slow to answer.

She studied his face, wishing things would stay in focus and not move back and forth, like they were currently doing. "Royce?" she prodded him.

"I think so."

She would have nodded, but she remembered at the last second that it would hurt to move. "Son of a bitch."

"Sorry about the head. You and Kathleen seem to be feeling the effects the strongest."

"Being smaller, the effect would be stronger and longer lasting." She rolled over slightly. "Would have been much better if I'd thrown it all up last night."

"We didn't figure it out until everyone was unconscious." His big hand slowly stroked her back and shoulder. "I'm just glad you're awake. You're the last one."

She smiled weakly. "I did enjoy the wine."

He laughed lightly. "I wonder if you will again."

"Not sure I'll ever drink again."

"Speaking of which, you need to sit up and get down some water." He helped her into a sitting position, then held up a glass of water for her to drink.

It took some effort, but she managed to get half of it down. Then he helped her lie back.

She sighed. "It feels better to be horizontal."

"How about we get you downstairs? You can wait there."

"Wait for what?" She groaned, as she sat up again. Only she already knew. She studied his grim expression, the gathering darkness in his eyes. "The cops?"

He nodded. "We called them early, and they've been here for the last hour." He motioned to the noise on the other side of the railing and down below. Now that it was pointed out to her, she heard the loud noises, the extra voices. The string of words floating up to her.

"You'll likely be last."

"Poison?"

"Hate."

"Angry."

"Jealous."

None of those words made any sense, not when said to the friends she'd known for years. "They think one of us did it?"

"It's the only real answer."

Stifling a groan, she pushed herself up again and sat with crossed legs. Her head hurt just from that movement. She couldn't imagine trying to go down the stairs and being nice while being questioned. But she'd do it. It was part of what she did anyway. "Can you help me up, please?" she asked in a shaky voice.

He grabbed her elbows and gently tugged her to her feet. Vertical, she swayed in place. The room spun around her. "I don't think I can make it downstairs."

"I'll help." He smiled, and, in an easy move, he carefully scooped her up into his arms, and, moving slowly, he walked over to the stairs and headed down. As he reached the bottom step, there were cries from the others.

"Yay, she's awake."

"Welcome to the land of dry throats and massive headaches, Stacy."

She groaned. "I hear you there. That's one club I could do without a membership to."

That elicited a few responding groans of laughter.

"How are you feeling, Miss Carter?" the uniformed police officer asked in concern.

"I'm okay. At least I hope I'll be okay." She wasn't so sure, but, if she looked like the rest of them, she was dead already.

Royce lowered her to the couch, where she sat in the middle, with Stevie on the left and Geoffrey on the right. Royce headed to the kitchen. He returned a moment later with a full glass of water for her. She thanked him and sipped it. It felt like she would never get enough, yet she was full. Or at least her stomach said she was too full. At the same time, she was desperate to have more.

She sighed and sank back.

Stevie muttered, "Yeah, you got the same problem." He held up the glass in his hand. "I want to drink. It tastes so great that I want to drain the glass over and over again. But, at the same time, I'm full. My stomach says it'll upchuck if I throw anything else down there."

"Me too," said Geoffrey. "Sucks."

"Have you all given statements?" the uniformed cop asked the two men beside Stacy.

They both nodded. "We have. I think you just have Stacy left."

"*Great*," Stacy quipped. "Nice to know I'm on time for something."

The uniformed officer sat down in front of her on the coffee table. "I just need to ask you a few questions."

She nodded. "To be expected. Although I have no idea how I can help."

"Did you open any of the wine bottles yourself?"

She frowned. "No, I don't think so."

"Did you watch anyone else open a bottle?"

She thought about it and said slowly, "I must have, but I can't say that I remember who or when or even what bottles." She looked over at Stevie. "You filled my glass last, as you said something about it helping me to sleep. Helping me to forget about Yvonne."

"Did I?" He dropped his head backward on the back of the couch. "I don't remember much about the end of the evening. I understand that Royce got me to my bed, and I crashed, fully dressed."

"Nice," Stacy said, with a grin. "At least I managed to get into my PJs before collapsing."

"On the other side of that coin," Stevie said, "I'm fully dressed now, but you, my dear, are *still* in your pajamas. And you'll have to make it back upstairs and get dressed." At her groan, he laughed. "See? There is a method to my madness."

"No," she said. "You're just lazy."

"Well, now that you two are working through the merits of sleeping in your clothes or having to get changed twice," Geoffrey snapped, "maybe we can get back to the questions for Stacy, so we can get to the bottom of this mess."

Hearing and echoing his frustration in her mind, Stacy turned back to the policeman. "Sorry," she said. "It helps to lighten the worry with humor."

"Understood. As long as we are joking around though, the longer this will take to get through."

That wiped the laughter off her face. "Sorry. Please continue."

He quickly ran through the questions. She answered the best she could.

When he asked her about the afternoon and supposedly feeling as if her belongings had been disturbed, the others turned to her with interest.

"I can't really explain it, except that I noticed the clothing wasn't exactly as I'd left it. I'm a bit of a neat freak," she said apologetically. "My clothes weren't packed as I'd packed them."

"Do you know of any reason why anyone would do that?"

"I wondered if one of the women might have needed monthly supplies unexpectedly, and, not being here to ask, they just looked for themselves. Other than that, I can't imagine. Unless a stranger entered and was looking for money or other small valuables."

"But would a stranger who'd come into the cabin on the off chance that it was empty care about replacing the clothing in the same order? Wouldn't they have just dumped the bags and sorted through to find what they wanted? And was there anything missing?"

At the rush of questions, she had to stop, marshal her thoughts, then answer them in order. "I don't know. I imagine, and no."

By the time the police had finished questioning everyone, Stacy felt marginally better. The coffee helped, as did getting up and walking around, followed by a hot shower. When she came out dressed and feeling warm, her stomach gurgled loudly. Someone had made pancakes, and the group sat down at the table in silence to eat. She joined them, reaching for a stack to transfer to her plate. No one said a word. That usually meant there was no good news, but she needed to know.

Finally, after a few moments, she had to ask the one question that hadn't been brought up. "Has anyone heard anything of Yvonne?"

Silence.

They glanced around at each other, while she watched. She caught George's gaze, and he shook his head. She nodded. Search and rescue would have been back out at first light. That her group was not joining them said much about the shape they were in today after the drugs. And how impaired the drugs made them feel. She waited a few moments, before bringing it up again. After several bites of the light, fluffy treat, she asked, "Do you think it is related?"

Silence.

She kept eating, wishing she understood the undercurrents.

"Well, I highly doubt she'd have drugged the wine and then pulled a disappearing act," Geoffrey said. "Especially not because Royce here turned her down."

Stacy's head jerked up, her gaze going from Geoffrey to Royce's bent head.

"Oh, you missed that part," Geoffrey said. "Apparently that's the conclusion these two brilliant men came up with."

"No, not really," Royce said patiently, "but it's a possibility that we have to consider."

"Right." Geoffrey subsided into sullen silence. The only sounds were the occasional *clang* of cutlery against the plates.

"Or the same person drugged us and had something to do with Yvonne's disappearance," Stacy suggested. "Not that I am looking at a worst-case scenario but …"

Geoffrey stared at her. "You have a dark mind."

She shrugged. "Maybe."

How could she explain the stuff she saw and heard every day? Cases that were the worst of what mankind could do to each other. "Or it was a prank," she suggested. "Maybe this was meant to be a joke, and the drugs were more powerful than they thought."

"You're reaching there, sis."

She nodded, as she ate another bite. "Occupational hazard." She had to think about the issue carefully. "Two issues here. My question is, are they related?"

"Three issues, if we're counting everyone's belongings were searched."

A few nods came around the table, but no one said much of anything. She lifted her cup of coffee to her mouth, when her phone went off. She pulled it out and read the text. It was from James, another coworker. He'd gotten the information for her on the male they'd found by contacting the RCMP here in Canada.

All indications said he'd been drugged before freezing to death. The drugs were still frozen in his bloodstream. Tox screen was in progress. She appreciated the professional courtesy.

Her heart sinking, she sat back slightly, so she could ask him to connect with the police here, explaining about the missing woman and the drugs in their wine.

She looked up, caught her brother's gaze, and gave a subtle head motion toward the other room. She stood and took her coffee with her. Thankfully she'd finished eating. "I'm going to sit by the fire." She turned her back and walked casually to the living room, where she chose a seat farthest away from the others. She heard footsteps and knew her brother was coming. She had her phone out and decided to give James a few other details and explained more about Yvonne's disappearance and their belongings being searched. She knew he'd freak. That Stevie and Mark were being super quiet told her they already understood how big a mess they were mired in.

George sat down beside her. Royce came and sat on the other side. She should have known.

"What's up, Stacy?" her brother asked.

"The man we found?" She glanced between them to make sure, with all that had happened, that they remembered whom she spoke about.

They both nodded.

"He was drugged but ultimately died from exposure."

Royce sat back, a gentle "*Shit*" slipping from his lips.

George stared at her. "Drugged?" he asked softly. "Do we know what drugs?"

"Not yet. I've told James about what just happened to us. He's in contact with local law enforcement here. They'll try to see if the drugs were the same as the ones we were given. He's also limited to the goodwill of the local police. Remember. We're in a different country."

"So are we thinking that man was murdered?"

"Well, if he was drugged and then died, he sure as hell was," George said. "Yet that doesn't mean it was intentional. If any of us had gone outside last night, it could have ended up with the same result."

"Are we really thinking we have ... what? ... A serial drugging going on here?" Royce shook his head. "That sounds too bizarre."

"I suspect the drugging is just a means to an end," Stacy said quietly. "I just don't know what the end result is." But she was afraid she did. Kidnapping. But for what purpose, she had no clue.

"And Yvonne?"

She shook her head. "I don't know. Maybe she opened a bottle of wine and had several glasses before going back out for a few runs."

"Hell," Royce whispered. "That's all too possible."

"So what gives?" Geoffrey asked.

They'd been talking so low that she hadn't realized the rest of their friends had come to stand around them, worry on their faces.

George quickly filled them in.

Instead of surprised shock, there was mostly silence.

After a moment, Stevie said, "Not good."

"Are we thinking that the drugs were more of a prank then? With this dead guy just deciding to go for a walk in his drunken, drugged stupor? Neither scenario is likely, surely?" Kathleen asked, curling up close to George. She shuddered. George tugged her closer.

"I'm not sure yet," Stacy said seriously. "First, we're checking that the drugs used on him were the same that were used on us."

"That's horrible." Stevie threw himself onto the closest chair. "I came for a chance to rip down some runs, not get my ass drugged," he mumbled.

Stacy snorted. "And I came to finally get a vacation."

"A busman's vacation," Geoffrey said, with a snigger.

No arguing that.

ROYCE HATED THE thought of what was going on. They needed to shift the energy of the place, but, at the same time, he wanted to do a thorough search of everyone's stuff himself. He figured he might get a little resistance on that. George would agree with him. Unless they would all leave and not know any better. The cops were likely to come back here as well.

Then Stacy did it. "I'll take my camera outside and find something beautiful to photograph. Maybe that will make me feel better."

"Not alone," Royce snapped.

She glared at him. "I didn't get a chance to finish. I was going to suggest that we all get out. Go boarding. Catch a few runs. Something to change this depressed energy we are all feeling."

"If we have energy for that," Geoffrey said sharply, "then we have energy to rejoin the search for Yvonne."

"We aren't allowed to," George said quietly. "They don't know the effects of the drugs. They don't want us out there, in case they have to turn around and rescue us."

"Then, for the same reason, boarding and skiing are out."

Stevie looked at George for confirmation. At his nod, he groaned. "This is not the vacation I planned."

"It's not the vacation any of us planned," Kathleen said. "What about driving to the village and spending the afternoon walking around, have lunch out, do coffee? Something to get us out of here but not enough to zap our strength?"

"Another consideration," Christine said, "is the police. Are we allowed to go anywhere, or do we have to stay cooped up here?"

Silence.

"Damn if I know," Stacy said. "I'm presuming they got what they needed from us, so we can leave. If they need more, they'll come back or contact us at home. In the meantime, I need some fresh air." She got up and walked over to the boot room. "I know it would be foolish to go alone, so does anyone want to go with me?"

"I'm coming," Royce said in a hard voice.

She shrugged. "Fine, thank you."

"Aren't you going to bring your camera?" he asked curiously. "It's still upstairs, isn't it?"

She exhaled noisily. "Damn it."

He raised his eyebrows. "You might want to acknowledge that you aren't 100 percent yet."

"I know, but I need to get out. To get away." She motioned to the somber group sitting around the fire. "I don't want to do that all day."

"I'll go get your bag." He could get there easier than she could. He figured he'd take her out to the hillside, and they could sit in the sun and enjoy a few minutes respite. "Then we'll take a walk."

Up in the loft, he grabbed her stuff, took a quick look around to see if there was anything else she needed, and saw something odd sticking out from under Stacy's blankets. He bent down for a closer look.

A syringe. He pulled his sleeve down over his hand and picked it up. He sniffed the tip end but couldn't smell anything. He held it up to the tiny bit of light and realized there was still a little bit left inside. Stacy had a travel pack of tissues on her bed, and he carefully placed the syringe inside, then dumped her makeup bag and hid it all in there. He didn't want the others to know about it.

He knew Stacy wouldn't have been the one spiking the wine bottles, but that was likely to be the immediate reasoning of the rest of the group. She knew drugs. She'd been here all afternoon, so she had opportunity.

He did too, if he looked at it that way. Some could say he'd tucked it under Stacy's bed to throw suspicion on her, whereas sleeping up here, like he had last night, gave him access to her sleeping space. He hated to think of his friends turning on him, but no doubt he was questioning those he'd called a *friend* himself.

Except George. He would never hurt his sister, and he'd been furious that anyone might hurt Kathleen. Stevie and Mark on the other hand had just as much knowledge of drugs as Stacy did. They could have come back anytime and spiked the wine bottles themselves.

But why? The two men worked with Stacy every day. They would have had lots of opportunity to drug her.

Then he remembered the stalker that Stacy had felt in the bushes yesterday. What if that person was making sure she was out there and not in the cabin, so they could put the drugs in the wine? And through a syringe, no less. He slipped the makeup bag under his shirt and walked downstairs.

"Oh, Royce has it bad. Now he's even the gopher," Christine teased.

Royce laughed. "We won't be long, and we'll keep the cabin in sight the whole time we're out," he promised. "If anyone cares to join us, feel free."

"As if we'd be welcome," scoffed Stevie.

"Actually you would be," Stacy said, from the boot room doorway. "Especially if you come in an hour or so and bring coffee."

STUPID IDIOTS. LOOK at them, too scared to do anything. Looking

sideways at each other, wondering if one of their friends had just fucked them over.

He smiled inside.

Oh happy days. This was an extra bit of fun he hadn't expected.

Well worth repeating though. Watching this close-knit group slowly fall apart. Soon they'd turn on each other, like rabid dogs, and start attacking.

He couldn't wait.

They had no idea what was coming.

But they would soon.

Fools.

Chapter 25

S TACY STOPPED AT the crest of the hill and breathed deep. Then did it again. She couldn't believe how stifling the cabin had begun to feel. How difficult the atmosphere. She suspected that, with her and Royce gone, there'd be talk about them. As long as no one suspected them for this wine-doping scenario, she was fine with the talk. Expected it even. After all, humans loved to gossip.

"Feel better?" Royce asked quietly.

"Much." She tilted her head back and let the sun hit her face. "It was getting hard to take in there."

"I agree."

She stilled at an odd note in his tone. Without trying to make it obvious, she studied his face. Worry tensed his features, as he stared blankly ahead. Something was going on behind those magnetic eyes. "What's wrong?" she asked. He opened his mouth to say something, and she cut him off. "Don't lie."

The look on his face was both comical and affronted.

"Sorry," she rushed to assure him. "I didn't mean that quite the way it sounded. I would just prefer to know everything. I can't deal if I don't have all the facts."

In a subtle furtive movement, he checked around them to make sure they were alone.

She watched him curiously. "What is it?"

"When I went to get your camera bag," he said, pulling out her makeup bag from inside his coat, "I found this almost under your bed. As if you may have dropped it."

"My makeup bag?" She frowned. "I thought I left it on my bed."

"You did. I dumped the contents on the bed so I could use the bag." He motioned toward it. "Open carefully."

She unzipped the pouch, while he continued to watch the area. And saw the syringe stuffed into her Kleenex travel pack. "Oh my God." She blinked several times as she processed the implications. "Is it possible I was injected with the drugs?" she wondered.

"Possible, but, unless you can find an injection site, I doubt it. I figured it was likely the method of getting the drugs in the sealed wine bottles. People might have noticed an uncorked bottle or one that had been opened and recorked. However, with so many of us in the cabin, they would have assumed someone else opened it. But no one would have noticed a tiny pinprick through the cork."

She closed her eyes. "Shit. That took some planning. And do you think leaving this bit of evidence beside my bed was on purpose? Or did it fall from the perp's pocket while searching my room?"

With a shrug, he said, "Could be either."

Now it was her turn to look around the area to make sure they were alone. Yet she hoped the police were driving up to ask more questions. Instead the snowy area was calm, the air still. Nothing moved but the two of them. "We need to get this to the police."

"I know. I wasn't so sure I should let the others know what I found."

"Thank you for that." She smiled wryly. "And for trusting that I'm not the bad guy here."

"I never suspected you," he said. "It's not your way."

"Really? You don't think I could freeze someone to death?" she joked. "Look. He's even making it easy on them by drugging them first."

That gaze latched on to her face and narrowed. "Put that way, I wonder if that was the end that he hoped for the rest of us."

"On average, most poisoners are women."

"But we weren't poisoned," he corrected. "We were drugged."

"And, for some people, there is no difference."

He looked at her. "So do we have a woman then? Are we back to thinking it was Yvonne?"

"No." Stacy stared down at the cabin. "I actually don't."

"Why is that?"

Yeah, why did she think that? She studied the cabin, thinking about the sequence of events, even as she tucked the small bag into Royce's coat pocket. "I don't think she'd have left her gear behind like that. I can't see a motive for turning on everyone just because she was upset at you."

He protested. "She wasn't upset."

"Maybe she just didn't show it."

His hand whipped up and ran through his hair in a gesture she was starting to recognize as his instinctive reaction to stressful news.

"She wasn't upset," he reiterated. "I do understand women, and she was not seriously coming on to me, and she was not feeling rejected."

"On the off chance you are correct, what do you think happened to her?"

He glared at her. "I am correct."

After studying the look in his eyes for a long moment and wondering how any woman could not feel affected by a brush-off from him, Stacy willed it to the back of her mind and shifted her gaze away. "Fine. That doesn't change the fact that she is missing."

He took a step forward and grasped Stacy's face between his hands. "I need you to trust me."

Frowning, her gaze locked on to his. Searching. "I never said I didn't."

"No, you haven't." He stared at the sky over her head, as if wrestling with something. "But I don't hear that you do either."

That magnetic gaze of his locked onto hers again, willing her to give him what he wanted. Needed. She wanted to pull away but somehow found it impossible to break the hold he had on her. "I do trust you."

"Do you? You're out here in the woods with me, but do you trust that I wasn't the one to tamper with the wine? I had the opportunity. You did too. I trust you. But, if I did it, of course I would trust you. And you would never know."

Something hard was in his voice. Almost mean. As if she'd done something to piss him off. Instead of making her nervous by his harshness or the tension in his hands, her anger soared. She leaned forward and glared at him. "I wouldn't be out here if I didn't trust you."

The light in his eyes deepened. In a surprise move, he lowered his head and blocked the bright sun from her eyes. The cool touch of his lips surprised her. But the banked heat didn't. It had always been there. Barely leashed, sitting just under the surface. Waiting to ignite. She shivered. Her body remembered the touch of his hands, the tone of his muscles. The warmth of his breath.

He deepened the kiss, heat flaring between them, as he bent her over his arm. Her arms clutched him tightly, as her world spun, inside and out. She moaned deep in the back of her throat.

Suddenly she was back on her feet and set apart from him. She struggled to keep her balance in the world suddenly gone awry. She gasped for breath.

"I'm sorry," he finally got out, his chest heaving, his breathing raspy and deep. He rubbed his face. "I shouldn't have done that."

She blinked, struggling to adjust to the sudden change in his manner. She'd have done a lot for him to grab her and kiss her again, but … he looked guilty. *Why?* "Why did you then?" she asked in what she thought was a reasonable voice.

"Because I wanted to, damn it."

Her mouth dropped open.

"Oh, for God's sake. You know how I feel about you." He raised his hands in frustration and turned away.

It was hard to know what to say. She decided the truth might be the best way forward. "I don't know how you feel about me."

He spun and glared. "Bullshit. Of course you do. Hell, everyone does."

"I'd heard something from a couple people, but more of a joke—"

"It is a big joke to them. They all know."

"Know what?" she asked, her voice steady, her gaze direct, questioning. She had to know. Had to get to the root of this. It was too important to just gloss over.

He snorted, shaking his head, glaring at her. "Never mind." He motioned to the gorgeous scenery around them. "Take your damn pictures. I'll stand guard."

Shit. She wanted to push the issue. Get him to open up and to say exactly what he wanted from her. But a tiny part of her didn't really want to know. She'd kept him out of her life by pushing him away and by closing the door between them.

Because she didn't want to open it.

Hadn't wanted to open it.

Keeping it closed had been easier.

And slamming him for his behavior had given her some righteous logic for keeping the door closed. Excuses to not let him into her heart.

Because he'd break it.

And she was so weak that she didn't want to be hurt again. So she kept the door closed.

She was a coward.

REALLY? THEY WERE standing on the hillside in a lover's clench. For everyone to see. As if they were a couple. As if they had a right to such a relationship. Bull. They had the right to nothing.

Sunshine shone down on them, like a lover's kiss, and he hated it.

She was not for him. He was not for her. Neither should be allowed to live. That was obscene. Royce went with anyone. He was a rabid dog in heat. Everyone knew that. But even that bastard should have standards. Obviously he didn't.

Disgusting.

And out in the open like that.

Oh wait, what's this? Trouble in paradise. He watched as the two separated, as if Royce flung her away.

"Good boy, Royce. I knew you had more sense than that." He chuckled at the temper showing in the line of Royce's shoulders and back, as he faced the cabin. Stacy stood behind him, her hand out toward him.

And Royce ignored her. Good. He couldn't see them clear enough to see the expressions on their faces or to hear the words exchanged, but he could see their silhouettes, and that was enough. For the moment, that was enough.

This might be a winter paradise setting here, but there was no paradise on this mountain today. This week. This lifetime. At least not for them.

Only for him.

ROYCE REFUSED TO turn around. He locked down the emotions he'd stuffed inside a long time ago. He shouldn't have kissed her. Not because of her but because of him. The taste of such sweet honey, a passion so thick and wild—once tasted, it was hard to forget, and having stirred it all up again would make it that much harder to stomp back inside again.

Bitterness clawed at his throat. He wanted to make love to her until they were both stupid, but, since that wouldn't happen, no point in wishing things were different.

He'd tried so damn hard to be there for her. Now look. It was all gone again. Resolve stretched inside him. He needed to turn a new leaf after this nightmare. He needed to walk away forever. Be friends with her, sure, because he wouldn't forfeit his best friend, George. But it was time to grow up. Realize some dreams were hang-ups from previous days. Previous years. Previous lives.

No, it was time to move on.

And leave her behind.

He took a deep breath, feeling better as the cool air hit his lungs.

Bullshit. He felt worse. Fresh air wouldn't make any difference in his life. Only one thing would.

And that ain't happening.

Then he felt a hand slide into his and lace their fingers together.

His resolve, his anger, his bitterness evaporated in an instant, and he knew he could no more walk away from her than he could walk away from his heart.

It was impossible.

They were the same.

Chapter 26

S TACY STARED DOWN at her hand. Had it actually crept out and done what she thought it might have done? Betrayed her? His hands squeezed over hers so tightly that she thought he'd surely break something. But it didn't hurt. Instead, it was as if, by that very pressure, something inside her was building, an inner tension that needed him to squeeze harder and harder. Maybe finally breaking through the barriers she'd erected against him so long ago. Against the world so long ago. Against fate so long ago.

He turned slowly, and she almost gasped at the pain in his gaze as he studied her. His eyes open, full of hope, and yet expecting so much less.

Damn, she was a fool. And a bitch to cause so much agony. "I'm sorry," she said.

He shuttered his gaze, his shoulders slumping slightly. He nodded. "Not to worry. I'm a big boy." He went to drop her hand, but she hung on.

"No," she cried. "You don't understand."

He stilled, then slowly turned back to face her. "What don't I understand?"

"Why I'm sorry."

A light opened in his gaze, letting her see inside for the first time. Not too far in. But maybe enough.

She dropped her gaze. "It was hard for me. That weekend. I was desperate to know there was a purpose to living. To have a reason to get up every day. When I lost my friends, well, my world collapsed. When I lost them, I was like a ship that had run aground. No way to float away."

She shivered against the chill inside.

"Nothing to do but be beaten by the times of change, and I felt like I couldn't move. When I saw you that weekend, something clicked. I needed to be held. Needed to be connected at least in some way to someone else. To the rest of the world."

She stopped, unsure of what to say next and a little embarrassed by the outpouring already. Yet she needed to get it all out. "I was looking to find a purpose to continue with life. I wasn't suicidal. I just didn't feel anything." She gave a small deprecating movement. "I don't mean to make so much about it, but I thought, if you understood how I felt, maybe you'd understand my reaction."

When she didn't continue for a long moment, he nudged her gently. "And your reaction afterward?" he asked cautiously. "I do understand your reasons for that weekend. We've all had that need to be close to someone. But afterward ..." Sadness once again glanced off his tone. "What was that all about?"

Instinctively she tried to pull her hand away, only he held her fast, letting her know he wanted answers and he wanted them now.

She opened her mouth, then closed it. He narrowed his gaze at her. She gave him a lopsided smile and the truth. "I was scared."

That dark, mysterious gaze widened, and the light inside that she'd seen before slowly flared back into life.

"Scared?" He shook his head. "How the devil could you be scared of me after that weekend? You had to know by then that I'd never hurt you."

"Not scared of you. Scared of getting hurt again. Scared of caring and losing again. Scared of falling so far off the grid that next time I might not survive. Scared of what could be—knowing I didn't deserve it. Or you."

His mouth dropped open.

She continued. "Scared of your lifestyle. It could kill you, you know? Scared of your quick and easy girlfriends because I didn't want to become one—and yet I just had been. I'd never done anything like that before. Promised myself I never would. I held myself accountable to a specific standard."

"And fell into the ghetto by spending that weekend with me?" This time, his tone was incredulous and so was the hurt.

Damn, all she seemed to do was hurt him.

But she had to get it all out. Then he'd realize that they wouldn't be any good together. That he could move on. That it was better that he did so.

"For having that weekend that I'd always wanted. I wasn't like you. I wasn't like your string of girlfriends, and I didn't want to be like them. I wanted to have longer than three-day relationships. To care about the people I went to bed with. Sex was never casual for me."

Her voice dropped. "That weekend I needed you. I wanted you. I took what you offered, and then I walked away." Her voice broke. "I'd always thought I was better than one of your weekend flings, only I ended up falling there anyway. Ended up worse than the other women. They'd at least been honest about why they were in your bed and what they wanted. Me? I just lied to you. To me. Because I was where I'd always wanted to be," she admitted, "since forever. And I couldn't even be honest about it."

He stared at her in shocked silence, obviously not getting it.

"Don't you understand?" she cried out. "I'm not good enough. I don't deserve you or to be happy. I couldn't give you what you needed." She snorted in disgust. "I should have done more to stop Janice and Francine. More to warn them. Maybe if I'd gone with them, I might have been able to save them. I lost them, and I survived." Tears clouded her vision. "Why me? They were so full of life. They shouldn't have died."

"Ah hell," he snapped, exasperation in every line of his body. "Did you really put me through these last few years, *us* through these last few years, out of guilt? Survivor's guilt?"

Her gaze widened in response.

"Damn it." He reached out and snatched her into his arms. "To think of all the pain I've gone through—"

"Exactly," she cried out, trying to step back out of his arms. "I put you through all that—"

"For being one the smartest women I know, you are the st—"

"Don't say it," she warned.

"Ha. I know the answer to this problem." And he took her mouth with a force that surprised them both. The bite of pain, the hard pressure of his lips, the clamped arms around her back ...

And she barely noticed. She kissed him back with all the longing she'd held inside for so long. Finally having the freedom to take a little and to give a lot, she tried to show him how sorry she was. How much she wanted this. How desperately glad she was to be back in his arms.

Until she tasted salt. As in salty tears.

Her own.

"Jesus." He pulled back slightly, his thumb reaching to stroke her swollen lips. The look on his face was one of dismay and shame. "I'm so sorry," he whispered, replacing his thumb with his lips, as he dropped delicate kisses along her mouth, her chin, and up to her nose and her drenched eyes. "I'm so sorry."

She shook her head. "I'm fine. You didn't hurt me."

"This"—he dropped a tender kiss on her lips, then at the corner of her eyes—"and this say otherwise."

She smiled through the tears. "No. It's an outpouring of emotions but not pain." Then she corrected herself immediately. "Outpouring of pain held in for too long."

"In that case …" He pulled her closer and cuddled her against his chest. "Cry away."

And damn if his permission didn't bring on the waterworks. And she bawled. With shaking shoulders, her face buried against his coat, she released the last few years of what she'd thought she'd been handling, only to now realize she'd avoided it and had instead stuffed the pain and hurt deep inside.

ROYCE HELD HER close, his heart full, his mind overwhelmed. Stacy was an incredibly strong woman. She lived in her head so much that she'd used that space to disconnect from her heart. And now that that bridge had been rebuilt, the floodgates opened up between them.

It might take her a bit to reconcile the new connection.

He'd be there to help her.

If she would let him.

He knew she'd take a huge step back if she could right now, just because it would be more comfortable for her. And she had to be feeling raw.

As he worked through his next step, he noted her shoulders were no longer shaking and her sobs had been reduced to sniffles. He couldn't help himself—he cuddled her even closer, his cheek resting on top of her head. She'd said a lot that he would have to consider, not the least about his own behavior. How it looked to others hadn't been a consideration before. From her perspective, he could understand her hesitancy to go in that direction. He'd had similar thoughts earlier. He didn't particularly like her assessment, but he understood it. By the same twisted measure, he was incredibly happy she hadn't led his same lifestyle. How did that work?

Except to make him not feel too good about his own standards.

"What are you thinking?" she asked, her voice low, hesitant.

He sighed. It would take her some time to feel secure at this new place in her life.

"I'm thinking that I'm guilty of the same judgment. I'm personally very happy that you've been more restrained with your relationships," he admitted. "And that's not something I expected to feel. It's never mattered before."

That startled a gurgle of laughter from her.

He grinned, loving the sound and loving her.

Loving her. He paused. Did he?

He hadn't quite taken the thought process that far. He'd been obsessed with her for a long time. Loved being with her. Loved making love to her. But did he love her? Hell, yes. And had probably spent more than half of his life in love with her.

A shout from behind had them both turning around.

Stevie. With two travel mugs full of coffee.

"Oops," Stacy said, "I guess our hour is up." She wiped the tears from her eyes and smiled at Stevie.

Royce? He just glared at his friend, who was giving them that all-too-knowing grin.

Damn friends.

Couldn't live with them and couldn't live without them.

Chapter 27

STACY SMILED AT Stevie, ignoring his wry grin. She knew her crying jag still showed on her face. There wasn't much she could do about it. Besides, Stevie was a romantic. He'd love to think of her and Royce settling their differences. There hadn't been an open war between them, but there'd been a definite cold front.

She accepted the cup of coffee with relief. "Thank you," she murmured. She twisted off the lid and breathed in the aromatic steam. "This smells divine."

"Nothing like a great cup of java to help you overcome all that relationship angst."

"What would you know?" she countered, with a smile. "Your relationships last all of ten minutes."

Royce gave a great shout of laughter at that, while Stevie gave her a wounded look, but, in the end, his eyes were twinkling. "And that's because you won't go out with me," he cried out in a piteous voice. "Now if you would …"

"Ha," she said, with a big grin, "Then what?"

"I might manage twenty!"

On that note of laughter, she turned to smile down at the cabin, knowing most of them had likely seen her and Royce make up. Oh well. Let them. She felt better. That's what counted. And that Royce should feel better. She slid a sideways glance his way and realized he was frowning.

She followed the direction of his gaze.

A person stumbled through the trees. Fell. Got up and stumbled forward, headed for the cabin.

"Good Lord. Who is that?" she cried out.

Stevie turned to stare. Then they all galvanized into action.

They raced across the hill, only to watch the person fall again, and this time he didn't get up.

Royce reached him first, Stevie and Stacy on his heels.

Royce picked up the stranger and ran to the cabin. Stacy pulled out her phone and called for medical assistance. She gave what little details she had, watching as Stevie peeled past Royce to get to the cabin in preparation.

She came barreling in to see Royce lay the stranger in front of the fire, everyone crowding around, as he tried to warm him up.

A scarf was wrapped around his head, and he wore a coat that appeared to be too big.

Royce gently undressed him.

And they all stopped in shock.

Stacy ran up to squeeze in between her brother and Kathleen.

"What's wrong?" she cried.

"It's Yvonne," Royce said, his voice grave. "Only this is not her coat."

Stacy came down beside Yvonne and picked up her icy hand. "I've called it in. Where could she have been all this time?"

"Given she's wearing someone else's coat, do we want to assume she was alone?" George asked in a hard voice, his gaze looking out the window and the mountain behind them. "I suggest a group search the direction she came from and make sure another person isn't in trouble."

Stacy nodded. "Please do. We'll try to get her warm, until the ambulance arrives."

She heard most of them splitting off and getting dressed to search. While Stevie and Royce worked on Yvonne, she stripped off the wet outer clothing and boots. Once Yvonne was wrapped up in blankets, Stacy carried the clothing to the kitchen table and carefully went through the pockets. It was a man's coat. She continued to work her way through the pockets and folds, looking for anything to indicate what had happened and who the other party was. Inside the breast pocket of the big coat was a business card. She pulled it out. "Brian Hennessey."

"What?"

"Inside the pocket is a business card with that name on it."

"Repeat the name," Royce said. She walked over and showed the card to him. He shrugged. "I've never heard it."

She turned it for Stevie to look at, and he shook his head. "Me neither." He turned his attention back to Yvonne.

Next Stacy returned to the boots that Yvonne wore and searched both, including lifting the sole of one and then the other. Nothing. However, they were an expensive leather brand by a high-end company. And new from the looks of them. The coat was 100 percent wool and looked more appropriate for a stroll around town than in a winter resort. However, it wasn't impossible.

She checked the pants and shirt next. Yvonne still had on her long underwear. And all four items were ones Stacy recognized. So she'd been in her own clothes but wearing a man's coat. That wasn't even all that odd.

"Did you find anything, Stacy?" Royce asked.

"No. Nothing useful." She kept the oddities out of the conversation for the moment. She turned back to the men. "How is she?"

"In bad shape."

In the background, she heard the sirens of an incoming emergency vehicle. She raced to the door.

The police SUV pulled up behind the first responder. Yvonne was quickly loaded up and taken away, leaving the three of them to face the police. When they explained who was in the emergency vehicle, Stacy was delighted to see the relief on the cops' faces. No one had expected her disappearance to turn out so well. Stacy showed them the clothing they'd taken off her and the business card.

At the card, the first officer asked, "Do you know this name?"

Stacy shook her head. "No."

"Are you sure?"

"Yes. I might know his face, but I don't know his name."

"He's the man you found frozen in the snow."

She stared at him in shock. "What? But that means Yvonne was possibly with him? As she's wearing his coat. Only …"

Royce finished her thought. "Only he died before she went missing."

ROYCE DIDN'T LIKE this turn of events. Arms crossed, he stood in front of the fire, as he listened to Stacy and the cop work things back and forth. The problem was, there was no easy way to work it. They'd found a dead man. Two days later, a friend of theirs went missing and turned up the next day, wearing the dead man's coat.

That didn't make sense, not any way he tried to fit the pieces together. He'd also taken one of the policemen aside and handed over the syringe. The cop hadn't been impressed at not being called right away but asked a few more questions and packed up the syringe for testing.

As the cops made a move to leave, they looked up the hill to see the rest of his group coming back.

George reached them first. "No sign of anyone else," he said, gasping for breath. "We tracked her a long way up but need snowmobiles to go any farther."

"We have someone on the way already. Thanks for checking." The cop pulled out the business card found in Yvonne's coat. "Do you know this name?"

George read the card, a frown on his face, as he replied, "No, should I?"

"It was in the pocket of the man's coat Yvonne was wearing," Stacy said.

He looked over at her, a question in his eyes.

It was the cop who answered. "The card belongs to the dead man you found in the snow a few days ago."

"What?" George reacted in shock. "How is that possible she was wearing his coat then?" He frowned at the others. "Maybe he took it off in his confusion, and she found it while she was in trouble and put it on. It's the only thing that makes sense."

"We'll see," the cop said noncommittally. "There will be an answer."

"There always is," Royce said quietly, his gaze on Stacy, whose gaze hadn't left the business card in the cop's hand. What did she know?

Chapter 28

THE SNOWMOBILES ARRIVED before the police were out of sight. There were two. The drivers stopped, asked for what little information was available, then took off in a rush. There were still a few hours of daylight left.

Stacy turned to Royce. "I'd like to go up there and take a look for myself."

He frowned, instinctively shaking his head.

She nodded. "I know we can't go as fast or as far as the sled, but I'd like to see the trail she made to determine where she was coming from."

"The backside of the mountain."

"But she wasn't wearing her boarding gear, so why was she down there?" Stacy countered. "I'd just like to go."

Royce gave in. He knew she wouldn't give up. She wasn't considered hardheaded and stubborn for nothing. She geared up for a trek outdoors, then turned and said, "George, would you mind grabbing my camera bag, please?"

She waited while he fetched it for her, then, with that over her shoulder, Royce at her side, they headed out. As several snowmobiles had traveled the same track, the walking was easier now. Trudging uphill for the first part, she had a hard time holding back the knot of nervousness inside. She had a horrible feeling this was all connected to something so much bigger but knew they didn't have all the pieces yet. She didn't know if the snowmobile guys would find something, but she wanted to double-check that she hadn't missed something herself.

"So do you want to tell me what we're really doing?" Royce asked.

"I saw something the other day. It was stunning, eerie, and incredibly beautiful. Now I'm wondering if there wasn't something more sinister."

She felt his sharp gaze but didn't take her gaze off the hillside ahead of her.

"I want to know if the direction Yvonne came from was in the same area as what I photographed earlier. If it wasn't, that's great then, so what I saw before was Mother Nature at her best. If it is where Yvonne came from, however, then we need to inspect it closer."

"Do I get to know what 'it' is?" he asked calmly.

"I don't have a problem telling you, but I'd prefer to see your initial reaction, in case it's not the same as mine. I could be imagining this. I just can't be sure."

"Good enough. Where is this place?"

"Where we were the day we were late because I was taking pictures."

"I don't think she came from that direction," he said slowly.

"It depends how far away she might have been."

With that, she fell silent. She needed to save her energy. At the top, she took several deep breaths, as she regained her strength. Ahead, she noted the snowmobile tracks, heading to the right and up. She studied the ridge ahead.

The images she'd seen earlier were around the corner.

ROYCE STUDIED STACY'S face, as she looked at the snowy ridge ahead of them. Concentration glowed from those blue eyes, as she picked out one geographical marker, then zipped across, looking for another. She chewed on her bottom lip—an action guaranteed to drive him nuts. He wanted to tell her to stop it. That her lips were swollen from the abuse. But then he wanted to soothe them with his own lips.

And that she wasn't ready for. At least he didn't think so.

But he could hope.

Then she turned to face him, a question in her gaze. He smiled, shrugged, and turned to study the mountain. She so wasn't ready to know what he'd been thinking.

But that didn't mean he'd stop thinking about it.

Chapter 29

CRAZY THOUGHTS TWISTED inside Stacy's head. Could other cabins be in the backwoods? Could Yvonne have been trying to come home? Was there a cabin close by that they didn't know about? Just because she didn't know about such a place didn't mean it didn't exist. It was a huge resort. This area had been settled for over one hundred years, with many private lots. Cabins dotted the area—out of the way but close enough to all the amenities of the resort. Still, the authorities would know. The search and rescue team as well.

As they trudged forward, Stacy removed her camera from her bag and pulled up the pictures she'd taken the other day.

"What's going on?" Royce asked. "What are you looking for?"

"I thought I saw something the other day," she said, flicking through the strip of photos. "Remember when I was out here for so long?"

"Right, and you appeared to be fascinated with that waterfall?"

"Yes, I was, but what fascinates me now is what's beside it. There was opaqueness to the ice, as if a big black space were behind it."

"Like a cave or something?"

"*Hmm ...*" she murmured, carefully studying the image in front of her. "I just wondered if maybe there was a cabin or a dwelling of some kind here, likely very old, that maybe Yvonne and whoever she was with—if she was with someone—tripped into and spent the night, then tried to find their way back out again in the morning."

"If they were snowmobiling and broke down, they might have taken refuge, but I can't imagine any other scenario where that would make sense."

"I know." She motioned at the image to the left of the hillside, where the shadow was. An odd-shaped shadow. "Doesn't that look different along there?"

He peered at it, shrugged, and said, "Honestly, not really."

She laughed. "Let's go take a closer look."

It took another ten minutes of slogging through the snow on the tracks that were just crusted enough to hold their weight, until they went to take the next step, at which point they broke through to the soft snow below.

By the time they got to where she had stood before, she was sweating freely and wondering just how healthy she truly was. She groaned, opening her jacket to let in some fresh air. "That's hard work today," she said.

"It is."

She stared up at the left side of the hill adjacent to the frozen waterfall.

She turned to study the scene.

The shadow was as high as the right side. The slope easier. There didn't appear to be any way up, but, of course, there never was, unless you knew the routes.

Royce headed over to the area she'd pointed out, and Stacy fell in behind him. They were halfway there when she heard the snowmobiles.

She couldn't see them yet, but their engines were loud enough to hear over the blanket of snow separating them. She understood they were coming farther off to the left. Renewing her excitement that maybe she was correct, she and Royce kept climbing, finally cresting the small rise, as the sleds bounded toward them.

Up top was a flat stretch of long pristine snow, marred by a set of tracks. The snowmobiles came to a stop. One of the search and rescue team noted that they'd followed the tracks to this area, but it had stopped in the trees. The snow had been trampled in many places, but they hadn't found anything or anyone else.

"Do you two want a lift back?" the first man asked.

Stacy did. Desperately. But she wanted to take a look around her first. Then hearing that the snowmobiles were going back now and not in fifteen minutes, she declined. She stood at the top of the hill and watched them slash their way across the hillside below, heading for the cabin and everyone who waited there. Resolutely she turned. Now that she was here, she had no idea what she expected to find. She was aware of Royce watching her.

Finally he said, "If you tell me what you're looking for, maybe I could help you look."

"It's kind of stupid. I was just thinking there might be a way inside."

"Inside?" he asked cautiously. "Inside what?"

"I think a big cavern is here. A cave. Something."

"And?"

"I was just wondering if that's where Yvonne had been all night."

"And why would she have?"

She could tell he was trying not to say she was being crazy.

"I don't know. But I thought I saw a person in the ice images when I had my camera out before. I had my zoom lens and could see so much but had trouble capturing it. Now it doesn't look the same," she cried out in frustration. "I can't find what I saw before."

"A man?"

She stopped, her temper igniting. "Yes. A man."

He threw up his hands. "Hey, that's fine. Maybe you did see someone here. But what difference does that make?"

She really hated having to tell him. It was her line of work that immediately saw all the good things in life and the bad that were right beside them. In this case, inside them. She refused to answer, instead walking to a small depression in the snow. A tree above them, with its overhung branches, kept them pretty well protected, but new snow had fallen from its boughs above. Hiding whatever was below. She walked closer.

And fell.

Through the snow.

Through the ice.

Through the air to the ground.

She screamed as her world flipped. Cold sharp shards of ice bit at her, and she flailed her arms and legs, trying to stop her fall. Her landing was fast and hard. Stars slammed into her mind.

Dimly in the background, she heard Royce yelling for her.

She groaned.

"Stacy? Don't move. I'm coming down."

She whispered, "Don't." Then realizing he couldn't hear her, she called out, "Don't, it's too dangerous."

"Right," he called out, humor in his voice. "So I'm supposed to just leave you?"

Of course he wouldn't. She knew that. Neither did she want him crashing down with her. They hadn't brought any rescue gear, so he'd need to go back and get some rope. She'd just lie here and rest until he returned.

In the back of her mind, she realized he was talking to someone. Good. Someone else to help. But she also realized that what she really wanted was to roll over and sleep. It would feel *sooo* good. She shifted, trying to get more comfortable, and moaned when she moved her head.

That shifted the sleepy cobwebs from her mind. She had to move. Had to get up. It was the head injury making her want to lie here. She reached up and checked the sore spot, but her fingers weren't sticky, so the wound hadn't broken through the skin. Good. It was just a stunner of a crack. She shifted gently onto her hands and knees and managed to sit on her haunches and look around. Fallen snow and ice were everywhere. She snatched up her camera, grateful to see it still in good working order. She glanced up at Royce, who slowly came down the snowslide, making a rough set of steps as he came.

"I'm okay," she said. "I just saw stars for a moment."

He kept working his way toward her, his gaze intent. "Even small cracks like that can kill you."

"I do know that," she said in a conversational tone. All too well. The last case on her table had been a woman who'd fallen while skiing and had refused medical attention. She'd not been wearing a helmet at the time of the accident, and she'd retreated to her hotel room. She was dead the next day from a small bleed in the brain.

"*Right.*"

She laughed. "I will get checked over. I won't be stupid about this. I'm just telling you that nothing is broken and that I'm feeling well. It was just a small tumble."

"Doesn't matter how small. In these conditions, it still counts."

He'd almost reached her by the time she'd decided to try standing up. That worked. She was a little shaky, but being on her feet felt much better. She checked herself over and shook out her arms and legs. "I'm actually quite fine," she said to him as he reached her.

"Better than fine." And he gently tugged her into his arms.

She relaxed against him, happy to know that she could now. Falling was scary, but knowing she wasn't alone and had someone responsible enough to help was even better. That it was Royce was perfect.

After a moment she pushed back slightly, looked up into his warm eyes, and saw the relief and care in his gaze. She reached up and kissed him gently. "Thank you."

"For what?" he asked, his gaze quizzical.

"For being here."

A beautiful light flickered to life in those beautiful brown eyes of his. He tugged her back into his arms and cuddled her close. "Thanks for letting me," he whispered against her hair.

She smiled. She couldn't see much of what they were standing on from where she was. She twisted, still in the circle of his arms, and tried to look around. "What is this place?"

"Likely just another trap waiting for an unsuspecting person to find it." He laughed. "Congratulations for being that lucky person."

"Ha, I should buy a lottery ticket." The walls were fallen snow that had tumbled in with her. With the sun shining down into her pit and reflecting on the snow, it was so blinding she had to use her hands to stop the glare. She slid her boot back and forth and looked down to see a hard sheet of ice under the fallen snow. At least the hollow was big enough to walk a few feet forward and back.

"Do you think you can try getting out," he asked, "or do you want me to call for help?"

She glanced back the way he'd come down. Coming down had been easy. She wasn't so sure she'd get up the same way. There were no visible steps as they'd crumbled under his weight. But she might still be able to climb up. Stepping carefully, as her balance still wasn't perfect, she made it to the bottom of where he'd half-climbed, half-slid down. Standing at the bottom looking up, it appeared much steeper— and much higher than she expected.

"We'll wait for the crew to come," Royce said cheerfully. "I'm not up to climbing that sucker."

"You would manage that easily," she said. "I don't think I can." She stepped up and tried to grab onto a boulder in front of her. It crumbled under the pressure. "There's nothing to grasp. Nothing to step on." As she said that, the first snow step under her boots sank, giving emphasis to her words.

"Exactly. So we wait."

"I wonder how far this fault goes." She took a few steps toward him.

He reached out to steady her, tucking her up closer. "I doubt very far. We could be at ground level where we're standing and the walls on either side of us are just a big snow dump from the cliff above."

"That's possible." She looked up and saw the top of the waterfall and the bare rock. She motioned in the direction where she'd originally fallen. "It looked like an opening was down there."

"Doesn't matter if there is," he said. "We're not exploring." He gave her a stern look. "We've had enough excitement for one day."

Under a hooded glance, she wondered what the chances were of changing his mind.

"No," he said sternly. "We're not looking."

Just then they heard shouts from the rescue team. Stevie's voice was the loudest, as he called out to them.

"See?" Royce smiled. "For once, he has perfect timing."

ROYCE LET OUT a sigh of relief when he and Stacy were back on top of the pit. He wasn't exactly sure what kind of fault had created that trap, but he was so glad Stacy hadn't been alone. Maybe that was what had happened to Yvonne. Except where would she have gotten the coat?

Stacy said, "A heartfelt *thank you* to everyone."

"Let's go," Royce said. "Hot rum toddies sound like the perfect end to a very rough day."

The group slowly trekked down the hillside, Stacy and Royce safely ensconced in the middle. Royce carried one of the ropes that had been used to help them climb back up, as the sides continuously caved in on them, hampering their efforts. Now all he wanted was to be home. Not back in the cabin, although that would be a good place to start, but home in Seattle and his cozy apartment—or in Stacy's cedar-and-glass converted loft would be much better. And her bed.

He wouldn't push her, but, once they were alone, the air would spark and fire between them, with no help from him. They'd be tearing up the sheets in no time. He doubted she was ready for that at the cabin, due to a lack of privacy.

But, after all the accidents and weird events, he wouldn't let her sleep alone. Good thing he'd moved his stuff up there last night. They were supposed to stay a few more days, but he could see this curtailing the festivities. Personally he'd go home tomorrow, if he could get Stacy to go too.

Then again, if they could get a fun day out of this, it would end the vacation on a much better note, even if they did cut it short by a day or so.

Stacy's cheeks were bright red by the time they made it to the cabin, shedding their outerwear and their boots in the boot room first. Just one step inside the main cabin, and Royce smelled the wonderful aromas. Kathleen had stayed behind and had made coffee and had a thick beef stew simmering. Just the smell alone was heavenly. After standing in the cold as long as they had, Royce was chilled and starving. He doubted Stacy was feeling any differently.

She was likely worse. He could see the fatigue in her eyes again. Damn it, she was supposed to rest while here. Regain her strength.

"I'm fine. Stop worrying."

"Not going to happen," he muttered. "This vacation has been nothing but hell."

There was an odd silence beside him. He turned to look at her, wondering what he'd said or didn't say. "What?"

"It certainly has had some low points, but there have also been a few highlights." She squeezed his hand.

Damn. He lifted her hand and kissed the back of it. "That there has been," he whispered, hoping it was only loud enough for her to hear.

It wasn't.

"That's enough mushy stuff, you two. Keep walking."

Geoffrey and Stevie gave the two of them a gentle push deeper toward the living room. Stacy rubbed her hands together, appreciating the warmth of being inside and out of the elements. Standing in front of the fire was heavenly. Royce headed for the kitchen and got two big mugs. He made hot mochas and laced them with rum, before taking them back to Stacy. She sat on the couch, her feet in front of the fire.

He knew that, with a hot meal, a hot drink, and a hot fire, she'd be asleep in no time. He envied her.

She was talking to Stevie in a low voice, as Royce approached. "I know I saw something. I'll go back up there tomorrow."

He stopped in front of her. "You're not going anywhere near back there." His voice was hard, cold. Damn it. When would she quit?

She smiled sweetly and said nothing.

He didn't trust her. Taking the spot next to her, he leaned his head back and waited. But she surprised him by letting the subject drop.

She sipped her hot drink, stopped, and sipped again. "This is really good."

That was an understatement. But he sipped his, just glad to be under cover and safe. The wind was picking up, and, sure enough, there'd be a snowstorm again tonight. Then again, that's partly why they came here. Winter playtime.

Only, so far, there hadn't been much fun.

UNBELIEVABLE. HE COULDN'T *understand how he'd gotten so lucky. Unlucky to begin with, then lucky. And he'd stick with the lucky part. It was crazy good, but, at the same time, he couldn't hold his hot rum toddy*

in his hands, as they trembled so badly that it would be noticeable. And this wasn't the time for a show of nerves.

Unless they were nerves of steel. Odd that he was reacting to today's close call so badly. Why this time?

Because it was the closest anyone had come to his space. His private space. He had never shared that part of the mountain. Well, except for one other. That person understood a part of him. He loved to snowboard down that strip, climb the frozen waterfall, and enjoy his surroundings.

He had never intended to share that pristine wilderness.

If Stacy went back up—oh, yeah, he'd heard her talking about it—well, she may have gotten off lucky today, but she wouldn't have the same luck the second time.

He'd make sure of it.

Chapter 30

STACY TOOK HER bowl back to the kitchen and filled the sink with hot water. She'd do the dishes now, in case she crashed early. She could feel her energy disappearing with the tick of the clock. Too many shocks and adrenaline rushes today. Her system was on overload and would shut down soon.

She felt it draining with each dish she washed. Finally she was done. She needed to talk to Royce about what she'd seen and what she'd thought she'd opened up there, but she knew he wouldn't be receptive, and she wasn't up for the fight.

If she went to bed soon, she could review the pictures she'd taken, some from the other day and others from today.

She visited for a few minutes longer and then said good night. Within minutes, she was ready for bed and climbing the stairs to the loft. Alone, she pulled out her camera and flicked through to the set of images she took earlier. She wished she had her laptop or tablet, but she didn't, so she could only look on the small screen. Not ideal.

She shifted to the images she took today and went back and forth several times, trying to figure out what she'd seen. After a few moments, her eyelids started to droop.

With the images still up, she crawled into bed and studied them. When she couldn't hold the camera anymore, she closed her eyes and rested. Something was bugging her. Something she wished she could pull out from the back of her mind.

But she was too tired.

As she was drifted off to sleep, she heard someone climbing the stairs. Royce. Her eyes flew open. Or was it? Her muscles tensed as she waited.

He was so quiet, she wasn't sure. She rolled over, so she could look at him. And found Royce staring down at her.

"Hey." He sat down on the side of her bed. "I had hoped you would be asleep by now."

"I was looking at my pictures," she said sleepily. "Seeing if I could figure out what was bugging me."

"And did you?" He stroked his fingers down her cheeks, soothing, caressing.

She made a tiny shaking movement of her head.

"See? It's probably not there."

She gave a sleepy smile. "Maybe."

"So forget about it right now. And sleep."

"Can't. I keep seeing the image in my head."

He reached down and picked up the camera, flicking through the images one by one. He stopped at one, then another. He held up the one and turned it, so she could see what he was looking at. "This one?"

"No." She grabbed it and moved through the images again. "These."

He looked at the images and then down at her, before returning to study the images. He angled the camera slightly toward the light, frowned, went to the next one, and then the next one. Finally he sat back. "*Huh.*"

"Yeah. What do you see?"

"Maybe a cave behind a thin layer of ice. Maybe nothing. Maybe a person." He looked at her again. "What lens did you have for this? It's super close-up, but I've never seen anything this clear."

"I took those that day you were watching, waiting for me." She pushed herself up on one elbow and twisted so she could point out the first image. "I have a wonderful zoom that I used to get these. You can see magnification with each image."

"I can. And this last one is close but not enough to make anything out. This is why you wanted to go today and see that area again? Did you figure it out when you were there today?"

"No. I was hoping to, but then I fell."

"How close to this blackness were we when you fell?" he asked, studying the latest images with a frown on his face.

"Almost right on top."

ROYCE STUDIED THE pictures, his frown deepening. He wasn't sure he liked any of this. There was definitely a dark spot. It could be a woman. Why would anyone be there? It was likely just a trick of the light.

But he didn't like it.

If someone was hiding, why? Was she hurt? Or in trouble? Stacy had taken these days ago. Was it the man they'd found dead? Had he been caught there like that? Or was it someone with a cabin close by? This cabin was remote, so it was all too plausible that there were others around.

What was there at the frozen waterfall?

Now that he could see what Stacy had seen, he wanted to go back too.

He settled back slightly and couldn't take his gaze from her. "Do you think this has something to do with Yvonne's disappearance?"

She winced. "I don't know. What I do know is that, if a space is there, if a person is there, maybe Yvonne was too."

"Honey, you can't save everyone." He reached down and pulled her into his arms. He held her close, cradled her in his arms, and held her tight. "We'll talk about it in the morning. And I don't want us going up there alone. There might be someone in trouble who needs our help or there might be someone causing trouble. We don't go alone. Got it?"

"Yes."

"Good." He lay her back down. "Now get some sleep. I'll keep watch to make sure that tumble didn't cause more damage than we suspect." He leaned over and kissed her. She threw her arms around his head and chest and pulled him closer.

Just like last time, heat flashed out of control, as she pressed herself against him, her hands hungry, as they held him close.

His lips plundered, and she was greedy in response.

God, he'd never gotten enough before. And he didn't think he could get enough now. She was dynamite. And, for once, she was his.

She heard snickers and laughter from the group below. She motioned with her head, her gaze regretful.

"I'm sorry," he whispered.

Her lips quirked. "Me too."

"Go back to sleep," he said quietly. "Tomorrow is a new day."

She shifted to the far side of her bed and threw back the covers, then patted the space beside her.

His eyes lit up. "Are you sure?" he asked, his voice low, his gaze searching.

She nodded. "I'm so tired that you won't disturb me."

He stood and returned to his bed, where he quickly got changed. Leaving his clothes on his bed, he returned to her side of the loft and slid under the covers.

He tugged her up close to his chest and shifted them both, so they fit on the bed and with each other. She smiled, snuggled in, and closed her eyes.

Listening to her soft breathing, as it deepened and slowed, he realized he didn't want to sleep. His body needed it. His mind and heart, however, didn't want to miss this moment. He was afraid he'd wake up and find the previous day had been a dream, and she would still be holding him at arm's length.

Right now, with her in his arms, he was happy.

LOOK AT THEM. All of a sudden they were a couple. Just like that. From enemies to lovers. He couldn't hear anything from the loft at this point, but knowing they were up there together made his blood boil. He tossed back his laced hot chocolate and smiled at the others. "All right, I'm turning in. I'm tired myself."

"We all are," someone murmured from the corner.

He couldn't determine which of the three crashed males had spoken. They all were stretched over the furniture, as if the thought of getting up and shifting to their beds was the last thing on their minds.

"You all would get a better night if you slept in your beds and not on the couches."

"*Mmm,*" came a mumble from the corner.

"Your loss." *He walked past a pair of splayed legs, and he wasn't sure, but that looked like Kathleen asleep on the floor.*

Whatever.

The more trusting they were, the easier it would be to set his plans in motion.

Except he needed sleep himself. Then he'd take the next step.

Chapter 31

SOMETIME IN THE middle of the night, Stacy woke to heat, fire, and ice. Warm hands inside the back of her shirt and a chill to the air.

She opened her eyes, shifting back slightly to look at Royce's face. And saw his heated gaze staring down at her. "About time you woke up," he murmured thickly and lowered his head.

With her arms around him, she abandoned herself to the moment and his embrace. He deepened the kiss. Her lips parted, letting him inside. She moaned, the tiny sound catching in the back of her throat.

"*Shh,*" he whispered, his lips trailing down her cheek. "It's after midnight. The others are asleep."

Her gaze widened, and she froze. The heat from his breath bathed her neck and throat, sending shivers down her spine. She thought about protesting—until his wicked fingers slid around her ribs, before climbing a little higher. When his hand closed around her breast, she gasped and arched.

"*Shh.*"

The effort to hold back, when her nerves were screaming into awareness, was excruciating. He bent his head and took her nipple into his mouth and suckled.

She whimpered once, twice, then again, her body twisting in the dark of the night. She couldn't hear anyone else up, but she couldn't really hear anything over the pounding of her heart and the rasp of her shirt, as he lifted it up and over her head. Cold air hit her fevered body. She wanted him. Oh God, she wanted him. She slid her hands down his hard body, realizing he'd already divested himself of all clothing.

She wanted to explore him, as his hands were making mincemeat of her. In front of her own eyes, she had turned into a mewling kitten, desperate for more. She stroked his back, his chest, and his long powerful arms, before sliding her hands down to his buttocks, where they rested for a long moment, loving the feel of the muscles, hard and hot, beneath her fingers. He shifted his attention from her breast, as his fingers slid down to the curls already damp with need, her pajama bottoms having somehow disappeared long ago. She parted her thighs, giving those devilish fingers access. And shuddered with the effort of holding back her cries, as he gently parted the folds and slid one finger in. She dug her nails into the taut muscles of his back, tugging him closer.

He shifted, settling himself between her legs.

She gasped, her back arching, his lips coming down on hers to hold in her cries. He settled in such a perfect spot and yet ... not. She almost couldn't bear it.

Supported on his elbows, he slid his hands up to hold her head still, while he dropped kisses on her chin and nose, as she wiggled frantically beneath him. He kissed her again, but it was tiny teasing kisses, ... so not what she wanted.

He held his hips back and away just enough ...

Enough. Her hands, eager and hot, slipped between their bodies to stroke him.

"Oh no you don't," he whispered, reaching down to grab her hand. Instantly she lifted up and kissed him with all the passion she'd kept pent-up.

He shuddered, pulled her hand up to rest on the pillow beside her head, and sank into her willing, waiting, wet body.

She opened her mouth to cry out her joy. Instantly he sealed her mouth with his own. He stroked in and out, slowly, lightly. Going a tiny bit deeper each time.

She lost track of time. She couldn't see anything. She could only feel, as her body raced to the end of the road. It knew what was coming, knew the end would be something glorious, and she couldn't hold it back. Couldn't prolong the moment. It. Had. To. Be. Now.

Her climax ripped through her. Silent. Powerful. Explosive.

She floated in the rainbow of sensations, dimly aware of Royce's own explosive release, right before he collapsed beside her. She slipped her arms around him, holding him close.

"Are you okay?" he asked a few moments later, worry in his voice. He kissed the corner of her eyes, and she realized that she was crying. Tears of release. Tears of relief. Tears of rejoicing.

Best thing ever.

SO GOOD. ROYCE lay in bed, listening to Stacy's heavy breathing, as she slipped back into dreamland. At least he hoped her dreams would be sweet and joyful. He knew his would be. He was so damn happy right now. Emotions swamped him, and he held back the sudden burning in the corner of his eyes. But damn it, he wanted to cry. For joy. She'd never left his heart. He'd wanted her back in his arms for so long. Wanted her back in his bed for so long. His arms squeezed convulsively.

She murmured a gentle protest. He immediately relaxed and dropped kisses on her head, "It's fine—sleep," he whispered.

She snuggled closer and swelled his heart.

He had no idea what time it was. The cabin was dark. He couldn't see the top of the stairs from where he lay, and no light shone from the windows below. And he would have seen light in the room if dawn had arrived.

He heard a few sounds below. An odd rustle. Someone snoring. That made him grin. That would be Stevie. That guy could move mountains with the force of his snore.

There were a few other gentler noises, but nothing out of the ordinary.

With Stacy slumbering gently in his arms, he felt his own worries slip away. Surely they were all safe for the night?

THEY'D NEVER BE safe.

Or maybe it was more a case of some of them would rest forever. Soon. At least one of them.

It was all in the planning and in the execution. The reason he hadn't been caught? He was careful. Damn careful. And, no matter the temptation, he'd wait until the timing was right to make his move. In the meantime, he'd continue to imagine the possibilities.

After all, an artist was only as good as his or her imagination.

And he'd never come up short yet.

He wasn't about to start now.

Chapter 32

S TACY COULDN'T KEEP the smile off her face the next morning. George teased her mercilessly. Thankfully he kept it generic, so not everyone would know, but, from others' hidden grins, most did. Stevie had given her a hug in the morning, an unusual thing for him to do.

He'd whispered in her hair, "Another one bites the dust."

She wasn't sure if he'd been referring to her or to Royce. She'd hoped Royce, considering the laments Stevie had poured out over the years, about losing his boarding buddies to women. More to the point, the women had usually added to the men's life, but, to Stevie, there was something completely male about going to the mountain and blasting down at psychotic speeds in conqueror mode.

Not that she saw Stevie as a conqueror type. But he did.

She could see Royce fitting that role. She perked up. That would be a good thing in her opinion. He was on his way to becoming a lawyer. Something he never advertised. It was seriously hard work, and few recognized it. He'd also had a later start than most.

Stacy understood. Getting her degrees had been nothing short of brutal—but with a difference. She'd at least enjoyed the knowledge, the learning, the problem solving. And the puzzles. She'd always loved puzzles as a kid. They'd been a highlight on her Saturday evenings to do one with her grandpa. Nostalgia hit, as she thought about those evenings so long ago.

Her gramps had died close to ten years ago now. His death had hit her harder than expected.

Then there'd been more deaths, like her aunt, followed by her grandmother. All older people, all dying well past the first bloom of life.

She shouldn't have been as distressed by those deaths as others, but they'd had an accumulated effect that had been blown out of proportion with the sudden and tragic loss of her two best friends.

Her job was separate from her personal life. She excelled in death at work and was terrified of it at home. She'd become a workaholic, burying herself in death to avoid the reality of what death really was. She was sure a shrink would have a heyday with her crazy mind-set. But death at work was fine. Death at home was not. She honored death at the one, so she didn't have to deal with it at the other.

It was as if she'd gone into this line of work, thinking that would garner her a special pass from death in her private life.

When it hadn't, she'd felt betrayed.

Stupid.

But enlightened. She'd have to ruminate on that a little longer. Maybe find another few truths that were a little too close to home for comfort but were the better for being brought into the light.

"Thoughts?" Royce asked beside her. She threw him a sunny smile. "Nothing special."

He quirked an eyebrow, but she turned away. Most of the others would try to find some sunshine and empty runs before the day became too busy. They'd all decided to stay for one more day, just to see if they could leave on a good note.

George had called the hospital to check on Yvonne, but she was in a coma. Still, she was alive. That's what counted at this stage. She'd pulled through the night, and every extra night gave her body a chance to heal.

"Okay, we're ready to head out. Everyone got cell phones? We've had enough problems this week, let's have no more." Geoffrey turned to look at Stacy, as if to say he knew she'd be the one to have problems.

She smiled and waved at him.

He sighed, turned, and headed out the door into the bright sunshine.

Stacy grabbed the pot of coffee and refilled her mug. Being up late meant most of the others had eaten and had their fill of coffee, long before she'd even made it down. Royce and George had been speaking quietly in the corner. She had a good idea about what. Now that George was walking out, she could relax alone with Royce. Although, as she turned to the bedrooms, she realized she hadn't seen Kevin. "Where is Kevin?" she asked Royce.

He looked at her and shrugged. "No idea. I didn't get downstairs much before you did, and he wasn't here."

"He must have gone out already then."

She turned to stare at the back bedrooms. "Unless he is still asleep?" She walked down the hallway, checking the doorways as she came to them. There was one closed door. She wondered about opening it. She turned back to Royce and motioned. "Do we open it? He could still be asleep."

"True." Royce grabbed the doorknob, turned it gently, peered inside, and then withdrew. Kevin was still sleeping.

"Oh good." Stacy stepped back, as he closed the door. "Kevin was pretty exhausted last night."

"Hell, we all were."

"True." She returned to the living room. "I need food. What about you?"

"Yes." Together, they made up a hearty bacon-and-egg breakfast. Happy in the glow of a new relationship, with the added warmth of knowing this was their time, Stacy fought back the worry that the bubble might burst.

She deserved happiness.

But it felt fleeting. As if it wouldn't last. She figured that her previous experience with Royce was behind it all and tried to toss away the feeling.

They polished off their breakfast and did the dishes.

"Do you want to go skiing?"

She smiled at him. "I want to go back to that corner."

"Well, as that's not happening, at least not right now, how about a few hours of skiing instead?"

She sighed and agreed. It took a short while to get dressed for the weather, to grab their gear, and make their way to the lifts.

The sun was shining. The sky was blue. The wait lines for the lift were short.

It was a perfect ski morning. They sat on the chair, climbing up the mountain, loving the moment. At the top, they slid off the chair, cut around the people standing at the top, and dove off the edge of the run. Royce was a scary boarder, and he loved to play in the parks, whereas Stacy was a great skier and loved doing runs through the trees.

Together they found a middle ground and raced, laughed, and raced some more. By the time they had several runs under their belt, Royce suggested they try a couple different ones. And for the next couple hours they skidded, swerved, and explored new terrain.

Her cheeks were cold and her lips chapped by the time they decided to take a break. She didn't want to go to a restaurant. Maybe the cabin was empty, and they could have it to themselves.

Royce pointed out the break in the trees. "Shall we go back for some food?"

She nodded. They cut into the side run and came to a peak. She recognized the area. She motioned toward where they'd been yesterday. He frowned, considered it, then shrugged his shoulders. They wouldn't get far because of the angle they were coming in from. She led the way, trying to stay high, and that also meant she couldn't ski fast. She was going almost uphill. Royce held his speed a little better. Finally they were across the top and could descend to the other side.

They were still not at the place where she'd fallen, when Royce pointed to the right. "Stacy," Royce called out. "Look."

She studied the area, the dark shadow that she had to consider was open space behind the rock face. But nothing was different about it today. Her gaze shifted higher to the area where she had fallen.

"Damn it," she whispered beside him. "Someone is up there."

ROYCE ADMITTED TO being curious about what they'd see today, when back at this spot. Especially after Stacy's images were caught on camera. But to see someone walking around up there was odd indeed. They were too far way to identify who it was, and he couldn't even be sure whether it was a man or a woman.

"Could it be the search and rescue team putting up warning barriers?" Stacy asked in a reasonable tone.

"Hell, this whole area is out-of-bounds." They only came this way because it led to the cabin, without having to drive around the roads.

He glanced over at her to see her frowning up at the ridge. He turned back to stare himself. And sucked in his breath. As he watched, the man disappeared from view.

"He's gone down that damn hole," she whispered. "If he's alone, he might get stuck."

"First, we can't see what he's done. Second, he's obviously brought gear and set it up to get out on his own if that's the case or …" But he couldn't think of an *or*.

Stacy had. "Or he knows the area and has another way out."

They waited to see if the man would surface again.

He didn't.

The two returned to the cabin in silence. With their winter gear off and drying by the heater stove, Stacy rummaged in the kitchen to warm up leftover stew. It didn't take long. And that, with a couple buns and a fresh pot of coffee, was lunch.

They never said a word. They both sat down on the couch and ate in silence. When Royce finished his bowl, he set it down on the table and said, "We'd better go check."

He glanced over at Stacy, still eating her stew, the rosy flush on her cheeks calming down. He knew the combination of heavy activity in the cold, followed by a hot meal, would have a deadly effect on her energy. She'd likely need a nap. But he couldn't get what he'd seen out of his mind. He also didn't want to drag Stacy back up that hill. Not that she would allow herself to be left behind.

Leaving her alone here wasn't an option. He glanced down the hallway to where Kevin had been sleeping. The door was ajar. Good. So he'd gotten up and probably hit the slopes. It was a perfect day for it.

He turned his attention back to Stacy, her bowl now on the coffee table beside his. She was curled into a ball beside him. He wondered if he should go alone.

"I'm going to power nap for twenty minutes, then we'll go."

He glanced at his watch and considered that. It was just after one-thirty, so lots of daylight still left yet, and they'd be out in the better part of the afternoon. So that worked. While she slept, he got up and cleaned away the lunch mess.

They still had lots of food, particularly if they were cutting the trip short. There was talk of one or two people staying behind, if the others left early, but no decisions had been made, and the further away they were from the incidents, the more people were inclined to stay for the rest of the week.

For all the sadness and difficulties of these last few days, Royce couldn't regret coming. And, if he had to leave early, at least he knew he'd be leaving with Stacy. He could always come back another week.

When he was finished, he went up to the loft and removed his heavy sweater. He wouldn't need it this afternoon.

When he came down, Stacy was already sitting up and rubbing the sleep out of her eyes.

"Hey, how was your nap?" he asked, sitting down beside her and tugging her into his arms. He kissed her gently, wishing they hadn't seen that man earlier. Royce wouldn't be going anywhere but to bed right now otherwise. And that's so where he wanted to be.

She gave him a bright-eyed smile. "It was good. I'm ready to go." She motioned to the coffeepot on the stove. "Any left? We could take a thermos up with us."

"I'll get it," he volunteered, hopping to his feet. She was right. A thermos of coffee up there would be good. "Are you taking your camera?" he called back to her.

"Absolutely, the view of the cabin and the whole valley is spectacular from there."

"Too bad we don't have a snowmobile. It would make this trip a piece of cake."

"What's the matter, tired?" she teased from the doorway, a bright smile on her face.

"Ha. Tired of the problems, yes. Physically tired, no." And he waggled his eyebrows.

"Down, boy." She laughed. "Let's go. The others could come in at any time."

He stopped and considered her words. "That's actually a good idea. Then we'd have backup."

"No, we won't have enough time, if they don't get here soon enough," she said. "We'll text them all and leave a note behind." She turned around and headed to the living room, calling back, "George left his scratch pad here. I'll write him one on that."

Royce took the thermos out to the boot room, where he started getting dressed to go outside again. Stacy joined him, and, within minutes, they were fully dressed and back out in the winter wonderland.

Chapter 33

S TACY LED THE way back to the frozen waterfall. With the sun melting the top layer, they still had an icy layer underneath to contend with, but, in her winter hikers, she had good traction. She wasn't as tired as she expected to be right now, and it was too beautiful out to be anything but amazed at Mother Nature's artwork.

With the bright sun twinkling off the white canvas, and the ice reflecting and refracting at will, the colors of the cold air could be glimpsed in some unexpected spots. It was amazing. She stopped to take several photographs as they walked.

Royce stood at her side. He never asked her to speed it up or what she was looking at, seemingly content to let her take her time.

Something she appreciated.

"That's probably good for here." She took several steps forward and exclaimed over a large snowflake pattern frozen into the top of a melted, then refrozen surface. "I can't resist." *Click. Click.* She sighed happily and turned to look at how far they'd come. As she studied the distance, something caught her attention from the corner of her eye. Stevie and Kevin were walking down the slope toward the cabin.

"Stevie!"

Sure enough, he turned, saw her, waved, and veered toward them.

"Where are you two heading at this hour?" he asked. He was covered in snow, as if he'd tumbled through a few snow banks, but he wore a big smile.

"We're going back up to where I fell in," Stacy said, holding up her camera. "I want to take a few shots."

Stevie rolled his eyes and grinned. "Figures. Please don't fall in again."

Royce shook the coil of rope he carried over one shoulder. "Just in case. She does seem to get into trouble a lot."

"Hey, that's not fair," she protested. "It's not my fault."

"It isn't, but it is," Royce said, by way of cryptic answer.

"As if that makes any sense," she scoffed. She turned back to the cabin and motioned at it to Stevie. "Are you cutting the day short? That's not like you."

"Yeah, I argued with a tree back there." He gave her a sheepish, lopsided grin. "Figured it might be a good time to call it quits for the day. I've been going strong since early morning. Besides"—he patted his stomach—"I'm starving."

"Me too," Kevin said, nudging Stevie down the hill. "I am not used to days like these. I didn't prepare enough."

"Prepare?" Royce asked, eyeing Kevin's big grin. "Prepare how?"

"I woke up and realized everyone had left, so I ran out the door, without eating breakfast," he said, laughing. "Time to fix that."

With that comment, the two took off down the mountain, creating a new path in the snow. Stacy couldn't resist. She pulled out her camera and took several shots of the two friends sauntering down to the cabin. She could just imagine all kinds of captions for these photos.

Still grinning, she turned back to find that Royce had started to climb the slope, slashing across the hillside. "We're almost there," he called back.

"I'm coming."

The rest of the climb was harder work, but she made it to the top without too much effort. After a moment to catch her breath, she took off her jacket and cooled down.

Royce watched her. "Just be sure you don't catch a chill."

She nodded. "I won't, but walking into the sun was harder than I expected today."

"We've also put in a good day's work already. You should be tired." He walked a couple steps toward the crevasse, stopping a safe distance away. "Good. No one is here. Take your look, snap a few photos, then let's head back."

It was a good idea. Now that they were here, it was hard to see anything menacing in the area—except for the pit itself. Since no one was lying unconscious or injured below, the man they'd seen had to have left safely. He probably worked for the resort. Snowmobile tracks were around, but it was hard to tell how old they were.

She took several pictures, careful to stand back. If she were higher, looking down, she could take better shots, but there wasn't much option to do that. She gave the pit a wide berth, as she walked around. "Do you see tracks from whomever we saw earlier?" she asked.

"There were lots of people here yesterday," Royce said, looking at the trampled snow. "Who can tell?"

She walked farther out, looking for any sign that someone had approached from a different direction. The two snowmobiles had raced over the top of some tracks, almost obliterating them. "True enough. It's hard to see anything anymore."

"Not to mention the temperatures today were much warmer, with some melting going on."

She nodded. Still, she couldn't help take a few photographs of the snowmobiles' tracks and the trampled ground around the hole. "It's deeper than I remember."

"No wonder. You fell in and didn't really get a good look at it afterward. You were hustled down to the cabin to warm up."

She stared down the crevasse and wondered why it bothered her so badly. She glanced up at the frozen waterfall then back down at the deep slice in the snow pack. She'd come here to solve one problem, and instead she'd opened up another. Loathe to leave just yet, but knowing Royce was getting impatient, she walked for a last time to the far side.

And saw the blackness behind the fallen snow. She'd had to see it just right. The stack of snow hid the shadow. Even if they didn't explore what was behind it, that snow should be collapsed, so that someone else didn't fall in. "Royce, we need to do something about this."

He walked over to stand at her side. She studied his face to see if he saw what she saw and noted his narrowed gaze, as he caught sight of the blackness. A long tree branch lay to the side. She dimly remembered seeing someone using it to test the edges of the fault line.

Royce picked it up and knocked down the tower of fallen snow protecting the space behind. He frowned. He tried knocking more snow off the top so the space would open up, but instead his branch hit something hard. They rushed over and approached from the side, his stick carefully brushing the snow of the side. It was an overhang made of rock. But what was under it?

"I want to see what's down there."

Royce glanced over at her. "It's likely nothing."

"Likely, yes," she admitted. "That, however, isn't the same thing as knowing for sure. We saw someone jump down here. There's no sign of anyone. Where did he go?"

They both studied the darkness. "He probably used a rope and climbed back out. I'll go," Royce said. "I'll set up the ropes first, then I can climb back out, if need be."

He attached the one end to the big tree standing guard for so many years, then threw the rest over the edge.

He'd brought a rope ladder.

She hadn't seen one in ages. "I didn't realize that's what you were carrying."

"I figured it was the easiest way to get out, when the sides keep crumbling in on us here."

"Good thinking," she said. And it was. It was brilliant. Then Royce thrived on this kind of thing. He was a definite Boy Scout and followed the *be prepared for anything* motto very well. She'd always been amazed at the things he'd pulled off with her brother. Some were stupid, and some were damn good. Now he carefully skittered down the slope into the narrow ravine and called back. "I'm down."

"Test your ladder first," she said.

"A little late to test if I'm already here," he teased. "But I will, if it makes you feel better."

Under her watchful gaze, he climbed up several rungs easily. "See?"

"Good. Then I'll come down too."

"No need. You stay up and keep watch. I'll check out this cave, and then we can leave."

"I want to see too," she complained.

"You do realize that you could be making a big deal out of nothing. I'll see a rock wall and turn around and come right back up there." He glared at her. "Stay where you are, and I'll check. If there's anything to find, you'll see it when I knock back the snow."

He turned his back on her and started doing just that. It was evident very quickly that he would need a couple minutes to clear a path.

She watched and waited from up above. Every once in a while she turned around to find the pristine countryside empty and untouched. No one was out here but the two of them. It should have made her feel better, but instead it was too empty. No bird flew past, no songs or warbles sounded on the air. It was still, watchful. Waiting.

She hated that her imagination was on overdrive, but it didn't seem fanciful that Royce just might find something that the birds already knew about.

ROYCE WORKED STEADILY to drop the snow to a reasonable-size pile that he could get around and see what was behind the mass. He'd seen many different footprints, which made no sense. After all, there wasn't—or shouldn't have been—anyone down here. Except for the man they'd seen.

Maybe it was just curiosity, but …

Stacy didn't believe it, and her nervousness made him question his own assumptions. The footprints added to his concern.

After a moment, he peered in. All he could see was black. He pulled out his flashlight and turned it on. The light shone deep into the cavern. And it was huge. And there were more footprints.

Damn.

He puzzled over it.

It wasn't criminal to have come in here. It wasn't even abnormal. This was a hugely popular resort for skiing, snowboarding, snowmobiling, spelunkers, and climbers of all kinds every month of the year.

Yet why the secrecy?

Or was anything secret about it? He backed up slightly, so that he could turn to talk to Stacy, only to rear back as she stood right beside him. In exasperation, he asked, "Do you do anything that you are told to do?"

"Sure," she said, with a big grin. "Lots. But only the ones I like."

"Really?" He shook his head. "I doubt it."

"Wow." She bent forward and peered into the blackness. "What is this?"

"It's a cavern of some kind." He turned the flashlight to cast the flare of light across the darkness.

"It's huge," she cried out.

"It does appear to be."

He looked at her and then stepped around the snow pile inside the cavern.

"What an amazing space." She quickly followed him. "Footprints."

He stopped in front of her and shone the light down on it. "It's just one set, I think."

"One set in and one set out," she said. "Or is he still in here? We saw him jump down a few hours ago, if you remember."

"True. But remember that stack of snow I had to knock down to get in here?"

She didn't note that the stranger could have stacked this pile up to hide his tracks in or out regardless of which way he went. "*Hmm.* Maybe not. Maybe he found another exit."

"Maybe," Royce said. "We don't know enough at this point. No way to sort out the tracks." Particularly as they'd just stomped over them too.

"True. The ground is a bit of a mess."

Taking a step forward, she realized they would lose all the natural daylight from outside if they carried on any farther.

And she wasn't sure she wanted to do that.

"Are we going in or going back?" Royce asked.

She winced. "I guess we have to check." She turned to look back the way they'd come. "We should make sure that others know we are here."

"Good point." Royce walked back a couple steps and kicked the rest of the snow away from the entrance so that it would be open and clean. Then he made an arrow in the snow pointing to the cavern. And a big *R*.

She laughed. "Well, if this opening isn't enough of a message, that should do it. We'll have to remember to remove that, just so someone doesn't come upon it later and think we or some other poor person whose name starts with an *R* is in there."

He grinned. "Good point."

As he walked past, she turned to follow him.

Chapter 34

STACY WAS DAMN glad she wasn't alone.

She followed Royce deeper into the cavern. An eerie silence surrounded them, punctuated by the crisp, staccato noise of Royce's footsteps on the icy ground. It was creepy. And scary. She'd seen some rough places in her time, but she'd never done any caving. She didn't like dark places. Or confined spaces. Again she reminded herself of the joy of having Royce with her. He stopped suddenly, and she bumped into him. "What is it?"

"The pathway splits here."

"Where do the footprints lead?"

"Both directions." An odd tone filled his words.

There wasn't room to get past him. She tried to peer around his shoulder but couldn't see much. "Is there a path more traveled?"

"No. I'm thinking they're both well used."

"Recently?" she asked incredulously. "Really? How is that possible?" She slipped closer to him. "That is so bizarre."

"I know." He hesitated. "I don't like it."

Relief flooded her. "Neither do I. I'm just not sure what to do about it."

The silence lengthened, as they considered the ramification of going deeper.

"Leave?" she suggested. "Come back with more people? It just seems a little ..." She couldn't find the word she wanted. "I don't know how to describe it. But I don't like it. At all."

"Back up then, be careful of your steps, and just turn around."

"I am." And she was. "Maybe we should tell the others?"

"I'm not sure which of them to talk to."

She put out her hand to use the wall for support. And heard something behind her. She spun around. "What was that?"

Royce was already walking toward the noise they'd both heard. "No idea." He walked forward with purpose.

She followed, her heart in her throat and her pulse pounding. She knew she'd been the one who had pushed to come here, but, at this point, she'd give a lot to just turn around and go home.

Still, if anyone injured was in here, crying out for help, then they needed to render aid. She'd been in trouble herself more than once, and she couldn't walk away.

But, damn, she wanted to.

Royce turned to the left. She winced. She was thinking turning right was the best bet. But he was closer and might have heard the noise better.

He paused and cocked an ear and listened intently.

She followed but heard nothing. She waited to see what Royce would do.

At first it seemed like he did nothing, but then he crept forward.

Crap. She followed close on his heels. As she took the next step, her foot slipped, and she flailed before going down. "*Ohm,*" she cried out.

Royce spun around, his arm out to catch her, but it was too late. She fell to the ground, her elbow cracking hard on the rock. She sat on the cold floor and held her arm against her chest.

Crouching in front of her, Royce whispered, "Are you okay?"

"Yes, I'm fine." She winced, as she tried to straighten her arm. "It hurts, but I don't think it's broken."

"Here. Grab my hand," he said. With his help, she stood up slowly. There she made a slow check of the rest of her. Everything was fine. Sore, but not too bad. "I'm fine."

"Good. Do you want to go onward or shall I take you back outside?"

"You're not going in any farther alone," she said. "I'll keep going."

He stood, undecided, in front of her. Then he pulled out his cell phone and typed on it. "I'm texting George. And Stevie."

She brightened. "You might as well text them all." That was the best idea yet. Then she heard another noise, this time from behind her to the right.

"What is that?"

"I don't know." Royce stood still, then groaned. "If it weren't for the footprints, I'd be concerned it was bears."

She gasped. "And it still might be."

"Not likely at this point." He nudged her toward the cave entrance. "But we're not taking the chance."

"Ok—"

And then came a louder noise, and, damn it, something that almost sounded like a human moan. But on the right.

"Shit." She looked at Royce's undecided expression and said, "The others are coming, but we need to see what or who that is. Someone might need our help." She walked forward confidently, trying to not nurse her arm. She'd be fine. Someone else wasn't.

There were no more noises to follow, but she kept stepping forward. "Royce, have you heard from anyone yet? We don't want to be sending texts and not have the messages go anywhere."

"I heard from Stevie. Kevin went back boarding, so Stevie is contacting the others and coming up alone. Maybe a half hour."

"Good." Feeling more confident, she turned to go down the right-hand path this time, walking carefully as she went. Royce kept a hand on her shoulder.

"Take it easy."

She stopped. "Shine your light up ahead, will you?"

He obliged and lit up the pathway a little farther down the darkness. She couldn't see anything up ahead. Taking a chance, she said, "Hello? Is anyone there?"

Silence.

She cast a worried look at Royce but kept on going. "Surely someone would have responded."

"Unless they can't."

She twisted her lips and remembered the footprints that came in but didn't leave, and she took another step. The ice was treacherous.

"Go slow." At her look, he grinned. "I know you are. We can also wait for the others to get here."

At that, she turned away and kept moving forward. And heard the noise from straight ahead. She had no idea what it was, but she was determined to find out. She turned another corner, amazed and worried at the depth they were traveling into this cavern.

Royce grabbed her shoulder and pulled her to a stop. "Wait."

She stopped in place. He shone the light ahead again, from one side to the other, revealing an antechamber of some kind. She marveled at the beauty of what she could see. And the chill that had settled into her bones. It was so damn cold in here. The natural light couldn't reach this far, and there didn't appear to be any opening up top. Although there likely were some—but covered in ice.

She walked up to the entrance to the larger room and stopped. In front of her, lying on the ground ...

Kathleen.

"Oh my God! Royce, look." She ran forward and dropped to Kathleen's side. "Oh no. She's in rough shape."

Royce was already taking off his coat and wrapping it around the injured woman's shoulders. "She needs medical help and fast."

"I'll make the calls." Taking the flashlight, she returned as close to the entrance as she could go, mindful of the treacherous footing, making sure she went far enough to get through on her phone.

"Emergency, we've found an injured woman. She's in rough shape. We'll need a rescue team here immediately." She quickly explained the location, adding, "The others from our group are supposed to be on their way up here too."

After hanging up, she looked for Stevie, but, since she was under the rock overhang, there was no way to know how close he was. She returned to Royce's side, as carefully as she could. Stacy couldn't begin to understand how or why Kathleen was here. She was also damn lucky to be found.

Back at Royce's side, she dropped to her knees. "I got through. They are sending a team."

"Good. Let's hope they get here soon."

He was busy rubbing Kathleen's arms and legs, trying to get the circulation going. Stacy took off her coat, and they rolled her on top of it. Kathleen opened her eyes and tried to open her mouth.

Stacy said, "*Shh.* We've found you now. A team is coming to help. Stay strong. Keep fighting." She rubbed Kathleen's cheeks. "Don't give up."

Her head rolled to the side, and she closed her eyes.

"No!" snapped Stacy.

Kathleen opened her eyes and tried to focus on Stacy's face. Then struggled to move.

"Good, she's still got some movement," Stacy said. "Don't try to move. You'll burn through too much energy. You need to conserve your strength and try to warm up."

Her mind churned. Why was Kathleen here? There was no reason for it. She and George had headed out early this morning to go boarding. That they hadn't returned yet was no biggie. They were still well within normal times. She hadn't texted or spoken to her brother at all today, but again that was not unusual.

Besides, she'd been with Royce. She hadn't wanted anyone—or anything—to intrude on their private time.

Now she stared down at the one girlfriend she thought her brother loved, a woman Stacy admired and liked and would be quite happy to have in the family. She couldn't help but worry that something had happened to her brother.

She looked over at Royce. In a low voice, she asked, "Any idea what happened to her? Why she'd be here?"

Royce shook his head. "Tuck up against her back, will you?" He'd pulled Kathleen close to his body, but the opposite side of Kathleen was open to the cold. Stacy sat down on the ground and wrapped her arms around them both. "Did you bring a thermal blanket in that pocket of yours?" she asked. "I left my pack behind." Of course it had emergency weather gear, but they'd only planned to be out for an hour or so.

Best laid plans and all those other mistakes people made on a regular basis.

"And where's George?" she asked fiercely.

"No idea," Royce whispered quietly, letting his warm breath bathe Kathleen's icy face. "He hasn't answered my text."

"Oh God." Stacy was torn between trying to help save Kathleen and going to search for her brother. It was likely that, if one was here, then the other was as well. She glanced into the dark shadows around them.

"You aren't leaving," Royce said in a low voice. "We don't know what happened to Kathleen. If she was attacked, then he could still be here."

"Does she have any injuries?"

"Head wound."

Stacy frowned. "I need to see it."

He shifted slightly and turned on the flashlight. Stacy moved so she could examine the injury. No longer bleeding, but it had bled originally. She explored the injury carefully. A definite skull fracture. She studied the angle and depression. "From what I can see, she was hit from behind by someone taller than her," she said quietly, her stomach knotting and her heart sinking. "This is so not good."

"There's no chance she could have fallen and hit a rock on her way down?"

"I'd have to see in better light, but the blow came from above. If a rock came down from the ceiling, then maybe."

"It only matters in that we might be looking for someone who wanted her dead."

"You think this was deliberate?" She kept her voice light. She couldn't see any other scenario herself but hoped there was one. "Her attacker might not have known the damage the blow caused."

"Or he might be coming back to make sure it had done exactly what he'd planned."

"Good," Stacy said in a hard voice. "Let him. We have lots of people coming too." There was a long silence. She sighed. "What now?"

She stared at him in the gloomy darkness, the flashlight pointed toward the entrance to help guide the others to the right place. He wrapped an arm around her, pulling her close, Kathleen sandwiched between them. After a moment he said, "You do realize that we may have sent out the SOS call to the very person who attacked her in the first place?"

She hesitated, hating the suspicion. The doubts. She knew everyone in their group. They were close to Royce as well. It was tough to glance at people—many you've known for a long time—and wonder if they were trying to kill you.

She whispered, "I know."

ROYCE WATCHED STACY carefully. The last thing he wanted was to have Stacy go off half-cocked and decide she wanted to search for her brother.

His phone jangled in his pocket. He reached down and pulled it out. "Stevie is at the top of the pit."

"Maybe I should guide him down here," she said quietly, staring in the direction where the light shone toward the entrance.

"He should be able to find the rope down." Royce was busy texting him directions. The next text came in. "He found the rope, and he heard from Geoffrey. He and George are boarding together."

"Thank God." Stacy could feel some of the tension in her shoulders ease back now that she knew her brother was okay. "Stevie should be here in no time."

Royce studied Kathleen's face, hating the pallor. "Damn it, I wish I'd just picked her up and carried her out of here."

"She's better off here and being taken out on a stretcher. We're doing the best we can do for her. The rescuers will be here in minutes."

"We could have her halfway down to the cabin by now."

"And cause her more harm in the process. Here we're warming her as much as we can."

He knew she was right. The cavalry was on its way. He needed to keep Kathleen still and warm. And safe.

The icy floor was starting to creep into his bones. He welcomed it. It kept in check the raging anger that had heated his blood to the boiling point.

No point in losing his head. He had to figure this out. It occurred to him that someone just might be picking them off one by one.

He knew that the biggest group of suspects was his own friend group. That choked him, but he was trying to stay cool and collected. Many other people knew the group was staying here. And many more were finding out every day. That opened up the suspect pool.

"What are you thinking?" Stacy asked.

"Trying to figure out who did this. And why."

"The *why* is particularly disturbing," Stacy said. "I can't see that all of us could possibly have done something to piss off one person."

He gazed at her. "It wouldn't have to be all of us involved. I'm not sure this person cares about there being roadkill. People who got in the way would be secondary. Like in the drugging."

"You think it was the same person?"

His lopsided grin slipped out. "Could you imagine that we've pissed off more than one person during the last while?"

"Not likely."

"Then again …" Royce frowned. "I'm trying to remember if there were any major dissensions about this trip. Some people weren't impressed that you were coming. The timing was also an issue."

Stacy gasped. "Really? I could have stayed behind."

"No," he said sharply. "Don't ever think that. The concerns were more that you might be depressing to the group, if you weren't handling life well on your first time back."

Even in the dim light, he saw the wince ripple across her face. He was sorry for that, but they needed to get to the bottom of the truth here.

"That's fair," she said quietly. "Was anyone very upset?"

"No. Not at all."

"What about ex-girlfriends?" she asked, her voice hesitant.

"None serious for a very long time. None casual for awhile," he said, not even attempting to hold back the humor. "After tasting moonlight, there was no going back to the regular fare."

And her smile lit up the cavern.

He opened his mouth to say something when a shout sounded at the mouth of the tunnel.

"We're here," Royce called out.

Stacy hopped to her feet and ran in the direction of the noise, before Royce had a chance to stop her.

Then he heard Stevie's voice and knew it was all fine.

REALLY? MORE SHIT happening that wasn't supposed to happen. Jesus. His heart pounded, his hands were sweaty, and he knew he was in serious danger of spending the rest of his life behind bars.

Shit. Shit. Shit.

He couldn't think.

He had to act. Had to find a way out.

Kathleen was to blame. First, she saw him in the kitchen; then she said something to George in front of him about him playing with the wine bottles. Like what the hell? Now he had to deal with both of them. They'd found Kathleen already. Unbelievable. That wasn't supposed to happen. She was supposed to be dead.

Dead people don't talk.

He'd gone to find George. Make sure he plugged that hole. Surely Kathleen would have been fine here for a few moments. Like how long had he been gone? Forty minutes max? He swore it wasn't longer. Surely not.

Just long enough for that meddling bitch and her stud to get in the way. How the hell had they found his secret place? What could he have possibly done wrong?

Now it didn't matter, damn it. Unless Kathleen died. He brightened. That was the trick. She needed to die. For real this time.

Except considering the number of people here trying to help her, he wouldn't get close enough to finish the job. He had to hope that Mother Nature had already done the damage for him.

Chapter 35

S TACY RUSHED TOWARD the voice. "Hello? Hello?" she cried out. There was Stevie. "There you are."

She rushed into his arms, so damn happy that help had arrived.

"Easy, easy. I'm here."

"Oh thank God." She stepped back and smiled up at him. "Where are the others? She needs to get to the hospital now."

"Is she hurt?" he asked, splaying the flashlight behind her.

"A head wound," she said. Looking behind Stevie, she frowned and repeated, "Where are the others?"

"I couldn't find anyone else," he said. "I came and hoped the others would follow as they came in."

"Oh no." She ran out to the crevasse and stared up at the waning sun. "Surely they'd be at the cabin by now?"

"They should be there soon," he said, worry in his tone. "But even Kevin went back for a couple more runs."

"Hell." She turned. "Come on. She's not doing well at all." She led the way back to Royce. "Where is the search and rescue team?" she fretted. "I called it in myself."

"They'll be here," Stevie said. "You know they are reliable."

"Unless someone called it off," she snapped darkly. "Kathleen has been hit in the head. She didn't do it to herself."

"Whoa, what?"

She spun around, slipped, and almost went down. Stevie reached out and caught her before she hit the ground, but her knee still wrenched, as she tried to save herself.

"Take it easy. We don't need another accident."

"No." She straightened slowly and winced. "I twisted my knee."

"Badly?"

"No." She tested her weight, limping forward gingerly. "I think it will be fine, but Kathleen is unconscious."

"What is she doing in here?" He looked around, as they slowly made their way forward. "And what is this place?"

"No idea. I thought I saw something like this in the waterfall pictures I took. As we're beside the same area, maybe a series of tunnels are connected inside."

"Good Lord. If it weren't for the circumstances, this would be a really cool find."

"*Cool* is not the word I'd use," she muttered. "But the temperature is definitely working against us at the moment." She pulled out her phone and turned it on, hoping to see a text from someone. There was nothing. "Damn it, where is everyone?" She called out, "Royce, you there?"

There was a faint echo all around them. She hated the fear sitting on the edge of her nerves. She didn't dare move faster.

"Are you lost?" Stevie asked. "Surely you didn't go too deep into this place on the off chance someone was in here."

So much disapproval filled his tone that she sighed. "I thought I heard something, so we ventured inside." She headed down the right-hand passageway. "Royce?"

She wanted to run, but her knee was hurting and complaining. She made it another twenty steps forward and called out again. "Royce."

This time she thought she heard something. She moved faster. And, sure enough, there was Royce, seated on the ground ahead of her.

She dropped to the ground beside him. "How is she?"

He shook his head. "Worse. We need her out of here."

Stevie took one look and opened his bag, tossing down thermal heater blankets. Stacy opened it up, and, with Royce's help, they removed their coats and bundled Kathleen into the first blanket. With the second blanket he'd brought, they repeated the action. Stacy snagged her coat and put it on. Instantly her body warmed. Royce put his on, then bent and lifted Kathleen into his arms.

"Are you su—"

"We must move her. If nobody else is here, we have to get her there ourselves. Lead the way, Stacy," Royce said.

She snorted. "Really? I almost got us lost finding you."

He grinned. "I wondered what took you so long."

She smiled and headed back toward the front entrance.

The light changed the closer they got to the outside. Instead of a bright light, there was only a muted glow. "Shit." She ran to the edge to find a wall of snow piled in front.

As the three stared, they realized what had happened. And that this was likely why the others hadn't come inside. "The snow from that tree must have fallen," she exclaimed. "And remember the pile on the ledge?"

"Yeah. Shitty timing."

While Royce held Kathleen in his arms, Stevie and Stacy kicked away at the snow. Stevie had his little shovel out now, and they managed to punch through enough for them to see outside where the search and rescue team waited, having no idea where they were supposed to be.

Stacy called out, "We're here."

A round of cheers went up.

Royce handed over his burden to the paramedics and stepped back. The men surrounded Kathleen and quickly had her vitals checked and monitored, before packing her up in the sled. They were on their way in minutes. There were two other snowmobiles. Royce insisted that Stacy catch a ride down to the cabin. He'd walk with Stevie. It wasn't far, and there wasn't room for all three of them to ride back. The sun was low and getting lower behind the mountain. The shadowy long fingers stretched across the pristine white snow.

They started down the slope. Royce lifted his face to the cool air and took several deep breaths. "It's good to be alive."

"It is at that." Stevie walked a few more steps, then the words exploded from him. "What the hell is going on?"

"I don't know," Royce admitted. "I think one of us is hunting either all of us or one or two of us."

"Shit." Stevie glared at him. "You think one of us is killing people in our group?"

"I think so. I can't imagine a stranger drugging our wine. It just doesn't fit."

"But anyone could have had access. We don't leave a guard on watch."

"True, but they'd have to know where the wine was and who'd be drinking it."

"Or they didn't care. Maybe they were after the women. One went missing, and one is injured."

"Maybe." Royce pondered that. "But why?"

"The oldest reason in the world maybe."

"Sex? Rape? I didn't see any evidence of a sexual attack on Kathleen." Royce came to a dead stop. "Shit. What about George? He doesn't know yet. What if he's in that damn cave?"

"I saw them both together earlier. They were heading to the peak," Stevie said, staring up at the hillside and the fading light.

Royce stopped and stared. "He left Kathleen to go home on her own? I find that hard to believe."

"She wasn't with him there. And he wouldn't have let her leave alone. She must have come with someone from our group. Someone George trusted. No way he would let her go off alone otherwise." Stevie frowned. "Are you thinking that the person she came back to the cabin with is the one who attacked her?"

"I don't know what else to think," Royce admitted. "I doubt that she went in that cavern on her own. She hates dark spaces. She wanted to go home yesterday, but George wanted to stay."

"Shit." Stevie groaned. "And, if she doesn't wake up, no way to know why she came here."

"George might know. Maybe?"

"And maybe not. In which case no way to know who in our group is doing this, allowing him to sit among us."

"I know. Interesting dilemma, isn't it?"

"No, it's bloody awful."

HE COULD ONLY hope Kathleen died instead of waking up. Damn bitch. Damn interfering bitch. Now what the hell was he to do?

Part of him knew he needed to just pack in his plan this time around and play it safe. Just walk away. And yet … he couldn't quite do that.

He'd waited years for this. And, after this week, he had no idea when he'd get such a chance again.

It was risky.

Shitty odds.

But he couldn't let it pass by.

He'd just have to figure out a way to make this work.

Chapter 36

S TACY CLIMBED OFF the snowmobile and thanked the rescue team.
"Are you sure you'll be okay?"

"I'm fine now that I'm back here, safe and sound," she said, with a reassuring smile. "If no one is here, I'll get the fire going and get a meal together. Thank you so much for coming to the aid of my friend."

"Glad we got to her on time."

"Me too," she said, heartfelt relief in her voice. With a wave, the two snowmobiles took off.

She watched them go. The chill she'd never quite rid herself of flared into an icy awareness again. She turned to look up the hillside, delighted to see that both Stevie and Royce were in sight. She waved up at them and smiled when they both waved back; then she headed inside. The cabin was empty.

And cold.

She'd had enough of being cold. The heater stove had been turned down, but there were still embers. She opened it up and had a roaring fire in no time. It immediately chased the chill from the cabin, adding cheery comfort. She filled the coffeepot and put it on the stove to warm up. Then she wandered into the kitchen to see what food was left to put a meal together. They'd lost track of the menu days ago, and, with the odd schedule and problems, bits and pieces of different food items were left.

The big kielbasa sausages fired her culinary imagination, and she quickly started a Hungarian stew. With lots of peppers, onions, and tomatoes, she could make this happen in time for dinner. She found a partial package of uncooked pasta to use up as well.

Working and happy to be doing so, she chopped, diced, and stirred the basics together. When she heard the men at the outside door, she started in on the smoked sausages. They'd add a major boost to the dish. Actually they were an integral part. A few potatoes sat off to the side. She had to wonder whether they were needed for breakfast or she could add them as substance to the stew. Making an executive decision, she snatched them up.

"Something smells good, Stacy," Royce said, coming into the kitchen.

"Food," Stevie cried out. "Is that cooked?" He reached out and nicked a chunk of sausage and chewed on it, before she had a chance to answer.

"These are smoked." She reached for another one to cut up and found those pieces disappearing from her board faster than she could cut. She held up her knife in a mocking, threatening motion. "Go check on the coffee," she snapped lightly. "And let me get this on to cook."

"The others should be here soon." Royce sat at the table beside her. "Can I help?"

"No, I've got this," she said, happy to be doing something. "It just needs to simmer for an hour, if we can."

"An hour is likely fine," Royce said. "Everyone will have coffee, when they get here. They might need a snack though."

She pointed to the box of food off to the side. "Check in there. Likely to be chips still, maybe bagels that could be toasted. Possibly some crackers and cheese."

He hopped up and started digging through the box. He pulled out everything that appealed to him.

"If you open packages and set out the food onto platters, then we can hand them out when everyone gets in."

He nodded.

She felt his gaze on her, but she kept her head down and on her work.

She didn't want to talk about what was going on. The danger they were all in. She knew a killer was among them. Maybe Kathleen would survive, but maybe she wouldn't. Stacy had to consider that Kathleen's attacker hadn't expected her to. At the very least, he would not be pleased to find out that Kathleen had been found.

Stacy couldn't deal with it all at the moment. She was focusing on what she could do right now. The rest was too much.

"Stacy?"

The warm, caring concern in Royce's voice made her stop, and she realized she'd taken the first pepper and had basically diced it into nothing.

She bowed her head. "I want to go home."

Warm hands slid around her shoulders and tugged her backward. The tears burned the back of her eyes.

"Understood," he said against her ear.

And damn if that didn't start the tears flowing. "And," she said, her voice choked up as she fought the emotions clogging her throat and heart, "I know that I came to face the mountain, the loss of my friends, my fears, grief, you, any number of other issues, but I don't think I want to come back. *Ever.*"

He tightened his arms around her. She dropped the knife, turned into his arms, and let a damn hiccough escape.

God, she was tired. She didn't know what the hell was going on here, but it was scary and deadly. When would this stop? And would it stop before anyone else got hurt?

She didn't want that to be Royce. Or anyone else she knew.

It hurt to consider one of the people she'd known for years was doing this.

And made her wonder just how well she knew any of them.

A heavy pounding came on the cabin door. Royce released her. "I'll get it."

She brushed her eyes and turned back to finish what she was doing. All the pieces could join the pot on the stove and just simmer.

She heard voices in the living room, as she dumped in the last of the ingredients. She grabbed a cloth to clean up, then poured two cups of coffee and carried them out to see who was there.

She stopped in the doorway.

It was the police. One cop stationed himself at the doorway and watched the proceedings. The second cop was the same man she'd spoken to earlier. He looked over at her. The serious look in his eyes had her nerves jangling. "Do you have news about Kathleen?" Her lips trembled. In a faint voice, she asked, "Is she dead?"

The cop shook his head. "She's still fighting. They took her to Vancouver General. Your other friend is there too."

"Oh thank God." Stacy walked forward and handed the coffee to Royce and Stevie. She asked the two policemen if they wanted some, but both shook their heads. She rushed back into the kitchen to get herself a cup.

Royce patted the couch beside him for her to sit.

"Now. Please tell us how you happened to find her."

"There's so little to tell, it's scary," Stacy said. "I'm going to have nightmares for years worrying about the 'what ifs.'"

"Explain," the cop asked, his gaze intent.

She sighed. She rubbed her forehead as she tried to figure out how to best say this. "I'm …" And she stopped.

Royce reached out a hand and squeezed hers.

"Okay, let's go back a bit." She glanced over at Stevie and Royce, saw the compassion in their faces, and took a deep breath.

"Three years ago, I came here with two best friends and many others. A group similar to the one here today. We were all excellent boarders and skiers, young and stupid."

"Stupid?"

Of course the cop picked up on that word. "The other two were more reckless, had little respect for rules, and felt that they could do what they wanted, if it wouldn't affect anyone else."

God, this was hard. She hated to say anything negative about the dead, but, dammit, that's what they'd been like. She swallowed a sip of coffee. "They wanted me to go on the backside of Gopher Run one morning, and I said hell no. The avalanche risk was high, and it was out-of-bounds, and I'm a much more cautious skier. I talked them out of it. I hadn't been feeling all that great and wanted to cut the afternoon short." She stared at the cop but saw instead the young adventurous faces of her friends. "I left."

And she saw the understanding in the cop's face. "I went into the village and did a bit of shopping, then thought maybe I'd meet up with them again. I went up the lift to midstation and texted my girlfriends to meet me. We met up, talked for a few moments, then my brother and his friends joined us. My brother and his friends took off downhill, and I went to follow him, thinking the women were behind me. They weren't."

She gripped her cup, the whites of her knuckles showing. But all she could see was the white from that day. "I turned back to find them …"

She faltered. Stevie came and sat down beside her and held her other hand. She gave him a grateful smile and returned to her story. "I crested over the top of the mountain, and, by that time, I knew where they were. I was on top, looking down, and I could see them way below, having a wonderful time." She smiled wistfully. Then her smile fell away, and she gazed at the man waiting, memories haunting her. "Then an avalanche started."

She stopped and swallowed. "I screamed at them. Of course they couldn't hear me." She turned to stare at the cabin walls. The same cabin they'd stayed at during that vacation. A cabin she'd sworn never to return to. "It hit them hard. They were picked up and swallowed like tiny krill eaten by a blue whale." She sighed and fell silent a moment. "The avalanche went over a cliff and just kept going. Their bodies were never recovered."

There was an odd silence, as the cops digested that. Heavy in the air was the hanging question of how anything that happened a few years ago connected to the series of bizarre events now.

Her smile was crooked, when she answered that unspoken question. "So you see? The reason that I went in that cave is because I'm obsessed. I see those women's faces everywhere on this mountain. I saw a spectacular series of light refracting into women's faces on the frozen waterfall when we were at the other day, and I took a lot of pictures of it." She felt more than saw Royce stand up and return with her camera.

"I hated to come back here again, but, at the same time, I can't get rid of the feeling that I might be able to find my friends and to bring them home." Her voice faltered. "I feel compelled to search everywhere, under every rock, inside every hollow. Even though I know I'm nowhere near where they fell, I can't let go of that little bit of hope."

"You were very close to these friends, I presume?" the cop asked.

She nodded, wiping the tears from her eyes. "Very. It was always the three of us. We were a matched set. Just very different personalities. Janice was the daredevil, and I was the opposite, while Francine was in the middle, but she could be persuaded to go either way."

She paused, and the room was silent, as if they were all waiting for her to say more. When she spoke again, her voice cracked. "I've been lost since."

"Here are the images she saw on the waterfall," Royce said, holding out the camera. Everyone crowded around. There were a few exclamations at the beauty in the ice.

"Wow."

The second cop stepped forward. "I know you. You're the artist who photographs the faces of Mother Nature."

Stacy nodded. "Yes, that's me. Now you know why faces are my focus."

He nodded, staring at the images. The cop clicked through them, until Royce said, "Stop." He pointed at the image. "This is the one that had us going back to look."

In the image was an eerie blackness in the ice, as if a cave were behind it.

"Then she fell in the crevasse yesterday and thought she'd seen something more." He looked over at Stacy for confirmation, then continued. "After we saw what appeared to be a man jump into the same crevasse, we went back and found that cavern opening."

"Did you know that it opened up, Stacy?" the cop asked.

"The geographical layout said it *could* connect to the cave behind the waterfall, and, once I saw that dark shadow at the end of the pit I'd fallen into, I couldn't get it out of my mind." She shrugged. "I insisted on going back."

"Damn good thing," the cop said. "Kathleen would be dead by now if you hadn't."

She knew that. "But why was she there in the first place?"

Royce piped up, "And how much does this have to do with the drugged wine and Yvonne?"

As the second cop returned to his position at the door, the other cop looked from one to the other. "They have to be connected. Too much going on with the ten of you for it not to be connected."

"Eight," Stacy corrected sadly. "There are only eight of us here in the cabin now."

ROYCE LISTENED TO Stacy and her teary explanation. He had known she'd been badly affected by the loss of her friends, but he hadn't *really* known. How could he? She hadn't shared very much with him. Then again, he sat back thinking, three years ago he'd just come out of a short-term relationship with Janice. And likely Janice had told Stacy. Royce should have too. No wonder she refused to see him. To go out with him. Every time she'd looked at him, she would've felt the loss of her friends all over again.

He damned himself for that weekend. He'd often wondered why bright, vivacious, man-eater Janice had come on to him at that time. Just after he'd asked Stacy out and had been laughingly told off as not being serious. Only he had been serious. And the rejection hadn't been easy.

Accepting Janice's offer had been easier, had filled a need to be wanted after too many rejections that had driven down his self-esteem. Part of his pattern back then. After that fateful weekend three years ago, he knew he'd have to change to make something long-lasting with

Stacy. They'd both taken years to get to this point. And now it was all rearing its ugly head yet again.

He could only hope she wouldn't push him away. He squeezed her hand, unable to break contact with her, just in case.

The first cop spoke in a quiet voice, "So you saw someone up there, and he disappeared into the same crevasse that you fell into?"

"As far as I could see."

She looked up at Royce, and he nodded. "I saw him too."

"Him? For sure? Not Kathleen?"

"Oh." Stacy shook her head. "No, it wasn't Kathleen I saw up there. At least, I don't think so."

The cop nodded and wrote down a few more notes. "What are everyone's plans at the moment?"

"I'd like to go home," Stacy said. "But, given the time of day, the weather, that won't likely be until morning, and that was our original plan." And she was worried about George. Very worried. Usually he was with Kathleen.

"A storm is coming in tonight, so, if you are leaving, you need to leave now, but not before we have all your contact information."

"We can't leave now. Half our group isn't back yet." Royce checked his watch. "They should be soon though."

Stevie's cell phone went off at that point. "That's George. He and Geoffrey are on the way back."

"No one has told him about Kathleen, have they?" Stacy asked. "He'll want to leave immediately to be at her side."

"If they don't get back soon ..." Royce noted, "he may not be able to."

"Speaking of which," the cop said, "we're heading back to the station. If you leave, let us know who and when, so we can keep track of you. And please stick together. Let's have no one else go missing."

Royce stood. "We'll let you know what we decide."

The cop nodded and walked to his partner's side at the door. He turned back once he reached the doorway and gave them a stern look. "Stay safe."

It was a grim warning in light of what was going on. But a sensible one. Royce shook his hand. "Are you sure it's safe for us to stay here?"

The cop stared at him. "I'm not sure it's safe for any of you anywhere. If you split up and head off to separate homes, you won't know who's been attacked, who's gone missing, or who is doing these attacks. If you stay here together, maybe someone will show their hand."

And, with that, they left.

Chapter 37

S TACY SAT IN front of the fire, using the hot mug of coffee to warm her cold hands. The conversation ranged from anger to disbelief. And her brother had yet to make it back. He'd texted several times to say they were coming. The weather had shifted, and high winds were slowing their return trip.

She'd held back telling him anything. She wanted him here, safe and sound. Royce had called the hospital to find that Kathleen had made it there safely, and they were slowly raising her body temperature and were optimistic about her chances. There was no change in Yvonne's condition.

For Stacy, that wasn't good enough. She knew the worst would be telling her brother what had happened. She stood up and stirred the stew, then added the prepped potatoes and some more seasoning. Somehow the dish had grown large enough to feed a dozen, so she hoped the men were all hungry. She was anything but.

Of course, her stomach was still nursing the caffeine she'd poured down to keep her going.

Royce sat on the couch and waited for her to join him. "Are you okay to stay the night?"

She nodded. "I am." She glanced over at him. "As long as I'm not sleeping alone."

"Not going to happen." He slid an arm around her shoulders. "We need to keep an eye on everyone tonight."

"In more ways than one," she added in a low voice. He hugged her gently. Outside, she heard noises over the wind. "Hopefully that's George and Geoffrey."

"I'll go see." Royce stood, handed her his coffee, and stepped out to the boot room area. She hears the raised voices, as the men came in. Relief flooded her heart. Her brother was home safe. She felt so sorry for him for what she knew was to come.

She waited, her body tense. The loud voices shut off to almost complete silence, followed by yelling like she hadn't heard before. Then a hard bounce, as if her brother had picked up Royce and slammed him against a wall. Her brother was quite capable of that. And, given the circumstances, Royce would likely take it as well.

More shouting and more pounding shook the whole cabin.

When the silence hit again, she got up and walked over. Her brother sat on the bench, his head bowed and his shoulders shaking. Mark and Kevin stood there, looking at the ground, shaking their heads in disbelief. Geoffrey sat in stunned silence.

She didn't hesitate. She walked up to George and wrapped her arms around her brother. Immediately he buried his head against her and held her tight. She held on, until the storm of George's rage had passed. When he was calmer, she sat down beside him and gave him the update that she'd gotten from the hospital. "She's going to pull through, George."

He nodded, his face in his hands. When he looked up at her, she saw the ravaged soul of a guilty conscience.

She reached out and grabbed his hand. "Tell me."

"She wanted to go home today. Get away from here. I wanted to stay one more day. Enjoy the mountain. Make something good to take away."

"I wanted to go too, but, at the same time, I didn't need more bad memories to overcome the good," Stacy replied. "So I stayed for the same reason you did."

"Except she wouldn't have been hurt if we'd left," he said bitterly. "If I'd listened to her, she'd—we'd be safe at home and thankful to be there."

"And now she's safe in the hospital, with staff who know what they are doing."

He gazed at her sorrowfully. "Did she say anything?"

Stacy shook her head. "No. Not that I could hear." She looked over at Royce, who shook his head as well. "Come inside, get warm, and grab some coffee. Dinner is almost ready. We can discuss what to do then."

George let Stacy lead him into the other room, where everyone watched his slow, unsteady steps. Learning of Kathleen's attack had hit him at a level she'd never seen before. And she didn't want to see it ever again.

The blow was too much even for a strong man.

She served him coffee, before returning to the kitchen to stir the pot, simmering away. Then she realized something else. She turned and faced the others. Where was Christine?

"It smells good, Stacy," Royce said.

"Who cares about food?" Kevin said. "I just want to go home." He held up his phone. "I can't raise Christine on the phone. She has friends here, but she should have checked in by now."

"Oh no. Not again," Stacy said. "I was just going to ask where she was."

Kevin shrugged. "But I don't know that it is a problem. Her phone could have just died. She was really upset at what was going on. Said it was bad voodoo or something and planned to find another place to stay. I didn't say anything to you guys, figured you'd be pissed."

"But we'd understand," Stacy said. "I sure do."

"I think that goes for most of us," Royce said. "We'll have to pack and clean up tonight to leave in the morning. If anyone wants to put in a few runs tomorrow, we can discuss it then."

"I don't," George snapped. "Maybe never again."

Stacy felt the same way, but she wasn't about to join this discussion. She had more reason to never want to return than anyone. Yet, for some reason, she wasn't having the same reaction the others were.

Odd.

Well, not really. She knew why. It had come up when she'd been talking to the cop. About the *what if* that plagued her. "For the moment, I presume she's found some place to stay. Keep trying to reach her and get confirmation."

Kevin nodded. "Will do."

"What are the police doing about that hazard?" Stevie asked.

"Good point." Kevin leaned forward.

"What can they do?" Mark asked. "The area is riddled with them."

"I think they are looking to check it out early tomorrow, if they haven't already," Stacy said. "We gave them all the information we knew about it today."

Mark nodded. "Interesting."

"I did tell them that I took a look around but didn't see anything or anyone else up there." Royce lifted his coffee cup and took a sip. "I don't think that space went anywhere."

"These mountains are riddled with caves," Stevie said. "It's not unusual to see something like this. It's only because we found it that makes it unusual. If it had been mapped, then we'd have thought nothing of it."

True enough, and something Stacy hadn't thought about.

"Dinner is ready," she said. "Royce, can you please carry it to the table?"

He hopped up and carried over the large pot. The others, appetites returning, crowded around, dishing up full bowls. She walked into the kitchen and pulled out the last of the French bread, sliced it up, and took it out to the table. Everyone grabbed a slice, and silence prevailed.

But it was a good sound. Stacy ate slowly, enjoying the hot meal. Just being inside, safe, was a comfort. Knowing that she would be leaving tomorrow was another comfort. And, as much as she didn't want to look at everyone around this table with suspicion, she didn't know how not to.

After dinner, the group slowly did dishes together, no one moving quickly or happily. The conversation stayed muted and centered around generic issues. Stacy stood in the kitchen and wondered what to do with all the food. Was it worth packing up tonight or should she wait until the morning, after they'd all eaten?

"Leave it for now, Stacy." Royce stood in the doorway. "Everyone is likely to want a snack later tonight, and we still need a meal in the morning."

"I'd just decided on that too." She filled the teakettle and put it on the stove. "I'd like a cup of tea."

"You could have a drink," he said. "There'll be a lot of that flowing this evening."

She shuddered. "No thanks. And I wouldn't trust any of those bottles, and neither would I want to lose my wits to any degree tonight."

"I should have said that"—he walked closer—"if you wanted a drink, I'd watch over you."

She smiled up at him. "You aren't going to drink?"

He shook his head. "No."

Clear. Firm. Decisive. She liked that. But she still wouldn't have a drink from anything.

ROYCE HELD OUT his arms, smiling when she stepped into them. He hugged her close. The two of them stayed quiet until the teakettle whistled. She stepped back and walked over to the stove and the kettle.

"Do you want a cup of tea?" Stacy asked him.

"No thanks." He waited for her to make tea, then stayed behind her, until she walked out to the main living room, where the rest of them sat.

She might not have connected the dots. He wondered how long before she realized that she was the last woman left in the group, although Christine had disappeared on her own—at least as far as anyone could figure.

Only Stacy was left, and he planned on watching over her like a hawk. He wouldn't drink or eat anything, unless Stacy or he had made it. That wouldn't guarantee his safety, but it would give him a better chance. He wondered about the Hungarian stew, but the only time Stacy had left it unguarded was when they were in the boot room with George, and Royce had stood in the doorway to keep an eye on the others.

Now it was late but not late enough for bed. They had a few hours to kill.

He winced at that phrase. So not what he needed to think about right now.

Standing beside the fire, he studied the others around the room. He couldn't believe any were cold-blooded killers. Still, maybe Kathleen's had been an accident. Yvonne? Well, who knew? Christine? No one had heard from her, but hopefully she'd found a safer place to stay.

Kathleen's attacker could have been anyone. A stranger.

Not one of his friends. They'd never shown any tendency toward violence. A few had tempers, but then so did he. A few got mouthy when drunk, while others were adrenaline junkies. He used to be one of them.

No, he couldn't believe it of his group. Someone else had to be responsible.

His mind worked the issues. What if this friend of Kathleen's had been responsible for her accident? Maybe they'd had a falling out. It could even have been Christine. She was conveniently missing. Maybe she'd lured Kathleen to the cave. They fought. Then Christine had run.

Possibly getting revenge on something Kathleen had said or done. He glanced over at George. Had George ever had an affair with Christine? If so, could that be why? Not that such a thing warranted killing the woman.

He sat down beside George and asked him in a low voice.

George stared at him in confusion, before a tinge of anger flared in his gaze.

"I'm just wondering if she'd be holding a grudge against Kathleen." George still stared at him, but at least there was spark of awareness.

"What if Christine isn't missing? What if she planned this? Then found a chance to get her revenge on Kathleen and took it?"

George shook his head. "Christine isn't like that."

Royce shrugged. "Maybe not, but I'd have sworn none of us were."

"Kevin came in late," George muttered in a barely there whisper. "Maybe it was him."

"But why?"

"For the same reason I have to consider Stevie." At that, George stared at Royce hard, as if willing him to understand his reasoning.

Royce sat back and stared at Kevin and Stevie, without trying to make it look like he was. They'd both been friends with the group for years. So had Mark for that matter. Mark sat in the corner and nursed a bottle of whiskey. Royce wondered. Had Kevin or Mark ever made a play for Kathleen? He dimly remembered that Stevie had. Somehow he felt he could discount that. Stevie made a play for every woman.

Had Christine, though, made a play for George? His friend hadn't answered that query. He repeated his question and watched George's gaze slide away.

Ah, shit. "How long ago?"

George sighed and sat back, his shoulders slumped. "A month before I hooked up with Kathleen. Christine came on to me, but I said no. I was into Kathleen by then."

ALL HIS PLANS were falling to pieces. He couldn't have that. Not at this stage. He'd wanted this for so long that he wanted to cry. Like a baby, with a long-promised treat snatched out from under him, he wanted to scream and rage.

But he'd grown up a long time ago.

And this? Well, this was something he needed. What the other two needed. It was completing the circle. Something that had to happen this time around.

Who knew when he'd get another chance? No, he couldn't let this time slip away. They had no idea. A weird save on Kathleen, but, other than that, no one had any reason to suspect him. At all.

That Irish luck of his grandmother's was still holding.

Nice timing with Christine gone missing to mix up the issue too.

He felt his nerves jangling. His heart racing. Damn it. How could he make this happen and in such a short time?

Everyone was leaving tomorrow … or maybe not. An idea sparked in the back of his worried mind. An idea that just might be doable.

But he might need help. Only asking for that help might cause him to lose the prize. He knew where Stacy belonged but knew his buddy wanted her too. And his plans were different. Ugly.

That couldn't happen.

His own vision was beautiful. So how could he make this work?

Chapter 38

S TACY WANTED TO go to bed and sleep, but she knew she'd never close her eyes long enough to get there. Who could? Too much was unknown, and too much was suspected. She knew Royce and her brother couldn't have had anything to do with this. But, in the back of her mind, she could see file upon file of morgue cases, where men and women had said the same thing about their loved ones. Did you ever really know someone?

She didn't want Royce to have anything to do with them. She trusted him.

And many a woman had lost their lives doing the same thing, trusting the wrong person.

She tried to look at this scientifically. Who had the opportunity? As Royce had been with her all day, neither of them had attacked Kathleen. George had left Kathleen to go to the peak with Geoffrey. That should then clear both of them.

According to Kevin, the rest of them were going to the village for lunch, when Kathleen got a text. She said she would stay, until a friend caught up with her. Then they'd both come to find him for a cup of coffee. She'd been standing in the middle of the crowd, texting away. He hadn't caught the name of the person she was meeting. And he hadn't thought to ask.

Her cell phone wasn't with Kathleen when she was found. It was easy to assume that her friend was the attacker and had removed the evidence of the meeting.

No one had seen her again. And, they admitted, they hadn't worried about it or her. She'd met a friend. They were all on vacation, so who knew how long the two had gotten to talking? Maybe they'd decided to go to a restaurant, or, if they were both into snowboarding, maybe do a couple runs. If it was George she was meeting, they were likely coming to the cabin for a few moments of privacy. They hadn't seriously thought anything of it.

Until they'd found her, George hadn't even known she'd been missing. Mark and Stevie were together boarding until Stevie hit the tree. Kevin joined Mark for a couple runs, before going off on his own, then back for more runs. They confirmed that George and Geoffrey were together, up to where they split with Kathleen. Then Kevin had joined them, and he and Kathleen went for coffee. George and Geoffrey had gone out boarding again. They may have lost sight of each other on the runs, but they'd always met up at the bottom. And, yes, they were boarding on this side of the mountain.

Stevie frowned. "This sucks. I hate to think we are all sitting here, wondering if one of us attacked Kathleen."

"I'm not worried," Geoffrey said. "I was boarding with George all afternoon."

"And you never once lost sight of him? You never did runs in different directions or lost each other only to meet up on the top of the mountain again, where you both laughed and took off down one more time?" Stevie sneered, more than a little bitterness in his voice.

Stacy studied Geoffrey's face as he reacted to Stevie's accusation.

"No, we did not," he snapped. "We did all the runs together. You know what the peak is like. That's not a place to go alone or to lose sight of your buddy."

"Hell, we've all done that peak on our own," argued Stevie. "And we've all pulled stunts where we ditched our buddy to go left and take a series of jumps."

"Regardless of small things like that, we weren't out of each other's sight for more than a few minutes." George glared at Stevie. "To get to where Kathleen was found and to come back would have taken thirty minutes at least. More likely forty minutes."

Geoffrey subsided into his chair, anger vibrating through his long lanky frame. "I had nothing to do with her attack." He stared at the shot of scotch in his hand and refused to say any more.

Stacy looked over at Royce. She knew this was important. They needed to know where everyone was, but, at the same time, it was damn scary.

Just when she thought the conversation would die down, Mark piped up, "You know, just because Stacy and Royce found her, that doesn't mean they weren't the ones who knocked her out."

Stacy stared at someone she'd known and worked with for years and felt that inside center that kept her stable and calm start to crumble. Could they really be accusing her?

Royce, as if knowing how the comment had unsettled her, said calmly, "But it's not likely, is it?"

"You could have had an argument and pushed her. The crack in her head from the fall was worse than Stacy realized. When she never showed up, you knew exactly where to go and find her. Nice and easy."

Stacy stayed still, waiting to see if anyone else would jump on that bandwagon. She could have said the evidence would say Kathleen had been lying in the cold for a couple hours, but, since she and Royce had been together all day and mostly alone, Mark's theory was plausible.

"Motive?" Royce asked, curiosity in his voice. "What could we possibly have fought about?"

"Well, let's look at this rationally. Honestly, the best people to figure this out is us. We don't need the police poking into our lives any more than they are already," George said quietly. "We'll all analytically dissect everyone here and what motive or where they were at the time Kathleen was attacked. We know she was with me until twelve-thirty, and, no, I wasn't alone with her. There were a good half-dozen witnesses."

"Then, as you've already started on Royce and me," Stacy said, "let's finish and move on to each of you."

The others nodded.

"So motive for me to have attacked Kathleen?" Stacy asked, her voice steady, feeling an unreal sensation at what was happening.

"Maybe you were jealous?" Stevie said, shrugging. "Maybe it was an argument over George?"

"Why would there be an argument over George?"

Stevie looked at George and then away. He stayed silent. Stacy contemplated Stevie's face, then turned to look at her brother. "George, what don't I know?"

"Nothing much."

"Much?" She pounced on that word. "But there is something?"

"I just wanted you to come on this trip to help you move past your grief. She thought I spent too much time and effort on it."

"But you've only been together for what, six, seven months? I've been dealing with this for three years. Why would that cause her any jealousy?"

"She felt that because she was related to the winter sport side of my life that you weren't being accepting of her. We've talked marriage, and that was an issue for her. That I felt you still needed me so much and that she felt like you didn't want anything to do with her."

"Good Lord." Stacy sat back in shock. "First, I like Kathleen.

Then I also really liked Anna, Sarah, and Jessica." At that comment, the place erupted in laughter. "If I'm not all over her, it's more a case of I'm afraid she'll go by the wayside, as all the others have. It's hard on me too when you break up with them, you know? I make friends with your partners, and the partners disappear, and I'm on the receiving end of that loss too."

George stared at her, his mouth open. With difficulty, he closed it. "I never thought of that."

"No, of course not," she muttered. "And, for the record, you don't need to hover over me, nor do I resent her because she's associated with winter sports …" She rolled her eyes at that one. "But you and I are close. I expect to be close with your partner. I'd just not like to make and lose a dozen friends before you decide on the right one."

More laughter broke through the crowd, and even George grinned at her. "But trying out that dozen is so much fun," he said, laughing.

The humor helped ease the tension in the room.

"Anyone else got any reason why there'd be a problem that would cause me to attack Kathleen and then leave her? Only to turn around, presumably out of remorse, to save her?"

One by one, they all shook their heads. She sighed with relief. "Well, that's good to know. I was with Royce all day, so he's my alibi."

"Which," Royce pointed out, "just means we can alibi each other."

She nodded. "Also problematic." She smiled. "So let's analyze Royce next."

Now the group, feeling a little more at ease, fell into the game. For Royce, all they could determine was a potential prior relationship with Kathleen or an argument where she'd determined to cause problems with him and Stacy.

As nothing made any sense there, they moved on around the circle.

When they fell silent, Stevie said, "That didn't help."

"Yes, it did," Stacy said. "Now we aren't looking at each other as if we'll try to murder each other while we sleep."

He grinned. "So true. Besides, if you were going to kill me, it would be at work. There you threaten me all the time."

"And me," Mark said, laughing.

She smiled at him. He'd been snowboarding with Stevie all morning, and they'd done a few runs on their own on the other mountain, but he'd seen George at lunchtime too. It appeared, if he were telling the truth, he was off the hook at this point. Then again, they all were.

"One person we aren't mentioning is Christine," Royce said. "She's unaccounted for right now. Had she fallen down a crevasse like Stacy and had no one to help her? Was she attacked and is lying lost for someone to find down the road? Did she find a place to stay and would like to not know us this trip?"

"Wasn't she good friends with Kathleen?" Stevie asked. "I thought that's how she came to be here this weekend?" He glanced from one blank face to the other. "If so, what if they had an argument, and it was Christine who left Kathleen in there?"

There was a moment of heavy silence, as if the thought of the two women fighting could end up in one of them almost dying.

Stacy knew it happened all the time.

But no one ever wanted to consider it happening to two women they knew. Kevin had called the police and had let them know she hadn't checked in. They were trying to locate Christine, but they were overwhelmed with the weather causing trouble and hampering their efforts. Given it was one of the members of their group, the police were taking her disappearance seriously.

George suggested, "Maybe the same person who attacked Kathleen also took out Christine?"

"Why though?" Stacy asked, her heart shuddering at the thought.

"And Christine is probably sitting in someone's private pool, grateful to have found a spot for the weekend," Kevin snapped. "She'd really not like us discussing her this way."

"If something happened to both women, and if they were both in the same location," Stacy said quietly, "then I'd say the two women either saw something, overheard something, or found something that someone wanted to protect."

Silence.

ROYCE WATCHED STACY'S bomb drop into the vast well of silence. She could be right. But there was one thing that no one was bringing up. He would in a moment, if no one else did, but he was wondering if it had occurred to anyone else. All of them had been together for a long time. They'd gone on trips at various times through the years, with various group configurations, depending on who could come. They often had people come and go in between, as work schedules allowed people to get away. But, in three years, there was only one change this time.

Kevin shook his head. "Don't go there. Christine is fine. Let's keep her out of this."

"I think it all centers around Stacy," Stevie said. "Regardless of what the two women may or may not have seen, Stacy's the common denominator."

Stacy stared at her coworker in shock. "I'm what?"

Royce sat back to listen. This was what he'd been expecting.

"We've never had a problem before this trip. We've done many similar trips with no problem." Stevie leaned forward, his hands clasped in front of him, as if trying to straighten out his thoughts. "Now three women have been attacked or have gone missing, Stacy is the fourth and last one standing. We've found a missing man no one knows anything about. And we've been drugged." He looked from one curious face to the other, finally landing on Stacy. "So what's different this time? Stacy is here."

Her gaze widened, and Royce could see her mind spinning. "Glad you brought that up," Royce said. "The question here is really about whether she made this happen or if her presence acted as a catalyst to make this happen."

"That's such a fine difference, isn't it?" George asked. "How are they any different?"

"Did the trouble come *with* me? Or did it happen because I'm actually here?" Stacy leaned back. "That really sucks. Thanks for that, Stevie."

"Not trying to make you feel bad. I'm just saying that your presence is about the only difference that I can see from all the other trips in recent years."

"Not quite true," George said. "There is a shortage of women this time, and one of them is in a more committed relationship this time around."

"So sex being a motive then?" Kevin shrugged. "Women have never been an issue. We're all well-known for picking up someone for a night or two."

"And yet we haven't done that in years," Stevie pointed out. "In fact, I can't remember the last time I did."

Stacy smirked.

He caught sight of it and narrowed his gaze at her. "I haven't since Janice and Francine. I loved them as much as any friend, and losing them changed my attitude."

Royce felt her gasp of pain. He was already holding her hand but needed to do more. He reached his arm around her shoulders and tugged her up against him. She came, ever-so-slightly stiff, as if from a blow, but she relaxed into his arms. "It was a tough time back then," she said. "We were all such great friends. Their loss was difficult to get over."

"I certainly changed."

"So did I," Mark said quietly. "It took a long time to not expect them to be around every corner, pranking us at every opportunity."

Stacy smiled, her eyes overly bright. "They were always so vivacious."

Geoffrey said, "I understand that you've all lost someone important to you, but exactly what does that have to do with the scenario right now?"

"Maybe it doesn't," Stevie said, "but we lost two women that week. And now we came here this week—the first time Stacy is actually back with us—and two more women are also taken out."

"Oh God." Stacy slid down on the couch and burst into tears.

Chapter 39

S TACY TRIED TO rally from the emotional blows, but the last comparison was stunning and painful.

In the background, she heard George protest. "Surely that's just a coincidence. Besides, if Christine is missing, then the numbers don't work. That's just stupid. There's no connection to what happened on that trip and this time."

"Just Stacy," repeated Stevie in a subdued voice. "God, I'm sorry for bringing it up, Stacy."

She nodded, but the motion made the nausea rise in the back of her throat. She shifted to drop her head between her knees, while she fought to not lose her dinner.

"That's gross," Kevin said. "I'm going to be really glad when this trip is over with."

"Same here," Stevie said, standing up. He walked to where the open bottle of scotch stood and filled his glass. "I'm tempted to drive out of here tonight. Except Mother Nature is making sure we can't do that."

"Easy, Stevie," Royce said.

"I am taking it easy." Stevie gave a broken laugh. "What the hell is wrong with me?"

"Nothing," Stacy said loyally. "Nothing at all."

He snorted. "Really? Well, you wouldn't go out with me, so there must be something." He threw back half the glass of scotch in his hand and wheezed as the hot liquor burned its way down his throat.

The others waited for him to stop coughing, keeping a careful eye on him. Stacy had forgotten this part. The maudlin side to Stevie's character that always came out when he got drunk. Something he didn't do often. Considering the circumstances, she'd love to find oblivion herself.

But she didn't dare. She stayed quiet, hating that anything of this trip would be connected to her last trip here. She'd come to honor her friends and the memories they'd had together and to get past it, so they would not hold her back from enjoying the rest of her life.

To a certain extent, she'd done that. She would feel much better if their bodies were found, but, at the same time, she could deal with the reality of their grave. To think that someone had somehow connected the two trips in their mind was incredibly unsettling.

If it were true, if her brother and her friends had been worried about Stacy's mind-set these last few years, had they all missed someone else's deteriorating mind-set as well? Someone maybe who'd been alone through tough times? She'd been blessed to have her brother watching over her.

She had no idea who it could be. Stevie had been devastated. Mark less so. George had felt guilty. She herself had gone to pieces.

She knew now that there was no saving Janice or Francine. And, if it hadn't been the avalanche, it would have likely been something else. Those two were hotheaded, rash, and careless. Stacy doubted either would have reached their thirties.

She'd often wondered why the three had been such great friends. Stacy had been the staid, safe, shy contrast to their bubbling, outgoing adventurousness.

God, she missed them.

"Stacy?"

She glanced over at Royce. He nodded toward Stevie, who tossed back another hefty slug of scotch, while she watched. Time to put aside her own grief. She stood and walked over to Stevie and took away the bottle of scotch. "Bedtime, buddy."

He glared at her. "Not ready to sleep."

She smirked. "Lie down, and you'll be out like a light in no time."

A heavy sigh slid from his chest. "I hurt, Stacy," he muttered. "I miss them."

She knew how he felt. She wrapped her arm around him. "Come on. Let's get you to your room."

With stumbling steps, she walked him down the hallway to his bed. He stared at it and took a couple steps forward. She turned him around, gave him a little push, and he sat down with a heavy sigh.

"I miss them so much," he said again, as he flopped sideways, his head hitting the pillow. She bent down and lifted his feet, until he was stretched out. He never was one to make his bed, and this morning was no different. That was a good thing, as his covers—an open sleeping bag—had been shoved along the back wall. She reached over and dragged it forward, covering him up.

She started to walk away, when he reached out and grabbed her hand. "Don't you miss them too, Stacy?"

"I do, Stevie. So much." She bent down, gave him a goodnight kiss on his cheek, and said, "Now sleep. We'll go home in the morning, so we have to be up in good time to pack."

"Don't wanna," he whined, but it was more of a whisper. He followed that with a huge jaw-cracking yawn. "So tired."

"Then sleep."

She watched him for a long moment, as he fell deeper and deeper into a nice peaceful slumber. "At least you'll sleep tonight, buddy."

Royce spoke from the doorway. "The others are heading to bed too."

"Good." She walked toward him, her hand out for his. "How is George?"

"He's sitting beside the fire."

"Then that's where I'm going first." Still holding hands, she walked over to her brother and sat down beside him. "Will you sleep tonight?"

He shook his head. "Not likely. I should be at the hospital."

"And that can't happen, so you might as well get some sleep so you're in decent shape to watch over her tomorrow."

"A good idea in theory, but the last thing I feel like doing is putting myself at risk here," he said in a low voice. "I don't know if we're in danger, but what if one of us did attack those women?"

Royce sat down beside her. "I understand, but I'm not sure how we're supposed to solve that issue."

"I want to solve it. I figure, if I beat everyone up, at least I'll be assured of getting the right guy in the mix."

She snorted. "Thanks, but no thanks."

"You're exempt," George said. He ran his hand over his weary face. "I feel like shit. I keep thinking that, if I hadn't gone up to the peak, she'd be sitting beside me right now. But no—I had to do one last run. Damn it." He glared at the two of them, as if they could turn back time and give him a chance to make the right decision. "Why do I always have to push it? She was tired. I was tired. I knew that. But I also knew that our time was coming to an end and that I still had enough energy for a couple last runs. Plus, she doesn't like the peak, and I wanted to hit that run at least once."

"So what? There's no way to know that you could have stopped this anyway. You didn't have a crystal ball to say this would happen,"

Stacy said. "You can't know everything."

"But we all knew it could happen." He curled his hands into fists, as his voice broke. "And I ignored it."

Stacy didn't know how to help him. He needed rest. They had a lot to do in the morning to get ready to leave, and she knew he'd want to go at the first break in the weather. Hell, if it wasn't for that storm out there, they'd be driving toward Kathleen right now.

"I know your emotions are all over the place," she said quietly, "but you need to be wide awake and alert to help us in the morning. Plus, it's a long drive."

"I'll be fine." He brushed off her concerns with a wave of his hands. "Go to bed. I'll stay here for a while and doze if I need to."

She reached over and kissed his cheek. "Okay, but if you can sleep, please do."

He looked over at her and smiled. "Go and rest."

She rolled her eyes at him and got up. With her brother still up to watch the fire, she checked that all the food had been put away, then carried on to the stairs. The others had gone to their rooms. As she passed the room George had been sleeping in with Kathleen, her footsteps slowed. That's why he didn't want to go to bed. He'd be surrounded with reminders of her.

Royce nudged her forward again. "Let him stay up. He'll be fine."

She nodded and kept moving up the stairs to the loft. She was too keyed up to sleep, yet, at the same time, she was exhausted. So much going on. So much turmoil. And the grief, … the fear, … it was all so crippling.

And it made her tired. A bone-deep weariness that she couldn't recharge because that same tension sat inside, nagging at her. Not allowing her to ever let her guard down. How could she? Someone had attacked her friends. Was maybe still looking to assault her. None of it made sense. And her head ached, trying to figure it out.

"Stop thinking about it," Royce said. "Get into bed and at least rest."

She nodded and quickly changed her clothing. She wanted to lie down before she dropped. She tugged on her long johns and crawled up to her pillow and crashed.

ROYCE WATCHED HER settle down on top of the blankets. "Hey, Stacy," he said quietly, trying to roll her over so he could tug the blankets free. She murmured and rolled where he wanted, but it was like rolling a sleeping child, only much larger. Finally he had the covers out from under her and could cover her up.

He hadn't realized she was so tired, but she'd hit that bed and was out like a light. He sat protectively at her side and stared over the railing. He saw George nursing a beer on the couch, where they'd left him. It would be a while before he forgot his role or lack of role in today's events. Royce knew Kathleen had a good chance of recovering, but if they'd been any later ... The medical center at the resort was top-notch and knew how to handle cases like hers. That she'd been flown out to the closest hospital meant they were doing the best for her. It was up to her to fight for survival now. She'd done that in the cave; he just hoped she still had a little more fight left in her.

For George's sake too.

Royce was tired but had no plans to sleep. Someone had to watch over Stacy. She was the only female left. And he had a bad feeling about why that was. He could well believe Christine wanted nothing to do with them now. Royce wanted to go home and to spend his life becoming reacquainted with Stacy. Not regretting that he hadn't done enough.

He heard no movements from the others below him. He didn't know whether they were lying wide-eyed in bed or sleeping. He hoped sleeping. Stevie needed to sleep off the booze. But, if it gave him a good night's rest, then so be it. There were worse things one could do. Royce stared down at his empty hands, thinking he should have brought up a bottle himself. But he wouldn't want to lose control.

God, what a nightmare.

He shifted to lean back against the railing. Stacy slumbered gently beside him. Lord, it would be a long night.

WHAT A SILLY air-clearing bonding session. Did anyone believe the lies they'd all told? Stacy and Royce might have been together the whole time— except for when Stacy left Royce alone with Kathleen to go to the front of the cavern for help. He smiled, his teeth flashing in the darkness. He'd seriously considered taking out Royce right then and there. Yet he had nothing against the guy. Royce was good people, and the world needed more like him.

But the opportunity to finish off that nosy bitch Kathleen would have been perfect. He could only hope the cold did the job for him. Then Royce had been rejoined by Stacy and Stevie, and he'd lost his opportunity. How damn wrong.

So close and yet so far.

Still, it was what it was.

He was in the clear and still moving forward to his goal.

But he was running out of time. Or was he?

He thought about the vehicle configurations as to who was leaving with whom, wondering if he could change the seating arrangements. Isolate the one person he needed to isolate—and preferably in a place where there were lots of people to confuse the issue again. He needed suspects. Lots and lots of suspects.

He fell into a deep sleep, as his mind worked on options.

It was all good.

Chapter 40

S TACY WOKE THE next morning, tears clogging her throat and burning her eyes. She'd dreamed of her beautiful friends all night. Painful memories. Emotional memories. She wiped away the tears and sniffled. Instantly a warm hand landed on her shoulder and tugged her close.

Damn if that didn't turn on the waterworks. No, she was stronger than this. She'd never had anyone to hold her close before and was scared to come to rely on it now. She couldn't stand it if that was pulled away from her. The loss would be so difficult.

"Wake up, Stacy," Royce's sleepy voice murmured in her ear. "You're having another bad dream."

She smiled through her tears and nestled against his bare chest. Another bad dream? Had he been watching over her all night? Of course he had. That was Royce. Why had she pushed him away for so long? All the reasons seemed so frivolous right now. So not important. His history was his alone, and his behavior? Well, she wasn't sure it was ever as bad as she'd made it out to be.

She'd believed it to keep him at a distance and hadn't yet updated her vision of the old Royce to the new Royce. He'd lost that big playboy act years ago, but she wouldn't let herself acknowledge it. If she did, she wouldn't have a reason to keep pushing him away. And without that, she'd have to acknowledge the feelings she'd kept locked down inside since forever. To let those feelings out meant to actually honor them and to feel them, and that would mean being vulnerable. A possibility of getting hurt. If she lost him, that would be something she might never recover from. Look how she'd gone off the deep end with losing her friends.

To have Royce in a relationship where she gave everything was frightening to her. To lose him would be to lose herself.

And that couldn't happen. Not again.

She lay here, tears gathering in the back of her eyes. God, she was such a coward.

How had that happened? She'd always been the cautious one, but she'd assumed that was because she was the sensible one. Now, as she looked at her brother's wild lifestyle, her friends' crazy lifestyles, and what she'd assumed Royce's to be back then, it wasn't the commonsense side of her that drove her actions; it was the cowardly side. She could lose so many people she cared about because of their lifestyle choices that she'd put up walls, had locked herself down, and had refused to let them in any further.

After losing her two girlfriends, well, she'd damn-near slammed the door to her heart closed forever.

Maybe George was right. Maybe Kathleen had felt a wall up between her and Stacy. It was also true that Kathleen was like the twelfth girlfriend in that long string of George's girlfriends, but, at the same time, Stacy had shut the door to letting her in, fearing she would lose Kathleen too. As Stacy had all of George's other girlfriends. As she thought deeper and deeper about it, she realized she hadn't let anyone new into her life in these last few years at all.

At work, she was polite and professional. Mark and Stevie were there, and they'd known her since before the accident and had refused to be kicked out of her inner circle. But it had closed around them, not letting anyone else in. Royce was someone who had managed to get in, and she could see that, over time, Kathleen would make it too, but she hadn't yet because dear, safe, cowardly Stacy was still protecting her heart.

Fool.

She wondered how many times Royce had woken her up last night to calm her down, as her subconscious worked on her grief and fears. She wished she'd woken up with energy and a sense of closure, and, maybe for her two friends, she had. She knew she'd never see them again. That they would never walk into her room, regaling her with tales of their colorful evenings and the games the two of them had gotten up to. There'd been no malice to either of them, but there'd not been much substance either, as her father would have said. "Flighty, frippery women" he would have called them. And maybe he had been correct, but that in no way devalued who they were. The world was a big place and had space for people of all kinds—even fireflies.

As she lay here, it slowly dawned on her that it was almost light in the cabin. Noises were happening downstairs, and she should get up. She wanted to leave, but, safe in Royce's arms, she didn't want to move.

She slowly disentangled herself from his arms and sat up.

He shifted beside her. "Is it time to get up?"

She looked down at the sprawled conqueror in her bed and thought, *What a waste.* "Someone else is up too."

He sighed. "Well, the sooner we get moving, the faster we can get home."

"I hear you there." Whoever was moving around downstairs hadn't been up long, as the fire crackled cheerfully, but the warmth hadn't reached the loft yet. Moving quickly against the bite of cold air, she pulled on her wool socks, pants, and a heavy sweater. Her eyes had a gritty feel to them. A combination of a lack of sleep, too many tears, and dry air.

She turned back to Royce, who hadn't moved, bent to kiss him, and found herself tugged down on top of his broad chest. She laughed.

"You could stay here for a little bit," he murmured against her lips.

Her own curved in response. "It wouldn't be a 'little bit,' as you know. Wait until we're home. Then we'll have all the time in the world. I don't go back to work until Monday."

"So the rest of today and tomorrow is mine, right?"

"It's a date. But I get a hot bubble bath when I get home first."

He looked interested in that concept, then said with a wicked grin, "Is the tub big enough for the two of us?" His gaze heated as he stared at her, waiting for her answer.

Images of the two of them flooded her mind, making it hard to breathe. "Deadly. You are so deadly."

She got up, plucking her sweater away from her chest, as if to cool herself off, and walked to the stairway.

"Wait," he called softly, "you didn't answer my question."

She smirked. "That's because I don't know. I guess we'll find out though."

And she headed downstairs.

ROYCE LAY BACK down. He couldn't stop grinning. Despite everything that had happened, life was damn good. Now to pack up and get home. That hot bath for two sounded pretty damn fine.

Checking the time, he sat up and quickly got dressed. It was damn cold, but he couldn't hear the wind outside anymore. That was a good thing. There were no windows in the loft, so he couldn't see out, and what he could see from the downstairs windows was nothing but sheer white. He realized they would likely have to shovel the vehicles out this morning.

Given that, he quickly packed up his gear and left his single bag beside Stacy's unpacked belongings. She wouldn't need more than a few minutes to collect her stuff. He walked downstairs and lifted his nose appreciatively. Nothing like the heady aroma of coffee on a chilly morning in the mountains. And, from the intensity of that smell, it was almost ready to drink. He wandered into the kitchen to find Stacy already pouring.

"Hey, sleepyhead," she said, as she handed him a mug. "Just in time."

"As you only came down five minutes ago, it's hard to call me a sleepyhead," he protested.

"Ha, it wasn't hard at all." She grinned and walked past him toward the fireplace.

She sat down in the living room on the couch where she usually sat; he took up the spot beside her.

"So who's already up?"

She looked down the hallway. "No idea. The fire was lit and the coffee on when I came down. I presume that person is packing up right now to leave."

That made sense. "I'm packed. I put my bag beside yours."

She nodded. "Okay, after this cup, I'll go collect my stuff, and both bags can go into the vehicle right away. Then we have to sort out the winter gear."

"I'll do that. I'm more concerned with how much work there will be to dig out the vehicles."

"I've already been outside shoveling," George said, walking down the hallway, carrying his and Kathleen's bags. "And Kathleen is responding well. The doctors are optimistic. They also suspect she might have drugs in her system. The tox screen is pending."

Royce stared. "What?"

George nodded. "That's actually good news, as some of her symptoms were due to drugs and not to the severity of her condition."

Stacy leaned forward, her gaze intent. "Really? But that changes everything."

Royce stared at her. "How? Nothing has changed. Someone drugged her. And attacked her and left her for dead."

Stacy was shaking her head at them, her hair sliding from side to side. "No. He likely drugged her. She realized something was wrong, fought to get away, and was struck from behind. Left there because Mother Nature would finish the job after the drugs and the blow to the head."

HE LISTENED TO *the three of them talk. Shit. Shit.* Shit. *He shouldn't have waited. Shouldn't have let events develop to this point.*

Who could have foreseen that Kathleen would be found in time to be saved? Or that the damn doctors would consider checking for drugs? Shit. When they realized the drugs were the same as in the wine, they'd connect her attacker to this group.

Their lives would be torn apart by the cops at that point.

His mind raced. What options did he have? He considered saving his ass and giving up on his plan, only to realize that the plan dominated. His matched set had to be complete. That was his goal. His purpose. If he got to continue his life as before with that goal complete, then it would be a perfect finish.

So how could he get Stacy away from the others?

Chapter 41

STACY PACKED UP the kitchen. She'd done it many times before, but she wasn't sure she'd ever done it alone. There were mostly empty coolers, lots of opened packages, and a shortage of tie clips to keep them closed. Breakfast had been a hodgepodge of leftovers that needed to be eaten. She'd had leftover Hungarian stew herself. A hot meal, although spicy, had seemed to fit the bill for the long drive ahead. She washed up the dishes, hearing sounds of the others packing and putting the cabin back to the way it was. It was a process they'd all done many times over.

"Okay, that's our bags in the boot room with our gear." Royce walked to where she was stacking up the last of the dishes. She would have to rinse any coffee cups, once they were done packing up. Usually everyone sat, had a last mug of coffee, and ran through the checklist a final time.

"Are you sure you don't want to do a few runs before we head out?" Royce asked.

She turned to look at him, surprise lighting her face. "I actually hadn't considered that. Is someone staying here?"

"Both Stevie and Mark are going to. We could go back with them."

She frowned, thinking about it. She wanted to go home but— and she knew he'd be frustrated at this—she also kind of wanted to go back to where they'd found Kathleen. She couldn't get it out of her mind that she'd been in that location for a reason. Besides, it would be completely safe, now with all the mountain crews out posting warning signs and with all the officials involved.

George walked in. "Stacy, you two do what you want to do. I'm going straight to the hospital to see Kathleen."

She nodded. "Understood. I presume you'll be staying there with her for a while."

He nodded. "I won't stay all day, but it could be a good couple hours."

She'd expected no less. She pulled the plug in the sink, letting the soapy water drain. "Royce, as we don't have our own wheels, we have three choices, I presume."

"Right. Ride with George and stay at the hospital, until he's ready to go home." He ticked off his fingers. "Stay with Stevie and Mark and either board with them for a couple hours or go into the town and just walk around and have coffee."

"That's possible." She was here, and, as much as she wanted to go straight home, that wasn't an option. She had a few hours to kill no matter what.

"And third is to go with Geoffrey and Kevin."

"I don't see them here. Do we know what their plans are?" she asked, hoping that maybe they'd be heading straight back and wishing she'd brought her own transportation. "And did Kevin hear from Christine?"

"Geoffrey is getting a few runs in while Kevin is heading to the search and rescue office first to find out more about Christine. I doubt he'll leave without knowing something." George's grin slid out sideways, and he shrugged. "If he gets answers, he's likely to meet up with Geoffrey for a run or two. After all, our passes are still good for today."

She nodded in understanding. And these guys lived for this. "Okay, so a few hours to kill no matter what. Sit at a hospital, ski, or walk the town."

"If you're coming with me, you need to be ready to leave in a few minutes," George said, filling his travel mug. "I've got the SUV dug out and warming up."

Stacy looked over at Royce. He gazed back at her. She dropped her gaze. She knew what she wanted to do, but, hell, it's not likely that it would happen. But she would always wonder. And the part of her that was so good at her job was rearing its ugly head.

"I guess another choice is to stay in the cabin or to grab my camera and wait for the first group to come back and leave with them," she said, raising an eyebrow at Royce.

He nodded in surprise. "That can happen too."

She turned to her brother. "Go. I know you're rushing to get away. Please drive carefully and let me know when you get there."

He grabbed her in a big hug. "Will do." He turned to Royce, slapped him on the back, and said, "Keep her safe."

"You know it," Royce said quietly.

And, with that, George was gone.

ROYCE WATCHED GEORGE leave with misgivings. He couldn't help but feel that Stacy should have gone with him. She'd be out of this mess then. Safe. She, for some reason, hadn't chosen that option.

Likely it was knowing that the trip would stall at the hospital—possibly for the rest of the day or even overnight. That did not hold any appeal for him either.

What was it about the bright light of day that made everything seem less sinister and more positive? Then he glanced at her staring down at the floor and realized she had something else on her mind. His stomach sank. Damn that woman. He had a bad feeling that she would want to go back to the cave, where they'd found Kathleen.

Even though the search and rescue people were doing their jobs, it wouldn't likely be enough for Stacy. Although, with so many people around the area, it should be safe enough.

He sighed.

As the others got ready to put on their outdoor gear, he leaned against the kitchen counter and asked in a low voice, so the others couldn't hear, "You want to go back up there and look around, don't you?"

She glanced under her lashes at him, as if trying to gauge his reaction, but she made no attempt to not understand his meaning. "I can't get rid of the feeling that there is something more to this. Why would Kathleen have been there in the first place? It makes no sense. And Christine hasn't checked in. Maybe she's avoiding us, and maybe she truly is missing. Kathleen either walked in there on her own or had been carried. And, yes"—she held up a hand to forestall his response—"maybe that was just to keep her out of sight."

He nodded and stayed quiet, waiting.

She returned to staring at the floor. Then, with a little sigh, she said, "I could never go back to where I lost my friends. I almost lost this one because we weren't going in any deeper. Now I just need to confirm that we checked everything and know that Christine isn't in there too. That no one else is either."

"It's not good enough that we found Kathleen? That search and rescue have been notified that Christine didn't check in with us?" he asked, a thin thread of humor in his voice.

"Yes and no." Then she shrugged. "I can't explain it. But I need to go back."

She motioned outside. "The others are boarding. George is gone. We have a couple hours to kill, and I have my camera on a bright sunny day. Is it so wrong to go in, take a moment to walk the space, then leave so I really know for sure that all is well?" Her smile turned up a notch. "It should be safe with the officials all over the area now."

He studied her earnest face for a long moment. "Will you leave it alone after this?"

She smiled a bright, glorious smile and said, "Yes, I will."

Chapter 42

KEVIN AND GEOFFREY packed their vehicle up fully and drove into the village and parked at the main gondola. They would snowboard from that location, then head home when they were ready, further reducing Stacy's options.

Emotional goodbyes were par for the course—especially this time. With words of warning to be careful and to let them know if they heard from Christine, Stacy waved them off. She hoped they had a fantastic day. Now that she was alone with Royce, there was a keyed-up restlessness inside. She wanted to go to the cavern, then leave—and leave it all behind. Stevie and Mark had gone snowboarding, promising to be back by noon, so they could leave and get home in good time. She looked down at her watch. It was almost nine. They had three hours. Not tons of time, but enough. She looked up at Royce. "Ready?"

He nodded. They lifted their packs and ropes, determined to not get into any trouble on this quick trip, then back to the cabin to be ready when the guys returned. She had enough food to create some hefty sandwiches for while they were on the road. She couldn't wait to get back home. She planned on convincing Royce to stay at her place for the rest of the weekend. Monday, and their jobs would come soon enough. So be it. Her world was rosy again. And she loved it.

They walked quickly in the well-packed snow. A light dusting was on top from last night's storm, but as much as had blown in appeared to have been picked up and blown out again. They created new steps as they traveled. It was a gorgeous day out.

"I'm glad the weather will be nice for the drive home," she said, as they walked at a steady pace. Royce appeared to be deep in thought, his gaze on the path ahead but his attention elsewhere.

She waited a moment, then asked, "What are you thinking?"

He glanced down at her, then gave a noncommittal shrug. "Just thinking timelines. Now knowing that Kathleen had been drugged, it means she hadn't been in that place very long, so I'm rethinking everyone's alibi based on the new information."

Ugh. She walked beside him, her mind going over what Stevie had said he'd been doing. And Mark. Then Geoffrey and George. She couldn't remember what Kevin had said. "It would still take a good half hour to get to this place, deal with Kathleen, then another half hour to get back, all without being seen," she said. "That's a big chunk of time to be missing."

"I know. But someone attacked her." He turned to study her. "And Christine hasn't turned up."

"I know," she said quietly. "And that's just one of the issues bugging me. If Kathleen had already been drugged, why attack her?"

"The most likely reason is the drugs weren't taking effect fast enough, and she was fighting her attacker."

The hill was just up ahead. It was a little harder to climb with the loose snow under her feet, but they were at the top before long. She wandered closer to the out-of-bounds tape and saw a churning up of the snow below. There might have been some fresh snow, but, with the blowing and lifting in the wind, very little had landed down below. Myriad prints remained from yesterday. And the snowmobile tracks were all over the top of the pit. "Looks like some of the team came back and checked on the place," she said, pointing to the newer tracks.

"They said they would."

She caught the hint of long-suffering patience in his voice and had to grin. "Did I say *thank you* for coming with me today?"

"You did. Let's get on with it."

He dropped the rope ladder over the ledge, tied it off around a tree, and went down first. She scurried after him. Down in the darker depths, she remembered the eerie chill she'd felt last time. "It's like something old and dark is about this place."

"It *is* old. I doubt this ice has ever seen the sun's warming rays."

The trail to the cave was completely flattened now. Good. It was less scary as when it had seemed to have been deliberately hidden.

He walked inside first, ducking to go under the overhang. He turned on his strong flashlight, the bright beam casting a long shadow over the exterior. "Interesting place," he said, studying the icy walls and bits of rock showing through. He walked in deeper, Stacy following.

Suddenly they were at the place where they'd found Kathleen.

She turned around slowly. Now that it was early in the day, and, with the beam of the flashlight, she could see that they weren't actually far from the entrance. Kathleen might have stumbled in here on her own, if she were trying to get way from someone, or someone could have easily carried her that short distance.

Grimly, she looked at the blood on the ground. Given these temperatures, it would be here forever. Royce carefully searched the small space. She walked to the closest wall, and, with him pointing the flashlight so she could see, she put out her hand to touch the wall and walked the room, just so she didn't miss anything.

Ice was like a mirror and was equally deceptive. She walked all the way around and realized nothing was here. Her heart bloomed with relief. "Oh thank heavens," she murmured. "I was so afraid."

"Afraid of what?" Royce asked.

"That I'd find something much worse." But she refused to elaborate. She returned to where the corridor split and stared down the left-hand path, then realized she had to know. She motioned him ahead of her. "Let's check this one out."

"Stacy—"

"Please," she said, desperation in her voice. "I have to know."

He strode forward silently. There was another room, bigger and higher here. She did the same thing. She put her hand on the left side and proceeded to walk the chamber, the light leading the way and letting her ensure nothing was here to be worried about.

On the left side, she stopped. There was another cut in the wall, almost like a hallway. "Royce, come look."

He walked closer. "Damn it."

His flashlight shone on the smooth icy sides and the rock ceiling. Stacy grabbed his arm and lowered the blaze of light to the ground, she saw the bits of fresh snow on the path that had fallen from someone's boots. It was likely from this morning.

She froze. Her mind instantly went on alert. It could have been one of the search and rescue team making sure the cavern was empty—but it didn't feel like it.

Stacy deliberately and very quietly said, "Let's go."

And she walked forward, silently following whoever had come before them into this icy place this morning.

"WAIT," ROYCE SAID, his voice low. He had his cell phone out and texted George, even though he knew he'd be driving. He wasn't sure who else he could trust at this point. **In the cavern. Found some-**

thing odd. **If you don't hear from us every ten minutes for the next hour, we are in trouble and need help. Send the cavalry. Hell, send everyone anyway. This is bad.**

Then he put away his phone, stepped in front of her, and walked down the corridor. They came to another widening in the chamber, and they both came to a sudden stop.

Stevie sat in the middle of the room, huge fat tears falling down his cheeks. He looked over at them, his face a complete wreck.

Whatever was going on here had finished him. He pointed to the wall to the right of them. "I can't believe it. I just found them. They can't be here. It's too grotesque. It's so wrong."

Royce shone the light on the wall.

Stacy cried and ran forward.

There, suspended by wires, holding the two women in a pseudo graceful midair display, as delicate as multiple broken bones and torn clothing could make them, were the two women who had been killed by an avalanche—her best friends—Janice and Francine.

They'd been hung in place, forever on display in their icy art museum.

Chapter 43

S TACY VOMITED.

She dropped to her knees, as projectile vomit leaped from her throat to hurl onto the icy ground. She heard sounds dimly in the background, but she was too busy shaking and trembling on her knees. Her mind screamed against the abomination, the grotesqueness of what she could see in front of her.

Her friends—real-life dolls.

Frozen for eternity.

So lifelike that she wanted them to jump down—to rush over and to give her a hug and an explanation for why'd they'd been hiding for so long.

Until she saw the dead eyes. The hard marble flesh. The broken teeth in the grimace of a smile.

The only consolation was that her friends weren't alive when this had been done to them. Determined to take a closer look and to know the worst, she stood up shakily, Royce's firm hand on her elbow.

Or maybe not so firm, as she sensed the tremors running through him. He had his phone out; he'd taken several pictures and was sending them somewhere. Hopefully to get help for her friends.

She took a deep breath, dug deep, and tried to get into professional mode and do what she did naturally. Now that she was a little calmer, or maybe just frozen, she analyzed the scene. Both women had sustained multiple broken bones. Janice's knee was twisted, the kneecap not quite right. Some attempts had been made to straighten it the way it would be normally. Stacy noted in a dispassionate way that the tiny wires were used to hold her leg in a close approximation to the right location and position.

She studied the twisted ends of the wire that had been fashioned into locking closures.

An elaborate setup held the women in the most natural positions possible, as if they were flying down the mountain on snowboards—

just as they'd been before the avalanche had wiped them out. Their frozen knees bent, their arms out for balance, their bodies showing a natural grace of movement. Both women had been gifted snowboarders, taking to the sport easily.

This macabre display puzzled Stacy. Although broken, so many attempts had been made to place them in a natural position. A display of some kind. An artist's rendering? A memorial?

The person who'd done this had tried to reenact that wonderful free spirit both women had in life. She felt her tears sliding down her face, as she stepped in front of Janice. Her face had a dead flat-white look of having been frozen for a long time.

With a start, she realized a layer of color had been applied over her icy complexion, as if someone had used blush and possibly eyeliner to give the woman a more alive look.

Well, it was beyond anything Stacy had seen before. She walked over to Francine, noting the same attempts with the makeup, the broken arm wired together, the tear in her snow pants that had been crudely mended, and something was off in the neck and head alignment.

To see what her friends had suffered through with their deaths. The fear. The pain. The awareness at the last moment ... Stacy bowed her head, struggling to hold back the waves of emotions threatening to send her in a tailspin. After a long moment, the icy silence around her filtered into her mind. She shook her head and stepped back, distancing herself.

With a heavy sigh, she turned back to Royce—and Stevie, the blubbering ball of emotional distress on the floor. She walked over to him, compassion and sadness filling her head. Was he distressed at having just seen this, or had he done this and was now overwrought at being caught? She remembered him talking about the two missing friends and how he missed them. A mantra he'd said over and over again these last few years. She bent down and wrapped her arms around him, holding him tight. He hung on and cried and cried. "Easy, Stevie."

He shook his head. "It's not right."

"I know."

She really hoped he'd had nothing to do with this.

"They look so beautiful," he whispered, staring in agony at the two women, poised on a snow bank in mid-dash down the mountain. "And so wrong."

She nodded, agreeing silently. She glanced over at Royce, but he stood staring at something beside the two women, a muscle in his jaw twitching in a hard staccato manner. He was furious. She knew he would have already sent out a distress call, and it was only a matter of time before the place was overrun with police and crime scene people. In this case, she could easily pinpoint the time of death. That horrific avalanche off the cliff face three years ago.

Still, someone had gone to a lot of time and trouble to find these women and to bring them here.

"Stacy." Royce's voice was cold, clear, direct. A command. Not a request. She patted Stevie on the shoulders and tried to stand up.

"No, don't go over there," Stevie said, clutching at her.

"It's okay, Stevie. Royce needs to show me something."

Stevie hung on harder, but she managed to step out of his grasp, and, as if understanding he'd lost the chance to stop her, he collapsed into a pile of weeping jelly again.

Concerned, she stared down at her friend, wondering if he'd done this.

"Stacy."

She turned and walked over to where Royce stood. She stepped to his side and asked, "What?"

He pointed to the spot higher up on the small hill of snow the artist had created as part of the slope the women were snowboarding on. He then pointed to the spot above the two women. Janice's name was on a large card. Beside her was a card bearing Francine's name.

Stacy sighed. Then realized he was pointing to a third and empty spot. A spot waiting for another model—a third art piece to be put into position.

There was a name on that last label too.

Stacy.

AS SAD AND so psychologically heartbreaking as the display in front of him was, Royce's stomach had wanted to follow Stacy's massive upchuck when he saw the third name card. He barely managed to hold it back.

He'd known both women. Just not as well as the others in their group. They'd been Stacy's best friends. And Stevie's very close friends. He glanced over at Stevie, wondering what the hell his role in this was.

God, what a sick thought.

They'd never thought to find the women's bodies after the massive search had been called off. The whole area had been too danger-ous, as more avalanches had threatened to go off.

Obviously someone hadn't been able to let them go. Royce couldn't imagine the effort required to reclaim the bodies from the mountain. Someone must have seen the two women as they were tossed in the avalanche or maybe caught sight of one of them as the storm of snow had finally abated. Maybe that had given him a starting place, and he'd lucked into actually finding the one, then had persevered to find the second one. There was no doubt the women had died that day, but to do this to them …

Royce shook his head. He couldn't imagine the mind-set of the person who couldn't let them go.

And then he'd seen the name cards. And found Stacy's over the empty spot. Was she supposed to have died that day? Had someone set off that avalanche on purpose? It could happen, but it wasn't all that easy to do. Or had someone decided that the three women belonged together?

"What was it Mark, or had that been Geoffrey, who'd said some-thing about matched sets?" Royce asked in a low voice. He frowned. What else had he said? Something about *The three women had done everything together.*

Did either of those men have the expertise to pull this off? Then he realized the expertise would have been in recovering the bodies, but the rest was all about muscle and rope knowledge. So both did. Actually they'd all done courses in search and rescue work. The wire was crude but effective. All the men in their group were big enough to manhandle the bodies onto sleds and into this space. He had to wonder if there wasn't another entrance, as Stacy had suggested early on. This display would never have been found, if Stacy hadn't fallen down that crevasse in the first place.

Stacy, pale and shaky looking, hovered protectively over a dis-traught Stevie. She would recover now. She'd been looking for her friends, but he doubted she'd expected to find them and had certainly never expected to find them like this.

He glanced at his watch. He was loathe to leave the two of them, but surely there should be a rescue team here by now? The police? Their friends? He'd texted damn-near everyone he knew. Had this person despaired of Stacy ever joining the other two and had decided that Kathleen fit the bill as well, or had Kathleen stumbled onto this by accident and had been taken out?

He kept watch, knowing all too well that this was not over. Not until they were surrounded by the police and the "artist" caught.

And where was Christine? He'd wondered if she could be here as well. It didn't necessarily fit, but no normal mind would say this was logical either. Christine and Kathleen to join Janice and Francine. Then Stacy for a perfect set?

He had to wonder just how far over the edge this person had actually gone. Was he even now murdering women to add to his collection?

Royce, now thoroughly chilled by death, returned to the other entrance and cocked an ear, listening for the others.

Surely they should be here by now?

Chapter 44

S TACY STEPPED BACK from Stevie, her heart sore, her mind almost numb. She didn't know if Stevie had done this, but he was in no shape to be questioned about it now. The police would take care of it. Although she had no idea what the charges would be in this case—if any. Had he attacked Kathleen as well?

If so, then everything changed. She got up and walked closer to her friends, unable to leave them alone like this. Her body fought the chill that had settled deep inside. She'd wanted to find her friends since forever. Have their bodies sent home for burial. Find closure. Obviously someone else had needed closure as well. She shook her head at the enormity of this.

Did the person come back and forth all the time and visit with the women?

She spotted a box to one side. She walked over and opened the lid, making sure to use her gloves. Inside were candles and flashlights. Emergency rations. If Kathleen had found these, she would have been a little better off, but nothing would have staved off that mind-numbing cold for long. Stacy studied the items, wondering what they said about the person who owned it. Could she identify the owner of the box by the contents?

Every one of the men she'd come to the cabin with would have kept candles and matches in here. A few would have put in a small something for warmth as well. She dug into the box farther and, sure enough, found a couple emergency blankets and even several granola bars. Just in case. She sat back on her heels. Just in case, what? That they got caught out here in the cold? Chose to stay beside her friends? To watch over them? To be with them? Were they lost without them?

"Stacy? What did you find?" Royce called out.

"A box with supplies," she called back. They weren't far away from each other, but the sound of their voices echoed weirdly in the small chamber.

With the flashlight she found in the box, she turned it on and used it to search further. There was an odd travel bag to the one side. She frowned, recognizing it. She turned around. "I think Christine's bag is here," she said, her voice rising.

"What? Just her bag?"

"I don't know. I can't see anything else." She already had the bag open. "Makeup, a hairbrush, her wallet."

No response from Royce.

"Royce?" she called back. Where the hell was he? This was too important. Still crouched, she spun around, shining her flashlight across the darkened room. Royce's flashlight wasn't on. Shit. She turned hers off and moved quickly to the side. She could dimly see Stevie in the center of the room, still crying. But it was more of a deep wrenching sob. She knew he'd loved the two women but had no idea they'd been this close. Then again, Stevie had always been a big teddy bear.

Unlike Mark, who had always worshipped them from a distance. Lusting after women he couldn't have. Adoring models and movie starlets with a passion. He almost set up a shrine to each and every one, as they shifted through his consciousness and his life. He was fickle too. He adored one woman, then moved on. Even though he never knew them personally, it was as if they didn't measure up, and he had to go look for another one to idolize.

He'd always been like that. He'd wanted Stacy for a while, but she'd made it clear that it wasn't in the cards. As she remembered, he'd been after Janice. She thought Janice had spent a weekend with him for fun, then no more. It was so Janice's style. Francine had been the same. When Janice had been done with him, then Francine had stepped in. Hell, they'd both done the rounds with every male in the group. Including Royce and her brother, for sure. It had been part of the lifestyle. One Stacy hadn't been a part of.

She took another step back, her heart in her throat, and fear started to cut off her ability to think. There was no sign of Royce. No sound to say he was anywhere close.

And yet she heard heavy breathing. Heavy breathing she recognized.

And she thought she knew.

Please not.

Please let her be wrong.

She swallowed and closed her eyes. Her heart pounded, as her blood rushed through her body. She could barely breathe.

Where the hell was Royce?

ROYCE COULDN'T CATCH his breath. He'd been sucker punched from behind so fast that he not only hadn't seen it, he hadn't felt it, until his ribs could no longer expand to gasp for air. He couldn't groan. He couldn't move. Someone had snuck up on him and taken him out so damn easily.

Anger filled his brain, and the rest of him was so full of pain.

Physical pain. He had to move. If he'd been taken out that fast, not even leaving him a clue as to who had done him in or his intentions, then what would they do to Stevie and Stacy?

He could still hear Stevie sobbing. Had he been the one to rig up the women? He'd been completely devastated when they'd gone missing. He'd come here for several vacations to be close to them. In a twisted way, Royce could understand Stevie keeping the women here like this. But he couldn't see Stevie attacking Kathleen or Yvonne. And Christine? That made no sense.

So who else?

He rolled over and gasped, willing himself to get to his knees. The shards of pain almost dropped him. Black mist filled his eyes, and his head dropped. Christ.

Stacy. He had to keep going for her.

He used the wall to stand upright. He hit vertical. Dizziness took over, and he sagged. He had no idea what the guy had done to him, but it was lethal.

Lethal? He frowned, considering what he was up against. Who he was up against? Did he know anyone with that kind of training? The man had moved too smoothly. Too quickly. It was a practiced move. He'd known what to do and where to hit. Royce had to consider that there might be a few other people hanging here than just the two women. He would hate to think so, but, if he'd been dropped so easily, his attacker could pick off any of the winter enthusiasts without much trouble.

Although there weren't many missing people from the area.

But they'd found a dead man, who hadn't been reported missing too.

Royce took a deep breath, straightened his shoulders, and hobbled a couple steps forward. Only darkness surrounded him. He didn't dare turn on the flashlight. He searched the shadows. Where was Stacy?

Silently huddling close to the wall, he sent a message, screaming for help to George, the only one not here and the only one he could then trust. George would help. And fast.

As soon as he was finished, he crouched and waited. Up ahead in the deep darkness in front of him, an odd sound tinkled through the space. An odd sound, discordant to the surroundings. And too damn perfect in timing. He froze.

It was a cell phone.

And it played George's favorite ringtone.

OH, WHAT FUN. Now the cat was out of the bag. Or was it? They had no idea whose phone went off. Ringtones were fun and easy to change. He smiled. He didn't even bother looking at the text—but he'd have to remember to thank the sender. It was a great time to get a text.

He wasn't nuts, although more than a few people might think so.

He wondered if Stacy recognized the ringtone. She was incredibly brilliant in one way but in others? ... Not so much. Still, she was about to take a very different career path.

One she'd been destined for a long time ago. He felt that sense of accomplishment well up inside him.

This was working out perfectly.

They were all here. He had no idea what to do with the sniveling Stevie. God, the man was a mess. A coward and just a wimp.

Not like him. He wasn't a wimp himself. He'd never been one. He loved women. Of all kinds. Some men kept mementos. So what if he kept the women? He'd been hearing news stories of all kinds of men out there keeping women as sex slaves in their basements. He wasn't that bad. Geesh. He did love to look at them though.

He knew where they all were. They hadn't found his *collection yet. The matched set was front and center. And that one wasn't even his.*

He'd been forced to find another stage to play on. A happy sigh slipped out.

Creativity was inspiring. He could do so much. None of these women would mind. Even if they were still alive, they wouldn't. He knew them. Knew what they were like under the skin. The two showcase specimens took the highest position, and that's where both of them would say they deserved to be. They'd also put Stacy slightly below them both, whether she'd understood that about her friends or not.

They considered her an oddity, someone below them in life. Not as good as they were.

And her place was ready and waiting for her.

At least for a little while.

Chapter 45

THAT RINGTONE.

    Stacy's heart froze. Then shattered. Blow after blow. How many more could she take and still stay upright? This wasn't right. This couldn't be. There had to be another explanation. Her mind struggled to grasp any logical reason her brother's ringtone should have sounded in the dark space. She'd curled up tight against the corner, beside her friends. Hoping, praying she was wrong. Maybe whoever it was had changed his ringtone, so that he'd be mistaken for George. Or, and her heart seized at the idea, maybe George didn't have his phone because this asshole had taken him out and retrieved the phone. Maybe George had left it behind.

    She knew she was grasping at straws. Only so many options were ahead of her, and none of them looked good.

    And none of them addressed why Royce wasn't responding.

    Her mind kept asking, *Was she sure it wasn't Royce?* He could have taken George's phone before George pulled out this morning. It's not like her brother had been organized or collected. No, it had to be someone else. Royce would never do that. Janice's snowboard was only inches away from her hand. She wanted to reach out and touch it, to ensure it was real, to confirm she wasn't caught in some psychotic drug-induced nightmare.

    But the thought of touching her friend—board, boot, clothing—three years dead, was too much, even for her. On her table? Yes. In the field to get the answers needed? Yes. Here and now? No.

    She dropped her head to her knees. There had to be a way out of this. *Think, damn it. Think, before there'd be no thinking left.* She could just imagine this asshole taking out Stevie and Royce. No one would ever find them. No one would ever find her best friends. Or find her.

    She'd not believed in God in a very long time. Now she couldn't help but hope she'd been wrong. Only she suspected He helped those who helped themselves, rather than stepping into a scenario like this at the last moment.

A scrape rasped across the ice on her left. Shit. She had no weapon. Nothing.

And, for all she knew, she was the last one capable of saving anyone.

Then she heard something that made the hairs on the back of her neck stand up.

Heavy raspy breathing, ... from the right ...

She tried to shrink smaller.

A flashlight turned on, blinding her. "There you are."

She stared. In shock.

Stevie. She scrambled to her feet in relief. "Oh, thank God. I got so turned around, I didn't know who was here and who wasn't. Who was the good guy and who wasn't." She threw herself into his arms and hung on.

"Stacy?"

She paused, turned. "Royce! Oh, I'm so glad to see you." She slipped away from Stevie and gave him a huge smile. "I was so scared."

"Uh, Stacy," Royce said, "come here, please."

She took a step toward him, a little puzzled at the odd tone to his voice.

"Ac—" She choked back a scream, as an arm came around her throat and locked across her windpipe. She was dragged backward, her chest screaming for air, red swimming before her eyes. She couldn't focus. Everything was focused on the pain in her throat—the air her lungs were struggling to lock onto.

Her feet slid out from under her, as she was dragged farther backward.

And she finally heard the words being exchanged.

"Don't hurt her, Stevie." Royce's voice broke. "Please don't hurt her."

"I'm not going to hurt her," Stevie said, his voice a chilling singsong tone. "She's finally going to be with her friends. They're best friends, you know? Stacy has been lost without them. She's going to love being with them again."

Stacy tried to say no, tried to tell him that she didn't want to be with them. But he wasn't listening. As she heard the weird pitch in his voice, she realized that he would likely not hear her anyway. He was in his own world.

She tried to cry out for help. Tried to let Royce know she was choking to death.

"Stevie," she choked out. "I can't breathe."

Instantly the choke hold around her neck eased up, but he still held her tight, so she couldn't get free. She gasped, gulping madly for air.

"There. See? She's fine, Royce." Stevie turned Stacy to face Janice. "See, Stacy? They are waiting for you. All this time. They will be so happy to have you with them. I'll just put you up into the right position, so you can look at each other for eternity. You'll look perfect again."

"Is that what you're trying to do, Stevie?" Stacy asked, feeling hot tears in her eyes. She coughed, still trying to get air back into her lungs. "Give the three of us a chance to be together again?"

"Of course. They've been waiting for you. I tried to make them look right as they were …" He looked at Janice, frustration and worry on his pale features. "But they never looked right. Something was missing. Incomplete. And I finally knew why." A beatific smile shone from his face. "They were missing you, Stacy."

He pinned her in place with his arms. "And Stacy was missing the women. You've been missing them so much, haven't you, Stacy?"

"I do miss …" Her voice came out like a frog. She cleared her throat and tried again. "I do miss them, Stevie, but I don't want to join them."

With a wary glance at where she'd last seen Royce, she tried to shuffle slightly away from Stevie, but, backed up as she was to where Janice hung in the macabre horror show, she had nowhere to go.

"Yes, you do," he crooned in a soft voice. "I'll let you visit with them, until the cold puts you to sleep permanently." He looked at the hooks and wires he had waiting. "You'll like that. But I have to get you into position before you freeze." Frustration entered his voice. "It's really difficult to fix the position after you're frozen."

Oh God. "Stevie, don't you want to visit with me over the next many years? We've had such fun together."

"Oh, I will be here a lot. Now that I have you to visit too," he exclaimed lovingly.

His voice sent shivers through her. She hurt for him. She understood that, as much as she'd retreated from life for a while to deal with her losses, he hadn't been able to. He'd become obsessed with finding the women, and, once he had, he couldn't let them go.

She understood.

But she didn't want to join them in this sad gallery. She didn't know how all this worked with the other crap that had been going on, but she needed to find that out if she could. If she was lucky, someone was listening in. Even if they couldn't protect her, maybe the truth would come out.

"Stevie, did you drug everyone?"

"Me? No." He looked so outraged at her, she was taken aback. "Why would you think I'd do that? I'd never hurt you."

She blinked but managed to not look at her hanging friends. He hadn't killed them. He just couldn't let them go. "I didn't think so," she said in a soft voice. "I know that's not you." When he appeared to relax, slightly mollified, she added, "Do you know who would have done it?"

He shook his head. "Damn asshole. My head was killing me for days."

She nodded, as if she understood. And really she did. She'd suffered from that as well. But, if he hadn't drugged everyone, then who had?

"Have you had anyone else here to admire your work?" she asked, trying to keep her voice light and interested.

"Just one."

Oh no. She so needed to know who that was.

"But he told me that you wouldn't appreciate it. That I shouldn't show you." He looked at her brokenly. "But you understand, don't you? You miss them as much as I do."

Oh dear God. "I do." She hesitated, struggling to keep her voice calm. "Did someone help you do this?" She couldn't stop the hysteria rising in her tone.

"Do this?" His voice rose. "What do you mean by *this*?"

She fought for control. "Did someone help you create this display?" She didn't know what else to call it.

"Ah, yes, but just a little bit. He said I inspired him to try something similar."

There was almost disgust in his voice. She wondered what the hell she'd missed. "You don't like his work?"

"It's all right, but mine has heart. I'm doing something that *needs* to happen. Something that completes these lost souls."

"And what is his?" She was trying to keep him talking. To pretend interest in his work. He loved his work because he loved his subjects—literally. But who else was here? And how dangerous was he?

If he was here with Stevie and knew about her friends, then he was no friend to her. She had to expect him to be dangerous. More so than Stevie. He wanted her to hang to complete the matched set, as they'd always been called, but this other guy? … What was he up to?

Royce had to be here somewhere. But maybe so was someone else.

ROYCE FROZE AS he heard Stevie's words. Someone else who knew about this nightmare? And he hadn't turned Stevie in? *Shit.*

He looked around the darkness, grateful his eyes had adjusted. Not enough to see clearly, but with Stevie swinging around the flashlight, Royce was getting an idea of the room. There appeared to be another room off the far side.

Was that where the other person kept his work? And, if it was, did Royce really want to see it? Or would it be just as gruesome as this nightmare?

He heard a sound coming around the corner toward Stevie. He shrank back out of sight.

There might be a way to come around behind these two. Now if only he had a weapon. He didn't want to think of going hand-to-hand against the man who'd already taken him down once. However, they'd used tools to do this work, so what were the chances they'd left something behind?

Trying to keep an eye on the newcomer and Stacy, Royce crawled along the outside edge of the floor.

And heard a voice that made his blood curdle.

AH, LOOK AT this. His little boy Stevie was moving up in life. He had Stacy, and she was still alive. For Stevie, that was big.

It was also likely to make him cross that fine line into insanity. Stevie didn't do this work because he was compelled to find pure expression of his art form. He did it because he was lost. Lost in his love of the friends who he'd cared for so deeply.

See? That was just the wrong reason.

He, on the other hand, loved this work. He operated on a completely different motivational level because of it. As Stevie became weaker and more mentally unbalanced, he himself got stronger. Too bad for Stevie. Good job for him.

Now wait until Stacy got a good look at him. She'd never believe it. He couldn't wait.

And he stepped into the limelight, where every great achiever deserved to be.

And heard her gasp.

Only it wasn't as big a one as he'd hoped. It wasn't as shocked as he'd hoped. In fact, it was more of an element in proving her theory correct.

And that just pissed him off. If she'd guessed it had been him, then she was damn wrong.

No one knew him that well. He made sure they didn't. In fact, he made dead *sure.*

Chapter 46

STACY LOOKED INTO Mark's eyes, and what she saw was scarier than Stevie's blind and misguided devotion. His actions were understandable, if you saw the fractured mind behind it all.

Mark's eyes, on the other hand, were the opposite. This was fun for him. This was something he planned, looked forward to, and didn't give a damn about the outcome—because he was sure he'd be the winner. This wasn't a game. Couldn't be one—there couldn't be anyone out there that was strong enough, good enough to beat him.

Because he was better than everyone. He'd always had that superior arrogance. It had gotten him in trouble several times at work, but he'd always skimmed past the trouble, just shy of any of it sticking to him.

Now as she stared at the two best friends, the two men she'd worked with for close to eight years, she wondered if she'd ever really known them. She hadn't seen Stevie's decline, and she should have. She hadn't seen the psychopath in Mark, and she should have.

She collapsed to the cold floor at Stevie's feet, her butt numb, but her head on fire, as she realized the number of times the two men had alibied each other. "Why the drugs, Mark?"

He laughed. "Why not? It was fun watching you bump around in the dark, trying to figure it out. And getting nowhere. I had to throw things into confusion. Make Yvonne play into the mess. God, I hated her. As much as I wanted her to suffer, I didn't want her here forever with the others." He shrugged. "I drugged her and kept her here just long enough for her to wake up and to try to escape. Should have given her more drugs apparently. Still, I got what I wanted."

Stacy frowned. "What you wanted or who?"

"Oh, very good." He grinned and walked closer, pulling her to her feet. "Come and see for yourself."

She really didn't want to, but he dragged her forward regardless, Stevie trailing behind, crying out, "Don't hurt her."

"I'm not going to hurt her, Stevie, but, since you got to show her your work, I get to show her mine." And he thrust her forward, turning the commercial flashlight in his hands on full beam.

The sight slammed into her brain, and she squeezed her eyes closed in horror, her breath catching in her chest. She shuddered and opened her eyes to stare at the macabre scene. Poor Christine hung in an awkward angle, her neck obviously broken. Instead of trying to make his victims look alive and in action, like Stevie had managed, Mark's victims looked terrified and bore the marks of multiple injuries with bruising, indicating they'd been inflicted while they were still alive.

Stacy's hope that they would find Christine alive, as they had Kathleen, just died. Christine had most likely been killed soon after she hadn't checked in the first time. Likely when Kathleen had been attacked. Damn it. They hadn't even known. No one had gone to look for her. Had Mark been in this room the whole time—with Christine? While they were trying to save Kathleen?

Had she been alive long? Hoping someone would come and save her, as they had Kathleen?

Grief choked Stacy. And anger. And hatred.

He shone the light around to show her several other women in unfortunate positions, as he arranged them to suit him. Some were dressed, one was not. She didn't recognize the woman, but she'd been arranged in a sexually explicit manner.

"How many?" she asked in a hoarse voice, her eyes burning with unshed tears. So many women. They couldn't have all come from here. No way. He must have been picking them up from other locations and driving them here. Those poor women.

"I'm up to eleven now," he said casually. "I planned several more for this piece. Of course a couple weren't quite right." He shrugged. "I'd have kept Kathleen though. I had to do something when she saw me with the wine bottles. She wasn't sure what she'd seen, but, once she mentioned it to George, I knew she had to go."

Stacy closed her eyes, not wanting to know what he'd done with those discards.

Then she remembered the man they'd found. The one with the cowboy boots.

"Don't tell me. The cowboy boots didn't fit?"

Mark gave a bark of laughter. "Actually I was considering another sculpture with men, but it didn't feel right. I let him escape weeks ago. Figured he wouldn't get far. His girlfriend now though …" He shone his light on a stunning redhead on the left, a very broken doll-like redhead.

Stacy choked back the questions bubbling up. So many victims. She didn't want to know what this scene in front of her was supposed to represent—but knew it would have special meaning to Mark. It always did. She couldn't see any theme or reason why the women were in these positions. And she didn't want to know. All she wanted was to get the hell out of here and never come back. Ever.

"Even then," Mark added, "I haven't kept all the women. I let Yvonne go too. I hadn't expected her to survive though." He smirked. "Too bad she's still alive. Although, from what I hear, she's not likely to make it anyway."

Stacy's stomach heaved. There shouldn't have been anything left inside to eject, but her body was proving her wrong. She bent over, collapsing to her knees, as she vomited again.

"Oh gross. Not again." Stevie danced backward. "I'll get the shovel again and clean up."

He disappeared, and she was grateful. She didn't think she had much chance of getting out of here alive, but, if she messed up their display, she would at least have accomplished something. Gasping for breath, she asked in a low voice, "Is there water?"

A bottle was thrust into her hand, and she took a drink, then rinsed her mouth.

"I gather you don't appreciate our work," Mark said, a rough edge to his voice.

"It's a bit much to take in all at once."

"Isn't it though?" He kicked some snow over her acidic spewing. "Stevie? Where the hell are you with that damn shovel?"

"I guess it made it more fun to have a partner for all this."

"Ha, it certainly made it easier," Mark said in a conversational tone. "I saw what he'd done and couldn't believe what our Stevie boy had accomplished all on his own. It was like a challenge to try my hand."

She nodded, as if she understood. Like hell. Who could?

Her gaze landed on several tools tossed on the ground ahead of her. As if they'd been working and had just dropped them when they heard sounds. She didn't know what he expected from her, but she wasn't going down without a fight.

"Get up. I have to find Stevie."

She shifted forward, getting hold of a hammer and sliding it along her grip.

He glared in the direction Stevie had gone. She must hurry. She swung, aiming for his temple. Hard. And danced back. Then flew forward and smashed him in the same spot again. And again.

He yelled, his one hand going for her throat, his other hand going to the side of his head that gushed blood. She danced out of his way, shifted to his other side, and, with both hands, she used the hammer like a baseball bat and took out his knee.

He went down screaming. One of his hands was splayed out flat on the ice, trying to support himself. She danced in and smashed his fingers as hard as she could. With his martial arts skills, she'd be lucky to get away from him, even if he had only one hand and one knee. She dared not let him get his hands on her.

Hammer ready, she danced just out of reach, her breathing panicked. She wanted to go in and hit him over and over again, until he was nothing but hamburger, but she didn't kill people. She wasn't him. She refused to become him.

"Stacy?"

Royce. "Oh my God." She threw the hammer down and ran into his arms. "Are you okay? I was so afraid they'd gotten to you."

"Mark here did. But I managed to recover long enough to hear what was going on. Stevie is out cold and ..." He motioned toward where Mark had crumpled on the ground. "Apparently you handled this guy all by yourself."

"Nothing like knowing you were the next specimen to be put on display to give you strength and courage," she said, with a grimace. She pointed to the wall of women. "He's killed eleven."

Royce stared in grim horror at the room of his victims. "I'd like to hit him eleven times just for these poor souls."

Noises behind them had them both spinning around, expecting the worst, only to have the room fill with cops and rescue personnel. As one, they came to a sudden stop inside the big cavern and stared.

"Oh dear God. Those poor women."

"A serial killer?"

"He killed all of them? There must be a dozen women here."

"He ..." Stacy pointed out Mark, where he lay moaning on the ground. "He has killed eleven. But they are not all here in this room."

"And that horrific snowboarding scene we just walked past?" one of the men asked incredulously. "What about those two?"

Stacy looked at him sadly. "They both died in an avalanche three years ago." She ran her hand down the side of her head, not surprised to see her hand shaking badly. "Stevie, the man Royce knocked out

733

cold here, he's responsible for finding their bodies and arranging them in that display. They were our best friends," she said gently, sadly. "He couldn't handle losing them."

"So he found them and kept them here as what? Mementos that he could come and visit?" one of the men asked, staring at the room of horror, his voice trembling and thin. "I can't believe this has been going on for so long."

"A memorial, I think. The two women died three years ago, so they weren't here longer than that. The other women less so, as Mark started his collection after he saw Stevie's work."

"Stevie had to finish the job he started—for the women's sake. So they could be together again," Mark defended his friend. "Can't you appreciate that?"

Stacy could. But she had no idea how to even contemplate Mark's actions. And she didn't want to.

The authorities stared at Mark, then at each other.

They turned their backs on him and started to process the scene. Two cops were in the mix. One walked over and grabbed Mark's arms and tugged them behind his back, ignoring his screams as they handcuffed him. In a smooth movement, the cops lifted him to his feet. He continued to scream that he was injured. "Stacy beat me with a hammer," he said, crying out. "I wasn't doing anything to her."

One of the men turned and asked her, "Did you?"

She nodded faintly. "I did. Several times. Self-defense. He was trying to make me his twelfth victim."

"Too bad you didn't hit him some more. Then he'd be dead, and we wouldn't have the problem of a trial."

She searched his gaze, then admitted softly, "I hit him several times in the temple. I'm not sure he'll survive anyway."

The guy's eyes widened. He grinned. "You're Stacy Carter, aren't you? I attended a talk you gave last year in Vancouver."

"I love Vancouver." She gave him a wan smile. "I hope I acquitted myself well."

"That talk was great." He turned to look at the chaos around him. "I'm glad to see you can handle yourself in the field too." He nodded and moved on.

She turned to Royce. "Are you ready to leave?"

His lopsided smile slipped out. "If you remember, I never wanted to come here."

Teary-eyed, she stepped into his arms. "That may be true, but I am very glad to finally have this at rest."

Burrowing his head against hers, he hugged her tight. Then he turned in the direction of the exit. "Let's get going."

They walked back out to the crevasse, walking around a dozen people. "This place will be a busy hub for days," she said.

"And our ride is now gone too. I presume they will take Mark's truck and impound it?"

She sighed. "They will. We'll have to find a ride home on our own."

"Or not." Royce pointed up to the top of the hill.

George, a worried frown on his face, stood waiting for them. As soon as they reached him, he grabbed Stacy and hugged her tight. "I went in and saw," he said, "then came right back out and puked." He shook his head. "Jesus. Stevie and Mark?"

"Yeah, but we've got them now," Stacy said. "Unfortunately Christine is dead."

Holding her tight, George kept repeating, "Dear God. I almost lost you too."

"I'm safe." She pulled back slightly, her exhausted gaze going from one man to the other. "However, I don't think I'll ever let you talk me into another winter vacation here again."

"You?" Royce said, "Hell, I won't ever come back myself."

"Ditto."

The three hooked arms and carefully made their way back to the cabin and George's waiting Land Rover.

"Can we leave?" Royce asked, as they loaded up their bags.

"Yes, they'll get a hold of us tomorrow for full statements," George said. "I was going through Squamish when I started getting your texts, so I still haven't seen Kathleen, but she's awake and talking. Maybe she can leave today too. Yvonne has woken from the coma, but she'll be a couple days yet."

"Good, then home it is. There's a bathtub with my name on it," he said, with a big grin on his face. "At Stacy's place."

"A bathtub, *huh*?" George turned to look at his sister. "Is that okay with you?"

"Oh yeah," she said. "It's got my name on it too."

And she couldn't wait. Her future looked the best she'd ever seen it.

This concludes Books 1–3 of By Death.

Read the first chapter of Tuesday's Child: Psychic Visions, Book 1

Psychic Visions: Tuesday's Child (Book #1)
Chapter 1

March 18 at 2:35 a.m.

S AMANTHA BLAIR STRUGGLED against phantom restraints. *No, not again.*

This wasn't her room or her bed, and it sure as hell wasn't her body. Tears welled and trickled slowly from eyes not her own. Then the pain started. Still she couldn't move. She could only endure. Terror clawed at her soul, while dying nerves screamed.

The attack became a frenzy of stabs and slices, snatching away all thought. Her body jerked and arched in a macabre dance. Black spots blurred her vision, and still the slaughter continued.

Sam screamed. The terror was hers, but the cracked, broken voice was not.

Confusion reigned, as her mind grappled with reality. What was going on?

Understanding crashed in on her. With it came despair and horror.

She'd become a visitor in someone else's nightmare. Locked inside a horrifying energy warp, she'd linked to this poor woman, whose life dripped away from multiple gashes.

Another psychic vision.

The knife slashed down, impaling the woman's abdomen, splitting her wide from rib cage to pelvis. Her agonized scream echoed on forever in Sam's mind. She cringed.

The other woman slipped into unconsciousness. Sam wasn't offered the same gift. Now the pain was Sam's alone. The stab wounds and broken bones became Sam's to experience, even though they weren't hers.

The woman's head cocked to one side, her cheek resting on the blood-soaked bedding. From the new vantage point, Sam's horrified gaze locked on a bloody knife, held high by a man dressed in black from the top of his head down. Only his eyes showed, glowing with feverish delight. She shuddered. *Please, dear God, let it end soon.*

The attacker's fury died suddenly. A fine tremor shook his arm, as fatigue set in. "Shit." He removed his glove and scratched the exposed skin.

In the waning moonlight, from the corner of her eye, Sam caught the metallic glint of a ring on his finger. It mattered. She knew it did. She struggled to imprint the image before the opportunity was lost. Her eyes drifted closed. In the darkness of her mind, the wait for Death was endless.

Sam's soul wept. Oh, God, she hated this. Why? Why was she here? She couldn't help the woman. She couldn't even help herself.

Sam welcomed the next blow—so light, only a minor flinch undulated through the dreadfully damaged body of this woman. Maybe the poor woman had passed on. Sam's tortured spirit stirred deep within the rolling waves of blackness, struggling for freedom from this nightmare.

With one last surge of energy, the woman opened her eyes and locked on to the killer's gaze staring back from within the mask. In ever-slowing heartbeats, her—and Sam's—circle of vision narrowed, until the two soulless orbs blended into one small band, before it blinked out altogether. The silence, when it came, was absolute.

Gratefully Sam relaxed into the woman's death.

Twenty minutes later, Sam bolted upright in her own bed. Survival instincts screamed at her to run. White agony dropped her in place.

"*Ooooh*," she cried out. Fearing more pain, she slid her hands over her belly. Her fingers slipped along the raw edges of a deep slash. Searing pain made her gasp and twist away. Hot tears poured. Warm sticky fluid coated her fingers. "Oh, God. Oh, God. Oh, God," she chanted.

Staring in confusion around her, fear, panic, and finally recognition seeped into her dazed mind. Early morning rays highlighted the water stains on the ceiling, shining through the slapdash coat of whitewash on there, and Sam's banged-up suitcases, open on the floor. An empty room—an empty life. A remnant of a foster-care childhood.

She was home.

Memories swamped her, flooding her senses with yet more hurt.

Sam broke down. Like an animal, she tried to curl into a tiny ball, only to scream again as pain jackknifed through her. Torn edges of muscle tissue and flesh rubbed against each other, and broken ribs creaked with her slightest movement. Blood slipped over her torn breasts to soak the sheets below.

The smell. Wet wool fought with the unique and unforgettable smell of fresh blood.

Sam caught her breath and froze, her face hot, tight with agony. "Shit, shit, and shit!" She swore under her breath, like a mantra.

Tremors wracked her tiny frame, keeping the pain alive, as she morphed through realities. *Transition time.* What a joke. That always brought images of New Age mumbo jumbo to mind. Nothing light and airy could describe this. Each blow leveled at the victim had manifested in Sam's own body. This was hard-core healing time for Sam—time when bones knitted, sliced ligaments and muscle tissue grew back together, and skin stitched itself closed.

Sam understood her injuries had something to do with her imperfect control, paired with her inability to accept her gifts. Apparently, if she could surmount the latter, the first would diminish. She didn't quite understand how or why. Or what to do about it. Her body somehow always healed; the physical and mental scars always remained. She was a mess.

The physical process usually took anywhere from ten to twenty minutes—depending on the injuries. The mental confusion, disconnectedness, sense of isolation took longer to disappear. She paid a high price for moving too soon. Shuddering, Sam reached for the frayed edges of her control. It wouldn't be much longer. She hoped.

Nothing could stop the hot tears, leaking from her closed eyelids.

This session had been bad. Apart from the broken ribs, there were so many stab wounds. She'd never experienced one death so physically damaging. Nervously she wondered at the extent of her blood loss. If she didn't learn how to disconnect, these visions could be the end of her—literally.

Just like that poor woman.

Sam hated that these episodes were changing, growing, developing. So powerful and so ugly, they made her sick to her soul.

Several minutes later, Sam raised her head to survey the bed. The pain was manageable, although she wouldn't move her limbs yet. Blood had soaked the top of the many Thrift Store blankets piled high on the bed. Her hollowed belly had become a vessel for the cooling puddle of blood. Shit. The stuff was everywhere.

The metallic taste clung to her lips and teeth. She rolled the disgusting spit around the inside of her mouth, waiting. She wanted to run away—from the memories, the visions, her life. But knowing that pain simmered beneath the surface, waiting to rip her apart, stopped her. Weary, ageless patience added to the bleakness in her heart.

Ten more minutes passed. Now she should be good to go. Lifting her head, she spat the bloody gob onto the waiting wad of tissue and noted the time.

Transition had taken fifteen minutes this morning.

She was improving.

Oh, God. Sam broke into sobs again. When would this end? Other psychics found things or heard things. Many of them saw events before they happened. She saw violence—not only saw it but experienced it too.

Occasional shudders racked her frame from the coldness that seemed destined to live in her veins. The odd straggling sniffle escaped. She couldn't remember when she'd last been warm. Dropping the top blood-soaked blanket to the floor, Sam tugged the motley collection of covers tighter around her skinny frame. Warmth was a comfort that belonged to others.

She wasn't so lucky.

She walked with one foot on the dark side—whether she liked it or not. And that was the problem. She'd been running for a long time. Then she'd landed at this cabin and had been hiding ever since. That was no answer either.

Her resolve firmed. Enough was enough. It was time to gain control of her *gift*. Time to do something, even if just reading more books on psychics, maybe finding one she could talk to. This monster had to be stopped.

Plus, Christ, she was tired of waking up dead.

Book 1 is available now!

To find out more visit Dale Mayer's website.

https://geni.us/Dmtuesdayuniversal

Simon Says... HIDE: Kate Morgan (Book #1)

Welcome to a new thriller series from *USA Today* Best-Selling Author Dale Mayer. Set in Vancouver, BC, the team of Detective Kate Morgan and Simon St. Laurant, an unwilling psychic, marries all the elements of Dale's work that you've come to love, plus so much more.

Detective Kate Morgan, newly promoted to the Vancouver PD Homicide Department, stands for the victims in her world. She was once a victim herself, just as her mother had been a victim, and then her brother—an unsolved missing child's case—was yet another victim. She can't stand those who take advantage of others, and the worst ones are those who prey on the hopes of desperate people to line their own pockets.

So, when she finds a connection between a current case and more than a half-dozen cold cases, where a child's life hangs in the balance, Kate would make a deal with the devil himself to find the culprit and to save the child.

Simon St. Laurant's grandmother had the Sight and had warned him that, once he used it, he could never walk away. Until now, her caution had made it easy to avoid that first step. But, when nightmares of his own past are triggered, Simon can't stand back and watch child after child be abused. Not without offering his help to those chasing the monsters.

Even if it means dealing with the cranky and critical Detective Kate Morgan …

Find Simon Says… Hide here!
To find out more visit Dale Mayer's website.
https://geni.us/DMSSHideUniversal

Simon Says... HIDE: Kate Morgan (Book #1)
Chapter 1

Vancouver, First Monday in June ...

NEWLY MINTED HOMICIDE detective Kate Morgan sat on one of the many benches positioned in this child-friendly park, watching the kids play on the swings in downtown Vancouver. She'd passed her first three months in her new position amid the craziness of too many murder cases to count. Vancouver, BC, was like any big city around the world and had its share of criminal activity. The city had its issues—just being on the coast and blending many different nationalities—yet somehow it all worked. Plus it was home for her. Always had been.

Because of those life-and-death issues, Vancouver had three homicide units, usually with six or seven detectives in each unit. She chuckled. At one time, the two other units called themselves Team Canuck or Team Flames, showing how hockey crazy Canada got. She didn't know what her unit used to call themselves, as she was the odd-one-out still. New enough to know her place and not so new to misunderstand the team needed time to meld.

Her ever-assessing gaze watched two men on a bench on the far side of the park. One got up, tossed a bright yellow ball at the other and then, with a raised hand, turned and walked away.

Her focus flitted to the storm approaching in the distance, assessed its threat, and dismissed it. Rain was part of the reality when living on the coast. The more pressing threats in her world were the two-legged predators. She'd known the dangers ever since her younger brother had disappeared, even now, twenty-five years later with still no trace of him. She kept a copy of his file on her desk, as a reminder of the work she'd dedicated herself to. Timmy was always close to her heart. She could only hope to get closure, as she worked to give closure to others.

Sudden movement on her left had her watching a lean man of average height, walking into the park and staring at the kids on the swing. Something about his gaze set her nerves on edge. He was slightly turned away from her, only letting her see his jeans and well-worn jacket with the upturned collar. He perched on a nearby bench seat, seemingly fascinated by the boys' antics.

The single male on the far side stood suddenly and strode her way, tossing the yellow ball and catching it smoothly with every step. He gazed at the street beside her, unconcerned for the kids or other adults. His focus was internal. From the power suit he wore, business deals most likely.

As she turned back to the other man, he'd disappeared. Her gaze zipped to the boys at the swings. They were still there. Relaxing slightly, she studied the park exits. Both men had left at the same time. From opposite sides of the park.

It shouldn't have meant anything.

But it felt like it did.

Her phone rang just then. Rodney, one of her team. "We found another one. Prepare yourself. It's a little boy."

Tuesday

SIMON ST. LAURANT had had a bad week. He twisted in bed, kicking off the blanket. His body shimmered with sweat. He drifted in and out of sleep. He'd been up until two in the morning in one of his friendlier gambling games and had crashed soon afterward. Now it was five in the morning, and the last thing he wanted was to be awake. He rolled over, pulled the sheet over his sweating body, and closed his eyes.

As he tried to fall asleep again, he drifted down the same godforsaken dark street, just a halo of light coming from the streetlamps across on the other side. A small man, holding the hand of a very young boy at his side, walked quietly down the street. The little boy asked, "When will we be there?"

"We'll be there soon," the older man promised.

Something was just so damn wrong about that picture that Simon kept telling the little boy to run, wanting to reach out and drag him to safety. But, even as Simon reached out a hand, he saw that it wasn't real, that he wasn't there, that he couldn't grab that little boy and escape. As the older man walked under the streetlamp, Simon caught the hungry look on the man's face. A predator's look. Yet not clear enough to identify him.

Simon woke immediately, sat up, and groaned in frustration. "Why that same goddamn freaking nightmare?" he cried out, before flopping to his back yet again.

He was exhausted, his mind overwhelmed, as he drifted once again into the deepness of sleep. This time he landed in a small room, with lots of toys on the bed and on the floor. A bed that broke his heart because it had a plastic sheet for the little kids who might wet themselves. A blanket was atop the bed but was otherwise empty. Simon's mind knew that a light was on the side of the room and that Simon would see the child soon, but he didn't want to go there. He kicked himself out of the dream, sitting up again, shuddering in the dark. "Damn it," he muttered, rubbing his eyes. "What fresh hell is this?"

Almost as if by asking that question, his body stiffened. He fell backward again, and this time he was in a different room, and the bed was bigger. It had little pink roses around the base and unicorns across the headboard. A little girl sobbed her eyes out, curled up into a tiny ball, hugging a teddy bear. The problem was that fancy little bed was completely out of place, surrounded by bare concrete walls and old cracked floors. The lack of carpet or any other niceties suggested this would not be a nice little home for her.

Instead Simon saw the bloodstains on the mattress around her, the pain and the terror in her heart, and the loneliness in her soul. He wanted to hold her and to tell her that it would be okay. But the same words rippled through his mind: *Hide. He's coming.*

Then everything went dark …

When he woke again, he lay in his bed, staring at the ceiling, dry-eyed, but felt as if he'd bawled his entire life away. Every part of his body hurt, especially his soul. He sat up, felt like he was thirty years older than his thirty-seven years on this planet. Thirty-seven years of pain and fighting to get the upper hand, trying to ensure that he wouldn't be a victim in this world again.

Years ago he'd sworn to be a victor instead. He played the game, but he didn't let others play him. That wasn't part of his new reality. Not anymore—not for a long time. He looked down at his bed, the bottom sheet literally pulled off the mattress and twisted beneath him, while the top sheet was crumpled on the floor beside him.

"Looks like I had a party—and not the fun kind," he muttered, as he slowly straightened. He stretched, turned to get the kinks out of his neck and his back. A bad night had the effect of turning his spine into a pretzel that he could spend hours trying to untwist. He needed a hot shower to complete the job. Yet every time he went under the water, he kept seeing images of the boy that he'd seen in the first nightmare this morning.

It made no sense, when he'd seen many other children throughout his lifetime of nightmares, but, for some reason, he identified with that one. That night terror always upset him because he didn't know that child. It wasn't Simon as a child, and he didn't understand the dialogue, didn't remember it from his own life. What he did know was that these nightmares had to stop.

If he had a friend who was a doctor, he might have talked to him or her, but unfortunately he didn't even have that. In truth, speaking out loud of this weakness, … in the wrong hands, that knowledge could crush Simon. As he walked naked to the shower, he knew something had to change; he couldn't keep going on this way. The nightmares had restarted suddenly, for no current reason, and they were getting stronger, clearer, and more traumatic to view.

He should get away for a few days. Book a gambling cruise to take his mind off this mess. Maybe see Yale there. Simon's gaze caught sight of the yellow child's ball that Yale had tossed to Simon, the two men out of the blue both at the park yesterday.

Simon often walked that corridor and had come upon his old friend, looking sad and depressed. It had been nice to see Yale unexpectedly. Normally they'd be in on the same poker games or cruises, but he hadn't seen his old college friend in over six months.

Much happier after their visit, Yale had laughed, as he'd tossed him the ball, and said, "For old times' sake."

With a shrug, Simon stepped under the rain showerhead and let the hot water slosh over his head and down his back to the tiles below.

As soon as he was dry and dressed in lightweight pants with a linen shirt, perfect for summers in Vancouver, he picked up his blazer, flipped it over his shoulder, and headed out. He needed coffee in a big way, but he also had to escape the solitude of his own thoughts, preferably out in public, where he could disappear into the crowds. He walked off the elevator, crossed the lobby, and headed toward the front door, held open by the doorman.

Once outside, he stopped for a long moment, lifted his head, and sniffed the early morning Vancouver air. The nearby harbor, with that scent of salt, plus the noise and the bustle of city life, all of it melded together beautifully. With a smile he turned and headed toward his favorite coffee shop.

Find Simon Says… Hide here!
To find out more visit Dale Mayer's website.
https://geni.us/DMSSHideUniversal

Author's Note

Thank you for reading By Death Books 1–3! If you enjoyed my book, I'd appreciate it if you'd leave a review.

Dear reader,

I love to hear from readers, and you can contact me at my website: www.dalemayer.com or at my Facebook author page. To be informed of new releases and special offers, sign up for my newsletter or follow me on BookBub. And if you are interested in joining Dale Mayer's Reader Group, here is the Facebook sign up page.
http://geni.us/DaleMayerFBGroup

Cheers,
Dale Mayer

About the Author

Dale Mayer is a *USA Today* best-selling author, best known for her SEALs military romances, her Psychic Visions series, and her Lovely Lethal Garden cozy series. Her contemporary romances are raw and full of passion and emotion (Broken But … Mending, Hathaway House series). Her thrillers will keep you guessing (Kate Morgan, By Death series), and her romantic comedies will keep you giggling (*It's a Dog's Life*, a stand-alone novella; and the Broken Protocols series, starring Charming Marvin, the cat).

Dale honors the stories that come to her—and some of them are crazy, break all the rules and cross multiple genres!

To go with her fiction, she also writes nonfiction in many different fields, with books available on résumé writing, companion gardening, and the US mortgage system. All her books are available in print and ebook format.

Connect with Dale Mayer Online

Also by Dale Mayer

Published Adult Books:

Shadow Recon
Magnus, Book 1

Bullard's Battle
Ryland's Reach, Book 1
Cain's Cross, Book 2
Eton's Escape, Book 3
Garret's Gambit, Book 4
Kano's Keep, Book 5
Fallon's Flaw, Book 6
Quinn's Quest, Book 7
Bullard's Beauty, Book 8
Bullard's Best, Book 9
Bullard's Battle, Books 1–2
Bullard's Battle, Books 3–4
Bullard's Battle, Books 5–6
Bullard's Battle, Books 7–8

Terkel's Team
Damon's Deal, Book 1
Wade's War, Book 2
Gage's Goal, Book 3
Calum's Contact, Book 4
Rick's Road, Book 5
Scott's Summit, Book 6
Brody's Beast, Book 7

Psychic Vision Series

Eye of the Falcon
Itsy-Bitsy Spider
Unmasked
Deep Beneath
From the Ashes
Stroke of Death
Ice Maiden
Snap, Crackle…
What If…
Talking Bones
String of Tears
Inked Forever
Psychic Visions Books 1–3
Psychic Visions Books 4–6
Psychic Visions Books 7–9

By Death Series

Touched by Death
Haunted by Death
Chilled by Death
By Death Books 1–3

Broken Protocols – Romantic Comedy Series

Cat's Meow
Cat's Pajamas
Cat's Cradle
Cat's Claus
Broken Protocols 1-4

Broken and… Mending

Skin
Scars
Scales (of Justice)
Broken but… Mending 1-3

Glory

Biker Blues

SEALs of Honor

Heroes for Hire

SEALs of Steel

The Mavericks

Jax, Book 3
Beau, Book 4
Asher, Book 5
Ryker, Book 6
Miles, Book 7
Nico, Book 8
Keane, Book 9
Lennox, Book 10
Gavin, Book 11
Shane, Book 12
Diesel, Book 13
Jerricho, Book 14
Killian, Book 15
Hatch, Book 16
Corbin, Book 17
Aiden, Book 18
The Mavericks, Books 1–2
The Mavericks, Books 3–4
The Mavericks, Books 5–6
The Mavericks, Books 7–8
The Mavericks, Books 9–10
The Mavericks, Books 11–12

Standalone Novellas
It's a Dog's Life
Riana's Revenge
Second Chances

Published Young Adult Books:

Family Blood Ties Series
Vampire in Denial
Vampire in Distress
Vampire in Design
Vampire in Deceit

Vampire in Defiance

Vampire in Conflict

Vampire in Chaos

Vampire in Crisis

Vampire in Control

Vampire in Charge

Family Blood Ties Set 1–3

Family Blood Ties Set 1–5

Family Blood Ties Set 4–6

Family Blood Ties Set 7–9

Sian's Solution, A Family Blood Ties Series Prequel Novelette

Design series

Dangerous Designs

Deadly Designs

Darkest Designs

Design Series Trilogy

Standalone

In Cassie's Corner

Gem Stone (a Gemma Stone Mystery)

Time Thieves

Published Non-Fiction Books:

Career Essentials

Career Essentials: The Résumé

Career Essentials: The Cover Letter

Career Essentials: The Interview

Career Essentials: 3 in 1

Printed in the USA
CPSIA information can be obtained
at www.ICGtesting.com
LVHW021402251023
762104LV00007B/152

9 781988 315